I0784937

J. M. Barrie

SENTIMENTAL TOMMY & Its Sequel, Tommy and Grizel
(Illustrated Edition)

OK Publishing 2021

J. M. Barrie
SENTIMENTAL TOMMY & Its Sequel, Tommy and Grizel

(Illustrated Edition)

Tale of a Young Orphan Boy Growing up in London & Scotland

Published by
MUSAICUM
Books

- Advanced Digital Solutions & High-Quality book Formatting -

musaicumbooks@okpublishing.info

2021 OK Publishing

ISBN 978-80-272-7635-6

Contents

Sentimental Tommy

Chapter I
Tommy Contrives to Keep One Out

The celebrated Tommy first comes into view on a dirty London stair, and he was in sexless garments, which were all he had, and he was five, and so though we are looking at him, we must do it sideways, lest he sit down hurriedly to hide them. That inscrutable face, which made the clubmen of his later days uneasy and even puzzled the ladies while he was making love to them, was already his, except when he smiled at one of his pretty thoughts or stopped at an open door to sniff a potful. On his way up and down the stair he often paused to sniff, but he never asked for anything; his mother had warned him against it, and he carried out her injunction with almost unnecessary spirit, declining offers before they were made, as when passing a room, whence came the smell of fried fish, he might call in, "I don't not want none of your fish," or "My mother says I don't not want the littlest bit," or wistfully, "I ain't hungry," or more wistfully still, "My mother says I ain't hungry." His mother heard of this and was angry, crying that he had let the neighbors know something she was anxious to conceal, but what he had revealed to them Tommy could not make out, and when he questioned her artlessly, she took him with sudden passion to her flat breast, and often after that she looked at him long and woefully and wrung her hands.

The only other pleasant smell known to Tommy was when the water-carts passed the mouth of his little street. His street, which ended in a dead wall, was near the river, but on the doleful south side of it, opening off a longer street where the cabs of Waterloo station sometimes found themselves when they took the wrong turning; his home was at the top of a house of four floors, each with accommodation for at least two families, and here he had lived with his mother since his father's death six months ago. There was oil-cloth on the stair as far as the second floor; there had been oil-cloth between the second floor and the third-Tommy could point out pieces of it still adhering to the wood like remnants of a plaster.

This stair was nursery to all the children whose homes opened on it, not so safe as nurseries in the part of London that is chiefly inhabited by boys in sailor suits, but preferable as a centre of adventure, and here on an afternoon sat two. They were very busy boasting, but only the smaller had imagination, and as he used it recklessly, their positions soon changed; sexless garments was now prone on a step, breeches sitting on him.

Shovel, a man of seven, had said, "None on your lip. You weren't never at Thrums yourself."

Tommy's reply was, "Ain't my mother a Thrums woman?"

Shovel, who had but one eye, and that bloodshot, fixed it on him threateningly.

"The Thames is in London," he said.

"'Cos they wouldn't not have it in Thrums," replied Tommy.

"'Amstead 'Eath's in London, I tell yer," Shovel said.

"The cemetery is in Thrums," said Tommy.

"There ain't no queens in Thrums, anyhow."

"There's the auld licht minister."

"Well, then, if you jest seed Trafalgar Square!"

"If you jest seed the Thrums town-house!"

"St. Paul's ain't in Thrums."

"It would like to be."

After reflecting, Shovel said in desperation, "Well, then, my father were once at a hanging."

Tommy replied instantly, "It were my father what was hanged."

There was no possible answer to this save a knock-down blow, but though Tommy was vanquished in body, his spirit remained stanch; he raised his head and gasped, "You should see how they knock down in Thrums!" It was then that Shovel sat on him.

Such was their position when an odd figure in that house, a gentleman, passed them without a word, so desirous was he to make a breath taken at the foot of the close stair last him to the top. Tommy merely gaped after this fine sight, but Shovel had experience, and "It's a kid or a coffin." he said sharply, knowing that only birth or death brought a doctor here.

Watching the doctor's ascent, the two boys strained their necks over the rickety banisters, which had been polished black by trousers of the past, and sometimes they lost him, and then they saw his legs again.

"Hello, it's your old woman!" cried Shovel. "Is she a deader?" he asked, brightening, for funerals made a pleasant stir on the stair.

The question had no meaning for bewildered Tommy, but he saw that if his mother was a deader, whatever that might be, he had grown great in his companion's eye. So he hoped she was a deader.

"If it's only a kid," Shovel began, with such scorn that Tommy at once screamed, "It ain't!" and, cross-examined, he swore eagerly that his mother was in bed when he left her in the morning, that she was still in bed at dinner-time, also that the sheet was over her face, also that she was cold.

Then she was a deader and had attained distinction in the only way possible in that street. Shovel did not shake Tommy's hand warmly, the forms of congratulation varying in different parts of London, but he looked his admiration so plainly that Tommy's head waggled proudly. Evidently, whatever his mother had done redounded to his glory as well as to hers, and somehow he had become a boy of mark. He said from his elevation that he hoped Shovel would believe his tales about Thrums now, and Shovel, who had often cuffed Tommy for sticking to him so closely, cringed in the most snobbish manner, craving permission to be seen in his company for the next three days. Tommy, the upstart, did not see his way to grant this favor for nothing, and Shovel offered a knife, but did not have it with him; it was his sister Ameliar's knife, and he would take it from her, help his davy. Tommy would wait there till Shovel fetched it. Shovel, baffled, wanted to know what Tommy was putting on hairs for. Tommy smiled, and asked whose mother was a deader. Then Shovel collapsed, and his wind passed into Tommy.

The reign of Thomas Sandys, nevertheless, was among the shortest, for with this question was he overthrown: "How did yer know she were cold?"

"Because," replied Tommy, triumphantly, "she tell me herself."

Shovel only looked at him, but one eye can be so much more terrible than two, that plop, plop, plop came the balloon softly down the steps of the throne and at the foot shrank pitifully, as if with Ameliar's knife in it.

"It's only a kid arter all!" screamed Shovel, furiously. Disappointment gave him eloquence, and Tommy cowered under his sneers, not understanding them, but they seemed to amount to this, that in having a baby he had disgraced the house.

"But I think," he said, with diffidence, "I think I were once one."

Then all Shovel could say was that he had better keep it dark on that stair.

Tommy squeezed his fist into one eye, and the tears came out at the other. A good-natured impulse was about to make Shovel say that though kids are undoubtedly humiliations, mothers and boys get used to them in time, and go on as brazenly as before, but it was checked by Tommy's unfortunate question, "Shovel, when will it come?"

Shovel, speaking from local experience, replied truthfully that they usually came very soon after the doctor, and at times before him.

"It ain't come before him," Tommy said, confidently.

"How do yer know?"

"'Cos it weren't there at dinner-time, and I been here since dinner-time."

The words meant that Tommy thought it could only enter by way of the stair, and Shovel quivered with delight. "H'st!" he cried, dramatically, and to his joy Tommy looked anxiously down the stair, instead of up it.

"Did you hear it?" Tommy whispered.

Before he could control himself Shovel blurted out: "Do you think as they come on their feet?"

"How then?" demanded Tommy; but Shovel had exhausted his knowledge of the subject. Tommy, who had begun to descend to hold the door, turned and climbed upwards, and his tears were now but the drop left in a cup too hurriedly dried. Where was he off to? Shovel called after him; and he answered, in a determined whisper: "To shove of it out if it tries to come in at the winder."

This was enough for the more knowing urchin, now so full of good things that with another added he must spill, and away he ran for an audience, which could also help him to bait Tommy, that being a game most sportive when there are several to fling at once. At the door he knocked over, and was done with, a laughing little girl who had strayed from a more fashionable street. She rose solemnly, and kissing her muff, to reassure it if it had got a fright, toddled in at the first open door to be out of the way of unmannerly boys.

Tommy, climbing courageously, heard the door slam, and looking down he saw —a strange child. He climbed no higher. It had come.

After a long time he was one flight of stairs nearer it. It was making itself at home on the bottom step; resting, doubtless, before it came hopping up. Another dozen steps, and-It was beautifully dressed in one piece of yellow and brown that reached almost to its feet, with a bit left at the top to form a hood, out of which its pert face peeped impudently; oho, so they came in their Sunday clothes. He drew so near that he could hear it cooing: thought itself as good as upstairs, did it!

He bounced upon her sharply, thinking to carry all with a high hand. "Out you go!" he cried, with the action of one heaving coals.

She whisked round, and, "Oo boy or oo girl?" she inquired, puzzled by his dress.

"None of your cheek!" roared insulted manhood.

"Oo boy," she said, decisively.

With the effrontery of them when they are young, she made room for him on her step, but he declined the invitation, knowing that her design was to skip up the stair the moment he was off his guard.

"You don't needn't think as we'll have you," he announced, firmly. "You had best go away to-go to —" His imagination failed him. "You had best go back," he said.

She did not budge, however, and his next attempt was craftier. "My mother," he assured her, "ain't living here now;" but mother was a new word to the girl, and she asked gleefully, "Oo have mother?" expecting him to produce it from his pocket. To coax him to give her a sight of it she said, plaintively, "Me no have mother."

"You won't not get mine," replied Tommy doggedly.

She pretended not to understand what was troubling him, and it passed through his head that she had to wait there till the doctor came down for her. He might come at any moment.

A boy does not put his hand into his pocket until every other means of gaining his end has failed, but to that extremity had Tommy now come. For months his only splendid possession had been a penny despised by trade because of a large round hole in it, as if (to quote Shovel) some previous owner had cut a farthing out of it. To tell the escapades of this penny (there are no adventurers like coin of the realm) would be one way of exhibiting Tommy to the curious, but it would be a hard-hearted way. At present the penny was doubly dear to him, having been long lost and lately found. In a noble moment he had dropped it into a charity box hanging forlorn against the wall of a shop, where it lay very lonely by itself, so that when Tommy was that way he could hear it respond if he shook the box, as acquaintances give each other the time of day in passing. Thus at comparatively small outlay did he spread his benevolence over weeks and feel a glow therefrom, until the glow went, when he and Shovel recaptured the penny with a thread and a bent pin.

This treasure he sadly presented to the girl, and she accepted it with glee, putting it on her finger, as if it were a ring, but instead of saying that she would go now she asked him, coolly,

"Oo know tories?"

"Stories!" he exclaimed, "I'll —I'll tell you about Thrums," and was about to do it for love, but stopped in time. "This ain't a good stair for stories," he said, cunningly. "I can't not tell stories on this stair, but I —I know a good stair for stories."

The ninny of a girl was completely hoodwinked; and see, there they go, each with a hand in the muff, the one leering, oh, so triumphantly; the other trusting and gleeful. There was an exuberance of vitality about her as if she lived too quickly in her gladness, which you may remember in some child who visited the earth for but a little while.

How superbly Tommy had done it! It had been another keen brain pitted against his, and at first he was not winning. Then up came Thrums, and-But the thing has happened before; in a word, Blücher. Nevertheless, Tommy just managed it, for he got the girl out of the street and on to another stair no more than in time to escape a ragged rabble, headed by Shovel, who, finding their quarry gone, turned on their leader viciously, and had gloomy views of life till his cap was kicked down a sewer, which made the world bright again.

Of the tales told by Tommy that day in words Scotch and cockney, of Thrums, home of heroes and the arts, where the lamps are lit by a magician called Leerie-leerie-licht-the-lamps (but he is also friendly, and you can fling stones at him), and the merest children are allowed to set the spinning-wheels a-whirling, and dagont is the swear, and the stairs are so fine that the houses wear them outside for show, and you drop a pail at the end of a rope down a hole, and sometimes it comes up full of water, and sometimes full of fairies-of these and other wonders, if you would know, ask not a dull historian, nor even go to Thrums, but to those rather who have been boys and girls there and now are exiles. Such a one Tommy knows, an unhappy woman, foolish, not very lovable, flung like a stone out of the red quarry upon a land where it cannot grip, and tearing her heart for a sight of the home she shall see no more. From her Tommy had his pictures, and he colored them rarely.

Never before had he such a listener. "Oh, dagont, dagont!" he would cry in ecstasy over these fair scenes, and she, awed or gurgling with mirth according to the nature of the last, demanded "'Nother, 'nother!" whereat he remembered who and what she was, and showing her a morsel of the new one, drew her to more distant parts, until they were so far from his street that he thought she would never be able to find the way back.

His intention had been, on reaching such a spot, to desert her promptly, but she gave him her hand in the muff so confidingly that against his judgment he fell a-pitying the trustful mite who was wandering the world in search of a mother, and so easily diddled on the whole that the chances were against her finding one before morning. Almost unconsciously he began to look about him for a suitable one.

They were now in a street much nearer to his own home than the spurts from spot to spot had led him to suppose. It was new to him, but he recognized it as the acme of fashion by those two sure signs; railings with most of their spikes in place, and cards scored with, the word "Apartments." He had discovered such streets as this before when in Shovel's company, and they had watched the toffs go out and in, and it was a lordly sight, for first the toff waggled a rail that was loose at the top and then a girl, called the servant, peeped at him from below, and then he pulled the rail again, and then the door opened from the inside, and you had a glimpse of wonder-land with a place for hanging hats on. He had not contemplated doing anything so handsome for the girl as this, but why should he not establish her here? There were many possible mothers in view, and thrilling with a sense of his generosity he had almost fixed on one but mistrusted the glint in her eye and on another when she saved herself by tripping and showing an undarned heel.

He was still of an open mind when the girl of a sudden cried, gleefully, "Ma-ma, ma-ma!" and pointed, with her muff, across the street. The word was as meaningless to Tommy as mother had been to her, but he saw that she was drawing his attention to a woman some thirty yards away.

"Man-man!" he echoed, chiding her ignorance; "no, no, you blether, that ain't a man, that's a woman; that's woman-woman."

"Ooman-ooman," the girl repeated, docilely, but when she looked again, "Ma-ma, ma-ma," she insisted, and this was Tommy's first lesson that however young you catch them they will never listen to reason.

She seemed of a mind to trip off to this woman, and as long as his own mother was safe, it did not greatly matter to Tommy whom she chose, but if it was this one, she was going the wrong way about it. You cannot snap them up in the street.

The proper course was to track her to her house, which he proceeded to do, and his quarry, who was looking about her anxiously, as if she had lost something, gave him but a short chase. In the next street to the one in which they had first seen her, a street so like it that Tommy might have admired her for knowing the difference, she opened the door with a key and entered, shutting the door behind her. Odd to tell, the child had pointed to this door as the one she would stop at, which surprised Tommy very much.

On the steps he gave her his final instructions, and she dimpled and gurgled, obviously full of admiration for him, which was a thing he approved of, but he would have liked to see her a little more serious.

"That is the door. Well, then, I'll waggle the rail as makes the bell ring, and then I'll run."

That was all, and he wished she had not giggled most of the time. She was sniggering, as if she thought him a very funny boy, even when he rang the bell and bolted.

From a safe place he watched the opening of the door, and saw the frivolous thing lose a valuable second in waving the muff to him. "In you go!" he screamed beneath his breath. Then she entered and the door closed. He waited an hour, or two minutes, or thereabout, and she had not been ejected. Triumph!

With a drum beating inside him Tommy strutted home, where, alas, a boy was waiting to put his foot through it.

To Tommy, a swaggerer, came Shovel sour-visaged; having now no cap of his own, he exchanged with Tommy, would also have bled the blooming mouth of him, but knew of a revenge that saves the knuckles: announced, with jeers and offensive finger exercise, that "it" had come.

Shovel was a liar. If he only knowed what Tommy knowed!

If Tommy only heard what Shovel had heard!

Tommy was of opinion that Shovel hadn't not heard anything.

Shovel believed as Tommy didn't know nuthin.

Tommy wouldn't listen to what Shovel had heard.

Neither would Shovel listen to what Tommy knew.

If Shovel would tell what he had heard, Tommy would tell what he knew.

Well, then, Shovel had listened at the door, and heard it mewling.

Tommy knowed it well, and it never mewled.

How could Tommy know it?

'Cos he had been with it a long time.

Gosh! Why, it had only comed a minute ago.

This made Tommy uneasy, and he asked a leading question cunningly. A boy, wasn't it?

No, Shovel's old woman had been up helping to hold it, and she said it were a girl.

Shutting his mouth tightly; which was never natural to him, the startled Tommy mounted the stair, listened and was convinced. He did not enter his dishonored home. He had no intention of ever entering it again. With one salt tear he renounced —a child, a mother.

On his way downstairs he was received by Shovel and party, who planted their arrows neatly. Kids cried steadily, he was told, for the first year. A boy one was bad enough, but a girl one was oh lawks. He must never again expect to get playing with blokes like what they was. Already she had got round his old gal who would care for him no more. What would they say about this in Thrums?

Shovel even insisted on returning him his cap, and for some queer reason, this cut deepest. Tommy about to charge, with his head down, now walked away so quietly that Shovel, who could not help liking the funny little cuss, felt a twinge of remorse, and nearly followed him with a magnanimous offer: to treat him as if he were still respectable.

Tommy lay down on a distant stair, one of the very stairs where *she* had sat with him. Ladies, don't you dare to pity him now, for he won't stand it. Rage was what he felt, and a man in a rage (as you may know if you are married) is only to be soothed by the sight of all womankind in terror of him. But you may look upon your handiwork, and gloat, an you will, on the wreck you have made. A young gentleman trusted one of you; behold the result. O! O! O! O! now do you understand why we men cannot abide you?

If she had told him flat that his mother, and his alone, she would have, and so there was an end of it. Ah, catch them taking a straight road. But to put on those airs of helplessness, to wave him that gay good-by, and then the moment his back was turned, to be off through the air on-perhaps on her muff, to the home he had thought to lure her from. In a word, to be diddled by a girl when one flatters himself he is diddling! S'death, a dashing fellow finds it hard to bear. Nevertheless, he has to bear it, for oh, Tommy, Tommy, 'tis the common lot of man.

His hand sought his pocket for the penny that had brought him comfort in dark hours before now; but, alack, she had deprived him even of it. Never again should his pinkie finger go through that warm hole, and at the thought a sense of his forlornness choked him and he cried. You may pity him a little now.

Darkness came and hid him even from himself. He is not found again until a time of the night that is not marked on ornamental clocks, but has an hour to itself on the watch which a hundred thousand or so of London women carry in their breasts; the hour when men steal homewards trickling at the mouth and drawing back from their own shadows to the wives they once went a-maying with, or the mothers who had such travail at the bearing of them, as if for great ends. Out of this, the drunkard's hour, rose the wan face of Tommy, who had waked up somewhere clammy cold and quaking, and he was a very little boy, so he ran to his mother.

Such a shabby dark room it was, but it was home, such a weary worn woman in the bed, but he was her son, and she had been wringing her hands because he was so long in coming, and do you think he hurt her when he pressed his head on her poor breast, and do you think she grudged the heat his cold hands drew from her warm face? He squeezed her with a violence that put more heat into her blood than he took out of it.

And he was very considerate, too: not a word of reproach in him, though he knew very well what that bundle in the back of the bed was.

She guessed that he had heard the news and stayed away through jealousy of his sister, and by and by she said, with a faint smile, "I have a present for you, laddie." In the great world without, she used few Thrums words now; you would have known she was Scotch by her accent only, but when she and Tommy were together in that room, with the door shut, she always spoke as if her window still looked out on the bonny Marywellbrae. It is not really bonny, it is gey an' mean an' bleak, and you must not come to see it. It is just a steep wind-swept street, old and wrinkled, like your mother's face.

She had a present for him, she said, and Tommy replied, "I knows," with averted face.

"Such a bonny thing."

"Bonny enough," he said bitterly.

"Look at her, laddie."

But he shrank from the ordeal, crying, "No, no, keep her covered up!"

The little traitor seemed to be asleep, and so he ventured to say, eagerly, "It wouldn't not take long to carry all our things to another house, would it? Me and Shovel could near do it ourselves."

"And that's God's truth," the woman said, with a look round the room.
"But what for should we do that?"

"Do you no see, mother?" he whispered excitedly. "Then you and me could slip away, and-and leave her-in the press."

The feeble smile with which his mother received this he interpreted thus, "Wherever we go'd to she would be there before us."

"The little besom!" he cried helplessly.

His mother saw that mischievous boys had been mounting him on his horse, which needed only one slap to make it go a mile; but she was a spiritless woman, and replied indifferently, "You're a funny litlin."

Presently a dry sob broke from her, and thinking the child was the cause, soft-hearted Tommy said, "It can't not be helped, mother; don't cry, mother, I'm fond on yer yet, mother; I —I took her away. I found another woman-but she would come."

"She's God's gift, man," his mother said, but she added, in a different tone, "Ay, but he hasna sent her keep."

"God's gift!" Tommy shuddered, but he said sourly, "I wish he would take her back. Do you wish that, too, mother?"

The weary woman almost said she did, but her arms-they gripped the baby as if frightened that he had sent for it. Jealous Tommy, suddenly deprived of his mother's hand, cried, "It's true what Shovel says, you don't not love me never again; you jest loves that little limmer!"

"Na, na," the mother answered, passionate at last, "she can never be to me what you hae been, my laddie, for you came to me when my hame was in hell, and we tholed it thegither, you and me.'"

This bewildered though it comforted him. He thought his mother might be speaking about the room in which they had lived until six months ago, when his father was put into the black box, but when he asked her if this were so, she told him to sleep, for she was dog-tired. She always evaded him in this way when he questioned her about his past, but at times his mind would wander backwards unbidden to those distant days, and then he saw flitting dimly through them the elusive form of a child. He knew it was himself, and for moments he could see it clearly, but when he moved a step nearer it was not there. So does the child we once were play hide and seek with us among the mists of infancy, until one day he trips and falls into the daylight. Then we seize him, and with that touch we two are one. It is the birth of self-consciousness.

Hitherto he had slept at the back of his mother's bed, but to-night she could not have him there, the place being occupied, and rather sulkily he consented to lie crosswise at her feet, undressing by the feeble fire and taking care, as he got into bed, not to look at the usurper. His mother watched him furtively, and was relieved to read in his face that he had no recollection of ever having slept at the foot of a bed before. But soon after he fell asleep he awoke, and was afraid to move lest his father should kick him. He opened his eyes stealthily, and this was neither the room nor the bed he had expected to see.

The floor was bare save for a sheepskin beside the bed. Tommy always stood on the sheepskin while he was dressing because it was warm to the feet, though risky, as your toes sometimes caught in knots in it. There was a deal table in the middle of the floor with some dirty crockery on it and a kettle that would leave a mark, but they had been left there by Shovel's old girl, for Mrs. Sandys usually kept her house clean. The chairs were of the commonest, and the press door would not remain shut unless you stuck a knife between its halves; but there, was a gay blue wardrobe, spotted white where Tommy's mother had scraped off the mud that had once bespattered it during a lengthy sojourn at the door of a shop; and on the mantelpiece was a clock in a little brown and yellow house, and on the clock a Bible that had been in Thrums. But what Tommy was proudest of was his mother's kist, to which the chests of Londoners are not to be compared, though like it in appearance. On the inside of the lid of this kist was pasted, after a Thrums custom, something that his mother called her marriage lines, which she forced Shovel's mother to come up and look at one day, when that lady had made an innuendo Tommy did not understand, and Shovel's mother had looked, and though she could not read, was convinced, knowing them by the shape.

Tommy lay at the foot of the bed looking at this room, which was his home now, and trying to think of the other one, and by and by the fire helped him by falling to ashes, when darkness came in, and packing the furniture in grotesque cloths, removed it piece by piece, all but the clock. Then the room took a new shape. The fireplace was over there instead of here, the torn yellow blind gave way to one made of spars of green wood, that were bunched up at one side, like a lady out for a walk. On a round table there was a beautiful blue cloth, with very few gravy marks, and here a man ate beef when a woman and a boy ate bread, and near the fire was the man's big soft chair, out of which you could pull hairs, just as if it were Shovel's sister.

Of this man who was his father he could get no hold. He could feel his presence, but never see him. Yet he had a face. It sometimes pressed Tommy's face against it in order to hurt him, which it could do, being all short needles at the chin.

Once in those days Tommy and his mother ran away and hid from some one. He did not know from whom nor for how long, though it was but for a week, and it left only two impressions on his mind, the one that he often asked, "Is this starving now, mother?" the other that before turning a corner she always peered round it fearfully. Then they went back again to the man and he laughed when he saw them, but did not take his feet off the mantelpiece. There came a time when the man was always in bed, but still Tommy could not see his face. What he did see was the man's clothes lying on the large chair just as he had placed them there when he undressed for the last time. The black coat and worsted waistcoat which he could take off together were on the seat, and the light trousers hung over the side, the legs on the hearthrug, with the red socks still sticking in them: a man without a body.

But the boy had one vivid recollection of how his mother received the news of his father's death. An old man with a white beard and gentle ways, who often came to give the invalid physic, was standing at the bedside, and Tommy and his mother were sitting on the fender. The old man came to her and said, "It is all over," and put her softly into the big chair. She covered her face with her hands, and he must have thought she was crying, for he tried to comfort her. But as soon as he was gone she rose, with such a queer face, and went on tiptoe to the bed, and looked intently at her husband, and then she clapped her hands joyously three times.

At last Tommy fell asleep with his mouth open, which is the most important thing that has been told of him as yet, and while he slept day came and restored the furniture that night had stolen. But when the boy woke he did not even notice the change; his brain traversed the hours it had lost since he lay down as quickly as you may put on a stopped clock, and with his first tick he was thinking of nothing but the deceiver in the back of the bed. He raised his head, but could only see that she had crawled under the coverlet to escape his wrath. His mother was asleep. Tommy sat up and peeped over the edge of the bed, then he let his eyes wander round the room; he was looking for the girl's clothes, but they were nowhere to be seen. It is distressing to have to tell that what was in his mind was merely the recovery of his penny. Perhaps as they were Sunday clothes she had hung them up in the wardrobe? He slipped on to the floor and crossed to the wardrobe, but not even the muff could he find. Had she been tired, and gone to bed in them? Very softly he crawled over his mother, and pulling the coverlet off the child's face, got the great shock of his childhood.

It was another one!

Chapter III
Showing How Tommy was Suddenly Transformed Into a Young Gentleman

It would have fared ill with Mrs. Sandys now, had her standoffishness to her neighbors been repaid in the same coin, but they were full of sympathy, especially Shovel's old girl, from whom she had often drawn back offensively on the stair, but who nevertheless waddled up several times a day with savory messes, explaining, when Mrs. Sandys sniffed, that it was not the tapiocar but merely the cup that smelt of gin. When Tommy returned the cups she noticed not only that they were suspiciously clean, but that minute particles of the mess were adhering to his nose and chin (perched there like shipwrecked mariners on a rock, just out of reach of the devouring element), and after this discovery she brought two cupfuls at a time. She was an Irish, woman who could have led the House of Commons, and in walking she seldom raised her carpet shoes from the ground, perhaps because of her weight, for she had an expansive figure that bulged in all directions, and there were always bits of her here and there that she had forgotten to lace. Round the corner was a delightful eating-house, through whose window you were allowed to gaze at the great sweating dumplings, and Tommy thought Shovel's mother was rather like a dumpling that had not been a complete success. If he ever knew her name he forgot it. Shovel, who probably had another name also, called her his old girl or his old woman or his old lady, and it was a sight to see her chasing him across the street when she was in liquor, and boastful was Shovel of the way she could lay on, and he was partial to her too, and once when she was giving it to him pretty strong with the tongs, his father (who followed many professions, among them that of finding lost dogs), had struck her and told her to drop it, and then Shovel sauced his father for interfering, saying she should lick him as long as she blooming well liked, which made his father go for him with a dog-collar; and that was how Shovel lost his eye.

For reasons less unselfish than his old girl's Shovel also was willing to make up to Tommy at this humiliating time. It might be said of these two boys that Shovel knew everything but Tommy knew other things, and as the other things are best worth hearing of Shovel liked to listen to them, even when they were about Thrums, as they usually were. The very first time Tommy told him of the wondrous spot, Shovel had drawn a great breath, and said, thoughtfully:

"I allers knowed as there were sich a beauty place, but I didn't jest know its name."

"How could yer know?" Tommy asked jealously.

"I ain't sure," said Shovel, "p'raps I dreamed on it."

"That's it," Tommy cried. "I tell yer, everybody dreams on it!" and Tommy was right; everybody dreams of it, though not all call it Thrums.

On the whole, then, the coming of the kid, who turned out to be called Elspeth, did not ostracize Tommy, but he wished that he had let the other girl in, for he never doubted that her admittance would have kept this one out. He told neither his mother nor his friend of the other girl, fearing that his mother would be angry with him when she learned what she had missed, and that Shovel would crow over his blundering, but occasionally he took a side glance at the victorious infant, and a poorer affair, he thought, he had never set eyes on. Sometimes it was she who looked at him, and then her chuckle of triumph was hard to bear. As long as his mother was there, however, he endured in silence, but the first day she went out in a vain search for work (it is about as difficult to get washing as to get into the Cabinet), he gave the infant a piece of his mind, poking up her head with a stick so that she was bound to listen.

"You thinks as it was clever on you, does yer? Oh, if I had been on the stair!

"You needn't not try to get round me. I likes the other one five times better; yes, three times better.

"Thievey, thievey, thief, that's her place you is lying in. What?

"If you puts out your tongue at me again —! What do yer say?

"She was twice bigger than you. You ain't got no hair, nor yet no teeth. You're the littlest I ever seed. Eh? Don't not speak then, sulks!"

Prudence had kept him away from the other girl, but he was feeling a great want: someone to applaud him. When we grow older we call it sympathy. How Reddy (as he called her because she had beautiful red-brown hair) had appreciated him! She had a way he liked of opening her eyes very wide when she looked at him. Oh, what a difference from that thing in the back of the bed!

Not the mere selfish desire to see her again, however, would take him in quest of Reddy. He was one of those superior characters, was Tommy, who got his pleasure in giving it, and therefore gave it. Now, Reddy was a worthy girl. In suspecting her of overreaching him he had maligned her: she had taken what he offered, and been thankful. It was fitting that he should give her a treat: let her see him again.

His mother was at last re-engaged by her old employers, her supplanter having proved unsatisfactory, and as the work lay in a distant street, she usually took the kid with her, thus leaving no one to spy on Tammy's movements. Reddy's reward for not playing him false, however, did not reach her as soon as doubtless she would have liked, because the first two or three times he saw her she was walking with the lady of his choice, and of course he was not such a fool as to show himself. But he walked behind them and noted with satisfaction that the lady seemed to be reconciled to her lot and inclined to let bygones be bygones; when at length Reddy and her patron met, Tommy thought this a good sign too, that Ma-ma (as she would call the lady) had told her not to go farther away than the lamp-post, lest she should get lost again. So evidently she had got lost once already, and the lady had been sorry. He asked Reddy many shrewd questions about how Ma-ma treated her, and if she got the top of the Sunday egg and had the licking of the pan and wore flannel underneath and slept at the back; and the more he inquired, the more clearly he saw that he had got her one of the right kind.

Tommy arranged with her that she should always be on the outlook for him at the window, and he would come sometimes, and after that they met frequently, and she proved a credit to him, gurgling with mirth at his tales of Thrums, and pinching him when he had finished, to make sure that he was really made just like common human beings. He was a thin, pale boy, while she looked like a baby rose full blown in a night because her time was short; and his movements were sluggish, but if she was not walking she must be dancing, and sometimes when there were few people in the street, the little armful of delight that she was jumped up and down like a ball, while Tommy kept the time, singing "Thrummy, Thrummy, Thrum Thrum Thrummy." They must have seemed a quaint pair to the lady as she sat at her window watching them and beckoning to Tommy to come in.

One day he went in, but only because she had come up behind and taken his hand before he could run. Then did Tommy quake, for he knew from Reddy how the day after the mother-making episode, Ma-ma and she had sought in vain for his door, and he saw that the object had been to call down curses on his head. So that head was hanging limply now.

You think that Tommy is to be worsted at last, but don't be too sure; you just wait and see. Ma-ma and Reddy (who was clucking rather heartlessly) first took him into a room prettier even than the one he had lived in long ago (but there was no bed in it), and then, because someone they were in search of was not there, into another room without a bed (where on earth did they sleep?) whose walls were lined with books. Never having seen rows of books before except on sale in the streets, Tommy at once looked about him for the barrow. The table was strewn with sheets of paper of the size that they roll a quarter of butter in, and it was an amazing thick table, a solid square of wood, save for a narrow lane down the centre for the man to put his legs in-if he had legs, which unfortunately there was reason to doubt. He was a formidable man, whose beard licked the table while he wrote, and he wore something like a brown blanket, with a rope tied round it at the middle. Even more uncanny than himself were three busts on a shelf, which Tommy took to be deaders, and he feared the blanket might blow open and show that the man also ended at the waist. But he did not, for presently he turned round to see who had come in (the seat of his chair turning with him in the most startling way) and then Tommy was relieved to notice two big feet far away at the end of him.

"This is the boy, dear," the lady said. "I had to bring him in by force."

Tommy raised his arm instinctively to protect his face, this being the kind of man who could hit hard. But presently he was confused, and also, alas, leering a little. You may remember that Reddy had told him she must not go beyond the lamp-post, lest she should be lost again. She had given him no details of the adventure, but he learned now from Ma-ma and Papa (the man's name was Papa) that she had strayed when Ma-ma was in a shop and that some good kind boy had found her and brought her home; and what do you say to this, they thought Tommy was that boy! In his amazement he very nearly blurted out that he was the other boy, but just then the lady asked Papa if he had a shilling, and this abruptly closed Tommy's mouth. Ever afterwards he remembered Papa as the man that was not sure whether he had a shilling until he felt his pockets —a new kind of mortal to Tommy, who grabbed the shilling when it was offered to him, and then looked at Reddy imploringly, he was so afraid she would tell. But she behaved splendidly, and never even shook her head at him. After this, as hardly need be told, his one desire was to get out of the house with his shilling before they discovered their mistake, and it was well that they were unsuspicious people, for he was making strange hissing sounds in his throat, the result of trying hard to keep his sniggers under control.

There were many ways in which Tommy could have disposed of his shilling. He might have been a good boy and returned it next day to Papa. He might have given Reddy half of it for not telling. It could have carried him over the winter. He might have stalked with it into the shop where the greasy puddings were and come rolling out hours afterwards. Some of these schemes did cross his little mind, but he decided to spend the whole shilling on a present to his mother, and it was to be something useful. He devoted much thought to what she was most in need of, and at last he bought her a colored picture of Lord Byron swimming the Hellespont.

He told her that he got his shilling from two toffs for playing with a little girl, and the explanation satisfied her; but she could have cried at the waste of the money, which would have been such a God-send to her. He cried altogether, however, at sight of her face, having expected it to look so pleased, and then she told him, with caresses, that the picture was the one thing she had been longing for ever since she came to London. How had he known this, she asked, and he clapped his hands gleefully, and said he just knowed when he saw it in the shop window.

"It was noble of you," she said, "to spend all your siller on me."

"Wasn't it, mother?" he crowed "I'm thinking there ain't many as noble as I is!"

He did not say why he had been so good to her, but it was because she had written no letters to Thrums since the intrusion of Elspeth; a strange reason for a boy whose greatest glory at one time had been to sit on the fender and exultingly watch his mother write down words that would be read aloud in the wonderful place. She was a long time in writing a letter, but that only made the whole evening romantic, and he found an arduous employment in keeping his tongue wet in preparation for the licking of the stamp.

But she could not write to the Thrums folk now without telling them of Elspeth, who was at present sleeping the sleep of the shameless in the hollow of the bed, and so for his sake, Tommy thought, she meant to write no more. For his sake, mark you, not for her own. She had often told him that some day he should go to Thrums, but not with her; she would be far away from him then in a dark place she was awid to be lying in. Thus it seemed, to Tommy that she denied herself the pleasure of writing to Thrums lest the sorry news of Elspeth's advent should spoil his reception when he went north.

So grateful Tommy gave her the picture, hoping that it would fill the void. But it did not. She put it on the mantelpiece so that she might just sit and look at it, she said, and he grinned at it from every part of the room, but when he returned to her, he saw that she was neither looking at it nor thinking of it. She was looking straight before her, and sometimes her lips twitched, and then she drew them into her mouth to keep them still. It is a kind of dry weeping that sometimes comes to miserable ones when their minds stray into the happy past, and Tommy sat and watched her silently for a long time, never doubting that the cause of all her woe was that she could not write to Thrums.

He had seldom seen tears on his mother's face, but he saw one now. They had been reluctant to come for many a day, and this one formed itself beneath her eye and sat there like a blob of blood.

His own began to come more freely. But she needn't not expect him to tell her to write nor to say that he didn't care what Thrums thought of him so long as she was happy.

The tear rolled down his mother's thin cheek and fell on the grey shawl that had come from Thrums.

She did not hear her boy as he dragged a chair to the press and standing on it got something down from the top shelf. She had forgotten him, and she started when presently the pen was slipped into her hand and Tommy said, "You can do it, mother, I wants yer to do it, mother, I won't not greet, mother!"

When she saw what he wanted her to do she patted his face approvingly, but without realizing the extent of his sacrifice. She knew that he had some maggot in his head that made him regard Elspeth as a sore on the family honor, but ascribing his views to jealousy she had never tried seriously to change them. Her main reason for sending no news to Thrums of late had been but the cost of the stamp, though she was also a little conscience-stricken at the kind of letters she wrote, and the sight of the materials lying ready for her proved sufficient to draw her to the table.

"Is it to your grandmother you is writing the letter?" Tommy asked, for her grandmother had brought Mrs. Sandys up and was her only surviving relative. This was all Tommy knew of his mother's life in Thrums, though she had told him much about other Thrums folk, and not till long afterwards did he see that there must be something queer about herself, which she was hiding from him.

This letter was not for her granny, however, and Tommy asked next, "Is it to Aaron Latta?" which so startled her that she dropped the pen.

"Whaur heard you that name?" she said sharply. "I never spoke it to you."

"I've heard you saying it when you was sleeping, mother."

"Did I say onything but the name? Quick, tell me."

"You said, 'Oh, Aaron Latta, oh, Aaron, little did we think, Aaron,' and things like that. Are you angry with me, mother?"

"No," she said, relieved, but it was some time before the desire to write came back to her. Then she told him "The letter is to a woman that was gey cruel to me," adding, with a complacent pursing of her lips, the curious remark, "That's the kind I like to write to best."

The pen went scrape, scrape, but Tommy did not weary, though he often sighed, because his mother would never read aloud to him what she wrote. The Thrums people never answered her letters, for the reason, she said, that those she wrote to could not write, which seemed to simple Tommy to be a sufficient explanation. So he had never heard the inside of a letter talking, though a postman lived in the house, and even Shovel's old girl got letters; once when her uncle died she got a telegram, which Shovel proudly wheeled up and down the street in a barrow, other blokes keeping guard at the side. To give a letter to a woman who had been cruel to you struck Tommy as the height of nobility.

"She'll be uplifted when she gets it!" he cried.

"She'll be mad when she gets it," answered his mother, without looking up.

This was the letter: —

"MY DEAR ESTHER, —I send you these few scrapes to let you see I have not forgot you, though my way is now grand by yours. A spleet new black silk, Esther, being the second in a twelvemonth, as I'm a living woman. The other is no none tashed yet, but my gudeman fair insisted on buying a new one, for says he 'Rich folk like as can afford to be mislaird, and nothing's ower braw for my bonny Jean.' Tell Aaron Latta that. When I'm sailing in my silks, Esther, I sometimes picture you turning your wincey again, for I'se uphaud that's all the new frock you've ha'en the year. I dinna want to give you a scunner of your man, Esther, more by token they said if your mither had not took him in hand you would never have kent the color of his nightcap, but when you are wraxing ower your kail-pot in a plot of heat, just picture me ringing the bell for my servant, and saying, with a wave of my hand, 'Servant, lay the dinner.' And ony bonny afternoon when your man is cleaning out stables and you're at the tub in a short gown, picture my man taking me and the children out a ride in a carriage, and I sair doubt your bairns was never in nothing more genteel than a coal cart. For bairns is yours, Esther, and children is mine, and that's a burn without a brig till't.

"Deary me, Esther, what with one thing and another, namely buying a sofa, thirty shillings as I'm a sinner, I have forgot to tell you about my second, and it's a girl this time, my man saying he would like a change. We have christened her Elspeth after my grandmamma, and if my auld granny's aye living, you can tell her that's her. My man is terrible windy of his two beautiful children, but he says he would have been the happiest gentleman in London though he had just had me, and really his fondness for me, it cows, Esther, sitting aside me on the bed, two pounds without the blankets, about the time Elspeth was born, and feeding me with the fat of the land, namely, tapiocas and sherry wine. Tell Aaron Latta that.

"I pity you from the bottom of my heart, Esther, for having to bide in Thrums, but you have never seen no better, your man having neither the siller nor the desire to take yon jaunts, and I'm thinking that is just as well, for if you saw how the like of me lives it might disgust you with your own bit house. I often laugh, Esther, to think that I was once like you, and looked upon Thrums as a bonny place. How is the old hole? My son makes grand sport of the onfortunate bairns as has to bide in Thrums, and I see him doing it the now to his favorite companion, which is a young gentleman of ladylike manners, as bides in our terrace. So no more at present, for my man is sitting ganting for my society, and I daresay yours is crying to you to darn his old socks. Mind and tell Aaron Latta."

This letter was posted next day by Tommy, with the assistance of Shovel, who seems to have been the young gentleman of ladylike manners referred to in the text.

Chapter IV
The End of an Idyll

Tommy never saw Reddy again owing to a fright he got about this time, for which she was really to blame, though a woman who lived in his house was the instrument.

It is, perhaps, idle to attempt a summary of those who lived in that house, as one at least will be off, and another in his place, while we are giving them a line apiece. They were usually this kind who lived through the wall from Mrs. Sandys, but beneath her were the two rooms of Hankey, the postman, and his lodger, the dreariest of middle-aged clerks except when telling wistfully of his ambition, which was to get out of the tea department into the coffee department, where there is an easier way of counting up the figures. Shovel and family were also on this floor, and in the rooms under them was a newly married couple. When the husband was away at his work, his wife would make some change in the furniture, taking the picture from this wall, for instance, and hanging it on that wall, or wheeling the funny chair she had lain in before she could walk without a crutch, to the other side of the fireplace, or putting a skirt of yellow paper round the flower pot, and when he returned he always jumped back in wonder and exclaimed: "What an immense improvement!" These two were so fond of one another that Tommy asked them the reason, and they gave it by pointing to the chair with the wheels, which seemed to him to be no reason at all. What was this young husband's trade Tommy never knew, but he was the only prettily dressed man in the house, and he could be heard roaring in his sleep, *"And the next article?"* The meanest looking man lived next door to him. Every morning this man put on a clean white shirt, which sounds like a splendid beginning, but his other clothes were of the seediest, and he came and went shivering, raising his shoulders to his ears and spreading his hands over his chest as if anxious to hide his shirt rather than to display it. He and the happy husband were nicknamed Before and After, they were so like the pictorial advertisement of Man before and after he has tried Someone's lozenges. But it is rash to judge by outsides; Tommy and Shovel one day tracked Before to his place of business, and it proved to be a palatial eating-house, long, narrow, padded with red cushions; through the door they saw the once despised, now in beautiful black clothes, the waistcoat a mere nothing, as if to give his shirt a chance at last, a towel over his arm, and to and fro he darted, saying "Yessirquitesosir" to the toffs on the seats, shouting "Twovegonebeef-onebeeronetartinahurry" to someone invisible, and pocketing twopences all day long, just like a lord. On the same floor as Before and After lived the large family of little Pikes, who quarrelled at night for the middle place in the bed, and then chips of ceiling fell into the room below, tenant Jim Ricketts and parents, lodger the young woman we have been trying all these doors for. Her the police snapped up on a charge; that made Tommy want to hide himself-child-desertion.

Shovel was the person best worth listening to on the subject (observe him, the centre of half a dozen boys), and at first he was for the defence, being a great stickler for the rights of mothers. But when the case against the girl leaked out, she need not look to him for help. The police had found the child in a basket down an area, and being knowing ones they pinched it to make it cry, and then they pretended to go away. Soon the mother, who was watching hard by to see if it fell into kind hands, stole to her baby to comfort it, "and just as she were a kissing on it and blubbering, the perlice copped her."

"The slut!" said disgusted Shovel, "what did she hang about for?" and in answer to a trembling question from Tommy he replied, decisively, "Six months hard."

"Next case" was probably called immediately, but Tommy vanished, as if he had been sentenced and removed to the cells.

Never again, unless he wanted six months hard, must he go near Reddy's home, and so he now frequently accompanied his mother to the place where she worked. The little room had a funny fireplace called a stove, on which his mother made tea and the girls roasted chestnuts, and it had no other ordinary furniture except a long form. But the walls were mysterious. Three of them were covered with long white cloths, which went to the side when you tugged them, and then you could see on rails dozens of garments that looked like nightgowns. Beneath the form were scores of little shoes, most of them white or brown. In this house Tommy's mother spent eight hours daily, but not all of them in this room. When she arrived the first thing she did was to put Elspeth on the floor, because you cannot fall off a floor; then she went upstairs with a bucket and a broom to a large bare room, where she stayed so long that Tommy nearly forgot what she was like.

While his mother was upstairs Tommy would give Elspeth two or three shoes to eat to keep her quiet, and then he played with the others, pretending to be able to count them, arranging them in designs, shooting them, swimming among them, saying "bow-wow" at them and then turning sharply to see who had said it. Soon Elspeth dropped her shoes and gazed in admiration at him, but more often than not she laughed in the wrong place, and then he said ironically: "Oh, in course I can't do nothin'; jest let's see you doing of it, then, cocky!"

By the time the girls began to arrive, singly or in twos and threes, his mother was back in the little room, making tea for herself or sewing bits of them that had been torn as they stepped out of a cab, or helping them to put on the nightgowns, or pretending to listen pleasantly to their chatter and hating them all the time. There was every kind of them, gorgeous ones and shabby ones, old tired ones and dashing young ones, but whether they were the Honorable Mrs. Something or only Jane Anything, they all came to that room for the same purpose: to get a little gown and a pair of shoes. Then they went upstairs and danced to a stout little lady, called the Sylph, who bobbed about like a ball at the end of a piece of elastic. What Tommy never forgot was that while they danced the Sylph kept saying, "One, two, three, four; one, two, three, four," which they did not seem to mind, but when she said "One, two, three, four, *picture!*" they all stopped and stood motionless, though it might be with one foot as high as their head and their arms stretched out toward the floor, as if they had suddenly seen a halfpenny there.

In the waiting-room, how they joked and pirouetted and gossiped, and hugged and scorned each other, and what slang they spoke and how pretty they often looked next moment, and how they denounced the one that had just gone out as a cat with whom you could not get in a word edgeways, and oh, how prompt they were to give a slice of their earnings to any "cat" who was hard up! But still, they said, she had talent, but no genius. How they pitied people without genius.

Have you ever tasted an encore or a reception? Tommy never had his teeth in one, but he heard much about them in that room, and concluded that they were some sort of cake. It was not the girls who danced in groups, but those who danced alone, that spoke of their encores and receptions, and sometimes they had got them last night, sometimes years ago. Two girls met in the room, one of whom had stolen the other's reception, and-but it was too dreadful to write about. Most of them carried newspaper cuttings in their purses and read them aloud to the others, who would not listen. Tommy listened, however, and as it was all about how one house had risen at the girls and they had brought another down, he thought they led the most adventurous lives.

Occasionally they sent him out to buy newspapers or chestnuts, and then he had to keep a sharp eye on the police lest they knew about Reddy. It was a point of honor with all the boys he knew to pretend that the policeman was after them. To gull the policeman into thinking all was well they blackened their faces and wore their jackets inside out; their occupation was a constant state of readiness to fly from him, and when he tramped out of sight, unconscious of their existence, they emerged from dark places and spoke in exultant whispers. Tommy had been proud to join them, but he now resented their going on in this way; he felt that he alone had the right to fly from the law. And once at least while he was flying something happened to him that he was to remember better, far better, than his mother's face.

What set him running on this occasion (he had been sent out to get one of the girls' shoes soled) was the grandest sight to be seen in London-an endless row of policemen walking in single file, all with the right leg in the air at the same time, then the left leg. Seeing at once that they were after him, Tommy ran, ran, ran until in turning a corner he found himself wedged between two legs. He was of just sufficient size to fill the aperture, but after a momentary look he squeezed through, and they proved to be the gate into an enchanted land.

The magic began at once. "Dagont, you sacket!" cried some wizard.

A policeman's hand on his shoulder could not have taken the wind out of Tommy more quickly. In the act of starting a-running again he brought down his hind foot with a thud and stood stock still. Can any one wonder? It was the Thrums tongue, and this the first time he had heard it except from his mother.

It was a dull day, and all the walls were dripping wet, this being the part of London where the fogs are kept. Many men and women were passing to and fro, and Tommy, with a wild exultation in his breast, peered up at the face of this one and that; but no, they were only ordinary people, and he played rub-a-dub with his feet on the pavement, so furious was he with them for moving on as if nothing had happened. Draw up, ye carters; pedestrians, stand still; London, silence for a moment, and let Tommy Sandys listen!

Being but a frail plant in the way of a flood, Tommy was rooted up and borne onward, but he did not feel the buffeting. In a passion of grief he dug his fists in his eyes, for the glory had been his for but a moment. It can be compared to nothing save the parcel (attached to a concealed string) which Shovel and he once placed on the stair for Billy Hankey to find, and then whipped away from him just as he had got it under his arm. But so near the crying, Tommy did not cry, for even while the tears were rushing to his aid he tripped on the step of a shop, and immediately, as if that had rung the magic bell again, a voice, a woman's voice this time, said shrilly, "Threepence ha'penny, and them jimply as big as a bantam's! Na, na, but I'll gi'e you five bawbees."

Tommy sat down flop on the step, feeling queer in the head. Was it-was it-was it Thrums? He knew he had been running a long time.

The woman, or fairy, or whatever you choose to call her, came out of the shop and had to push Tommy aside to get past. Oh, what a sweet foot to be kicked by. At the time, he thought she was dressed not unlike the women of his own stair, but this defect in his vision he mended afterward, as you may hear. Of course, he rose and trotted by her side like a dog, looking up at her as if she were a cathedral; but she mistook his awe for impudence and sent him sprawling, with the words, "Tak that, you glowering partan!"

Do you think Tommy resented this? On the contrary he screamed from where he lay, "Say it again! say it again!"

She was gone, however, but only, as it were, to let a window open, from which came the cry, "Davit, have you seen my man?"

A male fairy roared back from some invisible place, "He has gone yont to Petey's wi' the dambrod."

"I'll dambrod him!" said the female fairy, and the window shut.

Tommy was now staggering like one intoxicated, but he had still some sense left him, and he walked up and down in front of this house, as if to take care of it. In the middle of the street some boys were very busy at a game, carts and lorries passing over them occasionally. They came to the pavement to play marbles, and then Tommy noticed that one of them wore what was probably a glengarry bonnet. Could he be a Thrums boy?

At first he played in the stupid London way, but by and by he had to make a new ring, and he did it by whirling round on one foot. Tommy knew from his mother that it is only done in this way in Thrums. Oho! Oho!

By this time he was prancing round his discovery, saying, "I'm one, too-so am I —dagont, does yer hear? dagont!" which so alarmed the boy that he picked up his marble and fled, Tommy, of course, after him. Alas! he must have been some mischievous sprite, for he lured his pursuer back into London and then vanished, and Tommy, searching in vain for the enchanted street, found his own door instead.

His mother pooh-poohed his tale, though he described the street exactly as it struck him on reflection, and it bore a curious resemblance to the palace of Aladdin that Reddy had told him about, leaving his imagination to fill in the details, which it promptly did, with a square, a town-house, some outside stairs, and an auld licht kirk. There was no such street, however, his mother assured him; he had been dreaming. But if this were so, why was she so anxious to make him promise never to look for the place again?

He did go in search of it again, daily for a time, always keeping a look-out for bow-legs, and the moment he saw them, he dived recklessly between, hoping to come out into fairyland on the other side. For though he had lost the street, he knew that this was the way in.

Shovel had never heard of the street, nor had Bob. But Bob gave him something that almost made him forget it for a time. Bob was his favorite among the dancing girls, and she-or should it be he? The odd thing about these girls was that a number of them were really boys-or at least were boys at Christmas-time, which seemed to Tommy to be even stranger than if they had been boys all the year round. A friend of Bob's remarked to her one day, "You are to be a girl next winter, ain't you, Bob?" and Bob shook her head scornfully.

"Do you see any green in my eye, my dear?" she inquired.

Her friend did not look, but Tommy looked, and there was none. He assured her of this so earnestly that Bob fell in love with him on the spot, and chucked him under the chin, first with her thumb and then with her toe, which feat was duly reported to Shovel, who could do it by the end of the week.

Did Tommy, Bob wanted to know, still think her a mere woman?

No, he withdrew the charge, but-but-She was wearing her outdoor garments, and he pointed to them, "Why does yer wear them, then?" he demanded.

"For the matter of that," she replied, pointing at his frock, "why do you wear them?" Whereupon Tommy began to cry.

"I ain't not got no right ones," he blubbered. Harum-scarum Bob, who was a trump, had him in her motherly arms immediately, and the upshot of it was that a blue suit she had worn when she was Sam Something changed owners. Mrs. Sandys "made it up," and that is how Tommy got into trousers.

Many contingencies were considered in the making, but the suit would fit Tommy by and by if he grew, or it shrunk, and they did not pass each other in the night. When proud Tommy first put on his suit the most unexpected shyness overcame him, and having set off vaingloriously he stuck on the stair and wanted to hide. Shovel, who had been having an argument with his old girl, came, all boastful bumps, to him, and Tommy just stood still with a self-conscious simper on his face. And Shovel, who could have damped him considerably, behaved in the most honorable manner, initiating him gravely into the higher life, much as you show the new member round your club.

It was very risky to go back to Reddy, whom he had not seen for many weeks; but in trousers! He could not help it. He only meant to walk up and down her street, so that she might see him from the window, and know that this splendid thing was he; but though he went several times into the street, Reddy never came to the window.

The reason he had to wait in vain at Reddy's door was that she was dead; she had been dead for quite a long time when Tommy came back to look for her. You mothers who have lost your babies, I should be a sorry knave were I to ask you to cry now over the death of another woman's child. Reddy had been lent to two people for a very little while, just as your babies were, and when the time was up she blew a kiss to them and ran gleefully back to God, just as your babies did. The gates of heaven are so easily found when we are little, and they are always standing open to let children wander in.

But though Reddy was gone away forever, mamma still lived in that house, and on a day she opened the door to come out, Tommy was standing there-she saw him there waiting for Reddy. Dry-eyed this sorrowful woman had heard the sentence pronounced, dry eyed she had followed the little coffin to its grave; tears had not come even when waking from illusive dreams she put out her hand in bed to a child who was not there; but when she saw Tommy waiting at the door for Reddy, who had been dead for a month, her bosom moved and she could cry again.

Those tears were sweet to her husband, and it was he who took Tommy on his knee in the room where the books were, and told him that there was no Reddy now. When Tommy knew that Reddy was a deader he cried bitterly, and the man said, very gently, "I am glad you were so fond of her."

"'T ain't that," Tommy answered with a knuckle in his eye, "'t ain't that as makes me cry." He looked down at his trousers and in a fresh outburst of childish grief he wailed, "It's them!"

Papa did not understand, but the boy explained. "She can't not never see them now," he sobbed, "and I wants her to see them, and they has pockets!"

It had come to the man unexpectedly. He put Tommy down almost roughly, and raised his hand to his head as if he felt a sudden pain there.

But Tommy, you know, was only a little boy.

Chapter V
The Girl with Two Mothers

Elspeth at last did something to win Tommy's respect; she fell ill of an ailment called in Thrums the croop. When Tommy first heard his mother call it croop, he thought she was merely humoring Elspeth, and that it was nothing more distinguished than London whooping-cough, but on learning that it was genuine croop, he began to survey the ambitious little creature with a new interest.

This was well for Elspeth, as she had now to spend most of the day at home with him, their mother, whose health was failing through frequent attacks of bronchitis, being no longer able to carry her through the streets. Of course Elspeth took to repaying his attentions by loving him, and he soon suspected it, and then gloomily admitted it to himself, but never to Shovel. Being but an Englishman, Shovel saw no reason why relatives should conceal their affection for each other, but he played on this Scottish weakness of Tommy's with cruel enjoyment.

"She's fond on yer!" he would say severely.

"You's a liar."

"Gar long! I believe as you're fond on her!"

"You jest take care, Shovel."

"Ain't yer?"

"Na-o!"

"Will yer swear?"

"So I will swear."

"Let's hear yer."

"Dagont!"

So for a time the truth was kept hidden, and Shovel retired, casting aspersions, and offering to eat all the hair on Elspeth's head for a penny.

This hair was white at present, which made Tommy uneasy about her future, but on the whole he thought he might make something of her if she was only longer. Sometimes he stretched her on the floor, pulling her legs out straight, for she had a silly way of doubling them up, and then he measured her carefully with his mother's old boots. Her growth proved to be distressingly irregular, as one day she seemed to have grown an inch since last night, and then next day she had shrunk two inches.

After her day's work Mrs. Sandys was now so listless that, had not Tommy interfered, Elspeth would have been a backward child. Reddy had been able to walk from the first day, and so of course had he, but this little slow-coach's legs wobbled at the joints, like the blade of a knife without a spring. The question of questions was How to keep her on end?

Tommy sat on the fender revolving this problem, his head resting on his hand: that favorite position of mighty intellects when about to be photographed, Elspeth lay on her stomach on the floor, gazing earnestly at him, as if she knew she was in his thoughts for some stupendous purpose. Thus the apple may have looked at Newton before it fell.

Hankey, the postman, compelled the flowers in his window to stand erect by tying them to sticks, so Tommy took two sticks from a bundle of firewood, and splicing Elspeth's legs to them, held her upright against the door with one hand. All he asked of her to-day was to remain in this position after he said "One, two, three, four, *picture!*" and withdrew his hand, but down she flopped every time, and he said, with scorn,

"You ain't got no genius: you has just talent."

But he had her in bed with the scratches nicely covered up before his mother came home.

He tried another plan with more success. Lost dogs, it may be remembered, had a habit of following Shovel's father, and he not only took the wanderers in, but taught them how to beg and shake hands and walk on two legs. Tommy had sometimes been present at these agreeable exercises, and being an inventive boy he-But as Elspeth was a nice girl, let it suffice to pause here and add shyly, that in time she could walk.

He also taught her to speak, and if you need to be told with what luscious word he enticed her into language you are sentenced to re-read the first pages of his life.

"Thrums," he would say persuasively, "Thrums, Thrums. You opens your mouth like this, and shuts it like this, and that's it." Yet when he had coaxed her thus for many days, what does she do but break her long silence with the word "Tommy!" The recoil knocked her over.

Soon afterward she brought down a bigger bird. No Londoner can say "Auld licht," and Tommy had often crowed over Shovel's "Ol likt." When the testing of Elspeth could be deferred no longer, he eyed her with the look a hen gives the green egg on which she has been sitting twenty days, but Elspeth triumphed, saying the words modestly even, as if nothing inside her told her she had that day done something which would have baffled Shakespeare, not to speak of most of the gentlemen who sit for Scotch constituencies.

"Reddy couldn't say it!" Tommy cried exultantly, and from that great hour he had no more fears for Elspeth.

Next the alphabet knocked for admission; and entered first *M* and *P*, which had prominence in the only poster visible from the window. Mrs. Sandys had taught Tommy his letters, but he had got into words by studying posters.

Elspeth being able now to make the perilous descent of the stairs, Tommy guided her through the streets (letting go hurriedly if Shovel hove in sight), and here she bagged new letters daily. With Catlings something, which is the best, she got into capital _C_s; _y_s are found easily when you know where to look for them (they hang on behind); _N_s are never found singly, but often three at a time; *Q* is so aristocratic that even Tommy had only heard of it, doubtless it was there, but indistinguishable among the masses like a celebrity in a crowd; on the other hand, big *A* and little *e* were so dirt cheap, that these two scholars passed them with something very like a sneer.

The printing-press is either the greatest blessing or the greatest curse of modern times, one sometimes forgets which. Elspeth's faith in it was absolute, and as it only spoke to her from placards, here was her religion, at the age of four:

"PRAY WITHOUT CEASING. HAPPY ARE THEY WHO NEEDING KNOW THE
PAINLESS POROUS PLASTER."

Of religion, Tommy had said many fine things to her, embellishments on the simple doctrine taught him by his mother before the miseries of this world made her indifferent to the next. But the meaning of "Pray without ceasing," Elspeth, who was God's child always, seemed to find out for herself, and it cured all her troubles. She prayed promptly for every one she saw doing wrong, including Shovel, who occasionally had words with Tommy on the subject, and she not only prayed for her mother, but proposed to Tommy that they should buy her a porous plaster. Mrs. Sandys had been down with bronchitis again.

Tommy raised the monetary difficulty.

Elspeth knew where there was some money, and it was her very own.

Tommy knew where there was money, and it was his very own.

Elspeth would not tell how much she had, and it was twopence halfpenny.

Neither would Tommy tell, and it was twopence.

Tommy would get a surprise on his birthday.

So would Elspeth get a surprise on her birthday.

Elspeth would not tell what the surprise was to be, and it was to be a gun.

Tommy also must remain mute, and it was to be a box of dominoes.

Elspeth did not want dominoes.

Tommy knew that, but he wanted them.

Elspeth discovered that guns cost fourpence, and dominoes threepence halfpenny; it seemed to her, therefore, that Tommy was defrauding her of a halfpenny.

Tommy liked her cheek. You got the dominoes for threepence halfpenny, but the price on the box is fivepence, so that Elspeth would really owe him a penny.

This led to an agonizing scene in which Elspeth wept while Tommy told her sternly about Reddy. It had become his custom to tell the tale of Reddy when Elspeth was obstreperous.

Then followed a scene in which Tommy called himself a scoundrel for frightening his dear Elspeth, and swore that he loved none but her. Result: reconciliation, and agreed, that instead of a gun and dominoes, they should buy a porous plaster. You know the shops where the plasters are to be obtained by great colored bottles in their windows, and, as it was advisable to find the very best shop, Tommy and Elspeth in their wanderings came under the influence of the bottles, red, yellow, green, and blue, and color entered into their lives, giving them many delicious thrills. These bottles are the first poem known to the London child, and you chemists who are beginning to do without them in your windows should be told that it is a shame.

In the glamour, then, of the romantic battles walked Tommy and Elspeth hand in hand, meeting so many novelties that they might have spared a tear for the unfortunate children who sit in nurseries surrounded by all they ask for, and if the adventures of these two frequently ended in the middle, they had probably begun another while the sailor-suit boy was still holding up his leg to let the nurse put on his little sock. While they wandered, they drew near unwittingly to the enchanted street, to which the bottles are a colored way, and at last they were in it, but Tommy recognized it not; he did not even feel that he was near it, for there were no outside stairs, no fairies strolling about, it was a short street as shabby as his own.

But someone had shouted "Dinna haver, lassie; you're blethering!"

Tommy whispered to Elspeth, "Be still; don't speak," and he gripped her hand tighter and stared at the speaker. He was a boy of ten, dressed like a Londoner, and his companion had disappeared. Tommy never doubting but that he was the sprite of long ago, gripped him by the sleeve. All the savings of Elspeth and himself were in his pocket, and yielding to impulse, as was his way, he thrust the fivepence halfpenny into James Gloag's hand. The new millionaire gaped, but not at his patron, for the why and wherefore of this gift were trifles to James beside the tremendous fact that he had fivepence halfpenny. "Almichty me!" he cried and bolted. Presently he returned, having deposited his money in a safe place, and his first remark was perhaps the meanest on record. He held out his hand and said greedily, "Have you ony mair?"

This, you feel certain, must have been the most important event of that evening, but strange to say, it was not. Before Tommy could answer James's question, a woman in a shawl had pounced upon him and hurried him and Elspeth out of the street. She had been standing at a corner looking wistfully at the window blinds behind which folk from Thrums passed to and fro, hiding her face from people in the street, but gazing eagerly after them. It was Tommy's mother, whose first free act on coming to London had been to find out that street, and many a time since them site had skulked through it or watched it from dark places, never daring to disclose herself, but sometimes recognizing familiar faces, sometimes hearing a few words in the old tongue that is harsh and ungracious to you, but was so sweet to her, and bearing them away with her beneath her shawl as if they were something warm to lay over her cold heart.

For a time she upbraided Tommy passionately for not keeping away from this street, but soon her hunger for news of Thrums overcame her prudence, and she consented to let him go back if he promised never to tell that his mother came from Thrums. "And if ony-body wants to ken your name, say it's Tommy, but dinna let on that it's Tommy Sandys."

"Elspeth," Tommy whispered that night, "I'm near sure there's something queer about my mother and me and you." But he did not trouble himself with wondering what the something queer might be, so engrossed was he in the new and exciting life that had suddenly opened to him.

Chapter VI
The Enchanted Street

In Thrums Street, as it ought to have been called, herded at least one-half of the Thrums folk in London, and they formed a colony, of which the grocer at the corner sometimes said wrathfully that not a member would give sixpence for anything except Bibles or whiskey. In the streets one could only tell they were not Londoners by their walk, the flagstones having no grip for their feet, or, if they had come south late in life, by their backs, which they carried at the angle on which webs are most easily supported. When mixing with the world they talked the English tongue, which came out of them as broad as if it had been squeezed through a mangle, but when the day's work was done, it was only a few of the giddier striplings that remained Londoners. For the majority there was no raking the streets after diversion, they spent the hour or two before bed-time in reproducing the life of Thrums. Few of them knew much of London except the nearest way between this street and their work, and their most interesting visitor was a Presbyterian minister, most of whose congregation lived in much more fashionable parts, but they were almost exclusively servant girls, and when descending area-steps to visit them he had been challenged often and jocularly by policemen, which perhaps was what gave him a subdued and furtive appearance.

The rooms were furnished mainly with articles bought in London, but these became as like Thrums dressers and seats as their owners could make them, old Petey, for instance, cutting the back off a chair because he felt most at home on stools. Drawers were used as baking-boards, pails turned into salt-buckets, floors were sanded and hearthstones ca'med, and the popular supper consisted of porter, hot water, and soaked bread, after every spoonful of which, they groaned pleasantly, and stretched their legs. Sometimes they played at the dambrod, but more often they pulled down the blinds on London and talked of Thrums in their mother tongue. Nevertheless few of them wanted to return to it, and their favorite joke was the case of James Gloag's father, who being home-sick flung up his situation and took train for Thrums, but he was back in London in three weeks.

Tommy soon had the entry to these homes, and his first news of the inmates was unexpected. It was that they were always sleeping. In broad daylight he had seen Thrums men asleep on beds, and he was somewhat ashamed of them until he heard the excuse. A number of the men from Thrums were bakers, the first emigrant of this trade having drawn others after him, and they slept great part of the day to be able to work all night in a cellar, making nice rolls for rich people. Baker Lumsden, who became a friend of Tommy, had got his place in the cellar when his brother died, and the brother had succeeded Matthew Croall when he died.

They die very soon, Tommy learned from Lumsden, generally when they are eight and thirty. Lumsden was thirty-six, and when he died his nephew was to get the place. The wages are good.

Then there were several masons, one of whom, like the first baker, had found work for all the others, and there were men who had drifted into trades strange to their birthplace, and there was usually one at least who had come to London to "better himself" and had not done it as yet. The family Tommy liked best was the Whamonds, and especially he liked old Petey and young Petey Whamond. They were a large family of women and men, all of whom earned their living in other streets, except the old man, who kept house and was a famous knitter of stockings, as probably his father had been before him. He was a great one, too, at telling what they would be doing at that moment in Thrums, every corner of which was as familiar to him as the ins and outs of the family hose. Young Petey got fourteen shillings a week from a hatter, and one of his duties was to carry as many as twenty band-boxes at a time through fashionable streets; it is a matter for elation that dukes and statesmen had often to take the curb-stone, because young Petey was coming. Nevertheless young Petey was not satisfied, and never would be (such is the Thrums nature) until he became a salesman in the shop to which he acted at present as fetch and carry, and he used to tell Tommy that this position would be his as soon as he could sneer sufficiently at the old hats. When gentlemen come into the shop and buy a new hat, he explained, they put it on, meaning to tell you to send the old one to their address, and the art of being a fashionable hatter lies in this: you must be able to curl your lips so contemptuously at the old hat that they tell you guiltily to keep it, as they have no further use for it. Then they retire ashamed of their want of moral courage and you have made an extra half-guinea.

"But I aye snort," young Petey admitted, "and it should be done without a sound." When he graduated, he was to marry Martha Spens, who was waiting for him at Tillyloss. There was a London seamstress whom he preferred, and she was willing, but it is safest to stick to Thrums.

When Tommy was among his new friends a Scotch word or phrase often escaped his lips, but old Petey and the others thought he had picked it up from them, and would have been content to accept him as a London waif who lived somewhere round the corner. To trick people so simply, however, is not agreeable to an artist, and he told them his name was Tommy Shovel, and that his old girl walloped him, and his father found dogs, all which inventions Thrums Street accepted as true. What is much more noteworthy is that, as he gave them birth, Tommy half believed them also, being already the best kind of actor.

Not all the talking was done by Tommy when he came home with news, for he seldom mentioned a Thrums name, of which his mother could not tell him something more. But sometimes she did not choose to tell, as when he announced that a certain Elspeth Lindsay, of the Marywellbrae, was dead. After this she ceased to listen, for old Elspeth had been her grandmother, and she had now no kin in Thrums.

"Tell me about the Painted Lady," Tommy said to her. "Is it true she's a witch?" But Mrs. Sandys had never heard of any woman so called: the Painted Lady must have gone to Thrums after her time.

"There ain't no witches now," said Elspeth tremulously; Shovel's mother had told her so.

"Not in London," replied Tommy, with contempt; and this is all that was said of the Painted Lady then. It is the first mention of her in these pages.

The people Mrs. Sandys wanted to hear of chiefly were Aaron Latta and Jean Myles, and soon Tommy brought news of them, but at the same time he had heard of the Den, and he said first:

"Oh, mother, I thought as you had told me about all the beauty places in Thrums, and you ain't never told me about the Den."

His mother heaved a quick breath. "It's the only place I hinna telled you o'," she said.

"Had you forget, it mother?"

Forget the Den! Ah, no, Tommy, your mother had not forgotten the Den.

"And, listen, Elspeth, in the Den there's a bonny spring of water called the Cuttle Well. Had you forgot the Cuttle Well, mother?"

No, no; when Jean Myles forgot the names of her children she would still remember the Cuttle Well. Regardless now of the whispering between Tommy and Elspeth, she sat long over the fire, and it is not difficult to fathom her thoughts. They were of the Den and the Cuttle Well.

Into the life of every man, and no woman, there comes a moment when he learns suddenly that he is held eligible for marriage. A girl gives him the jag, and it brings out the perspiration. Of the issue elsewhere of this stab with a bodkin let others speak; in Thrums its commonest effect is to make the callant's body take a right angle to his legs, for he has been touched in the fifth button, and he backs away broken-winded. By and by, however, he is at his work-among the turnip-shoots, say-guffawing and clapping his corduroys, with pauses for uneasy meditation, and there he ripens with the swedes, so that by the back-end of the year he has discovered, and exults to know, that the reward of manhood is neither more nor less than this sensation at the ribs. Soon thereafter, or at worst, sooner or later (for by holding out he only puts the women's dander up), he is led captive to the Cuttle Well. This well has the reputation of being the place where it is most easily said.

The wooded ravine called the Den is in Thrums rather than on its western edge, but is so craftily hidden away that when within a stone's throw you may give up the search for it; it is also so deep that larks rise from the bottom and carol overhead, thinking themselves high in the heavens before they are on a level with Nether Drumley's farmland. In shape it is almost a semicircle, but its size depends on you and the maid. If she be with you, the Den is so large that you must rest here and there; if you are after her boldly, you can dash to the Cuttle Well, which was the trysting-place, in the time a stout man takes to lace his boots; if you are of those self-conscious ones who look behind to see whether jeering blades are following, you may crouch and wriggle your way onward and not be with her in half an hour.

Old Petey had told Tommy that, on the whole, the greatest pleasure in life on a Saturday evening is to put your back against a stile that leads into the Den and rally the sweethearts as they go by. The lads, when they see you, want to go round by the other stile, but the lasses like it, and often the sport ends spiritedly with their giving you a clout on the head.

Through the Den runs a tiny burn, and by its side is a pink path, dyed this pretty color, perhaps, by the blushes the ladies leave behind them. The burn as it passes the Cuttle Well, which stands higher and just out of sight, leaps in vain to see who is making that cooing noise, and the well, taking the spray for kisses, laughs all day at Romeo, who cannot get up. Well is a name it must have given itself, for it is only a spring in the bottom of a basinful of water, where it makes about as much stir in the world as a minnow jumping at a fly. They say that if a boy, by making a bowl of his hands, should suddenly carry off all the water, a quick girl could thread her needle at the spring. But it is a spring that will not wait a moment.

Men who have been lads in Thrums sometimes go back to it from London or from across the seas, to look again at some battered little house and feel the blasts of their bairnhood playing through the old wynds, and they may take with them a foreign wife. They show her everything, except the Cuttle Well; they often go there alone. The well is sacred to the memory of first love. You may walk from the well to the round cemetery in ten minutes. It is a common walk for those who go back.

First love is but a boy and girl playing at the Cuttle Well with a bird's egg. They blow it on one summer evening in the long grass, and on the next it is borne away on a coarse laugh, or it breaks beneath the burden of a tear. And yet—I once saw an aged woman, a widow of many years, cry softly at mention of the Cuttle Well. "John was a good man to you," I said, for John had been her husband. "He was a leal man to me," she answered with wistful eyes, "ay, he was a leal man to me-but it wasna John I was thinking o'. You dinna ken what makes me greet so sair," she added, presently, and though I thought I knew now I was wrong. "It's because I canna mind his name," she said.

So the Cuttle Well has its sad memories and its bright ones, and many of the bright memories have become sad with age, as so often happens to beautiful things, but the most mournful of all is the story of Aaron Latta and Jean Myles. Beside the well there stood for long a great pink stone, called the Shoaging, Stone, because it could be rocked like a cradle, and on it lovers used to cut their names. Often Aaron Latta and Jean Myles sat together on the Shoaging Stone, and then there came a time when it bore these words cut by Aaron Latta:

HERE LIES THE MANHOOD OF AARON LATTA, A FOND SON, A FAITHFUL FRIEND AND A TRUE LOVER, WHO VIOLATED THE FEELINGS OF SEX ON THIS SPOT, AND IS NOW THE SCUNNER OF GOD AND MAN

Tommy's mother now heard these words for the first time, Aaron having cut them on the stone after she left Thrums, and her head sank at each line, as if someone had struck four blows at her.

The stone was no longer at the Cuttle Well. As the easiest way of obliterating the words, the minister had ordered it to be broken, and of the pieces another mason had made stands for watches, one of which was now in Thrums Street.

"Aaron Latta ain't a mason now," Tommy rattled on: "he is a warper, because he can warp in his own house without looking on mankind or speaking to mankind. Auld Petey said he minded the day when Aaron Latta was a merry loon, and then Andrew McVittie said, 'God behears, to think that Aaron Latta was ever a merry man!' and Baker Lumsden said, 'Curse her!'"

His mother shrank in her chair, but said nothing, and Tommy explained: "It was Jean Myles he was cursing; did you ken her, mother? she ruined Aaron Latta's life."

"Ay, and wha ruined Jean Myles's life?" his mother cried passionately.

Tommy did not know, but he thought that young Petey might know, for young Petey had said: "If I had been Jean Myles I would have spat in Aaron's face rather than marry him."

Mrs. Sandys seemed pleased to hear this.

"They wouldna tell me what it were she did," Tommy went on; "they said it was ower ugly a story, but she were a bad one, for they stoned her out of Thrums. I dinna know where she is now, but she were stoned out of Thrums!"

"No alane?"

"There was a man with her, and his name was-it was —"

His mother clasped her hands nervously while Tommy tried to remember the name. "His name was Magerful Tam," he said at length.

"Ay," said his mother, knitting her teeth, "that was his name."

"I dinna mind any more," Tommy concluded. "Yes, I mind they aye called Aaron Latta 'Poor Aaron Latta.'"

"Did they? I warrant, though, there wasna one as said 'Poor Jean Myles'?"

She began the question in a hard voice, but as she said "Poor Jean Myles" something caught in her throat, and she sobbed, painful dry sobs.

"How could they pity her when she were such a bad one?" Tommy answered briskly.

"Is there none to pity bad ones?" said his sorrowful mother.

Elspeth plucked her by the skirt. "There's God, ain't there?" she said, inquiringly, and getting no answer she flopped upon her knees, to say a babyish prayer that would sound comic to anybody except to Him to whom it was addressed.

"You ain't praying for a woman as was a disgrace to Thrums!" Tommy cried, jealously, and he was about to raise her by force, when his mother stayed his hand.

"Let her alane," she said, with a twitching mouth and filmy eyes. "Let her alane. Let my bairn pray for Jean Myles."

Chapter VII
Comic Overture to a Tragedy

"Jean Myles bides in London" was the next remarkable news brought by Tommy from Thrums Street. "And that ain't all, Magerful Tam is her man; and that ain't all, she has a laddie called Tommy and that ain't all, Petey and the rest has never seen her in London, but she writes letters to Thrums folks and they writes to Petey and tells him what she said. That ain't all neither, they canna find out what street she bides in, but it's on the bonny side of London, and it's grand, and she wears silk clothes, and her Tommy has velvet trousers, and they have a servant as calls him 'sir.' Oh, I would just like to kick him! They often looks for her in the grand streets, but they're angry at her getting on so well, and Martha Scrymgeour said it were enough to make good women like her stop going reg'lar to the kirk."

"Martha said that!" exclaimed his mother, highly pleased. "Heard you anything of a woman called Esther Auld? Her man does the orra work at the Tappit Hen public in Thrums."

"He's head man at the Tappit Hen public now," answered Tommy; "and she wishes she could find out where Jean Myles bides, so as she could write and tell her that she is grand too, and has six hair-bottomed chairs."

"She'll never get the satisfaction," said his mother triumphantly. "Tell me more about her."

"She has a laddie called Francie, and he has yellow curls, and she nearly greets because she canna tell Jean Myles that he goes to a school for the children of gentlemen only. She is so mad when she gets a letter from Jean Myles that she takes to her bed."

"Yea, yea!" said Mrs. Sandys cheerily.

"But they think Jean Myles has been brought low at last," continued Tommy, "because she hasna wrote for a long time to Thrums, and Esther Auld said that if she knowed for certain as Jean Myles had been brought low, she would put a threepenny bit in the kirk plate."

"I'm glad you've telled me that, laddie," said Mrs. Sandys, and next day, unknown to her children, she wrote another letter. She knew she ran a risk of discovery, yet it was probable that Tommy would only hear her referred to in Thrums Street by her maiden name, which he had never heard from her, and as for her husband he had been Magerful Tam to everyone. The risk was great, but the pleasure —

Unsuspicious Tommy soon had news of another letter from Jean Myles, which had sent Esther Auld to bed again.

"Instead of being brought low," he announced, "Jean Myles is grander than ever. Her Tommy has a governess."

"That would be a doush of water in Esther's face?" his mother said, smiling.

"She wrote to Martha Scrymgeour," said Tommy, "that it ain't no pleasure to her now to boast as her laddie is at a school for gentlemen's children only. But what made her maddest was a bit in Jean Myles's letter about chairs. Jean Myles has give all her hair-bottomed chairs to a poor woman and buyed a new kind, because hair-bottomed ones ain't fashionable now. So Esther Auld can't not bear the sight of her chairs now, though she were windy of them till the letter went to Thrums."

"Poor Esther!" said Mrs. Sandys gaily.

"Oh, and I forgot this, mother. Jean Myles's reason for not telling where she bides in London is that she's so grand that she thinks if auld Petey and the rest knowed where the place was they would visit her and boast as they was her friends. Auld Petey stamped wi' rage when he heard that, and Martha Scrymgeour said, 'Oh, the pridefu' limmer!'"

"Ay, Martha," muttered Mrs. Sandys, "you and Jean Myles is evens now."

But the passage that had made them all wince the most was one giving Jean's reasons for making no calls in Thrums Street. "You can break it to Martha Scrymgeour's father and mither," the letter said, "and to Petey Whamond's sisters and the rest as has friends in London, that I have seen no Thrums faces here, the low part where they bide not being for the like of me to file my feet in. Forby that, I could not let my son mix with their bairns for fear they should teach him the vulgar Thrums words and clarty his blue-velvet suit. I'm thinking you have to dress your laddie in corduroy, Esther, but you see that would not do for mine. So no more at present, and we all join in compliments, and my little velvets says he wishes I would send some of his toys to your little corduroys. And so maybe I will, Esther, if you'll tell Aaron Latta how rich and happy I am, and if you're feared to say it to his face, tell it to the roaring farmer of Double Dykes, and he'll pass it on."

"Did you ever hear of such a woman?" Tommy said indignantly, when he had repeated as much of this insult to Thrums as he could remember.

But it was information his mother wanted.

"What said they to that bit?" she asked.

At first, it appears, they limited their comments to "Losh, losh," "keeps a'," "it cows," "my eertie," "ay, ay," "sal, tal," "dagont" (the meaning of which is obvious). But by and by they recovered their breath, and then Baker Lamsden said, wonderingly:

"Wha that was at her marriage could have thought it would turn out so weel? It was an eerie marriage that, Petey!"

"Ay, man, you may say so," old Petey answered. "I was there; I was one o' them as went in ahint Aaron Latta, and I'm no' likely to forget it."

"I wasna there," said the baker, "but I was standing at the door, and I saw the hearse drive up."

"What did they mean, mother?" Tommy asked, but she shuddered and replied, evasively, "Did Martha Scrymgeour say anything?"

"She said such a lot," he had to confess, "that I dinna mind none on it. But I mind what her father in Thrums wrote to her; he wrote to her that if she saw a carriage go by, she was to keep her eyes on the ground, for likely as not Jean Myles would be in it, and she thought as they was all dirt beneath her feet. But Kirsty Ross-who is she?"

"She's Martha's mother. What about her?"

"She wrote at the end of the letter that Martha was to hang on ahint the carriage and find out where Jean Myles bides."

"Laddie, that was like Kirsty! Heard you what the roaring farmer o' Double Dykes said?"

No, Tommy had not heard him mentioned. And indeed the roaring farmer of Double Dykes had said nothing. He was already lying very quiet on the south side of the cemetery.

Tommy's mother's next question cost her a painful effort. "Did you hear," she asked, "whether they telled Aaron Latta about the letter?"

"Yes, they telled him," Tommy replied, "and he said a queer thing; he said, 'Jean Myles is dead, I was at her coffining.' That's what he aye says when they tell him there's another letter. I wonder what he means, mother?"

"I wonder!" she echoed, faintly. The only pleasure left her was to raise the envy of those who had hooted her from Thrums, but she paid a price for it. Many a stab she had got from the unwitting Tommy as he repeated the gossip of his new friends, and she only won their envy at the cost of their increased ill-will. They thought she was lording it in London, and so they were merciless; had they known how poor she was and how ill, they would have forgotten everything save that she was a Thrummy like themselves, and there were few but would have shared their all with her. But she did not believe this, and therefore you may pity her, for the hour was drawing near, and she knew it, when she must appeal to some one for her children's sake, not for her own.

No, not for her own. When Tommy was wandering the pretty parts of London with James Gloag and other boys from Thrums Street in search of Jean Myles, whom they were to know by her carriage and her silk dress and her son in blue velvet, his mother was in bed with bronchitis in the wretched room we know of, or creeping to the dancing school, coughing all the way.

Some of the fits of coughing were very near being her last, but she wrestled with her trouble, seeming at times to stifle it, and then for weeks she managed to go to her work, which was still hers, because Shovel's old girl did it for her when the bronchitis would not be defied. Shovel's old slattern gave this service unasked and without payment; if she was thanked it was ungraciously, but she continued to do all she could when there was need; she smelled of gin, but she continued to do all she could.

The wardrobe had been put upon its back on the floor, and so converted into a bed for Tommy and Elspeth, who were sometimes wakened in the night by a loud noise, which alarmed them until they learned that it was only the man in the next room knocking angrily on the wall because their mother's cough kept him from sleeping.

Tommy knew what death was now, and Elspeth knew its name, and both were vaguely aware that it was looking for their mother; but if she could only hold out till Hogmanay, Tommy said, they would fleg it out of the house. Hogmanay is the mighty winter festival of Thrums, and when it came round these two were to give their mother a present that would make her strong. It was not to be a porous plaster. Tommy knew now of something better than that.

"And I knows too!" Elspeth gurgled, "and I has threepence a'ready, I has."

"Whisht!" said Tommy, in an agony of dread, "she hears you, and she'll guess. We ain't speaking of nothing to give to you at Hogmanay," he said to his mother with great cunning. Then he winked at Elspeth and said, with his hand over his mouth, "I hinna twopence!" and Elspeth, about to cry in fright, "Have you spended it?" saw the joke and crowed instead, "Nor yet has I threepence!"

They smirked together, until Tommy saw a change come over Elspeth's face, which made him run her outside the door.

"You was a-going to pray!" he said, severely.

"'Cos it was a lie, Tommy. I does have threepence."

"Well, you ain't a-going to get praying about it. She would hear yer."

"I would do it low, Tommy."

"She would see yer."

"Oh, Tommy, let me. God is angry with me."

Tommy looked down the stair, and no one was in sight. "I'll let yer pray here," he whispered, "and you can say I have twopence. But be quick, and do it standing."

Perhaps Mrs. Sandys had been thinking that when Hogmanay came her children might have no mother to bring presents to, for on their return to the room her eyes followed them woefully, and a shudder of apprehension shook her torn frame. Tommy gave Elspeth a look that meant "I'm sure there's something queer about her."

There was also something queer about himself, which at this time had the strangest gallop. It began one day with a series of morning calls from Shovel, who suddenly popped his head over the top of the door (he was standing on the handle), roared "Roastbeef!" in the manner of a railway porter announcing the name of a station, and then at once withdrew.

He returned presently to say that vain must be all attempts to wheedle his secret from him, and yet again to ask irritably why Tommy was not coming out to hear all about it. Then did Tommy desert Elspeth, and on the stair Shovel showed him a yellow card with this printed on it: "S.R.J.C.—Supper Ticket;" and written beneath, in a lady's hand: "Admit Joseph Salt." The letters, Shovel explained, meant Society for the somethink of Juvenile Criminals, and the toffs what ran it got hold of you when you came out of quod. Then if you was willing to repent they wrote down your name and the place what you lived at in a book, and one of them came to see yer and give yer a ticket for the blow-out night. This was blow-out night, and that were Shovel's ticket. He had bought it from Hump Salt for fourpence. What you get at the blow-out was roast-beef, plum-duff, and an orange; but when Hump saw the fourpence he could not wait.

A favor was asked of Tommy. Shovel had been told by Hump that it was the custom of the toffs to sit beside you and question you about your crimes, and lacking the imagination that made Tommy such an ornament to the house, the chances were that he would flounder in his answers and be ejected. Hump had pointed this out to him after pocketing the fourpence. Would Tommy, therefore, make up things for him to say; reward, the orange.

This was a proud moment for Tommy, as Shovel's knowledge of crime was much more extensive than his own, though they had both studied it in the pictures of a lively newspaper subscribed to by Shovel, senior. He became patronizing at once and rejected the orange as insufficient.

Then suppose, after he got into the hall, Shovel dropped his ticket out at the window; Tommy could pick it up, and then it would admit him also.

Tommy liked this, but foresaw a danger: the ticket might be taken from Shovel at the door, just as they took them from you at that singing thing in the church he had attended with young Petey.

So help Shovel's davy, there was no fear of this. They were superior toffs, what trusted to your honor.

Would Shovel swear to this?

He would.

But would he swear dagont?

He swore dagont; and then Tommy had him. As he was so sure of it, he could not object to Tommy's being the one who dropped the ticket out at the window?

Shovel did object for a time, but after a wrangle he gave up the ticket, intending to take it from Tommy when primed with the necessary tale. So they parted until evening, and Tommy returned to Elspeth, secretive but elated. For the rest of the day he was in thought, now waggling his head smugly over some dark, unutterable design and again looking a little scared. In growing alarm she watched his face, and at last she slipped upon her knees, but he had her up at once and said, reproachfully:

"It were me as taught yer to pray, and now yer prays for me! That's fine treatment!"

Nevertheless, after his mother's return, just before he stole out to join Shovel, he took Elspeth aside and whispered to her, nervously:

"You can pray for me if you like, for, oh, Elspeth; I'm thinking as I'll need it sore!" And sore he needed it before the night was out.

Chapter VIII
The Boy with Two Mothers

"I love my dear father and my dear mother and all the dear little kids at 'ome. You are a kind laidy or gentleman. I love yer. I will never do it again, so help me bob. Amen."

This was what Shovel muttered to himself again and again as the two boys made their way across the lamp-lit Hungerford Bridge, and Tommy asked him what it meant.

"My old gal learned me that; she's deep," Shovel said, wiping the words off his mouth with his sleeve.

"But you got no kids at 'ome!" remonstrated Tommy. (Ameliar was now in service.)

Shovel turned on him with the fury of a mother protecting her young. "Don't you try for to knock none on it out," he cried, and again fell a-mumbling.

Said Tommy, scornfully: "If you says it all out at one bang you'll be done at the start."

Shovel sighed.

"And you should blubber when yer says it," added Tommy, who could laugh or cry merely because other people were laughing or crying, or even with less reason, and so naturally that he found it more difficult to stop than to begin. Shovel was the taller by half a head, and irresistible with his fists, but to-night Tommy was master.

"You jest stick to me, Shovel," he said airily. "Keep a grip on my hand, same as if yer was Elspeth."

"But what was we copped for, Tommy?" entreated humble Shovel.

Tommy asked him if he knew what a butler was, and Shovel remembered, confusedly, that there had been a portrait of a butler in his father's news-sheet.

"Well, then," said Tommy, inspired by this same source, "there's a room a butler has, and it is a pantry, so you and me we crawled through the winder and we opened the door to the gang. You and me was copped. They catched you below the table and me stabbing the butler."

"It was me what stabbed the butler," Shovel interposed, jealously.

"How could you do it, Shovel?"

"With a knife, I tell yer!"

"Why, you didn't have no knife," said Tommy, impatiently.

This crushed Shovel, but he growled sulkily:

"Well, I bit him in the leg."

"Not you," said selfish Tommy. "You forgets about repenting, and if I let yer bite him, you would brag about it. It's safer without, Shovel."

Perhaps it was. "How long did I get in quod, then, Tommy?"

"Fourteen days."

"So did you?" Shovel said, with quick anxiety.

"I got a month," replied Tommy, firmly.

Shovel roared a word that would never have admitted him to the hall. Then, "I'm as game as you, and gamer," he whined.

"But I'm better at repenting. I tell yer, I'll cry when I'm repenting." Tommy's face lit up, and Shovel could not help saying, with a curious look at it:

"You-you ain't like any other cove I knows," to which Tommy replied, also in an awe-struck voice:

"I'm so queer, Shovel, that when I thinks 'bout myself I'm —I'm sometimes near feared."

"What makes your face for to shine like that? Is it thinking about the blow-out?"

No, it was hardly that, but Tommy could not tell what it was. He and the saying about art for art's sake were in the streets that night, looking for each other.

The splendor of the brightly lighted hall, which was situated in one of the meanest streets of perhaps the most densely populated quarter in London, broke upon the two boys suddenly and hit each in his vital part, tapping an invitation on Tommy's brain-pan and taking Shovel coquettishly in the stomach. Now was the moment when Shovel meant to strip Tommy of the ticket, but the spectacle in front dazed him, and he stopped to tell a vegetable barrow how he loved his dear father and his dear mother, and all the dear kids at home. Then Tommy darted forward and was immediately lost in the crowd surging round the steps of the hall.

Several gentlemen in evening dress stood framed in the lighted doorway, shouting: "Have your tickets in your hands and give them up as you pass in." They were fine fellows, helping in a splendid work, and their society did much good, though it was not so well organized as others that have followed in its steps; but Shovel, you may believe, was in no mood to attend to them. He had but one thought: that the traitor Tommy was doubtless at that moment boring his way toward them, underground, as it were, and "holding his ticket in his hand." Shovel dived into the rabble and was flung back upside down. Falling with his arms round a full-grown man, he immediately ran up him as if he had been a lamp-post, and was aloft just sufficiently long to see Tommy give up the ticket and saunter into the hall.

The crowd tried at intervals to rush the door. It was mainly composed of ragged boys, but here and there were men, women, and girls, who came into view for a moment under the lights as the mob heaved and went round and round like a boiling potful. Two policemen joined the ticket-collectors, and though it was a good-humored gathering, the air was thick with such cries as these:

"I lorst my ticket, ain't I telling yer? Gar on, guv'nor, lemme in!"

"Oh, crumpets, look at Jimmy! Jimmy never done nothink, your honor; he's a himposter'"

"I'm the boy what kicked the peeler. Hie, you toff with the choker, ain't I to step up?"

"Tell yer, I'm a genooine criminal, I am. If yer don't lemme in I'll have the lawr on you."

"Let a poor cove in as his father drownded hisself for his country."

"What air yer torking about? Warn't I in larst year, and the cuss as runs the show, he says to me, 'Allers welcome,' he says. None on your sarse, Bobby. I demands to see the cuss what runs —"

"Jest keeping on me out 'cos I ain't done nothin'. Ho, this is a encouragement to honesty, I don't think."

Mighty in tongue and knee and elbow was an unknown knight, ever conspicuous; it might be but by a leg waving for one brief moment in the air. He did not want to go in, would not go in though they went on their blooming knees to him; he was after a viper of the name of Tommy. Half an hour had not tired him, and he was leading another assault, when a magnificent lady, such as you see in wax-works, appeared in the vestibule and made some remark to a policeman, who then shouted:

"If so there be hany lad here called Shovel, he can step forrard."

A dozen lads stepped forward at once, but a flail drove them right and left, and the unknown knight had mounted the parapet amid a shower of execrations. "If you are the real Shovel," the lady said to him, "you can tell me how this proceeds, 'I love my dear father and my dear mother —' Go on."

Shovel obeyed, tremblingly. "And all the dear little kids at 'ome. You are a kind laidy or gentleman. I love yer. I will never do it again, so help me bob. Amen."

"Charming!" chirped the lady, and down pleasant-smelling aisles she led him, pausing to drop an observation about Tommy to a clergyman: "So glad I came; I have discovered the most delightful little monster called Tommy." The clergyman looked after her half in sadness, half sarcastically; he was thinking that he had discovered a monster also.

At present the body of the hall was empty, but its sides were lively with gorging boys, among whom ladies moved, carrying platefuls of good things. Most of them were sweet women, fighting bravely for these boys, and not at all like Shovel's patroness, who had come for a sensation. Tommy falling into her hands, she got it.

Tommy, who had a corner to himself, was lolling in it like a little king, and he not only ordered roast-beef for the awe-struck Shovel, but sent the lady back for salt. Then he whispered, exultantly: "Quick, Shovel, feel my pocket" (it bulged with two oranges), "now the inside pocket" (plum-duff), "now my waistcoat pocket" (threepence); "look in my mouth" (chocolates).

When Shovel found speech he began excitedly: "I love my dear father and my dear —"

"Gach!" said Tommy, interrupting him contemptuously. "Repenting ain't no go, Shovel. Look at them other coves; none of them has got no money, nor full pockets, and I tell you, it's 'cos they has repented."

"Gar on!"

"It's true, I tells you. That lady as is my one, she's called her ladyship, and she don't care a cuss for boys as has repented," which of course was a libel, her ladyship being celebrated wherever paragraphs penetrate for having knitted a pair of stockings for the deserving poor.

"When I saw that," Tommy continued, brazenly, "I bragged 'stead of repenting, and the wuss I says I am, she jest says, 'You little monster,' and gives me another orange."

"Then I'm done for," Shovel moaned, "for I rolled off that 'bout loving my dear father and my dear mother, blast 'em, soon as I seen her."

He need not let that depress him. Tommy had told her he would say it, but that it was all flam.

Shovel thought the ideal arrangement would be for him to eat and leave the torking to Tommy. Tommy nodded. "I'm full, at any rate," he said, struggling with his waistcoat. "Oh, Shovel, I *am* full!"

Her ladyship returned, and the boys held by their contract, but of the dark character Tommy seems to have been, let not these pages bear the record. Do you wonder that her ladyship believed him? On this point we must fight for our Tommy. You would have believed him. Even Shovel, who knew, between the bites, that it was all whoppers, listened as to his father reading aloud. This was because another boy present half believed it for the moment also. When he described the eerie darkness of the butler's pantry, he shivered involuntarily, and he shut his eyes once-ugh! —that was because he saw the blood spouting out of the butler. He was turning up his trousers to show the mark of the butler's boot on his leg when the lady was called away, and then Shovel shook him, saying: "Darn yer, doesn't yer know as it's all your eye?" which brought Tommy to his senses with a jerk.

"Sure's death, Shovel," he whispered, in awe, "I was thinking I done it, every bit!"

Had her ladyship come back she would have found him a different boy. He remembered now that Elspeth, for whom he had filled his pockets, was praying for him; he could see her on her knees, saying, "Oh, God, I'se praying for Tommy," and remorse took hold of him and shook him on his seat. He broke into one hysterical laugh and then immediately began to sob. This was the moment when Shovel should have got him quietly out of the hall.

Members of the society discussing him afterwards with bated breath said that never till they died could they forget her ladyship's face while he did it. "But did you notice the boy's own face? It was positively angelic." "Angelic, indeed; the little horror was intoxicated." No, there was a doctor present, and according to him it was the meal that had gone to the boy's head; he looked half starved. As for the clergyman, he only said: "We shall lose her subscription; I am glad of it."

Yes, Tommy was intoxicated, but with a beverage not recognized by the faculty. What happened was this: Supper being finished, the time had come for what Shovel called the jawing, and the boys were now mustered in the body of the hall. The limited audience had gone to the gallery, and unluckily all eyes except Shovel's were turned to the platform. Shovel was apprehensive about Tommy, who was not exactly sobbing now; but strange, uncontrollable sounds not unlike the winding up of a clock proceeded from his throat; his face had flushed; there was a purposeful look in his usually unreadable eye; his fingers were fidgeting on the board in front of him, and he seemed to keep his seat with difficulty.

The personage who was to address the boys sat on the platform with clergymen, members of committee, and some ladies, one of them Tommy's patroness. Her ladyship saw Tommy and smiled to him, but obtained no response. She had taken a front seat, a choice that she must have regretted presently.

The chairman rose and announced that the. Rev. Mr. ——would open the proceedings with prayer. The Rev. Mr. —— rose to pray in a loud voice for the waifs in the body of the hall. At the same moment rose Tommy, and began to pray in a squeaky voice for the people on the platform.

He had many Biblical phrases, mostly picked up in Thrums Street, and what he said was distinctly heard in the stillness, the clergyman being suddenly bereft of speech. "Oh," he cried, "look down on them ones there, for, oh, they are unworthy of Thy mercy, and, oh, the worst sinner is her ladyship, her sitting there so brazen in the black frock with yellow stripes, and the worse I said I were the better pleased were she. Oh, make her think shame for tempting of a poor boy, for getting suffer little children, oh, why cumbereth she the ground, oh —"

He was in full swing before any one could act. Shovel having failed to hold him in his seat, had done what was perhaps the next best thing, got beneath it himself. The arm of the petrified clergyman was still extended, as if blessing his brother's remarks; the chairman seemed to be trying to fling his right hand at the culprit; but her ladyship, after the first stab, never moved a muscle. Thus for nearly half a minute, when the officials woke up, and squeezing past many knees, seized Tommy by the neck and ran him out of the building. All down the aisle he prayed hysterically, and for some time afterwards, to Shovel, who had been cast forth along with him.

At an hour of that night when their mother was asleep, and it is to be hoped they were the only two children awake in London, Tommy sat up softly in the wardrobe to discover whether Elspeth was still praying for him. He knew that she was on the floor in a night-gown some twelve sizes too large for her, but the room was as silent and black as the world he had just left by taking his fingers from his ears and the blankets off his face.

"I see you," he said mendaciously, and in a guarded voice, so as not to waken his mother, from whom he had kept his escapade. This had not the desired effect of drawing a reply from Elspeth, and he tried bluster.

"You needna think as I'll repent, you brat, so there! What?

"I wish I hadna told you about it!" Indeed, he had endeavored not to do so, but pride in his achievement had eventually conquered prudence.

"Reddy would have laughed, she would, and said as I was a wonder. Reddy was the kind I like. What?

"You ate up the oranges quick, and the plum-duff too, so you should pray for yoursel' as well as for me. It's easy to say as you didna know how I got them till after you eated them, but you should have found out. What?

"Do you think it was for my own self as I done it? I jest done it to get the oranges and plum-duff to you, I did, and the threepence too. Eh? Speak, you little besom.

"I tell you as I did repent in the hall. I was greeting, and I never knowed I put up that prayer till Shovel told me on it. We was sitting in the street by that time."

This was true. On leaving the hall Tommy had soon dropped to the cold ground and squatted there till he came to, when he remembered nothing of what had led to his expulsion. Like a stream that has run into a pond and only finds itself again when it gets out, he was but a continuation of the boy who when last conscious of himself was in the corner crying remorsefully over his misdeed; and in this humility he would have returned to Elspeth had no one told him of his prayer. Shovel, however, was at hand, not only to tell him all about it, but to applaud, and home strutted Tommy chuckling.

"I am sleeping," he next said to Elspeth, "so you may as well come to your bed."

He imitated the breathing of a sleeper, but it was the only sound to be heard in London, and he desisted fearfully. "Come away, Elspeth," he said, coaxingly, for he was very fond of her and could not sleep while she was cold and miserable.

Still getting no response he pulled his body inch by inch out of the bed-clothes, and holding his breath, found the floor with his feet stealthily, as if to cheat the wardrobe into thinking that he was still in it. But his reason was to discover whether Elspeth had fallen asleep on her knees without her learning that he cared to know. Almost noiselessly he worked himself along the floor, but when he stopped to bring his face nearer hers, there was such a creaking of his joints that if Elspeth did not hear it she-she must be dead! His knees played whack on the floor.

Elspeth only gasped once, but he heard, and remained beside her for a minute, so that she might hug him if such was her desire; and she put out her hand in the darkness so that his should not have far to travel alone if it chanced to be on the way to her. Thus they sat on their knees, each aghast at the hard-heartedness of the other.

Tommy put the blankets over the kneeling figure, and presently announced from the wardrobe that if he died of cold before repenting the blame of keeping him out of heaven would be Elspeth's. But the last word was muffled, for the blankets were tucked about him as he spoke, and two motherly little arms gave him the embrace they wanted to withhold. Foiled again, he kicked off the bed-clothes and said: "I tell yer I wants to die!"

This terrified both of them, and he added, quickly:

"Oh, God, if I was sure I were to die to-night I would repent at once." It is the commonest prayer in all languages, but down on her knees slipped Elspeth again, and Tommy, who felt that it had done him good, said indignantly: "Surely that is religion. What?"

He lay on his face until he was frightened by a noise louder than thunder in the daytime-the scraping of his eyelashes on the pillow. Then he sat up in the wardrobe and fired his three last shots.

"Elspeth Sandys, I'm done with yer forever, I am. I'll take care on yer, but I'll never kiss yer no more.

"When yer boasts as I'm your brother I'll say you ain't. I'll tell my mother about Reddy the morn, and syne she'll put you to the door smart.

"When you are a grown woman I'll buy a house to yer, but you'll have jest to bide in it by your lonely self, and I'll come once a year to speir how you are, but I won't come in, I won't —I'll jest cry up the stair."

The effect of this was even greater than he had expected, for now two were in tears instead of one, and Tommy's grief was the more heartrending, he was so much better at everything than Elspeth. He jumped out of the wardrobe and ran to her, calling her name, and he put his arms round her cold body, and the dear mite, forgetting how cruelly he had used her, cried, "Oh, tighter, Tommy, tighter; you didn't not mean it, did yer? Oh, you is terrible fond on me, ain't yer? And you won't not tell my mother 'bout Reddy, will yer, and you is no done wi' me forever, is yer? and you won't not put me in a house by myself, will yer? Oh, Tommy, is that the tightest you can do?"

And Tommy made it tighter, vowing, "I never meant it; I was a bad un to say it. If Reddy were to come back wanting for to squeeze you out, I would send her packing quick, I would. I tell yer what, I'll kiss you with folk looking on, I will, and no be ashamed to do it, and if Shovel is one of them what sees me, and he puts his finger to his nose, I'll blood the mouth of him, I will, dagont!"

Then he prayed for forgiveness, and he could always pray more beautifully than Elspeth. Even she was satisfied with the way he did it, and so, alack, was he.

"But you forgot to tell," she said fondly, when once more they were in the wardrobe to-gether —"you forgot to tell as you filled your pockets wif things to me."

"I didn't forget," Tommy replied modestly. "I missed it out, on purpose, I did, 'cos I was sure God knows on it without my telling him, and I thought he would be pleased if I didn't let on as I knowed it was good of me."

"Oh, Tommy," cried Elspeth, worshipping him, "I couldn't have doned that, I couldn't!" She was barely six, and easily taken in, but she would save him from himself if she could.

Chapter IX
Auld Lang Syne

What to do with her ladyship's threepence? Tommy finally decided to drop it into the charity-box that had once contained his penny. They held it over the slit together, Elspeth almost in tears because it was such a large sum to give away, but Tommy looking noble he was so proud of himself; and when he said "Three!" they let go.

There followed days of excitement centred round their money-box. Shovel introduced Tommy to a boy what said as after a bit you forget how much money was in your box, and then when you opened it, oh, Lor'! there is more than you thought, so he and Elspeth gave this plan a week's trial, affecting not to know how much they had gathered, but when they unlocked it, the sum was still only eightpence; so then Tommy told the liar to come on, and they fought while the horrified Elspeth prayed, and Tommy licked him, a result due to one of the famous Thrums left-handers then on exhibition in that street for the first time, as taught the victor by Petey Whamond the younger, late of Tillyloss.

The money did come in, once in spate (twopence from Bob in twenty-four hours), but usually so slowly that they saw it resting on the way, and then, when they listened intently, they could hear the thud of Hogmanay. The last halfpenny was a special aggravation, strolling about, just out of reach, with all the swagger of sixpence, but at last Elspeth had it, and after that, the sooner Hogmanay came the better.

They concealed their excitement under too many wrappings, but their mother suspected nothing. When she was dressing on the morning of Hogmanay, her stockings happened to be at the other side of the room, and they were such a long way off that she rested on the way to them. At the meagre breakfast she said what a heavy teapot that was, and Tommy thought this funny, but the salt had gone from the joke when he remembered it afterwards. And when she was ready to go off to her work she hesitated at the door, looking at her bed and from it to her children as if in two minds, and then went quietly downstairs.

The distance seems greater than ever to-day, poor woman, and you stop longer at the corners, where rude men jeer at you. Scarcely can you push open the door of the dancing-school or lift the pail; the fire has gone out, you must again go on your knees before it, and again the smoke makes you cough. Gaunt slattern, fighting to bring up the phlegm, was it really you for whom another woman gave her life, and thought it a rich reward to get dressing you once in your long clothes, when she called you her beautiful, and smiled, and smiling, died? Well, well; but take courage, Jean Myles. The long road still lies straight up hill, but your climbing is near an end. Shrink from the rude men no more, they are soon to forget you, so soon! It is a heavy door, but soon you will have pushed it open for the last time. The girls will babble still, but not to you, not of you. Cheer up, the work is nearly done. Her beautiful! Come, beautiful, strength for a few more days, and then you can leave the key of the leaden door behind you, and on your way home you may kiss your hand joyously to the weary streets, for you are going to die.

Tommy and Elspeth had been to the foot of the stair many times to look for her before their mother came back that evening, yet when she re-entered her home, behold, they were sitting calmly on the fender as if this were a day like yesterday or to-morrow, as if Tommy had not been on a business visit to Thrums Street, as if the hump on the bed did not mean that a glorious something was hidden under the coverlet. True, Elspeth would look at Tommy imploringly every few minutes, meaning that she could not keep it in much longer, and then Tommy would mutter the one word "Bell" to remind her that it was against the rules to begin before the Thrums eight-o'clock bell rang. They also wiled away the time of waiting by inviting each other to conferences at the window where these whispers passed —

"She ain't got a notion, Tommy."

"Dinna look so often at the bed."

"If I could jest get one more peep at it!"

"No, no; but you can put your hand on the top of it as you go by."

The artfulness of Tommy lured his unsuspecting mother into telling how they would be holding Hogmanay in Thrums to-night, how cartloads of kebbock cheeses had been rolling into the town all the livelong day ("Do you hear them, Elspeth?"), and in dark closes the children were already gathering, with smeared faces and in eccentric dress, to sally forth as guisers at the clap of eight, when the ringing of a bell lets Hogmanay loose. ("You see, Elspeth?") Inside the houses men and women were preparing (though not by fasting, which would have been such a good way that it is surprising no one ever thought of it) for a series of visits, at every one of which they would be offered a dram and kebbock and bannock, and in the grander houses "bridies," which are a sublime kind of pie.

Tommy had the audacity to ask what bridies were like. And he could not dress up and be a guiser, could he, mother, for the guisers sang a song, and he did not know the words? What a pity they could not get bridies to buy in London, and learn the song and sing it. But of course they could not! ("Elspeth, if you tumble off the fender again, she'll guess.")

Such is a sample of Tommy, but Elspeth was sly also, if in a smaller way, and it was she who said: "There ain't nothin' in the bed, is there, Tommy!" This duplicity made her uneasy, and she added, behind her teeth, "Maybe there is," and then, "O God, I knows as there is."

But as the great moment drew near there were no more questions; two children were staring at the clock and listening intently for the peal of a bell nearly five hundred miles away.

The clock struck. "Whisht! It's time, Elspeth! They've begun! Come on!"

A few minutes afterwards Mrs. Sandys was roused by a knock at the door, followed by the entrance of two mysterious figures. The female wore a boy's jacket turned outside in, the male a woman's bonnet and a shawl, and to make his disguise the more impenetrable he carried a poker in his right hand. They stopped in the middle of the floor and began to recite, rather tremulously,

> Get up, good wife, and binna sweir,
> And deal your bread to them that's here.
> For the time will come when you'll be dead,
> And then you'll need neither ale nor bread.

Mrs. Sandys had started, and then turned piteously from them; but when they were done she tried to smile, and said, with forced gayety, that she saw they were guisers, and it was a fine night, and would they take a chair. The male stranger did so at once, but the female said, rather anxiously: "You are sure as you don't know who we is?" Their hostess shook her head, and then he of the poker offered her three guesses, a daring thing to do, but all went well, for her first guess was Shovel and his old girl; second guess, Before and After; third guess, Napoleon Buonaparte and the Auld Licht minister. At each guess the smaller of the intruders clapped her hands gleefully, but when, with the third, she was unmuzzled, she putted with her head at Mrs. Sandys and hugged her, screaming, "It ain't none on them; it's jest me, mother, it's Elspeth!" and even while their astounded hostess was asking could it be true, the male conspirator dropped his poker noisily (to draw attention to himself) and stood revealed as Thomas Sandys.

Wasn't it just like Thrums, wasn't it just the very, very same? Ah, it was wonderful, their mother said, but, alas, there was one thing wanting: she had no Hogmanay to give the guisers.

Had she not? What a pity, Elspeth! What a pity, Tommy! What might that be in the bed, Elspeth? It couldn't not be their Hogmanay, could it, Tommy? If Tommy was his mother he would look and see. If Elspeth was her mother she would look and see.

Her curiosity thus cunningly aroused, Mrs. Sandys raised the coverlet of the bed and-there were three bridies, an oatmeal cake, and a hunk of kebbock. "And they comed from Thrums!" cried Elspeth, while Tommy cried, "Petey and the others got a lot sent from Thrums, and I bought the bridies from them, and they gave me the bannock and the kebbock for nuthin'!" Their mother did not utter the cry of rapture which Tommy expected so confidently that he could have done it for her; instead, she pulled her two children toward her, and the great moment was like to be a tearful rather than an ecstatic one, for Elspeth had begun to whimper, and even Tommy-but by a supreme effort he shouldered reality to the door.

"Is this my Hogmanay, guidwife?" he asked in the nick of time, and the situation thus being saved, the luscious feast was partaken of, the guisers listening solemnly as each bite went down. They also took care to address their hostess as "guidwife" or "mistress," affecting not to have met her lately, and inquiring genially after the health of herself and family. "How many have you?" was Tommy's masterpiece, and she answered in the proper spirit, but all the time she was hiding great part of her bridie beneath her apron, Hogmanay having come too late for her.

Everything was to be done exactly as they were doing it in Thrums Street, and so presently Tommy made a speech; it was the speech of old Petey, who had rehearsed it several times before him. "Here's a toast," said Tommy, standing up and waving his arms, "here's a toast that we'll drink in silence, one that maun have sad thoughts at the back o't to some of us, but one, my friends, that keeps the hearts of Thrums folk green and ties us all thegither, like as it were wi' twine. It's to all them, wherever they may be the night, wha' have sat as lads and lasses at the Cuttle Well."

To one of the listeners it was such an unexpected ending that a faint cry broke from her, which startled the children, and they sat in silence looking at her. She had turned her face from them, but her arm was extended as if entreating Tommy to stop.

"That was the end," he said, at length, in a tone of expostulation; "it's auld Petey's speech."

"Are you sure," his mother asked wistfully, "that Petey was to say *all* them as have sat at the Cuttle Well? He made no exception, did he?"

Tommy did not know what exception was, but he assured her that he had repeated the speech, word for word. For the remainder of the evening she sat apart by the fire, while her children gambled for crack-nuts, young Petey having made a teetotum for Tommy and taught him what the letters on it meant. Their mirth rang faintly in her ear, and they scarcely heard her fits of coughing; she was as much engrossed in her own thoughts as they in theirs, but hers were sad and theirs were jocund-Hogmanay, like all festivals, being but a bank from which we can only draw what we put in. So an hour or more passed, after which Tommy whispered to Elspeth: "Now's the time; they're at it now," and each took a hand of their mother, and she woke from her reverie to find that they had pulled her from her chair and were jumping up and down, shouting, excitedly, "For Auld Lang Syne, my dear, for Auld Lang Syne, Auld Lang Syne, my dear, Auld Lang Syne." She tried to sing the words with her children, tried to dance round with them, tried to smile, but —

It was Tommy who dropped her hand first. "Mother," he cried, "your face is wet, you're greeting sair, and you said you had forgot the way."

"I mind it now, man, I mind it now," she said, standing helplessly in the middle of the room.

Elspeth nestled against her, crying, "My mother was thinking about Thrums, wasn't she, Tommy?"

"I was thinking about the part o't I'm most awid to be in," the poor woman said, sinking back into her chair.

"It's the Den," Tommy told Elspeth.

"It's the Square," Elspeth told Tommy.

"No, it's Monypenny."

"No, it's the Commonty."

But it was none of these places. "It's the cemetery," the woman said, "it's the hamely, quiet cemetery on the hillside. Oh, there's mony a bonny place in my nain bonny toon, but there's nain so hamely like as the cemetery." She sat shaking in the chair, and they thought she was to say no more, but presently she rose excitedly, and with a vehemence that made them shrink from her she cried: "I winna lie in London! tell Aaron Latta that; I winna lie in London!"

For a few more days she trudged to her work, and after that she seldom left her bed. She had no longer strength to coax up the phlegm, and a doctor brought in by Shovel's mother warned her that her days were near an end. Then she wrote her last letter to Thrums, Tommy and Elspeth standing by to pick up the pen when it fell from her feeble hand, and in the intervals she told them that she was Jean Myles.

"And if I die and Aaron hasna come," she said, "you maun just gang to auld Petey and tell him wha you are."

"But how can you be Jean Myles?" asked astounded Tommy. "You ain't a grand lady and —"

His mother looked at Elspeth. "No' afore her," she besought him; but before he set off to post the letter she said: "Come canny into my bed the night, when Elspeth 's sleeping, and syne I'll tell you all there is to tell about Jean Myles."

"Tell me now whether the letter is to Aaron Latta?"

"It's for him," she said, "but it's no' to him. I'm feared he might burn it without opening it if he saw my write on the cover, so I've wrote it to a friend of his wha will read it to him."

"And what's inside, mother?" the boy begged, inquisitively. "It must be queer things if they'll bring Aaron Latta all the way from Thrums."

"There's but little in it, man," she said, pressing her hand hard upon her chest. "It's no muckle mair than 'Auld Lang Syne, my dear, for Auld Lang Syne.'"

Chapter X
The Favorite of the Ladies

That night the excited boy was wakened by a tap-tap, as of someone knocking for admittance, and stealing to his mother's side, he cried, "Aaron Latta has come; hearken to him chapping at the door!"

It was only the man through the wall, but Mrs. Sandys took Tommy into bed with her, and while Elspeth slept, told him the story of her life. She coughed feebly now, but the panting of the dying is a sound that no walls can cage, and the man continued to remonstrate at intervals. Tommy never recalled his mother's story without seeming, through the darkness in which it was told, to hear Elspeth's peaceful breathing and the angry tap-tap on the wall.

"I'm sweer to tell it to you," she began, "but tell I maun, for though it's just a warning to you and Elspeth no' to be like them that brought you into the world, it's all I have to leave you. Ay, and there's another reason: you may soon be among folk wha ken but half the story and put a waur face on it than I deserve."

She had spoken calmly, but her next words were passionate.

"They thought I was fond o'him," she cried; "oh, they were blind, blind! Frae the first I could never thole the sight o' him.

"Maybe that's no' true," she had to add. "I aye kent he was a black, but yet I couldna put him out o' my head; he took sudden grips o' me like an evil thought. I aye ran frae him, and yet I sair doubt that I went looking for him too."

"Was it Aaron Latta?" Tommy asked.

"No, it was your father. The first I ever saw of him was at Cullew, four lang miles frae Thrums. There was a ball after the market, and Esther Auld and me went to it. We went in a cart, and I was wearing a pink print, wi' a white bonnet, and blue ribbons that tied aneath the chin. I had a shawl abune, no' to file them. There wasna a more innocent lassie in Thrums, man, no, nor a happier one; for Aaron Latta-Aaron came half the way wi' us, and he was hauding my hand aneath the shawl. He hadna speired me at that time, but I just kent.

"It was an auld custom to choose a queen of beauty at the ball, but that night the men couldna 'gree wha should be judge, and in the tail-end they went out thegither to look for one, determined to mak' judge o' the first man they met, though they should have to tear him off a horse and bring him in by force. You wouldna believe to look at me now, man, that I could have had any thait o' being made queen, but I was fell bonny, and I was as keen as the rest. How simple we were, all pretending to one another that we didna want to be chosen! Esther Auld said she would hod ahint the tent till a queen was picked, and at the very time she said it, she was in a palsy, through no being able to decide whether she looked better in her shell necklace or wanting it. She put it on in the end, and syne when we heard the tramp o' the men, her mind misgave her, and she cried: 'For the love o' mercy, keep them out till I get it off again!' So we were a' laughing when they came in.

"Laddie, it was your father and Elspeth's that they brought wi' them, and he was a stranger to us, though we kent something about him afore the night was out. He was finely put on, wi' a gold chain, and a free w'y of looking at women, and if you mind o' him ava, you ken that he was fair and buirdly, wi' a full face, and aye a laugh ahint it. I tell ye, man, that when our een met, and I saw that triumphing laugh ahint his face, I took a fear of him, as if I had guessed the end.

"For years and years after that night I dreamed it ower again, and aye I heard mysel' crying to God to keep that man awa' frae me. But I doubt I put up no sic prayer at the time; his masterful look fleid me, and yet it drew me against my will, and I was trembling wi' pride as well as fear when he made me queen. We danced thegither and fought thegither a' through the ball, and my will was no match for his, and the worst o't was I had a kind o' secret pleasure in being mastered.

"Man, he kissed me. Lads had kissed me afore that night, but never since first I went wi' Aaron Latta to the Cuttle Well. Aaron hadna done it, but I was never to let none do it again except him. So when your father did it I struck him, but ahint the redness that came ower his face, I saw his triumphing laugh, and he whispered that he liked me for the blow. He said, 'I prefer the sweer anes, and the more you struggle, my beauty, the better pleased I'll be.' Almost his hinmost words to me was, 'I've been hearing of your Aaron, and that pleases me too!' I fired up at that and telled him what I thought of him, but he said, 'If you canna abide me, what made you dance wi' me so often?' and, oh, laddie, that's a question that has sung in my head since syne.

"I've telled you that we found out wha he was, and 'deed he made no secret of it. Up to the time he was twal year auld he had been a kent face in that part, for his mither was a Cullew woman called Mag Sandys, ay, and a single woman. She was a hard ane too, for when he was twelve year auld he flung out o' the house saying he would ne'er come back, and she said he shouldna run awa' wi' thae new boots on, so she took the boots off him and let him go.

"He was a grown man when more was heard o' him, and syne stories came saying he was at Redlintie, playing queer games wi' his father. His father was gauger there, that's exciseman, a Mr. Cray, wha got his wife out o' Thrums, and even when he was courting her (so they say) had the heart to be ower chief wi' this other woman. Weel, Magerful Tam, as he was called through being so masterful, cast up at Redlintie frae none kent where, gey desperate for siller, but wi' a black coat on his back, and he said that all he wanted was to be owned as the gauger's son. Mr. Cray said there was no proof that he was his son, and syne the queer sport began. Your father had noticed he was like Mr. Cray, except in the beard, and so he had his beard clippit the same, and he got hand o' some weel-kent claethes o' the gauger's that had been presented to a poor body, and he learned up a' the gauger's tricks of speech and walking, especially a droll w'y he had o' taking snuff and syne flinging back his head. They were as like as buckies after that, and soon there was a town about it, for one day ladies would find that they had been bowing to the son thinking he was the father, and the next they wouldna speak to the father, mistaking him for the son; and a report spread to the head office o' the excise that the gauger of Redlintie spent his evenings at a public house, singing 'The De'il's awa' wi' the Exciseman.' Tam drank nows and nans, and it ga'e Mr. Cray a turn to see him come rolling yont the street, just as if it was himsel' in a looking-glass. He was a sedate-living man now, but chiefly because his wife kept him in good control, and this sight brought back auld times so vive to him, that he a kind of mistook which ane he was, and took to dropping, forgetful-like, into public-houses again. It was high time Tam should be got out of the place, and they did manage to bribe him into leaving, though no easily, for it had been fine sport to him, and to make a sensation was what he valued above all things. We heard that he went back to Redlintie a curran years after, but both the gauger and his wife were dead, and I ken that he didna trouble the twa daughters. They were Miss Ailie and Miss Kitty, and as they werena left as well off as was expected they came to Thrums, which had been their mother's town, and started a school for the gentry there. I dinna doubt but what it's the school that Esther Auld's laddie is at.

"So after being long lost sight o' he turned up at Cullew, wi' what looked to simple folk a fortune in his pouches, and half a dozen untrue stories about how he made it. He had come to make a show o' himsel' afore his mither, and I dare say to give her some gold, for he was aye ready to give when he had, I'll say that for him; but she had flitted to some unkent place, and so he bade on some weeks at the Cullew public. He caredna whether the folk praised or blamed him so long as they wondered at him, and queer stories about his doings was aye on the road to Thrums. One was that he gave wild suppers to whaever would come; another that he went to the kirk just for the glory of flinging a sovereign into the plate wi' a clatter; another that when he lay sleeping on twa chairs, gold and silver dribbled out o' his trouser pouches to the floor.

"There was an ugly story too, about a lassie, that led to his leaving the place and coming to Thrums, after he had near killed the Cullew smith, in a fight. The first I heard o' his being in Thrums was when Aaron Latta walked into my granny's house and said there was a strange man at the Tappit Hen public standing drink to any that would tak', and boasting that he had but to waggle his finger to make me give Aaron up. I went wi' Aaron and looked in at the window, but I kent wha it was afore I looked. If Aaron had just gone in and struck him! All decent women, laddie, has a horror of being fought about. I'm no sure but what that's just the difference atween guid ones and ill ones, but this man had a power ower me; and if Aaron had just struck him! Instead o' meddling he turned white, and I couldna help contrasting them, and thinking how masterful your father looked. Fine I kent he was a brute, and yet I couldna help admiring him for looking so magerful.

"He bade on at the Tappit Hen, flinging his siller about in the way that made him a king at Cullew, but no molesting Miss Ailie and Miss Kitty, which all but me thought was what he had come to Thrums to do. Aaron and me was cried for the first time the Sabbath after he came, and the next Sabbath for the second time, but afore that he was aye getting in my road and speaking to me, but I ran frae him and hod frae him when I could, and he said the reason I did that was because I kent his will was stronger than mine. He was aye saying things that made me think he saw down to the bottom o' my soul; what I didna understand was that in mastering other women he had been learning to master me. Ay, but though I thought ower muckle about him, never did I speak him fair. I loo'ed Aaron wi' all my heart, and your father kent it; and that, I doubt, was what made him so keen, for, oh, but he was vain!

"And now we've come to the night I'm so sweer to speak about. She was a good happy lassie that went into the Den that moonlight night wi' Aaron's arm round her, but it was another woman that came out. We thought we had the Den to oursel's, and as we sat on the Shoaging Stane at the Cuttle Well, Aaron wrote wi' a stick on the ground 'Jean Latta,' and prigged wi' me to look at it, but I spread my hands ower my face, and he didna ken that I was keeking at it through my fingers all the time. We was so ta'en up with oursel's that we saw nobody coming, and all at once there was your father by the side o' us! 'You've written the wrong name, Aaron,' he said, jeering and pointing with his foot at the letters; 'it should be Jean Sandys.'

"Aaron said not a word, but I had a presentiment of ill, and I cried, 'Dinna let him change the name, Aaron!' Your father had been to change it himsel', but at that he had a new thait, and he said, 'No, I'll no' do it; your brave Aaron shall do it for me.'

"Laddie, it doesna do for a man to be a coward afore a woman that's fond o' him. A woman will thole a man's being anything except like hersel'. When I was sure Aaron was a coward I stood still as death, waiting to ken wha's I was to be.

"Aaron did it. He was loath, but your father crushed him to the ground, and said do it he should, and warned him too that if he did it he would lose me, bantering him and cowing him and advising him no' to shame me, all in a breath. He kent so weel, you see, what was in my mind, and aye there was that triumphing laugh ahint his face. If Aaron had fought and been beaten, even if he had just lain there and let the man strike away, if he had done anything except what he was bidden, he would have won, for it would have broken your father's power ower me. But to write the word! It was like dishonoring me to save his ain skin, and your father took good care he should ken it. You've heard me crying to Aaron in my sleep, but it wasna for him I cried, it was for his fire-side. All the love I had for him, and it was muckle, was skailed forever that night at the Cuttle Well. Without a look ahint me away I went wi' my master, and I had no more will to resist him-and oh, man, man, when I came to mysel' next morning I wished I had never been born!

"The men folk saw that Aaron had shamed them, and they werena quite so set agin me as the women, wha had guessed the truth, though they couldna be sure o't. Sair I pitied mysel', and sair I grat, but only when none was looking. The mair they miscalled me the higher I held my head, and I hung on your father's arm as if I adored him, and I boasted about his office and his clerk in London till they believed what I didna believe a word o' myself.

"But though I put sic a brave face on't, I was near demented in case he shouldna marry me, and he kent that and jokit me about it. Dinna think I was fond o' him; I hated him now. And dinna think his masterfulness had any more power ower me; his power was broken forever when I woke up that weary morning. But that was ower late, and to wait on by mysel' in Thrums for what might happen, and me a single woman —I daredna! So I flattered at him, and flattered at him, till I got the fool side o' him, and he married me.

"My granny let the marriage take place in her house, and he sent in so muckle meat and drink that some folk was willing to come. One came that wasna wanted. In the middle o' the marriage Aaron Latta, wha had refused to speak to anybody since that night, walked in wearing his blacks, wi' crape on them, as if it was a funeral, and all he said was that he had come to see Jean Myles coffined. He went away quietly as soon as we was married, but the crowd outside had fathomed his meaning, and abune the minister's words I could hear them crying, 'Ay, it's mair like a burial than a marriage!'

"My heart was near breaking wi' woe, but, oh, I was awid they shouldna ken it, and the bravest thing I ever did was to sit through the supper that night, making muckle o' your father, looking fond-like at him, laughing at his coarse jokes, and secretly hating him down to my very marrow a' the time. The crowd got word o' the ongoings, and they took a cruel revenge. A carriage had been ordered for nine o'clock to take us to Tilliedrum, where we should get the train to London, and when we heard it, as we thought, drive up to the door, out we went, me on your father's arm laughing, but wi' my teeth set. But Aaron's words had put an idea into their heads, though he didna intend it, and they had got out the hearse. It was the hearse they had brought to the door instead of a carriage.

"We got awa' in a carriage in the tail-end, and the stanes hitting it was all the good luck flung after me. It had just one horse, and I mind how I cried to Esther Auld, wha had been the first to throw, that when I came back it would be in a carriage and pair.

"Ay, I had pride! In the carriage your father told me as a joke that he had got away without paying the supper, and that about all the money he had now, forby what was to pay our tickets to London, was the half-sovereign on his watch-chain. But I was determined to have Thrums think I had married grand, and as I had three pound six on me, the savings o' all my days, I gave two pound of it to Malcolm Crabb, the driver, unbeknown to your father, but pretending it was frae him, and telled him to pay for the supper and the carriage with it. He said it was far ower muckle, but I just laughed, and said wealthy gentlemen like Mr. Sandys couldna be bothered to take back change, so Malcolm could keep what was ower. Malcolm was the man Esther Auld had just married, and I counted on this maddening her and on Malcolm's spreading the story through the town. Laddie, I've kent since syne what it is to be without bite or sup, but I've never grudged that siller."

The poor woman had halted many times in her tale, and she was glad to make an end. "You've forgotten what a life he led me in London," she said, "and it could do you no good to hear it, though it might be a lesson to thae lassies at the dancing-school wha think so much o' masterful men. It was by betting at horseraces that your father made a living, and whiles he was large o' siller, but that didna last, and I question whether he would have stuck to me if I hadna got work. Well, he's gone, and the Thrums folk'll soon ken the truth about Jean Myles now."

She paused, and then cried, with extraordinary vehemence: "Oh, man, how I wish I could keep it frae them for ever and ever!"

But presently she was calm again and she said: "What I've been telling you, you can understand little o' the now, but some of it will come back to you when you're a grown man, and if you're magerful and have some lassie in your grip, maybe for the memory of her that bore you, you'll let the poor thing awa'."

And she asked him to add this to his nightly prayer: "O God, keep me from being a magerful man!" and to teach this other prayer to Elspeth, "O God, whatever is to be my fate, may I never be one of them that bow the knee to magerful men, and if I was born like that and canna help it, oh, take me up to heaven afore I'm fil't."

The wardrobe was invisible in the darkness, but they could still hear Elspeth's breathing as she slept, and the exhausted woman listened long to it, as if she would fain carry away with her to the other world the memory of that sweet sound.

"If you gang to Thrums," she said at last, "you may hear my story frae some that winna spare me in the telling; but should Elspeth be wi' you at sic times, dinna answer back; just slip quietly away wi' her. She's so young that she'll soon forget all about her life in London and all about me, and that'll be best for her. I would like her lassiehood to be bright and free frae cares, as if there had never been sic a woman as me. But laddie, oh, my laddie, dinna you forget me; you and me had him to thole thegither, dinna you forget me! Watch ower your little sister by day and hap her by night, and when the time comes that a man wants her-if he be magerful, tell her my story at once. But gin she loves one that is her ain true love, dinna rub off the bloom, laddie, with a word about me. Let her and him gang to the Cuttle Well, as Aaron and me went, kenning no guile and thinking none, and with their arms round one another's waists. But when her wedding-day comes round —"

Her words broke in a sob and she cried: "I see them, I see them standing up thegither afore the minister! Oh! you lad, you lad that's to be married on my Elspeth, turn your face and let me see that you're no' a magerful man!"

But the lad did not turn his face, and when she spoke next it was to Tommy.

"In the bottom o' my kist there's a little silver teapot. It's no' real silver, but it's fell bonny. I bought it for Elspeth twa or three months back when I saw I couldna last the winter. I bought it to her for a marriage present. She's no' to see it till her wedding-day comes round. Syne you're to give it to her, man, and say it's with her mother's love. Tell her all about me, for it canna harm her then. Tell her of the fool lies I sent to Thrums, but dinna forget what a bonny place I thought it all the time, nor how I stood on many a driech night at the corner of that street, looking so waeful at the lighted windows, and hungering for the wring of a Thrums hand or the sound of the Thrums word, and all the time the shrewd blasts cutting through my thin trails of claithes. Tell her, man, how you and me spent this night, and how I fought to keep my hoast down so as no' to waken her. Mind that whatever I have been, I was aye fond o' my bairns, and slaved for them till I dropped. She'll have long forgotten what I was like, and it's just as well, but yet-Look at me, Tommy, look long, long, so as you'll be able to call up my face as it was on the far-back night when I telled you my mournful story. Na, you canna see in the dark, but haud my hand, haud it tight, so that, when you tell Elspeth, you'll mind how hot it was, and the skin loose on it; and put your hand on my cheeks, man, and feel how wet they are wi' sorrowful tears, and lay it on my breast, so that you can tell her how I was shrunk awa'. And if she greets for her mother a whiley, let her greet."

The sobbing boy hugged his mother. "Do you think I'm an auld woman?" she said to him.

"You're gey auld, are you no'?" he answered.

"Ay," she said, "I'm gey auld; I'm nine and twenty. I was seventeen on the day when Aaron Latta went half-road in the cart wi' me to Cullew, hauding my hand aneath my shawl. He hadna spiered me, but I just kent."

Tommy remained in his mother's bed for the rest of the night, and so many things were buzzing in his brain that not for an hour did he think it time to repeat his new prayer. At last he said reverently: "O God, keep me from being a magerful man!" Then he opened his eyes to let God see that his prayer was ended, and added to himself: "But I think I would fell like it."

Chapter XI
Aaron Latta

The Airlie post had dropped the letters for outlying farms at the Monypenny smithy and trudged on. The smith having wiped his hand on his hair, made a row of them, without looking at the addresses, on his window-sill, where, happening to be seven in number, they were almost a model of Monypenny, which is within hail of Thrums, but round the corner from it, and so has ways of its own. With the next clang on the anvil the middle letter fell flat, and now the likeness to Monypenny was absolute.

Again all the sound in the land was the melancholy sweet kink, kink, kink of the smith's hammer.

Across the road sat Dite Deuchars, the mole-catcher, a solitary figure, taking his pleasure on the dyke. Behind him was the flour-miller's field, and beyond it the Den, of which only some tree-tops were visible. He looked wearily east the road, but no one emerged from Thrums; he looked wearily west the road, which doubled out of sight at Aaron Latta's cottage, little more than a stone's throw distant. On the inside of Aaron's window an endless procession seemed to be passing, but it was only the warping mill going round. It was an empty day, but Dite, the accursed, was used to them; nothing ever happened where he was, but many things as soon as he had gone.

He yawned and looked at the houses opposite. They were all of one story; the smith's had a rusty plough stowed away on its roof; under a window stood a pew and bookboard, bought at the roup of an old church, and thus transformed into a garden-seat. There were many of them in Thrums that year. All the doors, except that of the smithy, were shut, until one of them blew ajar, when Dite knew at once, from the smell which crossed the road, that Blinder was in the bunk pulling the teeth of his potatoes. May Ann Irons, the blind man's niece, came out at this door to beat the cistern with a bass, and she gave Dite a wag of her head. He was to be married to her if she could get nothing better.

By and by the Painted Lady came along the road. She was a little woman, brightly dressed, so fragile that a collie might have knocked her over with his tail, and she had a beautiful white-and-pink face, the white ending of a sudden in the middle of her neck, where it met skin of a duller color. As she tripped along with mincing gait, she was speaking confidentially to herself, but when she saw Dite grinning, she seemed, first, afraid, and then sorry for herself, and then she tried to carry it off with a giggle, cocking her head impudently at him. Even then she looked childish, and a faded guilelessness, with many pretty airs and graces, still lingered about her, like innocent birds loath to be gone from the spot where their nest has been. When she had passed monotony again reigned, and Dite crossed to the smithy window, though none of the letters could be for him. He could read the addresses on six of them, but the seventh lay on its back, and every time he rose on his tip-toes to squint down at it, the spout pushed his bonnet over his eyes.

"Smith," he cried in at the door, "to gang hame afore I ken wha that letter's to is more than I can do."

The smith good-naturedly brought the letter to him, and then glancing at the address was dumfounded. "God behears," he exclaimed, with a sudden look at the distant cemetery, "it's to Double Dykes!"

Dite also shot a look at the cemetery. "He'll never get it," he said, with mighty conviction.

The two men gazed at the cemetery for some time, and at last Dite muttered, "Ay, ay, Double Dykes, you was aye fond o' your joke!"

"What has that to do wi' 't?" rapped out the smith, uncomfortably.

Dite shuddered. "Man," he said, "does that letter no bring Double Dykes back terrible vive again! If we was to see him climbing the cemetery dyke the now, and coming stepping down the fields in his moleskin waistcoat wi' the pearl buttons —"

Auchterlonie stopped him with a nervous gesture.

"But it couldna be the pearl buttons," Dite added thoughtfully, "for Betty Finlayson has been wearing them to the kirk this four year. Ay, ay, Double Dykes, that puts you farther awa' again."

The smith took the letter to a neighbor's house to ask the advice of old Irons, the blind tailor, who when he lost his sight had given himself the name of Blinder for bairns to play with.

"Make your mind easy, smith," was Blinder's counsel. "The letter is meant for the Painted Lady. What's Double Dykes? It's but the name of a farm, and we gave it to Sanders because he was the farmer. He's dead, and them that's in the house now become Double Dykes in his place."

But the Painted Lady only had the house, objected Dite; Nether Drumgley was farming the land, and so he was the real Double Dykes. True, she might have pretended to her friends that she had the land also.

She had no friends, the smith said, and since she came to Double Dykes from no one could find out where, though they knew her furniture was bought in Tilliedrum, she had never got a letter. Often, though, as she passed his window she had keeked sideways at the letters, as bairns might look at parlys. If he made a tinkle with his hammer at such times off she went at once, for she was as easily flichtered as a field of crows, that take wing if you tap your pipe on the loof of your hand. It was true she had spoken to him once; when he suddenly saw her standing at his smiddy door, the surprise near made him fall over his brot. She looked so neat and ladylike that he gave his hair a respectful pull before he remembered the kind of woman she was.

And what was it she said to him? Dite asked eagerly.

She had pointed to the letters on the window-sill, and said she, "Oh, the dear loves!" It was a queer say, but she had a bonny English word. The English word was no doubt prideful, but it melted in the mouth like a lick of sirup. She offered him sixpence for a letter, any letter he liked, but of course he refused it. Then she prigged with him just to let her hold one in her hands, for said she, bairnlike, "I used to get one every day." It so happened that one of the letters was to Mysy Bobbie; and Mysy was of so little importance that he thought there would be no harm in letting the Painted Lady hold her letter, so he gave it to her, and you should have seen her dawting it with her hand and holding it to her breast like a lassie with a pigeon. "Isn't it sweet?" she said, and before he could stop her she kissed it. She forgot it was no letter of hers, and made to open it, and then she fell a-trembling and saying she durst not read it, for you never knew whether the first words might not break your heart. The envelope was red where her lips had touched it, and yet she had an innocent look beneath the paint. When he took the letter from her, though, she called him a low, vulgar fellow for presuming to address a lady. She worked herself into a fury, and said far worse than that; a perfect guller of clarty language came pouring out of her. He had heard women curse many a time without turning a hair, but he felt wae when she did it, for she just spoke it like a bairn that had been in ill company.

The smith's wife, Suphy, who had joined the company, thought that men were easily taken in, especially smiths. She offered, however, to convey the letter to Double Dykes. She was anxious to see the inside of the Painted Lady's house, and this would be a good opportunity. She admitted that she had crawled to the east window of it before now, but that dour bairn of the Painted Lady's had seen her head and whipped down the blind.

Unfortunate Suphy! she could not try the window this time, as it was broad daylight, and the Painted Lady took the letter from her at the door. She returned crestfallen, and for an hour nothing happened. The mole-catcher went off to the square, saying, despondently, that nothing would happen until he was round the corner. No sooner had he rounded the corner than something did happen.

A girl who had left Double Dykes with a letter was walking quickly toward Monypenny. She wore a white pinafore over a magenta frock, and no one could tell her whether she was seven or eight, for she was only the Painted Lady's child. Some boys, her natural enemies, were behind; they had just emerged from the Den, and she heard them before they saw her, and at once her little heart jumped and ran off with her. But the halloo that told her she was discovered checked her running. Her teeth went into her underlip; now her head was erect. After her came the rabble with a rush, flinging stones that had no mark and epithets that hit. Grizel disdained to look over her shoulder. Little hunted child, where was succor to come from if she could not fight for herself?

Though under the torture she would not cry out. "What's a father?" was their favorite jeer, because she had once innocently asked this question of a false friend. One tried to snatch the letter from her, but she flashed him a look that sent him to the other side of the dyke, where, he said, did she think he was afraid of her? Another strutted by her side, mimicking her in such diverting manner that presently the others had to pick him out of the ditch. Thus Grizel moved onward defiantly until she reached Monypenny, where she tossed the letter in at the smithy door and immediately returned home. It was the letter that had been sent to her mother, now sent back, because it was meant for the dead farmer after all.

The smith read Jean Myles's last letter, with a face of growing gravity. "Dear Double Dykes," it said, "I send you these few scrapes to say I am dying, and you and Aaron Latta was seldom sindry, so I charge you to go to him and say to him 'Aaron Latta, it's all lies Jean Myles wrote to Thrums about her grandeur, and her man died mony year back, and it was the only kindness he ever did her, and if she doesna die quick, her and her starving bairns will be flung out into the streets.' If that doesna move him, say, 'Aaron Latta, do you mind yon day at Inverquharity and the cushie doos?' likewise, 'Aaron Latta, do you mind yon day at the Kaims of Airlie?' likewise, 'Aaron Latta, do you mind that Jean Myles was ower heavy for you to lift? Oh, Aaron, you could lift me so pitiful easy now.' And syne says you solemnly three times, 'Aaron Latta, Jean Myles is lying dying all alone in a foreign land; Aaron Latta, Jean Myles is lying dying all alone in a foreign land; Aaron Latta, Jean Myles is lying dying all alone in a foreign land.' And if he's sweer to come, just say, 'Oh, Aaron, man, you micht; oh, Aaron, oh, Aaron, are you coming?'"

The smith had often denounced this woman, but he never said a word against her again. He stood long reflecting, and then took the letter to Blinder and read it to him.

"She doesna say, 'Oh, Aaron Latta, do you mind the Cuttle Well?'" was the blind man's first comment.

"She was thinking about it," said Auchterlonie.

"Ay, and he's thinking about it," said Blinder, "night and day, night and day. What a town there'll be about that letter, smith!"

"There will. But I'm to take it to Aaron afore the news spreads. He'll never gang to London though."

"I think he will, smith."

"I ken him well."

"Maybe I ken him better."

"You canna see the ugly mark it left on his brow."

"I can see the uglier marks it has left in his breast."

"Well, I'll take the letter; I can do no more."

When the smith opened the door of Aaron's house he let out a draught of hot air that was glad to be gone from the warper's restless home. The usual hallan, or passage, divided the but from the ben, and in the ben a great revolving thing, the warping-mill, half filled the room. Between it and a pile of webs that obscured the light a little silent man was sitting on a box turning a handle. His shoulders were almost as high as his ears, as if he had been caught forever in a storm, and though he was barely five and thirty, he had the tattered, dishonored beard of black and white that comes to none till the glory of life has gone.

Suddenly the smith appeared round the webs. "Aaron," he said, awkwardly, "do you mind Jean Myles?"

The warper did not for a moment take his eyes off a contrivance with pirns in it that was climbing up and down the whirring mill.

"She's dead," he answered.

"She's dying," said the smith.

A thread broke, and Aaron had to rise to mend it.

"Stop the mill and listen," Auchterlonie begged him, but the warper returned to his seat and the mill again revolved.

"This is her dying words to you," continued the smith. "Did you speak?"

"I didna, but I wish you would take your arm off the haik."

"She's loath to die without seeing you. Do you hear, man? You shall listen to me, I tell you."

"I am listening, smith," the warper replied, without rancour. "It's but right that you should come here to take your pleasure on a shamed man." His calmness gave him a kind of dignity.

"Did I ever say you was a shamed man, Aaron?"

"Am I not?" the warper asked quietly; and Auchterlonie hung his head.

Aaron continued, still turning the handle, "You're truthful, and you canna deny it. Nor will you deny that I shamed you and every other mother's son that night. You try to hod it out o' pity, smith, but even as you look at me now, does the man in you no rise up against me?"

"If so," the smith answered reluctantly, "if so, it's against my will."

"It is so," said Aaron, in the same measured voice, "and it's right that it should be so. A man may thieve or debauch or murder, and yet no be so very different frae his fellow-men, but there's one thing he shall not do without their wanting to spit him out o' their mouths, and that is, violate the feelings of sex."

The strange words in which the warper described his fall had always an uncomfortable effect on those who heard him use them, and Auchterlonie could only answer in distress, "Maybe that's what it is."

"That's what it is. I have had twal lang years sitting on this box to think it out. I blame none but mysel'."

"Then you'll have pity on Jean in her sair need," said the smith. He read slowly the first part of the letter, but Aaron made no comment, and the mill had not stopped for a moment.

"She says," the smith proceeded, doggedly —"she says to say to you, 'Aaron Latta, do you mind yon day at Inverquharity and the cushie doos?'"

Only the monotonous whirr of the mill replied.

"She says, 'Aaron Latta, do you mind that Jean Myles was ower heavy for you to lift? Oh, Aaron, you could lift me so pitiful easy now.'"

Another thread broke and the warper rose with sudden fury.

"Now that you've eased your conscience, smith," he said, fiercely, "make your feet your friend."

"I'll do so," Auchterlonie answered, laying the letter on the webs, "but I leave this ahint me."

"Wap it in the fire."

"If that's to be done, you do it yoursel'. Aaron, she treated you ill, but —"

"There's the door, smith."

The smith walked away, and had only gone a few steps when he heard the whirr of the mill again. He went back to the door.

"She's dying, man!" he cried.

"Let her die!" answered Aaron.

In an hour the sensational news was through half of Thrums, of which Monypenny may be regarded as a broken piece, left behind, like the dot of quicksilver in the tube, to show how high the town once rose. Some could only rejoice at first in the down-come of Jean Myles, but most blamed the smith (and himself among them) for not taking note of her address, so that Thrums Street could be informed of it and sent to her relief. For Blinder alone believed that Aaron would be softened.

"It was twa threads the smith saw him break," the blind man said, "and Aaron's good at his work. He'll go to London, I tell you."

"You forget, Blinders, that he was warping afore I was a dozen steps frae the door."

"Ay, and that just proves he hadna burned the letter, for he hadna time. If he didna do it at the first impulse, he'll no do it now."

Every little while the boys were sent along the road to look in at Aaron's end window and report.

At seven in the evening Aaron had not left his box, and the blind man's reputation for seeing farther than those with eyes was fallen low.

"It's a good sign," he insisted, nevertheless. "It shows his mind's troubled, for he usually louses at six."

By eight the news was that Aaron had left his mill and was sitting staring at his kitchen fire.

"He's thinking o' Inverquharity and the cushie doos," said Blinder.

"More likely," said Dite Deuchars, "he's thinking o' the Cuttle Well."

Corp Shiach clattered along the road about nine to say that Aaron Latta was putting on his blacks as if for a journey.

At once the blind man's reputation rose on stilts. It fell flat, however, before the ten-o'clock bell rang, when three of the Auchterlonie children, each pulling the others back that he might arrive first, announced that Aaron had put on his corduroys again, and was back at the mill.

"That settles it," was everyone's good-night to Blinder, but he only answered thoughtfully, "There's a fierce fight going on, my billies."

Next morning when his niece was shaving the blind man, the razor had to travel over a triumphant smirk which would not explain itself to womankind, Blinder being a man who could bide his time. The time came when the smith looked in to say, "Should I gang yont to Aaron's and see if he'll give me the puir woman's address?"

"No, I wouldna advise that," answered Blinder, cleverly concealing his elation, "for Aaron Latta's awa' to London."

"What! How can you ken?"

"I heard him go by in the night."

"It's no possible!"

"I kent his foot."

"You're sure it was Aaron?"

Blinder did not consider the question worth answering, his sharpness at recognizing friends by their tread being proved. Sometimes he may have carried his pretensions too far. Many granted that he could tell when a doctor went by, when a lawyer, when a thatcher, when a herd, and this is conceivable, for all callings have their walk. But he was regarded as uncanny when he claimed not only to know ministers in this way, but to be able to distinguish between the steps of the different denominations.

He had made no mistake about the warper, however. Aaron was gone, and ten days elapsed before he was again seen in Thrums.

Chapter XII
A Child's Tragedy

No one in Thrums ever got a word from Aaron Latta about how he spent those ten days, and Tommy and Elspeth, whom he brought back with him, also tried to be reticent, but some of the women were too clever for them. Jean and Aaron did not meet again. Her first intimation that he had come she got from Shovel, who said that a little high-shouldered man in black had been inquiring if she was dead, and was now walking up and down the street, like one waiting. She sent her children out to him, but he would not come up. He had answered Tommy roughly, but when Elspeth slipped her hand into his, he let it stay there, and he instructed her to tell Jean Myles that he would bury her in the Thrums cemetery and bring up her bairns. Jean managed once to go to the window and look down at him, and by and by he looked up and saw her. They looked long at each other, and then he turned away his head and began to walk up and down again.

At Tilliedrum the coffin was put into a hearse and thus conveyed to Monypenny, Aaron and the two children sitting on the box-seat. Someone said, "Jean Myles boasted that when she came back to Thrums it would be in her carriage and pair, and she has kept her word," and the saying is still preserved in that Bible for week-days of which all little places have their unwritten copy, one of the wisest of books, but nearly every text in it has cost a life.

About a score of men put on their blacks and followed the hearse from the warper's house to the grave. Elspeth wanted to accompany Tommy, but Aaron held her back, saying, quietly, "In this part, it's only men that go to burials, so you and me maun bide at name," and then she cried, no one understood why, except Tommy. It was because he would see Thrums first; but he whispered to her, "I promise to keep my eyes shut and no look once," and so faithfully did he keep his promise on the whole that the smith held him by the hand most of the way, under the impression that he was blind.

But he had opened his eyes at the grave, when a cord was put into his hand, and then he wept passionately, and on his way back to Monypenny, whether his eyes were open or shut, what he saw was his mother being shut up in a black hole and trying for ever and ever to get out. He ran to Elspeth for comfort, but in the meantime she had learned from Blinder's niece that graves are dark and cold, and so he found her sobbing even like himself. Tommy could never bear to see Elspeth crying, and he revealed his true self in his way of drying her tears.

"It will be so cold in that hole," she sobbed.

"No," he said, "it's warm."

"It will be dark."

"No, it's clear."

"She would like to get out."

"No, she was terrible pleased to get in."

It was characteristic of him that he soon had Elspeth happy by arguments not one of which he believed himself; characteristic also that his own grief was soothed by the sound of them. Aaron, who was in the garret preparing their bed, had told the children that they must remain indoors to-day out of respect to their mother's memory (to-morrow morning they could explore Thrums); but there were many things in that kitchen for them to look at and exult over. It had no commonplace ceiling, the couples, or rafters, being covered with the loose flooring of a romantic garret, and in the rafters were several great hooks, from one of which hung a ham, and Tommy remembered, with a thrill which he communicated to Elspeth, that it is the right of Thrums children to snip off the ham as much as they can remove with their finger-nails and roast it on the ribs of the fire. The chief pieces of furniture were a dresser, a corner cupboard with diamond panes, two tables, one of which stood beneath the other, but would have to come out if Aaron tried to bake, and a bed with a door. These two did not know it, but the room was full of memories of Jean Myles. The corner cupboard had been bought by Aaron at a roup because she said she would like to have one; it was she who had chosen the six cups and saucers with the blue spots on them. A razor-strop, now hard as iron, hung on a nail on the wall; it had not been used since the last time Aaron strutted through the Den with his sweetheart. One day later he had opened the door of the bird-cage, which still stood in the window, and let the yellow yite go. Many things were where no woman would have left them: clothes on the floor with the nail they had torn from the wall; on a chair a tin basin, soapy water and a flannel rag in it; horn spoons with whistles at the end of them were anywhere-on the mantelpiece, beneath the bed; there were drawers that could not be opened because their handles were inside. Perhaps the windows were closed hopelessly also, but this must be left doubtful; no one had ever tried to open them.

The garret where Tommy and Elspeth were to sleep was reached by a ladder from the hallan; when you were near the top of the ladder your head hit a trap-door and pushed it open. At one end of the garret was the bed, and at the other end were piled sticks for firewood and curious dark-colored slabs whose smell the children disliked until Tommy said, excitedly, "Peat!" and then they sniffed reverently.

It was Tommy, too, who discovered the tree-tops of the Den, and Elspeth seeing him gazing in a transport out at the window cried, "What is it, Tommy? Quick!"

"Promise no to scream," he replied, warningly. "Well, then, Elspeth Sandys, that's where the Den is!"

Elspeth blinked with awe, and anon said, wistfully, "Tommy, do you see that there? That's where the Den is!"

"It were me what told you," cried Tommy, jealously.

"But let me tell you, Tommy!"

"Well, then, you can tell me."

"That there is the Den, Tommy!"

"Dagont!"

Oh, that to-morrow were here! Oh, that Shovel could see these two to-morrow!

Here is another splendid game, T. Sandys, inventor. The girl goes into the bed, the boy shuts the door on her, and imitates the sound of a train in motion. He opens the door and cries, "Tickets, please." The girl says, "What is the name of this place?" The boy replies, "It's Thrums!" There is more to follow, but the only two who have played the game always roared so joyously at this point that they could get no farther.

"Oh, to-morrow, come quick, quick!"

"Oh, poor Shovel!"

To-morrow came, and with it two eager little figures rose and gulped their porridge, and set off to see Thrums. They were dressed in the black clothes Aaron Latta had bought for them in London, and they had agreed just to walk, but when they reached the door and saw the tree-tops of the Den they-they ran. Would you not like to hold them back? It is a child's tragedy.

They went first into the Den, and the rocks were dripping wet, all the trees, save the firs, were bare, and the mud round a tiny spring pulled off one of Elspeth's boots.

"Tommy," she cried, quaking, "that narsty puddle can't not be the Cuttle Well, can it?"

"No, it ain't," said Tommy, quickly, but he feared it was.

"It's c-c-colder here than London," Elspeth said, shivering, and Tommy was shivering too, but he answered, "I'm —I'm —I'm warm."

The Den was strangely small, and soon they were on a shabby brae where women in short gowns came to their doors and men in night-caps sat down on the shafts of their barrows to look at Jean Myles's bairns.

"What does yer think?" Elspeth whispered, very doubtfully.

"They're beauties," Tommy answered, determinedly.

Presently Elspeth cried, "Oh, Tommy, what a ugly stair! Where is the beauty stairs as is wore outside for show?"

This was one of them and Tommy knew it. "Wait till you see the west town end," he said bravely; "it's grand." But when they were in the west town end, and he had to admit it, "Wait till you see the square," he said, and when they were in the square, "Wait," he said, huskily, "till you see the town-house." Alas, this was the town-house facing them, and when they knew it, he said hurriedly, "Wait till you see the Auld Licht Kirk."

They stood long in front of the Auld Licht Kirk, which he had sworn was bigger and lovelier than St. Paul's, but-well, it is a different style of architecture, and had Elspeth not been there with tears in waiting, Tommy would have blubbered. "It's —it's littler than I thought," he said desperately, "but-the minister, oh, what a wonderful big man he is!"

"Are you sure?" Elspeth squeaked.

"I swear he is."

The church door opened and a gentleman came out, a little man, boyish in the back, with the eager face of those who live too quickly. But it was not at him that Tommy pointed reassuringly; it was at the monster church key, half of which protruded from his tail pocket and waggled like the hilt of a sword.

Speaking like an old residenter, Tommy explained that he had brought his sister to see the church, "She's ta'en aback," he said, picking out Scotch words carefully, "because it's littler than the London kirks, but I told her —I told her that the preaching is better."

This seemed to please the stranger, for he patted Tommy on the head while inquiring, "How do you know that the preaching is better?"

"Tell him, Elspeth," replied Tommy modestly.

"There ain't nuthin' as Tommy don't know," Elspeth explained. "He knows what the minister is like too."

"He's a noble sight," said Tommy.

"He can get anything from God he likes," said Elspeth.

"He's a terrible big man," said Tommy.

This seemed to please the little gentleman less. "Big!" he exclaimed, irritably; "why should he be big?"

"He is big," Elspeth almost screamed, for the minister was her last hope.

"Nonsense!" said the little gentleman. "He is-well, I am the minister."

"You!" roared Tommy, wrathfully.

"Oh, oh, oh!" sobbed Elspeth.

For a moment the Rev. Mr. Dishart looked as if he would like to knock two little heads together, but he walked away without doing it.

"Never mind," Tommy whispered hoarsely to Elspeth. "Never mind, Elspeth, you have me yet."

This consolation seldom failed to gladden her, but her disappointment was so sharp to-day that she would not even look up.

"Come away to the cemetery, it's grand," he said; but still she would not be comforted.

"And I'll let you hold my hand-as soon as we're past the houses," he added.

"I'll let you hold it now," he said eventually; but even then Elspeth cried dismally, and her sobs were hurting him more than her.

He knew all the ways of getting round Elspeth, and when next he spoke it was with a sorrowful dignity. "I didna think," he said, "as yer wanted me never to be able to speak again; no, I didna think it, Elspeth."

She took her hands from her face and looked at him inquiringly.

"One of the stories mamma told me and Reddy," he said, "were about a man what saw such a beauty thing that he was struck dumb with admiration. Struck dumb is never to be able to speak again, and I wish I had been struck dumb when you wanted it."

"But I didn't want it!" Elspeth cried.

"If Thrums had been one little bit beautier than it is," he went on solemnly, "it would have struck me dumb. It would have hurt me sore, but what about that, if it pleased you!"

Then did Elspeth see what a wicked girl she had been, and when next the two were observed by the curious (it was on the cemetery road), they were once more looking cheerful. At the smallest provocation they exchanged notes of admiration, such as, "Oh, Tommy, what a bonny barrel!" or "Oh, Elspeth, I tell yer that's a dyke, and there's just walls in London," but sometimes Elspeth would stoop hastily, pretending that she wanted to tie her bootlace, but really to brush away a tear, and there were moments when Tommy hung very limp. Each was trying to deceive the other for the other's sake, and one of them was never good at deception. They saw through each other, yet kept up the chilly game, because they could think of nothing better, and perhaps the game was worth playing, for love invented it.

They sat down on their mother's grave. No stone was ever erected to the memory of Jean Myles, but it is enough for her that she lies at home. That comfort will last her to the Judgment Day.

The man who had dug the grave sent them away, and they wandered to the hill, and thence down the Roods, where there were so many outside stairs not put there for show that it was well Elspeth remembered how susceptible Tommy was to being struck dumb. For her sake he said, "They're bonny," and for his sake she replied, "I'm glad they ain't bonnier."

When within one turn of Monypenny they came suddenly upon some boys playing at capey-dykey, a game with marbles that is only known in Thrums. There are thirty-five ways of playing marbles, but this is the best way, and Elspeth knew that Tommy was hungering to look on, but without her, lest he should be accused of sweethearting. So she offered to remain in the background.

Was she sure she shouldn't mind?

She said falteringly that of course she would mind a little, but —

Then Tommy was irritated, and said he knew she would mind, but if she just pretended she didn't mind, he could leave her without feeling that he was mean.

So Elspeth affected not to mind, and then he deserted her, conscience at rest, which was his nature. But he should have remained with her. The players only gave him the side of their eye, and a horrid fear grew on him that they did not know he was a Thrums boy. "Dagont!" he cried to put them right on that point, but though they paused in their game, it was only to laugh at him uproariously. Let the historian use an oath for once; dagont, Tommy had said the swear in the wrong place!

How fond he had been of that word! Many a time he had fired it in the face of Londoners, and the flash had often blinded them and always him. Now he had brought it home, and Thrums would have none of it; it was as if these boys were jeering at their own flag. He tottered away from them until he came to a trance, or passage, where he put his face to the wall and forgot even Elspeth.

He had not noticed a girl pass the mouth of the trance, trying not very successfully to conceal a brandy-bottle beneath her pinafore, but presently he heard shouts, and looking out he saw Grizel, the Painted Lady's child, in the hands of her tormentors. She was unknown to him, of course, but she hit back so courageously that he watched her with interest, until-until suddenly he retreated farther into the trance. He had seen Elspeth go on her knees, obviously to ask God to stay the hands and tongues of these cruel boys.

Elspeth had disgraced him, he felt. He was done with her forever. If they struck her, serve her right.

Struck her! Struck little Elspeth! His imagination painted the picture with one sweep of its brush. Take care, you boys, Tommy is scudding back.

They had not molested Elspeth as yet. When they saw and heard her praying, they had bent forward, agape, as if struck suddenly in the stomach. Then one of them, Francie Crabb, the golden-haired son of Esther Auld, recovered and began to knead Grizel's back with his fists, less in viciousness than to show that the prayer was futile. Into this scene sprang Tommy, and he thought that Elspeth was the kneaded one. Had he taken time to reflect he would probably have used the Thrums feint, and then in with a left-hander, which is not very efficacious in its own country; but being in a hurry he let out with Shovel's favorite, and down went Francie Crabb.

"Would you!" said Tommy, threatening, when Francie attempted to rise.

He saw now that Elspeth was untouched, that he had rescued an unknown girl, and it cannot be pretended of him that he was the boy to squire all ladies in distress. In ordinary circumstances he might have left Grizel to her fate, but having struck for her, he felt that he would like to go on striking. He had also the day's disappointments to avenge. It is startling to reflect that the little minister's height, for instance, put an extra kick in him.

So he stood stridelegs over Francie, who whimpered, "I wouldna have struck this one if that one hadna prayed for me. It wasna likely I would stand that."

"You shall stand it," replied Tommy, and turning to Elspeth, who had risen from her knees, he said: "Pray away, Elspeth."

Elspeth refused, feeling that there would be something wrong in praying from triumph, and Tommy, about to be very angry with her, had a glorious inspiration. "Pray for yourself," he said to Francie, "and do it out loud."

The other boys saw that a novelty promised, and now Francie need expect no aid from them. At first he refused to pray, but he succumbed when Tommy had explained the consequences, and illustrated them.

Tommy dictated: "Oh, God, I am a sinner. Go on."

Francie not only said it, but looked it.

"And I pray to you to repent me, though I ain't worthy," continued Tommy.

"And I pray to you to repent me, though I ain't worthy," growled Francie. (It was the arrival of ain't in Thrums.)

Tommy considered, and then: "I thank Thee, O God," he said, "for telling this girl-this lassie-to pray for me."

Two gentle taps helped to knock this out of Francie.

Being an artist, Tommy had kept his best for the end (and made it up first). "And lastly," he said, "I thank this boy for thrashing me —I mean this here laddie. Oh, may he allus be near to thrash me when I strike this other lassie again. Amen."

When it was all over Tommy looked around triumphantly, and though he liked the expression on several faces, Grizel's pleased him best. "It ain't no wonder you would like to be me, lassie!" he said, in an ecstasy.

"I don't want to be you, you conceited boy," retorted the Painted Lady's child hotly, and her heat was the greater because the clever little wretch had read her thoughts aright. But it was her sweet voice that surprised him.

"You're English!" he cried.

"So are you," broke in a boy offensively, and then Tommy said to Grizel loftily, "Run away; I'll not let none on them touch you."

"I am not afraid of them," she rejoined, with scorn, "and I shall not let you help me, and I won't run." And run she did not; she walked off leisurely with her head in the air, and her dignity was beautiful, except once when she made the mistake of turning round to put out her tongue.

But, alas! in the end someone ran. If only they had not called him "English." In vain he fired a volley of Scotch; they pretended not to understand it. Then he screamed that he and Shovel could fight the lot of them. Who was Shovel? they asked derisively. He replied that Shovel was a bloke who could lick any two of them-and with one hand tied behind his back.

No sooner had he made this proud boast than he went white, and soon two disgraceful tears rolled down his cheeks. The boys saw that for some reason unknown his courage was gone, and even Francie Crabb began to turn up his sleeves and spit upon his hands.

Elspeth was as bewildered as the others, but she slipped her hand into his and away they ran ingloriously, the foe too much astounded to jeer. She sought to comfort him by saying (and it brought her a step nearer womanhood), "You wasn't feared for yourself, you wasn't; you was just feared they would hurt me."

But Tommy sobbed in reply, "That ain't it. I bounced so much about the Thrums folk to Shovel, and now the first day I'm here I heard myself bouncing about Shovel to Thrums folk, and it were that what made me cry. Oh, Elspeth, it's —it's not the same what I thought it would be!"

Nor was it the same to Elspeth, so they sat down by the roadside and cried with their arms round each other, and any passer-by could look who had the heart. But when night came, and they were in their garret bed, Tommy was once more seeking to comfort Elspeth with arguments he disbelieved, and again he succeeded. As usual, too, the make-believe made him happy also.

"Have you forgot," he whispered, "that my mother said as she would come and see us every night in our bed? If yer cries, she'll see as we're terrible unhappy, and that will make her unhappy too."

"Oh, Tommy, is she here now?"

"Whisht! She's here, but they don't like living ones to let on as they knows it."

Elspeth kept closer to Tommy, and with their heads beneath the blankets, so as to stifle the sound, he explained to her how they could cheat their mother. When she understood, he took the blankets off their faces and said in the darkness in a loud voice:

"It's a grand place, Thrums!"

Elspeth replied in a similar voice, "Ain't the town-house just big!"

Said Tommy, almost chuckling, "Oh, the bonny, bonny Auld Licht Kirk!"

Said Elspeth, "Oh, the beauty outside stairs!"

Said Tommy, "The minister is so long!"

Said Elspeth, "The folk is so kind!"

Said Tommy, "Especially the laddies!"

"Oh, I is so happy!" cried Elspeth.

"Me too!" cried Tommy.

"My mother would be so chirpy if she could jest see us!" Elspeth said, quite archly.

"But she canna!" replied Tommy, slyly pinching Elspeth in the rib.

Then they dived beneath the blankets, and the whispering was resumed.

"Did she hear, does yer think?" asked Elspeth.

"Every word," Tommy replied. "Elspeth, we've done her!"

Chapter XIII
Shows How Tommy Took Care of Elspeth

Thus the first day passed, and others followed in which women, who had known Jean Myles, did her children kindnesses, but could not do all they would have done, for Aaron forbade them to enter his home except on business though it was begging for a housewife all day. Had Elspeth at the age of six now settled down to domestic duties she would not have been the youngest housekeeper ever known in Thrums, but she was never very good at doing things, only at loving and being loved, and the observant neighbors thought her a backward girl; they forgot, like most people, that service is not necessarily a handicraft. Tommy discovered what they were saying, and to shield Elspeth he took to housewifery with the blind down; but Aaron, entering the kitchen unexpectedly, took the besom from, him, saying:

"It's an ill thing for men folk to ken ower muckle about women's work."

"You do it yoursel'," Tommy argued.

"I said men folk," replied Aaron, quietly.

The children knew that remarks of this sort had reference to their mother, of whom he never spoke more directly; indeed he seldom spoke to them at all, and save when he was cooking or giving the kitchen a slovenly cleaning they saw little of him. Monypenny had predicted that their presence must make a new man of him, but he was still unsociable and morose and sat as long as ever at the warping-mill, of which he seemed to have become the silent wheel. Tommy and Elspeth always dropped their voices when they spoke of him, and sometimes when his mill stopped he heard one of them say to the other, "Whisht, he's coming!" Though he seldom, spoke sharply to them, his face did not lose its loneliness at sight of them. Elspeth was his favorite (somewhat to the indignation of both); they found this out without his telling them or even showing it markedly, and when they wanted to ask anything of him she was deputed to do it, but she did it quavering, and after drawing farther away from him instead of going nearer. A dreary life would have lain before them had they not been sent to school.

There were at this time three schools in Thrums, the chief of them ruled over by the terrible Cathro (called Knuckly when you were a street away from him). It was a famous school, from which a band of three or four or even six marched every autumn to the universities as determined after bursaries as ever were Highlandmen to lift cattle, and for the same reason, that they could not do without.

A very different kind of dominie was Cursing Ballingall, who had been dropped at Thrums by a travelling circus, and first became familiar to the town as, carrying two carpet shoes, two books, a pillow, and a saucepan, which were all his belongings, he wandered from manse to manse offering to write sermons for the ministers at circus prices. That scheme failing, he was next seen looking in at windows in search of a canny calling, and eventually he cut one of his braces into a pair of tawse, thus with a single stroke of the knife, making himself a school-master and lop-sided for life. His fee was but a penny a week, "with a bit o' the swine when your father kills," and sometimes there were so many pupils on a form that they could only rise as one. During the first half of the scholastic day Ballingall's shouts and pounces were for parents to listen to, but after his dinner of crowdy, which is raw meal and hot water, served in a cogie, or wooden bowl, languor overcame him and he would sleep, having first given out a sum in arithmetic and announced:

"The one as finds out the answer first, I'll give him his licks."

Last comes the Hanky School, which was for the genteel and for the common who contemplated soaring. You were not admitted to it in corduroys or bare-footed, nor did you pay weekly; no, your father called four times a year with the money in an envelope. He was shown into the blue-and-white room, and there, after business had been transacted, very nervously on Miss Ailie's part, she offered him his choice between ginger wine and what she falteringly called wh-wh-whiskey. He partook in the polite national manner, which is thus:

"You will take something, Mr. Cortachy?"

"No, I thank you, ma'am."

"A little ginger wine?"

"It agrees ill with me."

"Then a little wh-wh-whiskey?"

"You are ower kind."

"Then may I?"

"I am not heeding."

"Perhaps, though, you don't take?"

"I can take it or want it."

"Is that enough?"

"It will do perfectly."

"Shall I fill it up?"

"As you please, ma'am."

Miss Ailie's relationship to the magerful man may be remembered; she shuddered to think of it herself, for in middle-age she retained the mind of a young girl, but when duty seemed to call, this school-mistress could be brave, and she offered to give Elspeth her schooling free of charge. Like the other two hers was a "mixed" school, but she did not want Tommy, because she had seen him in the square one day, and there was a leer on his face that reminded her of his father.

Another woman was less particular. This was Mrs. Crabb, of the Tappit Hen, the Esther Auld whom Jean Myles's letters had so frequently sent to bed. Her Francie was still a pupil of Miss Ailie, and still he wore the golden hair, which, despite all advice, she would not crop. It was so beautiful that no common boys could see it without wanting to give it a tug in passing, and partly to prevent this, partly to show how high she had risen in the social scale, Esther usually sent him to school under the charge of her servant lass. She now proposed to Aaron that this duty should devolve on Tommy, and for the service she would pay his fees at the Hanky School.

"We maun all lend a hand to poor Jean's bairns," she said, with a gleam in her eye. "It would have been well for her, Aaron, if she had married you."

"Is that all you have to say?" asked the warper, who had let her enter no farther than the hallan.

"I would expect him to lift Francie ower the pools in wet weather; and it might be as well if he called him Master Francie."

"Is that all?"

"Ay, I ask no more, for we maun all help Jean's bairns. If she could only look down, Aaron, and see her little velvets, as she called him, lifting my little corduroys ower the pools!"

Aaron flung open the door. "Munt!" he said, and he looked so dangerous that she retired at once. He sent Tommy to Ballingall's, and accepted Miss Ailie's offer for Elspeth, but this was an impossible arrangement, for it was known to the two persons primarily concerned that Elspeth would die if she was not where Tommy was. The few boys he had already begun to know were at Cathro's or Ballingall's, and as they called Miss Ailie's a lassie school he had no desire to attend it, but where he was there also must Elspeth be. Daily he escaped from Ballingall's and hid near the Dovecot, as Miss Ailie's house was called, and every little while he gave vent to Shovel's whistle, so that Elspeth might know of his proximity and be cheered. Thrice was he carried back, kicking, to Ballingall's by urchins sent in pursuit, stern ministers of justice on the first two occasions; but on the third they made him an offer: if he would hide in Couthie's hen-house they were willing to look for him everywhere else for two hours.

Tommy's behavior seemed beautiful to the impressionable Miss Ailie, but it infuriated Aaron, and on the fourth day he set off for the parish school, meaning to put the truant in the hands of Cathro, from whom there was no escape. Vainly had Elspeth implored him to let Tommy come to the Dovecot, and vainly apparently was she trotting at his side now, looking up appealingly in his face. But when they reached the gate of the parish school-yard he walked past it because she was tugging him, and always when he seemed about to turn she took his hand again, and he seemed to have lost the power to resist Jean Myles's bairn. So they came to the Dovecot, and Miss Ailie gained a pupil who had been meant for Cathro. Tommy's arms were stronger than Elspeth's, but they could not hare done as much for him that day.

Thus did the two children enter upon the genteel career, to the indignation of the other boys and girls of Monypenny, all of whom were commoners.

Chapter XIV
The Hanky School

The Dovecot was a prim little cottage standing back from the steepest brae in Thrums and hidden by high garden walls, to the top of which another boy's shoulders were, for apple-lovers, but one step up. Jargonelle trees grew against the house, stretching their arms round it as if to measure its girth, and it was also remarkable for several "dumb" windows with the most artful blinds painted on them. Miss Ailie's fruit was famous, but she loved her flowers best, and for long a notice board in her garden said, appealingly: "Persons who come to steal the fruit are requested not to walk on the flower-beds." It was that old bachelor, Dr. McQueen, who suggested this inscription to her, and she could never understand why he chuckled every time he read it.

There were seven rooms in the house, but only two were of public note, the school-room, which was downstairs, and the blue-and-white room above. The school-room was so long that it looked very low in the ceiling, and it had a carpet, and on the walls were texts as well as maps. Miss Ailie's desk was in the middle of the room, and there was another desk in the corner; a cloth had been hung over it, as one covers a cage to send the bird to sleep. Perhaps Miss Ailie thought that a bird had once sung there, for this had been the desk of her sister, Miss Kitty, who died years before Tommy came to Thrums. Dainty Miss Kitty, Miss Kitty with the roguish curls, it is strange to think that you are dead, and that only Miss Ailie hears you singing now at your desk in the corner! Miss Kitty never sang there, but the playful ringlets were once the bright thing in the room, and Miss Ailie sees them still, and they are a song to her.

The pupils had to bring handkerchiefs to the Dovecot, which led to its being called the Hanky School, and in time these handkerchiefs may be said to have assumed a religious character, though their purpose was merely to protect Miss Ailie's carpet. She opened each scholastic day by reading fifteen verses from the Bible, and then she said sternly, "Hankies!" whereupon her pupils whipped out their handkerchiefs, spread them on the floor and kneeled on them while Miss Ailie repeated the Lord's Prayer. School closed at four o'clock, again with hankies.

Only on great occasions were the boys and girls admitted to the blue-and-white room, when they were given shortbread, but had to eat it with their heads flung back so that no crumbs should fall. Nearly everything in this room was blue or white, or both. There were white blinds and blue curtains, a blue table-cover and a white crumb-cloth, a white sheepskin with a blue footstool on it, blue chairs dotted with white buttons. Only white flowers came into this room, where there were blue vases for them, not a book was to be seen without a blue alpaca cover. Here Miss Ailie received visitors in her white with the blue braid, and enrolled new pupils in blue ink with a white pen. Some laughed at her, others remembered that she must have something to love after Miss Kitty died.

Miss Ailie had her romance, as you may hear by and by, but you would not have thought it as she came forward to meet you in the blue-and-white room, trembling lest your feet had brought in mud, but too much a lady to ask you to stand on a newspaper, as she would have liked dearly to do. She was somewhat beyond middle-age, and stoutly, even squarely, built, which gave her a masculine appearance; but she had grown so timid since Miss Kitty's death that when she spoke you felt that either her figure or her manner must have been intended for someone else. In conversation she had a way of ending a sentence in the middle which gave her a reputation of being "thro'ither," though an artificial tooth was the cause. It was slightly loose, and had she not at times shut her mouth suddenly, and then done something with her tongue, an accident might have happened. This tooth fascinated Tommy, and once when she was talking he cried, excitedly, "Quick, it's coming!" whereupon her mouth snapped close, and she turned pink in the blue-and-white room.

Nevertheless Tommy became her favorite, and as he had taught himself to read, after a fashion, in London, where his lesson-books were chiefly placards and the journal subscribed to by Shovel's father, she often invited him after school hours to the blue-and-white room, where he sat on a kitchen chair (with his boots off) and read aloud, very slowly, while Miss Ailie knitted. The volume was from the Thrums Book Club, of which Miss Ailie was one of the twelve members. Each member contributed a book every year, and as their tastes in literature differed, all sorts of books came into the club, and there was one member who invariably gave a ro-ro-romance. He was double-chinned and forty, but the school-mistress called him the dashing young banker, and for months she avoided his dangerous contribution. But always there came a black day when a desire to read the novel seized her, and she hurried home with it beneath her rokelay. This year the dashing banker's choice was a lady's novel called "I Love My Love with an A," and it was a frivolous tale, those being before the days of the new fiction, with its grand discovery that women have an equal right with men to grow beards. The hero had such a way with him and was so young (Miss Ailie could not stand them a day more than twenty) that the school-mistress was enraptured and scared at every page, but she fondly hoped that Tommy did not understand. However, he discovered one day what something printed thus, "D —n," meant, and he immediately said the word with such unction that Miss Ailie let fall her knitting. She would have ended the readings then had not Agatha been at that point in the arms of an officer who, Miss Ailie felt almost certain, had a wife in India, and so how could she rest till she knew for certain? To track the officer by herself was not to be thought of, to read without knitting being such shameless waste of time, and it was decided to resume the readings on a revised plan: Tommy to say "stroke" in place of the "D —ns," and "word we have no concern with" instead of "Darling" and "Little One."

Miss Ailie was not the only person at the Dovecot who admired Tommy. Though in duty bound, as young patriots, to jeer at him for having been born in the wrong place, the pupils of his own age could not resist the charm of his reminiscences; even Gav Dishart, a son of the manse, listened attentively to him. His great topic was his birthplace, and whatever happened in Thrums, he instantly made contemptible by citing something of the same kind, but on a larger scale, that had happened in London; he turned up his nose almost farther than was safe when they said Catlaw was a stiff mountain to climb. ("Oh, Gav, if you just saw the London mountains!") Snow! why they didn't know what snow was in Thrums. If they could only see St. Paul's or Hyde Park or Shovel! he couldn't help laughing at Thrums, he couldn't —Larfing, he said at first, but in a short time his Scotch was better than theirs, though less unconscious. His English was better also, of course, and you had to speak in a kind of English when inside the Hanky School; you got your revenge at "minutes." On the whole, Tommy irritated his fellow-pupils a good deal, but they found it difficult to keep away from him.

He also contrived to enrage the less genteel boys of Monypenny. Their leader was Corp Shiach, three years Tommy's senior, who had never been inside a school except once, when he broke hopefully into Ballingall's because of a stirring rumor (nothing in it) that the dominie had hangit himself with his remaining brace; then in order of merit came Birkie Fleemister; then, perhaps, the smith's family, called the Haggerty-Taggertys, they were such slovens. When school was over Tommy frequently stepped out of his boots and stockings, so that he no longer looked offensively genteel, and then Monypenny was willing to let him join in spyo, smuggle bools, kickbonnety, peeries, the preens, suckers pilly, or whatever game was in season, even to the baiting of the Painted Lady, but they would not have Elspeth, who should have been content to play dumps with the female Haggerty-Taggertys, but could enjoy no game of which Tommy was not the larger half. Many times he deserted her for manlier joys, but though she was out of sight he could not forget her longing face, and soon he sneaked off to her; he upbraided her, but he stayed with her. They bore with him for a time, but when they discovered that she had persuaded him (after prayer) to put back the spug's eggs which he had brought home in triumph, then they drove him from their company, and for a long time afterwards his deadly enemy was the hard-hitting Corp Shiach.

Elspeth was not invited to attend the readings of "I Love My Love with an A," perhaps because there were so many words in it that she had no concern with, but she knew they ended as the eight-o'clock bell began to ring, and it was her custom to meet Tommy a few yards from

Aaron's door. Farther she durst not venture in the gloaming through fear of the Painted Lady, for Aaron's house was not far from the fearsome lane that led to Double Dykes, and even the big boys who made faces at this woman by day ran from her in the dusk. Creepy tales were told of what happened to those on whom she cast a blighting eye before they could touch cold iron, and Tommy was one of many who kept a bit of cold iron from the smithy handy in his pocket. On his way home from the readings he never had occasion to use it, but at these times he sometimes met Grizel, who liked to do her shopping in the evenings when her persecutors were more easily eluded, and he forced her to speak to him. Not her loneliness appealed to him, but that look of admiration she had given him when he was astride of Francie Crabb. For such a look he could pardon many rebuffs; without it no praise greatly pleased him; he was always on the outlook for it.

"I warrant," he said to her one evening, "you want to have some man-body to take care of you the way I take care of Elspeth."

"No, I don't," she replied, promptly.

"Would you no like somebody to love you?"

"Do you mean kissing?" she asked.

"There's better things in it than that," he said guardedly; "but if you want kissing, I —I — Elspeth'll kiss you."

"Will she want to do it?" inquired Grizel, a little wistfully.

"I'll make her do it," Tommy said.

"I don't want her to do it," cried Grizel, and he could not draw another word from her. However he was sure she thought him a wonder, and when next they met he challenged her with it.

"Do you not now?"

"I won't tell you," answered Grizel, who was never known to lie.

"You think I'm a wonder," Tommy persisted, "but you dinna want me to know you think it."

Grizel rocked her arms, a quaint way she had when excited, and she blurted out, "How do you know?"

The look he liked had come back to her face, but he had no time to enjoy it, for just then Elspeth appeared, and Elspeth's jealousy was easily aroused.

"I dinna ken you, lassie," he said coolly to Grizel, and left her stamping her foot at him. She decided never to speak to Tommy again, but the next time they met he took her into the Den and taught her how to fight.

It is painful to have to tell that Miss Ailie was the person who provided him with the opportunity. In the readings they arrived one evening at the scene in the conservatory, which has not a single Stroke in it, but is so full of Words We have no Concern with that Tommy reeled home blinking, and next day so disgracefully did he flounder in his lessons that the gentle school-mistress cast up her arms in despair.

"I don't know what to say to you," she exclaimed.

"Fine I know what you want to say," he retorted, and unfortunately she asked, "What?"

"Stroke!" he replied, leering horridly.

"I Love My Love with an A" was returned to the club forthwith (whether he really did have a wife in India Miss Ailie never knew) and "Judd on the Shorter Catechism" took its place. But mark the result. The readings ended at a quarter to eight now, at twenty to eight, at half-past seven, and so Tommy could loiter on the way home without arousing Elspeth's suspicion. One evening he saw Grizel cutting her way through the Haggerty-Taggerty group, and he offered to come to her aid if she would say "Help me." But she refused.

When, however, the Haggerty-Taggertys were gone she condescended to say, "I shall never, never ask you to help me, but-if you like-you can show me how to hit without biting my tongue."

"I'll learn you Shovel's curly ones," replied Tommy, cordially, and he adjourned with her to the Den for that purpose. He said he chose the Den so that Corp Shiach and the others might not interrupt them, but it was Elspeth he was thinking of.

"You are like Miss Ailie with her cane when she is pandying," he told Grizel. "You begin well, but you slacken just when you are going to hit."

"It is because my hand opens," Grizel said.

"And then it ends in a shove," said her mentor, severely. "You should close your fists like this, with the thumbs inside, and then play dab, this way, that way, yon way. That's what Shovel calls, 'You want it, take it, you've got it.'"

Thus did the hunted girl get her first lesson in scientific warfare in the Den, and neither she nor Tommy saw the pathos of it. Other lessons followed, and during the rests Grizel told Tommy all that she knew about herself. He had won her confidence at last by-by swearing dagont that he was English also.

Chapter XV
The Man Who Never Came

"Is it true that your mother's a bonny swearer?"

Tommy wanted to find out all about the Painted Lady, and the best way was to ask.

"She does not always swear," Grizel said eagerly. "She sometimes says sweet, sweet things."

"What kind of things?"

"I won't tell you."

"Tell me one."

"Well, then, 'Beloved.'"

"Word We have no Concern with," murmured Tommy. He was shocked, but still curious. "Does she say 'Beloved' to you?" he inquired.

"No, she says it to him."

"Him! Wha is he?" Tommy thought he was at the beginning of a discovery, but she answered, uncomfortably,

"I don't know."

"But you've seen him?"

"No, he-he is not there."

"Not there! How can she speak to him if he's no there?"

"She thinks he is there. He-he comes on a horse."

"What is the horse like?"

"There is no horse."

"But you said —"

"She just thinks there is a horse. She hears it."

"Do you ever hear it?"

"No."

The girl was looking imploringly into Tommy's face as if begging it to say that these things need not terrify her, but what he wanted was information.

"What does the Painted Lady do," he asked, "when she thinks she hears the horse?"

"She blows kisses, and then-then she goes to the Den."

"What to do?"

"She walks up and down the Den, talking to the man."

"And him no there?" cried Tommy, scared.

"No, there is no one there."

"And syne what do you do?"

"I won't tell you."

Tommy reflected, and then he said, "She's daft."

"She is not always daft," cried Grizel. "There are whole weeks when she is just sweet."

"Then what do you make of her being so queer in the Den?"

"I am not sure, but I think —I think there was once a place like the Den at her own home in England, where she used to meet the man long ago, and sometimes she forgets that it is not long ago now."

"I wonder wha the man was?"

"I think he was my father."

"I thought you didna ken what a father was?"

"I know now. I think my father was a Scotsman."

"What makes you think that?"

"I heard a Thrums woman say it would account for my being called Grizel, and I think we came to Scotland to look for him, but it is so long, long ago."

"How long?"

"I don't know. We have lived here four years, but we were looking for him before that. It was not in this part of Scotland we looked for him. We gave up looking for him before we came here."

"What made the Painted Lady take a house here, then?"

"I think it was because the Den is so like the place she used to meet him in long ago."

"What was his name?"

"I don't know."

"Does the Painted Lady no tell you about yoursel'?"

"No, she is angry if I ask."

"Her name is Mary, I've heard?"

"Mary Gray is her name, but-but I don't think it is her real name."

"How, does she no use her real name?"

"Because she wants her own mamma to think she is dead."

"What makes her want that?"

"I am not sure, but I think it is because there is me. I think it was naughty of me to be born. Can you help being born?"

Tommy would have liked to tell her about Reddy, but forbore, because he still believed that he had acted criminally in that affair, and so for the time being the inquisition ended. But though he had already discovered all that Grizel knew about her mother and nearly all that curious Thrums ever ferreted out, he returned to the subject at the next meeting in the Den.

"Where does the Painted Lady get her money?"

"Oh," said Grizel, "that is easy. She just goes into that house called the bank, and asks for some, and they give her as much as she likes."

"Ay, I've heard that, but —"

The remainder of the question was never uttered. Instead,

"Hod ahint a tree!" cried Tommy, hastily, and he got behind one himself; but he was too late; Elspeth was upon them; she had caught them together at last.

Tommy showed great cunning. "Pretend you have eggs in your hand," he whispered to Grizel, and then, in a loud voice, he said: "Think shame of yoursel', lassie, for harrying birds' nests. It's a good thing I saw you, and brought you here to force you to put them back. Is that you, Elspeth? I caught this limmer wi' eggs in her hands (and the poor birds sic bonny singers, too!), and so I was forcing her to —"

But it would not do. Grizel was ablaze with indignation. "You are a horrid story-teller," she said, "and if I had known you were ashamed of being seen with me, I should never have spoken to you. Take him," she cried, giving Tommy a push toward Elspeth, "I don't want the mean little story-teller."

"He's not mean!" retorted Elspeth.

"Nor yet little!" roared Tommy.

"Yes, he is," insisted Grizel, "and I was not harrying nests. He came with me here because he wanted to."

"Just for the once," he said, hastily.

"This is the sixth time," said Grizel, and then she marched out of the Den. Tommy and Elspeth followed slowly, and not a word did either say until they were in front of Aaron's house. Then by the light in the window Tommy saw that Elspeth was crying softly, and he felt miserable.

"I was just teaching her to fight," he said humbly.

"You looked like it!" she replied, with the scorn that comes occasionally to the sweetest lady.

He tried to comfort her in various tender ways, but none of them sufficed this time, "You'll marry her as soon as you're a man," she insisted, and she would not let this tragic picture go. It was a case for his biggest efforts, and he opened his mouth to threaten instant self-destruction unless she became happy at once. But he had threatened this too frequently of late, even shown himself drawing the knife across his throat.

As usual the right idea came to him at the right moment. "If you just kent how I did it for your sake," he said, with gentle dignity, "you wouldna blame me; you would think me noble."

She would not help him with a question, and after waiting for it he proceeded. "If you just kent wha she is! And I thought she was dead! What a start it gave me when I found out it was her!"

"Wha is she?" cried Elspeth, with a sudden shiver.

"I was trying to keep it frae you," replied Tommy, sadly.

She seized his arm. "Is it Reddy?" she gasped, for the story of Reddy had been a terror to her all her days.

"She doesna ken I was the laddie that diddled her in London," he said, "and I promise you never to let on, Elspeth. I—I just went to the Den with her to say things that would put her off the scent. If I hadna done that she might have found out and ta'en your place here and tried to pack you off to the Painted Lady's."

Elspeth stared at him, the other grief already forgotten, and he thought he was getting on excellently, when she cried with passion, "I don't believe as it is Reddy!" and ran into the house.

"Dinna believe it, then!" disappointed Tommy shouted, and now he was in such a rage with himself that his heart hardened against her. He sought the company of old Blinder.

Unfortunately Elspeth had believed it, and her woe was the more pitiful because she saw at once, what had never struck Tommy, that it would be wicked to keep Grizel out of her rights. "I'll no win to Heaven now," she said, despairingly, to herself, for to offer to change places with Grizel was beyond her courage, and she tried some childish ways of getting round God, such as going on her knees and saying, "I'm so little, and I hinna no mother!" That was not a bad way.

Another way was to give Grizel everything she had, except Tommy. She collected all her treasures, the bottle with the brass top that she had got from Shovel's old girl, the "housewife" that was a present from Miss Ailie, the teetotum, the pretty buttons Tommy had won for her at the game of buttony, the witchy marble, the twopence she had already saved for the Muckley, these and some other precious trifles she made a little bundle of and set off for Double Dykes with them, intending to leave them at the door. This was Elspeth, who in ordinary circumstances would not have ventured near that mysterious dwelling even in daylight and in Tommy's company. There was no room for vulgar fear in her bursting little heart to-night.

Tommy went home anon, meaning to be whatever kind of boy she seemed most in need of, but she was not in the house, she was not in the garden; he called her name, and it was only Birkie Fleemister, mimicking her, who answered, "Oh, Tommy, come to me!" But Birkie had news for him.

"Sure as death," he said in some awe, "I saw Elspeth ganging yont the double dykes, and I cried to her that the Painted Lady would do her a mischief, but she just ran on."

Elspeth in the double dykes-alone-and at night! Oh, how Tommy would have liked to strike himself now! She must have believed his wicked lie after all, and being so religious she had gone to-He gave himself no time to finish the thought. The vital thing was that she was in peril, he seemed to hear her calling to him, "Oh, Tommy, come quick! oh, Tommy, oh, Tommy!" and in an agony of apprehension he ran after her. But by the time he got to the beginning of the double dykes he knew that she must be at the end of them, and in the Painted Lady's maw, unless their repute by night had blown her back. He paused on the Coffin Brig, which is one long narrow stone; and along the funnel of the double dykes he sent the lonely whisper, "Elspeth, are you there?" He tried to shout it, but no boy could shout there after nightfall in the Painted Lady's time, and when the words had travelled only a little way along the double dykes, they came whining back to him, like a dog despatched on uncanny work. He heard no other sound save the burn stealing on tiptoe from an evil place, and the uneasy rustling of tree-tops, and his own breathing.

The Coffin Brig remains, but the double dykes have fallen bit by bit into the burn, and the path they made safe is again as naked as when the Kingoldrum Jacobites filed along it, and sweer they were, to the support of the Pretender. It traverses a ridge and is streaked with slippery beech-roots which like to fling you off your feet, on the one side into a black burn twenty feet below, on the other down a pleasant slope. The double dykes were built by a farmer fond of his dram, to stop the tongue of a water-kelpie which lived in a pool below and gave him a turn every night he staggered home by shouting, "Drunk again, Peewitbrae!" and announcing, with a smack of the lips, that it had a bed ready for him in the burn. So Peewitbrae built two parallel dykes two feet apart and two feet high, between which he could walk home like a straight man. His cunning took the heart out of the brute, and water-kelpies have not been seen near Thrums since about that time.

By day even girls played at palaulays here, and it was a favorite resort of boys, who knew that you were a man when you could stand on both dykes at once. They also stripped boldly to the skin and then looked doubtfully at the water. But at night! To test your nerves you walked alone between the double dykes, and the popular practice was to start off whistling, which keeps up the courage. At the point where you turned to run back (the Painted Lady after you, or so you thought) you dropped a marked stone, which told next day how far you had ventured. Corp Shiach long held the championship, and his stone was ostentatiously fixed in one of the dykes with lime. Tommy had suffered at his hands for saying that Shovel's mark was thirty yards farther on.

With head bent to the level of the dykes, though it was almost a mirk night beneath the trees, and one arm outstretched before him straight as an elvint, Tommy faced this fearful passage, sometimes stopping to touch cold iron, but on the whole hanging back little, for Elspeth was in peril. Soon he reached the paling that was not needed to keep boys out of the Painted Lady's garden, one of the prettiest and best-tended flower-gardens in Thrums, and crawling through where some spars had fallen, he approached the door as noiseless as an Indian brave after scalps. There he crouched, with a heart that was going like a shuttle on a loom, and listened for Elspeth's voice.

On a night he had come nearly as far as this before, but in the tail of big fellows with a turnip lantern. Into the wood-work of the east window they had thrust a pin, to which a button was tied, and the button was also attached to a long string. They hunkered afar off and pulled this string, and then the button tapped the death-rap on the window, and the sport was successful, for the Painted Lady screamed. But suddenly the door opened and they were put to flight by the fierce barking of a dog. One said that the brute nabbed him in the leg, another saw the vive tongue of it, a third played lick at it with the lantern; this was before they discovered that the dog had been Grizel imitating one, brave Grizel, always ready to protect her mother, and never allowed to cherish the childish fears that were hers by birthright.

Tommy could not hear a sound from within, but he had startling proof that Elspeth was near. His foot struck against something at the door, and, stooping, he saw that it was a little bundle of the treasures she valued most. So she had indeed come to stay with the Painted Lady if Grizel proved merciless! Oh, what a black he had been!

Though originally a farm-house, the cottage was no larger than Aaron's, and of its two front windows only one showed a light, and that through a blind. Tommy sidled round the house in the hope that the small east window would be more hospitable, and just as he saw that it was blindless something that had been crouching rose between him and it.

"Let go!" he cried, feeling the Painted Lady's talons in his neck.

"Tommy!" was the answer.

"It's you, Elspeth?"

"Is it you, Tommy?"

"Of course. Whisht!"

"But say it is."

"It is."

"Oh, Tommy, I'm so fleid!"

He drew her farther from the window and told her it had all been a wicked lie, and she was so glad that she forgot to chide him, but he denounced himself, and he was better than

Elspeth even at that. However, when he learned what had brought her here he dried his eyes and skulked to the door again and brought back her belongings, and then she wanted him to come away at once. But the window fascinated him; he knew he should never find courage to come here again, and he glided toward it, signing to Elspeth to accompany him. They were now too near Double Dykes for speaking to be safe, but he tapped his head as a warning to her to remove her hat, for a woman's head-gear always reaches a window in front of its wearer, and he touched his cold iron and passed it to her as if it were a snuff-mull. Thus fortified, they approached the window fearfully, holding hands and stepping high, like a couple in a minuet.

Chapter XVI
The Painted Lady

It had been the ordinary dwelling room of the unknown poor, the mean little "end" —ah, no, no, the noblest chamber in the annals of the Scottish nation. Here on a hard anvil has its character been fashioned and its history made at rush-lights and its God ever most prominent. Always within reach of hands which trembled with reverence as they turned its broad page could be found the Book that is compensation for all things, and that was never more at home than on bare dressers and worm-eaten looms. If you were brought up in that place and have forgotten it, there is no more hope for you.

But though still recalling its past, the kitchen into which Tommy and Elspeth peered was trying successfully to be something else. The plate-rack had been a fixture, and the coffin-bed and the wooden bole, or board in the wall, with its round hole through which you thrust your hand when you wanted salt, and instead of a real mantelpiece there was a quaint imitation one painted over the fireplace. There were some pieces of furniture too, such as were usual in rooms of the kind, but most of them, perhaps in ignorance, had been put to novel uses, like the plate-rack, where the Painted Lady kept her many pretty shoes instead of her crockery. Gossip said she had a looking-glass of such prodigious size that it stood on the floor, and Tommy nudged Elspeth to signify, "There it is!" Other nudges called her attention to the carpet, the spinet, a chair that rocked like a cradle, and some smaller oddities, of which the queerest was a monster velvet glove hanging on the nail that by rights belonged to the bellows. The Painted Lady always put on this glove before she would touch the coals, which diverted Tommy, who knew that common folk lift coals with their bare hands while society uses the fringe of its second petticoat.

It might have been a boudoir through which a kitchen and bedroom had wandered, spilling by the way, but though the effect was tawdry, everything had been rubbed clean by that passionate housewife, Grizel. She was on her knees at present ca'ming the hearth-stone a beautiful blue, and sometimes looking round to address her mother, who was busy among her plants and cut flowers. Surely they were know-nothings who called this woman silly, and blind who said she painted. It was a little face all of one color, dingy pale, not chubby, but retaining the soft contours of a child's face, and the features were singularly delicate. She was clad in a soft gray, and her figure was of the smallest; there was such an air of youth about her that Tommy thought she could become a girl again by merely shortening her frock, not such a girl as gaunt Grizel, though, who would have looked a little woman had she let her frock down. In appearance indeed the Painted Lady resembled her plain daughter not at all, but in manner in a score of ways, as when she rocked her arms joyously at sight of a fresh bud or tossed her brown hair from her brows with a pretty gesture that ought, God knows, to have been for some man to love. The watchers could not hear what she and Grizel said, but evidently it was pleasant converse, and mother and child, happy in each other's company, presented a picture as sweet as it is common, though some might have complained that they were doing each other's work. But the Painted Lady's delight in flowers was a scandal in Thrums, where she would stand her ground if the roughest boy approached her with roses in his hand, and she gave money for them, which was one reason why the people thought her daft. She was tending her flowers now with experienced eye, smelling them daintily, and every time she touched them it was a caress.

The watchers retired into the field to compare impressions, and Elspeth said emphatically, "I like her, Tommy, I'm not none flcid at hei."

Tommy had liked her also, but being a man he said, "You forget that she's an ill one."

"She looks as if she didna ken that hersel'," answered Elspeth, and these words of a child are the best picture we can hope to get of the Painted Lady.

On their return to the window, they saw that Grizel had finished her ca'ming and was now sitting on the floor nursing a doll. Tommy had not thought her the kind to shut her eyes to the truth about dolls, but she was hugging this one passionately. Without its clothes it was of the nine-pin formation, and the painted eyes and mouth had been incorporated long since in loving Grizel's system; but it became just sweet as she swaddled it in a long yellow frock and slipped its bullet head into a duck of a pink bonnet. These articles of attire and the others that you begin with had all been made by Grizel herself out of the colored tissue-paper that shopkeepers wrap round brandy bottles. The doll's name was Griselda, and it was exactly six months old, and Grizel had found it, two years ago, lying near the Coffin Brig, naked and almost dead.

It was making the usual fuss at having its clothes put on, and Grizel had to tell it frequently that of all the babies-which shamed it now and again, but kept her so occupied that she forgot her mother. The Painted Lady had sunk into the rocking-chair, and for a time she amused herself with it, but by and by it ceased to rock, and as she sat looking straight before her a change came over her face. Elspeth's hand tightened its clutch on Tommy's; the Painted Lady had begun to talk to herself.

She was not speaking aloud, for evidently Grizel, whose back was toward her, heard nothing, but her lips moved and she nodded her head and smiled and beckoned, apparently to the wall, and the childish face rapidly became vacant and foolish. This mood passed, and now she was sitting very still, only her head moving, as she looked in apprehension and perplexity this way and that, like one who no longer knew where she was, nor who was the child by the fire. When at last Grizel turned and observed the change, she may have sighed, but there was no fear in her face; the fear was on the face of her mother, who shrank from her in unmistakable terror and would have screamed at a harsh word or a hasty movement. Grizel seemed to know this, for she remained where she was, and first she nodded and smiled reassuringly to her mother, and then, leaning forward, took her hand and stroked it softly and began to talk. She had laid aside her doll, and with the act become a woman again.

The Painted Lady was soothed, but her bewildered look came and went, as if she only caught at some explanation Grizel was making, to lose it in a moment. Yet she seemed most eager to be persuaded. The little watchers at this queer play saw that Grizel was saying things to her which she repeated docilely and clung to and lost hold of. Often Grizel illustrated her words by a sort of pantomime, as when she sat down on a chair and placed the doll in her lap, then sat down on her mother's lap; and when she had done this several times Tommy took Elspeth into the field to say to her:

"Do you no see? She means as she is the Painted Lady's bairn, just the same as the doll is her bairn."

If the Painted Lady needed to be told this every minute she was daft indeed, and Elspeth could peer no longer at the eerie spectacle. To leave Tommy, however, was equally difficult, so she crouched at his feet when he returned to the window, drawn there hastily by the sound of music.

The Painted Lady could play on the spinet beautifully, but Grizel could not play, though it was she who was trying to play now. She was running her fingers over the notes, producing noises from them, while she swayed grotesquely on her seat and made comic faces. Her object was to capture her mother's mind, and she succeeded for a short time, but soon it floated away from all control, and the Painted Lady fell a-shaking violently. Then Grizel seemed to be alarmed, and her arms rocked despairingly, but she went to her mother and took loving hold of her, and the woman clung to her child in a way pitiful to see. She was on Grizel's knee now, but she still shivered as if in a deadly chill, and her feet rattled on the floor, and her arms against the sides of the chair. Grizel pinned the trembling arms with her own and twisted her legs round her mother's, and still the Painted Lady's tremors shook them both, so that to Tommy they were as two people wrestling.

The shivering slowly lessened and at last ceased, but this seemed to make Grizel no less unhappy. To her vehement attempt to draw her mother's attention she got no response; the Painted Lady was hearkening intently for some sound other than Grizel's voice, and only once did she look at her child. Then it was with cruel, ugly eyes, and at the same moment she shoved Grizel aside so viciously that it was almost a blow. Grizel sat down sorrowfully beside her doll, like one aware that she could do no more, and her mother at once forgot her. What was she listening for so eagerly? Was it for the gallop of a horse? Tommy strained his ears.

"Elspeth-speak low-do you hear anything?"

"No; I'm ower fleid to listen."

"Whisht! do you no hear a horse?"

"No, everything's terrible still. Do you hear a horse?"

"I —I think I do, but far awa'."

His imagination was on fire. Did he hear a distant galloping or did he only make himself hear it? He had bent his head, and Elspeth, looking affrighted into his face, whispered, "I hear it too, oh, Tommy, so do I!"

And the Painted Lady had heard it. She kissed her hand toward the Den several times, and each time Tommy seemed to hear that distant galloping. All the sweetness had returned to her face now, and with it a surging joy, and she rocked her arms exultantly, but quickly controlled them lest Grizel should see. For evidently Grizel must be cheated, and so the Painted Lady became very sly. She slipped off her shoes to be able to make her preparations noiselessly, and though at all other times her face expressed the rapture of love, when she glanced at her child it was suspiciously and with a gleam of hatred. Her preparations were for going out. She was long at the famous mirror, and when she left it her hair was elaborately dressed and her face so transformed that first Tommy exclaimed "Bonny!" and then corrected himself with a scornful "Paint!" On her feet she put a foolish little pair of red shoes, on her head a hat too gay with flowers, and across her shoulders a flimsy white shawl at which the night air of Thrums would laugh. Her every movement was light and cautious and accompanied by side-glances at Grizel, who occasionally looked at her, when the Painted Lady immediately pretended to be tending her plants again. She spoke to Grizel sweetly to deceive her, and shot baleful glances at her next moment. Tommy saw that Grizel had taken up her doll once more and was squeezing it to her breast. She knew very well what was going on behind her back.

Suddenly Tommy took to his heels, Elspeth after him. He had seen the Painted Lady coming on her tip-toes to the window. They saw the window open and a figure in a white shawl creep out of it, as she had doubtless escaped long ago by another window when the door was barred. They lost sight of her at once.

"What will Grizel do now?" Tommy whispered, and he would have returned to his watching place, but Elspeth pointed to the window. Grizel was there closing it, and next moment the lamp was extinguished. They heard a key turn in the lock, and presently Grizel, carrying warm wraps, passed very near them and proceeded along the double dykes, not anxious apparently to keep her mother in view, but slowly, as if she knew where to find her. She went into the Den, where Tommy dared not follow her, but he listened at the stile and in the awful silence he fancied he heard the neighing of a horse.

The next time he met Grizel he was yearning to ask her how she spent that night, but he knew she would not answer; it would be a long time before she gave him her confidence again. He offered her his piece of cold iron, however, and explained why he carried it, whereupon she flung it across the road, crying, "You horrid boy, do you think I am frightened at my mamma!" But when he was out of sight she came back and slipped the cold iron into her pocket.

Chapter XVII
In Which Tommy Solves the Woman Problem

Pity made Elspeth want to like the Painted Lady's child now, but her own rules of life were all from a book never opened by Grizel, who made her religion for herself and thought God a swear; she also despised Elspeth for being so dependent on Tommy, and Elspeth knew it. The two great subjects being barred thus, it was not likely that either girl, despite some attempts on Elspeth's part, should find out the best that was in the other, without which friendship has no meaning, and they would have gone different ways had not Tommy given an arm to each. He, indeed, had as little in common with Grizel, for most conspicuous of his traits was the faculty of stepping into other people's shoes and remaining there until he became someone else; his individuality consisted in having none, while she could only be herself and was without tolerance for those who were different; he had at no time in his life the least desire to make other persons like himself, but if they were not like Grizel she rocked her arms and cried, "Why, why, why?" which is the mark of the "womanly" woman. But his tendency to be anyone he was interested in implied enormous sympathy (for the time being), and though Grizel spurned his overtures, this only fired his pride of conquest. We can all get whatever we want if we are quite determined to have it (though it be a king's daughter), and in the end Tommy vanquished Grizel. How? By offering to let her come into Aaron's house and wash it and dust it and ca'm it, "just as if you were our mother," an invitation she could not resist. To you this may seem an easy way, but consider the penetration he showed in thinking of it. It came to him one day when he saw her lift the smith's baby out of the gutter, and hug it with a passionate delight in babies.

"She's so awid to do it," he said basely to Elspeth, "that we needna let on how much we want it done." And he also mentioned her eagerness to Aaron as a reason why she should be allowed to do it for nothing.

For Aaron to hold out against her admittance would have been to defraud himself, for she transformed his house. When she saw the brass lining of the jelly-pan discolored, and that the stockings hanging from the string beneath the mantelpiece had given way where the wearers were hardest on them; when she found dripping adhering to a cold frying-pan instead of in a "pig," and the pitcher leaking and the carrot-grater stopped-when these and similar discoveries were made by Grizel, was it a squeal of horror she gave that such things should be, or a cry of rapture because to her had fallen the task of setting them right?

"She just made a jump for the besom," was Tommy's graphic description of how it all began.

You should have seen Grizel on the hoddy-table knocking nails into the wall. The hoddy-table is so called because it goes beneath the larger one at night, like a chicken under its mother, and Grizel, with the nails in her mouth, used them up so quickly that you would have sworn she swallowed half of them; yet she rocked her arms because she could not be at all four walls at once. She rushed about the room until she was dizzy, and Tommy knew the moment to cry "Grip her, she'll tumble!" when he and Elspeth seized her and put her on a stool.

It is on the hoddy-table that you bake and iron. "There's not a baking-board in the house," Elspeth explained. "There is!" cried Grizel, there and then converting a drawer into one.

Between her big bannocks she made baby ones, for no better reason than that she was so fond of babies, and she kissed the baby ones and said, "Oh, the loves, they are just sweet!" and she felt for them when Tommy took a bite. She could go so quickly between the board and the girdle that she was always at one end of the course or the other, but never gave you time to say at which end, and on the limited space round the fire she could balance such a number of bannocks that they were as much a wonder as the Lord's prayer written on a sixpence. Such a vigilant eye she kept on them, too, that they dared not fall. Yet she had never been taught to bake; a good-natured neighbor had now and again allowed her to look on.

Then her ironing! Even Aaron opened his mouth on this subject, Blinder being his confidant. "I thought there was a smell o' burning," he said, "and so I went butt the house; but man, as soon as my een lighted on her I minded of my mother at the same job. The crittur was so busy with her work that she looked as if, though the last trumpet had blawn, she would just have cried, 'I canna come till my ironing's done!' Ay, I went ben without a word."

But best of all was to see Grizel "redding up" on a Saturday afternoon. Where were Tommy and Elspeth then? They were shut up in the coffin-bed to be out of the way, and could scarce have told whether they fled thither or were wrapped into it by her energetic arms. Even Aaron dared not cross the floor until it was sanded. "I believe," he said, trying to jest, "you would like to shut me up in the bed too!" "I should just love it," she cried, eagerly; "will you go?" It is an inferior woman who has a sense of humor when there is a besom in her hand.

Thus began great days to Grizel, "sweet" she called them, for she had many of her mother's words, and a pretty way of emphasizing them with her plain face that turned them all into superlatives. But though Tommy and Elspeth were her friends now, her mouth shut obstinately the moment they mentioned the Painted Lady; she regretted ever having given Tommy her confidence on that subject, and was determined not to do so again. He did not dare tell her that he had once been at the east window of her home, but often he and Elspeth spoke to each other of that adventure, and sometimes they woke in their garret bed thinking they heard the horseman galloping by. Then they crept closer to each other, and wondered whether Grizel was cosey in her bed or stalking an eerie figure in the Den.

Aaron said little, but he was drawn to the girl, who had not the self-consciousness of Tommy and Elspeth in his presence, and sometimes he slipped a penny into her hand. The pennies were not spent, they were hoarded for the fair, or Muckle Friday, or Muckley, great day of the year in Thrums. If you would know how Tommy was making ready for this mighty festival, listen.

One of his sources of income was the *Mentor*, a famous London weekly paper, which seemed to visitors to be taken in by every person of position in Thrums. It was to be seen not only in parlors, but on the armchair at the Jute Bank, in the gauger's gig, in the Spittal factor's dog-cart, on a shoemaker's form, protruding from Dr. McQueen's tail pocket and from Mr. Duthie's oxter pocket, on Cathro's school-desk, in the Rev. Mr. Dishart's study, in half a dozen farms. Miss Ailie compelled her little servant, Gavinia, to read the *Mentor*, and stood over her while she did it; the phrase, "this week's," meant this week's *Mentor*. Yet the secret must be told: only one copy of the paper came to Thrums weekly; it was subscribed for by the whole reading public between them, and by Miss Ailie's influence Tommy had become the boy who carried it from house to house.

This brought him a penny a week, but so heavy were his incidental expenses that he could have saved little for the Muckley had not another organization given him a better chance. It was a society, newly started, for helping the deserving poor; they had to subscribe not less than a penny weekly to it, and at the end of the year each subscriber was to be given fuel, etc., to the value of double what he or she had put in. "The three Ps" was a nickname given to the society by Dr. McQueen, because it claimed to distribute "Peats and Potatoes with Propriety," but he was one of its heartiest supporters nevertheless. The history of this society in the first months of its existence not only shows how Tommy became a moneyed man, but gives a glimpse into the character of those it benefited.

Miss Ailie was treasurer, and the pennies were to be brought to her on Monday evenings between the hours of seven and eight. The first Monday evening found her ready in the school-room, in her hand the famous pencil that wrote red with the one end and blue with the other; by her side her assistant, Mr. T. Sandys, a pen balanced on his ear. For a whole hour did they wait, but though many of the worthiest poor had been enrolled as members, the few who appeared with their pennies were notoriously riff-raff. At eight Miss Ailie disconsolately sent Tommy home, but he was back in five minutes.

"There's a mask of them," he told her, excitedly, "hanging about, but feared to come in because the others would see them. They're ashamed to have it kent that they belong to a charity society, and Meggy Robbie is wandering round the Dovecot wi' her penny wrapped in a paper, and Watty Rattray and Ronny-On is walking up and down the brae pretending they dinna ken one another, and auld Connacher's Jeanie Ann says she has been four times round the town waiting for Kitty Elshioner to go away, and there's a one-leggit man hodding in the ditch, and Tibbie Birse is out wi' a lantern counting them."

Miss Ailie did not know what to do. "Here's Jeanie Ann's penny," Tommy continued, opening his hand, "and this is three bawbees frae Kitty Elshioner and you and me is no to tell a soul they've joined."

A furtive tapping was heard at the door. It was Ronny-On, who had skulked forward with twopence, but Gavinia answered his knock, so he just said, "Ay, Gavinia, it's yoursel'. Well, I'll be stepping," and would have retired had not Miss Ailie caught him. Even then he said, "Three bawbees is to you to lay by, and one bawbee to Gavinia no to tell."

To next Monday evening Miss Ailie now looked with apprehension, but Tommy lay awake that night until, to use a favorite crow of his, he "found a way." He borrowed the schoolmistress's blue-and-red pencil and sought the houses of the sensitive poor with the following effect. One sample will suffice; take him at the door of Meggy Robbie in the West Muir, which he flung open with the effrontery of a tax-collector.

"You're a three P," he said, with a wave of his pencil.

"I'm no sic thing!" cried the old lady.

"It winna do, woman," Tommy said sternly. "Miss Ailie told me you paid in your first penny on the chap of ten." He wetted the pencil on his tongue to show that it was vain to trifle with him, and Meggy bowed her head.

"It'll be through the town that I've joined," she moaned, but Tommy explained that he was there to save her.

"I'm willing to come to your house," he said, "and collect the money every week, and not a soul will I tell except the committee."

"Kitty Elshioner would see you coming," said Meggy.

"No, no, I'll creep yont the hedge and climb the hen-house."

"But it would be a' found out at any rate," she remembered, "when I go for the peats and things at Hogmanay."

"It needna be," eagerly replied Tommy. "I'll bring them to you in a barrow in the dead o' night."

"Could you?" she cried passionately, and he promised he would, and it may be mentioned here that he did.

"And what for yoursel'?" she inquired.

"A bawbee," he said, "the night afore the Muckley."

The bargain was made, but before he could get away, "Tell me, laddie," said Meggy, coaxingly, "has Kitty Elshioner joined?" They were all as curious to know who had joined as they were anxious to keep their own membership a secret; but Tommy betrayed none, at least none who agreed to his proposal. There were so many of these that on the night before the Muckley he had thirteen pence.

"And you was doing good all the time you was making the thirteen pence," Elspeth said, fondly. "I believe that was the reason you did it."

"I believe it was!" Tommy exclaimed. He had not thought of this before, but it was easy to him to believe anything.

Chapter XVIII
The Muckley

Every child in Thrums went to bed on the night before the Muckley hugging a pirly, or, as the vulgar say, a money-box; and all the pirlies were ready for to-morrow, that is to say, the mouths of them had been widened with gully knives by owners now so skilful at the jerk which sends their contents to the floor that pirlies they were no longer. "Disgorge!" was the universal cry, or, in the vernacular, "Out you come, you sweer deevils!"

Not a coin but had its history, not a boy who was unable to pick out his own among a hundred. The black one came from the 'Sosh, the bent lad he got for carrying in Ronny-On's sticks. Oh michty me, sure as death he had nearly forgotten the one with the warts on it. Which to spend first? The goldy one? Na faags, it was ower ill to come by. The scartit one? No, no, it was a lucky. Well, then, the one found in the rat's hole? (That was a day!) Ay, dagont, ay, we'll make the first blatter with it.

It was Tommy's first Muckley, and the report that he had thirteen pence brought him many advisers about its best investment. Even Corp Shiach (five pence) suspended hostilities for this purpose. "Mind this," he said solemnly, "there's none o' the candies as sucks so long as California's Teuch and Tasty. Other kinds may be sweeter, but Teuch and Tasty lasts the longest, and what a grip it has! It pulls out your teeth!" Corp seemed to think that this was a recommendation.

"I'm nane sure o' Teuch and Tasty," Birkie said. "If you dinna keep a watch on it, it slips ower when you're swallowing your spittle."

"Then you should tie a string to it," suggested Tommy, who was thought more of from that hour.

Beware of Pickpockets! Had it not been for placards with this glorious announcement (it is the state's first printed acknowledgment that boys and girls form part of the body politic) you might have thought that the night before the Muckley was absurdly like other nights. Not a show had arrived, not a strange dog, no romantic figures were wandering the streets in search of lodgings, no stands had sprung up in the square. You could pass hours in pretending to fear that when the morning came there would be no fairyland. And all the time you *knew*.

About ten o'clock Ballingall's cat was observed washing its face, a deliberate attempt to bring on rain. It was immediately put to death.

Tommy and Elspeth had agreed to lie awake all night; if Tommy nipped Elspeth, Elspeth would nip Tommy. Other children had made the same arrangement, though the experienced ones were aware that it would fail. If it was true that all the witches were dead, then the streets of stands and shows and gaming-tables and shooting-galleries were erected by human hands, and it followed that were you to listen through the night you must hear the hammers. But always in the watches the god of the Muckley came unseen and glued your eyes, as if with Teuch and Tasty, and while you slept-Up you woke with a start. What was it you were to mind as soon as you woke? Listen! That's a drum beating! It's the Muckley! They are all here! It has begun! Oh, michty, michty, michty, whaur's my breeks?

When Tommy, with Elspeth and Grizel, set off excitedly for the town, the country folk were already swarming in. The Monypenny road was thick with them, braw loons in blue bonnets with red bobs to them, tartan waistcoats, scarves of every color, woollen shirts as gay, and the strutting wearers in two minds-whether to take off the scarf to display the shirt, or hide the shirt and trust to the scarf. Came lassies, too, in wincey bodices they were like to burst through, and they were listening apprehensively as they ploughed onward for a tearing at the seams. There were red-headed lasses, yellow-chy-headed and black-headed, blue-shawled and red-shawled lasses; boots on every one of them, stockings almost as common, the skirt kilted up for the present, but down it should go when they were in the thick of things, and then it must take care of itself. All were solemn and sheepish as yet, but wait a bit.

The first-known face our three met was Corp. He was only able to sign to them, because Californy's specialty had already done its work and glued his teeth together. He was off to the smithy to be melted, but gave them to understand that though awkward it was glorious. Then came Birkie, who had sewn up the mouths of his pockets, all but a small slit in each, as a precaution against pickpockets, and was now at his own request being held upside down by the Haggerty-Taggertys on the chance that a halfpenny which had disappeared mysteriously might fall out. A more tragic figure was Francie Crabb (one and seven pence), who, like a mad, mad thing, had taken all his money to the fair at once. In ten minutes he had bought fourteen musical instruments.

Tommy and party had not yet reached the celebrated corner of the west town end where the stands began, but they were near it, and he stopped to give Grizel and Elspeth his final instructions: "(1) Keep your money in your purse, and your purse in your hand, and your hand in your pocket; (2) if you lose me, I'll give Shovel's whistle, and syne you maun squeeze and birse your way back to me."

Now then, are you ready? Bang! They were in it. Strike up, ye fiddlers; drums, break; tooters, fifers, at it for your lives; trumpets, blow; bagpipes, skirl; music-boxes, all together now-Tommy has arrived.

Even before he had seen Thrums, except with his mother's eye, Tommy knew that the wise begin the Muckley by measuring its extent. That the square and adjoining wynds would be crammed was a law of nature, but boyhood drew imaginary lines across the Roods, the west town end, the east town end, and the brae, and if the stands did not reach these there had been retrogression. Tommy found all well in two quarters, got a nasty shock on the brae, but medicine for it in the Roods; on the whole, yelled a hundred children, by way of greeting to each other, a better Muckley than ever.

From those who loved them best, the more notable Muckleys got distinctive names for convenience of reference. As shall be ostentatiously shown in its place, there was a Muckley called (and by Corp Shiach, too) after Tommy, but this, his first, was dubbed Sewster's Muckley, in honor of a seamstress who hanged herself that day in the Three-cornered Wood. Poor little sewster, she had known joyous Muckleys too, but now she was up in the Three-cornered Wood hanging herself, aged nineteen. I know nothing more of her, except that in her maiden days when she left the house her mother always came to the door to look proudly after her.

How to describe the scene, when owing to the throng a boy could only peer at it between legs or through the crook of a woman's arm? Shovel would have run up ploughmen to get his bird's-eye view, and he could have told Tommy what he saw, and Tommy could have made a picture of it in his mind, every figure ten feet high. But perhaps to be lost in it was best. You had but to dive and come up anywhere to find something amazing; you fell over a box of jumping-jacks into a new world.

Everyone to his taste. If you want Tommy's sentiments, here they are, condensed: "The shows surpass everything else on earth. Four streets of them in the square! The best is the menagerie, because there is the loudest roaring there. Kick the caravans and you increase the roaring. Admission, however, prohibitive (threepence). More economical to stand outside the show of the 'Mountain Maid and the Shepherd's Bride' and watch the merriman saying funny things to the monkey. Take care you don't get in front of the steps, else you will be pressed up by those behind and have to pay before you have decided that you want to go in. When you fling pennies at the Mountain Maid and the Shepherd's Bride they stop play-acting and scramble for them. Go in at night when there are drunk ploughmen to fling pennies. The Fat Wife with the Golden Locks lets you put your fingers in her arms, but that is soon over. 'The Slave-driver and his Victims.' Not worth the money; they are not blooding. To Jerusalem and Back in a Jiffy. This is a swindle. You just keek through holes."

But Elspeth was of a different mind. She liked To Jerusalem and Back best, and gave the Slave-driver and his Victims a penny to be Christians. The only show she disliked was the wax-work, where was performed the "Tragedy of Tiffano and the Haughty Princess." Tiffano loved the woodman's daughter, and so he would not have the Haughty Princess, and so she got a magician to turn him into a pumpkin, and then she ate him. What distressed Elspeth was that Tiffano could never get to heaven now, and all the consolation Tommy, doing his best, could give her was, "He could go, no doubt he could go, but he would have to take the Haughty Princess wi' him, and he would be sweer to do that."

Grizel reflected: "If I had a whip like the one the Slave-driver has shouldn't I lash the boys who hoot my mamma! I wish I could turn boys into pumpkins. The Mountain Maid wore a beautiful muslin with gold lace, but she does not wash her neck."

Lastly, let Corp have his say: "I looked at the outside of the shows, but always landed back at Californy's stand. Sucking is better nor near anything. The Teuch and Tasty is stickier than ever. I have lost twa teeth. The Mountain Maid is biding all night at Tibbie Birse's, and I went in to see her. She had a bervie and a boiled egg to her tea. She likes her eggs saft wi' a lick of butter in them. The Fat Wife is the one I like best. She's biding wi' Shilpit Kaytherine on the Tanage Brae. She weighs Jeems and Kaytherine and the sma' black swine. She had an ingin to her tea. The Slave-driver's a fushinless body. One o' the Victims gives him his licks. They a' bide in the caravan. You can stand on the wheel and keek in. They had herrings wi' the rans to their tea. I cut a hole in Jerusalem and Back, and there was no Jerusalem there. The man as ocht Jerusalem greets because the Fair Circassian winna take him. He is biding a' night wi' Blinder. He likes a dram in his tea."

Elspeth's money lasted till four o'clock. For Aaron, almost the only man in Thrums who shunned the revels that day, she bought a gingerbread house; and the miraculous powder which must be taken on a sixpence was to make Blinder see again, but unfortunately he forgot about putting it on the sixpence. And of course there was something for a certain boy. Grizel had completed her purchases by five o'clock, when Tommy was still heavy with threepence half-penny. They included a fluffy pink shawl, she did not say for whom, but the Painted Lady wore it afterwards, and for herself another doll.

"But that doll's leg is broken," Tommy pointed out.

"That was why I bought it," she said warmly, "I feel so sorry for it, the darling," and she carried it carefully so that the poor thing might suffer as little pain as possible.

Twice they rushed home for hasty meals, and were back so quickly that Tommy's shadow strained a muscle in turning with him. Night came on, and from a hundred strings stretched along stands and shows there now hung thousands of long tin things like trumpets. One burning paper could set a dozen of these ablaze, and no sooner were they lit than a wind that had been biding its time rushed in like the merriman, making the lamps swing on their strings, so that the flaring lights embraced, and from a distance Thrums seemed to be on fire.

Even Grizel was willing to hold Tommy's hand now, and the three could only move this way and that as the roaring crowd carried them. They were not looking at the Muckley, they were part of it, and at last Thrums was all Tommy's fancy had painted it. This intoxicated him, so that he had to scream at intervals, "We're here, Elspeth, I tell you, we're here!" and he became pugnacious and asked youths twice his size whether they denied that he was here, and if so, would they come on. In this frenzy he was seen by Miss Ailie, who had stolen out in a veil to look for Gavinia, but just as she was about to reprove him, dreadful men asked her was she in search of a lad, whereupon she fled home and barred the door, and later in the evening warned Gavinia, through the key-hole, taking her for a roystering blade, that there were policemen in the house, to which the astounding reply of Gavinia, then aged twelve, was, "No sic luck."

With the darkness, too, crept into the Muckley certain devils in the color of the night who spoke thickly and rolled braw lads in the mire, and egged on friends to fight and cast lewd thoughts into the minds of the women. At first the men had been bashful swains. To the women's "Gie me my faring, Jock," they had replied, "Wait, Jean, till I'm fee'd," but by night most had got their arles, with a dram above it, and he who could only guffaw at Jean a few hours ago had her round the waist now, and still an arm free for rough play with other kimmers. The Jeans were as boisterous as the Jocks, giving them leer for leer, running from them with a giggle, waiting to be caught and rudely kissed. Grand, patient, long-suffering fellows these men were, up at five, summer and winter, foddering their horses, maybe hours before there would be food for themselves, miserably paid, housed like cattle, and when the rheumatism seized them, liable to be flung aside like a broken graip. As hard was the life of the women: coarse food, chaff beds, damp clothes, their portion; their sweethearts in the service of masters who were reluctant to fee a married man. Is it to be wondered that these lads who could be faithful unto death drank soddenly on their one free day, that these girls, starved of opportunities for womanliness, of which they could make as much as the finest lady, sometimes woke after a Muckley to wish that they might wake no more? Our three brushed shoulders with the devils that had been let loose, but hardly saw them; they heard them, but did not understand their tongue. The eight-o'clock bell had rung long since, and though the racket was as great as ever, it was only because every reveller left now made the noise of two. Mothers were out fishing for their bairns. The Haggerty-Taggertys had straggled home hoarse as crows; every one of them went to bed that night with a stocking round his throat. Of Monypenny boys, Tommy could find none in the square but Corp, who, with another tooth missing, had been going about since six o'clock with his pockets hanging out, as a sign that all was over. An awkward silence had fallen on the trio; the reason, that Tommy had only threepence left and the smallest of them cost threepence. The reference of course is to the wondrous gold-paper packets of sweets (not unlike crackers in appearance) which are only seen at the Muckley, and are what every girl claims of her lad or lads. Now, Tommy had vowed to Elspeth-But he had also said to Grizel-In short, how could he buy for both with threepence?

Grizel, as the stranger, ought to get-But he knew Elspeth too well to believe that she would dry her eyes with that.

Elspeth being his sister-But he had promised Grizel, and she had been so ill brought up that she said nasty things when you broke your word.

The gold packet was bought. That is it sticking out of Tommy's inside pocket. The girls saw it and knew what was troubling him, but not a word was spoken now between the three. They set off for home self-consciously, Tommy the least agitated on the whole, because he need not make up his mind for another ten minutes. But he wished Grizel would not look at him sideways and then rock her arms in irritation. They passed many merry-makers homeward bound, many of them following a tortuous course, for the Scottish toper gives way first in the legs, the Southron in the other extremity, and thus between them could be constructed a man wholly sober and another as drunk as Chloe. But though the highway clattered with many feet, not a soul was in the double dykes, and at the easy end of that formidable path Grizel came to a determined stop.

"Good-night," she said, with such a disdainful glance at Tommy.

He had not made up his mind yet, but he saw that it must be done now, and to take a decisive step was always agony to him, though once taken it ceased to trouble. To dodge it for another moment he said, weakly: "Let's —let's sit down a whiley on the dyke."

But Grizel, while coveting the packet, because she had never got a present in her life, would not shilly-shally.

"Are you to give it to Elspeth?" she asked, with the horrid directness that is so trying to an intellect like Tommy's.

"N-no," he said.

"To Grizel?" cried Elspeth.

"N-no," he said again.

It was an undignified moment for a great boy, but the providence that watched over Tommy until it tired of him came to his aid in the nick of time. It took the form of the Painted Lady, who appeared suddenly out of the gloom of the Double Dykes. Two of the children jumped, and the third clenched her little fists to defend her mamma if Tommy cast a word at her. But he did not; his mouth remained foolishly open. The Painted Lady had been talking cheerfully to herself, but she drew back apprehensively, with a look of appeal on her face, and then-and then Tommy "saw a way." He handed her the gold packet, "It's to you," he said, "it's —it's your Muckley!"

For a moment she was afraid to take it, but when she knew that this sweet boy's gift was genuine, she fondled it and was greatly flattered, and dropped him the quaintest courtesy and then looked defiantly at Grizel. But Grizel did not take it from her. Instead, she flung her arms impulsively round Tommy's neck, she was so glad, glad, glad.

As Tommy and Elspeth walked away to their home, Elspeth could hear him breathing heavily, and occasionally he gave her a furtive glance.

"Grizel needna have done that," she said, sharply.

"No," replied Tommy.

"But it was noble of you," she continued, squeezing his hand, "to give it to the Painted Lady. Did you mean to give it to her a' the time?"

"Oh, Elspeth!"

"But did you?"

"Oh, Elspeth!"

"That's no you greeting, is it?" she asked, softly.

"I'm near the greeting," he said truthfully, "but I'm no sure what about." His sympathy was so easily aroused that he sometimes cried without exactly knowing why.

"It's because you're so good," Elspeth told him; but presently she said, with a complete change of voice, "No, Grizel needna have done that."

"It was a shameful thing to do," Tommy agreed, shaking his head. "But she did it!" he added triumphantly; "you saw her do it, Elspeth!"

"But you didna like it?" Elspeth asked, in terror.

"No, of course I didna like it, but —"

"But what, Tommy?"

"But I liked her to like it," he admitted, and by and by he began to laugh hysterically. "I'm no sure what I'm laughing at," he said, "but I think it's at mysel'." He may have laughed at himself before, but this Muckley is memorable as the occasion on which he first caught himself doing it. The joke grew with the years, until sometimes he laughed in his most emotional moments, suddenly seeing himself in his true light. But it had become a bitter laugh by that time.

Chapter XIX

Corp is Brought to Heel-Grizel Defiant

Corp Shiach was a bare-footed colt of a boy, of ungainly build, with a nose so thick and turned up that it was a certificate of character, and his hands were covered with warts, which he had a trick of biting till they bled. Then he rubbed them on his trousers, which were the picturesque part of him, for he was at present "serving" to the masons (he had "earned his keep" since long before he could remember), and so wore the white or yellow ducks which the dust of the quarry stains a rarer orange color than is known elsewhere. The orange of the masons' trousers, the blue of the hearthstones, these are the most beautiful colors to be seen in Thrums, though of course Corp was unaware of it. He was really very good-natured, and only used his fists freely because of imagination he had none, and thinking made him sweat, and consequently the simplest way of proving his case was to say, "I'll fight you." What might have been the issue of a conflict between him and Shovel was a problem for Tommy to puzzle over. Shovel was as quick as Corp was deliberate, and would have danced round him, putting in unexpected ones, but if he had remained just one moment too long within Corp's reach —

They nicknamed him Corp because he took fits, when he lay like one dead. He was proud of his fits, was Corp, but they were a bother to him, too, because he could make so little of them. They interested doctors and other carriage folk, who came to his aunt's house to put their fingers into him, and gave him sixpence, and would have given him more, but when they pressed him to tell them what he remembered about his fits, he could only answer dejectedly, "Not a damned thing."

"You might as well no have them ava," his wrathful aunt, with whom he lived, would say, and she thrashed him until his size forbade it.

Soon after the Muckley came word that the Lady of the Spittal was to be brought to see Corp by Mr. Ogilvy, the school-master of Glen Quharity, and at first Corp boasted of it, but as the appointed day drew near he became uneasy.

"The worst o't," he said to anyone who would listen, "is that my auntie is to be away frae hame, and so they'll put a' their questions to me."

The Haggerty-Taggertys and Birkie were so jealous that they said they were glad *they* never had fits, but Tommy made no such pretence.

"Oh, Corp, if I had thae fits of yours!" he exclaimed greedily.

"If they were mine to give awa'," replied Corp sullenly, "you could have them and welcome." Grown meek in his trouble, he invited Tommy to speak freely, with the result that his eyes were partially opened to the superiority of that boy's attainments. Tommy told him a number of interesting things to say to Mr. Ogilvy and the lady about his fits, about how queer he felt just before they came on, and the visions he had while he was lying stiff. But though the admiring Corp gave attentive ear, he said hopelessly next day, "Not a dagont thing do I mind. When they question me about my fits I'll just say I'm sometimes in them and sometimes out o' them, and if they badger me more, I can aye kick."

Tommy gave him a look that meant, "Fits are just wasted on you," and Corp replied with another that meant, "I ken they are." Then they parted, one of them to reflect.

"Corp," he said excitedly, when next they met, "has Mr. Ogilvy or the lady ever come to see you afore?"

They had not, and Corp was able to swear that they did not even know him by sight.

"They dinna ken me either," said Tommy.

"What does that matter?" asked Corp, but Tommy was too full to speak. He had "found a way."

The lady and Mr. Ogilvy found Corp such a success that the one gave him a shilling and the other took down his reminiscences in a note-book. But if you would hear of the rings of blue and white and yellow Corp saw, and of the other extraordinary experiences he described himself as having when in a fit, you need not search that note-book, for the page has been torn out. Instead of making inquiries of Mr. Ogilvy, try any other dominie in the district, Mr. Cathro, for instance, who delighted to tell the tale. This of course was when it leaked out that Tommy had personated Corp, by arrangement with the real Corp, who was listening in rapture beneath the bed.

Tommy, who played his part so well that he came out of it in a daze, had Corp at heel from that hour. He told him what a rogue he had been in London, and Corp cried admiringly, "Oh, you deevil! oh, you queer little deevil!" and sometimes it was Elspeth who was narrator, and then Tommy's noble acts were the subject; but still Corp's comment was "Oh, the deevil! oh, the queer little deevil!" Elspeth was flattered by his hero-worship, but his language shocked her, and after consulting Miss Ailie she advised him to count twenty when he felt an oath coming, at the end of which exercise the desire to swear would have passed away. Good-natured Corp willingly promised to try this, but he was never hopeful, and as he explained to Tommy, after a failure, "It just made me waur than ever, for when I had counted the twenty I said a big Damn, thoughtful-like, and syne out jumpit three little damns, like as if the first ane had cleckit in my mouth."

It was fortunate that Elspeth liked Corp on the whole, for during the three years now to be rapidly passed over, Tommy took delight in his society, though he never treated him as an equal; Corp indeed did not expect that, and was humbly grateful for what he got. In summer, fishing was their great diversion. They would set off as early as four in the morning, fishing wands in hand, and scour the world for trout, plodding home in the gloaming with stones in their fishing-basket to deceive those who felt its weight. In the long winter nights they liked best to listen to Blinder's tales of the Thrums Jacobites, tales never put into writing, but handed down from father to son, and proved true in the oddest of ways, as by Blinder's trick of involuntarily holding out his hands to a fire when he found himself near one, though he might be sweating to the shirt and the time a July forenoon. "I make no doubt," he told them, "as I do that because my forbear, Buchan Osler (called Buchan wi' the Haap after the wars was ower), had to hod so lang frae the troopers, and them so greedy for him that he daredna crawl to a fire once in an eight days."

The Lord of the Spittal and handsome Captain Body (whose being "out" made all the women anxious) marched through the Den, flapping their wings at the head of a fearsome retinue, and the Thrums folk looked so glum at them that gay Captain Body said he should kiss every lass who did not cheer for Charlie, and none cheered, but at the same time none ran away. Few in Thrums cared a doit for Charlie, but some hung on behind this troop till there was no turning back for them, and one of these was Buchan. He forced his wife to give Captain Body a white rose from her bush by the door, but a thorn in it pricked the gallant, and the blood from his fingers fell on the bush, and from that year it grew red roses.

"If you dinna believe me," Blinder said, "look if the roses is no red on the bush at Pyotdykes, which was a split frae Buchan's, and speir whether they're no named the blood rose."

"I believe you," Tommy would say breathlessly: "go on."

Captain Body was back in the Den by and by, but he had no thought of preeing lasses' mouths now. His face was scratched and haggard and his gay coat torn, and when he crawled to the Cuttle Well he caught some of the water in his bonnet and mixed meal with it, stirring the precious compound with his finger and using the loof of his hand as a spoon. Every stick of furniture Buchan and the other Thrums rebels possessed was seized by the government and rouped in the market-place of Thrums, but few would bid against the late owners, for whom the things were secretly bought back very cheaply.

To these and many similar stories Tommy listened open-mouthed, seeing the scene far more vividly than the narrator, who became alarmed at his quick, loud breathing, and advised him to forget them and go back to his lessons. But his lessons never interested Tommy, and he would go into the Den instead, and repeat Blinder's legends, with embellishments which made them so real that Corp and Elspeth and Grizel were afraid to look behind them lest the spectre of Captain Body should be standing there, leaning on a ghostly sword.

At such times Elspeth kept a firm grip of Tommy's hand, but one evening as they all ran panic-stricken from some imaginary alarm, she lost him near the Cuttle Well, and then, as it seemed to her, the Den became suddenly very dark and lonely. At first she thought she had it to herself, but as she stole timidly along the pink path she heard voices, and she cried "Tommy!" joyously. But no answer came, so it could not be Tommy. Then she thought it must be a pair of lovers, but next moment she stood transfixed with fear, for it was the Painted Lady, who was coming along the path talking aloud to herself. No, not to herself-to someone she evidently thought was by her side; she called him darling and other sweet names, and waited for his replies and nodded pleased assent to them, or pouted at them, and terrified Elspeth knew that she was talking to the man who never came.

When she saw Elspeth she stopped irresolutely, and the two stood looking in fear at each other. "You are not my brat, are you?" the Painted Lady asked.

"N-no," the child gasped.

"Then why don't you call me nasty names?"

"I dinna never call you names," Elspeth replied, but the woman still looked puzzled.

"Perhaps you are naughty also?" she said doubtfully, and then, as if making up her mind that it must be so, she came closer and said, with a voice full of pity: "I am so sorry."

Elspeth did not understand half of it, but the pitying voice, which was of the rarest sweetness, drove away much of her fear, and she said: "Do you no mind me? I was wi' Tommy when he gave you the gold packet on Muckley night."

Then the Painted Lady remembered. "He took such a fancy to me," she said, with a pleased simper, and then she looked serious again.

"Do you love him?" she asked, and Elspeth nodded.

"But is he all the world to you?"

"Yes," Elspeth said.

The Painted Lady took her by the arm and said impressively, "Don't let him know."

"But he does know," said Elspeth.

"I am so sorry," the Painted Lady said again. "When they know too well, then they have no pity."

"But I want Tommy to know," Elspeth insisted.

"That is the woeful thing," the Painted Lady said, rocking her arms in a way that reminded the child of Grizel. "We want them to know, we cannot help liking them to know!"

Suddenly she became confidential. "Do you think I showed my love too openly?" she asked eagerly. "I tried to hide it, you know. I covered my face with my hands, but he pulled them away, and then, of course, he knew."

She went on, "I kissed his horse's nose, and he said I did that because it was his horse. How could he know? When I asked him how he knew, he kissed me, and I pretended to be angry and ran away. But I was not angry, and I said to myself, 'I am glad, I am glad, I am glad!'

"I wanted so to be good, but-It is so difficult to refuse when you love him very much, don't you think?"

The pathos of that was lost on the girl, and the Painted Lady continued sadly: "It would be so nice, would it not, if they liked us to be good? I think it would be sweet." She bent forward and whispered emphatically, "But they don't, you know-it bores them.

"Never bore them-and they are so easily bored! It bores them if you say you want to be married. I think it would be sweet to be married, but you should never ask for a wedding. They give you everything else, but if you say you want a wedding, they stamp their feet and go away. Why are you crying, girl? You should not cry; they don't like it. Put on your prettiest gown and laugh and pretend you are happy, and then they will tell you naughty stories and give you these." She felt her ears and looked at her fingers, on which there may once have been jewels, but there were none now.

"If you cry you lose your complexion, and then they don't love you any more. I had always such a beautiful skin. Some ladies when they lose their complexion paint. Horrid, isn't it? I wonder they can do such a thing."

She eyed Elspeth suspiciously. "But of course you might do it just a little," she said, pleadingly —"just to make them go on loving you, don't you think?

"When they don't want to come any more they write you a letter, and you run with it to your room and kiss it, because you don't know what is inside. Then you open it, and that breaks your heart, you know." She nodded her head sagaciously and smiled with tears in her eyes. "Never, never, never open the letter. Keep it unopened on your breast, and then you can always think that he may come to-morrow. And if—"

Someone was approaching, and she stopped and listened. "My brat!" she cried, furiously, "she is always following me," and she poured forth a torrent of filthy abuse of Grizel, in the midst of which Tommy (for it was he) appeared and carried Elspeth off hastily. This was the only conversation either child ever had with the Painted Lady, and it bore bad fruit for Grizel. Elspeth told some of the Monypenny women about it, and they thought it their duty to point out to Aaron that the Painted Lady and her child were not desirable acquaintances for Tommy and Elspeth.

"I dinna ken," he answered sharply, "whether Tommy's a fit acquaintance for Grizel, but I'm very sure o' this, that she's more than a fit acquaintance for him. And look at what she has done for this house. I kenna what we should do if she didna come in nows and nans."

"You ken well, Aaron," they said, "that onything we could do in the way o' keeping your house in order we should do gladly."

"Thank you," he replied ungraciously, "but I would rather have her."

Nevertheless he agreed that he ought to forbid any intercourse with the Painted Lady, and unfortunately Grizel heard of this. Probably there never would have been any such intercourse; Grizel guarded against it more than anyone, for reasons she never spoke of, but she resented this veto proudly.

"Why must you not speak to my mamma?" she demanded of Tommy and Elspeth.

"Because-because she is a queer one," he said.

"She is not a queer one-she is just sweet."

He tried to evade the question by saying weakly, "We never see her to speak to at any rate, so it will make no difference. It's no as if you ever asked us to come to Double Dykes."

"But I ask you now," said Grizel, with flashing eyes.

"Oh, I darena!" cried Elspeth.

"Then I won't ever come into your house again," said Grizel, decisively.

"No to redd up?" asked Tommy, incredulously. "No to bake nor to iron? You couldna help it."

"Yes I could."

"Think what you'll miss!"

Grizel might have retorted, "Think what you will miss!" but perhaps the reply she did make had a sharper sting in it. "I shall never come again," she said loftily, "and my reason for not coming is that-that my mamma thinks your house is not respectable!" She flung this over her shoulder as she stalked away, and it may be that the tears came when there were none to see them, but hers was a resolute mind, and though she continued to be friendly with Tommy and Elspeth out of doors she never again crossed their threshold.

"The house is in a terrible state for want o' you," Tommy would say, trying to wheedle her. "We hinna sanded the floor for months, and the box-iron has fallen ahint the dresser, and my gray sark is rove up the back, and oh, you should just see the holes in Aaron's stockings!"

Then Grizel rocked her arms in agony, but no, she would not go in.

Chapter XX
The Shadow of Sir Walter

Tommy was in Miss Ailie's senior class now, though by no means at the top of it, and her mind was often disturbed about his future. On this subject Aaron had never spoken to anyone, and the problem gave Tommy himself so little trouble that all Elspeth knew was that he was to be great and that she was to keep his house. So the school-mistress braved an interview with Aaron for the sake of her favorite.

"You know he is a remarkable boy," she said.

"At his lessons, ma'am?" asked Aaron, quietly.

Not exactly at his lessons, she had to admit.

"In what way, then, ma'am?"

Really Miss Ailie could not say. There was something wonderful about Tommy, you felt it, but you could not quite give it a name. The warper must have noticed it himself.

"I've heard him saying something o' the kind to Elspeth," was Aaron's reply.

"But sometimes he is like a boy inspired," said the school-mistress. "You must have seen that?"

"When he was thinking o' himsel'," answered Aaron.

"He has such noble sentiments."

"He has."

"And I think, I really think," said Miss Ailie, eagerly, for this was what she had come to say, "that he has got great gifts for the ministry."

"I'm near sure o't," said Aaron, grimly.

"Ah, I see you don't like him."

"I dinna," the warper acknowledged quietly, "but I've been trying to do my duty by him for all that. It's no every laddie that gets three years' schooling straight on end."

This was true, but Miss Ailie used it to press her point. "You have done so well by him," she said, "that I think you should keep him at school for another year or two, and so give him a chance of carrying a bursary. If he carries one it will support him at college; if he does not-well, then I suppose he must be apprenticed to some trade."

"No," Aaron said, decisively; "if he gets the chance of a college education and flings it awa', I'll waste no more siller on his keep. I'll send him straight to the herding."

"And I shall not blame you," Miss Ailie declared eagerly.

"Though I would a hantle rather," continued the warper, "waur my money on Elspeth."

"What you spend on him," Miss Ailie argued, "you will really be spending on her, for if he rises in the world he will not leave Elspeth behind. You are prejudiced against him, but you cannot deny that."

"I dinna deny but what he's fond o' her," said Aaron, and after considering the matter for some days he decided that Tommy should get his chance. The school-mistress had not acted selfishly, for this decision, as she knew, meant that the boy must now be placed in the hands of Mr. Cathro, who was a Greek and Latin scholar. She taught Latin herself, it is true, but as cautiously as she crossed a plank bridge, and she was never comfortable in the dominie's company, because even at a tea-table he would refer familiarly to the ablative absolute instead of letting sleeping dogs lie.

"But Elspeth couldna be happy if we were at different schools," Tommy objected instantly.

"Yes, I could," said Elspeth, who had been won over by Miss Ailie; "it will be so fine, Tommy, to see you again after I hinna seen you for three hours."

Tommy was little known to Mr. Cathro at this time, except as the boy who had got the better of a rival teacher in the affair of Corp, which had delighted him greatly. "But if the sacket thinks he can play any of his tricks on me," he told Aaron, "there is an awakening before him," and he began the cramming of Tommy for a bursary with perfect confidence.

But before the end of the month, at the mere mention of Tommy's name, Mr. Cathro turned red in the face, and the fingers of his laying-on hand would clutch an imaginary pair of tawse. Already Tommy had made him self-conscious. He peered covertly at Tommy, and Tommy caught him at it every time, and then each quickly looked another way, and Cathro vowed never to look again, but did it next minute, and what enraged him most was that he knew Tommy noted his attempts at self-restraint as well as his covert glances. All the other pupils knew that a change for the worse had come over the dominie's temper. They saw him punish Tommy frequently without perceptible cause, and that he was still unsatisfied when the punishment was over. This apparently was because Tommy gave him a look before returning to his seat. When they had been walloped they gave Cathro a look also, but it merely meant, "Oh, that this was a dark road and I had a divot in my hand!" while his look was unreadable, that is unreadable to them, for the dominie understood it and writhed. What it said was, "You think me a wonder, and therefore I forgive you."

"And sometimes he fair beats Cathro!" So Tommy's schoolmates reported at home, and the dominie had to acknowledge its truth to Aaron. "I wish you would give that sacket a thrashing for me," he said, half furiously, yet with a grin on his face, one day when he and the warper chanced to meet on the Monypenny road.

"I'll no lay a hand on bairn o' Jean Myles," Aaron replied. "Ay, and I understood you to say that he should meet his match in you."

"Did I ever say that, man? Well, well, we live and learn."

"What has he been doing now?"

"What has he been doing!" echoed Cathro. "He has been making me look foolish in my own class-room. Yes, sir, he has so completely got the better of me (and not for the first time) that when I tell the story of how he diddled Mr. Ogilvy, Mr. Ogilvy will be able to cap it with the story of how the little whelp diddled me. Upon my soul, Aaron, he is running away with all my self-respect and destroying my sense of humor."

What had so crushed the dominie was the affair of Francie Crabb. Francie was now a pupil, like Gavin Dishart and Tommy, of Mr. Cathro's, who detested the boy's golden curls, perhaps because he was bald himself. They were also an incentive to evil-doing on the part of other boys, who must give them a tug in passing, and on a day the dominie said, in a fury, "Give your mother my compliments, Francie, and tell her I'm so tired of seeing your curls that I mean to cut them off to-morrow morning."

"Say he shall not," whispered Tommy.

"You shanna!" blurted out Francie.

"But I will," said Cathro; "I would do it now if I had the shears."

It was only an empty threat, but an hour afterwards the dominie caught Tommy wagering in witchy marbles and other coin that he would not do it, and then instead of taking the tawse to him he said, "Keep him to his bargains, laddies, for whatever may have been my intention at the time, I mean to be as good as my word now."

He looked triumphantly at Tommy, who, however, instead of seeming crestfallen, continued to bet, and now the other boys were eager to close with him, for great was their faith in Cathro. These transactions were carried out on the sly, but the dominie knew what was going on, and despite his faith in himself he had his twitches of uneasiness.

"However, the boy can only be trusting to fear of Mrs. Crabb restraining me," he decided, and he marched into the school-room next morning, ostentatiously displaying his wife's largest scissors. His pupils crowded in after him, and though he noticed that all were strangely quiet and many wearing scared faces, he put it down to the coming scene. He could not resist giving one triumphant glance at Tommy, who, however, instead of returning it, looked modestly down. Then —"Is Francie Crabb here?" asked Mr. Cathro, firmly.

"He's hodding ahint the press," cried a dozen voices.

"Come forward, Francie," said the dominie, clicking the shears to encourage him.

There was a long pause, and then Francie emerged in fear from behind the press. Yes, it was Francie, but his curls were gone!

The shears fell to the floor. "Who did this?" roared the terrible Cathro.

"It was Tommy Sandys," blurted out Francis, in tears.

The school-master was unable to speak, and, alarmed at the stillness, Francie whined, "He said it would be done at ony rate, and he promised me half his winnings."

It is still remembered by bearded men and married women who were at school that day how Cathro leaped three forms to get at Tommy, and how Tommy cried under the tawse and yet laughed ecstatically at the same time, and how subsequently he and Francie collected so many dues that the pockets of them stood out like brackets from their little persons.

The dominie could not help grinning a little at his own discomfiture as he told this story, but Aaron saw nothing amusing in it. "As I telled you," he repeated, "I winna touch him, so if you're no content wi' what you've done yoursel', you had better put Francie's mither on him."

"I hear she has taken him in hand already," Mr. Cathro replied dryly. "But, Aaron, I wish you would at least keep him closer to his lessons at night, for it is seldom he comes to the school well prepared."

"I see him sitting lang ower his books," said Aaron.

"Ay, maybe, but is he at them?" responded the dominie with a shake of the head that made Aaron say, with his first show of interest in the conversation, "You have little faith in his carrying a bursary, I see."

But this Mr. Cathro would not admit, for if he thought Tommy a numskull the one day he often saw cause to change his mind the next, so he answered guardedly, "It's too soon to say, Aaron, for he has eighteen months' stuffing to undergo yet before we send him to Aberdeen to try his fortune, and I have filled some gey toom wimes in eighteen months. But you must lend me a hand."

The weaver considered, and then replied stubbornly, "No, I give him his chance, but I'll have nocht to do wi' his use o't. And, dominie, I want you to say not another word to me about him atween this and examination time, for my mind's made up no to say a word to him. It's well kent that I'm no more fit to bring up bairns than to have them (dinna conter me, man, for the thing was proved lang syne at the Cuttle Well), and so till that time I'll let him gang his ain gait. But if he doesna carry a bursary, to the herding he goes. I've said it and I'll stick to it."

So, as far as Aaron was concerned, Tommy was left in peace to the glory of collecting his winnings from those who had sworn by Cathro, and among them was Master Gavin Ogilvy Dishart, who now found himself surrounded by a debt of sixpence, a degrading position for the son of an Auld Licht minister.

Tommy would not give him time, but was willing to take his copy of "Waverley" as full payment.

Gavin offered him "Ivanhoe" instead, because his mother had given a read of "Waverley" to Gavinia, Miss Ailie's servant, and she read so slowly, putting her finger beneath each word, that she had not yet reached the middle. Also, she was so enamoured of the work that she would fight anyone who tried to take it from her.

Tommy refused "Ivanhoe," as it was not about Jacobites, but suggested that Gavinia should be offered it in lieu of "Waverley," and told that it was a better story.

The suggestion came too late, as Gavinia had already had a loan of "Ivanhoe," and read it with rapture, inch by inch. However, if Tommy would wait a month, or —

Tommy was so eager to read more about the Jacobites that he found it trying to wait five minutes. He thought Gavin's duty was to get his father to compel Gavinia to give the book up.

Was Tommy daft? Mr. Dishart did not know that his son possessed these books. He did not approve of story books, and when Mrs. Dishart gave them to Gavin on his birthday she-she had told him to keep them out of his father's sight. (Mr. and Mrs. Dishart were very fond of each other, but there were certain little matters that she thought it unnecessary to trouble him about.)

So if Tommy was to get "Waverley" at once, he must discover another way. He reflected, and then set off to Miss Ailie's (to whom he still read sober works of an evening, but novels never), looking as if he had found a way.

For some time Miss Ailie had been anxious about her red-armed maid, who had never before given pain unless by excess of willingness, as when she offered her garter to tie Miss Ailie's parcels with. Of late, however, Gavinia had taken to blurting out disquieting questions, to the significance of which she withheld the key, such as —

"Is there ony place nowadays, ma'am, where there's tourniements? And could an able-bodied lassie walk to them? and what might be the charge to win in?"

Or, "Would you no like to be so michty beautiful, ma'am, that as soon as the men saw your bonny face they just up wi' you in their arms and ran?"

Or again, "What's the heaviest weight o' a woman a grand lusty man could carry in his arms as if she were an infant?"

This method of conveyance seemed to have a peculiar fascination for Gavinia, and she got herself weighed at the flesher's. On another occasion she broke a glass candlestick, and all she said to the pieces was, "Wha carries me, wears me."

This mystery was troubling the school-mistress sadly when Tommy arrived with the key to it. "I'm doubting Gavinia's reading ill books on the sly," he said.

"Never!" exclaimed Miss Ailie, "she reads nothing but the *Mentor*."

Tommy shook his head, like one who would fain hope so, but could not overlook facts. "I've been hearing," he said, "that she reads books as are full o' Strokes and Words We have no Concern with."

Miss Ailie could not believe it, but she was advised to search the kitchen, and under Gavinia's mattress was found the dreadful work.

"And you are only fifteen!" said Miss Ailie, eying her little maid sorrowfully.

"The easier to carry," replied Gavinia, darkly.

"And you named after a minister!" Miss Ailie continued, for her maid had been christened Gavinia because she was the first child baptized in his church after the Rev. Gavin Dishart came to Thrums. "Gavinia, I must tell him of this. I shall take this book to Mr. Dishart this very day."

"The right man to take it to," replied the maid, sullenly, "for it's his ain."

"Gavinia!"

"Well, it was Mrs. Dishart that lended it to me."

"I —I never saw it on the manse shelves."

"I'm thinking," said the brazen Gavinia, "as there's hoddy corners in manses as well as in blue-and-white rooms."

This dark suggestion was as great a shock to the gentle school-mistress as if out of a clear sky had come suddenly the word —

Stroke!

She tottered with the book that had so demoralized the once meek Gavinia into the blue-and-white room, where Tommy was restlessly awaiting her, and when she had told him all, he said, with downcast eyes:

"I was never sure o' Mrs. Dishart. When I hand her the *Mentor* she looks as if she didna care a stroke for't —"

"Tommy!"

"I'm doubting," he said sadly, "that she's ower fond o' Words We have no Concern with."

Miss Ailie would not listen to such talk, but she approved of the suggestion that "Waverley" should be returned not to the minister, but to his wife, and she accepted gratefully Tommy's kindly offer to act as bearer. Only happening to open the book in the middle, she —

"I'm waiting," said Tommy, after ten minutes.

She did not hear him.

"I'm waiting," he said again, but she was now in the next chapter.

"Maybe you would like to read it yoursel'!" he cried, and then she came to, and, with a shudder handed him the book. But after he had gone she returned to the kitchen to reprove Gavinia at greater length, and in the midst of the reproof she said faintly: "You did not happen to look at the end, did you?"

"That I did," replied Gavinia.

"And did she-did he —"

"No," said Gavinia, sorrowfully.

Miss Ailie sighed. "That's what I think too," said Gavinia.

"Why didn't they?" asked the school-mistress.

"Because he was just a sumph," answered Gavinia, scornfully. "If he had been like Fergus, or like the chield in 'Ivanhoe,' he wouldna have ta'en a 'no.' He would just have whipped her up in his arms and away wi' her. That's the kind for me, ma'am."

"There is a fascination about them," murmured Miss Ailie.

"A what?"

But again Miss Ailie came to. "For shame, Gavinia, for shame!" she said, severely; "these are disgraceful sentiments."

In the meantime Tommy had hurried with the book, not to the manse, but to a certain garret, and as he read, his imagination went on fire. Blinder's stories had made him half a Jacobite, and now "Waverley" revealed to him that he was born neither for the ministry nor the herding, but to restore to his country its rightful king. The first to whom he confided this was Corp, who immediately exclaimed: "Michty me! But what will the police say?"

"I ken a wy," answered Tommy, sternly.

Chapter XXI
The Last Jacobite Rising

On the evening of the Queen's birthday, bridies were eaten to her honor in a hundred Thrums homes, and her health was drunk in toddy, Scotch toddy and Highland toddy. Patullo, the writer, gave a men's party, and his sole instructions to his maid were "Keep running back and forrit wi' the hot water." At the bank there was a ladies' party and ginger wine. From Cathro's bedroom-window a flag was displayed with *Vivat Regina* on it, the sentiment composed by Cathro, the words sewn by the girls of his McCulloch class. The eight-o'clock bell rang for an hour, and a loyal crowd had gathered in the square to shout. To a superficial observer, such as the Baron Bailie or Todd, the new policeman, all seemed well and fair.

But a very different scene was being enacted at the same time in the fastnesses of the Den, where three resolute schemers had met by appointment. Their trysting-place was the Cuttle Well, which is most easily reached by the pink path made for that purpose; but the better to further their dark and sinister design, the plotters arrived by three circuitous routes, one descending the Reekie Broth Pot, a low but dangerous waterfall, the second daring the perils of the crags, and the third walking stealthily up the burn.

"Is that you, Tommy?"

"Whist! Do you mind the password?"

"Stroke!"

"Right. Have you heard Gav Dishart coming?"

"I hinna. I doubt his father had grippit him as he was slinking out o' the manse."

"I fear it, Corp. I'm thinking his father is in the Woman's pay."

"What woman?"

"The Woman of Hanover?"

"That's the queen, is it no?"

"She'll never get me to call her queen."

"Nor yet me. I think I hear Gav coming."

Gav Dishart was the one who had come by the burn, and his boots were cheeping like a field of mice. He gave the word "Stroke," and the three then looked at each other firmly. The lights of the town were not visible from the Cuttle Well, owing to an arm of cliff that is outstretched between, but the bell could be distinctly heard, and occasionally a shout of revelry.

"They little ken!" said Tommy, darkly.

"They hinna a notion," said Corp, but he was looking somewhat perplexed himself.

"It's near time I was back for family exercise," said Gav, uneasily, "so we had better do it quick, Tommy."

"Did you bring the wineglasses?" Tommy asked him.

"No," Gav said, "the press was lockit, but I've brought egg-cups."

"Stand round then."

The three boys now presented a picturesque appearance, but there was none save the man in the moon to see them. They stood round the Cuttle Well, each holding an egg-cup, and though the daring nature of their undertaking and the romantic surroundings combined to excite them, it was not fear but soaring purpose that paled their faces and caused their hands to tremble, when Tommy said solemnly, "Afore we do what we've come here to do, let's swear."

"Stroke!" he said.

"Stroke!" said Gav.

"Stroke!" said Corp.

They then filled their cups and holding them over the well, so that they clinked, they said:

"To the king ower the water!"

"To the king ower the water!"

"To the king ower the water!"

When they had drunk Tommy broke his cup against a rock, for he was determined that
it should never be used to honor a meaner toast, and the others followed his example, Corp
briskly, though the act puzzled him, and Gav with a gloomy look because he knew that the
cups would be missed to-morrow.

"Is that a' now?" whispered Corp, wiping his forehead with his sleeve.

"All!" cried Tommy. "Man, we've just begood."

As secretly as they had entered it, they left the Den, and anon three figures were standing
in a dark trance, cynically watching the revellers in the square.

"If they just kent!" muttered the smallest, who was wearing his jacket outside in to escape
observation.

"But they little ken!" said Gav Dishart.

"They hinna a notion!" said Corp, contemptuously, but still he was a little puzzled, and
presently he asked softly: "Lads, what just is it that they dinna ken?"

Had Gav been ready with an answer he could not have uttered it, for just then a terrible little
man in black, who had been searching for him in likely places, seized him by the cuff of the
neck, and, turning his face in an easterly direction, ran him to family worship. But there was
still work to do for the other two. Walking home alone that night from Mr. Patullo's party, Mr.
Cathro had an uncomfortable feeling that he was being dogged. When he stopped to listen,
all was at once still, but the moment he moved onward he again heard stealthy steps behind.
He retired to rest as soon as he reached his house, to be wakened presently by a slight noise at
the window, whence the flag-post protruded. It had been but a gust of wind, he decided, and
turned round to go to sleep again, when crash! the post was plucked from its place and cast
to the ground. The dominie sprang out of bed, and while feeling for a light, thought he heard
scurrying feet, but when he looked out at the window no one was to be seen; *Vivat Regina* lay
ignobly in the gutters. That it could have been the object of an intended theft was not probable,
but the open window might have tempted thieves, and there was a possible though risky way
up by the spout. The affair was a good deal talked about at the time, but it remained shrouded
in a mystery which even we have been unable to penetrate.

On the heels of the Queen's birthday came the Muckley, the one that was to be known to
fame, if fame was willing to listen to Corp, as Tommy's Muckley. Unless he had some grand
aim in view never was a boy who yielded to temptations more blithely than Tommy, but when
he had such aim never was a boy so firm in withstanding them. At this Muckley he had a
mighty reason for not spending money, and with ninepence in his pocket clamoring to be out he
spent not one halfpenny. There was something uncanny in the sight of him stalking unscathed
between rows of stands and shows, everyone of them aiming at his pockets. Corp and Gav, of
course, were in the secret and did their humble best to act in the same unnatural manner, but
now and again a show made a successful snap at Gav, and Corp had gloomy fears that he would
lose his head in presence of the Teuch and Tasty, from which humiliation indeed he was only
saved by the happy idea of requesting Tommy to shout "Deuteronomy!" in a warning voice,
every time they drew nigh Californy's seductive stand.

Was there nothing for sale, then, that the three thirsted to buy? There were many things,
among them weapons of war, a pack of cards, more properly called Devil's books, blue bonnets
suitable for Highland gentlemen, feathers for the bonnets, a tin lantern, yards of tartan cloth,
which the deft fingers of Grizel would convert into warriors' sashes. Corp knew that these
purchases were in Tommy's far-seeing eye, but he thought the only way to get them was to
ask the price and then offer half. Gav, the scholar, who had already reached daylight through
the first three books of Euclid, and took a walk every Saturday morning with his father and
Herodotus, even Gav, the scholar, was as thick-witted as Corp.

"We'll let other laddies buy them," Tommy explained in his superior way, "and then after
the Muckley is past, we'll buy them frae them."

The others understood now. After a Muckley there was always a great dearth of pence, and a
moneyed man could become owner of Muckley purchases at a sixth part of the Muckley price.

"You crittur!" exclaimed Corp, in abject admiration.

But Gav saw an objection. "The feck of them," he pointed out, "will waur their siller on shows and things to eat, instead of on what we want them to buy."

"So they will, the nasty sackets!" cried Corp.

"You couldna blame a laddie for buying Teuch and Tasty," continued Gav with triumph, for he was a little jealous of Tommy.

"You couldna," agreed Corp, "no, I'll be dagont, if you could," and his hand pressed his money feverishly.

"Deuteronomy!" roared Tommy, and Corp's hand jumped as if it had been caught in some other person's, pocket.

"But how are we to do?" he asked. "If you like, I'll take Birkie and the Haggerty-Taggertys round the Muckley and fight ilka ane that doesna buy —"

"Corp," said Tommy, calmly, "I wonder at you. Do you no ken yet that the best plan is to leave a thing to me?"

"Blethering gowks that we are, of course it is!" cried Corp, and he turned almost fiercely upon Gav. "Lippen all to him," he said with grand confidence, "he'll find a wy."

And Tommy found a way. Birkie was the boy who bought the pack of cards. He saw Tommy looking so-woe-begone that it was necessary to ask the reason.

"Oh, Birkie, lend me threepence," sobbed Tommy, "and I'll give you sixpence the morn."

"You're daft," said Birkie, "there's no a laddie in Thrums that will have one single lonely bawbee the morn."

"Him that buys the cards," moaned Tommy, "will never be without siller, for you tell auld folks fortunes on them at a penny every throw. Lend me threepence, Birkie. They cost a sic, and I have just —"

"Na, na," said greedy Birkie, "I'm no to be catched wi' chaff. If it's true, what you say, I'll buy the cards mysel'."

Having thus got hold of him, Tommy led Birkie to a stand where the King of Egypt was telling fortunes with cards, and doing a roaring trade among the Jocks and Jennys. He also sold packs at sixpence each, and the elated Birkie was an immediate purchaser.

"You're no so clever as you think yoursel'!" he said triumphantly to Tommy, who replied with his inscrutable smile. But to his satellites he said, "Not a soul will buy a fortune frae Birkie. I'll get thae cards for a penny afore next week's out."

Francie Crabb found Tommy sniggering to himself in the back wynd. "What are you goucking at?" asked Francie, in surprise, for, as a rule, Tommy only laughed behind his face.

"I winna tell you," chuckled Tommy, "but what a bar, oh, what a divert!"

"Come on, tell me."

"Well, it's at the man as is swallowing swords ahint the menagerie."

"I see nothing to laugh at in that."

"I'm no laughing at that. I'm laughing at him for selling the swords for ninepence the piece. Oh, what ignorant he is, oh, what a bar!"

"Ninepence is a mislaird price for a soord," said Francie. "I never gave ninepence."

Tommy looked at him in the way that always made boys fidget with their fists.

"You're near as big a bar as him," he said scornfully. "Did you ever see the sword that's hanging on the wall in the backroom at the post-office?"

"No, but my father has telled me about it. It has a grand name."

"It's an Andrea Ferrara, that's what it is."

"Ay, I mind the name now; there has been folk killed wi' that soord."

This was true, for the post-office Andrea Ferrara has a stirring history, but for the present its price was the important thing. "Dr. McQueen offered a pound note for it," said Tommy.

"I ken that, but what has it to do wi' the soord-swallower?"

"Just this; that the swords he is selling for ninepence are Andrea Ferraras, the same as the post-office ones, and he could get a pound a piece for them if he kent their worth. Oh, what a bar, oh, what —"

Francie's eyes lit up greedily, and he looked at his two silver shillings, and took two steps in the direction of the sword-swallower's, and faltered and could not make up his agitated mind. Tommy set off toward the square at a brisk walk.

"Whaur are you off to?" asked Francie, following him.

"To tell the man what his swords is worth. It would be ill done no to tell him." To clinch the matter, off went Tommy at a run, and off went Francie after him. As a rule Tommy was the swifter, but on this occasion he lagged of fell purpose, and reached the sword-swallower's tent just in time to see Francie emerge elated therefrom, carrying two Andrea Ferraras. Francie grinned when they met.

"What a bar!" he crowed.

"What a bar!" agreed Tommy, and sufficient has now been told to show that he had found a way. Even Gav acknowledged a master, and, when the accoutrements of war were bought at second hand as cheaply as Tommy had predicted, applauded him with eyes and mouth for a full week, after which he saw things in a new light. Gav of course was to enter the bursary lists anon, and he had supposed that Cathro would have the last year's schooling of him; but no, his father decided to send him for the grand final grind to Mr. Ogilvy of Glen Quharity, a famous dominie between whom and Mr. Dishart existed a friendship that none had ever got at the root of. Mr. Cathro was more annoyed than he cared to show, Gav being of all the boys of that time the one likeliest to do his teacher honor at the university competitions, but Tommy, though the decision cost him an adherent, was not ill-pleased, for he had discovered that Gav was one of those irritating boys who like to be leader. Gav, as has been said, suddenly saw Tommy's victory over Messrs. Birkie, Francie, etc., in a new light; this was because when he wanted back the shilling which he had contributed to the funds for buying their purchases, Tommy replied firmly:

"I canna give you the shilling, but I'll give you the lantern and the tartan cloth we bought wi' it."

"What use could they be to me at Glen Quharity?" Gav protested.

"Oh, if they are no use to you," Tommy said sweetly, "me and Corp is willing to buy them off you for threepence."

Then Gav became a scorner of duplicity, but he had to consent to the bargain, and again Corp said to Tommy, "Oh, you crittur!" But he was sorry to lose a fellow-conspirator. "There's just the twa o' us now," he sighed.

"Just twa!" cried Tommy. "What are you havering about, man? There's as many as I like to whistle for."

"You mean Grizel and Elspeth, I ken, but —"

"I wasna thinking of the womenfolk," Tommy told him, with a contemptuous wave of the hand. He went closer to Corp, and said, in a low voice, "The McKenzies are waiting!"

"Are they, though?" said Corp, perplexed, as he had no notion who the McKenzies might be.

"And Lochiel has twa hunder spearsmen."

"Do you say so?"

"Young Kinnordy's ettling to come out, and I meet Lord Airlie, when the moon rises, at the Loups o' Kenny, and auld Bradwardine's as spunky as ever, and there's fifty wild Highlandmen lying ready in the muckle cave of Clova."

He spoke so earnestly that Corp could only ejaculate, "Michty me!"

"But of course they winna rise," continued Tommy, darkly, "till he lands."

"Of course no," said Corp, "but-wha is he?"

"Himsel'," whispered Tommy, "the Chevalier!"

Corp hesitated. "But, I thought," he said diffidently, "I thought you —"

"So I am," said Tommy.

"But you said he hadna landed yet?"

"Neither he has."

"But you —"

"Well?"

"You're here, are you no?"

Tommy stamped his foot in irritation. "You're slow in the uptak," he said. "I'm no here. How can I be here when I'm at St. Germains?"

"Dinna be angry wi' me," Corp begged. "I ken you're ower the water, but when I see you, I kind of forget; and just for the minute I think you're here."

"Well, think afore you speak."

"I'll try, but that's teuch work. When do you come to Scotland?"

"I'm no sure; but as soon as I'm ripe."

At nights Tommy now sometimes lay among the cabbages of the school-house watching the shadow of Black Cathro on his sitting-room blind. Cathro never knew he was there. The reason Tommy lay among the cabbages was that there was a price upon his head.

"But if Black Cathro wanted to get the blood-money," Corp said apologetically, "he could nab you any day. He kens you fine."

Tommy smiled meaningly. "Not him," he answered, "I've cheated him bonny, he hasna a notion wha I am. Corp, would you like a good laugh?"

"That I would."

"Weel, then, I'll tell you wha he thinks I am. Do you ken a little house yont the road a bitty irae Monypenny?"

"I ken no sic house," said Corp, "except Aaron's."

"Aaron's the man as bides in it," Tommy continued hastily, "at least I think that's the name. Well, as you ken the house, you've maybe noticed a laddie that bides there too?"

"There's no laddie," began Corp, "except —"

"Let me see," interrupted Tommy, "what was his name? Was it Peter? No. Was it Willie? Stop, I mind, it was Tommy."

He glared so that Corp dared not utter a word.

"Have you notitched him?"

"I've —I've seen him," Corp gasped.

"Well, this is the joke," said Tommy, trying vainly to restrain his mirth, "Cathro thinks I'm that laddie! Ho! ho! ho!"

Corp scratched his head, then he bit his warts, then he spat upon his hands, then he said "Damn."

The crisis came when Cathro, still ignorant that the heather was on fire, dropped some disparaging remarks about the Stuarts to his history class. Tommy said nothing, but-but one of the school-windows was without a snib, and next morning when the dominie reached his desk he was surprised to find on it a little cotton glove. He raised it on high, greatly puzzled, and then, as ever when he suspected knavery, his eyes sought Tommy, who was sitting on a form, his arms proudly folded. That the whelp had put the glove there, Cathro no longer doubted, and he would have liked to know why, but was reluctant to give him the satisfaction of asking. So the gauntlet-for gauntlet it was-was laid aside, the while Tommy, his head humming like a beeskep, muttered triumphantly through his teeth, "But he lifted it, he lifted it!" and at closing time it was flung in his face with this fair tribute:

"I'm no a rich man, laddie, but I would give a pound note to know what you'll be at ten years from now."

There could be no mistaking the dire meaning of these words, and Tommy hurried, pale but determined, to the quarry, where Corp, with a barrow in his hands, was learning strange phrases by heart, and finding it a help to call his warts after the new swears.

"Corp," cried Tommy, firmly, "I've set sail!"

On the following Saturday evening Charles Edward landed in the Den. In his bonnet was the white cockade, and round his waist a tartan sash; though he had long passed man's allotted span his face was still full of fire, his figure lithe and even boyish. For state reasons he had assumed the name of Captain Stroke. As he leapt ashore from the bark, the Dancing Shovel, he was received right loyally by Corp and other faithful adherents, of whom only two, and these of a sex to which his House was ever partial, were visible, owing to the gathering gloom. Corp of that Ilk sank on his knees at the water's edge, and kissing his royal master's hand said, fervently, "Welcome, my prince, once more to bonny Scotland!" Then he rose and whispered, but with scarcely less emotion, "There's an egg to your tea."

Chapter XXII
The Siege of Thrums

The man in the moon is a native of Thrums, who was put up there for hacking sticks on the Sabbath, and as he sails over the Den his interest in the bit placey is still sufficient to make him bend forward and cry "Boo!" at the lovers. When they jump apart you can see the aged reprobate grinning. Once out of sight of the den, he cares not a boddle how the moon travels, but the masterful crittur enrages him if she is in a hurry here, just as he is cleverly making out whose children's children are courting now. "Slow, there!" he cries to the moon, but she answers placidly that they have the rest of the world to view to-night. "The rest of the world be danged!" roars the man, and he cranes his neck for a last glimpse of the Cuttle Well, until he nearly falls out of the moon.

Never had the man such a trying time as during the year now before him. It was the year when so many scientific magnates sat up half the night in their shirts, spying at him through telescopes. But every effort to discover why he was in such a fidget failed, because the spy-glasses were never levelled at the Thrums den. Through the whole of the incidents now to tell, you may conceive the man (on whom sympathy would be wasted) dagoning horribly, because he was always carried past the den before he could make head or tail of the change that had come over it.

The spot chosen by the ill-fated Stuart and his gallant remnant for their last desperate enterprise was eminently fitted for their purpose. Being round the corner from Thrums, it was commanded by no fortified place save the farm of Nether Drumgley, and on a recent goustie night nearly all the trees had been blown down, making a hundred hiding-places for bold climbers, and transforming the Den into a scene of wild and mournful grandeur. In no bay more suitable than the flooded field called the Silent Pool could the hunted prince have cast anchor, for the Pool is not only sheltered from observation, but so little troubled by gales that it had only one drawback: at some seasons of the year it was not there. This, however, did not vex Stroke, as it is cannier to call him, for he burned his boats on the night he landed (and a dagont, tedious job it was too), and pointed out to his followers that the drouth which kept him in must also keep the enemy out. Part of the way to the lair they usually traversed in the burn, because water leaves no trace, and though they carried turnip lanterns and were armed to the teeth, this was often a perilous journey owing to the lovers close at hand on the pink path, from which the trees had been cleared, for lads and lasses must walk whate'er betide. Ronny-On's Jean and Peter Scrymgeour, little Lisbeth Doak and long Sam'l from Pyotdykes were pairing that year, and never knew how near they were to being dirked by Corp of Corp, who, lurking in the burn till there were no tibbits in his toes, muttered fiercely, "Cheep one single cheep, and it will be thy hinmost, methinks!" under the impression that Methinks was a Jacobite oath.

For this voluntary service, Stroke clapped Corp of Corp on the shoulder with a naked sword, and said, "Rise, Sir Joseph!" which made Corp more confused than ever, for he was already Corp of Corp, Him of Muckle Kenny, Red McNeil, Andrew Ferrara, and the Master of Inverquharity (Stroke's names), as well as Stab-in-the-Dark, Grind-them-to-Mullins, and Warty Joe (his own), and which he was at any particular moment he never knew, till Stroke told him, and even then he forgot and had to be put in irons.

The other frequenters of the lair on Saturday nights (when alone the rebellion was active) were the proud Lady Grizel and Widow Elspeth. It had been thought best to make Elspeth a widow, because she was so religious.

The lair was on the right bank of the burn, near the waterfall, and you climbed to it by ropes, unless you preferred an easier way. It is now a dripping hollow, down which water dribbles from beneath a sluice, but at that time it was hidden on all sides by trees and the huge clods of sward they had torn from the earth as they fell. Two of these clods were the only walls of the lair, which had at times a ceiling not unlike Aaron Latta's bed coverlets, and the chief furniture was two barrels, marked "Usquebach" and "Powder." When the darkness of Stroke's fortunes sat like a pall upon his brow, as happened sometimes, he sought to drive it away by playing cards on one of these barrels with Sir Joseph, but the approach of the Widow made him pocket them quickly with a warning sign to his trusty knight, who did not understand, and asked what had become of them, whereupon Elspeth cried, in horror:

"Cards! Oh, Tommy, you promised —"

But Stroke rode her down with, "Cards! Wha has been playing cards? You, Muckle Kenny, and you, Sir Joseph, after I forbade it! Hie, there, Inverquharity, all of you, seize those men."

Then Corp blinked, came to his senses and marched himself off to the prison on the lonely promontory called the Queen's Bower, saying ferociously, "Jouk, Sir Joseph, and I'll blaw you into posterity."

It is sable night when Stroke and Sir Joseph reach a point in the Den whence the glimmering lights of the town are distinctly visible. Neither speaks. Presently the distant eight-o'clock bell rings, and then Sir Joseph looks anxiously at his warts, for this is the signal to begin, and as usual he has forgotten the words.

"Go on," says someone in a whisper. It cannot be Stroke, for his head is brooding on his breast. This mysterious voice haunted all the doings in the Den, and had better be confined in brackets.

("Go on.")

"Methinks," says Sir Joseph, "methinks the borers —"

("Burghers.")

"Methinks the burghers now cease from their labors."

"Ay," replied Stroke, "'tis so, would that they ceased from them forever!"

"Methinks the time is at hand."

"Ha!" exclaims Stroke, looking at his lieutenant curiously, "what makest thou say so? For three weeks these fortifications have defied my cannon, there is scarce a breach yet in the walls of yonder town."

"Methinks thou wilt find a way."

"It may be so, my good Sir Joseph, it may be so, and yet, even when I am most hopeful of success, my schemes go a gley."

"Methinks thy dark —"

("Dinna say Methinks so often.")

("Tommy, I maun. If I dinna get that to start me off, I go through other.")

("Go on.")

"Methinks thy dark spirit lies on thee to-night."

"Ay, 'tis too true. But canst thou blame me if I grow sad? The town still in the enemy's hands, and so much brave blood already spilt in vain. Knowest thou that the brave Kinnordy fell last night? My noble Kinnordy!"

Here Stroke covers his face with his hands, weeping silently, and-and there is an awkward pause.

("Go on —'Still have me.'")

("So it is.") "Weep not, my royal scone —"

("Scion.")

"Weep not, my royal scion, havest thou not still me?"

"Well said, Sir Joseph," cries Stroke, dashing the sign of weakness from his face. "I still have many brave fellows, and with their help I shall be master of this proud town."

"And then ghost we to fair Edinburgh?"

"Ay, 'tis so, but, Sir Joseph, thinkest thou these burghers love the Stuart not?"

"*Nay*, methinks they are true to thee, but their starch commander —(give me my time, this is a lang ane,) but their arch commander is thy bitterest foe. Vile spoon that he is! (It's no spoon, it's spawn.)"

"Thou meanest the craven Cathro?"

"Methinks ay. (I like thae short anes.)"

"'Tis well!" says Stroke, sternly. "That man hath ever slipped between me and my right. His time will come."

"He floppeth thee-he flouteth thee from the battlements."

"Ha, 'tis well!"

("You've said that already.")

("I say it twice.")

("That's what aye puts me wrang.) Ghost thou to meet the proud Lady Grizel to-night?"

"Ay."

"Ghost thou alone?"

"Ay."

("What easy anes you have!) I fear it is not chancey for thee to go."

"I must dree my dreed."

"These women is kittle cattle."

"The Stuart hath ever a soft side for them. Ah, my trusty foster-brother, knowest thou not what it is to love?"

"Alas, I too have had my fling. (Does Grizel kiss your hand yet?)"

"(No, she winna, the limmer.) Sir Joseph, I go to her."

"Methinks she is a haughty onion. I prithee go not to-night."

"I have given my word."

"Thy word is a band."

"Adieu, my friend."

"Methinks thou ghost to thy damn. (Did we no promise Elspeth there should be no swearing?)"

The raft Vick Lan Vohr is dragged to the shore, and Stroke steps on board, a proud solitary figure. "Farewell!" he cries hoarsely, as he seizes the oar.

"Farewell, my leech," answers Corp, and then helps him to disembark. Their hands chance to meet, and Stroke's is so hot that Corp quails.

"Tommy," he says, with a shudder, "do you-you dinna think it's a' true, do you?" But the ill-fated prince only gives him a warning look and plunges into the mazes of the forest. For a long time silence reigns over the Den. Lights glint fitfully, a human voice imitates the plaintive cry of the peewit, cautious whistling follows, comes next the clash of arms, and the scream of one in the death-throes, and again silence falls. Stroke emerges near the Reekie Broth Pot, wiping his sword and muttering, "Faugh! it drippeth!" At the same moment the air is filled with music of more than mortal-well, the air is filled with music. It seems to come from but a few yards away, and pressing his hand to his throbbing brow the Chevalier presses forward till, pushing aside the branches of a fallen fir, he comes suddenly upon a scene of such romantic beauty that he stands rooted to the ground. Before him, softly lit by a half-moon (the man in it perspiring with curiosity), is a miniature dell, behind which rise threatening rocks, overgrown here and there by grass, heath, and bracken, while in the centre of the dell is a bubbling spring called the Cuttle Well, whose water, as it overflows a natural basin, soaks into the surrounding ground and so finds a way into the picturesque stream below. But it is not the loveliness of the spot which fascinates the prince; rather is it the exquisite creature who sits by the bubbling spring, a reed from a hand-loom in her hands, from which she strikes mournful sounds, the while she raises her voice in song. A pink scarf and a blue ribbon are crossed upon her breast, her dark tresses kiss her lovely neck, and as she sits on the only dry stone, her face raised as if in wrapt communion with the heavens, and her feet tucked beneath her to avoid the mud, she seems not a human being, but the very spirit of the place and hour. The royal wanderer remains spellbound, while she strikes her lyre and sings (with but one trivial alteration) the song of MacMurrough: —

> Awake on your hills, on your islands awake,
> Brave sons of the mountains, the frith and the lake!
> 'Tis the bugle-but not for the chase is the call;
> 'Tis the pibroch's shrill summons-but not to the hall.
> 'Tis the summons of heroes for conquest or death,
> When the banners are blazing on mountain and heath;
> They call to the dirk, the claymore and the targe,
> To the march and the muster, the line and the charge.
> Be the brand of each Chieftain like Stroke's in his ire!
> May the blood through his veins flow like currents of fire!
> Burst the base foreign yoke as your sires did of yore,
> Or die like your sires, and endure it no more.

As the fair singer concluded, Stroke, who had been deeply moved, heaved a great sigh, and immediately, as if in echo of it, came a sigh from the opposite side of the dell. In a second of time three people had learned that a certain lady had two lovers. She starts to her feet, still carefully avoiding the puddles, but it is not she who speaks.

("Did you hear me?")

("Ay.")

("You're ready?")

("Ca' awa'.")

Stroke dashes to the girl's side, just in time to pluck her from the arms of a masked man. The villain raises his mask and reveals the face of-it looks like Corp, but the disguise is thrown away on Stroke.

"Ha, Cathro," he exclaims joyfully, "so at last we meet on equal terms!"

"Back, Stroke, and let me pass."

"Nay, we fight for the wench."

"So be it. The prideful onion is his who wins her."

"Have at thee, caitiff!"

A terrible conflict ensues. Cathro draws first blood. 'Tis but a scratch. Ha! well thrust, Stroke. In vain Cathro girns his teeth. Inch by inch he is driven back, he slips, he recovers, he pants, he is apparently about to fling himself down the steep bank and so find safety in flight, but he comes on again.

("What are you doing? You run now.")

("I ken, but I'm sweer!")

("Off you go.")

Even as Stroke is about to press home, the cowardly foe flings himself down the steep bank and rolls out of sight. He will give no more trouble to-night; and the victor turns to the Lady Grizel, who had been repinning the silk scarf across her breast, while the issue of the combat was still in doubt.

("Now, then, Grizel, you kiss my hand.")

("I tell you I won't.")

("Well, then, go on your knees to me.")

("You needn't think it.")

("Dagon you! Then ca' awa' standing.")

"My liege, thou hast saved me from the wretch Cathro."

"May I always be near to defend thee in time of danger, my pretty chick."

("Tommy, you promised not to call me by those silly names.")

("They slip out, I tell you. That was aye the way wi' the Stuarts.")

("Well, you must say 'Lady Grizel.') Good, my prince, how can I thank thee?"

"By being my wife. (Not a word of this to Elspeth.)"

"Nay, I summoned thee here to tell thee that can never be. The Grizels of Grizel are of ancient lineage, but they mate not with monarchs. My sire, the nunnery gates will soon close on me forever."

"Then at least say thou lovest me."

"Alas, I love thee not."

("What haver is this? I telled you to say 'Charles, would that I loved thee less.'")

("And I told you I would not.")

("Well, then, where are we now?")

("We miss out all that about my wearing your portrait next my heart, and put in the rich apparel bit, the same as last week.")

("Oh! Then I go on?) Bethink thee, fair jade —"

("Lady.")

"Bethink thee, fair lady, Stuart is not so poor but that, if thou come with him to his lowly lair, he can deck thee with rich apparel and ribbons rare."

"I spurn thy gifts, unhappy man, but if there are holes in —"

("Miss that common bit out. I canna thole it.")

("I like it.) If there are holes in the garments of thy loyal followers, I will come and mend them, and have a needle and thread in my pocket. (Tommy, there is another button off your shirt! Have you got the button?")

"(It's down my breeks.) So be it, proud girl, come!"

It was Grizel who made masks out of tin rags, picked up where tinkers had passed the night, and musical instruments out of broken reeds that smelled of caddis and Jacobite head-gear out of weaver's night-caps; and she kept the lair so clean and tidy as to raise a fear that intruders might mistake its character. Elspeth had to mind the pot, which Aaron Latta never missed, and Corp was supposed to light the fire by striking sparks from his knife, a trick which Tommy considered so easy that he refused to show how it was done. Many strange sauces were boiled in that pot, a sort of potato-turnip pudding often coming out even when not expected, but there was an occasional rabbit that had been bowled over by Corp's unerring hand, and once Tommy shot a —a haunch of venison, having first, with Corp's help, howked it out of Ronny-On's swine, then suspended head downward, and open like a book at the page of contents, steaming, dripping, a tub beneath, boys with bladders in the distance. When they had supped they gathered round the fire, Grizel knitting a shawl for they knew whom, but the name was never mentioned, and Tommy told the story of his life at the French court, and how he fought in the '45 and afterward hid in caves, and so did he shudder, as he described the cold of his bracken beds, and so glowed his face, for it was all real to him, that Grizel let the wool drop on her knee, and Corp whispered to Elspeth, "Dinna be fleid for him; I'se uphaud he found a wy." Those quiet evenings were not the least pleasant spent in the Den.

But sometimes they were interrupted by a fierce endeavor to carry the lair, when boys from Cathro's climbed to it up each other's backs, the rope, of course, having been pulled into safety at the first sound, and then that end of the Den rang with shouts, and deeds of valor on both sides were as common as pine needles, and once Tommy and Corp were only saved from captors who had them down, by Grizel rushing into the midst of things with two flaring torches, and another time bold Birkie, most daring of the storming party, was seized with two others and made to walk the plank. The plank had been part of a gate, and was suspended over the bank of the Silent Pool, so that, as you approached the farther end, down you went. It was not a Jacobite method, but Tommy feared that rows of bodies, hanging from the trees still standing in the Den, might attract attention.

Less alarming but more irritating was the attempt of the youth of Monypenny and the West town end, to establish a rival firm of Jacobites (without even being sure of the name). They started business (Francie Crabb leader, because he had a kilt) on a flagon of porter and an ounce of twist, which they carried on a stick through the Den, saying "Bowf!" like dogs, when they met anyone, and then laughing doubtfully. The twist and porter were seized by Tommy and his followers, and Haggerty-Taggerty, Major, arrived home with his head so firmly secured in the flagon that the solder had to be melted before he saw the world again. Francie was in still worse plight, for during the remainder of the evening he had to hide in shame among the brackens, and Tommy wore a kilt.

One cruel revenge the beaten rivals had. They waylaid Grizel, when she was alone, and thus assailed her, she answering not a word.

"What's a father?"

"She'll soon no have a mither either!"

"The Painted Lady needs to paint her cheeks no longer!"

"Na, the red spots comes themsels now."

"Have you heard her hoasting?"

"Ay, it's the hoast o' a dying woman."

"The joiner heard it, and gave her a look, measuring her wi' his eye for the coffin. 'Five and a half by one and a half would hold her snod,' he says to himsel'."

"Ronny-On's auld wife heard it, and says she, 'Dinna think, my leddy, as you'll be buried in consecrated ground.'"

"Na, a'body kens she'll just be hauled at the end o' a rope to the hole where the witches was shooled in."

"Wi' a paling spar through her, to keep her down on the day o' judgment."

Well, well, these children became men and women in time, one of them even a bit of a hero, though he never knew it.

Are you angry with them? If so, put the cheap thing aside, or think only of Grizel, and perhaps God will turn your anger into love for her.

Great-hearted, solitary child! She walked away from them without flinching, but on reaching the Den, where no one could see her-she lay down on the ground, and her cheeks were dry, but little wells of water stood in her eyes.

She would not be the Lady Grizel that night. She went home instead, but there was something she wanted to ask Tommy now, and the next time she saw him she began at once. Grizel always began at once, often in the middle, she saw what she was making for so clearly.

"Do you know what it means when there are red spots in your cheeks, that used not to be there?"

Tommy knew at once to whom she was referring, for he had heard the gossip of the youth of Monypenny, and he hesitated to answer.

"And if, when you cough, you bring up a tiny speck of blood?"

"I would get a bottle frae the doctor," said Tommy, evasively.

"She won't have the doctor," answered Grizel, unguardedly, and then with a look dared Tommy to say that she spoke of her mother.

"Does it mean you are dying?"

"I —I —oh, no, they soon get better."

He said this because he was so sorry for Grizel. There never was a more sympathetic nature than Tommy's. At every time of his life his pity was easily roused for persons in distress, and he sought to comfort them by shutting their eyes to the truth as long as possible. This sometimes brought relief to them, but it was useless to Grizel, who must face her troubles.

"Why don't you answer truthfully?" she cried, with vehemence. "It is so easy to be truthful!"

"Well, then," said Tommy, reluctantly, "I think they generally die."

Elspeth often carried in her pocket a little Testament, presented to her by the Rev. Mr. Dishart for learning by heart one of the noblest of books, the Shorter Catechism, as Scottish children do or did, not understanding it at the time, but its meaning comes long afterwards and suddenly, when you have most need of it. Sometimes Elspeth read aloud from her Testament to Grizel, who made no comment, but this same evening, when the two were alone, she said abruptly:

"Have you your Testament?"

"Yes," Elspeth said, producing it.

"Which is the page about saving sinners?"

"It's all about that."

"But the page when you are in a hurry?"

Elspeth read aloud the story of the Crucifixion, and Grizel listened sharply until she heard what Jesus said to the malefactor: "To-day shalt thou be with me in Paradise."

"And was he?"

"Of course."

"But he had been wicked all his life, and I believe he was only good, just that minute, because they were crucifying him. If they had let him come down. —"

"No, he repented, you know. That means he had faith, and if you have faith you are saved. It doesna matter how bad you have been. You have just to say 'I believe' before you die, and God lets you in. It's so easy, Grizel," cried Elspeth, with shining eyes.

Grizel pondered. "I don't believe it is so easy as that," she said, decisively.

Nevertheless she asked presently what the Testament cost, and when Elspeth answered "Fourpence," offered her the money.

"I don't want to sell it," Elspeth remonstrated.

"If you don't give it to me, I shall take it from you," said Grizel, determinedly.

"You can buy one."

"No, the shop people would guess."

"Guess what?"

"I won't tell you."

"I'll lend it to you."

"I won't take it that way." So Elspeth had to part with her Testament, saying wonderingly, "Can you read?"

"Yes, and write too. Mamma taught me."

"But I thought she was daft," Elspeth blurted out.

"She is only daft now and then," Grizel replied, without her usual spirit. "Generally she is not daft at all, but only timid."

Next morning the Painted Lady's child paid three calls, one in town, two in the country. The adorable thing is that, once having made up her mind, she never flinched, not even when her hand was on the knocker.

The first gentleman received her in his lobby. For a moment he did not remember her; then suddenly the color deepened on his face, and he went back and shut the parlor-door.

"Did anybody see you coming here?" he asked, quickly.

"I don't know."

"What does she want?"

"She did not send me, I came myself."

"Well?"

"When you come to our house —"

"I never come to your house."

"That is a lie."

"Speak lower!"

"When you come to our house you tell me to go out and play. But I don't.
I go and cry."

No doubt he was listening, but his eyes were on the parlor-door.

"I don't know why I cry, but you know, you wicked man! Why is it?"

"Why is it?" she demanded again, like a queen-child, but he could only fidget with his gold chain and shuffle uneasily in his parnella shoes.

"You are not coming to see my mamma again."

The gentleman gave her an ugly look.

"If you do," she said at once, "I shall come straight here and open that door you are looking at, and tell your wife."

He dared not swear. His hand —

"If you offer me money," said Grizel, "I shall tell her now."

He muttered something to himself.

"Is it true?" she asked, "that mamma is dying?"

This was a genuine shock to him, for he had not been at Double Dykes since winter, and then the Painted Lady was quite well.

"Nonsense!" he said, and his obvious disbelief brought some comfort to the girl. But she asked, "Why are there red spots on her cheeks, then?"

"Paint," he answered.

"No," cried Grizel, rocking her arms, "it is not paint now. I thought it might be and I tried to rub it off while she was sleeping, but it will not come off. And when she coughs there is blood on her handkerchief."

He looked alarmed now, and Grizel's fears came back. "If mamma dies," she said determinedly, "she must be buried in the cemetery."

"She is not dying, I tell you."

"And you must come to the funeral."

"Are you gyte?"

"With crape on your hat."

His mouth formed an emphatic "No."

"You must," said Grizel, firmly, "you shall! If you don't —" She pointed to the parlor-door.

Her remaining two visits were to a similar effect, and one of the gentlemen came out of the ordeal somewhat less shamefully than the first, the other worse, for he blubbered and wanted to kiss her. It is questionable whether many young ladies have made such a profound impression in a series of morning calls.

The names of these gentlemen are not known, but you shall be told presently where they may be found. Every person in Thrums used to know the place, and many itched to get at the names, but as yet no one has had the nerve to look for them.

Not at this time did Grizel say a word of these interviews to her friends, though Tommy had to be told of them later, and she never again referred to her mother at the Saturday evenings in the Den. But the others began to know a queer thing, nothing less than this, that in their absence the lair was sometimes visited by a person or persons unknown, who made use of their stock of firewood. It was a startling discovery, but when they discussed it in council, Grizel never contributed a word. The affair remained a mystery until one Saturday evening, when Tommy and Elspeth, reaching the lair first, found in it a delicate white shawl. They both recognized in it the pretty thing the Painted Lady had pinned across her shoulders on the night they saw her steal out of Double Dykes, to meet the man of long ago.

Even while their eyes were saying this, Grizel climbed in without giving the password, and they knew from her quick glance around that she had come for the shawl. She snatched it out of Tommy's hand with a look that prohibited questions.

"It's the pair o' them," Tommy said to Elspeth at the first opportunity, "that sometimes comes here at nights and kindles the fire and warms themsels at the gloze. And the last time they came they forgot the shawl."

"I dinna like to think the Painted Lady has been up here, Tommy."

"But she has. You ken how, when she has a daft fit, she wanders the Den trysting the man that never comes. Has she no been seen at all hours o' the night, Grizel following a wee bit ahint, like as if to take tent o her?"

"They say that, and that Grizel canna get her to go home till the daft fit has passed."

"Well, she has that kechering hoast and spit now, and so Grizel brings her up here out o' the blasts."

"But how could she be got to come here, if she winna go home?"

"Because frae here she can watch for the man."

Elspeth shuddered. "Do you think she's here often, Tommy?" she asked.

"Just when she has a daft fit on, and they say she's wise sax days in seven."

This made the Jacobite meetings eerie events for Elspeth, but Tommy liked them the better; and what were they not to Grizel, who ran to them with passionate fondness every Saturday night? Sometimes she even outdistanced her haunting dreads, for she knew that her mother did not think herself seriously ill; and had not the three gentlemen made light of that curious cough? So there were nights when the lair saw Grizel go riotous with glee, laughing, dancing, and shouting over-much, like one trying to make up for a lost childhood. But it was also noticed that when the time came to leave the Den she was very loath, and kissed her hands to the places where she had been happiest, saying, wistfully, and with pretty gestures that were foreign to Thrums, "Good-night, dear Cuttle Well! Good-by, sweet, sweet Lair!" as if she knew it could not last. These weekly risings in the Den were most real to Tommy, but it was Grizel who loved them best.

Chapter XXIV
A Romance of Two Old Maids and a Stout Bachelor

Came Gavinia, a burgess of the besieged city, along the south shore of the Silent Pool. She was but a maid seeking to know what love might be, and as she wandered on, she nibbled dreamily at a hot sweet-smelling bridie, whose gravy oozed deliciously through a bursting paper-bag.

It was a fit night for dark deeds.

"Methinks she cometh to her damn!"

The speaker was a masked man who had followed her-he was sniffing ecstatically-since she left the city walls.

She seemed to possess a charmed life. He would have had her in Shovel Gorge, but just then Ronny-On's Jean and Peter Scrymgeour turned the corner.

Suddenly Gavinia felt an exquisite thrill: a man was pursuing her. She slipped the paper-bag out of sight, holding it dexterously against her side with her arm, so that the gravy should not spurt out, and ran. Lights flashed, a kingly voice cried "Now!" and immediately a petticoat was flung over her head. (The Lady Griselda looked thin that evening.)

Gavinia was dragged to the Lair, and though many a time they bumped her, she still tenderly nursed the paper-bag with her arm, or fondly thought she did so, for when unmuffled she discovered that it had been removed, as if by painless surgery. And her captors' tongues were sweeping their chins for stray crumbs.

The wench was offered her choice of Stroke's gallant fellows, but "Wha carries me wears me," said she, promptly, and not only had he to carry her from one end of the Den to the other, but he must do it whistling as if barely conscious that she was there. So after many attempts (for she was always willing to let them have their try) Corp of Corp, speaking for Sir Joseph and the others, announced a general retreat.

Instead of taking this prisoner's life, Stroke made her his tool, releasing her on condition that every seventh day she appeared at the Lair with information concerning the doings in the town. Also, her name was Agnes of Kingoldrum, and, if she said it was not, the plank. Bought thus, Agnes proved of service, bringing such bags of news that Stroke was often occupied now in drawing diagrams of Thrums and its strongholds, including the residence of Cathro, with dotted lines to show the direction of proposed underground passages.

And presently came by this messenger disquieting rumors indeed. Another letter, being the third in six months, had reached the Dovecot, addressed, not to Miss Ailie, but to Miss Kitty. Miss Kitty had been dead fully six years, and Archie Piatt, the post, swore that this was the eighteenth, if not the nineteenth, letter he had delivered to her name since that time. They were all in the same hand, a man's, and there had been similar letters while she was alive, but of these he kept no record. Miss Ailie always took these letters with a trembling hand, and then locked herself in her bedroom, leaving the key in such a position in its hole that you might just as well go straight back to the kitchen. Within a few hours of the arrival of these ghostly letters, tongues were wagging about them, but to the two or three persons who (after passing a sleepless night) bluntly asked Miss Ailie from whom they came, she only replied by pursing her lips. Nothing could be learned at the post-office save that Miss Ailie never posted any letters there, except to two Misses and a Mrs., all resident in Redlintie. The mysterious letters came from Australy or Manchester, or some such part.

What could Stroke make of this? He expressed no opinion, but oh, his face was grim. Orders were immediately given to double the sentinels. A barrel was placed in the Queen's Bower. Sawdust was introduced at immense risk into the Lair. A paper containing this writing, "248xho317 Oxh4591AWS314dd5," was passed round and then solemnly burned. Nothing was left to chance.

Agnes of Kingoldrum (Stroke told her) did not know Miss Ailie, but she was commanded to pay special attention to the gossip of the town regarding this new move of the enemy. By next Saturday the plot had thickened. Previous letters might have reddened Miss Ailie's eyes for an hour or two, but they gladdened her as a whole. Now she sat crying all evening with this one on her lap; she gave up her daily walk to the Berlin wool shop, with all its romantic possibilities; at the clatter of the tea-things she would start apprehensively; she had let a red shawl lie for two days in the blue-and-white room.

Stroke never blanched. He called his faithful remnant around him, and told them the story of Bell the Cat, with its application in the records of his race. Did they take his meaning? This Miss Ailie must be watched closely. In short, once more, in Scottish history, someone must bell the cat. Who would volunteer?

Corp of Corp and Sir Joseph stepped forward as one man.

"Thou couldst not look like Gavinia," the prince said, shaking his head.

"Wha wants him to look like Gavinia?" cried an indignant voice.

"Peace, Agnes!" said Stroke.

"Agnes, why bletherest thou?" said Sir Joseph.

"If onybody's to watch Miss Ailie," insisted the obstinate woman, "surely it should be me!"

"Ha!" Stroke sprang to his feet, for something in her voice, or the outline of her figure, or perhaps it was her profile, had given him an idea. "A torch!" he cried eagerly and with its aid he scanned her face until his own shone triumphant.

"He kens a wy, methinks!" exclaimed one of his men.

Sir Joseph was right. It had been among the prince's exploits to make his way into Thrums in disguise, and mix with the people as one of themselves, and on several of these occasions he had seen Miss Ailie's attendant. Agnes's resemblance to her now struck him for the first time. It should be Agnes of Kingoldrum's honorable though dangerous part to take this Gavinia's place.

But how to obtain possession of Gavinia's person? Agnes made several suggestions, but was told to hold her prating peace. It could only be done in one way. They must kidnap her. Sir Joseph was ordered to be ready to accompany his liege on this perilous enterprise in ten minutes. "And mind," said Stroke, gravely, "we carry our lives in our hands."

"In our hands!" gasped Sir Joseph, greatly puzzled, but he dared ask no more, and when the two set forth (leaving Agnes of Kingoldrum looking very uncomfortable), he was surprised to see that Stroke was carrying nothing. Sir Joseph carried in his hand his red hanky, mysteriously knotted.

"Where is yours?" he whispered.

"What meanest thou?"

Sir Joseph replied, "Oh, nothing," and thought it best to slip his handkerchief into his trouser-pocket, but the affair bothered him for long afterwards.

When they returned through the Den, there still seemed (to the unpiercing eye) to be but two of them; nevertheless, Stroke re-entered the Lair to announce to Agnes and the others that he had left Gavinia below in charge of Sir Joseph. She was to walk the plank anon, but first she must be stripped that Agnes might don her garments. Stroke was every inch a prince, so he kept Agnes by his side, and sent down the Lady Griselda and Widow Elspeth to strip the prisoner, Sir Joseph having orders to stand back fifty paces. (It is a pleasure to have to record this.)

The signal having been given that this delicate task was accomplished, Stroke whistled shrilly, and next moment was heard from far below a thud, as of a body falling in water, then an agonizing shriek, and then again all was still, save for the heavy breathing of Agnes of Kingoldrum.

Sir Joseph (very wet) returned to the Lair, and Agnes was commanded to take off her clothes in a retired spot and put on those of the deceased, which she should find behind a fallen tree.

"I winna be called the deceased," cried Agnes hotly, but she had to do as she was bid, and when she emerged, from behind the tree she was the very image of the ill-fated Gavinia. Stroke showed her a plan of Miss Ailie's backdoor, and also gave her a kitchen key (when he produced this, she felt in her pockets and then snatched it from him), after which she set out for the Dovecot in a scare about her own identity.

"And now, what doest thou think about it a'?" inquired Sir Joseph eagerly, to which Stroke made answer, looking at him fixedly.

"The wind is in the west!"

Sir Joseph should have kept this a secret, but soon Stroke heard Inverquharity prating of it, and he called his lieutenant before him. Sir Joseph acknowledged humbly that he had been unable to hide it from Inverquharity, but he promised not to tell Muckle Kenny, of whose loyalty there were doubts. Henceforth, when the faithful fellow was Muckle Kenny, he would say doggedly to himself, "Dinna question me, Kenny. I ken nocht about it."

Dark indeed were now the fortunes of the Pretender, but they had one bright spot. Miss Ailie had been taken in completely by the trick played on her, and thus Stroke now got full information of the enemy's doings. Cathro having failed to dislodge the Jacobites, the seat of war had been changed by Victoria to the Dovecot, whither her despatches were now forwarded. That this last one, of which Agnes of Kingoldrum tried in vain to obtain possession, doubled the price on the Pretender's head, there could be no doubt; but as Miss Ailie was a notorious Hanoverian, only the hunted prince himself knew why this should make her cry.

He hinted with a snigger something about an affair he had once had with the lady.

The Widow and Sir Joseph accepted this explanation, but it made Lady Griselda rock her arms in irritation.

The reports about Miss Ailie's behavior became more and more alarming. She walked up and down her bedroom now in the middle of the night. Every time the knocker clanked she held herself together with both hands. Agnes had orders not to answer the door until her mistress had keeked through the window.

"She's expecting a veesitor, methinks," said Corp. This was his bright day.

"Ay," answered Agnes, "but is't a man-body, or just a woman-body?"

Leaving the rebels in the Lair stunned by Victoria's latest move, we now return to Thrums, where Miss Ailie's excited state had indeed been the talk of many. Even the gossips, however, had underestimated her distress of mind, almost as much as they misunderstood its cause. You must listen now (will you?) to so mild a thing as the long thin romance of two maiden ladies and a stout bachelor, all beginning to be old the day the three of them first drank tea together, and that was ten years ago.

Miss Ailie and Miss Kitty, you may remember, were not natives of Thrums. They had been born and brought up at Redlintie, and on the death of their parents they had remained there, the gauger having left them all his money, which was just sufficient to enable them to live like ladies, if they took tiny Magenta Cottage, and preferred an inexperienced maid. At first their life was very quiet, the walk from eleven to one for the good of fragile Miss Kitty's health its outstanding feature. When they strolled together on the cliffs, Miss Ailie's short thick figure, straight as an elvint, cut the wind in two, but Miss Kitty was swayed this way and that, and when she shook her curls at the wind, it blew them roguishly in her face, and had another shot at them, as soon as they were put to rights. If the two walked by the shore (where the younger sometimes bathed her feet, the elder keeping a sharp eye on land and water), the sea behaved like the wind, dodging Miss Ailie's ankles and snapping playfully at Miss Kitty's. Thus even the elements could distinguish between the sisters, who nevertheless had so much in common that at times Miss Ailie would look into her mirror and sigh to think that some day Miss Kitty might be like this. How Miss Ailie adored Miss Kitty! She trembled with pleasure if you said Miss Kitty was pretty, and she dreamed dreams in which she herself walked as bridesmaid only. And just as Miss Ailie could be romantic, Miss Kitty, the romantic, could be prim, and the primness was her own as much as the curls, but Miss Ailie usually carried it for her, like a cloak in case of rain.

Not often have two sweeter women grown together on one stem. What were the men of Redlintie about? The sisters never asked each other this question, but there were times when, apparently without cause, Miss Ailie hugged Miss Kitty vehemently, as if challenging the world, and perhaps Miss Kitty understood.

Thus a year or more passed uneventfully, until the one romance of their lives befell them. It began with the reappearance in Redlintie of Magerful Tarn, who had come to torment his father into giving him more money, but, finding he had come too late, did not harass the sisters. This is perhaps the best thing that can be told of him, and, as if he knew this, he had often told it himself to Jean Myles, without however telling her what followed. For something to his advantage did follow, and it was greatly to the credit of Miss Ailie and Miss Kitty, though they went about it as timidly as if they were participating in a crime. Ever since they learned of the sin which had brought this man into the world their lives had been saddened, for on the same day they realized what a secret sorrow had long lain at their mother's heart. Alison Sibbald was a very simple, gracious lady, who never recovered from the shock of discovering that she had married a libertine; yet she had pressed her husband to do something for his son, and been greatly pained when he refused with a coarse laugh. The daughters were very like her in nature, and though the knowledge of what she had suffered increased many fold their love for her, so that in her last days their passionate devotion to her was the talk of Redlintie, it did not blind them to what seemed to them to be their duty to the man. As their father's son, they held, he had a right to a third of the gauger's money, and to withhold it from him, now that they knew his whereabouts, would have been a form of theft. But how to give T. his third? They called him T. from delicacy, and they had never spoken to him. When he passed them in the streets, they turned pale, and, thinking of their mother, looked another way. But they knew he winked.

At last, looking red in one street, and white in another, but resolute in all, they took their business to the office of Mr. John McLean, the writer, who had once escorted Miss Kitty home from a party without anything coming of it, so that it was quite a psychological novel in several volumes. Now Mr. John happened to be away at the fishing, and a reckless maid showed them into the presence of a strange man, who was no other than his brother Ivie, home for a year's holiday from India, and naturally this extraordinary occurrence so agitated them that Miss Ailie had told half her story before she realized that Miss Kitty was titting at her dress. Then indeed she sought to withdraw, but Ivie, with the alarming yet not unpleasing audacity of his sex, said he had heard enough to convince him that in this matter he was qualified to take his brother's place. But he was not, for he announced, "My advice to you is not to give T. a halfpenny," which showed that he did not even understand what they had come about.

They begged permission to talk to each other behind the door, and presently returned, troubled but brave. Miss Kitty whispered "Courage!" and this helped Miss Ailie to the deed.

"We have quite made up our minds to let T. have the money," she said, "but-but the difficulty is the taking it to him. Must we take it in person?"

"Why not?" asked Ivie, bewildered.

"It would be such a painful meeting to us." said Miss Ailie.

"And to him," added simple Miss Kitty.

"You see we have thought it best not to-not to know him," said Miss Ailie, faintly.

"Mother —" faltered Miss Kitty, and at the word the eyes of both ladies began to fill.

Then, of course, Mr. McLean discovered the object of their visit, and promised that his brother should take this delicate task off their hands, and as he bowed them out he said, "Ladies, I think you are doing a very foolish thing, and I shall respect you for it all my life." At least Miss Kitty insisted that respect was the word, Miss Ailie thought he said esteem.

That was how it began, and it progressed for nearly a year at a rate that will take away your breath. On the very next day he met Miss Kitty in High Street, a most awkward encounter for her ("for, you know, Ailie, we were never introduced, so how could I decide all in a moment what to do?"), and he raised his hat (the Misses Croall were at their window and saw the whole thing). But we must gallop, like the friendship. He bowed the first two times, the third time he shook hands (by a sort of providence Miss Kitty had put on her new mittens), the fourth, fifth, and sixth times he conversed, the seventh time he-they replied that they really could not trouble him so much, but he said he was going that way at any rate; the eighth time, ninth time, and tenth time the figures of two ladies and a gentleman might have been observed, etc., and either the eleventh or twelfth time ("Fancy our not being sure, Ailie" —"It has all come so quickly, Kitty") he took his first dish of tea at Magenta Cottage.

There were many more walks after this, often along the cliffs to a little fishing village, over which the greatest of magicians once stretched his wand, so that it became famous forever, as all the world saw except himself; and tea at the cottage followed, when Ivie asked Miss Kitty to sing "The Land o' the Leal," and Miss Ailie sat by the window, taking in her merino, that it might fit Miss Kitty, cutting her sable muff (once Alison Sibbald's) into wristbands for Miss Kitty's astrakhan; they did not go quite all the way round, but men are blind.

Ivie was not altogether blind. The sisters, it is to be feared, called him the dashing McLean, but he was at this time nearly forty years old, an age when bachelors like to take a long rest from thinking of matrimony, before beginning again. Fifteen years earlier he had been in love, but the girl had not cared to wait for him, and, though in India he had often pictured himself returning to Redlintie to gaze wistfully at her old home, when he did come back he never went, because the house was a little out of the way. But unknown to him two ladies went, to whom he had told this as a rather dreary joke. They were ladies he esteemed very much, though having a sense of humor he sometimes chuckled on his way home from Magenta Cottage, and he thought out many ways of adding little pleasures to their lives. It was like him to ask Miss Kitty to sing and play, though he disliked music. He understood that it is a hard world for single women, and knew himself for a very ordinary sort of man. If it ever crossed his head that Miss Kitty would be willing to marry him, he felt genuinely sorry at the same time that she had not done better long ago. He never flattered himself that he could be accepted now, save for the good home he could provide (he was not the man to blame women for being influenced by that), for like most of his sex he was unaware that a woman is never too old to love or to be loved; if they do know it, the mean ones among them make a jest of it, at which (God knows why) their wives laugh. Mr. McLean had been acquainted with the sisters for months before he was sure even that Miss Kitty was his favorite. He found that out one evening when sitting with an old friend, whose wife and children were in the room, gathered round a lamp and playing at some child's game. Suddenly Ivie McLean envied his friend, and at the same moment he thought tenderly of Miss Kitty. But the feeling passed. He experienced it next and as suddenly when arriving at Bombay, where some women were waiting to greet their husbands.

Before he went away the two gentlewomen knew that he was not to speak. They did not tell each other what was in their minds. Miss Kitty was so bright during those last days, that she must have deceived anyone who did not love her, and Miss Ailie held her mouth very tight, and if possible was straighter than ever, but oh, how gentle she was with Miss Kitty! Ivie's last two weeks in the old country were spent in London, and during that time Miss Kitty liked to go away by herself, and sit on a rock and gaze at the sea. Once Miss Ailie followed her and would have called him a —

"Don't, Ailie!" said Miss Kitty, imploringly. But that night, when Miss Kitty was brushing her hair, she said, courageously, "Ailie, I don't think I should wear curls any longer. You know I —I shall be thirty-seven in August." And after the elder sister had become calm again. Miss Kitty said timidly, "You don't think I have been unladylike, do you, Ailie?"

Such a trifle now remains to tell. Miss Kitty was the better business woman of the two, and kept the accounts, and understood, as Miss Ailie could not understand, how their little income was invested, and even knew what consols were, though never quite certain whether it was their fall or rise that is matter for congratulation. And after the ship had sailed, she told Miss Ailie that nearly all their money was lost, and that she had known it for a month.

"And you kept it from me! Why?"

"I thought, Ailie, that you, knowing I am not strong-that you-would perhaps tell him."

"And I would!" cried Miss Ailie.

"And then," said Miss Kitty, "perhaps he, out of pity, you know!"

"Well, even if he had!" said Miss Ailie.

"I could not, oh, I could not," replied Miss Kitty, flushing; "it-it would not have been la-dylike, Ailie."

Thus forced to support themselves, the sisters decided to keep school genteelly, and, hearing that there was an opening in Thrums, they settled there, and Miss Kitty brushed her hair out now, and with a twist and a twirl ran it up her fingers into a net, whence by noon some of it had escaped through the little windows and was curls again. She and Miss Ailie were happy in Thrums, for time took the pain out of the affair of Mr. McLean, until it became not merely a romantic memory, but, with the letters he wrote to Miss Kitty and her answers, the great quiet pleasure of their lives. They were friendly letters only, but Miss Kitty wrote hers out in pencil first and read them to Miss Ailie, who had been taking notes for them.

In the last weeks of Miss Kitty's life Miss Ailie conceived a passionate unspoken hatred of Mr. McLean, and her intention was to write and tell him that he had killed her darling. But owing to the illness into which she was flung by Miss Kitty's death, that unjust letter was never written.

But why did Mr. McLean continue to write to Miss Kitty?

Well, have pity or be merciless as you choose. For several years Mr. McLean's letters had been the one thing the sisters looked forward to, and now, when Miss Ailie was without Miss Kitty, must she lose them also? She never doubted, though she may have been wrong, that, if Ivie knew of Miss Kitty's death, one letter would come in answer, and that the last. She could not tell him. In the meantime he wrote twice asking the reason of this long silence, and at last Miss Ailie, whose handwriting was very like her sister's, wrote him a letter which was posted at Tilliedrum and signed "Katherine Cray." The thing seems monstrous, but this gentle lady did it, and it was never so difficult to do again. Latterly, it had been easy.

This last letter of Mr. McLean's announced to Miss Kitty that he was about to start for home "for good," and he spoke in it of coming to Thrums to see the sisters, as soon as he reached Redlintie. Poor Miss Ailie! After sleepless nights she trudged to the Tilliedrum post-office with a full confession of her crime, which would be her welcome home to him when he arrived at his brother's house. Many of the words were written on damp blobs. After that she could do nothing but wait for the storm, and waiting she became so meek, that Gavinia, who loved her because she was "that simple," said sorrowfully:

"How is't you never rage at me now, ma'am? I'm sure it keepit you lightsome, and I likit to hear the bum o't."

"And instead o' the raging I was prigging for," the soft-hearted maid told her friends, "she gave me a flannel petticoat!" Indeed, Miss Ailie had taken to giving away her possessions at this time, like a woman who thought she was on her death-bed. There was something for each of her pupils, including-but the important thing is that there was a gift for Tommy, which had the effect of planting the Hanoverian Woman (to whom he must have given many uneasy moments) more securely on the British Throne.

Elspeth conveyed the gift to Tommy in a brown paper wrapping, and when it lay revealed as an aging volume of *Mamma's Boy*, a magazine for the Home, nothing could have looked more harmless. But, ah, you never know. Hungrily Tommy ran his eye through the bill of fare for something choice to begin with, and he found it. "The Boy Pirate" it was called. Never could have been fairer promise, and down he sat confidently.

It was a paper on the boys who have been undone by reading pernicious fiction. It gave their names, and the number of pistols they had bought, and what the judge said when he pronounced sentence. It counted the sensational tales found beneath the bed, and described the desolation of the mothers and sisters. It told the color of the father's hair before and afterwards.

Tommy flung the thing from him, picked it up again, and read on uneasily, and when at last he rose he was shrinking from himself. In hopes that he might sleep it off he went early to bed, but his contrition was still with him in the morning. Then Elspeth was shown the article which had saved him, and she, too, shuddered at what she had been, though her remorse was but a poor display beside his, he was so much better at everything than Elspeth. Tommy's distress of mind was so genuine and so keen that it had several hours' start of his admiration of it; and it was still sincere, though he himself had become gloomy, when he told his followers that they were no more. Grizel heard his tale with disdain, and said she hated Miss Ailie for giving him the silly book, but he reproved these unchristian sentiments, while admitting that Miss Ailie had played on him a scurvy trick.

"But you're glad you've repented, Tommy," Elspeth reminded him, anxiously.

"Ay, I'm glad," he answered, without heartiness.

"Well, gin you repent I'll repent too," said Corp, always ready to accept Tommy without question.

"You'll be happier," replied Tommy, sourly.

"Ay, to be good's the great thing," Corp growled; "but, Tommy, could we no have just one michty blatter, methinks, to end up wi'?"

This, of course, could not be, and Saturday forenoon found Tommy wandering the streets listlessly, very happy, you know, but inclined to kick at any one who came near, such, for instance, as the stranger who asked him in the square if he could point out the abode of Miss Ailie Cray.

Tommy led the way, casting some converted looks at the gentleman, and judging him to be the mysterious unknown in whom the late Captain Stroke had taken such a reprehensible interest. He was a stout, red-faced man, stepping firmly into the fifties, with a beard that even the most converted must envy, and a frown sat on his brows all the way, proving him possibly ill-tempered, but also one of the notable few who can think hard about one thing for at least five consecutive minutes. Many took a glint at him as he passed, but missed the frown, they were wondering so much why the fur of his heavy top-coat was on the inside, where it made little show, save at blasty corners.

Miss Ailie was in her parlor, trying to give her mind to a blue and white note-book, but when she saw who was coming up the garden she dropped the little volume and tottered to her bedroom. She was there when Gavinia came up to announce that she had shown a gentleman into the blue-and-white room, who gave the name of Ivie McLean. "Tell him —I shall come down-presently," gasped Miss Ailie, and then Gavinia was sure this was the man who was making her mistress so unhappy.

"She's so easily flichtered now," Gavinia told Tommy in the kitchen, "that for fear o' starting her I never whistle at my work without telling her I'm to do't, and if I fall on the stair, my first thought is to jump up and cry, 'It was just me tum'ling.' And now I believe this brute'll be the death o' her."

"But what can he do to her?"

"I dinna ken, but she's greeting sair, and yon can hear how he's rampaging up and down the blue-and-white room. Listen to his thrawn feet! He's raging because she's so long in coming down, and come she daurna. Oh, the poor crittur!"

Now, Tommy was very fond of his old school-mistress, and he began to be unhappy with Gavinia.

"She hasna a man-body in the world to take care o' her," sobbed the girl.

"Has she no?" cried Tommy, fiercely, and under one of the impulses that so easily mastered him he marched into the blue-and-white room.

"Well, my young friend, and what may you want?" asked Mr. McLean, impatiently.

Tommy sat down and folded his arms. "I'm going to sit here and see what you do to Miss Ailie," he said, determinedly.

Mr. McLean said "Oh!" and then seemed favorably impressed, for he added quietly: "She is a friend of yours, is she? Well, I have no intention of hurting her."

"You had better no," replied Tommy, stoutly.

"Did she send you here?"

"No; I came mysel'."

"To protect her?"

There was the irony in it that so puts up a boy's dander. "Dinna think," said Tommy, hotly, "that I'm fleid at you, though I have no beard-at least, I hinna it wi' me."

At this unexpected conclusion a smile crossed Mr. McLean's face, but was gone in an instant. "I wish you had laughed," said Tommy, on the watch; "once a body laughs he canna be angry no more," which was pretty good even for Tommy. It made Mr. McLean ask him why he was so fond of Miss Ailie.

"I'm the only man-body she has," he answered.

"Oh? But why are you her man-body?"

The boy could think of no better reason than this: "Because-because she's so sair in need o' are." (There were moments when one liked Tommy.)

Mr. McLean turned to the window, and perhaps forgot that he was not alone. "Well, what are you thinking about so deeply?" he asked by and by.

"I was trying to think o' something that would gar you laugh," answered Tommy, very earnestly, and was surprised to see that he had nearly done it.

The blue and white note-book was lying on the floor where Miss Ailie had dropped it. Often in Tommy's presence she had consulted this work, and certainly its effect on her was the reverse of laughter; but once he had seen Dr. McQueen pick it up and roar over every page. With an inspiration Tommy handed the book to Mr. McLean. "It made the doctor laugh," he said persuasively.

"Go away," said Ivie, impatiently; "I am in no mood for laughing."

"I tell you what," answered Tommy, "I'll go, if you promise to look at it," and to be rid of him the man agreed. For the next quarter of an hour Tommy and Gavinia were very near the door of the blue-and-white room, Tommy whispering dejectedly, "I hear no laughing," and Gavinia replying, "But he has quieted down."

Mr. McLean had a right to be very angry, but God only can say whether he had a right to be as angry as he was. The book had been handed to him open, and he was laying it down unread when a word underlined caught his eye. It was his own name. Nothing in all literature arrests our attention quite so much as that. He sat down to the book. It was just about this time that Miss Ailie went on her knees to pray.

It was only a penny pass-book. On its blue cover had been pasted a slip of white paper, and on the paper was written, in blue ink, "Alison Cray," with a date nearly nine years old. The contents were in Miss Ailie's prim handwriting; jottings for her own use begun about the time when the sisters, trembling at their audacity, had opened school, and consulted and added to fitfully ever since. Hours must have been spent in erasing the blots and other blemishes so carefully. The tiny volume was not yet full, and between its two last written pages lay a piece of blue blotting-paper neatly cut to the size of the leaf.

Some of these notes were transcripts from books, some contained the advice of friends, others were doubtless the result of talks with Miss Kitty (from whom there were signs that the work had been kept a secret), many were Miss Ailie's own. An entry of this kind was frequent: "If you are uncertain of the answer to a question in arithmetic, it is advisable to leave the room on some pretext and work out the sum swiftly in the passage." Various pretexts were suggested, and this one (which had an insufficient line through it) had been inserted by Dr. McQueen on that day when Tommy saw him chuckling, "You pretend that your nose is bleeding and putting your handkerchief to it, retire hastily, the supposition being that you have gone to put the key of the blue-and-white room down your back." Evidently these small deceptions troubled Miss Ailie, for she had written, "Such subterfuge is, I hope, pardonable, the object being the maintenance of scholastic discipline." On another page, where the arithmetic was again troubling her, this appeared: "If Kitty were aware that the squealing of the slate-pencils gave me such headaches, she would insist on again taking the arithmetic class, though it always makes her ill. Surely, then, I am justified in saying that the sound does not distress me." To this the doctor had added, "You are a brick."

There were two pages headed NEVER, which mentioned ten things that Miss Ailie must never do; among them, *"Never* let the big boys know you are afraid of them. To awe them, stamp with the foot, speak in a loud ferocious voice, and look them unflinchingly in the face."

"Punishments" was another heading, but she had written it small, as if to prevent herself seeing it each time she opened the book. Obviously her hope had been to dispose of Punishment in a few lines, but it would have none of that, and Mr. McLean found it stalking from page to page. Miss Ailie favored the cane in preference to tawse, which, "often flap round your neck as yon are about to bring them down." Except in desperate cases "it will probably be found sufficient to order the offender to bring the cane to you." Then followed a note about rubbing the culprit's hand "with sweet butter or dripping" should you have struck too hard.

Dispiriting item, that on resuming his seat the chastised one is a hero to his fellows for the rest of the day. Item, that Master John James Rattray knows she hurts her own hand more than his. Item, that John James promised to be good throughout the session if she would let him thrash the bad ones. Item, that Master T. Sandys, himself under correction, explained to her (the artistic instinct again) how to give the cane a waggle when descending, which would double its nip. Item, that Elsie Dundas offered to receive Francie Crabb's punishment for two snaps. Item, that Master Gavin Dishart, for what he considered the honor of his school, though aware he was imperilling his soul, fought Hendry Dickie of Cathro's for saying Miss Ailie could not draw blood with one stroke.

The effect on Miss Ailie of these mortifying discoveries could be read in the paragraph headed A MOTHER'S METHOD, which was copied from a newspaper. Mrs. E — —, it seems, was the mother of four boys (residing at D — —), and she subjected them frequently to corporal chastisement without permanent spiritual result. Mrs. E — —, by the advice of another lady, Mrs. K — — (mother of six), then had recourse to the following interesting experiment. Instead of punishing her children physically when they misbehaved, she now in their presence wounded herself by striking her left hand severely with a ruler held in the right. Soon their better natures were touched, and the four implored her to desist, promising with tears never to offend again. From that hour Mrs. E — — had little trouble with her boys.

It was recorded in the blue and white book how Miss Ailie gave this plan a fair trial, but her boys must have been darker characters than Mrs. E — —'s, for it merely set them to watching each other, so that they might cry out, "Pandy yourself quick, Miss Ailie; Gavin Dishart's drawing the devil on his slate." Nevertheless, when Miss Ailie announced a return to more conventional methods, Francie was put up (with threats) to say that he suffered agonies of remorse every time she pandied herself for him, but the thing had been organized in a hurry and Francie was insufficiently primed, and on cross-examination he let out that he thought remorse was a swelling of the hands.

Miss Ailie was very humble-minded, and her entries under THE TEACHER TAUGHT were all admonitions for herself. Thus she chided herself for cowardice because "Delicate private reasons have made me avoid all mention of India in the geography classes. Kitty says quite calmly that this is fair neither to our pupils nor to I — — M — —. The courage of Kitty in this matter is a constant rebuke to me." Except on a few occasions Mr. McLean found that he was always referred to as I — — M — —.

Quite early in the volume Miss Ailie knew that her sister's hold on life was loosening. "How bright the world suddenly seems," Mr. McLean read, "when there is the tiniest improvement in the health of an invalid one loves." Is it laughable that such a note as this is appended to a recipe for beef-tea? "It is surely not very wicked to pretend to Kitty that I keep some of it for myself; she would not take it all if she knew I dined on the beef it was made from." Other entries showed too plainly that Miss Ailie stinted herself of food to provide delicacies for Miss Kitty. No doubt her expenses were alarming her when she wrote this: "An interesting article in the *Mentor* says that nearly all of us eat and drink too much. Were we to mortify our stomachs we should be healthier animals and more capable of sustained thought. The word animal in this connection is coarse, but the article is most impressive, and a crushing reply to Dr. McQueen's assertion that the editor drinks. In the school-room I have frequently found my thoughts of late wandering from classwork, and I hastily ascribed it to sitting up during the night with Kitty or to my habit of listening lest she should be calling for me. Probably I had over-eaten, and I must mortify the stomach. A glass of hot water with half a spoonful of sugar in it is highly recommended as a light supper."

"How long ago it may seem since yesterday!" Do you need to be told on what dark day Miss Ailie discovered that? "I used to pray that I should be taken first, but I was both impious and selfish, for how could fragile Kitty have fought on alone?"

In time happiness again returned to Miss Ailie; of all our friends it is the one most reluctant to leave us on this side of the grave. It came at first disguised, in the form of duties, old and new; and stealthily, when Miss Ailie was not looking, it mixed with the small worries and joys that had been events while Miss Kitty lived, and these it converted once more into events, where Miss Ailie found it lurking, and at first she would not take it back to her heart, but it crept in without her knowing. And still there were I — — M — —'s letters. "They are all I have to look forward to," she wrote in self-defence. "I shall never write to I — — M — — again," was another entry, but Mr. McLean found on the same page, "I have written to I — — M — —, but do not intend posting it," and beneath that was, "God forgive me, I have posted it."

The troubles with arithmetic were becoming more terrible. "I am never *really* sure about the decimals," she wrote.

A Professor of Memory had appeared at the Muckley, and Miss Ailie admits having given him half-a-crown to explain his system to her. But when he was gone she could not remember whether you multiplied everything by ten before dividing by five and subtracting a hundred, or began by dividing and doing something underhand with the cube root. Then Mr. Dishart, who had a microscope, wanted his boy to be taught science, and several experiments were described at length in the book, one of them dealing with a penny, *H*, and a piston, *X Y*, and you do things to the piston "and then the penny comes to the surface." "But it never does," Miss Ailie wrote sorrowfully; perhaps she was glad when Master Dishart was sent to another school.

"Though I teach the girls the pianoforte I find that I cannot stretch my fingers as I used to do. Kitty used to take the music, and I often remember this suddenly when superintending a lesson. It is a pain to me that so many wish to acquire 'The Land o' the Leal,' which Kitty sang so often to I — — M — — at Magenta Cottage."

Even the French, of which Miss Ailie had once been very proud, was slipping from her. "Kitty and I kept up our French by translating I — — M — —'s letters and comparing our versions, but now that this stimulus is taken away I find that I am forgetting my French. Or is it only that I am growing old? too old to keep school?" This dread was beginning to haunt Miss Ailie, and the pages between which the blotting-paper lay revealed that she had written to the editor of the *Mentor* asking up to what age he thought a needy gentlewoman had a right to teach. The answer was not given, but her comment on it told everything. "I asked him to be severely truthful, so that I cannot resent his reply. But if I take his advice, how am I to live? And if I do not take it, I fear I am but a stumbling-block in the way of true education."

That is a summary of what Mr. McLean read in the blue and white book; remember, you were warned not to expect much. And Tommy and Gavinia listened, and Tommy said, "I hear no laughing," and Gavinia answered, "But he has quieted down," and upstairs Miss Ailie was on her knees. A time came when Mr. McLean could find something to laugh at in that little pass-book, but it was not then, not even when he reached the end. He left something on the last page instead. At least I think it must have been he: Miss Ailie's tears could not have been so long a-drying.

You may rise, now, Miss Ailie; your prayer is granted.

Mr. McLean wrote a few reassuring words to Miss Ailie, and having told Gavinia to give the note to her walked quietly out of the house; he was coming back after he had visited Miss Kitty's grave. Gavinia, however, did not knew this, and having delivered the note she returned dolefully to the kitchen to say to Tommy, "His letter maun have been as thraun as himsel', for as soon as she read it, down she plumped on her knees again."

But Tommy was not in the kitchen; he was on the garden-wall watching Miss Ailie's persecutor.

"Would it no be easier to watch him frae the gate?" suggested Gavinia, who had not the true detective instinct.

Tommy disregarded her womanlike question; a great change had come over him since she went upstairs; his bead now wobbled on his shoulders like a little balloon that wanted to cut its connection with earth and soar.

"What makes you look so queer?" cried the startled maid. "I thought you was converted."

"So I am," he shouted, "I'm more converted than ever, and yet I can do it just the same! Gavinia, I've found a wy!"

He was hurrying off on Mr. McLean's trail, but turned to say, "Gavinia, do you ken wha that man is?"

"Ower weel I ken," she answered, "it's Mr. McLean."

"McLean!" he echoed scornfully, "ay, I've heard that's one of the names he goes by, but hearken, and I'll tell you wha he really is. That's the scoundrel Stroke!"

No wonder Gavinia was flabbergasted. "Wha are you then?" she cried.

"I'm the Champion of Dames," he replied loftily, and before she had recovered from this he was stalking Mr. McLean in the cemetery.

Miss Kitty sleeps in a beautiful hollow called the Basin, but the stone put up to her memory hardly marks the spot now, for with a score of others it was blown on its face by the wind that uprooted so many trees in the Den, and as it fell it lies. From the Basin to the rough road that clings like a belt to the round cemetery dyke is little more than a jump, and shortly after Miss Kitty's grave had been pointed out to him. Mr. McLean was seen standing there hat in hand by a man on the road. This man was Dr. McQueen hobbling home from the Forest Muir; he did not hobble as a rule, but hobble everyone must on that misshapen brae, except Murdoch Gelatley, who, being short in one leg elsewhere, is here the only straight man. McQueen's sharp eyes, however, picked out not only the stranger but Tommy crouching behind Haggart's stone, and him did the doctor's famous crook staff catch in the neck and whisk across the dyke.

"What man is that you're watching, you mysterious loon?" McQueen demanded, curiously; but of course Tommy would not divulge so big a secret. Now the one weakness of this large-hearted old bachelor (perhaps it is a professional virtue) was a devouring inquisitiveness, and he would be troubled until he discovered who was the stranger standing in such obvious emotion by the side of an old grave. "Well, you must come back with me to the surgery, for I want you to run an errand for me," he said testily, hoping to pump the boy by the way, but Tommy dived beneath his stick and escaped. This rasped the doctor's temper, which was unfortunate for Grizel, whom he caught presently peeping in at his surgery window. A dozen times of late she had wondered whether she should ask him to visit her mamma, and though the Painted Lady had screamed in terror at the proposal, being afraid of doctors, Grizel would have ventured ere now, had it not been for her mistaken conviction that he was a hard man, who would only flout her. It had once come to her ears that he had said a woman like her mamma could demoralize a whole town, with other harsh remarks, doubtless exaggerated in the repetition, and so he was the last man she dared think of going to for help, when he should have been the first. Nevertheless she had come now, and a soft word from him, such as he gave most readily to all who were in distress, would have drawn her pitiful tale from her, but he was in a grumpy mood, and had heard none of the rumors about her mother's being ill, which indeed were only common among the Monypenny children, and his first words checked her confidences. "What are you hanging about my open window for?" he cried sharply.

"Did you think I wanted to steal anything?" replied the indignant child.

"I won't say but what I had some such thait."

She turned to leave him, but he hooked her with his staff. "As you're here," he said, "will you go an errand for me?"

"No," she told him promptly; "I don't like you."

"There's no love lost between us," he replied, "for I think you're the dourest lassie I ever clapped eyes on, but there's no other litlin handy, so you must do as you are bid, and take this bottle to Ballingall's."

"Is it a medicine bottle?" she asked, with sudden interest.

"Yes, it's medicine. Do you know Ballingall's house in the West town end?"

"Ballingall who has the little school?"

"The same, but I doubt he'll keep school no longer."

"Is he dying?"

"I'm afraid there's no doubt of it. Will you go?"

"I should love to go," she cried.

"Love!" he echoed, looking at her with displeasure. "You can't love to go, so talk no more nonsense, but go, and I'll give you a bawbee."

"I don't want a bawbee," she said. "Do you think they will let me go in to see Ballingall?"

The doctor frowned. "What makes you want to see a dying man?" he demanded.

"I should just love to see him!" she exclaimed, and she added determinedly, "I won't give up the bottle until they let me in."

He thought her an unpleasant, morbid girl, but "that is no affair of mine," he said shrugging his shoulders, and he gave her the bottle to deliver. Before taking it to Ballingall's, however, she committed a little crime. She bought an empty bottle at the 'Sosh, and poured into it some of the contents of the medicine bottle, which she then filled up with water. She dared try no other way now of getting medicine for her mother, and was too ignorant to know that there are different drugs for different ailments.

Grizel not only contrived to get in to see Ballingan but stayed by his side for several hours, and when she came out it was night-time. On her way home she saw a light moving in the Den, where she had expected to play no more, and she could not prevent her legs from running joyously toward it. So when Corp, rising out of the darkness, deftly cut her throat, she was not so angry as she should have been.

"I'm so glad we are to play again, after all, Corp," she said; but he replied grandly, "Thou little kennest wha you're speaking to, my gentle jade."

He gave a curious hitch to his breeches, but it only puzzled her. "I wear gallowses no more," he explained, lifting his waistcoat to show that his braces now encircled him as a belt, but even then she did not understand. "Know, then," said Corp, sternly, "I am Ben the Boatswain."

"And am I not the Lady Griselda any more?" she asked.

"I'm no sure," he confessed; "but if you are, there's a price on your head."

"What is Tommy?"

"I dinna ken yet, but Gavinia says he told her he's Champion of Damns. I kenna what Elspeth'll say to that."

Grizel was starting for the Lair, but he caught her by the skirt.

"Is he not at the Lair?" she inquired.

"We knowest it not," he answered gravely. "We're looking for't," he added with some awe; "we've been looking for't this three year." Then, in a louder voice, "If you can guide us to it, my pretty trifle, you'll be richly rewarded."

"But where is he? Don't you know?"

"Fine I knowest, but it wouldna be mous to tell you, for I kenna whether you be friend or foe. What's that you're carrying?"

"It is a—a medicine bottle."

"Gie me a sook!"

"No."

"Just one," begged Corp, "and I'll tell you where he is."

He got his way, and smacked his lips unctuously.

"Now, where is Tommy?"

"Put your face close to mine," said Corp, and then he whispered hoarsely, "He's in a spleet new Lair, writing out bills wi' a' his might, offering five hunder crowns reward for Stroke's head, dead or alive!"

* * * * *

The new haunt was a deserted house, that stood, very damp, near a little waterfall to the east of the Den. Bits of it well planted in the marsh adhere doggedly together to this day, but even then the roof was off and the chimney lay in a heap on the ground, like blankets that have slipped off a bed.

This was the good ship Ailie, lying at anchor, man-of-war, thirty guns, a cart-wheel to steer it by, T. Sandys, commander.

On the following Saturday, Ben the Boatswain piped all hands, and Mr. Sandys delivered a speech, of the bluff, straightforward kind that sailors love. Here, unfortunately, it must be condensed. He reminded them that three years had passed since their gracious queen (cheers) sent them into these seas to hunt down the Pretender (hisses). Their ship had been christened the Ailie, because its object was to avenge the insults offered by the Pretender to a lady of that name for whom everyone of them would willingly die. Like all his race the Pretender, or Stroke, as he called himself, was a torment to single women; he had not only stolen all this lady's wealth, but now he wanted to make her walk the plank, a way of getting rid of enemies the mere mention of which set the blood of all honest men boiling (cheers). As yet they had not succeeded in finding Stroke's Lair, though they knew it to be in one of the adjoining islands, but they had suffered many privations, twice their gallant vessel had been burned to the water's edge, once she had been sunk, once blown into the air, but had that dismayed them?

Here the Boatswain sent round a whisper, and they all cried loyally, "Ay, ay, sir."

He had now news for them that would warm their hearts like grog. He had not discovered the Lair, but he had seen Stroke, he had spoken to him! Disguised as a boy he had tracked the Jacobite and found him skulking in the house of the unhappy Ailie. After blustering for a little Stroke had gone on his knees and offered not only to cease persecuting this lady but to return to France. Mr. Sandys had kicked him into a standing posture and then left him. But this clemency had been ill repaid. Stroke had not returned to France. He was staying at the Quharity Arms, a Thrums inn, where he called himself McLean. It had gone through the town like wildfire that he had written to someone in Redlintie to send him on another suit of clothes and four dickies. No one suspected his real character, but all noted that he went to the unhappy Ailie's house daily, and there was a town about it. Ailie was but a woman, and women could not defend themselves "(Boatswain, put Grizel in irons if she opens her mouth)," and so the poor thing had been forced to speak to him, and even to go walks with him. Her life was in danger, and before now Mr. Sandys would have taken him prisoner, but the queen had said these words, "Noble Sandys, destroy the Lair," and the best way to discover this horrid spot was to follow Stroke night and day until he went to it. Then they would burn it to the ground, put him on board the Ailie, up with the jib-boom sail, and away to the Tower of London.

At the words "Tower of London," Ben cried "Tumble up there!" which was the signal for three such ringing cheers as only British tars are capable of. Three? To be exact only two and a half, for the third stopped in the middle, as if the lid had suddenly been put on.

What so startled them was the unexpected appearance in their midst of the very man Tommy had been talking of. Taking a stroll through the Den, Mr. McLean had been drawn toward the ruin by the first cheers, and had arrived in time to learn who and what he really was.

"Stroke!" gasped one small voice.

The presumptuous man folded his arms. "So, Sandys," he said, in hollow tones, "we meet again!"

Even Grizel got behind Tommy, and perhaps it was this that gave him spunk to say tremulously, "Wh-what are you doing her?"

"I have come," replied the ruddy Pretender, "to defy you, ay, proud Sandys, to challenge thee to the deed thou pratest of. I go from here to my Lair. Follow me, if thou darest!"

He brought his hand down with a bang upon the barrel, laughed disdainfully, and springing over the vessel's side was at once lost in the darkness. Instead of following, all stood transfixed, gazing at the barrel, on which lay five shillings.

"He put them there when he slammed it!"

"Losh behears! there's a shilling to ilka ane o' us."

"I winna touch the siller," said Sandys, moodily.

"What?" cried Gavinia.

"I tell you it's a bribe."

"Do you hear him?" screamed Gavinia. "He says we're no to lay hands on't! Corp, where's your tongue?"

But even in that trying moment Corp's trust in Tommy shone out beautiful and strong. "Dinna be feared, Gavinia," he whispered, "he'll find a wy."

"Lights out and follow Stroke!" was the order, and the crew at once scattered in pursuit, Mr. Sandys remaining behind a moment to-to put something in his pocket.

Mr. McLean gave them a long chase, walking demurely when lovers were in sight, but at other times doubling, jumping, even standing on eminences and crowing insultingly, like a cock, and not until he had only breath left to chuckle did the stout man vanish from the Den. Elspeth, now a cabin-boy, was so shaken by the realism of the night's adventures that Gavinia (able seaman) took her home, and when Mr. Sandys and his Boatswain met at the Cuttle Well neither could tell where Grizel was.

"She had no business to munt without my leave," Tommy said sulkily.

"No, she hadna. Is she the Lady Griselda yet?"

"Not her, she's the Commander's wife."

Ben shook his head, for this, he felt, was the one thing Tommy could not do. "Well, then," growled Tommy, "if she winna be that, she'll have to serve before the mast, for I tell you plain I'll have no single women on board."

"And what am I, forby Ben the Boatswain?"

"Nothing. Honest men has just one name."

"What! I'm just one single man?" Corp was a little crestfallen. "It's a come down," he said, with a sigh, "mind, I dinna grumble, but it's a come down."

"And you dinna have 'Methinks' now either," Tommy announced pitilessly.

Corp had dreaded this. "I'll be gey an' lonely without it," he said, with some dignity, "and it was the usefulest swear I kent o'. 'Methinks!' I used to roar at Mason Malcolm's collie, and the crittur came in ahint in a swite o' fear. Losh, Tommy, is that you blooding?"

There was indeed an ugly gash on Tommy's hand. "You've been hacking at yoursel' again," said the distressed Corp, who knew that in his enthusiasm Tommy had more than once drawn blood from himself. "When you take it a' so real as that," he said, uncomfortably "I near think we should give it up."

Tommy stamped his foot. "Take tent o' yoursel'!" he cried threateningly. "When I was tracking Stroke I fell in with one of his men, and we had a tussle. He pinked me in the hand, but 'tis only a scratch, bah! He was carrying treasure, and I took it from him."

Ben whistled. "Five shillings?" he asked, slapping his knee.

"How did you know?" demanded Tommy, frowning, and then they tried to stare each other down.

"I thought I saw you pouching it," Corp ventured to say.

"Boatswain!"

"I mean," explained Corp hurriedly, "I mean that I kent you would find a wy. Didest thou kill the Jacobite rebel?"

"He lies but a few paces off," replied Tommy, "and already the vultures are picking his bones."

"So perish all Victoria's enemies," said Ben the Boatswain, loyally, but a sudden fear made him add, with a complete change of voice, "You dinna chance to ken his name?"

"Ay, I had marked him before," answered Tommy, "he was called Corp of Corp."

Ben the Boatswain rose, sat down, rose again, "Tommy," he said, wiping his brow with his sleeve, "come awa' hame!"

Chapter XXVII
The Longer Catechism

In the meantime Mr. McLean was walking slowly to the Quharity Arms, fanning his face with his hat, and in the West town end he came upon some boys who had gathered with offensive cries round a girl in a lustre jacket. A wave of his stick put them to flight, but the girl only thanked him with a look, and entered a little house the window of which showed a brighter light than its neighbors. Dr. McQueen came out of this house a moment afterwards, and as the two men now knew each other slightly, they walked home together, McLean relating humorously how he had spent the evening. "And though Commander Sandys means to incarcerate me in the Tower of London," he said, "he did me a good service the other day, and I feel an interest in him."

"What did the inventive sacket do?" the doctor asked inquisitively; but McLean, who had referred to the incident of the pass-book, affected not to hear. "Miss Ailie has told me his history," he said, "and that he goes to the University next year."

"Or to the herding," put in McQueen, dryly.

"Yes, I heard that was the alternative, but he should easily carry a bursary; he is a remarkable boy."

"Ay, but I'm no sure that it's the remarkable boys who carry the bursaries. However, if you have taken a fancy to him you should hear what Mr. Cathro has to say on the subject; for my own part I have been more taken up with one of his band lately than with himself—a lassie, too."

"She who went into that house just before you came out?"

"The same, and she is the most puzzling bit of womankind I ever fell in with."

"She looked an ordinary girl enough," said Mr. McLean.

The doctor chuckled. "Man," he said, "in my time I have met all kinds of women except ordinary ones. What would you think if I told you that this ordinary girl had been spending three or four hours daily in that house entirely because there was a man dying in it?"

"Some one she had an affection for?"

"My certie, no! I'm afraid it is long since anybody had an affection for shilpit, hirpling, old Ballingall, and as for this lassie Grizel, she had never spoken to him until I sent her on an errand to his house a week ago. He was a single man (like you and me), without womenfolk, a school-master of his own making, and in the smallest way, and his one attraction to her was that he was on his death-bed. Most lassies of her age skirl to get away from the presence of death, but she prigged, sir, fairly prigged, to get into it!"

"Ah, I prefer less uncommon girls," McLean said. "They should not have let her have her wish; it can only do her harm."

"That is another curious thing," replied the doctor. "It does not seem to have done her harm; rather it has turned her from being a dour, silent crittur into a talkative one, and that, I take it, is a sign of grace."

He sighed, and added: "Not that I can get her to talk of herself and her mother. (There is a mystery about them, you understand.) No, the obstinate brat will tell me nothing on that subject; instead of answering my questions she asks questions of me-an endless rush of questions, and all about Ballingall. How did I know he was dying? When you put your fingers on their wrist, what is it you count? which is the place where the lungs are? when you tap their chest what do you listen for? are they not dying as long as they can rise now and then, and dress and go out? when they are really dying do they always know it themselves? If they don't know it, is that a sign that they are not so ill as you think them? When they don't know they are dying, is it best to keep it from them in case they should scream with terror? and so on in a spate of questions, till I called her the Longer Catechism."

"And only morbid curiosity prompted her?"

"Nothing else," said the confident doctor; "if there had been anything else I should have found it out, you may be sure. However, unhealthily minded though she be, the women who took their turn at Ballingall's bedside were glad of her help."

"The more shame to them," McLean remarked warmly; but the doctor would let no one, save himself, miscall the women of Thrums.

"Ca' canny," he retorted. "The women of this place are as overdriven as the men, from the day they have the strength to turn a pirn-wheel to the day they crawl over their bed-board for the last time, but never yet have I said, 'I need one of you to sit up all night wi' an unweel body,' but what there were half a dozen willing to do it. They are a grand race, sir, and will remain so till they find it out themselves."

"But of what use could a girl of twelve or fourteen be to them?"

"Use!" McQueen cried. "Man, she has been simply a treasure, and but for one thing I would believe it was less a morbid mind than a sort of divine instinct for nursing that took her to Ballingall's bedside. The women do their best in a rough and ready way; but, sir, it cowed to see that lassie easing a pillow for Ballingall's head, or changing a sheet without letting in the air, or getting a poultice on his back without disturbing the one on his chest. I had just to let her see how to do these things once, and after that Ballingall complained if any other soul touched him."

"Ah," said McLean, "then perhaps I was uncharitable, and the nurse's instinct is the true explanation."

"No, you're wrong again, though I might have been taken in as well as you but for the one thing I spoke of. Three days ago Ballingall had a ghost of a chance of pulling through, I thought, and I told the lassie that if he did, the credit would be mainly hers. You'll scarcely believe it, but, upon my word, she looked disappointed rather than pleased, and she said to me, quite reproachfully, 'You told me he was sure to die!' What do you make of that?"

"It sounds unnatural."

"It does, and so does what followed. Do you know what straiking is?"

"Arraying the corpse for the coffin, laying it out, in short, is it not?"

"Ay, ay. Well, it appears that Grizel had prigged with the women to let her be present at Ballingall's straiking, and they had refused."

"I should think so," exclaimed McQueen, with a shudder.

"But that's not all. She came to me in her difficulty, and said that if I didna promise her this privilege she would nurse Ballingall no more."

"Ugh! That shows at least that pity for him had not influenced her."

"No, she cared not a doit for him. I question if she's the kind that could care for anyone. It's plain by her thrawn look when you speak to her about her mother that she has no affection even for her. However, there she was, prepared to leave Ballingall to his fate if I did not grant her request, and I had to yield to her."

"You promised?"

"I did, sore against the grain, but I accept the responsibility. You are pained, but you don't know what a good nurse means to a doctor."

"Well?"

"Well, he died after all, and the straiking is going on now. You saw her go in."

"I think you could have been excused for breaking your word and turning her out."

"To tell the truth," said the doctor, "I had the same idea when I saw her enter, and I tried to shoo her to the door, but she cried, 'You promised, you *can't* break a promise!' and the morbid brat that she is looked so horrified at the very notion of anybody's breaking a promise that I slunk away as if she had right on her side."

"No wonder the little monster is unpopular," was McLean's comment. "The children hereabout seem to take to her as little as I do, for I had to drive away some who were molesting her. I am sorry I interfered now."

"I can tell you why they t'nead her," replied the doctor, and he repeated the little that was known in Thrums of the Painted Lady, "And you see the womenfolk are mad because they can find out so little about her, where she got her money, for instance, and who are the 'gentlemen' that are said to visit her at Double Dykes. They have tried many ways of drawing Grizel, from heckle biscuits and parlies to a slap in the face, but neither by coaxing nor squeezing will you get an egg out of a sweer hen, and so they found. 'The dour little limmer,' they say, 'stalking about wi' all her blinds down,' and they are slow to interfere when their laddies call her names. It's a pity for herself that she's not more communicative, for if she would just satisfy the women's curiosity she would find them full of kindness. A terrible thing, Mr. McLean, is curiosity. The Bible says that the love of money is the root of all evil, but we must ask Mr. Dishart if love of money is not a misprint for curiosity. And you won't find men boring their way into other folk's concerns; it is a woman's failing, essentially a woman's." This was the doctor's pet topic, and he pursued it until they had to part. He had opened his door and was about to enter when he saw Gavinia passing on her way home from the Den.

"Come here, my lass," he called to her, and then said inquisitively, "I'm told Mr. McLean is at his tea with Miss Ailie every day?"

"And it's true," replied Gavinia, in huge delight, "and what's more, she has given him some presents."

"You say so, lassie! What were they now?"

"I dinna ken," Gavinia had to admit, dejectedly. "She took them out o' the ottoman, and it has aye been kept looked."

McQueen looked very knowingly at her. "Will he, think you?" he asked mysteriously.

The maid seemed to understand, for she replied, promptly, "I hope he will."

"But he hasna spiered her as yet, you think?"

"No," she said, "no, but he calls her Ailie, and wi' the gentry it's but one loup frae that to spiering."

"Maybe," answered the doctor, "but it's a loup they often bogle at. I'se uphaud he's close on fifty, Gavinia?"

"There's no denying he is by his best," she said regretfully, and then added, with spirit, "but Miss Ailie's no heavy, and in thae grite arms o' his he could daidle her as if she were an infant."

This bewildered McQueen, and he asked, "What are you blethering about, Gavinia?" to which she replied, regally, "Wha carries me, wears me!" The doctor concluded that it must be Den language.

"And I hope he's good enough for her," continued Miss Ailie's warm-hearted maid, "for she deserves a good ane."

"She does," McQueen agreed heartily; "ay, and I believe he is, for he breathes through his nose instead of through his mouth; and let me tell you, Gavinia, that's the one thing to be sure of in a man before you take him for better or worse."

The astounded maid replied, "I'll ken better things than that about my lad afore I take him," but the doctor assured her that it was the box which held them all, "though you maun tell no one, lassie, for it's my one discovery in five and thirty years of practice."

Seeing that, despite his bantering tone, he was speaking seriously, she pressed him for his meaning, but he only replied sadly, "You're like the rest, Gavinia, I see it breaking out on you in spots."

"An illness!" she cried, in alarm.

"Ay, lassie, an illness called curiosity. I had just been telling Mr. McLean that curiosity is essentially a woman's ailment, and up you come ahint to prove it." He shook a finger at her reprovingly, and was probably still reflecting on woman's ways when Grizel walked home at midnight breathing through her nose, and Tommy fell asleep with his mouth open. For Tommy could never have stood the doctor's test of a man. In the painting of him, aged twenty-four, which was exhibited in the Royal Academy, his lips meet firmly, but no one knew save himself how he gasped after each sitting.

Chapter XXVIII

But It Should Have Been Miss Kitty

The ottoman whence, as Gavinia said, Miss Ailie produced the presents she gave to Mr. McLean, stood near the door of the blue-and-white room, with a reel of thread between, to keep them apart forever. Except on washing days it was of a genteel appearance, for though but a wooden kist, it had a gay outer garment with frills, which Gavinia starched, and beneath this was apparel of a private character that tied with tapes. When Miss Ailie, pins in her mouth, was on her knees arraying the ottoman, it might almost have been mistaken for a female child.

The contents of the ottoman were a few trivial articles sewn or knitted by Miss Kitty during her last illness, "just to keep me out of languor," she would explain wistfully to her sister. She never told Miss Ailie that they were intended for any special person; on the contrary, she said, "Perhaps you may find someone they will be useful to," but almost without her knowing it they always grew into something that would be useful to Ivie McLean.

"The remarkable thing is that they are an exact fit," the man said about the slippers, and Miss Ailie nodded, but she did not think it remarkable.

There were also two fluffy little bags, and Miss Ailie had to explain their use. "If you put your feet into them in bed," she faltered, "they-they keep you warm."

McLean turned hastily to something else, a smoking-cap. "I scarcely think this can have been meant for me," he said; "you have forgotten how she used to chide me for smoking."

Miss Ailie had not forgotten. "But in a way," she replied, flushing a little, "we-that is, Kitty-could not help admiring you for smoking. There is something so-so dashing about it."

"I was little worthy all the friendship you two gave me, Ailie," he told her humbly, and he was nearly saying something to her then that he had made up his mind to say. The time came a few days later. They had been walking together on the hill, and on their return to the Dovecot he had insisted, "in his old imperious way," on coming in to tea. Hearing talking in the kitchen Miss Ailie went along the passage to discover what company her maid kept; but before she reached the door, which was ajar, she turned as if she had heard something dreadful and hurried upstairs, signing to Mr. McLean, with imploring eyes, to follow her. This at once sent him to the kitchen door.

Gavinia was alone. She was standing in the middle of the floor, with one arm crooked as if making believe that another's arm rested on it, and over her head was a little muslin window-blind, representing a bride's veil. Thus she was two persons, but she was also a third, who addressed them in clerical tones.

"Ivie McLean," she said as solemnly as tho' she were the Rev. Mr. Dishart, "do you take this woman to be thy lawful wedded wife?" With almost indecent haste she answered herself, "I do."

"Alison Cray," she said next, "do you take this man to be thy lawful wedded husband?" "I do."

Just then the door shut softly; and Gavinia ran to see who had been listening, with the result that she hid herself in the coal-cellar.

While she was there, Miss Ailie and Mr. McLean were sitting in the blue-and-white room very self-conscious, and Miss Ailie was speaking confusedly of anything and everything, saying more in five minutes than had served for the previous hour, and always as she slackened she read an intention in his face that started her tongue upon another journey. But, "Timid Ailie," he said at last, "do you think you can talk me down?" and then she gave him a look of reproach that turned treacherously into one of appeal, but he had the hardihood to continue; "Ailie, do you need to be told what I want to say?"

Miss Ailie stood quite still now, a stiff, thick figure, with a soft, plain face and nervous hands. "Before you speak," she said, nervously, "I have something to tell you that-perhaps then you will not say it.

"I have always led you to believe," she began, trembling, "that I am forty-nine. I am fifty-one."

He would have spoken, but the look of appeal came back to her face, asking him to make it easier for her by saying nothing. She took a pair of spectacles from her pocket, and he divined what this meant before she spoke. "I have avoided letting you see that I need them," she said. "You-men don't like —" She tried to say it all in a rush, but the words would not come.

"I am beginning to be a little deaf," she went on. "To deceive you about that, I have sometimes answered you without really knowing what you said."

"Anything more, Ailie?"

"My accomplishments-they were never great, but Kitty and I thought my playing of classical pieces-my fingers are not sufficiently pliable now. And I —I forget so many things."

"But, Ailie —"

"Please let me tell you. I was reading a book, a story, last winter, and one of the characters, an old maid, was held up to ridicule in it for many little peculiarities that-that I recognized as my own. They had grown upon me without my knowing that they made me ridiculous, and now I —I have tried, but I cannot alter them."

"Is that all, Ailie?"

"No."

The last seemed to be the hardest to say. Dusk had come on, and they could not see each other well. She asked him to light the lamp, and his back was toward her while he did it, wondering a little at her request. When he turned, her hands rose like cowards to hide her head, but she pulled them down. "Do you not see?" she said.

"I see that you have done something to your hair," he answered, "I liked it best the other way."

Most people would have liked it best the other way. There was still a good deal of it, but the "bun" in which it ended had gone strangely small. "The rest was false," said Miss Ailie, with a painful effort; "at least, it is my own, but it came out when-when Kitty died."

She stopped, but he was silent. "That is all now," she said, softly; and she waited for him to speak if he chose. He turned his head away sharply, and Miss Ailie mistook his meaning. If she gave one little sob-Well, it was but one, and then all the glory of womanhood came rushing to her aid, and it unfurled its flag over her, whispering, "Now, sweet daughter, now, strike for me," and she raised her head gallantly, and for a moment in her life the old school-mistress was a queen. "I shall ring for tea," she said, quietly and without a tremor; "do you think there is anything so refreshing after a walk as a dish of tea?"

She rang the bell, but its tinkle only made Gavinia secede farther into the cellar, and that summons has not been answered to this day, and no one seems to care, for while the wires were still vibrating Mr. McLean had asked Miss Ailie to forgive him and marry him.

Miss Ailie said she would, but, "Oh," she cried, "ten years ago it might have been my Kitty. I would that it had been Kitty!"

Miss Ailie was dear to him now, and ten years is a long time, and men are vain. Mr. McLean replied, quite honestly, "I am not sure that I did not always like you best," but that hurt her, and he had to unsay the words.

"I was a thoughtless fool ten years ago," he said, bitterly, and Miss Ailie's answer came strangely from such timid lips. "Yes, you were!" she exclaimed, passionately, and all the wrath, long pent up, with very different feelings, in her gentle bosom, against the man who should have adored her Kitty, leapt at that reproachful cry to her mouth and eyes, and so passed out of her forever.

Chapter XXIX
Tommy the Scholar

So Miss Ailie could be brave, but what a poltroon she was also! Three calls did she make on dear friends, ostensibly to ask how a cold was or to instruct them in a new device in Shetland wool, but really to announce that she did not propose keeping school after the end of the term-because-in short, Mr. Ivie McLean and she-that is he-and so on. But though she had planned it all out so carefully, with at least three capital ways of leading up to it, and knew precisely what they would say, and pined to hear them say it, on each occasion shyness conquered and she came away with the words unspoken. How she despised herself, and how Mr. McLean laughed! He wanted to take the job off her hands by telling the news to Dr. McQueen, who could be depended on to spread it through the town, and Miss Ailie discovered with horror that his simple plan was to say, "How are you, doctor? I just looked in to tell you that Miss Ailie and I are to be married. Good afternoon." The audacity of this captivated Miss Ailie even while it outraged her sense of decency. To Redlintie went Mr. McLean, and returning next day drew from his pocket something which he put on Miss Ailie's finger, and then she had the idea of taking off her left glove in church, which would have announced her engagement as loudly as though Mr. Dishart had included it in his pulpit intimations. Religion, however, stopped her when she had got the little finger out, and the Misses Finlayson, who sat behind and knew she had an itchy something inside her glove, concluded that it was her threepenny for the plate. As for Gavinia, like others of her class in those days, she had never heard of engagement rings, and so it really seemed as if Mr. McLean must call on the doctor after all. But "No," said he, "I hit upon a better notion to-day in the Den," and to explain this notion he produced from his pocket a large, vulgar bottle, which shocked Miss Ailie, and indeed that bottle had not passed through the streets uncommented on.

Mr. McLean having observed this bottle afloat on the Silent Pool, had fished it out with his stick, and its contents set him chuckling. They consisted of a sheet of paper which stated that the bottle was being flung into the sea in lat. 20, long. 40, by T. Sandys, Commander of the Ailie, then among the breakers. Sandys had little hope of weathering the gale, but he was indifferent to his own fate so long as his enemy did not escape, and he called upon whatsoever loyal subjects of the Queen should find this document to sail at once to lat. 20, long. 40, and there cruise till they had captured the Pretender, *alias* Stroke, and destroyed his Lair. A somewhat unfavorable personal description of Stroke was appended, with a map of the coast, and a stern warning to all loyal subjects not to delay as one Ailie was in the villain's hands and he might kill her any day. Victoria Regina would give five hundred pounds for his head. The letter ended in manly style with the writer's sending an affecting farewell message to his wife and little children.

"And so while we are playing ourselves," said Mr. McLean to Miss Ailie, "your favorite is seeking my blood."

"Our favorite," interposed the school-mistress, and he accepted the correction, for neither of them could forget that their present relations might have been very different had it not been for Tommy's faith in the pass-book. The boy had shown a knowledge of the human heart, in Miss Ailie's opinion, that was simply wonderful; inspiration she called it, and though Ivie thought it a happy accident, he did not call it so to her. Tommy's father had been the instrument in bringing these two together originally, and now Tommy had brought them together again; there was fate in it, and if the boy was of the right stuff McLean meant to reward him.

"I see now," he said to Miss Ailie, "a way of getting rid of our fearsome secret and making my peace with Sandys at one fell blow." He declined to tell her more, but presently he sought Gavinia, who dreaded him nowadays because of his disconcerting way of looking at her inquiringly and saying "I do!"

"You don't happen to know, Gavinia," he asked, "whether the good ship Ailie weathered the gale of the 15th instant? If it did," he went on, "Commander Sandys will learn something to his advantage from a bottle that is to be cast into the ocean this evening."

Gavinia thought she heard the chink of another five shillings, and her mouth opened so wide that a chaffinch could have built therein. "Is he to look for a bottle in the pond?" she asked, eagerly.

"I do," replied McLean with such solemnity that she again retired to the coal-cellar.

That evening Mr. McLean cast a bottle into the Silent Pool, and subsequently called on Mr. Cathro, to whom he introduced himself as one interested in Master Thomas Sandys. He was heartily received, but at the name of Tommy, Cathro heaved a sigh that could not pass unnoticed. "I see you don't find him an angel," said Mr. McLean, politely.

"'Deed, sir, there are times when I wish he was an angel," the dominie replied so viciously that McLean laughed. "And I grudge you that laugh," continued Cathro, "for your Tommy Sandys has taken from me the most precious possession a teacher can have-my sense of humor."

"He strikes me as having a considerable sense of humor himself."

"Well he may, Mr. McLean, for he has gone off with all mine. But bide a wee till I get in the tumblers, and. I'll tell you the latest about him-if what you want to hear is just the plain exasperating truth.

"His humor that you spoke of," resumed the school-master presently, addressing his words to the visitor, and his mind to a toddy ladle of horn, "is ill to endure in a school where the understanding is that the dominie makes all the jokes (except on examination-day, when the ministers get their yearly fling), but I think I like your young friend worst when he is deadly serious. He is constantly playing some new part-playing is hardly the word though, for into each part he puts an earnestness that cheats even himself, until he takes to another. I suppose you want me to give you some idea of his character, and I could tell you what it is at any particular moment; but it changes, sir, I do assure you, almost as quickly as the circus-rider flings off his layers of waistcoats. A single puff of wind blows him from one character to another, and he may be noble and vicious, and a tyrant and a slave, and hard as granite and melting as butter in the sun, all in one forenoon. All you can be sure of is that whatever he is he will be it in excess."

"But I understood," said McLean, "that at present he is solely engaged on a war of extermination in the Den."

"Ah, those exploits, I fancy, are confined to Saturday nights, and unfortunately his Saturday debauch does not keep him sober for the rest of the week, which we demand of respectable characters in these parts. For the last day or two, for instance, he has been in mourning."

"I had not heard of that."

"No, I daresay not, and I'll give you the facts, if you'll fill your glass first. But perhaps —" here the dominie's eyes twinkled as if a gleam of humor had been left him after all —"perhaps you have been more used of late to ginger wine?"

The visitor received the shock impassively as if he did not know he had been hit, and Cathro proceeded with his narrative. "Well, for a day or two Tommy Sandys has been coming to the school in a black jacket with crape on the cuffs, and not only so, he has sat quiet and forlorn-like at his desk as if he had lost some near and dear relative. Now I knew that he had not, for his only relative is a sister whom you may have seen at the Hanky School, and both she and Aaron Latta are hearty. Yet, sir (and this shows the effect he has on me), though I was puzzled and curious I dared not ask for an explanation."

"But why not?" was the visitor's natural question.

"Because, sir, he is such a mysterious little sacket," replied Cathro, testily, "and so clever at leading you into a hole, that it's not chancey to meddle with him, and I could see through the corner of my eye that, for all this woeful face, he was proud of it, and hoped I was taking note. For though sometimes his emotion masters him completely, at other times he can step aside as it were, and take an approving look at it. That is a characteristic of him, and not the least maddening one."

"But you solved the mystery somehow, I suppose?"

"I got at the truth to-day by an accident, or rather my wife discovered it for me. She happened to call in at the school on a domestic matter I need not trouble you with (sal, she needna have troubled me with it either!), and on her way up the yard she noticed a laddie called Lewis Doig playing with other ungodly youths at the game of kickbonnety. Lewis's father, a gentleman farmer, was buried jimply a fortnight since, and such want of respect for his memory made my wife give the loon a dunt on the head with a pound of sugar, which she had just bought at the 'Sosh. He turned on her, ready to scart or spit or run, as seemed wisest, and in a klink her woman's eye saw what mine had overlooked, that he was not even wearing a black jacket. Well, she told him what the slap was for, and his little countenance cleared at once. 'Oh' says he, 'that's all right, Tommy and me has arranged it,' and he pointed blithely to a corner of the yard where Tommy was hunkering by himself in Lewis's jacket, and wiping his mournful eyes with Lewis's hanky. I daresay you can jalouse the rest, but I kept Lewis behind after the school skailed, and got a full confession out of him. He had tried hard, he gave me to understand, to mourn fittingly for his father, but the kickbonnety season being on, it was up-hill work, and he was relieved when Tommy volunteered to take it off his hands. Tommy's offer was to swop jackets every morning for a week or two, and thus properly attired to do the mourning for him."

The dominie paused, and regarded his guest quizzically. "Sir," he said at length, "laddies are a queer growth; I assure you there was no persuading Lewis that it was not a right and honorable compact."

"And what payment," asked McLean, laughing, "did Tommy demand from Lewis for this service?"

"Not a farthing, sir-which gives another uncanny glint into his character. When he wants money there's none so crafty at getting it, but he did this for the pleasure of the thing, or, as he said to Lewis, 'to feel what it would be like.' That, I tell you, is the nature of the sacket, he has a devouring desire to try on other folk's feelings, as if they were so many suits of clothes."

"And from your account he makes them fit him too."

"My certie, he does, and a lippie in the bonnet more than that."

So far the school-master had spoken frankly, even with an occasional grin at his own expense, but his words came reluctantly when he had to speak of Tommy's prospects at the bursary examinations. "I would rather say nothing on that head," he said, almost coaxingly, "for the laddie has a year to reform in yet, and it's never safe to prophesy."

"Still I should have thought that you could guess pretty accurately how the boys you mean to send up in a year's time are likely to do? You have had a long experience, and, I am told, a glorious one."

"'Deed, there's no denying it," answered the dominie, with a pride he had won the right to wear. "If all the ministers, for instance, I have turned out in this bit school were to come back together, they could hold the General Assembly in the square."

He lay back in his big chair, a complacent dominie again. "Guess the chances of my laddies!" he cried, forgetting what he had just said, and that there was a Tommy to bother him. "I tell you, sir, that's a matter on which I'm never deceived, I can tell the results so accurately that a wise Senatus would give my lot the bursaries I say they'll carry, without setting them down to examination-papers at all." And for the next half-hour he was reciting cases in proof of his sagacity.

"Wonderful!" chimed in McLean. "I see it is evident you can tell me how Tommy Sandys will do," but at that Cathro's rush of words again subsided into a dribble.

"He's the worst Latinist that ever had the impudence to think of bursaries," he groaned.

"And his Greek —" asked McLean, helping on the conversation as far as possible.

"His Greek, sir, could be packed in a pill-box."

"That does not sound promising. But the best mathematicians are sometimes the worst linguists."

"His Greek is better than his mathematics," said Cathro, and he fell into lamentation. "I have had no luck lately," he sighed. "The laddies I have to prepare for college are second-raters, and the vexing thing is, that when a real scholar is reared in Thrums, instead of his being handed over to me for the finishing, they send him to Mr. Ogilvy in Glenquharity. Did Miss Ailie ever mention Gavin Dishart to you-the minister's son? I just craved to get the teaching of that laddie, he was the kind you can cram with learning till there's no room left for another spoonful, and they bude send him to Mr. Ogilvy, and you'll see he'll stand high above my loons in the bursary list. And then Ogilvy will put on sic airs that there will be no enduring him. Ogilvy and I, sir, we are engaged in an everlasting duel; when we send students to the examinations, it is we two who are the real competitors, but what chance have I, when he is represented by a Gavin Dishart and my man is Tommy Sandys?"

McLean was greatly disappointed. "Why send Tommy up at all if he is so backward?" he said. "You are sure you have not exaggerated his deficiencies?"

"Well, not much at any rate. But he baffles me; one day I think him a perfect numskull, and the next he makes such a show of the small drop of scholarship he has that I'm not sure but what he may be a genius."

"That sounds better. Does he study hard?"

"Study! He is the most careless whelp that ever —"

"But if I were to give him an inducement to study?"

"Such as?" asked Cathro, who could at times be as inquisitive as the doctor.

"We need not go into that. But suppose it appealed to him?"

Cathro considered. "To be candid," he said, "I don't think he could study, in the big meaning of the word. I daresay I'm wrong, but I have a feeling that whatever knowledge that boy acquires he will dig out of himself. There is something inside him, or so I think at times, that is his master, and rebels against book-learning. No, I can't tell what it is; when we know that we shall know the real Tommy."

"And yet," said McLean, curiously, "you advise his being allowed to compete for a bursary. That, if you will excuse my saying so, sounds foolish to me."

"It can't seem so foolish to you," replied Cathro, scratching his head, "as it seems to me six days in seven."

"And you know that Aaron Latta has sworn to send him to the herding if he does not carry a bursary. Surely the wisest course would be to apprentice him now to some trade —"

"What trade would not be the worse of him? He would cut off his fingers with a joiner's saw, and smash them with a mason's mell; put him in a brot behind a counter, and in some grand, magnanimous mood he would sell off his master's things for nothing; make a clerk of him, and he would only ravel the figures; send him to the soldiering, and he would have a sudden impulse to fight on the wrong side. No, no, Miss Ailie says he has a gift for the ministry, and we must cling to that."

In thus sheltering himself behind Miss Ailie, where he had never skulked before, the dominie showed how weak he thought his position, and he added, with a brazen laugh, "Then if he does distinguish himself at the examinations I can take the credit for it, and if he comes back in disgrace I shall call you to witness that I only sent him to them at her instigation."

"All which," maintained McLean, as he put on his top-coat, "means that somehow, against your better judgment, you think he may distinguish himself after all."

"You've found me out," answered Cathro, half relieved, half sorry. "I had no intention of telling you so much, but as you have found me out I'll make a clean breast of it. Unless something unexpected happens to the laddie-unless he take to playing at scholarship as if it were a Jacobite rebellion, for instance-he shouldna have the ghost of a chance of a bursary, and if he were any other boy as ill-prepared I should be ashamed to send him up, but he is Tommy

Sandys, you see, and-it is a terrible thing to say, but it's Gospel truth, it's Gospel truth —I'm trusting to the possibility of his diddling the examiners!"

It was a startling confession for a conscientious dominie, and Cathro flung out his hands as if to withdraw the words, but his visitor would have no tampering with them. "So that sums up Tommy, so far as you know him," he said as he bade his host good-night.

"It does," Cathro admitted, grimly, "but if what you wanted was a written certificate of character I should like to add this, that never did any boy sit on my forms whom I had such a pleasure in thrashing."

Chapter XXX
End of the Jacobite Rising

In the small hours of the following night the pulse of Thrums stopped for a moment, and then went on again, but the only watcher remained silent, and the people rose in the morning without knowing that they had lost one of their number while they slept. In the same ignorance they toiled through a long day.

It was a close October day in the end of a summer that had lingered to give the countryside nothing better than a second crop of haws. Beneath the beeches leaves lay in yellow heaps like sliced turnip, and over all the strath was a pink haze; the fields were singed brown, except where a recent ploughing gave them a mourning border. From early morn men, women and children (Tommy among them) were in the fields taking up their potatoes, half-a-dozen gatherers at first to every drill, and by noon it seemed a dozen, though the new-comers were but stout sacks, now able to stand alone. By and by heavy-laden carts were trailing into Thrums, dog-tired toilers hanging on behind, not to be dragged, but for an incentive to keep them trudging, boys and girls falling asleep on top of the load, and so neglecting to enjoy the ride which was their recompense for lifting. A growing mist mixed with the daylight, and still there were a few people out, falling over their feet with fatigue; it took silent possession, and then the shadowy forms left in the fields were motionless and would remain there until carted to garrets and kitchen corners and other winter quarters on Monday morning. There were few gad-abouts that Saturday night. Washings were not brought in, though Mr. Dishart had preached against the unseemly sight of linen hanging on the line on the Sabbath-day. Innes, stravaiging the square and wynds in his apple-cart, jingled his weights in vain, unable to shake even moneyed children off their stools, and when at last he told his beast to go home they took with them all the stir of the town. Family exercise came on early in many houses, and as the gude wife handed her man the Bible she said entreatingly, "A short ane." After that one might have said that no earthly knock could bring them to their doors, yet within an hour the town was in a ferment.

When Tommy and Elspeth reached the Den the mist lay so thick that they had to feel their way through it to the *Ailie*, where they found Gavinia alone and scared. "Was you peeping in, trying to fleg me twa three minutes syne?" she asked, eagerly, and when they shook their heads, she looked cold with fear.

"As sure as death," she said, "there was some living thing standing there; I couldna see it for the rime, but I heard it breathing hard."

Tommy felt Elspeth's hand begin to tremble, and he said "McLean!" hastily, though he knew that McLean had not yet left the Quharity Arms. Next moment Corp arrived with another story as unnerving.

"Has Grizel no come yet?" he asked, in a troubled voice. "Tommy, hearken to this, a light has been burning in Double Dykes and the door swinging open a' day! I saw it mysel', and so did Willum Dods."

"Did you go close?"

"Na faags! Willum was hol'ing and I was lifting, so we hadna time in the daylight, and wha would venture near the Painted Lady's house on sic a night?"

Even Tommy felt uneasy, but when Gavinia cried, "There's something uncanny in being out the night; tell us what was in Mr. McLean's bottle, Tommy, and syne we'll run hame," he became Commander Sandys again, and replied, blankly, "What bottle?"

"The ane I warned you he was to fling into the water; dinna dare tell me you hinna got it."

"I know not what thou art speaking about," said Tommy; "but it's a queer thing, it's a queer thing, Gavinia" —here he fixed her with his terrifying eye —"I happen to have found a —another bottle," and still glaring at her he explained that he had found his bottle floating on the horizon. It contained a letter to him, which he now read aloud. It was signed "The Villain Stroke, his mark," and announced that the writer, "tired of this relentless persecution," had determined to reform rather than be killed. "Meet me at the Cuttle Well, on Saturday, when the eight-o'clock bell is ringing," he wrote, "and I shall there make you an offer for my freedom."

The crew received this communication with shouts, Gavinia's cry of "Five shillings, if no ten!" expressing the general sentiment, but it would not have been like Tommy to think with them. "You poor things," he said, "you just believe everything you're telled! How do I know that this is not a trick of Stroke's to bring me here when he is some other gait working mischief?"

Corp was impressed, but Gavinia said, short-sightedly, "There's no sign o't."

"There's ower much sign o't," retorted Tommy. "What's this story about Double Dykes? And how do we ken that there hasna been foul work there, and this man at the bottom o't? I tell you, before the world's half an hour older, I'll find out," and he looked significantly at Corp, who answered, quaking, "I winna gang by mysel', no, Tommy, I winna!"

So Tommy had to accompany him, saying, valiantly, "I'm no feared, and this rime is fine for hodding in," to which Corp replied, as firmly, "Neither am I, and we can aye keep touching cauld iron." Before they were half way down the Double Dykes they got a thrill, for they realized, simultaneously, that they were being followed. They stopped and gripped each other hard, but now they could hear nothing.

"The Painted Lady!" Corp whispered.

"Stroke!" Tommy replied, as cautiously. He was excited rather than afraid, and had the pluck to cry, "Wha's that? I see you!"—but no answer came back through the mist, and now the boys had a double reason for pressing forward.

"Can you see the house, Corp?"

"It should be here about, but it's smored in rime."

"I'm touching the paling. I ken the road to the window now."

"Hark! What's that?"

It sounded like devil's music in front of them, and they fell back until Corp remembered, "It maun be the door swinging open, and squealing and moaning on its hinges. Tommy, I take ill wi' that. What can it mean?"

"I'm here to find out." They reached the window where Tommy had watched once before, and looking in together saw the room plainly by the light of a lamp which stood on the spinet. There was no one inside, but otherwise Tommy noticed little change. The fire was out, having evidently burned itself done, the bed-clothes were in some disorder. To avoid the creaking door, the boys passed round the back of the house to the window of the other room. This room was without a light, but its door stood open and sufficient light came from the kitchen to show that it also was untenanted. It seemed to have been used as a lumber-room.

The boys turned to go, passing near the front of the empty house, where they shivered and stopped, mastered by a feeling they could not have explained. The helpless door, like the staring eyes of a dead person, seemed to be calling to them to shut it, and Tommy was about to steal forward for this purpose when Corp gripped him and whispered that the light had gone out. It was true, though Tommy disbelieved until they had returned to the east window to make sure.

"There maun be folk in the hoose, Tommy!"

"You saw it was toom. The lamp had gone out itself, or else-what's that?"

It was the unmistakable closing of a door, softly but firmly. "The wind has blown it to," they tried to persuade themselves, though aware that there was not sufficient wind for this. After a long period of stillness they gathered courage to go to the door and shake it. It was not only shut, but locked.

On their way back through the Double Dykes they were silent, listening painfully but hearing nothing. But when they reached the Coffin Brig Tommy said, "Dinna say nothing about this to Elspeth, it would terrify her;" he was always so thoughtful for Elspeth.

"But what do you think o't a'?" Corp said, imploringly.

"I winna tell you yet," replied Tommy, cautiously.

When they boarded the *Ailie*, where the two girls were very glad to see them again, the eight-o'clock bell had begun to ring, and thus Tommy had a reasonable excuse for hurrying his crew to the Cuttle Well without saying anything of his expedition to Double Dykes, save that he had not seen Grizel. At the Well they had not long to wait before Mr. McLean suddenly appeared out of the mist, and to their astonishment Miss Ailie was leaning on his arm. She was blushing and smiling too, in a way pretty to see, though it spoilt the effect of Stroke's statement.

The first thing Stroke did was to give up his sword to Tommy and to apologize for its being an umbrella on account of the unsettled state of the weather, and then Corp led three cheers, the captain alone declining to join in, for he had an uneasy feeling that he was being ridiculed.

"But I thought there were five of you," Mr. McLean said; "where is the fifth?"

"You ken best," replied Tommy, sulkily, and sulky he remained throughout the scene, because he knew he was not the chief figure in it. Having this knowledge to depress him, it is to his credit that he bore himself with dignity throughout, keeping his crew so well in hand that they dared not give expression to their natural emotions.

"As you are aware, Mr. Sandys," McLean began solemnly, "I have come here to sue for pardon. It is not yours to give, you reply, the Queen alone can pardon, and I grant it; but, sir, is it not well known to all of us that you can get anything out of her you like?"

Tommy's eyes roved suspiciously, but the suppliant proceeded in the same tone. "What are my offences? The first is that I have been bearing arms (unwittingly) against the Throne; the second, that I have brought trouble to the lady by my side, who has the proud privilege of calling you her friend. But, Sandys, such amends as can come from an erring man I now offer to make most contritely. Intercede with Her Majesty on my behalf, and on my part I promise to war against her no more. I am willing to settle down in the neighboring town as a law-abiding citizen, whom you can watch with eagle eye. Say, what more wouldst thou of the unhappy Stuart?"

But Tommy would say nothing, he only looked doubtfully at Miss Ailie, and that set McLean off again. "You ask what reparation I shall make to this lady? Sandys, I tell thee that here also thou hast proved too strong for me. In the hope that she would plead for me with you, I have been driven to offer her my hand in marriage, and she is willing to take me if thou grantest thy consent."

At this Gavinia jumped with joy, and then cried, "Up wi' her!" words whose bearing the school-mistress fortunately did not understand. All save Tommy looked at Miss Ailie, and she put her arm on Mr. McLean's, and, yes, it was obvious, Miss Ailie was a lover at the Cuttle Well at last, like so many others. She had often said that the Den parade was vulgar, but she never said it again.

It was unexpected news to Tommy, but that was not what lowered his head in humiliation now. In the general rejoicing he had been nigh forgotten; even Elspeth was hanging on Miss Ailie's skirts, Gavinia had eyes for none but lovers, Corp was rapturously examining five half-crowns that had been dropped into his hands for distribution. Had Tommy given an order now, who would have obeyed it? His power was gone, his crew would not listen to another word against Mr. McLean.

"Tommy thought Mr. McLean hated you!" said Elspeth to Miss Ailie.

"It was queer you made sic a mistake!" said Corp to Tommy.

"Oh, the tattie-doolie!" cried Gavinia.

So they knew that Mr. McLean had only been speaking sarcastically; of a sudden they saw through and despised their captain. Tears of mortification rose in Tommy's eyes, and kind-hearted Miss Ailie saw them, and she thought it was her lover's irony that made him smart. She had said little hitherto, but now she put her hand on his shoulder, and told them all that she did indeed owe the supreme joy that had come to her to him. "No, Gavinia," she said, blushing, "I will not give you the particulars, but I assure you that had it not been for Tommy, Mr. McLean would never have asked me to marry him."

Elspeth crossed proudly to the side of her noble brother (who could scarcely trust his ears), and Gavinia cried, in wonder, "What did he do?"

Now McLean had seen Tommy's tears also, and being a kindly man he dropped the satirist and chimed in warmly, "And if I had not asked Miss Ailie to marry me I should have lost the great happiness of my life, so you may all imagine how beholden I feel to Tommy."

Again Tommy was the centre-piece, and though these words were as puzzling to him as to his crew, their sincerity was unmistakable, and once more his head began to waggle complacently.

"And to show how grateful we are," said Miss Ailie, "we are to give him a —a sort of marriage present. We are to double the value of the bursary he wins at the university —" She could get no farther, for now Elspeth was hugging her, and Corp cheering frantically, and Mr. McLean thought it necessary to add the warning, "If he does carry a bursary, you understand, for should he fail I give him nothing."

"Him fail!" exclaimed Corp, with whom Miss Ailie of course agreed. "And he can spend the money in whatever way he chooses," she said, "what will you do with it, Tommy?"

The lucky boy answered, instantly, "I'll take Elspeth to Aberdeen to bide with me," and then Elspeth hugged him, and Miss Ailie said, in a delighted aside to Mr. McLean, "I told you so," and he, too, was well pleased.

"It was the one thing needed to make him work," the school-mistress whispered. "Is not his love for his sister beautiful?"

McLean admitted that it was, but half-banteringly he said to Elspeth: "What could you do in lodgings, you excited mite?"

"I can sit and look at Tommy," she answered, quickly.

"But he will be away for hours at his classes."

"I'll sit at the window waiting for him," said she.

"And I'll run back quick," said Tommy.

All this time another problem had been bewildering Gavinia, and now she broke in, eagerly: "But what was it he did? I thought he was agin Mr. McLean."

"And so did I," said Corp.

"I cheated you grandly," replied Tommy with the audacity he found so useful.

"And a' the time you was pretending to be agin him," screamed Gavinia, "was you-was you bringing this about on the sly?"

Tommy looked up into Mr. McLean's face, but could get no guidance from it, so he said nothing; he only held his head higher than ever. "Oh, the clever little curse!" cried Corp, and Elspeth's delight was as ecstatic, though differently worded. Yet Gavinia stuck to her problem, "How did you do it, what was it you did?" and the cruel McLean said: "You may tell her, Tommy; you have my permission."

It would have been an awkward position for most boys, and even Tommy-but next moment he said, quite coolly: "I think you and me and Miss Ailie should keep it to oursels, Gavinia's sic a gossip."

"Oh, how thoughtful of him!" cried Miss Ailie, the deceived, and McLean said: "How very thoughtful!" but now he saw in a flash why Mr. Cathro still had hopes that Tommy might carry a bursary.

Thus was the repentant McLean pardoned, and nothing remained for him to do save to show the crew his Lair, which they had sworn to destroy. He had behaved so splendidly that they had forgotten almost that they were the emissaries of justice, but not to destroy the Lair seemed a pity, it would be such a striking way of bringing their adventures in the Den to a close. The degenerate Stuart read this feeling in their faces, and he was ready, he said, to show them his Lair if they would first point it out to him; but here was a difficulty, for how could they do that? For a moment it seemed as if the negotiations must fall through; but Sandys, that captain of resource, invited McLean to step aside for a private conference, and when they rejoined the others McLean said, gravely, that he now remembered where the Lair was and would guide them to it.

They had only to cross a plank, invisible in the mist until they were close to it, and climb a slippery bank strewn with fallen trees. McLean, with a mock serious air, led the way, Miss Ailie on his arm. Corp and Gavinia followed, weighted and hampered by their new half-crowns, and Tommy and Elspeth, in the rear, whispered joyously of the coming life. And so, very unprepared for it, they moved toward the tragedy of the night.

Chapter XXXI
A Letter to God

"Do you keep a light burning in the Lair?" McLean turned to ask, forgetting for the moment that it was not their domicile, but his.

"No, there's no light," replied Corp, equally forgetful, but even as he spoke he stopped so suddenly that Elspeth struck against him. For he had seen a light. "This is queer!" he cried, and both he and Gavinia fell back in consternation. McLean pushed forward alone, and was back in a trice, with a new expression on his face. "Are you playing some trick on me?" he demanded suspiciously of Tommy. "There is some one there; I almost ran against a pair of blazing eyes."

"But there's nobody; there can be nobody there," answered Tommy, in a bewilderment that was obviously unfeigned, "unless-unless —" He looked at Corp, and the eyes of both finished the sentence. The desolate scene at Double Dykes, which the meeting with McLean and Miss Ailie had driven from their minds, again confronted them, and they seemed once more to hear the whimpering of the Painted Lady's door.

"Unless what?" asked the man, impatiently, but still the two boys only stared at each other. "The Den's no mous the night," said Corp at last, in a low voice, and his unspoken fears spread to the womankind, so that Miss Ailie shuddered and Elspeth gripped Tommy with both hands and Gavinia whispered, "Let's away hame, we can come back in the daylight."

But McLean chafed and pressed upward, and next moment a girl's voice was heard, crying: "It is no business of yours; I won't let you touch her."

"Grizel!" exclaimed Tommy and his crew, simultaneously, and they had no more fear until they were inside the Lair. What they saw had best be described very briefly. A fire was burning in a corner of the Lair, and in front of it, partly covered with a sheet, lay the Painted Lady, dead. Grizel stood beside the body guarding it, her hands clenched, her eyes very strange. "You sha'n't touch her!" she cried, passionately, and repeated it many times, as if she had lost the power to leave off, but Corp crept past her and raised the coverlet.

"She's straikit!" he shouted. "Did you do it yoursel', Grizel? God behears, she did it hersel'!"

A very long silence it seemed to be after that.

Miss Ailie would have taken the motherless girl to her arms, but first, at Corp's discovery, she had drawn back in uncontrollable repulsion, and Grizel, about to go to her, saw it, and turned from her to Tommy. Her eyes rested on him beseechingly, with a look he saw only once again in them until she was a woman, but his first thought was not for Grizel. Elspeth was clinging to him, terrified and sobbing, and he cried to her, "Shut your een," and then led her tenderly away. He was always good to Elspeth.

* * * * *

There was no lack of sympathy with Grizel when the news spread through the town, and unshod men with their gallowses hanging down, and women buttoning as they ran, hurried to the Den. But to all the questions put to her and to all the kindly offers made, as the body was carried to Double Dykes, she only rocked her arms, crying, "I don't want anything to eat. I shall stay all night beside her. I am not frightened at my mamma. I won't tell you why she was in the Den. I am not sure how long she has been dead. Oh, what do these little things matter?"

The great thing was that her mamma should be buried in the cemetery, and not in unconsecrated ground with a stake through her as the boys had predicted, and it was only after she was promised this that Grizel told her little tale. She had feared for a long time that her mamma was dying of consumption, but she told no one, because everybody was against her and her mamma. Her mamma never knew that she was dying, and sometimes she used to get so much better that Grizel hoped she would live a long time, but that hope never lasted long. The reason she sat so much with Ballingall was just to find out what doctors did to dying people to make them live a little longer, and she watched his straiking to be able to do it to her mamma when the time came. She was sure none of the women would consent to straik her mamma. On the previous night, she could not say at what hour, she had been awakened by a cold wind, and so she knew that the door was open. She put out her hand in the darkness and found that her mamma was not beside her. It had happened before, and she was not frightened. She had hidden the key of the door that night and nailed down the window, but her mamma had found the key. Grizel rose, lit the lamp, and, having dressed hurriedly, set off with wraps to the Den. Her mamma was generally as sensible as anybody in Thrums, but sometimes she had shaking fits, and after them she thought it was the time of long ago. Then she went to the Den to meet a man who had promised, she said, to be there, but he never came, and before daybreak Grizel could usually induce her to return home. Latterly she had persuaded her mamma to wait for him in the old Lair, because it was less cold there, and she had got her to do this last night. Her mamma did not seem very unwell, but she fell asleep, and she died sleeping, and then Grizel went back to Double Dykes for linen and straiked her.

Some say in Thrums that a spade was found in the Lair, but that is only the growth of later years. Grizel had done all she could do, and through the long Saturday she sat by the side of the body, helpless and unable to cry. She knew that it could not remain there much longer, but every time she rose to go and confess, fear of the indignities to which the body of her darling mamma might be subjected pulled her back. The boys had spoken idly, but hunted Grizel, who knew so much less and so much more than any of them, believed it all.

It was she who had stood so near Gavinia in the ruined house. She had only gone there to listen to human voices. When she discovered from the talk of her friends that she had left a light burning at Double Dykes and the door open, fear of the suspicions this might give rise to had sent her to the house on the heels of the two boys, and it was she who had stolen past them in the mist to put out the light and lock the door. Then she had returned to her mamma's side.

The doctor was among the listeners, almost the only dry-eyed one, but he was not dry-eyed because he felt the artless story least. Again and again he rose from his chair restlessly, and Grizel thought he scowled at her when he was really scowling at himself; as soon as she had finished he cleared the room brusquely of all intruders, and then he turned on her passionately.

"Think shame of yoursel'," he thundered, "for keeping me in the dark," and of course she took his words literally, though their full meaning was, "I shall scorn myself from this hour for not having won the poor child's confidence."

Oh, he was a hard man, Grizel thought, the hardest of them all. But she was used to standing up to hard men, and she answered, defiantly: "I did mean to tell you, that day you sent me with the bottle to Ballingall, I was waiting at the surgery door to tell you, but you were cruel, you said I was a thief, and then how could I tell you?"

This, too, struck home, and the doctor winced, but what he said was, "You fooled me for a whole week, and the town knows it; do you think I can forgive you for that?"

"I don't care whether you forgive me," replied Grizel at once.

"Nor do I care whether you care," he rapped out, all the time wishing he could strike himself; "but I'm the doctor of this place, and when your mother was ill you should have come straight to me. What had I done that you should be afraid of me?"

"I am not afraid of you," she replied, "I am not afraid of anyone, but mamma was afraid of you because she knew you had said cruel things about her, and I thought — I won't tell you what I thought." But with a little pressing she changed her mind and told him. "I was not sure whether you would come to see her, though I asked you, and if you came I knew you would tell her she was dying, and that would have made her scream. And that is not all, I thought you might tell her that she would be buried with a stake through her —"

"Oh, these blackguard laddies!" cried McQueen, clenching his fists.

"And so I dared not tell you," Grizel concluded calmly; "I am not frightened at you, but I was frightened you would hurt my dear darling mamma," and she went and stood defiantly between him and her mother.

The doctor moved up and down the room, crying, "How did I not know of this, why was I not told?" and he knew that the fault had been his own, and so was furious when Grizel told him so.

"Yes, it is," she insisted, "you knew mamma was an unhappy lady, and that the people shouted things against her and terrified her; and you must have known, for everybody knew, that she was sometimes silly and wandered about all night, and you are a big strong man, and so you should have been sorry for her; and if you had been sorry you would have come to see her and been kind to her, and then you would have found it all out."

"Have done, lassie!" he said, half angrily, half beseechingly, but she did not understand that he was suffering, and she went on, relentlessly: "And you knew that bad men used to come to see her at night-they have not come for a long time-but you never tried to stop their coming, and I could have stopped it if I had known they were bad; but I did not know at first, and I was only a little girl, and you should have told me."

"Have done!" It was all that he could say, for like many he had heard of men visiting the Painted Lady by stealth, and he had only wondered, with other gossips, who they were.

He crossed again to the side of the dead woman, "And Ballingall's was the only corpse you ever saw straiked?" he said in wonder, she had done her work so well. But he was not doubting her; he knew already that this girl was clothed in truthfulness.

"Was it you that kept this house so clean?" he asked, almost irritably, for he himself was the one undusted, neglected-looking thing in it, and he was suddenly conscious of his frayed wristband and of buttons hanging by a thread.

"Yes."

"What age are you?"

"I think I am thirteen."

He looked long at her, vindictively she thought, but he was only picturing the probable future of a painted lady's child, and he said mournfully to himself, "Ay, it does not even end here; and that's the crowning pity of it." But Grizel only heard him say, "Poor thing!" and she bridled immediately.

"I won't let you pity me," she cried.

"You dour brat!" he retorted. "But you need not think you are to have everything your own way still. I must get some Monypenny woman to take you till the funeral is over, and after that —"

"I won't go," said Grizel, determinedly, "I shall stay with mamma till she is buried."

He was not accustomed to contradiction, and he stamped his foot. "You shall do as you are told," he said.

"I won't!" replied Grizel, and she also stamped her foot.

"Very well, then, you thrawn tid, but at any rate I'll send in a woman to sleep with you."

"I want no one. Do you think I am afraid?"

"I think you will be afraid when you wake up in the darkness, and find yourself alone with-with it."

"I sha'n't, I shall remember at once that she is to be buried nicely in the cemetery, and that will make me happy."

"You unnatural —"

"Besides, I sha'n't sleep, I have something to do."

His curiosity again got the better of the doctor. "What can you have to do at such a time?" he demanded, and her reply surprised him:

"I am to make a dress."

"You!"

"I have made them before now," she said indignantly.

"But at such a time!"

"It is a black dress," she cried, "I don't have one, I am to make it out of mamma's."

He said nothing for some time, then "When did you think of this?"

"I thought of it weeks ago, I bought crape at the corner shop to be ready, and —"

She thought he was looking at her in horror, and stopped abruptly. "I don't care what you think," she said.

"What I do think," he retorted, taking up his hat, "is, that you are a most exasperating lassie. If I bide here another minute I believe you'll get round me."

"I don't want to get round you."

"Then what makes you say such things? I question if I'll get an hour's sleep to-night for thinking of you!"

"I don't want you to think of me!"

He groaned. "What could an untidy, hardened old single man like me do with you in his house?" he said. "Oh, you little limmer, to put such a thought into my head."

"I never did!" she exclaimed, indignantly.

"It began, I do believe it began," he sighed, "the first time I saw you easying Ballingall's pillows."

"What began?"

"You brat, you wilful brat, don't pretend ignorance. You set a trap to catch me, and —"

"Oh!" cried Grizel, and she opened the door quickly. "Go away, you horrid man," she said.

He liked her the more for this regal action, and therefore it enraged him. Sheer anxiety lest he should succumb to her on the spot was what made him bluster as he strode off, and "That brat of a Grizel," or "The Painted Lady's most unbearable lassie," or "The dour little besom" was his way of referring to her in company for days, but if any one agreed with him he roared "Don't be a fool, man, she's a wonder, she's a delight," or "You have a dozen yourself, Janet, but I wouldna neifer Grizel for the lot of them." And it was he, still denouncing her so long as he was contradicted, who persuaded the Auld Licht Minister to officiate at the funeral. Then he said to himself, "And now I wash my hands of her, I have done all that can be expected of me." He told himself this a great many times as if it were a medicine that must be taken frequently, and Grizel heard from Tommy, with whom she had some strange conversations, that he was going about denouncing her "up hill and down dale." But she did not care, she was so-so happy. For a hole was dug for the Painted Lady in the cemetery, just as if she had been a good woman, and Mr. Dishart conducted the service in Double Dykes before the removal of the body, nor did he say one word that could hurt Grizel, perhaps because his wife had drawn a promise from him. A large gathering of men followed the coffin, three of them because, as yon may remember, Grizel had dared them to stay away, but all the others out of sympathy with a motherless child who, as the procession started, rocked her arms in delight because her mamma was being buried respectably.

Being a woman, she could not attend the funeral, and so the chief mourner was Tommy, as you could see by the position he took at the grave, and by the white bands Grizel had sewn on his sleeves. He was looking very important, as if he had something remarkable in prospect, but little attention was given him until the cords were dropped into the grave, and a prayer offered up, when he pulled Mr. Dishart's coat and muttered something about a paper. Those who had been making ready to depart swung round again, and the minister told him if he had anything to say to speak out.

"It's a paper," Tommy said, nervous yet elated, and addressing all, "that Grizel put in the coffin. She told me to tell you about it when the cords fell on the lid."

"What sort of a paper?" asked Mr. Dishart, frowning.

"It's — it's a letter to God," Tommy gasped.

Nothing was to be heard except the shovelling of earth into the grave. "Hold your spade, John," the minister said to the gravedigger, and then even that sound stopped. "Go on," Mr. Dishart signed to the boy.

"Grizel doesna believe her mother has much chance of getting to heaven," Tommy said, "and she wrote the letter to God, so that when he opens the coffins on the last day he will find it and read about them."

"About whom?" asked the stern minister.

"About Grizel's father, for one. She doesna know his name, but the Painted Lady wore a locket wi' a picture of him on her breast, and it's buried wi' her, and Grizel told God to look at it so as to know him. She thinks her mother will be damned for having her, and that it winna be fair unless God damns her father too.”

“Go on,” said Mr. Dishart.

“There was three Thrums men —I think they were gentlemen —” Tommy continued, almost blithely, “that used to visit the Painted Lady in the night time afore she took ill. They wanted Grizel to promise no to tell about their going to Double Dykes, and she promised because she was ower innocent to know what they went for-but their names are in the letter.”

A movement in the crowd was checked by the minister’s uplifted arm. “Go on,” he cried.

“She wouldna tell me who they were, because it would have been breaking her promise,” said Tommy, “but” —he looked around him inquisitively —“but they’re here at the funeral.”

The mourners were looking sideways at each other, some breathing hard, but none dared to speak before the minister. He stood for a long time in doubt, but at last he signed to John to proceed with the filling in of the grave. Contrary to custom all remained. Not until the grave was again level with the sward did Mr. Dishart speak, and then it was with a gesture that appalled his hearers. “This grave,” he said, raising his arm, “is locked till the day of judgment.”

Leaving him standing there, a threatening figure, they broke into groups and dispersed, walking slowly at first, and then fast, to tell their wives.

Chapter XXXII
An Elopement

The solitary child remained at Double Dykes, awaiting the arrival of her father, for the Painted Lady's manner of leaving the world had made such a stir that the neighbors said he must have heard of it, even though he were in London, and if he had the heart of a stone he could not desert his bairn. They argued thus among themselves, less as people who were sure of it than to escape the perplexing question, what to do with Grizel if the man never claimed her? and before her they spoke of his coming as a certainty, because it would be so obviously the best thing for her. In the meantime they overwhelmed her with offers of everything she could need, which was kindly but not essential, for after the funeral expenses had been paid (Grizel insisted on paying them herself) she had still several gold pieces, found in her mamma's beautiful tortoise-shell purse, and there were nearly twenty pounds in the bank.

But day after day passed, and the man had not come. Perhaps he resented the Painted Lady's ostentatious death; which, if he was nicely strung, must have jarred upon his nerves. He could hardly have acknowledged Grizel now without publicity being given to his private concerns. Or he may never have heard of the Painted Lady's death, or if he read of it, he may not have known which painted lady in particular she was. Or he may have married, and told his wife all and she had forgiven him, which somehow, according to the plays and the novels, cuts the past adrift from a man and enables him to begin again at yesterday. Whatever the reason, Grizel's father was in no hurry to reveal himself, and though not to her, among themselves the people talked of the probability of his not coming at all. She could not remain alone at Double Dykes, they all admitted, but where, then, should she go? No fine lady in need of a handmaid seemed to think a painted lady's child would suit; indeed, Grizel at first sight had not the manner that attracts philanthropists. Once only did the problem approach solution; a woman in the Den-head was willing to take the child because (she expressed it) as she had seven she might as well have eight, but her man said no, he would not have his bairns fil't. Others would have taken her cordially for a few weeks or months, had they not known that at the end of this time they would be blamed, even by themselves, if they let her go. All, in short, were eager to show her kindness if one would give her a home, but where was that one to be found?

Much of this talk came to Grizel through Tommy, and she told him in the house of Double Dykes that people need not trouble themselves about her, for she had no wish to stay with them. It was only charity they brought her; no one wanted her for herself. "It is because I am a child of shame," she told him, dry-eyed.

He fidgeted on his chair, and asked, "What's that?" not very honestly.

"I don't know," she said, "no one will tell me, but it is something you can't love."

"You have a terrible wish to be loved," he said in wonder, and she nodded her head wistfully. "That is not what I wish for most of all, though," she told him, and when he asked what she wished for most of all, she said, "To love somebody; oh, it would be sweet!"

To Tommy, most sympathetic of mortals, she seemed a very pathetic little figure, and tears came to his eyes as he surveyed her; he could always cry very easily.

"If it wasna for Elspeth," he began, stammering, "I could love you, but you winna let a body do onything on the sly."

It was a vague offer, but she understood, and became the old Grizel at once. "I don't want you to love me," she said indignantly; "I don't think you know how to love."

"Neither can you know, then," retorted Tommy, huffily, "for there's nobody for you to love."

"Yes, there is," she said, "and I do love her and she loves me."

"But wha is she?"

"That girl." To his amazement she pointed to her own reflection in the famous mirror the size of which had scandalized Thrums. Tommy thought this affection for herself barely respectable, but he dared not say so lest he should be put to the door. "I love her ever so much," Grizel went on, "and she is so fond of me, she hates to see me unhappy. Don't look so sad, dearest, darlingest," she cried vehemently; "I love you, you know, oh, you sweet!" and with each epithet she kissed her reflection and looked defiantly at the boy.

"But you canna put your arms round her and hug her," he pointed out triumphantly, and so he had the last word after all. Unfortunately Grizel kept this side of her, new even to Tommy, hidden from all others, and her unresponsiveness lost her many possible friends. Even Miss Ailie, who now had a dressmaker in the blue-and-white room, sitting on a bedroom chair and sewing for her life (oh, the agony-or is it the rapture? —of having to decide whether to marry in gray with beads or brown plain to the throat), even sympathetic Miss Ailie, having met with several rebuffs, said that Grizel had a most unaffectionate nature, and, "Ay, she's hardy," agreed the town, "but it's better, maybe, for hersel'." There are none so unpopular as the silent ones.

If only Miss Ailie, or others like her, could have slipped noiselessly into Double Dykes at night, they would have found Grizel's pillow wet. But she would have heard them long before they reached the door, and jumped to the floor in terror, thinking it was her father's step at last. For, unknown to anyone, his coming, which the town so anxiously desired, was her one dread. She had told Tommy what she should say to him if he came, and Tommy had been awed and delighted, they were such scathing things; probably, had the necessity arisen, she would have found courage to say them, but they were made up in the daytime, and at night they brought less comfort. Then she listened fearfully and longed for the morning, wild ideas coursing through her head of flying before he could seize her; but when morning came it brought other thoughts, as of the strange remarks she had heard about her mamma and herself during the past few days. To brood over these was the most unhealthy occupation she could find, but it was her only birthright. Many of the remarks came unguardedly from lips that had no desire to pain her, others fell in a rage because she would not tell what were the names in her letter to God. The words that troubled her most, perhaps, were the doctor's, "She is a brave lass, but it must be in her blood." They were not intended for her ears, but she heard. "What did he mean?" she asked Miss Ailie, Mrs. Dishart, and others who came to see her, and they replied awkwardly, that it had only been a doctor's remark, of no importance to people who were well. "Then why are you crying?" she demanded, looking them full in the face with eyes there was no deceiving.

"Oh, why is everyone afraid to tell me the truth!" she would cry, beating her palms in anguish.

She walked into McQueen's surgery and said, "Could you not cut it out?" so abruptly that he wondered what she was speaking about.

"The bad thing that is in my blood," she explained. "Do cut it out, I sha'n't scream. I promise not to scream."

He sighed and answered, "If it could be cut out, lassie, I would try to do it, though it was the most dangerous of operations."

She looked in anguish at him. "There are cleverer doctors than you, aren't there?" she asked, and he was not offended.

"Ay, a hantle cleverer," he told her, "but none so clever as that. God help you, bairn, if you have to do it yourself some day."

"Can I do it myself?" she cried, brightening. "I shall do it now. Is it done with a knife?"

"With a sharper knife than a surgeon's," he answered, and then, regretting he had said so much, he tried to cheer her. But that he could not do. "You are afraid to tell me the truth too," she said, and when she went away he was very sorry for her, but not so sorry as she was for herself. "When I am grown up," she announced dolefully, to Tommy, "I shall be a bad woman, just like mamma."

"Not if you try to be good," he said.

"Yes, I shall. There is something in my blood that will make me bad, and I so wanted to be good. Oh! oh! oh!"

She told him of the things she had heard people say, but though they perplexed him almost as much as her, he was not so hopeless of learning their meaning, for here was just the kind of difficulty he liked to overcome. "I'll get it out o' Blinder," he said, with confidence in his ingenuity, "and then I'll tell you what he says." But however much he might strive to do so, Tommy could never repeat anything without giving it frills and other adornment of his own making, and Grizel knew this. "I must hear what he says myself," she insisted.

"But he winna speak plain afore you."

"Yes, he will, if he does not know I am there."

The plot succeeded, though only partially, for so quick was the blind man's sense of hearing that in the middle of the conversation he said, sharply, "Somebody's ahint the dyke!" and he caught Grizel by the shoulder. "It's the Painted Lady's lassie," he said when she screamed, and he stormed against Tommy for taking such advantage of his blindness. But to her he said, gently, "I daresay you egged him on to this, meaning well, but you maun forget most of what I've said, especially about being in the blood. I spoke in haste, it doesna apply to the like of you."

"Yes, it does," replied Grizel, and all that had been revealed to her she carried hot to the surgery, Tommy stopping at the door in as great perturbation as herself. "I know what being in the blood is now," she said, tragically, to McQueen, "there is something about it in the Bible. I am the child of evil passions, and that means that I was born with wickedness in my blood. It is lying sleeping in me just now because I am only thirteen, and if I can prevent its waking when I am grown up I shall always be good, but a very little thing will waken it; it wants so much to be wakened, and if it is once wakened it will run all through me, and soon I shall be like mamma."

It was all horribly clear to her, and she would not wait for words of comfort that could only obscure the truth. Accompanied by Tommy, who said nothing, but often glanced at her fascinated yet alarmed, as if expecting to see the ghastly change come over her at any moment- for he was as convinced as she, and had the livelier imagination-she returned to Monypenny to beg of Blinder to tell her one thing more. And he told her, not speaking lightly, but because his words contained a solemn warning to a girl who, he thought, might need it.

"What sort of thing would be likeliest to waken the wickedness?" she asked, holding her breath for the answer.

"Keeping company wi' ill men," said Blinder, gravely.

"Like the man who made mamma wicked, like my father?"

"Ay," Blinder replied, "fly from the like of him, my lass, though it should be to the other end of the world."

She stood quite still, with a most sorrowful face, and then ran away, ran so swiftly that when Tommy, who had lingered for a moment, came to the door she was already out of sight. Scarcely less excited than she, he set off for Double Dykes, his imagination in such a blaze that he looked fearfully in the pools of the burn for a black frock. But Grizel had not drowned herself; she was standing erect in her home, like one at bay, her arms rigid, her hands clenched, and when he pushed open the door she screamed.

"Grizel," said the distressed boy, "did you think I was him come for you?"

"Yes!"

"Maybe he'll no come. The folk think he winna come."

"But if he does, if he does!"

"Maybe you needna go wi' him unless you're willing?"

"I must, he can compel me, because he is my father. Oh! oh! oh!" She lay down on the bed, and on her eyes there slowly formed the little wells of water Tommy was to know so well in time. He stood by her side in anguish; for though his own tears came at the first call, he could never face them in others.

"Grizel," he said impulsively, "there's just one thing for you to do. You have money, and you maun run away afore he comes!"

She jumped up at that. "I have thought of it," she answered "I am always thinking about it, but how can I, oh, now can I? It would not be respectable."

"To run away?"

"To go by myself," said the poor girl, "and I do want to be respectable, it would be sweet."

In some ways Tommy was as innocent as she, and her reasoning seemed to him to be sound. She was looking at him woefully, and entreaty was on her face; all at once he felt what a lonely little crittur she was, and, in a burst of manhood, —

"But, dinna prig wi' me to go with you," he said, struggling.

"I have not!" she answered, panting, and she had not in words, but the mute appeal was still on her face.

"Grizel," he cried, "I'll come!"

Then she seized his hand and pressed it to her breast, saying, "Oh, Tommy, I am so fond of you!"

It was the first time she had admitted it, and his head wagged well content, as if saying for him, "I knew you would understand me some day." But next moment the haunting shadow that so often overtook him in the act of soaring fell cold upon his mind, and "I maun take Elspeth!" he announced, as if Elspeth had him by the leg.

"You sha'n't!" said Grizel's face.

"She winna let go," said Tommy's.

Grizel quivered from top to toe. "I hate Elspeth!" she cried, with curious passion, and the more moral Tommy was ashamed of her.

"You dinna ken how fond o' her I am," he said.

"Yes, I do."

"Then you shouldna want me to leave her and go wi' you."

"That is why I want it," Grizel blurted out, and now we are all ashamed of her. But fortunately Tommy did not see how much she had admitted in that hasty cry, and as neither would give way to the other they parted stiffly, his last words being "Mind, it wouldna be respectable to go by yoursel'," and hers "I don't care, I'm going." Nevertheless it was she who slept easily that night, and he who tossed about almost until cockcrow. She had only one ugly dream, of herself wandering from door to door in a strange town, asking for lodgings, but the woman who answered her weary knocks-there were many doors but it was invariably the same woman-always asked, suspiciously, "Is Tommy with you?" and Grizel shook her head, and then the woman drove her away, perceiving that she was not respectable. This woke her, and she feared the dream would come true, but she clenched her fists in the darkness, saying, "I can't help it, I am going, and I won't have Elspeth," and after that she slept in peace. In the meantime Tommy the imaginative-but that night he was not Tommy, rather was he Grizel, for he saw her as we can only see ourselves. Now she-or he, if you will-had been caught by her father and brought back, and she turned into a painted thing like her mother. She brandished a brandy bottle and a stream of foul words ran lightly from her mouth and suddenly stopped, because she was wailing "I wanted so to be good, it is sweet to be good!" Now a man with a beard was whipping her, and Tommy felt each lash on his own body, so that he had to strike out, and he started up in bed, and the horrible thing was that he had never been asleep. Thus it went on until early morning, when his eyes were red and his body was damp with sweat.

But now again he was Tommy, and at first even to think of leaving Elspeth was absurd. Yet it would be pleasant to leave Aaron, who disliked him so much. To disappear without a word would be a fine revenge, for the people would say that Aaron must have ill-treated him, and while they searched the pools of the burn for his body, Aaron would be looking on trembling, perhaps with a policeman's hand on his shoulder. Tommy saw the commotion as vividly as if the searchers were already out and he in a tree looking down at them; but in a second he also heard Elspeth skirling, and down he flung himself from the tree, crying, "I'm here, Elspeth, dinna greet; oh, what a brute I've been!" No, he could not leave Elspeth, how wicked of Grizel to expect it of him; she was a bad one, Grizel.

But having now decided not to go, his sympathy with the girl who was to lose him returned in a rush, and before he went to school he besought her to-it amounted to this, to be more like himself; that is, he begged her to postpone her departure indefinitely, not to make up her mind until to-morrow —or the day after-or the day after that. He produced reasons, as that she had only four pounds and some shillings now, while by and by she might get the Painted Lady's money, at present in the bank; also she ought to wait for the money that would come to her from the roup of the furniture. But Grizel waived all argument aside; secure in her four pounds and shillings she was determined to go to-night, for her father might be here to-morrow; she was going to London because it was so big that no one could ever find her there, and she would never, never write to Tommy to tell him how she fared, lest the letter put her father on her track. He implored her to write once, so that the money owing her might be forwarded, but even this bribe did not move her, and he set off for school most gloomily.

Cathro was specially aggravating that day, nagged him, said before the whole school that he was a numskull, even fell upon him with the tawse, and for no earthly reason except that Tommy would not bother his head with the *oratio obliqua*. If there is any kind of dominie more maddening than another, it is the one who will not leave you alone (ask any thoughtful boy). How wretched the lot of him whose life is cast among fools not capable of understanding him; what was that saying about entertaining angels unawares? London! Grizel had more than sufficient money to take two there, and once in London, a wonder such as himself was bound to do wondrous things. Now that he thought of it, to become a minister was abhorrent to him; to preach would be rather nice, oh, what things he should say (he began to make them up, and they were so grand that he almost wept), but to be good after the sermon was over, always to be good (even when Elspeth was out of the way), never to think queer unsayable things, never to say Stroke, never, in short, to "find a way" —he was appalled. If it had not been for Elspeth —

So even Elspeth did not need him. When he went home from school, thinking only of her, he found that she had gone to the Auld Licht manse to play with little Margaret. Very well, if such was her wish, he would go. Nobody wanted him except Grizel. Perhaps when news came from London of his greatness, they would think more of him. He would send a letter to Thrums, asking Mr. McLean to transfer his kindness to Elspeth. That would show them what a noble fellow he was. Elspeth would really benefit by his disappearance; he was running away for Elspeth's sake. And when he was great, which would be in a few years, he would come back for her.

But no, he —. The dash represents Tommy swithering once more, and he was at one or other end of the swither all day. When he acted sharply it was always on impulse, and as soon as the die was cast he was a philosopher with no regrets. But when he had time to reflect, he jumped miserably back and forward. So when Grizel was ready to start, he did not know in the least what he meant to do.

She was to pass by the Cuttle Well, on her way to Tilliedrum, where she would get the London train, he had been told coldly, and he could be there at the time-if he liked. The time was seven o'clock in the evening on a week-day, when the lovers are not in the Den, and Tommy arrived first. When he stole through the small field that separates Monypenny from the Den, his decision was-but on reaching the Cuttle Well, its nearness to the uncanny Lair chilled his courage, and now he had only come to bid her good-by. She was very late, and it suddenly struck him that she had already set off. "After getting me to promise to go wi' her!" he said to himself at once.

But Grizel came; she was only late because it had taken her such a long time to say good-by to the girl in the glass. She was wearing her black dress and lustre jacket, and carried in a bundle the few treasures she was taking with her, and though she did not ask Tommy if he was coming, she cast a quick look round to see if he had a bundle anywhere, and he had none. That told her his decision, and she would have liked to sit down for a minute and cry, but of course she had too much pride, and she bade him farewell so promptly that he thought he had a grievance. "I'm coming as far as the toll-house wi' you," he said, sulkily, and so they started together.

At the toll-house Grizel stopped. "It's a fine night," said Tommy, almost apologetically, "I'll go as far as the quarry o' Benshee."

When they came to the quarry he said, "We're no half-roads yet, I'll go wi' you as far as Padanarum." Now she began to wonder and to glance at him sideways, which made him more uncomfortable than ever. To prevent her asking him a question for which he had no answer, he said, "What makes you look so little the day?"

"I am not looking little," she replied, greatly annoyed, "I am looking taller than usual. I have let down my frock three inches so as to look taller-and older."

"You look younger than ever," he said cruelly.

"I don't! I look fifteen, and when you are fifteen you grow up very quickly. Do say I look older!" she entreated anxiously. "It would make me feel more respectable."

But he shook his head with surprising obstinacy, and then she began to remark on his clothes, which had been exercising her curiosity ever since they left the Den.

"How is it that you are looking so stout?" she asked.

"I feel cold, but you are wiping the sweat off your face every minute."

It was true, but he would have preferred not to answer. Grizel's questions, however, were all so straight in the face, that there was no dodging them. "I have on twa suits o' clothes, and a' my sarks," he had to admit, sticky and sullen.

She stopped, but he trudged on doggedly. She ran after him and gave his arm an impulsive squeeze with both hands, "Oh, you sweet!" she said.

"No, I'm not," he answered in alarm.

"Yes you are! You are coming with me."

"I'm not!"

"Then why did you put on so many clothes?"

Tommy swithered wretchedly on one foot. "I didna put them on to come wi' you," he explained, "I just put them on in case I should come wi' you."

"And are you not coming?"

"How can I ken?"

"But you must decide," Grizel almost screamed.

"I needna," he stammered, "till we're at Tilliedrum. Let's speak about some other thing."

She rocked her arms, crying, "It is so easy to make up one's mind."

"It's easy to you that has just one mind," he retorted with spirit, "but if you had as many minds as I have —!"

On they went.

Chapter XXXIII
There is Some One to Love Grizel at Last

Corp was sitting on the Monypenny dyke, spitting on a candlestick and then rubbing it briskly against his orange-colored trousers. The doctor passing in his gig, both of them streaked, till they blended, with the mud of Look-about-you road (through which you should drive winking rapidly all the way), saw him and drew up.

"Well, how is Grizel?" he asked. He had avoided Double Dykes since the funeral, but vain had been his attempts to turn its little inmate out of his mind; there she was, against his will, and there, he now admitted to himself angrily or with a rueful sigh, she seemed likely to remain until someone gave her a home. It was an almost ludicrous distrust of himself that kept him away from her; he feared that if he went to Double Dykes her lonely face would complete his conquest. For oh, he was reluctant to be got the better of, as he expressed it to himself. Maggy Ann, his maid, was the ideal woman for a bachelor's house. When she saw him coming she fled, guiltily concealing the hated duster; when he roared at her for announcing that dinner was ready, she left him to eat it half cold; when he spilled matches on the floor and then stepped upon them and set the rug on fire, she let him tell her that she should be more careful; she did not carry off his favorite boots to the cobbler because they were down at heel; she did not fling up her arms in horror and cry that she had brushed that coat just five minutes ago; nor did she count the treasured "dottels" on the mantelpiece to discover how many pipes he had smoked since morning; nor point out that he had stepped over the door-mat; nor line her shelves with the new *Mentor*; nor give him up his foot for sitting half the night with patients who could not pay-in short, he knew the ways of the limmers, and Maggy Ann was a jewel. But it had taken him a dozen years to bring her to this perfection, and well he knew that the curse of Eve, as he called the rage for the duster, slumbered in her rather than was extinguished. With the volcanic Grizel in the house, Maggy Ann would once more burst into flame, and the horrified doctor looked to right of him, to left of him, before him and behind him, and everywhere he seemed to see two new brooms bearing down. No, the brat, he would not have her; the besom, why did she bother him; the witches take her, for putting the idea into his head, nailing it into his head indeed. But nevertheless he was forever urging other people to adopt her, assuring them that they would find her a treasure, and even shaking his staff at them when they refused; and he was so uneasy if he did not hear of her several times a day that he made Monypenny the way to and from everywhere, so that he might drop into artful talk with those who had seen her last. Corp, accordingly, was not surprised at his "How is Grizel?" now, and he answered, between two spits, "She's fine; she gave me this."

It was one of the Painted Lady's silver candlesticks, and the doctor asked sharply why Grizel had given it to him.

"She said because she liked me," Corp replied, wonderingly. "She brought it to my auntie's door soon after I loused, and put it into my hand: ay, and she had a blue shawl, and she telled me to give it to Gavinia, because she liked her too."

"What else did she say?"

Corp tried to think. "I said, 'This cows, Grizel, but thank you kindly,'" he answered, much pleased with his effort of memory, but the doctor interrupted him rudely. "Nobody wants to hear what you said, you dottrel; what more did she say?" And thus encouraged Corp remembered that she had said she hoped he would not forget her. "What for should I forget her when I see her ilka day?" he asked, and was probably about to divulge that this was his reply to her, but without waiting for more, McQueen turned his beast's head and drove to the entrance to the Double Dykes. Here he alighted and hastened up the path on foot, but before he reached the house he met Dite Deuchars taking his ease beneath a tree, and Dite could tell him that Grizel was not at home. "But there's somebody in Double Dykes," he said, "though I kenna wha could be there unless it's the ghost of the Painted Lady hersel'. About an hour syne I saw Grizel come out o' the house, carrying a bundle, but she hadna gone many yards when she turned round and waved her hand to the east window. I couldna see wha was at it, but there maun have been somebody, for first the crittur waved to the window and next she kissed her hand to it, and syne she went on a bit, and syne she ran back close to the window and nodded and flung more kisses, and back and forrit she went a curran times as if she could hardly tear hersel' awa'. 'Wha's that you're so chief wi'?' I speired when she came by me at last, but she just said, 'I won't tell you,' in her dour wy, and she hasna come back yet."

Whom could she have been saying good-by to so demonstratively, and whither had she gone? With a curiosity that for the moment took the place of his uneasiness, McQueen proceeded to the house, the door of which was shut but not locked. Two glances convinced him that there was no one here, the kitchen was as he had seen it last, except that the long mirror had been placed on a chair close to the east window. The doctor went to the outside of the window, and looked in, he could see nothing but his own reflection in the mirror, and was completely puzzled. But it was no time, he felt, for standing there scratching his head, when there was reason to fear that the girl had gone. Gone where? He saw his selfishness now, in a glaring light, and it fled out of him pursued by curses.

He stopped at Aaron's door and called for Tommy, but Tommy had left the house an hour ago. "Gone with her, the sacket; he very likely put her up to this," the doctor muttered, and the surmise seemed justified when he heard that Grizel and Tommy had been seen passing the Fens. That they were running away had never struck those who saw them, and McQueen said nothing of his suspicions, but off he went in his gig on their track and ran them down within a mile of Tilliedrum. Grizel scurried on, thinking it was undoubtedly her father, but in a few minutes the three were conversing almost amicably, the doctor's first words had been so "sweet."

Tommy explained that they were out for a walk, but Grizel could not lie, and in a few passionate sentences she told McQueen the truth. He had guessed the greater part of it, and while she spoke he looked so sorry for her, such a sweet change had come over his manner, that she held his hand.

"But you must go no farther," he told her, "I am to take you back with me," and that alarmed her. "I won't go back," she said, determinedly, "he might come."

"There's little fear of his coming," McQueen assured her, gently, "but if he does come I give you my solemn word that I won't let him take you away unless you want to go."

Even then she only wavered, but he got her altogether with this: "And should he come, just think what a piece of your mind you could give him, with me standing by holding your hand."

"Oh, would you do that?" she asked, brightening.

"I would do a good deal to get the chance," he said.

"I should just love it!" she cried. "I shall come now," and she stepped light-heartedly into the gig, where the doctor joined her. Tommy, who had been in the background all this time, was about to jump up beside them, but McQueen waved him back, saying maliciously, "There's just room for two, my man, so I won't interfere with your walk."

Tommy, in danger of being left, very hot and stout and sulky, whimpered, "What have I done to anger you?"

"You were going with her, you blackguard," replied McQueen, not yet in full possession of the facts, for whether Tommy was or was not going with her no one can ever know.

"If I was," cried the injured boy, "it wasna because I wanted to go, it was because it wouldna have been respectable for her to go by hersel'."

The doctor had already started his shalt, but at these astonishing words he drew up sharply. "Say that again," ha said, as if thinking that his ears must have deceived him, and Tommy repeated his remark, wondering at its effect.

"And you tell me that you were going with her," the doctor repeated, "to make her enterprise more respectable?" and he looked from one to the other.

"Of course I was," replied Tommy, resenting his surprise at a thing so obvious; and "That's why I wanted him to come," chimed in Grizel.

Still McQueen's glance wandered from the boy to the girl and from the girl to the boy. "You are a pair!" he said at last, and he signed in silence to Tommy to mount the gig. But his manner had alarmed Grizel, ever watching herself lest she should stray into the ways of bad ones, and she asked anxiously, "There was nothing wrong in it, was there?"

"No," the doctor answered gravely, laying his hand on hers, "no, it was just sweet."

* * * * *

What McQueen had to say to her was not for Tommy's ears, and the conversation was but a makeshift until they reached Thrums, where he sent the boy home, recommending him to hold his tongue about the escapade (and Tommy of course saw the advisability of keeping it from Elspeth); but he took Grizel into his parlor and set her down on the buffet stool by the fire, where he surveyed her in silence at his leisure. Then he tried her in his old armchair, then on his sofa; then he put the *Mentor* into her hand and told her to hold it as if it were a duster, then he sent her into the passage, with instructions to open the door presently and announce "Dinner is ready;" then he told her to put some coals on the fire; then he told her to sit at the window, first with an open book in her hand, secondly as if she was busy knitting; and all these things she did wondering exceedingly, for he gave no explanation except the incomprehensible one, "I want to see what it would be like."

She had told him in the gig why she had changed the position of the mirror at Double Dykes, it was to let "that darling" wave good-by to her from the window; and now having experimented with her in his parlor he drew her toward his chair, so that she stood between his knees. And he asked her if she understood why he had gone to Double Dykes.

"Was it to get me to tell you what were the names in the letter?" she said, wistfully. "That is what everyone asks me, but I won't tell, no, I won't;" and she closed her mouth hard.

He, too, would have liked to hear the names, and he sighed, it must be admitted, at sight of that determined mouth, but he could say truthfully, "Your refusal to break your promise is one of the things that I admire in you."

Admire! Grizel could scarce believe that this gift was for her. "You don't mean that you really like me?" she faltered, but she felt sure all the time that he did, and she cried, "Oh, but why, oh, how can you!"

"For one reason," he said, "because you are so good."

"Good! Oh! oh! oh!" She clapped her hands joyously.

"And for another-because you are so brave."

"But I am not really brave," she said anxiously, yet resolved to hide nothing, "I only pretend to be brave, I am often frightened, but I just don't let on."

That, he told her, is the highest form of bravery, but Grizel was very, very tired of being brave, and she insisted impetuously, "I don't want to be brave, I want to be afraid, like other girls."

"Ay, it's your right, you little woman," he answered, tenderly, and then again he became mysterious. He kicked off his shoes to show her that he was wearing socks that did not match. "I just pull on the first that come to hand," he said recklessly.

"Oh!" cried Grizel.

On his dusty book-shelves he wrote, with his finger, "Not dusted since the year One."

"Oh! oh!" she cried.

He put his fingers through his gray, untidy hair. "That's the only comb I have that is at hand when I want it," he went on, regardless of her agony.

"All the stud-holes in my shirts," he said, "are now so frayed and large that the studs fall out, and I find them in my socks at night."

Oh! oh! he was killing her, he was, but what cared he? "Look at my clothes," said the cruel man, "I read when I'm eating, and I spill so much gravy that-that we boil my waistcoat once a month, and make soup of it!"

To Grizel this was the most tragic picture ever drawn by man, and he saw that it was time to desist. "And it's all," he said, looking at her sadly, "it's all because I am a lonely old bachelor

161

with no womankind to look after him, no little girl to brighten him when he comes home dog-tired, no one to care whether his socks are in holes and his comb behind the wash-stand, no soft hand to soothe his brow when it aches, no one to work for, no one to love, many a one to close the old bachelor's eyes when he dies, but none to drop a tear for him, no one to —"

"Oh! oh! oh! That is just like me. Oh! oh!" cried Grizel, and he pulled her closer to him, saying, "The more reason we should join thegither; Grizel, if you don't take pity on me, and come and bide with me and be my little housekeeper, the Lord Almighty only knows what is to become of the old doctor."

At this she broke away from him, and stood far back pressing her arms to her sides, and she cried, "It is not out of charity you ask me, is it?" and then she went a little nearer. "You would not say it if it wasn't true, would you?"

"No, my dawtie, it's true," he told her, and if he had been pitying himself a little, there was an end of that now.

She remembered something and cried joyously, "And you knew what was in my blood before you asked me, so I don't need to tell you, do I? And you are not afraid that I shall corrupt you, are you? And you don't think it a pity I didn't die when I was a tiny baby, do you? Some people think so, I heard them say it."

"What would have become of me?" was all he dared answer in words, but he drew her to him again, and when she asked if it was true, as she had heard some woman say, that in some matters men were all alike, and did what that one man had done to her mamma, he could reply solemnly, "No, it is not true; it's a lie that has done more harm than any war in any century."

She sat on his knee, telling him many things that had come recently to her knowledge but were not so new to him. The fall of woman was the subject, a strange topic for a girl of thirteen and a man of sixty. They don't become wicked in a moment, he learned; if they are good to begin with, it takes quite a long time to make them bad. Her mamma was good to begin with. "I know she was good, because when she thought she was the girl she used to be, she looked sweet and said lovely things." The way the men do is this, they put evil thoughts into the woman's head, and say them often to her, till she gets accustomed to them, and thinks they cannot be bad when the man she loves likes them, and it is called corrupting the mind.

"And then a baby comes to them," Grizel said softly, "and it is called a child of shame. I am a child of shame."

He made no reply, so she looked up, and his face was very old and sad. "I am sorry too," she whispered, but still he said nothing, and then she put her fingers on his eyes to discover if they were wet, and they were wet. And so Grizel knew that there was someone who loved her at last.

The mirror was the only article of value that Grizel took with her to her new home; everything else was rouped at the door of Double Dykes; Tommy, who should have been at his books, acting as auctioneer's clerk for sixpence. There are houses in Thrums where you may still be told who got the bed and who the rocking-chair, and how Nether Drumgley's wife dared him to come home without the spinet; but it is not by the sales that the roup is best remembered. Curiosity took many persons into Double Dykes that day, and in the room that had never been furnished they saw a mournful stack of empty brandy bottles, piled there by the auctioneer who had found them in every corner, beneath the bed, in presses, in boxes, whither they had been thrust by Grizel's mamma, as if to conceal their number from herself. The counting of these bottles was a labor, but it is not even by them that the roup is remembered. Among them some sacrilegious hands found a bundle of papers with a sad blue ribbon round them. They were the Painted Lady's love-letters, the letters she had written to the man. Why or how they had come back to her no one knew.

Most of them were given to Grizel, but a dozen or more passed without her leave into the kists of various people, where often since then they have been consulted by swains in need of a pretty phrase; and Tommy's school-fellows, the very boys and girls who hooted the Painted Lady, were in time-so oddly do things turn out-to be among those whom her letters taught how to woo. Where the kists did not let in the damp or careless fingers, the paper long remained clean, the ink but little faded. Some of the letters were creased, as if they had once been much folded, perhaps for slipping into secret hiding-places, but none of them bore any address or a date. "To my beloved," was sometimes written on the cover, and inside he was darling or beloved again. So no one could have arranged them in the order in which they were written, though there was a three-cornered one which said it was the first. There was a violet in it, clinging to the paper as if they were fond of each other, and Grizel's mamma had written, "The violet is me, hiding in a corner because I am so happy." The letters were in many moods, playful, reflective, sad, despairing, arch, but all were written in an ecstasy of the purest love, and most of them were cheerful, so that you seemed to see the sun dancing on the paper while she wrote, the same sun that afterwards showed up her painted cheeks. Why they came back to her no one ever discovered, any more than how she who slipped the violet into that three-cornered one and took it out to kiss again and wrote, "It is my first love-letter, and I love it so much I am reluctant to let it go," became in a few years the derision of the Double Dykes. Some of these letters may be in old kists still, but whether that is so or not, they alone have passed the Painted Lady's memory from one generation to another, and they have purified it, so that what she was died with her vile body, and what she might have been lived on, as if it were her true self.

Chapter XXXIV
Who Told Tommy to Speak

"Miss Alison Cray presents her compliments to-and requests the favor of their company at her marriage with Mr. Ivie McLean, on January 8th, at six o'clock."

Tommy in his Sabbath clothes, with a rose from the Dovecot hot-house for buttonhole (which he slipped into his pocket when he saw other boys approaching), delivered them at the doors of the aristocracy, where, by the way, he had been a few weeks earlier, with another circular.

"Miss Alison Cray being about to give up school, has pleasure in stating that she has disposed of the good-will of her establishment to Miss Jessy Langlands and Miss S. Oram, who will enter upon their scholastic duties on January 9th, at Hoods Cottage, where she most cordially," and so on.

Here if the writer dared (but you would be so angry) he would introduce at the length of a chapter two brand-new characters, the Misses Langlands and Oram, who suddenly present themselves to him in the most sympathetic light. Miss Ailie has been safely stowed to port, but their little boat is only setting sail, and they are such young ones, neither out of her teens, that he would fain turn for a time from her to them. Twelve pounds they paid for the good-will, and, oh, the exciting discussions, oh, the scraping to get the money together! If little Miss Langlands had not been so bold, big Miss Oram must have drawn back, but if Miss Oram had not had that idea about a paper partition, of what avail the boldness of Miss Langlands? How these two trumps of girls succeeded in hiring the Painted Lady's spinet from Nether Drumgley-in the absence of his wife, who on her way home from buying a cochin-china met the spinet in a cart-how the mother of one of them, realizing in a klink that she was common no more, henceforth wore black caps instead of mutches (but the father dandered on in the old plebeian way), what the enterprise meant to a young man in distant Newcastle, whose favorite name was Jessy, how the news travelled to still more distant Canada, where a family of emigrants which had left its Sarah behind in Thrums, could talk of nothing else for weeks-it is hard to have to pass on without dwelling on these things, and indeed-but pass on we must.

The chief figure at the wedding of Miss Ailie was undoubtedly Mr. T. Sandys. When one remembers his prominence, it is difficult to think that the wedding could have taken place without him. It was he (in his Sabbath clothes again, and now flaunting his buttonhole brazenly) who in insulting language ordered the rabble to stand back there. It was he who dashed out to the 'Sosh to get a hundred ha'pennies for the fifty pennies Mr. McLean had brought to toss into the air. It was he who went round in the carriage to pick up the guests and whisked them in and out, and slammed the door, and saw to it that the minister was not kept waiting, and warned Miss Ailie that if she did not come now they should begin without her. It was he who stood near her with a handkerchief ready in his hand lest she took to crying on her new brown silk (Miss Ailie was married in brown silk after all). As a crown to his audacity, it was he who told Mr. Dishart, in the middle of a noble passage, to mind the lamp.

These duties were Dr. McQueen's, the best man, but either demoralized by the bridegroom, who went all to pieces at the critical moment and was much more nervous than the bride, or in terror lest Grizel, who had sent him to the wedding speckless and most beautifully starched, should suddenly appear at the door and cry, "Oh, oh, take your fingers off your shirt!" he was through other till the knot was tied, and then it was too late, for Tommy had made his mark. It was Tommy who led the way to the school-room, where the feast was ready, it was Tommy who put the guests in their places (even the banker cringed to him), it was. Tommy who winked to Mr. Dishart as a sign to say grace. As you will readily believe, Miss Ailie could not endure the thought of excluding her pupils from the festivities, and they began to arrive as soon as the tables had been cleared of all save oranges and tarts and raisins. Tommy, waving Gavinia aside, showed them in, and one of them, curious to tell, was Corp, in borrowed blacks, and Tommy shook hands with him and called him Mr. Shiach, both new experiences to Corp, who knocked over a table in his anxiety to behave himself, and roared at intervals "Do you see the little deevil!" and bit his warts and then politely swallowed the blood.

As if oranges and tarts and raisins were not enough, came the Punch and Judy show, Tommy's culminating triumph. All the way to Redlintie had Mr. McLean sent for the Punch and Judy show, and nevertheless there was a probability of no performance, for Miss Ailie considered the show immoral. Most anxious was she to give pleasure to her pupils, and this she knew was the best way, but how could she countenance an entertainment which was an encouragement to every form of vice and crime? To send these children to the Misses Langlands and Oram, fresh from an introduction to the comic view of murder! It could not be done, now could it? Mr. McLean could make no suggestion. Mr. Dishart thought it would be advisable to substitute another entertainment; was there not a game called "The Minister's Cat"? Mrs. Dishart thought they should have the show and risk the consequences. So also thought Dr. McQueen. The banker was consulted, but saw no way out of the difficulty, nor did the lawyer, nor did the Misses Finlayson. Then Tommy appeared on the scene, and presently retired to find a way.

He found it. The performance took place, and none of the fun was omitted, yet neither Miss Ailie-tuts, tuts Mrs. McLean-nor Mr. Dishart could disapprove. Punch did chuck his baby out at the window (roars of laughter) in his jovial time-honored way, *but* immediately thereafter up popped the showman to say, "Ah, my dear boys and girls, let this be a lesson to you never to destroy your offsprings. Oh, shame on Punch, for to do the wicked deed; he will be catched in the end and serve him right." Then when Mr. Punch had wolloped his wife with the stick, amid thunders of applause, up again bobbed the showman, "Ah, my dear boys and girls, what a lesson is this we sees, what goings on is this? He have bashed the head of her as should ha' been the apple of his eye, and he does not care a —he does not care; but mark my words, his home it will now be desolate, no more shall she meet him at his door with kindly smile, he have done for her quite, and now he is a hunted man. Oh, be warned by his sad igsample, and do not bash the head of your loving wife." And there was a great deal more of the same, and simple Mrs. McLean almost wept tears of joy because her favorite's good heart had suggested these improvements.

Grizel was not at the wedding; she was invited, but could not go because she was in mourning. But only her parramatty frock was in mourning, for already she had been the doctor's housekeeper for two full months, and her father had not appeared to plague her (he never did appear, it may be told at once), and so how could her face be woeful when her heart leapt with gladness? Never had prisoner pined for the fields more than this reticent girl to be frank, and she poured out her inmost self to the doctor, so that daily he discovered something beautiful (and exasperating) about womanhood. And it was his love for her that had changed her. "You do love me, don't you?" she would say, and his answer might be "I have told you that fifty times already;" to which she would reply, gleefully, "That is not often, I say it all day to myself."

Exasperating? Yes, that was the word. Long before summer came, the doctor knew that he had given himself into the hands of a tyrant. It was idle his saying that this irregularity and that carelessness were habits that had become part of him; she only rocked her arms impatiently, and if he would not stand still to be put to rights, then she would follow him along the street, brushing him as he walked, a sight that was witnessed several times while he was in the mutinous stage.

"Talk about masterfulness," he would say, when she whipped off his coat or made a dart at the mud on his trousers; "you are the most masterful little besom I ever clapped eyes on."

But as he said it he perhaps crossed his legs, and she immediately cried, "You have missed two holes in lacing your boots!"

Of a morning he would ask her sarcastically to examine him from top to toe and see if he would do, and examine him she did, turning him round, pointing out that he had been sitting "again" on his tails, that oh, oh, he must have cut that buttonhole with his knife. He became most artful in hiding deficiencies from her, but her suspicions once roused would not sleep, and all subterfuge was vain. "Why have you buttoned your coat up tight to the throat to-day?" she would demand sternly.

"It is such a cold morning," he said.

"That is not the reason," she replied at once (she could see through broadcloth at a glance), "I believe you have on the old necktie again, and you promised to buy a new one."

"I always forget about it when I'm out," he said humbly, and next evening he found on his table a new tie, made by Grizel herself out of her mamma's rokelay.

It was related by one who had dropped in at the doctor's house unexpectedly, that he found Grizel making a new shirt, and forcing the doctor to try on the sleeves while they were still in the pin stage.

She soon knew his every want, and just as he was beginning to want it, there it was at his elbow. He realized what a study she had made of him when he heard her talking of his favorite dishes and his favorite seat, and his way of biting his underlip when in thought, and how hard he was on his left cuff. It had been one of his boasts that he had no favorite dishes, etc., but he saw now that he had been a slave to them for years without knowing it.

She discussed him with other mothers as if he were her little boy, and he denounced her for it. But all the time she was spoiling him. Formerly he had got on very well when nothing was in its place. Now he roared helplessly if he mislaid his razor.

He was determined to make a lady of her, which necessitated her being sent to school; she preferred hemming, baking and rubbing things till they shone, and not both could have had their way (which sounds fatal for the man), had they not arranged a compromise, Grizel, for instance, to study geography for an hour in the evening with Miss Langlands (go to school in the daytime she would not) so long as the doctor shaved every morning, but if no shave no geography; the doctor to wipe his pen on the blot-sheet instead of on the lining of his coat if she took three lessons a week from Miss Oram on the spinet. How happy and proud she was! Her glee was a constant source of wonder to McQueen. Perhaps she put on airs a little, her walk, said the critical, had become a strut; but how could she help that when the new joyousness of living was dancing and singing within her?

Had all her fears for the future rolled away like clouds that leave no mark behind? The doctor thought so at times, she so seldom spoke of them to him; he did not see that when they came she hid them from him because she had discovered that they saddened him. And she had so little time to brood, being convinced of the sinfulness of sitting still, that if the clouds came suddenly, they never stayed long save once, and then it was, mayhap, as well. The thunderclap was caused by Tommy, who brought it on unintentionally and was almost as much scared by his handiwork as Grizel herself. She and he had been very friendly of late, partly because they shared with McQueen the secret of the frustrated elopement, partly because they both thought that in that curious incident Tommy had behaved in a most disinterested and splendid way. Grizel had not been sure of it at first, but it had grown on Tommy, he had so thoroughly convinced himself of his intention to get into the train with her at Tilliedrum that her doubts were dispelled-easily dispelled, you say, but the truth must be told, Grizel was very anxious to be rid of them. And Tommy's were honest convictions, born full grown of a desire for happiness to all. Had Elspeth discovered how nearly he had deserted her, the same sentiment would have made him swear to her with tears that never should he have gone farther than Tilliedrum, and while he was persuading her he would have persuaded himself. Then again, when he met Grizel-well, to get him in doubt it would have been necessary to catch him on the way between these two girls.

So Tommy and Grizel were friends, and finding that it hurt the doctor to speak on a certain subject to him, Grizel gave her confidences to Tommy. She had a fear, which he shared on its being explained to him, that she might meet a man of the stamp of her father, and grow fond of him before she knew the kind he was, and as even Tommy could not suggest an infallible test which would lay them bare at the first glance, he consented to consult Blinder once more. He found the blind man by his fire-side, very difficult to coax into words on the important topic, but Tommy's "You've said ower much no to tell a bit more," seemed to impress him, and he answered the question, —

"You said a woman should fly frae the like o' Grizel's father though it should be to the other end of the world, but how is she to ken that he's that kind?"

"She'll ken," Blinder answered after thinking it over, "if she likes him and fears him at one breath, and has a sort of secret dread that he's getting a power ower her that she canna resist."

These words were a flash of light on a neglected corner to Tommy. "Now I see, now I ken," he exclaimed, amazed; "now I ken what my mother meant! Blinder, is that no the kind of man that's called masterful?"

"It's what poor women find them and call them to their cost," said Blinder.

Tommy's excitement was prodigious. "Now I ken, now I see!" he cried, slapping his leg and stamping up and down the room.

"Sit down!" roared his host.

"I canna," retorted the boy. "Oh, to think o't, to think I came to speir that question at you, to think her and me has wondered what kind he was, and I kent a' the time!" Without staying to tell Blinder what he was blethering about, he hurried off to Grizel, who was waiting for him in the Den, and to her he poured out his astonishing news.

"I ken all about them, I've kent since afore I came to Thrums, but though I generally say the prayer, I've forgot to think o' what it means." In a stampede of words he told her all he could remember of his mother's story as related to him on a grim night in London so long ago, and she listened eagerly. And when that was over, he repeated first his prayer and then Elspeth's, "O God, whatever is to be my fate, may I never be one of them that bow the knee to masterful man, and if I was born like that and canna help it, O take me up to heaven afore I'm fil't." Grizel repeated it after him until she had it by heart, and even as she said it a strange thing happened, for she began to draw back from Tommy, with a look of terror on her face.

"What makes you look at me like that?" he cried.

"I believe —I think-you are masterful," she gasped.

"Me!" he retorted indignantly.

"Now," she went on, waving him back, "now I know why I would not give in to you when you wanted me to be Stroke's wife. I was afraid you were masterful!"

"Was that it?" cried Tommy.

"Now," she proceeded, too excited to heed his interruptions, "now I know why I would not kiss your hand, now I know why I would not say I liked you. I was afraid of you, I —"

"Were you?" His eyes began to sparkle, and something very like rapture was pushing the indignation from his face. "Oh, Grizel, have I a power ower you?"

"No, you have not," she cried passionately. "I was just frightened that you might have. Oh, oh, I know you now!"

"To think o't, to think o't!" he crowed, wagging his head, and then she clenched her fist, crying, "Oh, you wicked, you should cry with shame!"

But he had his answer ready, "It canna be my wite, for I never kent o't till you told me. Grizel, it has just come about without either of us kenning!"

She shuddered at this, and then seized him by the shoulders. "It has not come about at all," she said, "I was only frightened that it might come, and now it can't come, for I won't let it."

"But can you help yoursel'?"

"Yes, I can. I shall never be friends with you again."

She had such a capacity for keeping her word that this alarmed him, and he did his best to extinguish his lights. "I'm no masterful, Grizel," he said, "and I dinna want to be, it was just for a minute that I liked the thought." She shook her head, but his next words had more effect. "If I had been that kind, would I have teached you Elspeth's prayer?"

"N-no, I don't think so," she said slowly, and perhaps he would have succeeded in soothing her, had not a sudden thought brought back the terror to her face.

"What is 't now?" he asked.

"Oh, oh, oh!" she cried, "and I nearly went away with you!" and without another word she fled from the Den. She never told the doctor of this incident, and in time it became a mere shadow in the background, so that she was again his happy housekeeper, but that was because she had found strength to break with Tommy. She was only an eager little girl, pathetically ignorant about what she wanted most to understand, but she saw how an instinct had been fighting for her, and now it should not have to fight alone. How careful she became! All Tommy's wiles were vain, she would scarcely answer if he spoke to her; if he had ever possessed a power over her it was gone, Elspeth's prayer had saved her.

Jean Myles had told Tommy to teach that prayer to Elspeth; but who had told him to repeat it to Grizel?

Chapter XXXV
The Branding of Tommy

Grizel's secession had at least one good effect: it gave Tommy more time in which to make a scholar of himself. Would you like a picture of Tommy trying to make a scholar of himself?

They all helped him in their different ways: Grizel, by declining his company; Corp, by being far away at Look-about-you, adding to the inches of a farm-house; Aaron Latta, by saying nothing but looking "college or the herding;" Mr. McLean, who had settled down with Ailie at the Dovecot, by inquiries about his progress; Elspeth by-but did Elspeth's talks with him about how they should live in Aberdeen and afterwards (when they were in the big house) do more than send his mind a-galloping (she holding on behind) along roads that lead not to Aberdeen? What drove Tommy oftenest to the weary drudgery was, perhaps, the alarm that came over him when he seemed of a sudden to hear the names of the bursars proclaimed and no Thomas Sandys among them. Then did he shudder, for well he knew that Aaron would keep his threat, and he hastily covered the round table with books and sat for hours sorrowfully pecking at them, every little while to discover that his mind had soared to other things, when he hauled it back, as one draws in a reluctant kite. On these occasions Aaron seldom troubled him, except by glances that, nevertheless, brought the kite back more quickly than if they had been words of warning. If Elspeth was present, the warper might sit moodily by the fire, but when the man and the boy were left together, one or other of them soon retired, as if this was the only way of preserving the peace. Though determined to keep his word to Jean Myles liberally, Aaron had never liked Tommy, and Tommy's avoidance of him is easily accounted for; he knew that Aaron did not admire him, and unless you admired Tommy he was always a boor in your presence, shy and self-distrustful. Especially was this so if you were a lady (how amazingly he got on in after years with some of you, what agony others endured till he went away!), and it is the chief reason why there are such contradictory accounts of him to-day.

Sometimes Mr. Cathro had hopes of him other than those that could only be revealed in a shameful whisper with the door shut. "Not so bad," he might say to Mr. McLean; "if he keeps it up we may squeeze him through yet, without trusting to-to what I was fool enough to mention to you. The mathematics are his weak point, there's nothing practical about him (except when it's needed to carry out his devil's designs) and he cares not a doit about the line A B, nor what it's doing in the circle K, but there's whiles he surprises me when we're at Homer. He has the spirit o't, man, even when he bogles at the sense."

But the next time Ivie called for a report—!

In his great days, so glittering, so brief (the days of the penny Life) Tommy, looking back to this year, was sure that he had never really tried to work. But he had. He did his very best, doggedly, wearily sitting at the round table till Elspeth feared that he was killing himself and gave him a melancholy comfort by saying so. An hour afterwards he might discover that he had been far away from his books, looking on at his affecting death and counting the mourners at the funeral.

Had he thought that Grizel's discovery was making her unhappy he would have melted at once, but never did she look so proud as when she scornfully passed him by, and he wagged his head complacently over her coming chagrin when she heard that he had carried the highest bursary. Then she would know what she had flung away. This should have helped him to another struggle with his lexicon, but it only provided a breeze for the kite, which flew so strong that he had to let go the string.

Aaron and the Dominie met one day in the square, and to Aaron's surprise Mr. Cathro's despondency about Tommy was more pronounced than before. "I wonder at that," the warper said, "for I assure you he has been harder 'at it than ever thae last nights. What's more, he used to look doleful as he sat at his table, but I notice now that he's as sweer to leave off as he's keen to begin, and the face of him is a' eagerness too, and he reads ower to himself what he has wrote and wags his head at it as if he thought it grand."

"Say you so?" asked Cathro, suspiciously; "does he leave what he writes lying about, Aaron?"

"No, but he takes it to you, does he no'?"

"Not him," said the Dominie, emphatically. "I may be mistaken, Aaron, but I'm doubting the young whelp is at his tricks again."

The Dominie was right, and before many days passed he discovered what was Tommy's new and delicious occupation.

For years Mr. Cathro had been in the habit of writing letters for such of the populace as could not guide a pen, and though he often told them not to come deaving him he liked the job, unexpected presents of a hen or a ham occasionally arriving as his reward, while the personal matters thus confided to him, as if he were a safe for the banking of private histories, gave him and his wife gossip for winter nights. Of late the number of his clients had decreased without his noticing it, so confident was he that they could not get on without him, but he received a shock at last from Andrew Dickie, who came one Saturday night with paper, envelope, a Queen's head, and a request for a letter for Bell Birse, now of Tilliedrum.

"You want me to speir in your name whether she'll have you, do you?" asked Cathro, with a flourish of his pen.

"It's no just so simple as that," said Andrew, and then he seemed to be rather at a loss to say what it was. "I dinna ken," he continued presently with a grave face, "whether you've noticed that I'm a gey queer deevil? Losh, I think I'm the queerest deevil I ken."

"We are all that," the Dominie assured him. "But what do you want me to write?"

"Well, it's like this," said Andrew, "I'm willing to marry her if she's agreeable, but I want to make sure that she'll take me afore I speir her. I'm a proud man, Dominie."

"You're a sly one!"

"Am I no!" said Andrew, well pleased. "Well, could you put the letter in that wy?"

"I wouldna," replied Mr. Cathro, "though I could, and I couldna though I would. It would defy the face of clay to do it, you canny lover."

Now, the Dominie had frequently declined to write as he was bidden, and had suggested alterations which were invariably accepted, but to his astonishment Andrew would not give in. "I'll be stepping, then," he said coolly, "for if you hinna the knack o't I ken somebody that has."

"Who?" demanded the irate Dominie.

"I promised no to tell you," replied Andrew, and away he went. Mr. Cathro expected him to return presently in humbler mood, but was disappointed, and a week or two afterwards he heard Andrew and Mary Jane Proctor cried in the parish church. "Did Bell Birse refuse him?" he asked the kirk officer, and was informed that Bell had never got a chance. "His letter was so cunning," said John, "that without speiring her, it drew ane frae her in which she let out that she was centred on Davit Allardyce."

"But who wrote Andrew's letter?" asked Mr. Cathro, sharply.

"I thought it had been yoursel'," said John, and the Dominie chafed, and lost much of the afternoon service by going over in his mind the names of possible rivals. He never thought of Tommy.

Then a week or two later fell a heavier blow. At least twice a year the Dominie had written for Meggy Duff to her daughter in Ireland a long letter founded on this suggestion, "Dear Kaytherine, if you dinna send ten shillings immediately, your puir auld mother will have neither house nor hame. I'm crying to you for't, Kaytherine; hearken and you'll hear my cry across the cauldriff sea." He met Meggy in the Banker's Close one day, and asked her pleasantly if the time was not drawing nigh for another appeal.

"I have wrote," replied the old woman, giving her pocket a boastful smack, which she thus explained, "And it was the whole ten shillings this time, and you never got more for me than five."

"Who wrote the letter for you?" he asked, lowering.

She, too, it seemed, had promised not to tell.

"Did you promise to tell nobody, Meggy, or just no to tell me," he pressed her, of a sudden suspecting Tommy.

"Just no to tell you," she answered, and at that.

"Da-a-a," began the Dominie, and then saved his reputation by adding "gont." The derivation of the word dagont has puzzled many, but here we seem to have it.

It is interesting to know what Tommy wrote. The general opinion was that his letter must have been a triumph of eloquent appeal, and indeed he had first sketched out several masterpieces, all of some length and in different styles, but on the whole not unlike the concoctions of Meggy's former secretary; that is, he had dwelt on the duties of daughters, on the hardness of the times, on the certainty that if Katherine helped this time assistance would never be needed again. This sort of thing had always satisfied the Dominie, but Tommy, despite his several attempts, had a vague consciousness that there was something second-rate about them, and he tapped on his brain till it responded. The letter he despatched to Ireland, but had the wisdom not to read aloud even to Meggy, contained nothing save her own words, "Dear Kaytherine, if you dinna send ten shillings immediately, your puir auld mother will have neither house nor hame. I'm crying to you for't, Kaytherine; hearken and you'll hear my cry across the cauldriff sea." It was a call from the heart which transported Katherine to Thrums in a second of time, she seemed to see her mother again, grown frail since last they met-and so all was well for Meggy. Tommy did not put all this to himself but he felt it, and after that he *could not* have written the letter differently. Happy Tommy! To be an artist is a great thing, but to be an artist and not know it is the most glorious plight in the world.

Other fickle clients put their correspondence into the boy's hands, and Cathro found it out but said nothing. Dignity kept him in check; he did not even let the tawse speak for him. So well did he dissemble that Tommy could not decide how much he knew, and dreaded his getting hold of some of the letters, yet pined to watch his face while he read them. This could not last forever. Mr. Cathro was like a haughty kettle which has choked its spout that none may know it has come a-boil, and we all know what in that event must happen sooner or later to the lid.

The three boys who had college in the tail of their eye had certain privileges not for the herd. It was taken for granted that when knowledge came their way they needed no overseer to make them stand their ground, and accordingly for great part of the day they had a back bench to themselves, with half a dozen hedges of boys and girls between them and the Dominie. From his chair Mr. Cathro could not see them, but a foot-board was nailed to it, and when he stood on this, as he had an aggravating trick of doing, softly and swiftly, they were suddenly in view. A large fire had been burning all day and the atmosphere was soporific. Mr. Cathro was so sleepy himself that the sight of a nodding head enraged him like a caricature, and he was on the foot-board frequently for the reason that makes bearded men suck peppermints in church. Against his better judgment he took several peeps at Tommy, whom he had lately suspected of writing his letters in school or at least of gloating over them on that back bench. To-day he was sure of it. However absorbing Euclid may be, even the forty-seventh of the first book does not make you chuckle and wag your head; you can bring a substantive in Virgil back to the verb that has lost it without looking as if you would like to exhibit them together in the square. But Tommy was thus elated until he gave way to grief of the most affecting kind. Now he looked gloomily before him as if all was over, now he buried his face in his hands, next his eyes were closed as if in prayer. All this the Dominie stood from him, but when at last he began to blubber —

At the blackboard was an arithmetic class, slates in hand, each member adding up aloud in turn a row of figures. By and by it was known that Cathro had ceased to listen. "Go on," his voice rather than himself said, and he accepted Mary Dundas's trembling assertion that four and seven make ten. Such was the faith in Cathro that even boys who could add promptly turned their eleven into ten, and he did not catch them at it. So obviously was his mind as well as his gaze on, something beyond, that Sandy Riach, a wit who had been waiting his chance for years, snapped at it now, and roared "Ten and eleven, nineteen" ("Go on," said Cathro), "and four, twenty," gasped Sandy, "and eight, sixteen," he added, gaining courage. "Very good," nmrmured the Dominie, whereupon Sandy clenched his reputation forever by saying, in one glorious mouthful, "and six, eleven, and two, five, and one, nocht."

There was no laughing at it then (though Sandy held a levee in the evening), they were all so stricken with amazement. By one movement they swung round to see what had fascinated Cathro, and the other classes doing likewise, Tommy became suddenly the centre of observation. Big tears were slinking down his face, and falling on some sheets of paper, which emotion prevented his concealing. Anon the unusual stillness in the school made him look up, but he was dazed, like one uncertain of his whereabouts, and he blinked rapidly to clear his eyes, as a bird shakes water from its wings.

Mr. Cathro first uttered what was afterward described as a kind of throttled skirl, and then he roared "Come here!" whereupon Tommy stepped forward heavily, and tried, as commanded, to come to his senses, but it was not easy to make so long a journey in a moment, and several times, as he seemed about to conquer his fears, a wave of feeling set them flowing again.

"Take your time," said Mr. Cathro, grimly, "I can wait," and this had such a helpful effect that Tommy was able presently to speak up for his misdeeds. They consisted of some letters written at home but brought to the school for private reading, and the Dominie got a nasty jar when he saw that they were all signed "Betsy Grieve." Miss Betsy Grieve, servant to Mr. Duthie, was about to marry, and these letters were acknowledgments of wedding presents. Now, Mr. Cathro had written similar letters for Betsy only a few days before.

"Did she ask you to write these for her?" he demanded, fuming, and Tommy replied demurely that she had. He could not help adding, though he felt the unwisdom of it, "She got some other body to do them first, but his letters didna satisfy her."

"Oh!" said Mr. Cathro, and it was such a vicious oh that Tommy squeaked tremblingly, "I dinna know who he was."

Keeping his mouth shut by gripping his underlip with his teeth, the Dominie read the letters, and Tommy gazed eagerly at him, all fear forgotten, soul conquering body. The others stood or sat waiting, perplexed as to the cause, confident of the issue. The letters were much finer productions than Cathro's, he had to admit it to himself as he read. Yet the rivals had started fair, for Betsy was a recent immigrant from Dunkeld way, and the letters were to people known neither to Tommy nor to the Dominie. Also, she had given the same details for the guidance of each. A lady had sent a teapot, which affected to be new, but was not; Betsy recognized it by a scratch on the lid, and wanted to scratch back, but politely. So Tommy wrote, "When you come to see me we shall have a cup of tea out of your beautiful present, and it will be like a meeting of three old friends." That was perhaps too polite, Betsy feared, but Tommy said authoritatively, "No, the politer the nippier."

There was a set of six cups and saucers from Peter something, who had loved Betsy in vain. She had shown the Dominie and Tommy the ear-rings given her long ago by Peter (they were bought with 'Sosh checks) and the poem he had written about them, and she was most anxious to gratify him in her reply. All Cathro could do, however, was to wish Peter well in some ornate sentences, while Tommy's was a letter that only a tender woman's heart could have indited, with such beautiful touches about the days which are no more alas forever, that Betsy listened to it with heaving breast and felt so sorry for her old swain that, forgetting she had never loved him, she all but gave Andrew the go-by and returned to Peter. As for Peter, who had been getting over his trouble, he saw now for the first time what he had lost, and he carried Betsy's dear letter in his oxter pocket and was inconsolable.

But the masterpiece went to Mrs. Dinnie, baker, in return for a flagon bun. Long ago her daughter, Janet, and Betsy had agreed to marry on the same day, and many a quip had Mrs. Dinnie cast at their romantic compact. But Janet died, and so it was a sad letter that Tommy had to write to her mother. "I'm doubting you're no auld enough for this ane," soft-hearted Betsy said, but she did not know her man. "Tell me some one thing the mother used often to say when she was taking her fun off the pair of you," he said, and "Where is she buried?" was a suggestive question, with the happy tag, "Is there a tree hanging over the grave?" Thus assisted, he composed a letter that had a tear in every sentence. Betsy rubbed her eyes red over it, and not all its sentiments were allowed to die, for Mrs. Dinnie, touched to the heart, printed the best of them in black licorice on short bread for funeral feasts, at which they gave rise to solemn reflections as they went down.

Nevertheless, this letter affected none so much as the writer of it. His first rough sketch became so damp as he wrote that he had to abandon his pen and take to pencil; while he was revising he had often to desist to dry his eyes on the coverlet of Aaron's bed, which made Elspeth weep also, though she had no notion what he was at. But when the work was finished he took her into the secret and read his letter to her, and he almost choked as he did so. Yet he smiled rapturously through his woe, and she knew no better than to be proud of him, and he woke next morning with a cold, brought on you can see how, but his triumph was worth its price.

Having read the letter in an uncanny silence, Mr. Cathro unbottled Tommy for the details, and out they came with a rush, blowing away the cork discretion. Yet was the Dominie slow to strike; he seemed to find more satisfaction in surveying his young friend with a wondering gaze that had a dash of admiration in it, which Tommy was the first to note.

"I don't mind admitting before the whole school," said Mr. Cathro, slowly, "that if these letters had been addressed to me they would have taken me in."

Tommy tried to look modest, but his chest would have its way.

"You little sacket," cried the Dominie, "how did you manage it?"

"I think I thought I was Betsy at the time," Tommy answered, with proper awe.

"She told me nothing about the weeping-willow at the grave," said the Dominie, perhaps in self-defence.

"You hadna speired if there was one," retorted Tommy, jealously.

"What made you think of it?"

"I saw it might come in neat." (He had said in the letter that the weeping-willow reminded him of the days when Janet's bonny hair hung down kissing her waist just as the willow kissed the grave.)

"Willows don't hang so low as you seem to think," said the Dominie.

"Yes, they do," replied Tommy, "I walked three miles to see one to make sure. I was near putting in another beautiful bit about weeping-willows."

"Well, why didn't you?"

Tommy looked up with an impudent snigger. "You could never guess," he said.

"Answer me at once," thundered his preceptor. "Was it because —"

"No," interrupted Tommy, so conscious of Mr. Cathro's inferiority that to let him go on seemed waste of time. "It was because, though it is a beautiful thing in itself, I felt a servant lassie wouldna have thought o't. I was sweer," he admitted, with a sigh; then firmly, "but I cut it out."

Again Cathro admired, reluctantly. The hack does feel the difference between himself and the artist. Cathro might possibly have had the idea, he could not have cut it out.

But the hack is sometimes, or usually, or nearly always the artist's master, and can make him suffer for his dem'd superiority.

"What made you snivel when you read the pathetic bits?" asked Cathro, with itching fingers.

"I was so sorry for Peter and Mrs. Dinnie," Tommy answered, a little puzzled himself now. "I saw them so clear."

"And yet until Betsy came to you, you had never heard tell of them?"

"No."

"And on reflection you don't care a doit about them?"

"N-no."

"And you care as little for Betsy?"

"No now, but at the time I a kind of thought I was to be married to Andrew."

"And even while you blubbered you were saying to yourself, 'What a clever billie I am!'"

Mr. Cathro had certainly intended to end the scene with the strap, but as he stretched out his hand for it he had another idea. "Do you know why Nether Drumgley's sheep are branded with the letters N.D.?" he asked his pupils, and a dozen replied, "So as all may ken wha they belong to."

"Precisely," said Mr. Cathro, "and similarly they used to brand a letter on a felon, so that all might know whom *he* belonged to." He crossed to the fireplace, and, picking up a charred stick, wrote with it on the forehead of startled Tommy the letters "S.T."

"Now," said the Dominie complacently, "we know to whom Tommy belongs."

All were so taken aback that for some seconds nothing could be heard save Tommy indignantly wiping his brow; then "Wha is he?" cried one, the mouthpiece of half a hundred.

"He is one of the two proprietors we have just been speaking of," replied Cathro, dryly, and turning again to Tommy, he said, "Wipe away, Sentimental Tommy, try hot water, try cold water, try a knife, but you will never get those letters off you; you are branded for ever and ever."

Chapter XXXVI

Of Four Ministers Who Afterwards Boasted That They Had Known Tommy Sandys

Bursary examination time had come, and to the siege of Aberdeen marched a hungry half-dozen —three of them from Thrums, two from the Glenuharity school. The sixth was Tod Lindertis, a ploughman from the Dubb of Prosen, his place of study the bothy after lousing time (Do you hear the klink of quoits?) or a one-roomed house near it, his tutor a dogged little woman, who knew not the accusative from the dative, but never tired of holding the book while Tod recited. Him someone greets with the good-natured jeer, "It's your fourth try, is it no, Tod?" and he answers cheerily, "It is, my lathie, and I'll keep kick, kick, kicking away to the _n_th time."

"Which means till the door flies open," says the dogged little woman, who is the gallant Tod's no less gallant wife, and already the mother of two. I hope Tod will succeed this time.

The competitors, who were to travel part of the way on their shanks, met soon after daybreak in Cathro's yard, where a little crowd awaited them, parents trying to look humble, Mr. Duthie and Ramsay Cameron thinking of the morning when they set off on the same errand-but the results were different, and Mr. Duthie is now a minister, and Ramsay is in the middle of another wob. Both dominies were present, hating each other, for that day only, up to the mouth, where their icy politeness was a thing to shudder at, and each was drilling his detachment to the last moment, but by different methods; for while Mr. Cathro entreated Joe Meldrum for God's sake to mind that about the genitive, and Willie Simpson to keep his mouth shut and drink even water sparingly, Mr. Ogilvy cracked jokes with Gav Dishart and explained them to Lauchlan McLauchlan. "Think of anything now but what is before you," was Mr. Ogilvy's advice. "Think of nothing else," roared Mr. Cathro. But though Mr. Ogilvy seemed outwardly calm it was base pretence; his dickie gradually wriggled through the opening of his waistcoat, as if bearing a protest from his inward parts, and he let it hang crumpled and conspicuous, while Grizel, on the outskirts of the crowd, yearned to put it right.

Grizel was not there, she told several people, including herself, to say good-by to Tommy, and oh, how she scorned Elspeth, for looking as if life would not be endurable without him. Knowing what Elspeth was, Tommy had decided that she should not accompany him to the yard (of course she was to follow him to Aberdeen if he distinguished himself-Mr. McLean had promised to bring her), but she told him of her dream that he headed the bursary list, and as this dream coincided with some dreams of his own, though not with all, it seemed to give her such fortitude that he let her come. An expressionless face was Tommy's, so that not even the experienced dominie of Glenquharity, covertly scanning his rival's lot, could tell whether he was gloomy or uplifted; he did not seem to be in need of a long sleep like Willie Simpson, nor were his eyes glazed like Gav Dishart's, who carried all the problems of Euclid before him on an invisible blackboard and dared not even wink lest he displaced them, nor did he, like Tod Lindertis, answer questions about his money pocket or where he had stowed his bread and cheese with

> "After envy, spare, obey,
> The dative put, remember, pray."

Mr. Ogilvy noticed that Cathro tapped his forehead doubtfully every time his eyes fell on Tommy, but otherwise shunned him, and he asked "What are his chances?"

"That's the laddie," replied Mr. Cathro, "who, when you took her ladyship to see Corp Shiach years ago impersona —"

"I know," Mr. Ogilvy interrupted him hastily, "but how will he stand, think you?"

Mr. Cathro coughed. "We'll see," he said guardedly.

Nevertheless Tommy was not to get round the corner without betraying a little of himself, for Elspeth having borne up magnificently when he shook hands, screamed at the tragedy of his back and fell into the arms of Tod's wife, whereupon Tommy first tried to brazen it out and then kissed her in the presence of a score of witnesses, including Grizel, who stamped her foot, though what right had she to be so angry? "I'm sure," Elspeth sobbed, "that the professor would let me sit beside you; I would just hunker on the floor and hold your foot and no say a word." Tommy gave Tod's wife an imploring look, and she managed to comfort Elspeth with predictions of his coming triumph and the reunion to follow. Grateful Elspeth in return asked Tommy to help Tod when the professors were not looking, and he promised, after which she had no more fear for Tod.

And now, ye drums that we all carry in our breasts, beat your best over the bravest sight ever seen in a small Scotch town of an autumn morning, the departure of its fighting lads for the lists at Aberdeen. Let the tune be the sweet familiar one you found somewhere in the Bible long ago, "The mothers we leave behind us" —leave behind us on their knees. May it dirl through your bones, brave boys, to the end, as you hope not to be damned. And now, quick march.

A week has elapsed, and now-there is no call for music now, for these are but the vanquished crawling back, Joe Meldrum and-and another. No, it is not Tod, he stays on in Aberdeen, for he is a twelve-pound tenner. The two were within a mile of Thrums at three o'clock, but after that they lagged, waiting for the gloaming, when they stole to their homes, ducking as they passed windows without the blinds down. Elspeth ran to Tommy when he appeared in the doorway, and then she got quickly between him and Aaron. The warper was sitting by the fire at his evening meal, and he gave the wanderer a long steady look, then without a word returned to his porridge and porter. It was a less hearty welcome home even than Joe's; his mother was among those who had wept to lose her son, but when he came back to her she gave him a whack on the head with the thieval.

Aaron asked not a question about those days in Aberdeen, but he heard a little about them from Elspeth. Tommy had not excused himself to Elspeth, he had let her do as she liked with his head (this was a great treat to her), and while it lay pressed against hers, she made remarks about Aberdeen professors which it would have done them good to hear. These she repeated to Aaron, who was about to answer roughly, and then suddenly put her on his knee instead.

"They didna ask the right questions," she told him, and when the warper asked if Tommy had said so, she declared that he had refused to say a word against them, which seemed to her to cover him with glory. "But he doubted they would make that mistake afore he started, she said brightly, so you see he saw through them afore ever he set eyes on them."

Corp would have replied admiringly to this "Oh, the little deevil!" (when he heard of Tommy's failure he wanted to fight Gav Dishart and Willie Simpson), but Aaron was another kind of confidant, and even when she explained on Tommy's authority that there are two kinds of cleverness, the kind you learn from books and a kind that is inside yourself, which latter was Tommy's kind, he only replied,

"He can take it wi' him to the herding, then, and see if it'll keep the cattle frae stravaiging."

"It's no that kind of cleverness either," said Elspeth, quaking, and quaked also Tommy, who had gone to the garret, to listen through the floor.

"No? I would like to ken what use his cleverness can be put to, then," said Aaron, and Elspeth answered nothing, and Tommy only sighed, for that indeed was the problem. But though to these three and to Cathro, and to Mr. and Mrs. McLean and to others more mildly interested, it seemed a problem beyond solution, there was one in Thrums who rocked her arms at their denseness, a girl growing so long in the legs that twice within the last year she had found it necessary to let down her parramatty frock. As soon as she heard that Tommy had come home vanquished, she put on the quaint blue bonnet with the white strings, in which she fondly believed she looked ever so old (her period of mourning was at an end, but she still wore her black dress) and forgetting all except that he was unhappy, she ran to a certain little house to comfort him. But she did not go in, for through the window she saw Elspeth petting him, and that somehow annoyed her. In the evening, however, she called on Mr. Cathro.

Perhaps you want to know why she, who at last saw Sentimental Tommy in his true light and spurned him accordingly, now exerted herself in his behalf instead of going on with the papering of the surgery. Well, that was the reason. She had put the question to herself before—not, indeed, before going to Monypenny but before calling on the Dominie—and decided that she wanted to send Tommy to college, because she disliked him so much that she could not endure the prospect of his remaining in Thrums. Now, are you satisfied?

She could scarcely take time to say good-evening to Mr. Cathro before telling him the object of her visit. "The letters Tommy has been writing for people are very clever, are they not?" she began.

"You've heard of them, have you?"

"Everybody has heard of them," she said injudiciously, and he groaned and asked if she had come to tell him this. But he admitted their cleverness, whereupon she asked, "Well, if he is clever at writing letters, would he not be clever at writing an essay?"

"I wager my head against a snuff mull that he would be, but what are you driving at?"

"I was wondering whether he could not win the prize I heard Dr. McQueen speaking about, the—is it not called the Hugh Blackadder?"

"My head against a buckie that he could! Sit down, Grizel, I see what you mean now. Ay, but the pity is he's not eligible for the Hugh Blackadder. Oh, that he was, oh, that he was! It would make Ogilvy of Glenquharity sing small at last! His loons have carried the Blackadder for the last seven years without a break. The Hugh Blackadder Mortification, the bequest is called, and, 'deed, it has been a sore mortification to me!"

Calming down, he told her the story of the bequest. Hugh Blackadder was a Thrums man who made a fortune in America, and bequeathed the interest of three hundred pounds of it to be competed for yearly by the youth of his native place. He had grown fond of Thrums and all its ways over there, and left directions that the prize should be given for the best essay in the Scots tongue, the ministers of the town and glens to be the judges, the competitors to be boys who were going to college, but had not without it the wherewithal to support themselves. The ministers took this to mean that those who carried small bursaries were eligible, and indeed it had usually gone to a bursar.

"Sentimental Tommy would not have been able to compete if he had got a bursary," Mr. Cathro explained, "because however small it was Mr. McLean meant to double it; and he can't compete without it, for McLean refuses to help him now (he was here an hour since, saying the laddie was obviously hopeless), so I never thought of entering Tommy for the Blackadder. No, it will go to Ogilvy's Lauchlan McLauchlan, who is a twelve-pounder, and, as there can be no competitors, he'll get it without the trouble of coming back to write the essay."

"But suppose Mr. McLean were willing to do what he promised if Tommy won the Blackadder?"

"It's useless to appeal to McLean. He's hard set against the laddie now and washes his hands of him, saying that Aaron Latta is right after all. He may soften, and get Tommy into a trade to save him from the herding, but send him to college he won't, and indeed he's right, the laddie's a fool."

"Not at writing let —"

"And what is the effect of his letter-writing, but to make me ridiculous? Me! I wonder you can expect me to move a finger for him, he has been my torment ever since his inscrutable face appeared at my door."

"Never mind him," said Grizel, cunningly. "But think what a triumph it would be to you if your boy beat Mr. Ogilvy's."

The Dominie rose in his excitement and slammed the table, "My certie, lassie, but it would!" he cried, "Ogilvy looks on the Blackadder as his perquisite, and he's surer of it than ever this year. And there's no doubt but Tommy would carry it. My head to a buckie preen he would carry it, and then, oh, for a sight of Ogilvy's face, oh, for —" He broke off abruptly. "But what's the good of thinking of it?" he said, dolefully, "Mr. McLean's a firm man when he makes up his mind."

Nevertheless, though McLean, who had a Scotchman's faith in the verdict of professors, and had been bitterly disappointed by Tommy's failure, refused to be converted by the Dominie's entreaties, he yielded to them when they were voiced by Ailie (brought into the plot *vice* Grizel retired), and Elspeth got round Aaron, and so it came about that with his usual luck, Tommy was given another chance, present at the competition, which took place in the Thrums school, the Rev. Mr. Duthie, the Rev. Mr. Dishart, the Rev. Mr. Gloag of Noran Side, the Rev. Mr. Lorrimer of Glenquharity (these on hair-bottomed chairs), and Mr. Cathro and Mr. Ogilvy (cane); present also to a less extent (that is to say, their faces at the windows), Corp and others, who applauded the local champion when he entered and derided McLauchlan. The subject of the essay was changed yearly, this time "A Day in Church" was announced, and immediately Lauchlan McLauchlan, who had not missed a service since his scarlet fever year (and too few then), smote his red head in agony, while Tommy, who had missed as many as possible, looked calmly confident. For two hours the competitors were put into a small room communicating with the larger one, and Tommy began at once with a confident smirk that presently gave way to a most holy expression; while Lauchlan gaped at him and at last got started also, but had to pause occasionally to rub his face on his sleeve, for like Corp he was one of the kind who cannot think without perspiring. In the large room the ministers gossiped about eternal punishment, and of the two dominies one sat at his ease, like a passenger who knows that the coach will reach the goal without any exertion on his part, while the other paced the floor, with many a despondent glance through the open door whence the scraping proceeded; and the one was pleasantly cool; and the other in a plot of heat; and the one made genial remarks about every-day matters, and the answers of the other stood on their heads. It was a familiar comedy to Mr. Ogilvy, hardly a variation on what had happened five times in six for many years: the same scene, the same scraping in the little room, the same background of ministers (black-aviced Mr. Lorrimer had begun to bark again), the same dominies; everything was as it had so often been, except that he and Cathro had changed places; it was Cathro who sat smiling now and Mr. Ogilvy who dolefully paced the floor.

To be able to write! Throughout Mr. Ogilvy's life, save when he was about one and twenty, this had seemed the great thing, and he ever approached the thought reverently, as if it were a maid of more than mortal purity. And it is, and because he knew this she let him see her face, which shall ever be hidden from those who look not for the soul, and to help him nearer to her came assistance in strange guise, the loss of loved ones, dolour unutterable; but still she was beyond his reach. Night by night, when the only light in the glen was the school-house lamp, of use at least as a landmark to solitary travellers-who miss it nowadays, for it burns no more-she hovered over him, nor did she deride his hopeless efforts, but rather, as she saw him go from black to gray and from gray to white in her service, were her luminous eyes sorrowful because she was not for him, and she bent impulsively toward him, so that once or twice in a long life he touched her fingers, and a heavenly spark was lit, for he had risen higher than himself, and that is literature.

He knew that oblivion was at hand, ready to sweep away his pages almost as soon as they were filled (Do we not all hear her besom when we pause to dip?), but he had done his best and he had a sense of humor, and perhaps some day would come a pupil of whom he could make what he had failed to make of himself. That prodigy never did come, though it was not for want of nursing, and there came at least, in succession most maddening to Mr. Cathro, a row of youths who could be trained to carry the Hugh Blackadder. Mr. Ogilvy's many triumphs in this competition had not dulled his appetite for more, and depressed he was at the prospect of a reverse. That it was coming now he could not doubt. McLauchlan, who was to be Rev., had a flow of words (which would prevent his perspiring much in the pulpit), but he could no more describe a familiar scene with the pen than a milkmaid can draw a cow. The Thrums representatives were sometimes as little gifted, it is true, and never were they so well exercised, but this Tommy had the knack of it, as Mr. Ogilvy could not doubt, for the story of his letter-writing had been through the glens.

"Keep up your spirits," Mr. Lorrimer had said to Mm as they walked together to the fray, "Cathro's loon may compose the better of the two, but, as I understand, the first years of his life were spent in London, and so he may bogle at the Scotch."

But the Dominie replied, "Don't buoy me up on a soap bubble. If there's as much in him as I fear, that should be a help to him instead of a hindrance, for it will have set him a-thinking about the words he uses."

And the satisfaction on Tommy's face when the subject of the essay was given out, with the business-like way in which he set to work, had added to the Dominie's misgivings; if anything was required to dishearten him utterly it was provided by Cathro's confident smile. The two Thrums ministers were naturally desirous that Tommy should win, but the younger of them was very fond of Mr. Ogilvy, and noticing his unhappy peeps through the door dividing the rooms, proposed that it should be closed. He shut it himself, and as he did so he observed that Tommy was biting his pen and frowning, while McLauchlan, having ceased to think, was getting on nicely. But it did not strike Mr. Dishart that this was worth commenting on.

"Are you not satisfied with the honors you have already got, you greedy man?" he said, laying his hand affectionately on Mr. Ogilvy, who only sighed for reply.

"It is well that the prize should go to different localities, for in that way its sphere of usefulness is extended," remarked pompous Mr. Gloag, who could be impartial, as there was no candidate from Noran Side. He was a minister much in request for church soirees, where he amused the congregations so greatly with personal anecdote about himself that they never thought much of him afterwards. There is one such minister in every presbytery.

"And to have carried the Hugh Blackadder seven times running is surely enough for any one locality, even though it be Glenquharity," said Mr. Lorrimer, preparing for defeat.

"There's consolation for you, sir," said Mr. Cathro, sarcastically, to his rival, who tried to take snuff in sheer bravado, but let it slip through his fingers, and after that, until the two hours were up, the talk was chiefly of how Tommy would get on at Aberdeen. But it was confined to the four ministers and one dominie. Mr. Ogilvy still hovered about the door of communication, and his face fell more and more, making Mr. Dishart quite unhappy.

"I'm an old fool," the Dominie admitted, "but I can't help being cast down. The fact is that —I have only heard the scrape of one pen for nearly an hour."

"Poor Lauchlan!" exclaimed Mr. Cathro, rubbing his hands gleefully, and indeed it was such a shameless exhibition that the Auld Licht minister said reproachfully, "You forget yourself, Mr. Cathro, let us not be unseemly exalted in the hour of our triumph."

Then Mr. Cathro sat upon his hands as the best way of keeping them apart, but the moment Mr. Dishart's back presented itself, he winked at Mr. Ogilvy. He winked a good deal more presently. For after all-how to tell it! Tommy was ignominiously beaten, making such a beggarly show that the judges thought it unnecessary to take the essays home with them for leisurely consideration before pronouncing Mr. Lauchlan McLauchlan winner. There was quite a commotion in the school-room. At the end of the allotted time the two competitors had been told to hand in their essays, and how Mr. McLauchlan was sniggering is not worth recording, so dumfounded, confused, and raging was Tommy. He clung to his papers, crying fiercely that the two hours could not be up yet, and Lauchlan having tried to keep the laugh in too long it exploded in his mouth, whereupon, said he, with a guffaw, "He hasna written a word for near an hour!"

"What! It was you I heard!" cried Mr. Ogilvy gleaming, while the unhappy Cathro tore the essay from Tommy's hands. Essay! It was no more an essay than a twig is a tree, for the gowk had stuck in the middle of his second page. Yes, stuck is the right expression, as his chagrined teacher had to admit when the boy was cross-examined. He had not been "up to some of his tricks," he had stuck, and his explanations, as you will admit, merely emphasized his incapacity.

He had brought himself to public scorn for lack of a word. What word? they asked testily, but even now he could not tell. He had wanted a Scotch word that would signify how many people were in church, and it was on the tip of his tongue but would come no farther. Puckle was nearly the word, but it did not mean so many people as he meant. The hour had gone by just like winking; he had forgotten all about time while searching his mind for the word.

When Mr. Ogilvy heard this he seemed to be much impressed, repeatedly he nodded his head as some beat time to music, and he muttered to himself, "The right word-yes, that's everything," and "'the time went by like winking' —exactly, precisely," and he would have liked to examine Tommy's bumps, but did not, nor said a word aloud, for was he not there in McLauchlan's interest?

The other five were furious; even Mr. Lorrimer, though his man had won, could not smile in face of such imbecility. "You little tattie doolie," Cathro roared, "were there not a dozen words to wile from if you had an ill-will to puckle? What ailed you at manzy, or —"

"I thought of manzy," replied Tommy, woefully, for he was ashamed of himself, "but-but a manse's a swarm. It would mean that the folk in the kirk were buzzing thegither like bees, instead of sitting still."

"Even if it does mean that," said Mr. Duthie, with impatience, "what was the need of being so particular? Surely the art of essay-writing consists in using the first word that comes and hurrying on."

"That's how I did," said the proud McLauchlan, who is now leader of a party in the church, and a figure in Edinburgh during the month of May.

"I see," interposed Mr. Gloag, "that McLauchlan speaks of there being a mask of people in the church. Mask is a fine Scotch word."

"Admirable," assented Mr. Dishart. "I thought of mask," whimpered Tommy, "but that would mean the kirk was crammed, and I just meant it to be middling full."

"Flow would have done," suggested Mr. Lorrimer.

"Flow's but a handful," said Tommy.

"Curran, then, you jackanapes!"

"Curran's no enough."

Mr. Lorrimer flung up his hands in despair.

"I wanted something between curran and mask," said Tommy, dogged, yet almost at the crying.

Mr. Ogilvy, who had been hiding his admiration with difficulty, spread a net for him. "You said you wanted a word that meant middling full. Well, why did you not say middling full-or fell mask?"

"Yes, why not?" demanded the ministers, unconsciously caught in the net.

"I wanted one word," replied Tommy, unconsciously avoiding it.

"You jewel!" muttered Mr. Ogilvy under his breath, but Mr. Cathro would have banged the boy's head had not the ministers interfered.

"It is so easy, too, to find the right word," said Mr. Gloag.

"It's no; it's as difficult as to hit a squirrel," cried Tommy, and again Mr. Ogilvy nodded approval.

But the ministers were only pained.

"The lad is merely a numskull," said Mr. Dishart, kindly.

"And no teacher could have turned him into anything else," said Mr. Duthie.

"And so, Cathro, you need not feel sore over your defeat," added Mr. Gloag; but nevertheless Cathro took Tommy by the neck and ran him out of the parish school of Thrums. When he returned to the others he found the ministers congratulating McLauchlan, whose nose was in the air, and complimenting Mr. Ogilvy, who listened to their formal phrases solemnly and accepted their hand-shakes with a dry chuckle.

"Ay, grin away, sir," the mortified dominie of Thrums said to him sourly, "the joke is on your side."

"You are right, sir," replied Mr. Ogilvy, mysteriously, "the joke is on my side, and the best of it is that not one of you knows what the joke is!"

And then an odd thing happened. As they were preparing to leave the school, the door opened a little and there appeared in the aperture the face of Tommy, tear-stained but excited. "I ken the word now," he cried, "it came to me a' at once; it is hantle!"

The door closed with a victorious bang, just in time to prevent Cathro —

"Oh, the sumph!" exclaimed Mr. Lauchlan McLauchlan, "as if it mattered what the word is now!"

And said Mr. Dishart, "Cathro, you had better tell Aaron Latta that the sooner he sends this nincompoop to the herding the better."

But Mr. Ogilvy giving his Lauchlan a push that nearly sent him sprawling, said in an ecstasy to himself, "He *had* to think of it till he got it-and he got it. The laddie is a genius!" They were about to tear up Tommy's essay, but he snatched it from them and put it in his oxter pocket. "I am a collector of curiosities," he explained, "and this paper may be worth money yet."

"Well," said Cathro, savagely, "I have one satisfaction, I ran him out of my school."

"Who knows," replied Mr. Ogilvy, "but what you may be proud to dust a chair for him when he comes back?"

Convinced of his own worthlessness, Tommy was sufficiently humble now, but Aaron Latta, nevertheless, marched to the square on the following market day and came back with the boy's sentence, Elspeth being happily absent.

"I say nothing about the disgrace you have brought on this house," the warper began without emotion, "for it has been a shamed house since afore you were born, and it's a small offence to skail on a clarty floor. But now I've done more for you than I promised Jean Myles to do, and you had your pick atween college and the herding, and the herding you've chosen twice. I call you no names, you ken best what you're fitted for, but I've seen the farmer of the Dubb of Prosen the day, and he was short-handed through the loss of Tod Lindertis, so you're fee'd to him. Dinna think you get Tod's place, it'll be years afore you rise to that, but it's right and proper that as he steps up, you should step down."

"The Dubb of Prosen!" cried Tommy in dismay. "It's fifteen miles frae here."

"It's a' that."

"But-but-but Elspeth and me never thought of my being so far away that she couldna see me. We thought of a farmer near Thrums."

"The farther you're frae her the better," said Aaron, uneasily, yet honestly believing what he said.

"It'll kill her," Tommy cried fiercely. With only his own suffering to consider he would probably have nursed it into a play through which he stalked as the noble child of misfortune, but in his anxiety for Elspeth he could still forget himself. "Fine you ken she canna do without me," he screamed.

"She maun be weaned," replied the warper, with a show of temper; he was convinced that the sooner Elspeth learned to do without Tommy the better it would be for herself in the end, but in his way of regarding the boy there was also a touch of jealousy, pathetic rather than forbidding. To him he left the task of breaking the news to Elspeth; and Tommy, terrified lest she should swoon under it, was almost offended when she remained calm. But, alas, the reason was that she thought she was going with him.

"Will we have to walk all the way to the Dubb of Prosen?" she asked, quite brightly, and at that Tommy twisted about in misery. "You are no-you canna —" he began, and then dodged the telling. "We-we may get a lift in a cart," he said weakly.

"And I'll sit aside you in the fields, and make chains o' the gowans, will I no? Speak, Tommy!"

"Ay-ay, will you," he groaned.

"And we'll have a wee, wee room to oursels, and —"

He broke down, "Oh, Elspeth," he cried, "it was ill-done of me no to stick to my books, and get a bursary, and it was waur o' me to bother about that word. I'm a scoundrel, I am, I'm a black, I'm a —"

But she put her hand on his mouth, saying, "I'm fonder o' you than ever, Tommy, and I'll like the Dubb o' Prosen fine, and what does it matter where we are when we're thegither?" which was poor comfort for him, but still he could not tell her the truth, and so in the end Aaron had to tell her. It struck her down, and the doctor had to be called in during the night to stop her hysterics. When at last she fell asleep Tommy's arm was beneath her, and by and by it was in agony, but he set his teeth and kept it there rather than risk waking her.

When Tommy was out of the way, Aaron did his clumsy best to soothe her, sometimes half shamefacedly pressing her cheek to his, and she did not repel him, but there was no response. "Dinna take on in that way, dawtie," he would say, "I'll be good to you."

"But you're no Tommy," Elspeth answered.

"I'm not, I'm but a stunted tree, blasted in my youth, but for a' that I would like to have somebody to care for me, and there's none to do't, Elspeth, if you winna. I'll gang walks wi' you, I'll take you to the fishing, I'll come to the garret at night to hap you up, I'll —I'll teach you the games I used to play mysel'. I'm no sure but what you might make something o' me yet, bairn, if you tried hard."

"But you're no Tommy," Elspeth wailed again, and when he advised her to put Tommy out of her mind for a little and speak of other things, she only answered innocently, "What else is there to speak about?"

Mr. McLean had sent Tommy a pound, and so was done with him, but Ailie still thought him a dear, though no longer a wonder, and Elspeth took a strange confession to her, how one night she was so angry with God that she had gone to bed without saying her prayers. She had just meant to keep Him in suspense for a little, and then say them, but she fell asleep. And that was not the worst, for when she woke in the morning, and saw that she was still living, she was glad she had not said them. But next night she said them twice.

And this, too, is another flash into her dark character. Tommy, who never missed saying his prayers and could say them with surprising quickness, told her, "God is fonder of lonely lassies than of any other kind, and every time you greet it makes Him greet, and when you're cheerful it makes Him cheerful too." This was meant to dry her eyes, but it had not that effect, for, said Elspeth, vindictively, "Well, then, I'll just make Him as miserable as I can."

When Tommy was merely concerned with his own affairs he did not think much about God, but he knew that no other could console Elspeth, and his love for her usually told him the right things to say, and while he said them, he was quite carried away by his sentiments and even wept over them, but within the hour he might be leering. They were beautiful, and were repeated of course to Mrs. McLean, who told her husband of them, declaring that this boy's love for his sister made her a better woman.

"But nevertheless," said Ivie, "Mr. Cathro assures me —"

"He is prejudiced," retorted Mrs. McLean warmly, prejudice being a failing which all women marvel at. "Just listen to what the boy said to Elspeth to-day. He said to her, 'When I am away, try for a whole day to be better than you ever were before, and think of nothing else, and then when prayer-time comes you will see that you have been happy without knowing it.' Fancy his finding out that."

"I wonder if he ever tried it himself?" said Mr. McLean.

"Ivie, think shame of yourself!"

"Well, even Cathro admits that he has a kind of cleverness, but —"

"Cleverness!" exclaimed Ailie, indignantly, "that is not cleverness, it is holiness;" and leaving the cynic she sought Elspeth, and did her good by pointing out that a girl who had such a brother should try to save him pain. "He is very miserable, dear," she said, "because you are so unhappy. If you looked brighter, think how that would help him, and it would show that you are worthy of him." So Elspeth went home trying hard to look brighter, but made a sad mess of it.

"Think of getting letters frae me every time the post comes in!" said Tommy, and then indeed her face shone.

And then Elspeth could write to him—yes, as often as ever she liked! This pleased her even more. It was such an exquisite thought that she could not wait, but wrote the first one before he started, and he answered it across the table. And Mrs. McLean made a letter bag, with two strings to it, and showed her how to carry it about with her in a safer place than a pocket.

Then a cheering thing occurred. Came Corp, with the astounding news that, in the Glenquharity dominie's opinion, Tommy should have got the Hugh Blackadder.

"He says he is glad he wasna judge, because he would have had to give you the prize, and he laughs like to split at the ministers for giving it to Lauchlan McLauchlan."

Now, great was the repute of Mr. Ogilvy, and Tommy gaped incredulous. "He had no word of that at the time," he said.

"No likely! He says if the ministers was so doited as to think his loon did best, it wasna for him to conter them."

"Man, Corp, you ca'me me aff my feet! How do you ken this?"

Corp had promised not to tell, and he thought he did not tell, but Tommy was too clever for him. Grizel, it appeared, had heard Mr. Ogilvy saying this strange thing to the doctor, and she burned to pass it on to Tommy, but she could not carry it to him herself, because-Why was it? Oh, yes, because she hated him. So she made a messenger of Corp, and warned him against telling who had sent him with the news.

Half enlightened, Tommy began to strut again. "You see there's something in me for all they say," he told Elspeth. "Listen to this. At the bursary examinations there was some English we had to turn into Latin, and it said, 'No man ever attained supreme eminence who worked for mere lucre; such efforts must ever be bounded by base mediocrity. None shall climb high but he who climbs for love, for in truth where the heart is, there alone shall the treasure be found.' Elspeth, it came ower me in a clink how true that was, and I sat saying it to myself, though I saw Gav Dishart and Willie Simpson and the rest beginning to put it into Latin at once, as little ta'en up wi' the words as if they had been about auld Hannibal. I aye kent, Elspeth, that I could never do much at the learning, but I didna see the reason till I read that. Syne I kent that playing so real-like in the Den, and telling about my fits when it wasna me that had them but Corp, and mourning for Lewis Doig's father, and writing letters for folk so grandly, and a' my other queer ploys that ended in Cathro's calling me Sentimental Tommy, was what my heart was in, and I saw in a jiffy that if thae things were work, I should soon rise to supreme eminence."

"But they're no," said Elspeth, sadly.

"No," he admitted, his face falling, "but, Elspeth, if I was to hear some day of work I could put my heart into as if it were a game! I wouldna be laug in finding the treasure syne. Oh, the blatter I would make!"

"I doubt there's no sic work," she answered, but he told her not to be so sure. "I thought there wasna mysel'," he said, "till now, but sure as death my heart was as ta'en up wi' hunting for the right word as if it had been a game, and that was how the time slipped by so quick. Yet it was paying work, for the way I did it made Mr. Ogilvy see I should have got the prize, and a' body kens there's more cleverness in him than in a cart-load o' ministers."

"But, but there are no more Hugh Blackadders to try for, Tommy?"

"That's nothing, there maun be other work o' the same kind. Elspeth, cheer up, I tell you, I'll find a wy!"

"But you didna ken yoursel' that you should have got the Hugh Blackadder?"

He would not let this depress him. "I ken now," he said. Nevertheless, why he should have got it was a mystery which he longed to fathom. Mr. Ogilvy had returned to Glenquharity, so that an explanation could not be drawn from him even if he were willing to supply it, which was improbable; but Tommy caught Grizel in the Banker's Close and compelled her to speak.

"I won't tell you a word of what Mr. Ogilvy said," she insisted, in her obstinate way, and, oh, how she despised Corp for breaking his promise.

"Corp didna ken he telled me," said Tommy, less to clear Corp than to exalt himself, "I wriggled it out o' him;" but even this did not bring Grizel to a proper frame of mind, so he said, to annoy her,

"At any rate you're fond o' me."

"I am not," she replied, stamping; "I think you are horrid."

"What else made you send Corp to me?"

"I did that because I heard you were calling yourself a blockhead."

"Oho," said he, "so you have been speiring about me though you winna speak to me!"

Grizel looked alarmed, and thinking to weaken his case, said, hastily, "I very nearly kept it from you, I said often to myself 'I won't tell him.'"

"So you have been thinking a lot about me!" was his prompt comment.

"If I have," she retorted, "I did not think nice things. And what is more, I was angry with myself for telling Corp to tell you."

Surely this was crushing, but apparently Tommy did not think so, for he said, "You did it against your will! That means I hae a power over you that you canna resist. Oho, oho!"

Had she become more friendly so should he, had she shed one tear he would have melted immediately; but she only looked him up and down disdainfully, and it hardened him. He said with a leer, "I ken what makes you hold your hands so tight, it's to keep your arms frae wagging;" and then her cry, "How do you know?" convicted her. He had not succeeded in his mission, but on his way home he muttered, triumphantly, "I did her, I did her!" and once he stopped to ask himself the question, "Was it because my heart was in it?" It was their last meeting till they were man and woman.

* * * * *

A blazing sun had come out on top of heavy showers, and the land reeked and smelled as of the wash-tub. The smaller girls of Monypenny were sitting in passages playing at fivey, just as Sappho for instance used to play it; but they heard the Dubb of Prosen cart draw up at Aaron Latta's door, and they followed it to see the last of Tommy Sandys. Corp was already there, calling in at the door every time he heard a sob; "Dinna, Elspeth, dinna, he'll find a wy," but Grizel had refused to come, though Tommy knew that she had been asking when he started and which road the cart would take. Well, he was not giving her a thought at any rate; his box was in the cart now, and his face was streaked with tears that were all for Elspeth. She should not have come to the door, but she came, and-it was such a pitiable sight that Aaron Latta could not look on. He went hurriedly to his workshop, but not to warp, and even the carter was touched and he said to Tommy, "I tell you what, man, I have to go round by Causeway End smiddy, and you and the crittur have time, if you like, to take the short cut and meet me at the far corner o' Caddam wood."

So Tommy and Elspeth, holding each other's hands, took the short cut and they came to the far end of Caddam, and Elspeth thought they had better say it here before the cart came; but Tommy said he would walk back with her through the wood as far as the Toom Well, and they could say it there. They tried to say it at the Well, but-Elspeth was still with him when he returned to the far corner of Caddam, where the cart was now awaiting him. The carter was sitting on the shaft, and he told them he was in no hurry, and what is more, he had the delicacy to turn his back on them and struck his horse with the reins for looking round at the sorrowful pair. They should have said it now, but first Tommy walked back a little bit of the way with Elspeth, and then she came back with him, and that was to be the last time, but he could not leave her, and so, there they were in the wood, looking woefully at each other, and it was not said yet.

They had said it now, and all was over; they were several paces apart. Elspeth smiled, she had promised to smile because Tommy said it would kill him if she was greeting at the very end. But what a smile it was! Tommy whistled, he had promised to whistle to show that he was happy as long as Elspeth could smile. She stood still, but he went on, turning round every few yards to-to whistle. "Never forget, day nor night, what I said to you," he called to her. "You're the only one I love, and I care not a hair for Grizel."

But when he disappeared, shouting to her, "I'll find a wy, I'll find a wy," she screamed and ran after him. He was already in the cart, and it had started. He stood up in it and waved his hand to her, and she stood on the dyke and waved to him, and thus they stood waving till a hollow in the road swallowed cart and man and boy. Then Elspeth put her hands to her eyes and went sobbing homeward.

When she was gone, a girl who had heard all that passed between them rose from among the broom of Caddam and took Elspeth's place on the dyke, where she stood motionless waiting for the cart to reappear as it climbed the other side of the hollow. She wore a black frock and a blue bonnet with white strings, but the cart was far away, and Tommy thought she was Elspeth, and springing to his feet again in the cart he waved and waved. At first she did not respond, for had she not heard him say, "You're the only one I love, and I care not a hair for Grizel?"

185

And she knew he was mistaking her for Elspeth. But by and by it struck her that he would be more unhappy if he thought Elspeth was too overcome by grief to wave to him. Her arms rocked passionately; no, no, she would not lift them to wave to him, he could be as unhappy as he chose. Then in a spirit of self-abnegation that surely raised her high among the daughters of men, though she was but a painted lady's child, she waved to him to save him pain, and he, still erect in the cart, waved back until nothing could be seen by either of them save wood and fields and a long, deserted road.

Tommy and Grizel

Part I

Chapter I
How Tommy Found a Way

O.P. Pym, the colossal Pym, that vast and rolling figure, who never knew what he was to write about until he dipped grandly, an author in such demand that on the foggy evening which starts our story his publishers have had his boots removed lest he slip thoughtlessly round the corner before his work is done, as was the great man's way-shall we begin with him, or with Tommy, who has just arrived in London, carrying his little box and leading a lady by the hand? It was Pym, as we are about to see, who in the beginning held Tommy up to the public gaze, Pym who first noticed his remarkable indifference to female society, Pym who gave him — —But alack! does no one remember Pym for himself? Is the king of the *Penny Number* already no more than a button that once upon a time kept Tommy's person together? And we are at the night when they first met! Let us hasten into Marylebone before little Tommy arrives and Pym is swallowed like an oyster.

This is the house, 22 Little Owlet Street, Marylebone, but which were his rooms it is less easy to determine, for he was a lodger who flitted placidly from floor to floor according to the state of his finances, carrying his apparel and other belongings in one great armful, and spilling by the way. On this particular evening he was on the second floor front, which had a fireplace in the corner, furniture all his landlady's and mostly horsehair, little to suggest his calling save a noble saucerful of ink, and nothing to draw attention from Pym, who lolled, gross and massive, on a sofa, one leg over the back of it, the other drooping, his arms extended, and his pipe, which he could find nowhere, thrust between the buttons of his waistcoat, an agreeable pipe-rack. He wore a yellow dressing-gown, or could scarcely be said to wear it, for such of it as was not round his neck he had converted into a cushion for his head, which is perhaps the part of him we should have turned to first It was a big round head, the plentiful gray hair in tangles, possibly because in Pym's last flitting the comb had dropped over the banisters; the features were ugly and beyond life-size, yet the forehead had altered little except in colour since the day when he was near being made a fellow of his college; there was sensitiveness left in the thick nose, humour in the eyes, though they so often watered; the face had gone to flabbiness at last, but not without some lines and dents, as if the head had resisted the body for a space before the whole man rolled contentedly downhill.

He had no beard. "Young man, let your beard grow." Those who have forgotten all else about Pym may recall him in these words. They were his one counsel to literary aspirants, who, according as they took it, are now bearded and prosperous or shaven and on the rates. To shave costs threepence, another threepence for loss of time-nearly ten pounds a year, three hundred pounds since Pym's chin first bristled. With his beard he could have bought an annuity or a cottage in the country, he could have had a wife and children, and driven his dog-cart, and been made a church-warden. All gone, all shaved, and for what? When he asked this question he would move his hand across his chin with a sigh, and so, bravely to the barber's.

Pym was at present suffering from an ailment that had spread him out on that sofa again and again-acute disinclination to work.

Meanwhile all the world was waiting for his new tale; so the publishers, two little round men, have told him. They have blustered, they have fawned, they have asked each other out to talk it over behind the door.

Has he any idea of what the story is to be about?

He has no idea.

Then at least, Pym-excellent Pym-sit down and dip, and let us see what will happen.

He declined to do even that. While all the world waited, this was Pym's ultimatum:

"I shall begin the damned thing at eight o'clock."

Outside, the fog kept changing at intervals from black to white, as lazily from white to black (the monster blinking); there was not a sound from the street save of pedestrians tapping with their sticks on the pavement as they moved forward warily, afraid of an embrace with the unknown; it might have been a city of blind beggars, one of them a boy.

At eight o'clock Pym rose with a groan and sat down in his stocking-soles to write his delicious tale. He was now alone. But though his legs were wound round his waste-paper basket, and he dipped often and loudly in the saucer, like one ringing at the door of Fancy, he could not get the idea that would set him going. He was still dipping for inspiration when T. Sandys, who had been told to find the second floor for himself, knocked at the door, and entered, quaking.

"I remember it vividly," Pym used to say when questioned in the after years about this his first sight of Tommy, "and I hesitate to decide which impressed me more, the richness of his voice, so remarkable in a boy of sixteen, or his serene countenance, with its noble forehead, behind which nothing base could lurk."

Pym, Pym! it is such as you that makes the writing of biography difficult. The richness of Tommy's voice could not have struck you, for at that time it was a somewhat squeaky voice; and as for the noble forehead behind which nothing base could lurk, how could you say that, Pym, you who had a noble forehead yourself?

No; all that Pym saw was a pasty-faced boy sixteen years old, and of an appearance mysteriously plain; hair light brown, and waving defiance to the brush; nothing startling about him but the expression of his face, which was almost fearsomely solemn and apparently unchangeable. He wore his Sunday blacks, of which the trousers might with advantage have borrowed from the sleeves; and he was so nervous that he had to wet his lips before he could speak. He had left the door ajar for a private reason; but Pym, misunderstanding, thought he did it to fly the more readily if anything was flung at him, and so concluded that he must be a printer's devil. Pym had a voice that shook his mantelpiece ornaments; he was all on the same scale as his ink-pot. "Your Christian name, boy?" he roared hopefully, for it was thus he sometimes got the idea that started him.

"Thomas," replied the boy.

Pym gave him a look of disgust "You may go," he said. But when he looked up presently, Thomas was still there. He was not only there, but whistling —a short, encouraging whistle that seemed to be directed at the door. He stopped quickly when Pym looked up, but during the remainder of the interview he emitted this whistle at intervals, always with that anxious glance at his friend the door; and its strained joviality was in odd contrast with his solemn face, like a cheery tune played on the church organ.

"Begone!" cried Pym.

"My full name," explained Tommy, who was speaking the English correctly, but with a Scots accent, "is Thomas Sandys. And fine you know who that is," he added, exasperated by Pym's indifference. "I'm the T. Sandys that answered your advertisement."

Pym knew who he was now. "You young ruffian," he gasped, "I never dreamt that you would come!"

"I have your letter engaging me in my pocket," said Tommy, boldly, and he laid it on the table. Pym surveyed it and him in comic dismay, then with a sudden thought produced nearly a dozen letters from a drawer, and dumped them down beside the other. It was now his turn to look triumphant and Tommy aghast.

Pym's letters were all addressed from the Dubb of Prosen Farm, near Thrums, N.B., to different advertisers, care of a London agency, and were Tommy's answers to the "wants" in a London newspaper which had found its way to the far North. "X Y Z" was in need of a chemist's assistant, and from his earliest years, said one of the letters, chemistry had been the study of studies for T. Sandys. He was glad to read, was T. Sandys, that one who did not object to long hours would be preferred, for it seemed to him that those who objected to long hours did not really love their work, their heart was not in it, and only where the heart is can the treasure be found.

"123" had a vacancy for a page-boy, "Glasgow Man" for a photographer; page-boy must not be over fourteen, photographer must not be under twenty. "I am a little over fourteen, but I look less," wrote T. Sandys to "123"; "I am a little under twenty," he wrote to "Glasgow Man," "but I look more." His heart was in the work.

To be a political organizer! If "H and H," who advertised for one, only knew how eagerly the undersigned desired to devote his life to political organizing!

In answer to "Scholastic's" advertisement for janitor in a boys' school, T. Sandys begged to submit his name for consideration.

Undoubtedly the noblest letter was the one applying for the secretaryship of a charitable society, salary to begin at once, but the candidate selected must deposit one hundred pounds. The application was noble in its offer to make the work a labour of love, and almost nobler in its argument that the hundred pounds was unnecessary.

"Rex" had a vacancy in his drapery department. T. Sandys had made a unique study of drapery.

Lastly, "Anon" wanted an amanuensis. "Salary," said "Anon," who seemed to be a humourist, "salary large but uncertain." He added with equal candour: "Drudgery great, but to an intelligent man the pickings may be considerable." Pickings! Is there a finer word in the language? T. Sandys had felt that he was particularly good at pickings. But amanuensis? The thing was unknown to him; no one on the farm could tell him what it was. But never mind; his heart was in it.

All this correspondence had produced one reply, the letter on which Tommy's hand still rested. It was a brief note, signed "O.P. Pym," and engaging Mr. Sandys on his own recommendation, "if he really felt quite certain that his heart (treasure included) was in the work." So far good, Tommy had thought when he received this answer, but there was nothing in it to indicate the nature of the work, nothing to show whether O.P. Pym was "Scholastic," or "123," or "Rex," or any other advertiser in particular. Stop, there was a postscript: "I need not go into details about your duties, as you assure me you are so well acquainted with them, but before you join me please send (in writing) a full statement of what you think they are."

There were delicate reasons why Mr. Sandys could not do that, but oh, he was anxious to be done with farm labour, so he decided to pack and risk it. The letter said plainly that he was engaged; what for he must find out slyly when he came to London. So he had put his letter firmly on Pym's table; but it was a staggerer to find that gentleman in possession of the others.

One of these was Pym's by right; the remainder were a humourous gift from the agent who was accustomed to sift the correspondence of his clients. Pym had chuckled over them, and written a reply that he flattered himself would stump the boy; then he had unexpectedly come into funds (he found a forgotten check while searching his old pockets for tobacco-crumbs), and in that glory T. Sandys escaped his memory. Result, that they were now face to face.

A tiny red spot, not noticeable before, now appeared in Tommy's eyes. It was never there except when he was determined to have his way. Pym, my friend, yes, and everyone of you who is destined to challenge Tommy, 'ware that red light!

"Well, which am I?" demanded Pym, almost amused, Tommy was so obviously in a struggle with the problem.

The saucer and the blank pages told nothing. "Whichever you are," the boy answered heavily, "it's not herding nor foddering cattle, and so long as it's not that, I'll put my heart in it, and where the heart is, there the treasure —"

He suddenly remembered that his host must be acquainted with the sentiment.

Easy-going Pym laughed, then said irritably, "Of what use could a mere boy be to me?"

"Then it's not the page-boy!" exclaimed Tommy, thankfully.

"Perhaps I am 'Scholastic,'" suggested Pym.

"No," said Tommy, after a long study of his face.

Pym followed this reasoning, and said touchily, "Many a schoolmaster has a red face."

"Not that kind of redness," explained Tommy, without delicacy.

"I am 'H and H,'" said Pym.

"You forget you wrote to me as one person," replied Tommy. "So I did. That was because I am the chemist; and I must ask you, Thomas, for your certificate."

Tommy believed him this time, and Pym triumphantly poured himself a glass of whisky, spilling some of it on his dressing-gown.

"Not you," said Tommy, quickly; "a chemist has a steady hand."

"Confound you!" cried Pym, "what sort of a boy is this?"

"If you had been the draper you would have wiped the drink off your gown," continued Tommy, thoughtfully, "and if you had been 'Glasgow Man' you would have sucked it off, and if you had been the charitable society you wouldn't swear in company." He flung out his hand. "I'll tell you who you are," he said sternly, "you're 'Anon.'"

Under this broadside Pym succumbed. He sat down feebly. "Right," he said, with a humourous groan, "and I shall tell you who you are. I am afraid you are my amanuensis!"

Tommy immediately whistled, a louder and more glorious note than before.

"Don't be so cocky," cried Pym, in sudden rebellion. "You are only my amanuensis if you can tell me what that is. If you can't —out you go!"

He had him at last! Not he!

"An amanuensis," said Tommy, calmly, "is one who writes to dictation. Am I to bring in my box? It's at the door."

This made Pym sit down again. "You didn't know what an amanuensis was when you answered my advertisement," he said.

"As soon as I got to London," Tommy answered, "I went into a bookseller's shop, pretending I wanted to buy a dictionary, and I looked the word up."

"Bring in your box," Pym said, with a groan.

But it was now Tommy's turn to hesitate. "Have you noticed," he asked awkwardly, "that I sometimes whistle?"

"Don't tell me," said Pym, "that you have a dog out there."

"It's not a dog," Tommy replied cautiously.

Pym had resumed his seat at the table and was once more toying with his pen. "Open the door," he commanded, "and let me see what you have brought with you."

Tommy obeyed gingerly, and then Pym gaped, for what the open door revealed to him was a tiny roped box with a girl of twelve sitting on it. She was dressed in some dull-coloured wincey, and looked cold and patient and lonely, and as she saw the big man staring at her she struggled in alarm to her feet, and could scarce stand on them. Tommy was looking apprehensively from her to Pym.

"Good God, boy!" roared Pym, "are you married?"

"No," cried Tommy, in agony, "she's my sister, and we're orphans, and did you think I could have the heart to leave Elspeth behind?" He took her stoutly by the hand.

"And he never will marry," said little Elspeth, almost fiercely; "will you, Tommy?"

"Never!" said Tommy, patting her and glaring at Pym.

But Pym would not have it. "Married!" he shouted. "Magnificent!" And he dipped exultantly, for he had got his idea at last. Forgetting even that he had an amanuensis, he wrote on and on and on.

"He smells o' drink," Elspeth whispered.

"All the better," replied Tommy, cheerily. "Make yourself at home, Elspeth; he's the kind I can manage. Was there ever a kind I couldna manage?" he whispered, top-heavy with conceit.

"There was Grizel," Elspeth said, rather thoughtlessly; and then Tommy frowned.

Chapter II
The Search for the Treasure

Six years afterwards Tommy was a famous man, as I hope you do not need to be told; but you may be wondering how it came about. The whole question, in Pym's words, resolves itself into how the solemn little devil got to know so much about women. It made the world marvel when they learned his age, but no one was quite so staggered as Pym, who had seen him daily for all those years, and been damning him for his indifference to the sex during the greater part of them.

It began while he was still no more than an amanuensis, sitting with his feet in the waste-paper basket, Pym dictating from the sofa, and swearing when the words would not come unless he was perpendicular. Among the duties of this amanuensis was to remember the name of the heroine, her appearance, and other personal details; for Pym constantly forgot them in the night, and he had to go searching back through his pages for them, cursing her so horribly that Tommy signed to Elspeth to retire to her tiny bedroom at the top of the house. He was always most careful of Elspeth, and with the first pound he earned he insured his life, leaving all to her, but told her nothing about it, lest she should think it meant his early death. As she grew older he also got good dull books for her from a library, and gave her a piano on the hire system, and taught her many things about life, very carefully selected from his own discoveries.

Elspeth out of the way, he could give Pym all the information wanted. "Her name is Felicity," he would say at the right moment; "she has curly brown hair in which the sun strays, and a blushing neck, and her eyes are like blue lakes."

"Height!" roared Pym. "Have I mentioned it?"

"No; but she is about five feet six."

"How the —— could you know that?"

"You tell Percy's height in his stocking-soles, and when she reached to his mouth and kissed him she had to stand on her tiptoes so to do."

Tommy said this in a most businesslike tone, but could not help smacking his lips. He smacked them again when he had to write: "Have no fear, little woman; I am by your side." Or, "What a sweet child you are!"

Pym had probably fallen into the way of making the Percys revel in such epithets because he could not remember the girl's name; but this delicious use of the diminutive, as addressed to full-grown ladies, went to Tommy's head. His solemn face kept his secret, but he had some narrow escapes; as once, when saying good-night to Elspeth, he kissed her on mouth, eyes, nose, and ears, and said: "Shall I tuck you in, little woman?" He came to himself with a start.

"I forgot," he said hurriedly, and got out of the room without telling her what he had forgotten.

Pym's publishers knew their man, and their arrangement with him was that he was paid on completion of the tale. But always before he reached the middle he struck for what they called his honorarium; and this troubled them, for the tale was appearing week by week as it was written. If they were obdurate, he suddenly concluded his story in such words as these:

"Several years have passed since these events took place, and the scene changes to a lovely garden by the bank of old Father Thames. A young man sits by the soft-flowing stream, and he is calm as the scene itself; for the storm has passed away, and Percy (for it is no other) has found an anchorage. As he sits musing over the past, Felicity steals out by the French window and puts her soft arms around his neck. 'My little wife!' he murmurs. *The End-unless you pay up by messenger.*"

This last line, which was not meant for the world (but little would Pym have cared though it had been printed), usually brought his employers to their knees; and then, as Tommy advanced in experience, came the pickings-for Pym, with money in his pockets, had important engagements round the corner, and risked intrusting his amanuensis with the writing of the next instalment, "all except the bang at the end."

Smaller people, in Tommy's state of mind, would have hurried straight to the love-passages; but he saw the danger, and forced his Pegasus away from them. "Do your day's toil first," he may be conceived saying to that animal, "and at evenfall I shall let you out to browse." So, with this reward in front, he devoted many pages to the dreary adventures of pretentious males, and even found a certain pleasure in keeping the lady waiting. But as soon as he reached her he lost his head again.

"Oh, you beauty! oh, you small pet!" he said to himself, with solemn transport.

As the artist in him was stirred, great problems presented themselves; for instance, in certain circumstances was "darling" or "little one" the better phrase? "Darling" in solitary grandeur is more pregnant of meaning than "little one," but "little" has a flavour of the patronizing which "darling" perhaps lacks. He wasted many sheets over such questions; but they were in his pocket when Pym or Elspeth opened the door. It is wonderful how much you can conceal between the touch on the handle and the opening of the door, if your heart is in it.

Despite this fine practice, however, he was the shyest of mankind in the presence of women, and this shyness grew upon him with the years. Was it because he never tried to uncork himself? Oh, no! It was about this time that he, one day, put his arm round Clara, the servant-not passionately, but with deliberation, as if he were making an experiment with machinery. He then listened, as if to hear Clara ticking. He wrote an admirable love-letter —warm, dignified, sincere-to nobody in particular, and carried it about in his pocket in readiness. But in love-making, as in the other arts, those do it best who cannot tell how it is done; and he was always stricken with a palsy when about to present that letter. It seemed that he was only able to speak to ladies when they were not there. Well, if he could not speak, he thought the more; he thought so profoundly that in time the heroines of Pym ceased to thrill him.

This was because he had found out that they were not flesh and blood. But he did not delight in his discovery: it horrified him; for what he wanted was the old thrill. To make them human so that they could be his little friends again-nothing less was called for. This meant slaughter here and there of the great Pym's brain-work, and Tommy tried to keep his hands off; but his heart was in it. In Pym's pages the ladies were the most virtuous and proper of their sex (though dreadfully persecuted), but he merely told you so at the beginning, and now and again afterwards to fill up, and then allowed them to act with what may be called rashness, so that the story did not really suffer. Before Tommy was nineteen he changed all that. Out went this because she would not have done it, and that because she could not have done it. Fathers might now have taken a lesson from T. Sandys in the upbringing of their daughters. He even sternly struck out the diminutives. With a pen in his hand and woman in his head, he had such noble thoughts that his tears of exaltation damped the pages as he wrote, and the ladies must have been astounded as well as proud to see what they were turning into.

That was Tommy with a pen in his hand and a handkerchief hard by; but it was another Tommy who, when the finest bursts were over, sat back in his chair and mused. The lady was consistent now, and he would think about her, and think and think, until concentration, which is a pair of blazing eyes, seemed to draw her out of the pages to his side, and then he and she sported in a way forbidden in the tale. While he sat there with eyes riveted, he had her to dinner at a restaurant, and took her up the river, and called her "little woman"; and when she held up her mouth he said tantalizingly that she must wait until he had finished his cigar. This queer delight enjoyed, back he popped her into the story, where she was again the vehicle for such glorious sentiments that Elspeth, to whom he read the best of them, feared he was becoming too good to live.

In the meantime the great penny public were slowly growing restive, and at last the two little round men called on Pym to complain that he was falling off; and Pym turned them out of doors, and then sat down heroically to do what he had not done for two decades-to read his latest work.

"Elspeth, go upstairs to your room," whispered Tommy, and then he folded his arms proudly. He should have been in a tremble, but latterly he had often felt that he must burst if he did not soon read some of his bits to Pym, more especially the passages about the hereafter; also the opening of Chapter Seventeen.

At first Pym's only comment was, "It is the same old drivel as before; what more can they want?"

But presently he looked up, puzzled. "Is this chapter yours or mine?" he demanded.

"It is about half and half," said Tommy.

"Is mine the first half? Where does yours begin?" "That is not exactly what I mean," explained Tommy, in a glow, but backing a little; "you wrote that chapter first, and then I—I—"

"You rewrote it!" roared Pym. "You dared to meddle with—" He was speechless with fury.

"I tried to keep my hand off," Tommy said, with dignity, "but the thing had to be done, and they are human now."

"Human! who wants them to be human? The fiends seize you, boy! you have even been tinkering with my heroine's personal appearance; what is this you have been doing to her nose?"

"I turned it up slightly, that's all," said Tommy.

"I like them down," roared Pym.

"I prefer them up," said Tommy, stiffly.

"Where," cried Pym, turning over the leaves in a panic, "where is the scene in the burning house?"

"It's out," Tommy explained, "but there is a chapter in its place about-it's mostly about the beauty of the soul being everything, and mere physical beauty nothing. Oh, Mr. Pym, sit down and let me read it to you."

But Pym read it, and a great deal more, for himself. No wonder he stormed, for the impossible had been made not only consistent, but unreadable. The plot was lost for chapters. The characters no longer did anything, and then went and did something else: you were told instead how they did it. You were not allowed to make up your own mind about them: you had to listen to the mind of T. Sandys; he described and he analyzed; the road he had tried to clear through the thicket was impassable for chips.

"A few more weeks of this," said Pym, "and we should all three be turned out into the streets."

Tommy went to bed in an agony of mortification, but presently to his side came Pym.

"Where did you copy this from?" he asked. "'It is when we are thinking of those we love that our noblest thoughts come to us, and the more worthy they are of our love the nobler the thought; hence it is that no one has done the greatest work who did not love God.'"

"I copied it from nowhere," replied Tommy, fiercely; "it's my own."

"Well, it has nothing to do with the story, and so is only a blot on it, and I have no doubt the thing has been said much better before. Still, I suppose it is true."

"It's true," said Tommy; "and yet—"

"Go on. I want to know all about it."

"And yet," Tommy said, puzzled, "I've known noble thoughts come to me when I was listening to a brass band."

Pym chuckled. "Funny things, noble thoughts," he agreed. He read another passage: "'It was the last half-hour of day when I was admitted, with several others, to look upon my friend's dead face. A handkerchief had been laid over it. I raised the handkerchief. I know not what the others were thinking, but the last time we met he had told me something, it was not much-only that no woman had ever kissed him. It seemed to me that, as I gazed, the wistfulness came back to his face. I whispered to a woman who was present, and stooping over him, she was about to-but her eyes were dry, and I stopped her. The handkerchief was replaced, and all left the room save myself. Again I raised the handkerchief. I cannot tell you how innocent he looked.'"

"Who was he?" asked Pym.

"Nobody," said Tommy, with some awe; "it just came to me. Do you notice how simple the wording is? It took me some time to make it so simple."

"You are just nineteen, I think?"

"Yes."

Pym looked at him wonderingly.

"Thomas," he said, "you are a very queer little devil."

He also said: "And it is possible you may find the treasure you are always talking about. Don't jump to the ceiling, my friend, because I say that. I was once after the treasure, myself; and you can see whether I found it."

From about that time, on the chances that this mysterious treasure might spring up in the form of a new kind of flower, Pym zealously cultivated the ground, and Tommy had an industrious time of it. He was taken off his stories, which at once regained their elasticity, and put on to exercises.

"If you have nothing to say on the subject, say nothing," was one of the new rules, which few would have expected from Pym. Another was: "As soon as you can say what you think, and not what some other person has thought for you, you are on the way to being a remarkable man."

"Without concentration, Thomas, you are lost; concentrate, though your coat-tails be on fire.

"Try your hand at description, and when you have done chortling over the result, reduce the whole by half without missing anything out.

"Analyze your characters and their motives at the prodigious length in which you revel, and then, my sonny, cut your analysis out. It is for your own guidance, not the reader's.

"'I have often noticed,' you are always saying. The story has nothing to do with you. Obliterate yourself. I see that will be your stiffest job.

"Stop preaching. It seems to me the pulpit is where you should look for the treasure. Nineteen, and you are already as didactic as seventy."

And so on. Over his exercises Tommy was now engrossed for so long a period that, as he sits there, you may observe his legs slowly lengthening and the coming of his beard. No, his legs lengthened as he sat with his feet in the basket; but I feel sure that his beard burst through prematurely some night when he was thinking too hard about the ladies.

There were no ladies in the exercises, for, despite their altercation about noses, Pym knew that on this subject Tommy's mind was a blank. But he recognized the sex's importance, and becoming possessed once more of a black coat, marched his pupil into the somewhat shoddy drawing-rooms that were still open to him, and there ordered Tommy to be fascinated for his future good. But it was as it had always been. Tommy sat white and speechless and apparently bored; could not even say, "You sing with so much expression!" when the lady at the pianoforte had finished.

"Shyness I could pardon," the exasperated Pym would roar; "but want of interest is almost immoral. At your age the blood would have been coursing through my veins. Love! You are incapable of it. There is not a drop of sentiment in your frozen carcass."

"Can I help that?" growled Tommy. It was an agony to him even to speak about women.

"If you can't," said Pym, "all is over with you. An artist without sentiment is a painter without colours. Young man, I fear you are doomed."

And Tommy believed him, and quaked. He had the most gallant struggles with himself. He even set his teeth and joined a dancing-class; though neither Pym nor Elspeth knew of it, and it never showed afterwards in his legs. In appearance he was now beginning to be the Sandys of the photographs: a little over the middle height and rather heavily built; nothing to make you uncomfortable until you saw his face. That solemn countenance never responded when he laughed, and stood coldly by when he was on fire; he might have winked for an eternity, and still the onlooker must have thought himself mistaken. In his boyhood the mask had descended scarce below his mouth, for there was a dimple in the chin to put you at ease; but now the short brown beard had come, and he was for ever hidden from the world.

He had the dandy's tastes for superb neckties, velvet jackets, and he got the ties instead of dining; he panted for the jacket, knew all the shop-windows it was in, but for years denied himself, with a moan, so that he might buy pretty things for Elspeth. When eventually he got it, Pym's friends ridiculed him. When he saw how ill his face matched it he ridiculed himself.

Often when Tommy was feeling that now at last the ladies must come to heel, he saw his face suddenly in a mirror, and all the spirit went out of him. But still he clung to his velvet jacket.

I see him in it, stalking through the terrible dances, a heroic figure at last. He shuddered every time he found himself on one leg; he got sternly into everybody's way; he was the butt of the little noodle of an instructor. All the social tortures he endured grimly, in the hope that at last the cork would come out. Then, though there were all kinds of girls in the class, merry, sentimental, practical, coquettish, prudes, there was no kind, he felt, whose heart he could not touch. In love-making, as in the favourite Thrums game of the dambrod, there are sixty-one openings, and he knew them all. Yet at the last dance, as at the first, the universal opinion of his partners (shop-girls, mostly, from the large millinery establishments, who had to fly like Cinderellas when the clock struck a certain hour) was that he kept himself to himself, and they were too much the lady to make up to a gentleman who so obviously did not want them.

Pym encouraged his friends to jeer at Tommy's want of interest in the sex, thinking it a way of goading him to action. One evening, the bottles circulating, they mentioned one Dolly, goddess at some bar, as a fit instructress for him. Coarse pleasantries passed, but for a time he writhed in silence, then burst upon them indignantly for their unmanly smirching of a woman's character, and swept out, leaving them a little ashamed. That was very like Tommy.

But presently a desire came over him to see this girl, and it came because they had hinted such dark things about her. That was like him also.

There was probably no harm in Dolly, though it is man's proud right to question it in ex-change for his bitters. She was tall and willowy, and stretched her neck like a swan, and returned you your change with disdainful languor; to call such a haughty beauty Dolly was one of the minor triumphs for man, and Dolly they all called her, except the only one who could have given an artistic justification for it.

This one was a bearded stranger who, when he knew that Pym and his friends were elsewhere, would enter the bar with a cigar in his mouth, and ask for a whisky-and-water, which was heroism again, for smoking was ever detestable to him, and whisky more offensive than quinine. But these things are expected of you, and by asking for the whisky you get into talk with Dolly; that is to say, you tell her several times what you want, and when she has served every other body you get it. The commercial must be served first; in the barroom he blocks the way like royalty in the street. There is a crown for us all somewhere.

Dolly seldom heard the bearded one's "good-evening"; she could not possibly have heard the "dear," for though it was there, it remained behind his teeth. She knew him only as the stiff man who got separated from his glass without complaining, and at first she put this down to forgetfulness, and did nothing, so that he could go away without drinking; but by and by, wherever he left his tumbler, cunningly concealed behind a water-bottle, or temptingly in front of a commercial, she restored it to him, and there was a twinkle in her eye.

"You little rogue, so you see through me!" Surely it was an easy thing to say; but what he did say was "Thank you." Then to himself he said, "Ass, ass, ass!"

Sitting on the padded seat that ran the length of the room, and surreptitiously breaking his cigar against the cushions to help it on its way to an end, he brought his intellect to bear on Dolly at a distance, and soon had a better knowledge of her than could be claimed by those who had Dollied her for years. He also wove romances about her, some of them of too lively a character, and others so noble and sad and beautiful that the tears came to his eyes, and Dolly thought he had been drinking. He could not have said whether he would prefer her to be good or bad.

These were but his leisure moments, for during the long working hours he was still at the exercises, toiling fondly, and right willing to tear himself asunder to get at the trick of writing. So he passed from exercises to the grand experiment.

It was to be a tale, for there, they had taken for granted, lay the treasure. Pym was most considerate at this time, and mentioned woman with an apology.

"I have kept away from them in the exercises," he said in effect, "because it would have been useless (as well as cruel) to force you to labour on a subject so uncongenial to you; and for the same reason I have decided that it is to be a tale of adventure, in which the heroine need be little more than a beautiful sack of coals which your cavalier carries about with him on his left shoulder. I am afraid we must have her to that extent, Thomas, but I am not asking much of you; dump her down as often as you like."

And Thomas did his dogged best, the red light in his eye; though he had not, and never could have had, the smallest instinct for story-writing, he knew to the finger-tips how it is done; but for ever he would have gone on breaking all the rules of the game. How he wrestled with himself! Sublime thoughts came to him (nearly all about that girl), and he drove them away, for he knew they beat only against the march of his story, and, whatever befall, the story must march. Relentlessly he followed in the track of his men, pushing the dreary dogs on to deeds of valour. He tried making the lady human, and then she would not march; she sat still, and he talked about her; he dumped her down, and soon he was yawning. This weariness was what alarmed him most, for well he understood that there could be no treasure where the work was not engrossing play, and he doubted no more than Pym that for him the treasure was in the tale or nowhere. Had he not been sharpening his tools in this belief for years? Strange to reflect now that all the time he was hacking and sweating at that novel (the last he ever attempted) it was only marching towards the waste-paper basket!

He had a fine capacity, as has been hinted, for self-deception, and in time, of course, he found a way of dodging the disquieting truth. This, equally of course, was by yielding to his impulses. He allowed himself an hour a day, when Pym was absent, in which he wrote the story as it seemed to want to write itself, and then he cut this piece out, which could be done quite easily, as it consisted only of moralizings. Thus was his day brightened, and with this relaxation to look forward to be plodded on at his proper work, delving so hard that he could avoid asking himself why he was still delving. What shall we say? He was digging for the treasure in an orchard, and every now and again he came out of his hole to pluck an apple; but though the apple was so sweet to the mouth, it never struck him that the treasure might be growing overhead. At first he destroyed the fruit of his stolen hour, and even after he took to carrying it about fondly in his pocket, and to rewriting it in a splendid new form that had come to him just as he was stepping into bed, he continued to conceal it from his overseer's eyes. And still he thought all was over with him when Pym said the story did not march.

"It is a dead thing," Pym would roar, flinging down the manuscript, —"a dead thing because the stakes your man is playing for, a woman's love, is less than a wooden counter to you. You are a fine piece of mechanism, my solemn-faced don, but you are a watch that won't go because you are not wound up. Nobody can wind the artist up except a chit of a girl; and how you are ever to get one to take pity on you, only the gods who look after men with a want can tell.

"It becomes more impenetrable every day," he said. "No use your sitting there tearing yourself to bits. Out into the street with you! I suspend these sittings until you can tell me you have kissed a girl."

He was still saying this sort of thing when the famous "Letters" were published —T. Sandys, author. "Letters to a Young Man About to be Married" was the full title, and another almost as applicable would have been "Bits Cut Out of a Story because They Prevented its Marching." If you have any memory you do not need to be told how that splendid study, so ennobling, so penetrating, of woman at her best, took the town. Tommy woke a famous man, and, except Elspeth, no one was more pleased than big-hearted, hopeless, bleary Pym.

"But how the —— has it all come about!" he kept roaring.

"A woman can be anything that the man who loves her would have her be," says the "Letters"; and "Oh," said woman everywhere, "if all men had the same idea of us as Mr. Sandys!"

"To meet Mr. T. Sandys." Leaders of society wrote it on their invitation cards. Their daughters, athirst for a new sensation, thrilled at the thought, "Will he talk to us as nobly as he writes?" And oh, how willing he was to do it, especially if their noses were slightly tilted!

Chapter III
Sandys on Woman

"Can you kindly tell me the name of the book I want?"

It is the commonest question asked at the circulating library by dainty ladies just out of the carriage; and the librarian, after looking them over, can usually tell. In the days we have now to speak of, however, he answered, without looking them over:

"Sandys's 'Letters,'"

"Ah, yes, of course. May I have it, please?"

"I regret to find that it is out."

Then the lady looked naughty. "Why don't you have two copies?" she pouted.

"Madam," said the librarian, "we have a thousand."

A small and very timid girl of eighteen, with a neat figure that shrank from observation, although it was already aware that it looked best in gray, was there to drink in this music, and carried it home in her heart. She was Elspeth, and that dear heart was almost too full at this time. I hesitate whether to tell or to conceal how it even created a disturbance in no less a place than the House of Commons. She was there with Mrs. Jerry, and the thing was recorded in the papers of the period in these blasting words: "The Home Secretary was understood to be quoting a passage from 'Letters to a Young Man,' but we failed to catch its drift, owing to an unseemly interruption from the ladies' gallery."

"But what was it you cried out?" Tommy asked Elspeth, when she thought she had told him everything. (Like all true women, she always began in the middle.)

"Oh, Tommy, have I not told you? I cried out, 'I'm his sister.'"

Thus, owing to Elspeth's behaviour, it can never be known which was the passage quoted in the House; but we may be sure of one thing-that it did the House good. That book did everybody good. Even Pym could only throw off its beneficent effects by a tremendous effort, and young men about to be married used to ask at the bookshops, not for the "Letters," but simply for "Sandys on Woman," acknowledging Tommy as the authority on the subject, like Mill on Jurisprudence, or Thomson and Tait on the Differential Calculus. Controversies raged about it. Some thought he asked too much of man, some thought he saw too much in women; there was a fear that young people, knowing at last how far short they fell of what they ought to be, might shrink from the matrimony that must expose them to each other, now that they had Sandys to guide them, and the persons who had simply married and risked it (and it was astounding what a number of them there proved to be) wrote to the papers suggesting that he might yield a little in the next edition. But Sandys remained firm.

At first they took for granted that he was a very aged gentleman; he had, indeed, hinted at this in the text; and when the truth came out ("And just fancy, he is not even married!") the enthusiasm was doubled. "Not engaged!" they cried. "Don't tell that to me. No unmarried man could have written such a eulogy of marriage without being on the brink of it." Perhaps she was dead? It ran through the town that she was dead. Some knew which cemetery.

The very first lady Mr. Sandys ever took in to dinner mentioned this rumour to him, not with vulgar curiosity, but delicately, with a hint of sympathy in waiting, and it must be remembered, in fairness to Tommy, that all artists love sympathy. This sympathy uncorked him, and our Tommy could flow comparatively freely at last. Observe the delicious change.

"Has that story got abroad?" he said simply. "The matter is one which, I need not say, I have never mentioned to a soul."

"Of course not," the lady said, and waited eagerly.

If Tommy had been an expert he might have turned the conversation to brighter topics, but he was not; there had already been long pauses, and in dinner talk it is perhaps allowable to fling on any faggot rather than let the fire go out. "It is odd that I should be talking of it now," he said musingly.

"I suppose," she said gently, to bring him out of the reverie into which he had sunk, "I suppose it happened some time ago?"

"Long, long ago," he answered. (Having written as an aged person, he often found difficulty in remembering suddenly that he was two and twenty.)

"But you are still a very young man."

"It seems long ago to me," he said with a sigh.

"Was she beautiful?"

"She was beautiful to my eyes."

"And as good, I am sure, as she was beautiful."

"Ah me!" said Tommy.

His confidante was burning to know more, and hoping they were being observed across the table; but she was a kind, sentimental creature, though stout, or because of it, and she said, "I am so afraid that my questions pain you."

"No, no," said Tommy, who was very, very happy.

"Was it very sudden?"

"Fever."

"Ah! but I meant your attachment."

"We met and we loved," he said with gentle dignity.

"That is the true way," said the lady.

"It is the only way," he said decisively.

"Mr. Sandys, you have been so good, I wonder if you would tell me her name?"

"Felicity," he said, with emotion. Presently he looked up. "It is very strange to me," he said wonderingly, "to find myself saying these things to you who an hour ago were a complete stranger to me. But you are not like other women."

"No, indeed!" said the lady, warmly.

"That," he said, "must be why I tell you what I have never told to another human being. How mysterious are the workings of the heart!"

"Mr. Sandys," said the lady, quite carried away, "no words of mine can convey to you the pride with which I hear you say that. Be assured that I shall respect your confidences." She missed his next remark because she was wondering whether she dare ask him to come to dinner on the twenty-fifth, and then the ladies had to retire, and by the time he rejoined her he was as tongue-tied as at the beginning. The cork had not been extracted; it had been knocked into the bottle, where it still often barred the way, and there was always, as we shall see, a flavour of it in the wine.

"You will get over it yet; the summer and the flowers will come to you again," she managed to whisper to him kind-heartedly, as she was going.

"Thank you," he said, with that inscrutable face. It was far from his design to play a part. He had, indeed, had no design at all, but an opportunity for sentiment having presented itself, his mouth had opened as at a cherry. He did not laugh afterwards, even when he reflected how unexpectedly Felicity had come into his life; he thought of her rather with affectionate regard, and pictured her as a tall, slim girl in white. When he took a tall, slim girl in white in to dinner, he could not help saying huskily:

"You remind me of one who was a very dear friend of mine. I was much startled when you came into the room."

"You mean some one who is dead?" she asked in awe-struck tones.

"Fever," he said.

"You think I am like her in appearance?"

"In every way," he said dreamily; "the same sweet—pardon me, but it is very remarkable. Even the tones of the voice are the same. I suppose I ought not to ask your age?"

"I shall be twenty-one in August." "She would have been twenty-one in August had she lived," Tommy said with fervour. "My dear young lady —"

This was the aged gentleman again, but she did not wince; he soon found out that they expect authors to say the oddest things, and this proved to be a great help to him.

"My dear young lady, I feel that I know you very well."

"That," she said, "is only because I resemble your friend outwardly. The real me (she was a bit of philosopher also) you cannot know at all."

He smiled sadly. "Has it ever struck you," he asked, "that you are very unlike other women?"

"Oh, how ever could you have found that out?" she exclaimed, amazed.

Almost before he knew how it came about, he was on terms of very pleasant sentiment with this girl, for they now shared between them a secret that he had confided to no other. His face, which had been so much against him hitherto, was at last in his favour; it showed so plainly that when he looked at her more softly or held her hand longer than is customary, he was really thinking of that other of whom she was the image. Or if it did not precisely show that, it suggested something or other of that nature which did just as well. There was a sweet something between them which brought them together and also kept them apart; it allowed them to go a certain length, while it was also a reason why they could never, never exceed that distance; and this was an ideal state for Tommy, who could be most loyal and tender so long as it was understood that he meant nothing in particular. She was the right kind of girl, too, and admired him the more (and perhaps went a step further) because he remained so true to Felicity's memory.

You must not think him calculating and cold-blooded, for nothing could be less true to the fact. When not engaged, indeed, on his new work, he might waste some time planning scenes with exquisite ladies, in which he sparkled or had a hidden sorrow (he cared not which); but these scenes seldom came to life. He preferred very pretty girls to be rather stupid (oh, the artistic instinct of the man!), but instead of keeping them stupid, as he wanted to do, he found himself trying to improve their minds. They screwed up their noses in the effort. Meaning to thrill the celebrated beauty who had been specially invited to meet him, he devoted himself to a plain woman for whose plainness a sudden pity had mastered him (for, like all true worshippers of beauty in women, he always showed best in the presence of plain ones). With the intention of being a gallant knight to Lady I-Won't-Tell-the-Name, a whim of the moment made him so stiff to her that she ultimately asked the reason; and such a charmingly sad reason presented itself to him that she immediately invited him to her riverside party on Thursday week. He had the conversations and incidents for that party ready long before the day arrived; he altered them and polished them as other young gentlemen in the same circumstances overhaul their boating costumes; but when he joined the party there was among them the children's governess, and seeing her slighted, his blood boiled, and he was her attendant for the afternoon.

Elspeth was not at this pleasant jink in high life. She had been invited, but her ladyship had once let Tommy kiss her hand for the first and last time, so he decided sternly that this was no place for Elspeth. When temptation was nigh, he first locked Elspeth up, and then walked into it.

With two in every three women he was still as shy as ever, but the third he escorted triumphantly to the conservatory. She did no harm to his work-rather sent him back to it refreshed. It was as if he were shooting the sentiment which other young men get rid of more gradually by beginning earlier, and there were such accumulations of it that I don't know whether he ever made up on them. Punishment sought him in the night, when he dreamed constantly that he was married-to whom scarcely mattered; he saw himself coming out of a church a married man, and the fright woke him up. But with the daylight came again his talent for dodging thoughts that were lying in wait, and he yielded as recklessly as before to every sentimental impulse. As illustration, take his humourous passage with Mrs. Jerry. Geraldine Something was her name, but her friends called her Mrs. Jerry.

She was a wealthy widow, buxom, not a day over thirty when she was merry, which might be at inappropriate moments, as immediately after she had expressed a desire to lead the higher life. "But I have a theory, my dear," she said solemnly to Elspeth, "that no woman is able to do it who cannot see her own nose without the help of a mirror." She had taken a great fancy to Elspeth, and made many engagements with her, and kept some of them, and the understanding was that she apprenticed herself to Tommy through Elspeth, he being too terrible to face by himself, or, as Mrs. Jerry expressed it, "all nose." So Tommy had seen very little of her, and thought less, until one day he called by passionate request to sign her birthday-book, and heard himself proposing to her instead!

For one thing, it was twilight, and she had forgotten to ring for the lamps. That might have been enough, but there was more: she read to him part of a letter in which her hand was solicited in marriage. "And, for the life of me," said Mrs. Jerry, almost in tears, "I cannot decide whether to say yes or no."

This put Tommy in a most awkward position. There are probably men who could have got out of it without proposing; but to him there seemed at the moment no other way open. The letter complicated matters also by beginning "Dear Jerry," and saying "little Jerry" further on-expressions which stirred him strangely.

"Why do you read this to me?" he asked, in a voice that broke a little.

"Because you are so wise," she said. "Do you mind?"

"Do I mind!" he exclaimed bitterly. ("Take care, you idiot!" he said to himself.)

"I was asking your advice only. Is it too much?"

"Not at all. I am quite the right man to consult at such a moment, am I not?"

It was said with profound meaning; but his face was as usual.

"That is what I thought," she said, in all good faith.

"You do not even understand!" he cried, and he was also looking longingly at his hat.

"Understand what?"

"Jerry," he said, and tried to stop himself, with the result that he added, "dear little Jerry!" ("What am I doing!" he groaned.)

She understood now. "You don't mean —" she began, in amazement.

"Yes," he cried passionately. "I love you. Will you be my wife?" ("I am lost!")

"Gracious!" exclaimed Mrs. Jerry; and then, on reflection, she became indignant. "I would not have believed it of you," she said scornfully. "Is it my money, or what? I am not at all clever, so you must tell me."

With Tommy, of course, it was not her money. Except when he had Elspeth to consider, he was as much a Quixote about money as Pym himself; and at no moment of his life was he a snob.

"I am sorry you should think so meanly of me," he said with dignity, lifting his hat; and he would have got away then (which, when you come to think of it, was what he wanted) had he been able to resist an impulse to heave a broken-hearted sigh at the door.

"Don't go yet, Mr. Sandys," she begged. "I may have been hasty. And yet-why, we are merely acquaintances!"

He had meant to be very careful now, but that word sent him off again. "Acquaintances!" he cried. "No, we were never that."

"It almost seemed to me that you avoided me."

"You noticed it!" he said eagerly. "At least, you do me that justice. Oh, how I tried to avoid you!"

"It was because —"

"Alas!"

She was touched, of course, but still puzzled. "We know so little of each other," she said.

"I see," he replied, "that you know me very little, Mrs. Jerry; but you-oh, Jerry, Jerry! I know you as no other man has ever known you!"

"I wish I had proof of it," she said helplessly.

Proof! She should not have asked Tommy for proof. "I know," he cried, "how unlike all other women you are. To the world you are like the rest, but in your heart you know that you are different; you know it, and I know it, and no other person knows it."

Yes, Mrs. Jerry knew it, and had often marvelled over it in the seclusion of her boudoir; but that another should have found it out was strange and almost terrifying.

"I know you love me now," she said softly. "Only love could have shown you that. But-oh, let me go away for a minute to think!" And she ran out of the room.

Other suitors have been left for a space in Tommy's state of doubt, but never, it may be hoped, with the same emotions. Oh, heavens! if she should accept him! He saw Elspeth sickening and dying of the news.

His guardian angel, however, was very good to Tommy at this time; or perhaps, like cannibals with their prisoner, the god of sentiment (who has a tail) was fattening him for a future feast; and Mrs. Jerry's answer was that it could never be.

Tommy bowed his head.

But she hoped he would let her be his very dear friend. It would be the proudest recollection of her life that Mr. Sandys had entertained such feelings for her.

Nothing could have been better, and he should have found difficulty in concealing his delight; but this strange Tommy was really feeling his part again. It was an unforced tear that came to his eye. Quite naturally he looked long and wistfully at her.

"Jerry, Jerry!" he articulated huskily, and whatever the words mean in these circumstances he really meant; then he put his lips to her hand for the first and last time, and so was gone, broken but brave. He was in splendid fettle for writing that evening. Wild animals sleep after gorging, but it sent this monster, refreshed, to his work.

Nevertheless, the incident gave him some uneasy reflections. Was he, indeed, a monster? was one that he could dodge, as yet; but suppose Mrs. Jerry told his dear Elspeth of what had happened? She had said that she would not, but a secret in Mrs. Jerry's breast was like her pug in her arms, always kicking to get free. "Elspeth," said Tommy, "what do you say to going north and having a sight of Thrums again?"

He knew what she would say. They had been talking for years of going back; it was the great day that all her correspondence with old friends in Thrums looked forward to.

"They made little of you, Tommy," she said, "when we left; but I'm thinking they will all be at their windows when you go back."

"Oh," replied Thomas, "that's nothing. But I should like to shake Corp by the hand again."

"And Aaron," said Elspeth. She was knitting stockings for Aaron at that moment.

"And Gavinia," Tommy said, "and the Dominie."

"And Ailie."

And then came an awkward pause, for they were both thinking of that independent girl called Grizel. She was seldom discussed. Tommy was oddly shy about mentioning her name; he would have preferred Elspeth to mention it: and Elspeth had misgivings that this was so, with the result that neither could say "Grizel" without wondering what was in the other's mind. Tommy had written twice to Grizel, the first time unknown to Elspeth, but that was in the days when the ladies of the penny numbers were disturbing him, and, against his better judgment (for well he knew she would never stand it), he had begun his letter with these mad words: "Dear Little Woman." She did not answer this, but soon afterwards she wrote to Elspeth, and he was not mentioned in the letter proper, but it carried a sting in its tail. "P.S.," it said "How is Sentimental Tommy?"

None but a fiend in human shape could have written thus, and Elspeth put her protecting arms round her brother. "Now we know what Grizel is," she said. "I am done with her now."

But when Tommy had got back his wind he said nobly: "I'll call her no names. If this is how she likes to repay me for-for all my kindnesses, let her. But, Elspeth, if I have the chance, I shall go on being good to her just the same."

Elspeth adored him for it, but Grizel would have stamped had she known. He had that comfort.

The second letter he never posted. It was written a few months before he became a celebrity, and had very fine things indeed in it, for old Dr. McQueen, Grizel's dear friend, had just died

at his post, and it was a letter of condolence. While Tommy wrote it he was in a quiver of
genuine emotion, as he was very pleased to feel, and it had a specially satisfying bit about death,
and the world never being the same again. He knew it was good, but he did not send it to her,
for no reason I can discover save that postscripts jarred on him.

Chapter IV
Grizel of the Crooked Smile

To expose Tommy for what he was, to appear to be scrupulously fair to him so that I might really damage him the more, that is what I set out to do in this book, and always when he seemed to be finding a way of getting round me (as I had a secret dread he might do) I was to remember Grizel and be obdurate. But if I have so far got past some of his virtues without even mentioning them (and I have), I know how many opportunities for discrediting him have been missed, and that would not greatly matter, there are so many more to come, if Grizel were on my side. But she is not; throughout those first chapters a voice has been crying to me, "Take care; if you hurt him you will hurt me"; and I know it to be the voice of Grizel, and I seem to see her, rocking her arms as she used to rock them when excited in the days of her innocent childhood. "Don't, don't, don't!" she cried at every cruel word I gave him, and she, to whom it was ever such agony to weep, dropped a tear upon each word, so that they were obliterated; and "Surely I knew him best," she said, "and I always loved him"; and she stood there defending him, with her hand on her heart to conceal the gaping wound that Tommy had made.

Well, if Grizel had always loved him there was surely something fine and rare about Tommy. But what was it, Grizel? Why did you always love him, you who saw into him so well and demanded so much of men? When I ask that question the spirit that hovers round my desk to protect Tommy from me rocks her arms mournfully, as if she did not know the answer; it is only when I seem to see her as she so often was in life, before she got that wound and after, bending over some little child and looking up radiant, that I think I suddenly know why she always loved Tommy. It was because he had such need of her.

I don't know whether you remember, but there were once some children who played at Jacobites in the Thrums Den under Tommy's leadership. Elspeth, of course, was one of them, and there were Corp Shiach, and Gavinia, and lastly, there was Grizel. Had Tommy's parents been alive she would not have been allowed to join, for she was a painted lady's child; but Tommy insisted on having her, and Grizel thought it was just sweet of him. He also chatted with her in public places, as if she were a respectable character; and oh, how she longed to be respectable! but, on the other hand, he was the first to point out how superbly he was behaving, and his ways were masterful, so the independent girl would not be captain's wife; if he said she was captain's wife he had to apologize, and if he merely looked it he had to apologize just the same.

One night the Painted Lady died in the Den, and then it would have gone hard with the lonely girl had not Dr. McQueen made her his little housekeeper, not out of pity, he vowed (she was so anxious to be told that), but because he was an old bachelor sorely in need of someone to take care of him. And how she took care of him! But though she was so happy now, she knew that she must be very careful, for there was something in her blood that might waken and prevent her being a good woman. She thought it would be sweet to be good.

She told all this to Tommy, and he was profoundly interested, and consulted a wise man, whose advice was that when she grew up she should be wary of any man whom she liked and mistrusted in one breath. Meaning to do her a service, Tommy communicated this to her; and then, what do you think? Grizel would have no more dealings with him! By and by the gods, in a sportive mood, sent him to labour on a farm, whence, as we have seen, he found a way to London, and while he was growing into a man Grizel became a woman. At the time of the doctor's death she was nineteen, tall and graceful, and very dark and pale. When the winds of the day flushed her cheek she was beautiful; but it was a beauty that hid the mystery of her face. The sun made her merry, but she looked more noble when it had set; then her pallor shone with a soft, radiant light, as though the mystery and sadness and serenity of the moon were in it. The full beauty of Grizel came out only at night, like the stars.

I had made up my mind that when the time came to describe Grizel's mere outward appearance I should refuse her that word "beautiful" because of her tilted nose; but now that the time has come, I wonder at myself. Probably when I am chapters ahead I shall return to this one and strike out the word "beautiful," and then, as likely as not, I shall come back afterwards and put it in again. Whether it will be there at the end, God knows. Her eyes, at least, were beautiful. They were unusually far apart, and let you look straight into them, and never quivered; they were such clear, gray, searching eyes, they seemed always to be asking for the truth. And she had an adorable mouth. In repose it was, perhaps, hard, because it shut so decisively; but often it screwed up provokingly at one side, as when she smiled, or was sorry, or for no particular reason; for she seemed unable to control this vagary, which was perhaps a little bit of babyhood that had forgotten to grow up with the rest of her. At those moments the essence of all that was characteristic and delicious about her seemed to have run to her mouth; so that to kiss Grizel on her crooked smile would have been to kiss the whole of her at once. She had a quaint way of nodding her head at you when she was talking. It made you forget what she was saying, though it was really meant to have precisely the opposite effect. Her voice was rich, with many inflections. When she had much to say it gurgled like a stream in a hurry; but its cooing note was best worth remembering at the end of the day. There were times when she looked like a boy. Her almost gallant bearing, the poise of her head, her noble frankness-they all had something in them of a princely boy who had never known fear.

I have no wish to hide her defects; I would rather linger over them, because they were part of Grizel, and I am sorry to see them go one by one. Thrums had not taken her to its heart. She was a proud-purse, they said, meaning that she had a haughty walk. Her sense of justice was too great. She scorned frailties that she should have pitied. (How strange to think that there was a time when pity was not the feeling that leaped to Grizel's bosom first!) She did not care for study. She learned French and the pianoforte to please the doctor; but she preferred to be sewing or dusting. When she might have been reading, she was perhaps making for herself one of those costumes that annoyed every lady of Thrums who employed a dressmaker; or, more probably, it was a delicious garment for a baby; for as soon as Grizel heard that there was a new baby anywhere, all her intellect deserted her, and she became a slave. Books often irritated her because she disagreed with the author; and it was a torment to her to find other people holding to their views when she was so certain that hers were right. In church she sometimes rocked her arms; and the old doctor by her side knew that it was because she could not get up and contradict the minister. She was, I presume, the only young lady who ever dared to say that she hated Sunday because there was so much sitting still in it.

Sitting still did not suit Grizel. At all other times she was happy; but then her mind wandered back to the thoughts that had lived too closely with her in the old days, and she was troubled. What woke her from these reveries was probably the doctor's hand placed very tenderly on her shoulder, and then she would start, and wonder how long he had been watching her, and what were the grave thoughts behind his cheerful face; for the doctor never looked more cheerful than when he was drawing Grizel away from the ugly past, and he talked to her as if he had noticed nothing; but after he went upstairs he would pace his bedroom for a long time; and Grizel listened, and knew that he was thinking about her. Then, perhaps, she would run up to him, and put her arms around his neck. These scenes brought the doctor and Grizel very close together; but they became rarer as she grew up, and then for once that she was troubled she was a hundred times irresponsible with glee, and "Oh, you dearest, darlingest," she would cry to him, "I must dance, —I must, I must! —though it is a fast-day; and you must dance with your mother this instant —I am so happy, so happy!" "Mother" was his nickname for her, and she delighted in the word. She lorded it over him as if he were her troublesome boy.

How could she be other than glorious when there was so much to do? The work inside the house she made for herself, and outside the doctor made it for her. At last he had found for nurse a woman who could follow his instructions literally, who understood that if he said five o'clock for the medicine the chap of six would not do as well, who did not in her heart despise the thermometer, and who resolutely prevented the patient from skipping out of bed to change her pillow-slips because the minister was expected. Such tyranny enraged every sufferer who had been ill before and got better; but what they chiefly complained of to the doctor (and he agreed with a humourous sigh) was her masterfulness about fresh air and cold water. Windows were opened that had never been opened before (they yielded to her pressure with a groan); and as for cold water, it might have been said that a bath followed her wherever she went-not, mark me, for putting your hands and face in, not even for your feet; but in you must go, the whole of you, "as if," they said indignantly, "there was something the matter with our skin."

She could not gossip, not even with the doctor, who liked it of an evening when he had got into his carpet shoes. There was no use telling her a secret, for she kept it to herself for evermore. She had ideas about how men should serve a woman, even the humblest, that made the men gaze with wonder, and the women (curiously enough) with irritation. Her greatest scorn was for girls who made themselves cheap with men; and she could not hide it. It was a physical pain to Grizel to hide her feelings; they popped out in her face, if not in words, and were always in advance of her self-control. To the doctor this impulsiveness was pathetic; he loved her for it, but it sometimes made him uneasy.

He died in the scarlet-fever year. "I'm smitten," he suddenly said at a bedside; and a week afterwards he was gone.

"We must speak of it now, Grizel," he said, when he knew that he was dying.

She pressed his hand. She knew to what he was referring. "Yes," she said, "I should love you to speak of it now."

"You and I have always fought shy of it," he said, "making a pretence that it had altogether passed away. I thought that was best for you."

"Dearest, darlingest," she said, "I know —I have always known."

"And you," he said, "you pretended because you thought it was best for me."

She nodded. "And we saw through each other all the time," she said.

"Grizel, has it passed away altogether now?"

Her grip upon his hand did not tighten in the least. "Yes," she could say honestly, "it has altogether passed away."

"And you have no more fear?"

"No, none."

It was his great reward for all that he had done for Grizel.

"I know what you are thinking of," she said, when he did not speak. "You are thinking of the haunted little girl you rescued seven years ago."

"No," he answered; "I was thanking God for the brave, wholesome woman she has grown into; and for something else, Grizel-for letting me live to see it."

"To do it," she said, pressing his hand to her breast.

She was a strange girl, and she had to speak her mind. "I don't think God has done it all," she said. "I don't even think that He told you to do it. I think He just said to you, 'There is a painted lady's child at your door. You can save her if you like.'

"No," she went on, when he would have interposed; "I am sure He did not want to do it all. He even left a little bit of it to me to do myself. I love to think that I have done a tiny bit of it myself. I think it is the sweetest thing about God that He lets us do some of it ourselves. Do I hurt you, darling?"

No, she did not hurt him, for he understood her. "But you are naturally so impulsive," he said, "it has often been a sharp pain to me to see you so careful."

"It was not a pain to me to be careful; it was a joy. Oh, the thousand dear, delightful joys I have had with you!"

"It has made you strong, Grizel, and I rejoice in that; but sometimes I fear that it has made you too difficult to win."

"I don't want to be won," she told him.

"You don't quite mean that, Grizel."

"No," she said at once. She whispered to him impulsively: "It is the only thing I am at all afraid of now."

"What?"

"Love."

"You will not be afraid of it when it comes."

"But I want to be afraid," she said.

"You need not," he answered. "The man on whom those clear eyes rest lovingly will be worthy of it all. If he were not, they would be the first to find him out."

"But need that make any difference?" she asked. "Perhaps though I found him out I should love him just the same."

"Not unless you loved him first, Grizel."

"No," she said at once again. "I am not really afraid of love," she whispered to him. "You have made me so happy that I am afraid of nothing."

Yet she wondered a little that he was not afraid to die, but when she told him this he smiled and said: "Everybody fears death except those who are dying." And when she asked if he had anything on his mind, he said: "I leave the world without a care. Not that I have seen all I would fain have seen. Many a time, especially this last year, when I have seen the mother in you crooning to some neighbour's child, I have thought to myself, 'I don't know my Grizel yet; I have seen her in the bud only,' and I would fain —" He broke off. "But I have no fears," he said. "As I lie here, with you sitting by my side, looking so serene, I can say, for the first time for half a century, that I have nothing on my mind.

"But, Grizel, I should have married," he told her. "The chief lesson my life has taught me is that they are poor critturs-the men who don't marry."

"If you had married," she said, "you might never have been able to help me."

"It is you who have helped me," he replied. "God sent the child; He is most reluctant to give any of us up. Ay, Grizel, that's what my life has taught me, and it's all I can leave to you." The last he saw of her, she was holding his hand, and her eyes were dry, her teeth were clenched; but there was a brave smile upon her face, for he had told her that it was thus he would like to see her at the end. After his death, she continued to live at the old house; he had left it to her ("I want it to remain in the family," he said), with all his savings, which were quite sufficient for the needs of such a manager. He had also left her plenty to do, and that was a still sweeter legacy.

And the other Jacobites, what of them? Hi, where are you, Corp? Here he comes, grinning, in his spleet new uniform, to demand our tickets of us. He is now the railway porter. Since Tommy left Thrums "steam" had arrived in it, and Corp had by nature such a gift for giving luggage the twist which breaks everything inside as you dump it down that he was inevitably appointed porter. There was no travelling to Thrums without a ticket. At Tilliedrum, which was the junction for Thrums, you showed your ticket and were then locked in. A hundred yards from Thrums. Corp leaped upon the train and fiercely demanded your ticket. At the station he asked you threateningly whether you had given up your ticket. Even his wife was afraid of him at such times, and had her ticket ready in her hand.

His wife was one Gavinia, and she had no fear of him except when she was travelling. To his face she referred to him as a doited sumph, but to Grizel pleading for him she admitted that despite his warts and quarrelsome legs he was a great big muckle sonsy, stout, buirdly well set up, wise-like, havering man. When first Corp had proposed to her, she gave him a clout on the head; and so little did he know of the sex that this discouraged him. He continued, however, to propose and she to clout him until he heard, accidentally (he woke up in church), of a man in the Bible who had wooed a woman for seven years, and this example he determined to emulate; but when Gavinia heard of it she was so furious that she took him at once. Dazed by his good fortune, he rushed off with it to his aunt, whom he wearied with his repetition of the great news.

"To your bed wi' you," she said, yawning.

"Bed!" cried Corp, indignantly. "And so, auntie, says Gavinia, 'Yes,' says she, 'I'll hae you.' Those were her never-to-be-forgotten words."

"You pitiful object," answered his aunt. "Men hae been married afore now without making sic a stramash."

"I daursay," retorted Corp; "but they hinna married Gavinia." And this is the best known answer to the sneer of the cynic.

He was a public nuisance that night, and knocked various people up after they had gone to bed, to tell them that Gavinia was to have him. He was eventually led home by kindly though indignant neighbours; but early morning found him in the country, carrying the news from farm to farm.

"No, I winna sit down," he said; "I just cried in to tell you Gavinia is to hae me." Six miles from home he saw a mud house on the top of a hill, and ascended genially. He found at their porridge a very old lady with a nut-cracker face, and a small boy. We shall see them again. "Auld wifie," said Corp, "I dinna ken you, but I've just stepped up to tell you that Gavinia is to hae me."

It made him the butt of the sportive. If he or Gavinia were nigh, they gathered their fowls round them and then said: "Hens, I didna bring you here to feed you, but just to tell you that Gavinia is to hae me." This flustered Gavinia; but Grizel, who enjoyed her own jokes too heartily to have more than a polite interest in those of other people, said to her: "How can you be angry! I think it was just sweet of him."

"But was it no vulgar?"

"Vulgar!" said Grizel. "Why, Gavinia, that is how every lady would like a man to love her."

And then Gavinia beamed. "I'm glad you say that," she said; "for, though I wouldna tell Corp for worlds, I fell likit it."

But Grizel told Corp that Gavinia liked it.

"It was the proof," she said, smiling, "that you have the right to marry her. You have shown your ticket. Never give it up, Corp."

About a year afterwards Corp, armed in his Sunday stand, rushed to Grizel's house, occasionally stopping to slap his shiny knees. "Grizel," he cried, "there's somebody come to Thrums without a ticket!" Then he remembered Gavinia's instructions. "Mrs. Shiach's compliments," he said ponderously, "and it's a boy."

"Oh, Corp!" exclaimed Grizel, and immediately began to put on her hat and jacket. Corp watched her uneasily. "Mrs. Shiach's compliments," he said firmly, "and he's ower young to be bathed yet; but she's awid to show him off to you," he hastened to add. "'Tell Grizel,' was her first words."

"Tell Grizel"! They were among the first words of many mothers. None, they were aware, would receive the news with quite such glee as she. They might think her cold and reserved with themselves, but to see the look on her face as she bent over a baby, and to know that the baby was yours! What a way she had with them! She always welcomed them as if in coming they had performed a great feat. That is what babies are agape for from the beginning. Had they been able to speak they would have said "Tell Grizel" themselves.

"And Mrs. Shiach's compliments," Corp remembered, "and she would be windy if you would carry the bairn at the christening."

"I should love it, Corp! Have you decided on the name?"

"Lang syne. Gin it were a lassie we were to call her Grizel —"

"Oh, how sweet of you!"

"After the finest lassie we ever kent," continued Corp, stoutly. "But I was sure it would be a laddie."

"Why?" "Because if it was a laddie it was to be called after Him," he said, with emphasis on the last word; "and thinks I to mysel', 'He'll find a way.' What a crittur he was for finding a way, Grizel! And he lookit so holy a' the time. Do you mind that swear word o' his —'stroke'? It just meant 'damn'; but he could make even 'damn' look holy."

"You are to call the baby Tommy?"

"He'll be christened Thomas Sandys Shiach," said Corp. "I hankered after putting something out o' the Jacobites intil his name; and I says to Gavinia, 'Let's call him Thomas Sandys Stroke Shiach,' says I, 'and the minister'll be nane the wiser'; but Gavinia was scandalized."

Grizel reflected. "Corp," she said, "I am sure Gavinia's sister will expect to be asked to carry the baby. I don't think I want to do it."

"After you promised!" cried Corp, much hurt. "I never kent you to break a promise afore."

"I will do it, Corp," she said, at once.

She did not know then that Tommy would be in church to witness the ceremony, but she knew before she walked down the aisle with T.S. Shiach in her arms. It was the first time that Tommy and she had seen each other for seven years. That day he almost rivalled his namesake in the interests of the congregation, who, however, took prodigious care that he should not see it-all except Grizel; she smiled a welcome to him, and he knew that her serene gray eyes were watching him.

Chapter V
The Tommy Myth

On the evening before the christening, Aaron Latta, his head sunk farther into his shoulders, his beard gone grayer, no other perceptible difference in a dreary man since we last saw him in the book of Tommy's boyhood, had met the brother and sister at the station, a barrow with him for their luggage. It was a great hour for him as he wheeled the barrow homeward, Elspeth once more by his side; but he could say nothing heartsome in Tommy's presence, and Tommy was as uncomfortable in his. The old strained relations between these two seemed to begin again at once. They were as self-conscious as two mastiffs meeting in the street; and both breathed a sigh of relief when Tommy fell behind.

"You're bonny, Elspeth," Aaron then said eagerly. "I'm glad, glad to see you again."

"And him too, Aaron?" Elspeth pleaded.

"He took you away frae me."

"He has brought me back." "Ay, and he has but to whistle to you and away you go wi' him again. He's ower grand to bide lang here now."

"You don't know him, Aaron. We are to stay a long time. Do you know Mrs. McLean invited us to stay with her? I suppose she thought your house was so small. But Tommy said, 'The house of the man who befriended us when we were children shall never be too small for us.'"

"Did he say that? Ay, but, Elspeth, I would rather hear what you said."

"I said it was to dear, good Aaron Latta I was going back, and to no one else."

"God bless you for that, Elspeth."

"And Tommy," she went on, "must have his old garret room again, to write as well as sleep in, and the little room you partitioned off the kitchen will do nicely for me."

"There's no a window in it," replied Aaron; "but it will do fine for you, Elspeth." He was almost chuckling, for he had a surprise in waiting for her. "This way," he said excitedly, when she would have gone into the kitchen, and he flung open the door of what had been his warping-room. The warping-mill was gone-everything that had been there was gone. What met the delighted eyes of Elspeth and Tommy was a cozy parlour, which became a bedroom when you opened that other door. "You are a leddy now, Elspeth," Aaron said, husky with pride, "and you have a leddy's room. Do you see the piano?"

He had given up the warping, having at last "twa three hunder'" in the bank, and all the work he did now was at a loom which he had put into the kitchen to keep him out of languor. "I have sorted up the garret, too, for you," he said to Tommy, "but this is Elspeth's room."

"As if Tommy would take it from me!" said Elspeth, running into the kitchen to hug this dear Aaron.

"You may laugh," Aaron replied vindictively, "but he is taking it frae you already"; and later, when Tommy was out of the way, he explained his meaning. "I did it all for you, Elspeth; 'Elspeth's room,' I called it. When I bought the mahogany arm-chair, 'That's Elspeth's chair,' I said to mysel'; and when I bought the bed, 'It's hers,' I said. Ay; but I was soon disannulled o' that thait, for, in spite of me, they were all got for him. Not a rissom in that room is yours or mine, Elspeth; every muhlen belongs to him."

"But who says so, Aaron? I am sure he won't."

"I dinna ken them. They are leddies that come here in their carriages to see the house where Thomas Sandys was born."

"But, Aaron, he was born in London!" "They think he was born in this house," Aaron replied doggedly, "and it's no for me to cheapen him."

"Oh, Aaron, you pretend ——"

"I was never very fond o' him," Aaron admitted, "but I winna cheapen Jean Myles's bairn, and when they chap at my door and say they would like to see the room Thomas Sandys was born in, I let them see the best room I have. So that's how he has laid hands on your parlor,

Elspeth. Afore I can get rid o' them they gie a squeak and cry, 'Was that Thomas Sandys's bed?' and I says it was. That's him taking the very bed frae you, Elspeth."

"You might at least have shown them his bed in the garret," she said.

"It's a shilpit bit thing," he answered, "and I winna cheapen him. They're curious, too, to see his favourite seat."

"It was the fender," she declared.

"It was," he assented, "but it's no for me to cheapen him, so I let them see your new mahogany chair. 'Thomas Sandys's chair,' they call it, and they sit down in it reverently. They winna even leave you the piano. 'Was this Thomas Sandys's piano?' they speir. 'It was,' says I, and syne they gowp at it." His under lip shot out, a sure sign that he was angry. "I dinna blame him," he said, "but he had the same masterful way of scooping everything into his lap when he was a laddie, and I like him none the mair for it"; and from this position Aaron would not budge.

"Quite right, too," Tommy said, when he heard of it. "But you can tell him, Elspeth, that we shall allow no more of those prying women to come in." And he really meant this, for he was a modest man that day, was Tommy. Nevertheless, he was, perhaps, a little annoyed to find, as the days went on, that no more ladies came to be turned away.

He heard that they had also been unable to resist the desire to shake hands with Thomas Sandys's schoolmaster. "It must have been a pleasure to teach him," they said to Cathro.

"Ah me, ah me!" Cathro replied enigmatically. It had so often been a pleasure to Cathro to thrash him!

"Genius is odd," they said. "Did he ever give you any trouble?"

"We were like father and son," he assured them. With natural pride he showed them the ink-pot into which Thomas Sandys had dipped as a boy. They were very grateful for his interesting reminiscence that when the pot was too full Thomas inked his fingers. He presented several of them with the ink-pot.

Two ladies, who came together, bothered him by asking what the Hugh Blackadder competition was. They had been advised to inquire of him about Thomas Sandys's connection therewith by another schoolmaster, a Mr. Ogilvy, whom they had met in one of the glens.

Mr. Cathro winced, and then explained with emphasis that the Hugh Blackadder was a competition in which the local ministers were the sole judges; he therefore referred the ladies to them. The ladies did go to a local minister for enlightenment, to Mr. Dishart; but, after reflecting, Mr. Dishart said that it was too long a story, and this answer seemed to amuse Mr. Ogilvy, who happened to be present.

It was Mr. McLean who retailed this news to Tommy. He and Ailie had walked home from church with the newcomers on the day after their arrival, the day of the christening. They had not gone into Aaron's house, for you are looked askance at in Thrums if you pay visits on Sundays, but they had stood for a long time gossiping at the door, which is permitted by the strictest. Ailie was in a twitter, as of old, and not able even yet to speak of her husband without an apologetic look to the ladies who had none. And oh, how proud she was of Tommy's fame! Her eyes were an offering to him.

"Don't take her as a sample of the place, though," Mr. McLean warned him, "for Thrums does not catch fire so readily as London." It was quite true. "I was at the school wi' him," they said up there, and implied that this damned his book.

But there were two faithful souls, or, more strictly, one, for Corp could never have carried it through without Gavinia's help. Tommy called on them promptly at their house in the Bellies Brae (four rooms, but a lodger), and said, almost before he had time to look, that the baby had Corp's chin and Gavinia's eyes. He had made this up on the way. He also wanted to say, so desirous was he of pleasing his old friends, that he should like to hold the baby in his arms; but it was such a thundering lie that even an author could not say it.

Tommy sat down in that house with a very warm heart for its inmates; but they chilled him—Gavinia with her stiff words, and Corp by looking miserable instead of joyous.

"I expected you to come to me first, Corp," said Tommy, reproachfully. "I had scarcely a word with you at the station."

"He couldna hae presumed," replied Gavinia, primly.

"I couldna hae presumed," said Corp, with a groan.

"Fudge!" Tommy said. "You were my greatest friend, and I like you as much as ever, Corp." Corp's face shone, but Gavinia said at once, "You werena sic great friends as that; were you, man?"

"No," Corp replied gloomily.

"Whatever has come over you both?" asked Tommy, in surprise. "You will be saying next, Gavinia, that we never played at Jacobites in the Den!"

"I dinna deny that Corp and me played," Gavinia answered determinedly, "but you didna. You said to us, 'Think shame,' you said, 'to be playing vulgar games when you could be reading superior books.' They were his very words, were they no, man?" she demanded of her unhappy husband, with a threatening look.

"They were," said Corp, in deepest gloom.

"I must get to the bottom of this," said Tommy, rising, "and as you are too great a coward, Corp, to tell the truth with that shameless woman glowering at you, out you go, Gavinia, and take your disgraced bairn with you. Do as you are told, you besom, for I am Captain Stroke again."

Corp was choking with delight as Gavinia withdrew haughtily. "I was sure you would sort her," he said, rubbing his hands, "I was sure you wasna the kind to be ashamed o' auld friends."

"But what does it mean?"

"She has a notion," Corp explained, growing grave again, "that it wouldna do for you to own the like o' us. 'We mauna cheapen him,' she said. She wanted you to see that we hinna been cheapening you." He said, in a sepulchral voice, "There has been leddies here, and they want to ken what Thomas Sandys was like as a boy. It's me they speir for, but Gavinia she just shoves me out o' sight, and says she, 'Leave them to me.'"

Corp told Tommy some of the things Gavinia said about Thomas Sandys as a boy: how he sat rapt in church, and, instead of going bird-nesting, lay on the ground listening to the beautiful little warblers overhead, and gave all his pennies to poorer children, and could repeat the Shorter Catechism, beginning at either end, and was very respectful to the aged and infirm, and of a yielding disposition, and said, from his earliest years, "I don't want to be great; I just want to be good."

"How can she make them all up?" Tommy asked, with respectful homage to Gavinia.

Corp, with his eye on the door, produced from beneath the bed a little book with coloured pictures. It was entitled "Great Boyhoods," by "Aunt Martha." "She doesna make them up," he whispered; "she gets them out o' this."

"And you back her up, Corp, even when she says I was not your friend!"

"It was like a t' knife intil me," replied loyal Corp; "every time I forswore you it was like a t' knife, but I did it, ay, and I'll go on doing it if you think my friendship cheapens you."

Tommy was much moved, and gripped his old lieutenant by the hand. He also called Gavinia ben, and, before she could ward him off, the masterful rogue had saluted her on the cheek. "That," said Tommy, "is to show you that I am as fond of the old times and my old friends as ever, and the moment you deny it I shall take you to mean, Gavinia, that you want another kiss."

"He's just the same!" Corp remarked ecstatically, when Tommy had gone.

"I dinna deny," Gavinia said, "but what he's fell taking"; and for a time they ruminated.

"Gavinia," said Corp, suddenly, "I wouldna wonder but what he's a gey lad wi' the women!"

"What makes you think that?" she replied coldly, and he had the prudence not to say. He should have followed his hero home to be disabused of this monstrous notion, for even while it was being propounded Tommy was sitting in such an agony of silence in a woman's presence that she could not resist smiling a crooked smile at him. His want of words did not displease Grizel; she was of opinion that young men should always be a little awed by young ladies.

He had found her with Elspeth on his return home. Would Grizel call and be friendly? he had asked himself many times since he saw her in church yesterday, and Elspeth was as curious. Each wanted to know what the other thought of her, but neither had the courage to inquire, they both wanted to know so much. Her name had been mentioned but casually, not a word to indicate that she had grown up since they saw her last. The longer Tommy remained silent, the more, he knew, did Elspeth suspect him. He would have liked to say, in a careless voice, "Rather pretty, isn't she?" but he felt that this little Elspeth would see through him at once.

For at the first glance he had seen what Grizel was, and a thrill of joy passed through him as he drank her in; it was but the joy of the eyes for the first moment, but it ran to his heart to say, "This is the little hunted girl that was!" and Tommy was moved with a manly gladness that the girl who once was so fearful of the future had grown into this. The same unselfish delight in her for her own sake came over him again when he shook hands with her in Aaron's parlor. This glorious creature with the serene eyes and the noble shoulders had been the hunted child of the Double Dykes! He would have liked to race back into the past and bring little Grizel here to look. How many boyish memories he recalled! and she was in every one of them. His heart held nothing but honest joy in this meeting after so many years; he longed to tell her how sincerely he was still her friend. Well, why don't you tell her, Tommy? It is a thing you are good at, and you have been polishing up the phrases ever since she passed down the aisle with Master Shiach in her arms; you have even planned out a way of putting Grizel at her ease, and behold, she is the only one of the three who is at ease. What has come over you? Does the reader think it was love? No, it was only that pall of shyness; he tried to fling it off, but could not. Behold Tommy being buried alive!

Elspeth showed less contemptibly than her brother, but it was Grizel who did most of the talking. She nodded her head and smiled crookedly at Tommy, but she was watching him all the time. She wore a dress in which brown and yellow mingled as in woods on an autumn day, and the jacket had a high collar of fur, over which she watched him. Let us say that she was watching to see whether any of the old Tommy was left in him. Yet, with this problem confronting her, she also had time to study the outer man, Tommy the dandy-his velvet jacket (a new one), his brazen waistcoat, his poetic neckerchief, his spotless linen. His velvet jacket was to become the derision of Thrums, but Tommy took his bonneting haughtily, like one who was glad to suffer for a Cause. There were to be meetings here and there where people told with awe how many shirts he sent weekly to the wash. Grizel disdained his dandy tastes; why did not Elspeth strip him of them? And oh, if he must wear that absurd waistcoat, could she not see that it would look another thing if the second button was put half an inch farther back? How sinful of him to spoil the shape of his silly velvet jacket by carrying so many letters in the pockets! She learned afterwards that he carried all those letters because there was a check in one of them, he did not know which, and her sense of orderliness was outraged. Elspeth did not notice these things. She helped Tommy by her helplessness. There is reason to believe that once in London, when she had need of a new hat, but money there was none, Tommy, looking very defiant, studied ladies' hats in the shop-windows, brought all his intellect to bear on them, with the result that he did concoct out of Elspeth's old hat a new one which was the admired of O.P. Pym and friends, who never knew the name of the artist. But obviously he could not take proper care of himself, and there is a kind of woman, of whom Grizel was one, to whose breasts this helplessness makes an unfair appeal. Oh, to dress him properly! She could not help liking to be a mother to men; she wanted them to be the most noble characters, but completely dependent on her.

Tommy walked home with her, and it seemed at first as if Elspeth's absence was to be no help to him. He could not even plagiarize from "Sandys on Woman." No one knew so well the kind of thing he should be saying, and no one could have been more anxious to say it, but a weight of shyness sat on the lid of Tommy. Having for half an hour raged internally at his misfortune, he now sullenly embraced it. "If I am this sort of an ass, let me be it in the superlative degree," he may be conceived saying bitterly to himself. He addressed Grizel coldly as "Miss McQueen," a name she had taken by the doctor's wish soon after she went to live with him.

"There is no reason why you should call me that," she said. "Call me Grizel, as you used to do."

"May I?" replied Tommy, idiotically. He knew it was idiotic, but that mood now had grip of him.

"But I mean to call you Mr. Sandys," she said decisively.

He was really glad to hear it, for to be called Tommy by anyone was now detestable to him (which is why I always call him Tommy in these pages). So it was like him to say, with a sigh, "I had hoped to hear you use the old name."

That sigh made her look at him sharply. He knew that he must be careful with Grizel, and that she was irritated, but he had to go on.

"It is strange to me," said Sentimental Tommy, "to be back here after all those years, walking this familiar road once more with you. I thought it would make me feel myself a boy again, but, heigh-ho, it has just the opposite effect: I never felt so old as I do to-day."

His voice trembled a little, I don't know why. Grizel frowned.

"But you never were as old as you are to-day, were you?" she inquired politely. It whisked Tommy out of dangerous waters and laid him at her feet. He laughed, not perceptibly or audibly, of course, but somewhere inside him the bell rang. No one could laugh more heartily at himself than Tommy, and none bore less malice to those who brought him to land.

"That, at any rate, makes me feel younger," he said candidly; and now the shyness was in full flight.

"Why?" asked Grizel, still watchful.

"It is so like the kind of thing you used to say to me when we were boy and girl. I used to enrage you very much, I fear," he said, half gleefully.

"Yes," she admitted, with a smile, "you did."

"And then how you rocked your arms at me, Grizel! Do you remember?"

She remembered it all so well! This rocking of the arms, as they called it, was a trick of hers that signified sudden joy or pain. They hung rigid by her side, and then shook violently with emotion.

"Do you ever rock them now when people annoy you?" he asked.

"There has been no one to annoy me," she replied demurely, "since you went away."

"But I have come back," Tommy said, looking hopefully at her arms.

"You see they take no notice of you."

"They don't remember me yet. As soon as they do they will cry out."

Grizel shook her head confidently, and in this she was pitting herself against Tommy, always a bold thing to do.

"I have been to see Corp's baby," he said suddenly; and this was so important that she stopped in the middle of the road.

"What do you think of him?" she asked, quite anxiously.

"I thought," replied Tommy, gravely, and making use of one of Grizel's pet phrases, "I thought he was just sweet."

"Isn't he!" she cried; and then she knew that he was making fun of her. Her arms rocked.

"Hurray!" cried Tommy, "they recognize me now! Don't be angry, Grizel," he begged her. "You taught me, long ago, what was the right thing to say about babies, and how could I be sure it was you until I saw your arms rocking?"

"It was so like you," she said reproachfully, "to try to make me do it."

"It was so unlike you," he replied craftily, "to let me succeed. And, after all, Grizel, if I was horrid in the old days I always apologized."

"Never!" she insisted.

"Well, then," said Tommy, handsomely, "I do so now"; and then they both laughed gaily, and I think Grizel was not sorry that there was a little of the boy who had been horrid left in Tommy-just enough to know him by.

"He'll be vain," her aged maid, Maggy Ann, said curiously to her that evening. They were all curious about Tommy.

"I don't know that he is vain," Grizel replied guardedly.

"If he's no vain," Maggy Ann retorted, "he's the first son of Adam it could be said o'. I jalouse it's his bit book."

"He scarcely mentioned it."

"Ay, then, it's his beard."

Grizel was sure it was not that.

"Then it'll be the women," said Maggy Ann.

"Who knows!" said Grizel of the watchful eyes; but she smiled to herself. She thought not incorrectly that she knew one woman of whom Mr. Sandys was a little afraid.

About the same time Tommy and Elspeth were discussing her. Elspeth was in bed, and Tommy had come into the room to kiss her good-night —he had never once omitted doing it since they went to London, and he was always to do it, for neither of them was ever to marry.

"What do you think of her?" Elspeth asked. This was their great time for confidences.

"Of whom?" Tommy inquired lightly.

"Grizel."

He must be careful.

"Rather pretty, don't you think?" he said, gazing at the ceiling.

She was looking at him keenly, but he managed to deceive her. She was much relieved, and could say what was in her heart. "Tommy," she said, "I think she is the most noble-looking girl I ever saw, and if she were not so masterful in her manner she would be beautiful." It was nice of Elspeth to say it, for she and Grizel were never very great friends.

Tommy brought down his eyes. "Did you think as much of her as that?" he said. "It struck me that her features were not quite classic. Her nose is a little tilted, is it not?"

"Some people like that kind of nose," replied Elspeth. "It is not classic," Tommy said sternly.

Chapter VI
Ghosts That Haunt the Den

Looking through the Tommy papers of this period, like a conscientious biographer, I find among them manuscripts that remind me how diligently he set to work at his new book the moment he went North, and also letters which, if printed, would show you what a wise and good man Tommy was. But while I was fingering those, there floated from them to the floor a loose page, and when I saw that it was a chemist's bill for oil and liniment I remembered something I had nigh forgotten. "Eureka!" I cried. "I shall tell the story of the chemist's bill, and some other biographer may print the letters."

Well, well! but to think that this scrap of paper should flutter into view to damn him after all those years!

The date is Saturday, May 28, by which time Tommy had been a week in Thrums without doing anything very reprehensible, so far as Grizel knew. She watched for telltales as for a mouse to show at its hole, and at the worst, I think, she saw only its little head. That was when Tommy was talking beautifully to her about her dear doctor. He would have done wisely to avoid this subject; but he was so notoriously good at condolences that he had to say it. He had thought it out, you may remember, a year ago, but hesitated to post it; and since then it had lain heavily within him, as if it knew it was a good thing and pined to be up and strutting.

He said it with emotion; evidently Dr. McQueen had been very dear to him, and any other girl would have been touched; but Grizel stiffened, and when he had finished, this is what she said, quite snappily:

"He never liked you."

Tommy was taken aback, but replied, with gentle dignity, "Do you think, Grizel, I would let that make any difference in my estimate of him?"

"But you never liked him," said she; and now that he thought of it, this was true also. It was useless to say anything about the artistic instinct to her; she did not know what it was, and would have had plain words for it as soon as he told her. Please to picture Tommy picking up his beautiful speech and ramming it back into his pocket as if it were a rejected manuscript.

"I am sorry you should think so meanly of me, Grizel," he said with manly forbearance, and when she thought it all out carefully that night she decided that she had been hasty. She could not help watching Tommy for backslidings, but oh, it was sweet to her to decide that she had not found any.

"It was I who was horrid," she announced to him frankly, and Tommy forgave her at once. She offered him a present: "When the doctor died I gave some of his things to his friends; it is the Scotch custom, you know. He had a new overcoat; it had been worn but two or three times. I should be so glad if you would let me give it to you for saying such sweet things about him. I think it will need very little alteration."

Thus very simply came into Tommy's possession the coat that was to play so odd a part in his history. "But oh, Grizel," said he, with mock reproach, "you need not think that I don't see through you! Your deep design is to cover me up. You despise my velvet jacket!"

"It does not —" Grizel began, and stopped.

"It is not in keeping with my doleful countenance," said Tommy, candidly; "that was what you were to say. Let me tell you a secret, Grizel: I wear it to spite my face. Sha'n't give up my velvet jacket for anybody, Grizel; not even for you." He was in gay spirits, because he knew she liked him again; and she saw that was the reason, and it warmed her. She was least able to resist Tommy when he was most a boy, and it was actually watchful Grizel who proposed that he and she and Elspeth should revisit the Den together. How often since the days of their childhood had Grizel wandered it alone, thinking of those dear times, making up her mind that if ever Tommy asked her to go into the Den again with him she would not go, the place was so much sweeter to her than it could be to him. And yet it was Grizel herself who was saying now, "Let us go back to the Den."

Tommy caught fire. "We sha'n't go back," he cried defiantly, "as men and women. Let us be boy and girl again, Grizel. Let us have that Saturday we missed long ago. I missed a Saturday on purpose, Grizel, so that we should have it now."

She shook her head wistfully, but she was glad that Tommy would fain have had one of the Saturdays back. Had he waxed sentimental she would not have gone a step of the way with him into the past, but when he was so full of glee she could take his hand and run back into it.

"But we must wait until evening," Tommy said, "until Corp is unharnessed; we must not hurt the feelings of Corp by going back to the Den without him."

"How mean of me not to think of Corp!" Grizel cried; but the next moment she was glad she had not thought of him, it was so delicious to have proof that Tommy was more loyal. "But we can't turn back the clock, can we, Corp?" she said to the fourth of the conspirators, to which Corp replied, with his old sublime confidence, "He'll find a way."

And at first it really seemed as if Tommy had found a way. They did not go to the Den four in a line or two abreast-nothing so common as that. In the wild spirits that mastered him he seemed to be the boy incarnate, and it was always said of Tommy by those who knew him best that if he leaped back into boyhood they had to jump with him. Those who knew him best were with him now. He took command of them in the old way. He whispered, as if Black Cathro were still on the prowl for him. Corp of Corp had to steal upon the Den by way of the Silent Pool, Grizel by the Queen's Bower, Elspeth up the burn-side, Captain Stroke down the Reekie Brothpot. Grizel's arms rocked with delight in the dark, and she was on her way to the Cuttle Well, the trysting-place, before she came to and saw with consternation that Tommy had been ordering her about.

She was quite a sedate young lady by the time she joined them at the well, and Tommy was the first to feel the change. "Don't you think this is all rather silly?" she said, when he addressed her as the Lady Griselda, and it broke the spell. Two girls shot up into women, a beard grew on Tommy's chin, and Corp became a father. Grizel had blown Tommy's pretty project to dust just when he was most gleeful over it; yet, instead of bearing resentment, he pretended not even to know that she was the culprit.

"Corp," he said ruefully, "the game is up!" And "Listen," he said, when they had sat down, crushed, by the old Cuttle Well, "do you hear anything?"

It was a very still evening. "I hear nocht," said Corp, "but the trickle o' the burn. What did you hear?"

"I thought I heard a baby cry," replied Tommy, with a groan. "I think it was your baby, Corp. Did you hear it, Grizel?"

She understood, and nodded.

"And you, Elspeth?"

"Yes."

"My bairn!" cried the astounded Corp.

"Yours," said Tommy, reproachfully; "and he has done for us. Ladies and gentlemen, the game is up."

Yes, the game was up, and she was glad, Grizel said to herself, as they made their melancholy pilgrimage of what had once been an enchanted land. But she felt that Tommy had been very forbearing to her, and that she did not deserve it. Undoubtedly he had ordered her about, but in so doing had he not been making half-pathetic sport of his old self-and was it with him that she was annoyed for ordering, or with herself for obeying? And why should she not obey, when it was all a jest? It was as if she still had some lingering fear of Tommy. Oh, she was ashamed of herself. She must say something nice to him at once. About what? About his book, of course. How base of her not to have done so already! but how good of him to have overlooked her silence on that great topic!

It was not ignorance of its contents that had kept her silent. To confess the horrid truth, Grizel had read the book suspiciously, looking as through a microscope for something wrong-hoping not to find it, but peering minutely. The book, she knew, was beautiful; but it was the writer of the book she was peering for-the Tommy she had known so well, what had he grown into? In her heart she had exulted from the first in his success, and she should have been still more glad (should she not?) to learn that his subject was woman; but no, that had irritated her. What was perhaps even worse, she had been still more irritated on hearing that the work was rich in sublime thoughts. As a boy, he had maddened her most in his grandest moments. I can think of no other excuse for her.

She would not accept it as an excuse for herself now. What she saw with scorn was that she was always suspecting the worst of Tommy. Very probably there was not a thought in the book that had been put in with his old complacent waggle of the head. "Oh, am I not a wonder!" he used to cry, when he did anything big; but that was no reason why she should suspect him of being conceited still. Very probably he really and truly felt what he wrote-felt it not only at the time, but also next morning. In his boyhood Mr. Cathro had christened him Sentimental Tommy; but he was a man now, and surely the sentimentalities in which he had dressed himself were flung aside for ever, like old suits of clothes. So Grizel decided eagerly, and she was on the point of telling him how proud she was of his book, when Tommy, who had thus far behaved so well, of a sudden went to pieces.

He and Grizel were together. Elspeth was a little in front of them, walking with a gentleman who still wondered what they meant by saying that they had heard his baby cry. "For he's no here," Corp had said earnestly to them all; "though I'm awid for the time to come when I'll be able to bring him to the Den and let him see the Jacobites' Lair."

There was nothing startling in this remark, so far as Grizel could discover; but she saw that it had an immediate and incomprehensible effect on Tommy. First, he blundered in his talk as if he was thinking deeply of something else; then his face shone as it had been wont to light up in his boyhood when he was suddenly enraptured with himself; and lastly, down his cheek and into his beard there stole a tear of agony. Obviously, Tommy was in deep woe for somebody or something.

It was a chance for a true lady to show that womanly sympathy of which such exquisite things are said in the first work of T. Sandys: but it merely infuriated Grizel, who knew that Tommy did not feel nearly so deeply as she this return to the Den, and, therefore, what was he in such distress about? It was silly sentiment of some sort, she was sure of that. In the old days she would have asked him imperiously to tell her what was the matter with him; but she must not do that now-she dare not even rock her indignant arms; she could only walk silently by his side, longing fervently to shake him.

He had quite forgotten her presence; indeed, she was not really there, for a number of years had passed, and he was Corp Shiach, walking the Den alone. To-morrow he was to bring his boy to show him the old Lair and other fondly remembered spots; to-night he must revisit them alone. So he set out blithely, but, to his bewilderment, he could not find the Lair. It had not been a tiny hollow where muddy water gathered; he remembered an impregnable fortress full of men whose armour rattled as they came and went; so this could not be the Lair. He had taken the wrong way to it, for the way was across a lagoon, up a deep-flowing river, then by horse till the rocky ledge terrified all four-footed things; no, up a grassy slope had never been the way. He came night after night, trying different ways; but he could not find the golden ladder, though all the time he knew that the Lair lay somewhere over there. When he stood still and listened he could hear the friends of his youth at play, and they seemed to be calling: "Are you coming, Corp? Why does not Corp come back?" but he could never see them, and when he pressed forward their voices died away. Then at last he said sadly to his boy: "I shall never be able to show you the Lair, for I cannot find the way to it." And the boy was touched, and he said: "Take my hand, father, and I will lead you to the Lair; I found the way long ago for myself."

It took Tommy about two seconds to see all this, and perhaps another half-minute was spent in sad but satisfactory contemplation of it. Then he felt that, for the best effect, Corp's home life was too comfortable; so Gavinia ran away with a soldier. He was now so sorry for Corp that the tear rolled down. But at the same moment he saw how the effect could be still further heightened by doing away with his friend's rude state of health, and he immediately jammed him between the buffers of two railway carriages, and gave him a wooden leg. It was at this point that a lady who had kept her arms still too long rocked them frantically, then said, with cutting satire: "Are you not feeling well, or have you hurt yourself? You seem to be very lame." And Tommy woke with a start, to see that he was hobbling as if one of his legs were timber to the knee.

"It is nothing," he said modestly. "Something Corp said set me thinking; that is all."

He had told the truth, and if what he imagined was twenty times more real to him than what was really there, how could Tommy help it? Indignant Grizel, however, who kept such a grip of facts, would make no such excuse for him.

"Elspeth!" she called.

"There is no need to tell her," said Tommy. But Grizel was obdurate.

"Come here, Elspeth," she cried vindictively. "Something Corp said a moment ago has made your brother lame."

Tommy was lame; that was all Elspeth and Corp heard or could think of as they ran back to him. When did it happen? Was he in great pain? Had he fallen? Oh, why had he not told Elspeth at once?

"It is nothing," Tommy insisted, a little fiercely.

"He says so," Grizel explained, "not to alarm us. But he is suffering horribly. Just before I called to you his face was all drawn up in pain."

This made the sufferer wince. "That was another twinge," she said promptly. "What is to be done, Elspeth?"

"I think I could carry him," suggested Corp, with a forward movement that made Tommy stamp his foot-the wooden one.

"I am all right," he told them testily, and looking uneasily at Grizel.

"How brave of you to say so!" said she.

"It is just like him," Elspeth said, pleased with Grizel's remark.

"I am sure it is," Grizel said, so graciously.

It was very naughty of her. Had she given him a chance he would have explained that it was all a mistake of Grizel's. That had been his intention; but now a devil entered into Tommy and spoke for him.

"I must have slipped and sprained my ankle," he said. "It is slightly painful; but I shall be able to walk home all right, Corp, if you let me use you as a staff."

I think he was a little surprised to hear himself saying this; but, as soon as it was said, he liked it. He was Captain Stroke playing in the Den again, after all, and playing as well as ever. Nothing being so real to Tommy as pretence, I daresay he even began to feel his ankle hurting him. "Gently," he begged of Corp, with a gallant smile, and clenching his teeth so that the pain should not make him cry out before the ladies. Thus, with his lieutenant's help, did Stroke manage to reach Aaron's house, making light of his mishap, assuring them cheerily that he should be all right to-morrow, and carefully avoiding Grizel's eye, though he wanted very much to know what she thought of him (and of herself) now.

There were moments when she did not know what to think, and that always distressed Grizel, though it was a state of mind with which Tommy could keep on very friendly terms. The truth seemed too monstrous for belief. Was it possible she had misjudged him? Perhaps he really had sprained his ankle. But he had made no pretence of that at first, and besides, —yes, she could not be mistaken, —it was the other leg.

She soon let him see what she was thinking. "I am afraid it is too serious a case for me," she said, in answer to a suggestion from Corp, who had a profound faith in her medical skill, "but, if you like," —she was addressing Tommy now, —"I shall call at Dr. Gemmell's, on my way home, and ask him to come to you."

"There is no necessity; a night's rest is all I need," he answered hastily.

"Well, you know best," she said, and there was a look on her face which Thomas Sandys could endure from no woman. "On second thoughts," he said, "I think it would be advisable to have a doctor. Thank you very much, Grizel. Corp, can you help me to lift my foot on to that chair? Softly-ah! —ugh!"

His eyes did not fall before hers. "And would you mind asking him to come at once, Grizel?" he said sweetly. She went straight to the doctor.

Chapter VII
The Beginning of the Duel

It was among old Dr. McQueen's sayings that when he met a man who was certified to be in no way remarkable he wanted to give three cheers. There are few of them, even in a little place like Thrums; but David Gemmell was one.

So McQueen had always said, but Grizel was not so sure. "He is very good-looking, and he does not know it," she would point out. "Oh, what a remarkable man!"

She had known him intimately for nearly six years now, ever since he became the old doctor's assistant on the day when, in the tail of some others, he came to Thrums, aged twenty-one, to apply for the post. Grizel had even helped to choose him; she had a quaint recollection of his being submitted to her by McQueen, who told her to look him over and say whether he would do-an odd position in which to place a fourteen-year-old girl, but Grizel had taken it most seriously, and, indeed, of the two men only Gemmell dared to laugh.

"You should not laugh when it is so important," she said gravely; and he stood abashed, although I believe he chuckled again when he retired to his room for the night. She was in that room next morning as soon as he had left it, to smell the curtains (he smoked), and see whether he folded his things up neatly and used both the brush and the comb, but did not use pomade, and slept with his window open, and really took a bath instead of merely pouring the water into it and laying the sponge on top (oh, she knew them!) —and her decision, after some days, was that, though far from perfect, he would do, if he loved her dear darling doctor sufficiently. By this time David was openly afraid of her, which Grizel noticed, and took to be, in the circumstances, a satisfactory sign.

She watched him narrowly for the next year, and after that she ceased to watch him at all. She was like a congregation become so sure of its minister's soundness that it can risk going to sleep. To begin with, he was quite incapable of pretending to be anything he was not. Oh, how unlike a boy she had once known! His manner, like his voice, was quiet. Being himself the son of a doctor, he did not dodder through life amazed at the splendid eminence he had climbed to, which is the weakness of Scottish students when they graduate, and often for fifty years afterwards. How sweet he was to Dr. McQueen, never forgetting the respect due to gray hairs, never hinting that the new school of medicine knew many things that were hidden from the old, and always having the sense to support McQueen when she was scolding him for his numerous naughty ways. When the old doctor came home now on cold nights it was not with his cravat in his pocket, and Grizel knew very well who had put it round his neck. McQueen never had the humiliation, so distressing to an old doctor, of being asked by patients to send his assistant instead of coming himself. He thought they preferred him, and twitted David about it; but Grizel knew that David had sometimes to order them to prefer the old man. She knew that when he said good-night and was supposed to have gone to his lodgings, he was probably off to some poor house where, if not he, a tired woman must sit the long night through by a sufferer's bedside, and she realized with joy that his chief reason for not speaking of such things was that he took them as part of his natural work and never even knew that he was kind. He was not specially skilful, he had taken no honours either at school or college, and he considered himself to be a very ordinary young man. If you had said that on this point you disagreed with him, his manner probably would have implied that he thought you a bit of an ass.

When a new man arrives in Thrums, the women come to their doors to see whether he is good-looking. They said No of Tommy when he came back, but it had been an emphatic Yes for Dr. Gemmell. He was tall and very slight, and at twenty-seven, as at twenty-one, despite the growth of a heavy moustache, there was a boyishness about his appearance, which is, I think, what women love in a man more than anything else. They are drawn to him by it, and they love him out of pity when it goes. I suppose it brings back to them some early, beautiful stage in the world's history when men and women played together without fear. Perhaps it lay in his smile, which was so winning that wrinkled old dames spoke of it, who had never met the word before, smiles being little known in Thrums, where in a workaday world we find it sufficient either to laugh or to look thrawn. His dark curly hair was what Grizel was most suspicious of; he must be vain of that, she thought, until she discovered that he was quite sensitive to its being mentioned, having ever detested his curls as an eyesore, and in his boyhood clipped them savagely to the roots. He had such a firm chin, if there had been another such chin going a-begging, I should have liked to clap it on to Tommy Sandys.

Tommy Sandys! All this time we have been neglecting that brave sufferer, and while we talk his ankle is swelling and swelling. Well, Grizel was not so inconsiderate, for she walked very fast and with an exceedingly determined mouth to Dr. Gemmell's lodgings. He was still in lodgings, having refused to turn Grizel out of her house, though she had offered to let it to him. She left word, the doctor not being in, that he was wanted at once by Mr. Sandys, who had sprained his ankle.

Now, then, Tommy!

For an hour, perhaps until she went to bed, she remained merciless. She saw the quiet doctor with the penetrating eyes examining that ankle, asking a few questions, and looking curiously at his patient; then she saw him lift his hat and walk out of the house.

It gave her pleasure; no, it did not. While she thought of this Tommy she despised, there came in front of him a boy who had played with her long ago when no other child would play with her, and now he said, "You have grown cold to me, Grizel," and she nodded assent, and little wells of water rose to her eyes and lay there because she had nodded assent.

She had never liked Dr. Gemmell so little as when she saw him approaching her house next morning. The surgery was still attached to it, and very often he came from there, his visiting-book in his hand, to tell her of his patients, even to consult her; indeed, to talk to Grizel about his work without consulting her would have been difficult, for it was natural to her to decide what was best for everybody. These consultations were very unprofessional, but from her first coming to the old doctor's house she had taken it as a matter of course that in his practice, as in affairs relating to his boots and buttons, she should tell him what to do and he should do it. McQueen had introduced his assistant to this partnership half-shamefacedly and with a cautious wink over the little girl's head; and Gemmell fell into line at once, showing her his new stethoscope as gravely as if he must abandon it at once should not she approve, which fine behaviour, however, was quite thrown away on Grizel, who, had he conducted himself otherwise, would merely have wondered what was the matter with the man; and as she was eighteen or more before she saw that she had exceeded her duties, it was then, of course, too late to cease doing it.

She knew now how good, how forbearing, he had been to the little girl, and that it was partly because he was acquainted with her touching history. The grave courtesy with which he had always treated her-and which had sometimes given her as a girl a secret thrill of delight, it was so sweet to Grizel to be respected-she knew now to be less his natural manner to women than something that came to him in her presence because he who knew her so well thought her worthy of deference; and it helped her more, far more, than if she had seen it turn to love. Yet as she received him in her parlor now-her too spotless parlor, for not even the ashes in the grate were visible, which is a mistake-she was not very friendly. He had discovered what Tommy was, and as she had been the medium she could not blame him for that, but how could he look as calm as ever when such a deplorable thing had happened?

"What you say is true; I knew it before I asked you to go to him, and I knew you would find it out; but please to remember that he is a man of genius, whom it is not for such as you to judge."

That was the sort of haughty remark she held ready for him while they talked of other cases; but it was never uttered, for by and by he said:

"And then, there is Mr. Sandys's ankle. A nasty accident, I am afraid."

Was he jesting? She looked at him sharply. "Have you not been to see him yet?" she asked.

He thought she had misunderstood him. He had been to see Mr. Sandys twice, both last night and this morning.

And he was sure it was a sprain?

Unfortunately it was something worse-dislocation; further mischief might show itself presently.

"Haemorrhage into the neighbouring joint on inflammation?" she asked scientifically and with scorn.

"Yes."

Grizel turned away from him. "I think not," she said.

Well, possibly not, if Mr. Sandys was careful and kept his foot from the ground for the next week. The doctor did not know that she was despising him, and he proceeded to pay Tommy a compliment. "I had to reduce the dislocation, of course," he told her, "and he bore the wrench splendidly, though there is almost no pain more acute."

"Did he ask you to tell me that?" Grizel was thirsting to inquire, but she forbore. Unwittingly, however, the doctor answered the question. "I could see," he said, "that Mr. Sandys made light of his sufferings to save his sister pain. I cannot recall ever having seen a brother and sister so attached."

That was quite true, Grizel admitted to herself. In all her recollections of Tommy she could not remember one critical moment in which Elspeth had not been foremost in his thoughts. It passed through her head, "Even now he must make sure that Elspeth is in peace of mind before he can care to triumph over me," and she would perhaps have felt less bitter had he put his triumph first.

His triumph! Oh, she would show him whether it was a triumph. He had destroyed for ever her faith in David Gemmell. The quiet, observant doctor, who had such an eye for the false, had been deceived as easily as all the others, and it made her feel very lonely. But never mind; Tommy should find out, and that within the hour, that there was one whom he could not cheat. Her first impulse, always her first impulse, was to go straight to his side and tell him what she thought of him. Her second, which was neater, was to send by messenger her compliments to Mr. and Miss Sandys, and would they, if not otherwise engaged, come and have tea with her that afternoon? Not a word in the note about the ankle, but a careful sentence to the effect that she had seen Dr. Gemmell to-day, and proposed asking him to meet them.

Maggy Ann, who had conveyed the message, came back with the reply. Elspeth regretted that they could not accept Grizel's invitation, owing to the accident to her brother being *very much more* serious than Grizel seemed to think. "I can't understand," Elspeth added, "why Dr. Gemmell did not tell you this when he saw you."

"Is it a polite letter?" asked inquisitive Maggy Ann, and Grizel assured her that it was most polite. "I hardly expected it," said the plain-spoken dame, "for I'm thinking by their manner it's more than can be said of yours."

"I merely invited them to come to tea."

"And him wi' his leg broke! Did you no ken he was lying on chairs?"

"I did not know it was so bad as that, Maggy Ann. So my letter seemed to annoy him, did it?" said Grizel, eagerly, and, I fear, well pleased.

"It angered her most terrible," said Maggy Ann, "but no him. He gave a sort of a laugh when he read it."

"A laugh!"

"Ay, and syne she says, 'It is most heartless of Grizel; she does not even ask how you are to-day; one would think she did not know of the accident'; and she says, 'I have a good mind to write her a very stiff letter.' And says he in a noble, melancholic voice, 'We must not hurt Grizel's feelings,' he says. And she says, 'Grizel thinks it was nothing because you bore it so cheerfully; oh, how little she knows you!' she says; and 'You are too forgiving,' she says. And says he, 'If I have anything to forgive Grizel for, I forgive her willingly.' And syne she quieted down and wrote the letter."

Forgive her! Oh, how it enraged Grizel! How like the Tommy of old to put it in that way. There never had been a boy so good at forgiving people for his own crimes, and he always looked so modest when he did it. He was reclining on his chairs at this moment, she was sure he was, forgiving her in every sentence. She could have endured it more easily had she felt sure that he was seeing himself as he was; but she remembered him too well to have any hope of that.

She put on her bonnet, and took it off again; a terrible thing, remember, for Grizel to be in a state of indecision. For the remainder of that day she was not wholly inactive. Meeting Dr. Gemmell in the street, she impressed upon him the advisability of not allowing Mr. Sandys to move for at least a week.

"He might take a drive in a day or two," the doctor thought, "with his sister."

"He would be sure to use his foot," Grizel maintained, "if you once let him rise from his chair; you know they all do." And Gemmell agreed that she was right. So she managed to give Tommy as irksome a time as possible.

But next day she called. To go through another day without letting him see how despicable she thought him was beyond her endurance. Elspeth was a little stiff at first, but Tommy received her heartily and with nothing in his manner to show that she had hurt his finer feelings. His leg (the wrong leg, as Grizel remembered at once) was extended on a chair in front of him; but instead of nursing it ostentatiously as so many would have done, he made humourous remarks at its expense. "The fact is," he said cheerily, "that so long as I don't move I never felt better in my life. And I daresay I could walk almost as well as either of you, only my tyrant of a doctor won't let me try." "He told me you had behaved splendidly," said Grizel, "while he was reducing the dislocation. How brave you are! You could not have endured more stoically though there had been nothing the matter with it."

"It was soon over," Tommy replied lightly. "I think Elspeth suffered more than I."

Elspeth told the story of his heroism. "I could not stay in the room," she said; "it was too terrible." And Grizel despised too tender-hearted Elspeth for that; she was so courageous at facing pain herself. But Tommy had guessed that Elspeth was trembling behind the door, and he had called out, "Don't cry, Elspeth; I am all right; it is nothing at all."

"How noble!" was Grizel's comment, when she heard of this; and then Elspeth was her friend again, insisted on her staying to tea, and went into the kitchen to prepare it. Aaron was out.

The two were alone now, and in the circumstances some men would have given the lady the opportunity to apologize, if such was her desire. But Tommy's was a more generous nature; his manner was that of one less sorry to be misjudged than anxious that Grizel should not suffer too much from remorse. If she had asked his pardon then and there, I am sure he would have replied, "Right willingly, Grizel," and begged her not to give another thought to the matter. What is of more importance, Grizel was sure of this also, and it was the magnanimity of him that especially annoyed her. There seemed to be no disturbing it. Even when she said, "Which foot is it?" he answered, "The one on the chair," quite graciously, as if she had asked a natural question.

Grizel pointed out that the other foot must be tired of being a foot in waiting. It had got a little exercise, Tommy replied lightly, last night and again this morning, when it had helped to convey him to and from his bed.

Had he hopped? she asked brutally.

No, he said; he had shuffled along. Half rising, he attempted to show her humourously how he walked nowadays-tried not to wince, but had to. Ugh, that was a twinge! Grizel sarcastically offered her assistance, and he took her shoulder gratefully. They crossed the room —a tedious journey. "Now let me see if you can manage alone," she says, and suddenly deserts him.

He looked rather helplessly across the room. Few sights are so pathetic as the strong man of yesterday feeling that the chair by the fire is a distant object to-day. Tommy knew how pathetic it was, but Grizel did not seem to know.

"Try it," she said encouragingly; "it will do you good."

"And clung to it, his teeth set."

He got as far as the table, and clung to it, his teeth set. Grizel clapped her hands. "Excellently done!" she said, with fell meaning, and recommended him to move up and down the room for a little; he would feel ever so much the better for it afterwards.

The pain-was-considerable, he said. Oh, she saw that, but he had already proved himself so good at bearing pain, and the new school of surgeons held that it was wise to exercise an injured limb.

Even then it was not a reproachful glance that Tommy gave her, though there was some sadness in it. He moved across the room several times, a groan occasionally escaping him. "Admirable!" said his critic. "Bravo! Would you like to stop now?"

"Not until you tell me to," he said determinedly, but with a gasp.

"It must be dreadfully painful," she replied coldly, "but I should like you to go on." And he went on until suddenly he seemed to have lost the power to lift his feet. His body swayed; there was an appealing look on his face. "Don't be afraid; you won't fall," said Grizel. But she had scarcely said it when he fainted dead away, and went down at her feet.

"Oh, how dare you!" she cried in sudden flame, and she drew back from him. But after a moment she knew that he was shamming no longer-or she knew it and yet could not quite believe it; for, hurrying out of the room for water, she had no sooner passed the door than she swiftly put back her head as if to catch him unawares; but he lay motionless.

The sight of her dear brother on the floor paralyzed Elspeth, who could only weep for him, and call to him to look at her and speak to her. But in such an emergency Grizel was as useful as any doctor, and by the time Gemmell arrived in haste the invalid was being brought to. The doctor was a practical man who did not ask questions while there was something better to do. Had he asked any as he came in, Grizel would certainly have said: "He wanted to faint to make me believe he really has a bad ankle, and somehow he managed to do it." And if the doctor had replied that people can't faint by wishing, she would have said that he did not know Mr. Sandys.

But, with few words, Gemmell got his patient back to the chairs, and proceeded to undo the bandages that were round his ankle. Grizel stood by, assisting silently. She had often assisted the doctors, but never before with that scornful curl of her lip. So the bandages were removed and the ankle laid bare. It was very much swollen and discoloured, and when Grizel saw this she gave a little cry, and the ointment she was holding slipped from her hand. For the first time since he came to Thrums, she had failed Gemmell at a patient's side.

"I had not expected it to be-like this," she said in a quivering voice, when he looked at her in surprise.

"It will look much worse to-morrow," he assured them, grimly. "I can't understand, Miss Sandys, how this came about."

"Miss Sandys was not in the room," said Grizel, abjectly, "but I was, and I —"

Tommy's face was begging her to stop. He was still faint and in pain, but all thought of himself left him in his desire to screen her. "I owe you an apology, doctor," he said quickly, "for disregarding your instructions. It was entirely my own fault; I would try to walk."

"Every step must have been agony," the doctor rapped out; and Grizel shuddered.

"Not nearly so bad as that," Tommy said, for her sake.

"Agony," insisted the doctor, as if, for once, he enjoyed the word. "It was a mad thing to do, as surely you could guess, Grizel. Why did you not prevent him?"

"She certainly did her best to stop me," Tommy said hastily; "but I suppose I had some insane fit on me, for do it I would. I am very sorry, doctor."

His face was wincing with pain, and he spoke jerkily; but the doctor was still angry. He felt that there was something between these two which he did not understand, and it was strange to him, and unpleasant, to find Grizel unable to speak for herself. I think he doubted Tommy from that hour. All he said in reply, however, was: "It is unnecessary to apologize to me; you yourself are the only sufferer."

But was Tommy the only sufferer? Gemmell left, and Elspeth followed him to listen to those precious words which doctors drop, as from a vial, on the other side of a patient's door; and then Grizel, who had been standing at the window with head averted, turned slowly round and looked at the man she had wronged. Her arms, which had been hanging rigid, the fists closed, went out to him to implore forgiveness. I don't know how she held herself up and remained dry-eyed, her whole being wanted so much to sink by the side of his poor, tortured foot, and bathe it in her tears.

So, you see, he had won; nothing to do now but forgive her beautifully. Go on, Tommy; you are good at it.

But the unexpected only came out of Tommy. Never was there a softer heart. In London the old lady who sold matches at the street corner had got all his pence; had he heard her, or any other, mourning a son sentenced to the gallows, he would immediately have wondered whether he might take the condemned one's place. (What a speech Tommy could have delivered from the scaffold!) There was nothing he would not jump at doing for a woman in distress, except, perhaps, destroy his note-book. And Grizel was in anguish. She was his suppliant, his brave, lonely little playmate of the past, the noble girl of to-day, Grizel whom he liked so much. As through a magnifying-glass he saw her top-heavy with remorse for life, unable to sleep of nights, crushed and ——

He was not made of the stuff that could endure it. The truth must out. "Grizel," he said impulsively, "you have nothing to be sorry for. You were quite right. I did not hurt my foot that night in the Den, but afterwards, when I was alone, before the doctor came. I wricked it here intentionally in the door. It sounds incredible; but I set my teeth and did it, Grizel, because you had challenged me to a duel, and I would not give in."

As soon as it was out he was proud of himself for having the generosity to confess it. He looked at Grizel expectantly.

Yes, it sounded incredible, and yet she saw that it was true. As Elspeth returned at that moment, Grizel could say nothing. She stood looking at him only over her high collar of fur. Tommy actually thought that she was admiring him.

Chapter VIII
What Grizel's Eyes Said

To be the admired of women-how Tommy had fought for it since first he drank of them in Pym's sparkling pages! To some it seems to be easy, but to him it was a labour of Sisyphus. Everything had been against him. But he concentrated. No labour was too Herculean; he was prepared, if necessary, to walk round the world to get to the other side of the wall across which some men can step. And he did take a roundabout way. It is my opinion, for instance, that he wrote his book in order to make a beginning with the ladies.

That as it may be, at all events he is on the right side of the wall now, and here is even Grizel looking wistfully at him. Had she admired him for something he was not (and a good many of them did that) he would have been ill satisfied. He wanted her to think him splendid because he was splendid, and the more he reflected the more clearly he saw that he had done a big thing. How many men would have had the courage to wrick their foot as he had done? (He shivered when he thought of it.) And even of these Spartans how many would have let the reward slip through their fingers rather than wound the feelings of a girl? These had not been his thoughts when he made confession; he had spoken on an impulse; but now that he could step out and have a look at himself, he saw that this made it a still bigger thing. He was modestly pleased that he had not only got Grizel's admiration, but earned it, and he was very kind to her when next she came to see him. No one could be more kind to them than he when they admired him. He had the most grateful heart, had our Tommy.

When next she came to see him! That was while his ankle still nailed him to the chair, a fortnight or so during which Tommy was at his best, sending gracious messages by Elspeth to the many who called to inquire, and writing hard at his new work, pad on knee, so like a brave soul whom no unmerited misfortune could subdue that it would have done you good merely to peep at him through the window. Grizel came several times, and the three talked very ordinary things, mostly reminiscences; she was as much a plain-spoken princess as ever, but often he found her eyes fixed on him wistfully, and he knew what they were saying; they spoke so eloquently that he was a little nervous lest Elspeth should notice. It was delicious to Tommy to feel that there was this little unspoken something between him and Grizel; he half regretted that the time could not be far distant when she must put it into words-as soon, say, as Elspeth left the room; an exquisite moment, no doubt, but it would be the plucking of the flower.

Don't think that Tommy conceived Grizel to be in love with him. On my sacred honour, that would have horrified him.

Curiously enough, she did not take the first opportunity Elspeth gave her of telling him in words how much she admired his brave confession. She was so honest that he expected her to begin the moment the door closed, and now that the artistic time had come for it, he wanted it; but no. He was not hurt, but he wondered at her shyness, and cast about for the reason. He cast far back into the past, and caught a little girl who had worn this same wistful face when she admired him most. He compared those two faces of the anxious girl and the serene woman, and in the wistfulness that sometimes lay on them both they looked alike. Was it possible that the fear of him which the years had driven out of the girl still lived a ghost's life to haunt the woman?

At once he overflowed with pity. As a boy he had exulted in Grizel's fear of him; as a man he could feel only the pain of it. There was no one, he thought, less to be dreaded of a woman than he; oh, so sure Tommy was of that! And he must lay this ghost; he gave his whole heart to the laying of it.

Few men, and never a woman, could do a fine thing so delicately as he; but of course it included a divergence from the truth, for to Tommy afloat on a generous scheme the truth was a buoy marking sunken rocks. She had feared him in her childhood, as he knew well; he therefore proceeded to prove to her that she had never feared him. She had thought him masterful, and all his reminiscences now went to show that it was she who had been the masterful one.

"You must often laugh now," he said, "to remember how I feared you. The memory of it makes me afraid of you still. I assure you, I joukit back, as Corp would say, that day I saw you in church. It was the instinct of self-preservation. 'Here comes Grizel to lord it over me again,' I heard something inside me saying. You called me masterful, and yet I had always to give in to you. That shows what a gentle, yielding girl you were, and what a masterful character I was!"

His intention, you see, was, without letting Grizel know what he was at, to make her think he had forgotten certain unpleasant incidents in their past, so that, seeing they were no longer anything to him, they might the sooner become nothing to her. And she believed that he had forgotten, and she was glad. She smiled when he told her to go on being masterful, for old acquaintance had made him like it. Hers, indeed, was a masterful nature; she could not help it; and if the time ever came when she must help it, the glee of living would be gone from her.

She did continue to be masterful-to a greater extent than Tommy, thus nobly behaving, was prepared for; and his shock came to him at the very moment when he was modestly expecting to receive the prize. She had called when Elspeth happened to be out; and though now able to move about the room with the help of a staff, he was still an interesting object. He saw that she thought so, and perhaps it made him hobble slightly more, not vaingloriously, but because he was such an artist. He ceased to be an artist suddenly, however, when Grizel made this unexpected remark:

"How vain you are!"

Tommy sat down, quite pale. "Did you come here to say that to me, Grizel?" he inquired, and she nodded frankly over her high collar of fur. He knew it was true as Grizel said it, but though taken aback, he could bear it, for she was looking wistfully at him, and he knew well what Grizel's wistful look meant; so long as women admired him Tommy could bear anything from them. "God knows I have little to be vain of," he said humbly.

"Those are the people who are most vain," she replied; and he laughed a short laugh, which surprised her, she was so very serious.

"Your methods are so direct," he explained. "But of what am I vain, Grizel? Is it my book?"

"No," she answered, "not about your book, but about meaner things. What else could have made you dislocate your ankle rather than admit that you had been rather silly?"

Now "silly" is no word to apply to a gentleman, and, despite his forgiving nature, Tommy was a little disappointed in Grizel.

"I suppose it was a silly thing to do," he said, with just a touch of stiffness.

"It was an ignoble thing," said she, sadly.

"I see. And I myself am the meaner thing than the book, am I?"

"Are you not?" she asked, so eagerly that he laughed again.

"It is the first compliment you have paid my book," he pointed out.

"I like the book very much," she answered gravely. "No one can be more proud of your fame than I. You are hurting me very much by pretending to think that it is a pleasure to me to find fault with you." There was no getting past the honesty of her, and he was touched by it. Besides, she did admire him, and that, after all, is the great thing.

"Then why say such things, Grizel?" he replied good-naturedly.

"But if they are true?"

"Still let us avoid them," said he; and at that she was most distressed.

"It is so like what you used to say when you were a boy!" she cried.

"You are so anxious to have me grow up," he replied, with proper dolefulness. "If you like the book, Grizel, you must have patience with the kind of thing that produced it. That night in the Den, when I won your scorn, I was in the preliminary stages of composition. At such times an author should be locked up; but I had got out, you see. I was so enamoured of my little fancies that I forgot I was with you. No wonder you were angry."

"I was not angry with you for forgetting me," she said sharply. (There was no catching Grizel, however artful you were.) "But you were sighing to yourself, you were looking as tragic as if some dreadful calamity had occurred —"

"The idea that had suddenly come to me was a touching one," he said.

"But you looked triumphant, too."

"That was because I saw I could make something of it." "Why did you walk as if you were lame?"

"The man I was thinking of," Tommy explained, "had broken his leg. I don't mind telling you that it was Corp."

He ought to have minded telling her, for it could only add to her indignation; but he was too conceited to give weight to that.

"Corp's leg was not broken," said practical Grizel.

"I broke it for him," replied Tommy; and when he had explained, her eyes accused him of heartlessness.

"If it had been my own," he said, in self-defence, "it should have gone crack just the same."

"Poor Gavinia! Had you no feeling for her?"

"Gavinia was not there," Tommy replied triumphantly. "She had run off with a soldier."

"You dared to conceive that?"

"It helped."

Grizel stamped her foot. "You could take away dear Gavinia's character with a smile!"

"On the contrary," said Tommy, "my heart bled for her. Did you not notice that I was crying?" But he could not make Grizel smile; so, to please her, he said, with a smile that was not very sincere: "I wish I were different, but that is how ideas come to me-at least, all those that are of any value."

"Surely you could fight against them and drive them away?"

This to Tommy, who held out sugar to them to lure them to him! But still he treated her with consideration.

"That would mean my giving up writing altogether, Grizel," he said kindly.

"Then why not give it up?"

Really! But she admired him, and still he bore with her.

"I don't like the book," she said, "if it is written at such a cost."

"People say the book has done them good, Grizel."

"What does that matter, if it does you harm?" In her eagerness to persuade him, her words came pell-mell. "If writing makes you live in such an unreal world, it must do you harm. I see now what Mr. Cathro meant, long ago, when he called you Senti———"

Tommy winced. "I remember what Mr. Cathro called me," he said, with surprising hauteur for such a good-natured man. "But he does not call me that now. No one calls me that now, except you, Grizel."

"What does that matter," she replied distressfully, "if it is true? In the definition of sentimentality in the dictionary—"

He rose indignantly. "You have been looking me up in the dictionary, have you, Grizel?"

"Yes, the night you told me you had hurt your ankle intentionally."

He laughed, without mirth now. "I thought you had put that down to vanity."

"I think," she said, "it was vanity that gave you the courage to do it." And he liked one word in this remark.

"Then you do give me credit for a little courage?"

"I think you could do the most courageous things," she told him, "so long as there was no real reason why you should do them."

It was a shot that rang the bell. Oh, our Tommy heard it ringing. But, to do him justice, he bore no malice; he was proud, rather, of Grizel's marksmanship. "At least," he said meekly, "it was courageous of me to tell you the truth in the end?" But, to his surprise, she shook her head.

"No," she replied; "it was sweet of you. You did it impulsively, because you were sorry for me, and I think it was sweet. But impulse is not courage."

So now Tommy knew all about it. His plain-spoken critic had been examining him with a candle, and had paid particular attention to his defects; but against them she set the fact that he had done something chivalrous for her, and it held her heart, though the others were in possession of the head. "How like a woman!" he thought, with a pleased smile. He knew them!

Still he was chagrined that she made so little of his courage, and it was to stab her that he said, with subdued bitterness: "I always had a suspicion that I was that sort of person, and it is pleasant to have it pointed out by one's oldest friend. No one will ever accuse you of want of courage, Grizel."

She was looking straight at him, and her eyes did not drop, but they looked still more wistful. Tommy did not understand the courage that made her say what she had said, but he knew he was hurting her; he knew that if she was too plain-spoken it was out of loyalty, and that to wound Grizel because she had to speak her mind was a shame-yes, he always knew that.

But he could do it; he could even go on: "And it is satisfactory that you have thought me out so thoroughly, because you will not need to think me out any more. You know me now, Grizel, and can have no more fear of me."

"When was I ever afraid of you?" she demanded. She was looking at him suspiciously now.

"Never as a girl?" he asked. It jumped out of him. He was sorry as soon as he had said it.

There was a long pause. "So you remembered it all the time," she said quietly. "You have been making pretence-again!" He asked her to forgive him, and she nodded her head at once. "But why did you pretend to have forgotten?"

"I thought it would please you, Grizel."

"Why should pretence please me?" She rose suddenly, in a white heat. "You don't mean to say that you think I am afraid of you still?"

He said No a moment too late. He knew it was too late.

"Don't be angry with me, Grizel," he begged her, earnestly. "I am so glad I was mistaken. It made me miserable. I have been a terrible blunderer, but I mean well; I misread your eyes."

"My eyes?"

"They have always seemed to be watching me, and often there was such a wistful look in them-it reminded me of the past."

"You thought I was still afraid of you! Say it," said Grizel, stamping her foot. But he would not say it. It was not merely fear that he thought he had seen in her eyes, you remember. This was still his comfort, and, I suppose, it gave the touch of complacency to his face that made Grizel merciless. She did not mean to be merciless, but only to tell the truth. If some of her words were scornful, there was sadness in her voice all the time, instead of triumph. "For years and years," she said, standing straight as an elvint, "I have been able to laugh at all the ignorant fears of my childhood; and if you don't know why I have watched you and been unable to help watching you since you came back, I shall tell you. But I think you might have guessed, you who write books about women. It is because I liked you when you were a boy. You were often horrid, but you were my first friend when every other person was against me. You let me play with you when no other boy or girl would let me play. And so, all the time you have been away, I have been hoping that you were growing into a noble man; and when you came back, I watched to see whether you were the noble man I wanted you so much to be, and you are not. Do you see now why my eyes look wistful? It is because I wanted to admire you, and I can't."

She went away, and the great authority on women raged about the room. Oh, but he was galled! There had been five feet nine of him, but he was shrinking. By and by the red light came into his eyes.

Chapter IX
Gallant Behaviour of T. Sandys

There were now no fewer than three men engaged, each in his own way, in the siege of Grizel, nothing in common between them except insulted vanity. One was a broken fellow who took for granted that she preferred to pass him by in the street. His bow was also an apology to her for his existence. He not only knew that she thought him wholly despicable, but agreed with her. In the long ago (yesterday, for instance) he had been happy, courted, esteemed; he had even esteemed himself, and so done useful work in the world. But she had flung him to earth so heavily that he had made a hole in it out of which he could never climb. There he lay damned, hers the glory of destroying him-he hoped she was proud of her handiwork. That was one Thomas Sandys, the one, perhaps, who put on the velvet jacket in the morning. But it might be number two who took that jacket off at night. He was a good-natured cynic, vastly amused by the airs this little girl put on before a man of note, and he took a malicious pleasure in letting her see that they entertained him. He goaded her intentionally into expressions of temper, because she looked prettiest then, and trifled with her hair (but this was in imagination only), and called her a quaint child (but this was beneath his breath). The third-he might be the one who wore the jacket-was a haughty boy who was not only done with her for ever, but meant to let her see it. (His soul cried, Oh, oh, for a conservatory and some of society's darlings, and Grizel at the window to watch how he got on with them!) And now that I think of it, there was also a fourth: Sandys, the grave author, whose life (in two vols. 8vo.) I ought at this moment to be writing, without a word about the other Tommies. They amused him a good deal. When they were doing something big he would suddenly appear and take a note of it.

The boy, who was stiffly polite to her (when Tommy was angry he became very polite), told her that he had been invited to the Spittal, the seat of the Rintoul family, and that he understood there were some charming girls there.

"I hope you will like them," Grizel said pleasantly.

"If you could see how they will like me!" he wanted to reply; but of course he could not, and unfortunately there was no one by to say it for him. Tommy often felt this want of a secretary.

The abject one found a glove of Grizel's, that she did not know she had lost, and put it in his pocket. There it lay, unknown to her. He knew that he must not even ask them to bury it with him in his grave. This was a little thing to ask, but too much for him. He saw his effects being examined after all that was mortal of T. Sandys had been consigned to earth, and this pathetic little glove coming to light. Ah, then, then Grizel would know! By the way, what would she have known? I am sure I cannot tell you. Nor could Tommy, forced to face the question in this vulgar way, have told you. Yet, whatever it was, it gave him some moist moments. If Grizel saw him in this mood, her reproachful look implied that he was sentimentalizing again. How little this chit understood him!

The man of the world sometimes came upon the glove in his pocket, and laughed at it, as such men do when they recall their callow youth. He took walks with Grizel without her knowing that she accompanied him; or rather, he let her come, she was so eager. In his imagination (for bright were the dreams of Thomas!) he saw her looking longingly after him, just as the dog looks; and then, not being really a cruel man, he would call over his shoulder, "Put on your hat, little woman; you can come." Then he conceived her wandering with him through the Den and Caddam Wood, clinging to his arm and looking up adoringly at him. "What a loving little soul it is!" he said, and pinched her ear, whereat she glowed with pleasure. "But I forgot," he would add, bantering her; "you don't admire me. Heigh-ho! Grizel wants to admire me, but she can't!" He got some satisfaction out of these flights of fancy, but it had a scurvy way of deserting him in the hour of greatest need; where was it, for instance, when the real Grizel appeared and fixed that inquiring eye on him?

He went to the Spittal several times, Elspeth with him when she cared to go; for Lady Rintoul and all the others had to learn and remember that, unless they made much of Elspeth, there could be no T. Sandys for them. He glared at anyone, male or female, who, on being introduced to Elspeth, did not remain, obviously impressed, by her side. "Give pleasure to Elspeth or away I go," was written all over him. And it had to be the right kind of pleasure, too. The ladies must feel that she was more innocent than they, and talk accordingly. He would walk the flower-garden with none of them until he knew for certain that the man walking it with little Elspeth was a person to be trusted. Once he was convinced of this, however, he was very much at their service, and so little to be trusted himself that perhaps they should have had careful brothers also. He told them, one at a time, that they were strangely unlike all the other women he had known, and held their hands a moment longer than was absolutely necessary, and then went away, leaving them and him a prey to conflicting and puzzling emotions.

Lord Rintoul, whose hair was so like his skin that in the family portraits he might have been painted in one colour, could never rid himself of the feeling that it must be a great thing to a writing chap to get a good dinner; but her ladyship always explained him away with an apologetic smile which went over his remarks like a piece of india-rubber, so that in the end he had never said anything. She was a slight, pretty woman of nearly forty, and liked Tommy because he remembered so vividly her coming to the Spittal as a bride. He even remembered how she had been dressed-her white bonnet, for instance.

"For long," Tommy said, musing, "I resented other women in white bonnets; it seemed profanation."

"How absurd!" she told him, laughing. "You must have been quite a small boy at the time."

"But with a lonely boy's passionate admiration for beautiful things," he answered; and his gravity was a gentle rebuke to her. "It was all a long time ago," he said, taking both her hands in his, "but I never forget, and, dear lady, I have often wanted to thank you." What he was thanking her for is not precisely clear, but she knew that the artistic temperament is an odd sort of thing, and from this time Lady Rintoul liked Tommy, and even tried to find the right wife for him among the families of the surrounding clergy. His step was sometimes quite springy when he left the Spittal; but Grizel's shadow was always waiting for him somewhere on the way home, to take the life out of him, and after that it was again, oh, sorrowful disillusion! oh, world gone gray! Grizel did not admire him. T. Sandys was no longer a wonder to Grizel. He went home to that as surely as the labourer to his evening platter.

And now we come to the affair of the Slugs. Corp had got a holiday, and they were off together fishing the Drumly Water, by Lord Rintoul's permission. They had fished the Drumly many a time without it, and this was to be another such day as those of old. The one who woke at four was to rouse the other. Never had either waked at four; but one of them was married now, and any woman can wake at any hour she chooses, so at four Corp was pushed out of bed, and soon thereafter they took the road. Grizel's blinds were already up. "Do you mind," Corp said, "how often, when we had boasted we were to start at four and didna get roaded till six, we wriggled by that window so that Grizel shouldna see us?"

"She usually did see us," Tommy replied ruefully. "Grizel always spotted us, Corp, when we had anything to hide, and missed us when we were anxious to be seen."

"There was no jouking her," said Corp. "Do you mind how that used to bother you?" a senseless remark to a man whom it was bothering still-or shall we say to a boy? For the boy came back to Tommy when he heard the Drumly singing; it was as if he had suddenly seen his mother looking young again. There had been a thunder-shower as they drew near, followed by a rush of wind that pinned them to a dike, swept the road bare, banged every door in the glen, and then sank suddenly as if it had never been, like a mole in the sand. But now the sun was out, every fence and farm-yard rope was a string of diamond drops. There was one to every blade of grass; they lurked among the wild roses; larks, drunken with song, shook them from their wings. The whole earth shone so gloriously with them that for a time Tommy ceased to care whether he was admired. We can pay nature no higher compliment.

But when they came to the Slugs! The Slugs of Kenny is a wild crevice through which the Drumly cuts its way, black and treacherous, into a lovely glade where it gambols for the rest of its short life; you would not believe, to see it laughing, that it had so lately escaped from prison. To the Slugs they made their way-not to fish, for any trout that are there are thinking for ever of the way out and of nothing else, but to eat their luncheon, and they ate it sitting on the mossy stones their persons had long ago helped to smooth, and looking at a roan-branch, which now, as then, was trailing in the water.

There were no fish to catch, but there was a boy trying to catch them. He was on the opposite bank; had crawled down it, only other boys can tell how, a barefooted urchin of ten or twelve, with an enormous bagful of worms hanging from his jacket button. To put a new worm on the hook without coming to destruction, he first twisted his legs about a young birch, and put his arms round it. He was after a big one, he informed Corp, though he might as well have been fishing in a treatise on the art of angling.

Corp exchanged pleasantries with him; told him that Tommy was Captain Ure, and that he was his faithful servant Alexander Bett, both of Edinburgh. Since the birth of his child, Corp had become something of a humourist. Tommy was not listening. As he lolled in the sun he was turning, without his knowledge, into one of the other Tommies. Let us watch the process.

He had found a half-fledged mavis lying dead in the grass. Remember also how the larks had sung after rain.

Tommy lost sight and sound of Corp and the boy. What he seemed to see was a baby lark that had got out of its nest sideways, a fall of half a foot only, but a dreadful drop for a baby. "You can get back this way," its mother said, and showed it the way, which was quite easy, but when the baby tried to leap, it fell on its back. Then the mother marked out lines on the ground, from one to the other of which it was to practise hopping, and soon it could hop beautifully so long as its mother was there to say every moment, "How beautifully you hop!" "Now teach me to hop up," the little lark said, meaning that it wanted to fly; and the mother tried to do that also, but in vain; she could soar up, up, up bravely, but could not explain how she did it. This distressed her very much, and she thought hard about how she had learned to fly long ago last year, but all she could recall for certain was that you suddenly do it. "Wait till the sun comes out after rain," she said, half remembering. "What is sun? What is rain?" the little bird asked. "If you cannot teach me to fly, teach me to sing." "When the sun comes out after rain," the mother replied, "then you will know how to sing." The rain came, and glued the little bird's wings together. "I shall never be able to fly nor to sing," it wailed. Then, of a sudden, it had to blink its eyes; for a glorious light had spread over the world, catching every leaf and twig and blade of grass in tears, and putting a smile into every tear. The baby bird's breast swelled, it did not know why; and it fluttered from the ground, it did not know how. "The sun has come out after the rain," it trilled. "Thank you, sun; thank you, thank you! Oh, mother, did you hear me? I can sing!" And it floated up, up, up, crying, "Thank you, thank you, thank you!" to the sun. "Oh, mother, do you see me? I am flying!" And being but a baby, it soon was gasping, but still it trilled the same ecstasy, and when it fell panting to earth it still trilled, and the distracted mother called to it to take breath or it would die, but it could not stop. "Thank you, thank you, thank you!" it sang to the sun till its little heart burst.

With filmy eyes Tommy searched himself for the little pocket-book in which he took notes of such sad thoughts as these, and in place of the book he found a glove wrapped in silk paper. He sat there with it in his hand, nodding his head over it so broken-heartedly you could not have believed that he had forgotten it for several days.

Death was still his subject; but it was no longer a bird he saw: it was a very noble young man, and his white, dead face stared at the sky from the bottom of a deep pool. I don't know how he got there, but a woman who would not admire him had something to do with it. No sun after rain had come into that tragic life. To the water that had ended it his white face seemed to be saying, "Thank you, thank you, thank you." It was the old story of a faithless woman. He had given her his heart, and she had played with it. For her sake he had striven to be famous; for her alone had he toiled through dreary years in London, the goal her lap, in which he should one day place his book —a poor, trivial little work, he knew (yet much admired by the best critics). Never had his thoughts wandered for one instant of that time to another woman; he had been as faithful in life as in death; and now she came to the edge of the pool and peered down at his staring eyes and laughed.

He had got thus far when a shout from Corp brought him, dazed, to his feet. It had been preceded by another cry, as the boy and the sapling he was twisted round toppled into the river together, uprooted stones and clods pounding after them and discolouring the pool into which the torrent rushes between rocks, to swirl frantically before it dives down a narrow channel and leaps into another caldron.

There was no climbing down those precipitous rocks. Corp was shouting, gesticulating, impotent. "How can you stand so still?" he roared.

For Tommy was standing quite still, like one not yet thoroughly awake. The boy's head was visible now and again as he was carried round in the seething water; when he came to the outer ring down that channel he must infallibly go, and every second or two he was in a wider circle.

Tommy was awake now, and he could not stand still and see a boy drown before his eyes. He knew that to attempt to save him was to face a terrible danger, especially as he could not swim; but he kicked off his boots. There was some gallantry in the man.

"You wouldna dare!" Corp cried, aghast.

Tommy hesitated for a moment, but he had abundance of physical courage. He clenched his teeth and jumped. But before he jumped he pushed the glove into Corp's hand, saying, "Give her that, and tell her it never left my heart." He did not say who she was; he scarcely knew that he was saying it. It was his dream intruding on reality, as a wheel may revolve for a moment longer after the spring breaks.

Corp saw him strike the water and disappear. He tore along the bank as he had never run before, until he got to the water's edge below the Slugs, and climbed and fought his way to the scene of the disaster. Before he reached it, however, we should have had no hero had not the sapling, the cause of all this pother, made amends by barring the way down the narrow channel. Tommy was clinging to it, and the boy to him, and, at some risk, Corp got them both ashore, where they lay gasping like fish in a creel.

The boy was the first to rise to look for his fishing-rod, and he was surprised to find no six-pounder at the end of it. "She has broke the line again!" he said; for he was sure then and ever afterwards that a big one had pulled him in.

Corp slapped him for his ingratitude; but the man who had saved this boy's life wanted no thanks. "Off to your home with you, wherever it is," he said to the boy, who obeyed silently; and then to Corp: "He is a little fool, Corp, but not such a fool as I am." He lay on his face, shivering, not from cold, not from shock, but in a horror of himself. I think it may fairly be said that he had done a brave if foolhardy thing; it was certainly to save the boy that he had jumped, and he had given himself a moment's time in which to draw back if he chose, which vastly enhances the merit of the deed. But sentimentality had been there also, and he was now shivering with a presentiment of the length to which it might one day carry him.

They lit a fire among the rocks, at which he dried his clothes, and then they set out for home, Corp doing all the talking. "What a town there will be about this in Thrums!" was his text; and he was surprised when Tommy at last broke silence by saying passionately: "Never speak about this to me again, Corp, as long as you live. Promise me that. Promise never to mention it to anyone. I want no one to know what I did to-day, and no one will ever know unless you tell; the boy can't tell, for we are strangers to him."

"He thinks you are a Captain Ure, and that I'm Alexander Bett, his servant," said Corp. "I telled him that for a divert."

"Then let him continue to think that."

Of course Corp promised. "And I'll go to the stake afore I break my promise," he swore, happily remembering one of the Jacobite oaths. But he was puzzled. They would make so much of Tommy if they knew. They would think him a wonder. Did he not want that?

"No," Tommy replied.

"You used to like it; you used to like it most michty."

"I have changed."

"Ay, you have; but since when? Since you took to making printed books?"

Tommy did not say, but it was more recently than that. What he was surrendering no one could have needed to be told less than he; the magnitude of the sacrifice was what enabled him to make it. He was always at home among the superlatives; it was the little things that bothered him. In his present fear of the ride that sentimentality might yet goad him to, he craved for mastery over self; he knew that his struggles with his Familiar usually ended in an embrace, and he had made a passionate vow that it should be so no longer. The best beginning of the new man was to deny himself the glory that would be his if his deed were advertised to the world. Even Grizel must never know of it-Grizel, whose admiration was so dear to him. Thus he punished himself, and again I think he deserves respect.

Chapter X
Gavinia on the Track

Corp, you remember, had said that he would go to the stake rather than break his promise; and he meant it, too, though what the stake was, and why such a pother about going to it, he did not know. He was to learn now, however, for to the stake he had to go. This was because Gavinia, when folding up his clothes, found in one of the pockets a glove wrapped in silk paper.

Tommy had forgotten it until too late, for when he asked Corp for the glove it was already in Gavinia's possession, and she had declined to return it without an explanation. "You must tell her nothing," Tommy said sternly. He was uneasy, but relieved to find that Corp did not know whose glove it was, nor even why gentlemen carry a lady's glove in their pocket.

At first Gavinia was mildly curious only, but her husband's refusal to answer any questions roused her dander. She tried cajolery, fried his take of trout deliciously for him, and he sat down to them sniffing. They were small, and the remainder of their brief career was in two parts. First he lifted them by the tail, then he laid down the tail. But not a word about the glove.

She tried tears. "Dinna greet, woman," he said in distress. "What would the bairn say if he kent I made you greet?"

Gavinia went on greeting, and the baby, waking up, promptly took her side.

"D — —n the thing!" said Corp.

"Your ain bairn!"

"I meant the glove!" he roared.

It was curiosity only that troubled Gavinia. A reader of romance, as you may remember, she had encountered in the printed page a score of ladies who, on finding such parcels in their husbands' pockets, left their homes at once and for ever, and she had never doubted but that it was the only course to follow; such is the power of the writer of fiction. But when the case was her own she was merely curious; such are the limitations of the writer of fiction. That there was a woman in it she did not believe for a moment. This, of course, did not prevent her saying, with a sob, "Wha is the woman?"

With great earnestness Corp assured her that there was no woman. He even proved it: "Just listen to reason, Gavinia. If I was sich a black as to be chief wi' ony woman, and she wanted to gie me a present, weel, she might gie me a pair o' gloves, but one glove, what use would one glove be to me? I tell you, if a woman had the impidence to gie me one glove, I would fling it in her face."

Nothing could have been clearer, and he had put it thus considerately because when a woman, even the shrewdest of them, is excited (any man knows this), one has to explain matters to her as simply and patiently as if she were a four-year-old; yet Gavinia affected to be unconvinced, and for several days she led Corp the life of a lodger in his own house.

"Hands off that poor innocent," she said when he approached the baby.

If he reproved her, she replied meekly, "What can you expect frae a woman that doesna wear gloves?"

To the baby she said: "He despises you, my bonny, because you hae no gloves. Ay, that's what maks him turn up his nose at you. But your mother is fond o' you, gloves or no gloves."

She told the baby the story of the glove daily, with many monstrous additions.

When Corp came home from his work, she said that a poor, love-lorn female had called with a boot for him, and a request that he should carry it in the pocket of his Sabbath breeks.

Worst of all, she listened to what he said in the night. Corp had a habit of talking in his sleep. He was usually taking tickets at such times, and it had been her custom to stop him violently; but now she changed her tactics: she encouraged him. "I would be lying in my bed," he said to Tommy, "dreaming that a man had fallen into the Slugs, and instead o' trying to save him I cried out, 'Tickets there, all tickets ready,' and first he hands me a glove and neist he hands me a boot and havers o' that kind sich as onybody dreams. But in the middle o' my dream it comes ower me that I had better waken up to see what Gavinia's doing, and I open my een, and there she is, sitting up, hearkening avidly to my every word, and putting sly questions to me about the glove."

"What glove?" Tommy asked coldly.

"The glove in silk paper."

"I never heard of it," said Tommy.

Corp sighed. "No," he said loyally, "neither did I"; and he went back to the station and sat gloomily in a wagon. He got no help from Tommy, not even when rumours of the incident at the Slugs became noised abroad.

"A'body kens about the laddie now," he said.

"What laddie?" Tommy inquired.

"Him that fell into the Slugs."

"Ah, yes," Tommy said; "I have just been reading about it in the paper. A plucky fellow, this Captain Ure who saved him. I wonder who he is."

"I wonder!" Corp said with a groan.

"There was an Alexander Bett with him, according to the papers," Tommy went on. "Do you know any Bett?"

"It's no a Thrums name," Corp replied thankfully. "I just made it up."

"What do you mean?" Tommy asked blankly.

Corp sighed, and went back again to the wagon. He was particularly truculent that evening when the six-o'clock train came in. "Tickets, there; look slippy wi' your tickets." His head bobbed up at the window of another compartment. "Tick — —" he began, and then he ducked.

The compartment contained a boy looking as scared as if he had just had his face washed, and an old woman who was clutching a large linen bag as if expecting some scoundrel to appear through the floor and grip it. With her other hand she held on to the boy, and being unused to travel, they were both sitting very self-conscious, humble, and defiant, like persons in church who have forgotten to bring their Bible. The general effect, however, was lost on Corp, for whom it was enough that in one of them he recognized the boy of the Slugs. He thought he had seen the old lady before, also, but he could not give her a name. It was quite a relief to him to notice that she was not wearing gloves.

He heard her inquiring for one Alexander Bett, and being told that there was no such person in Thrums, "He's married on a woman of the name of Gavinia," said the old lady; and then they directed her to the house of the only Gavinia in the place. With dark forebodings Corp skulked after her. He remembered who she was now. She was the old woman with the nut-cracker face on whom he had cried in, more than a year ago, to say that Gavinia was to have him. Her mud cottage had been near the Slugs. Yes, and this was the boy who had been supping porridge with her. Corp guessed rightly that the boy had remembered his unlucky visit. "I'm doomed!" Corp muttered to himself-pronouncing it in another way.

The woman, the boy, and the bag entered the house of Gavinia, and presently she came out with them. She was looking very important and terrible. They went straight to Ailie's cottage, and Corp was wondering why, when he suddenly remembered that Tommy was to be there at tea to-day.

Chapter XI
The Tea-Party

It was quite a large tea-party, and was held in what had been the school-room; nothing there now, however, to recall an academic past, for even the space against which a map of the world (Mercator's projection) had once hung was gone the colour of the rest of the walls, and with it had faded away the last relic of the Hanky School.

"It will not fade so quickly from my memory," Tommy said, to please Mrs. McLean. His affection for his old schoolmistress was as sincere as hers for him. I could tell you of scores of pretty things he had done to give her pleasure since his return, all carried out, too, with a delicacy which few men could rival, and never a woman; but they might make you like him, so we shall pass them by.

Ailie said, blushing, that she had taught him very little. "Everything I know," he replied, and then, with a courteous bow to the gentleman opposite, "except what I learned from Mr. Cathro."

"Thank you," Cathro said shortly. Tommy had behaved splendidly to him, and called him his dear preceptor, and yet the Dominie still itched to be at him with the tawse as of old. "And fine he knows I'm itching," he reflected, which made him itch the more.

It should have been a most successful party, for in the rehearsals between the hostess and her maid Christina every conceivable difficulty had been ironed out. Ailie was wearing her black silk, but without the Honiton lace, so that Miss Sophia Innes need not become depressed; and she had herself taken the chair with the weak back. Mr. Cathro, who, though a lean man, needed a great deal of room at table, had been seated far away from the spinet, to allow Christina to pass him without climbing. Miss Sophia and Grizel had the doctor between them, and there was also a bachelor, but an older one, for Elspeth. Mr. McLean, as stout and humoursome as of yore, had solemnly promised his wife to be jocular but not too jocular. Neither minister could complain, for if Mr. Dishart had been asked to say grace, Mr. Gloag knew that he was to be called on for the benediction. Christina, obeying strict orders, glided round the table leisurely, as if she were not in the least excited, though she could be heard rushing along the passage like one who had entered for a race. And, lastly, there was, as chief guest, the celebrated Thomas Sandys. It should have been a triumph of a tea-party, and yet it was not. Mrs. McLean could not tell why.

Grizel could have told why; her eyes told why every time they rested scornfully on Mr. Sandys. It was he, they said, who was spoiling the entertainment, and for the pitiful reason that the company were not making enough of him. He was the guest of the evening, but they were talking admiringly of another man, and so he sulked. Oh, how she scorned Tommy!

That other man was, of course, the unknown Captain Ure, gallant rescuer of boys, hero of all who admire brave actions except the jealous Sandys. Tommy had pooh-poohed him from the first, to Grizel's unutterable woe.

"Have you not one word of praise for such a splendid deed?" she had asked in despair.

"I see nothing splendid about it," he replied coldly.

"I advise you in your own interests not to talk in that way to others," she said. "Don't you see what they will say?"

"I can't help that," answered Tommy the just. "If they ask my opinion, I must give them the truth. I thought you were fond of the truth, Grizel." To that she could only wring her hands and say nothing; but it had never struck her that the truth could be so bitter.

And now he was giving his opinion at Mrs. McLean's party, and they were all against him, except, in a measure, Elspeth's bachelor, who said cheerily, "We should all have done it if we had been in Captain Ure's place; I would have done it myself, Miss Elspeth, though not fond of the water." He addressed all single ladies by their Christian name with a Miss in front of it. This is the mark of the confirmed bachelor, and comes upon him at one-and-twenty.

"I could not have done it," Grizel replied decisively, though she was much the bravest person present, and he explained that he meant the men only. His name was James Bonthron; let us call him Mr. James.

"Men are so brave!" she responded, with her eyes on Tommy, and he received the stab in silence. Had the blood spouted from the wound, it would have been an additional gratification to him. Tommy was like those superb characters of romance who bare their breast to the enemy and say, "Strike!"

"Well, well," Mr. Cathro observed, "none of us was on the spot, and so we had no opportunity of showing our heroism. But you were near by, Mr. Sandys, and if you had fished up the water that day, instead of down, you might have been called upon. I wonder what you would have done?"

Yes, Tommy was exasperating to him still as in the long ago, and Cathro said this maliciously, yet feeling that he did a risky thing, so convinced was he by old experience that you were getting in the way of a road-machine when you opposed Thomas Sandys.

"I wonder," Tommy replied quietly.

The answer made a poor impression, and Cathro longed to go on. "But he was always most dangerous when he was quiet," he reflected uneasily, and checked himself in sheer funk.

Mr. Gloag came, as he thought, to Tommy's defence. "If Mr. Sandys questions," he said heavily, "whether courage would have been vouchsafed to him at that trying hour, it is right and fitting that he should admit it with Christian humility."

"Quite so, quite so," Mr. James agreed, with heartiness. He had begun to look solemn at the word "vouchsafed."

"For we are differently gifted," continued Mr. Gloag, now addressing his congregation. "To some is given courage, to some learning, to some grace. Each has his strong point," he ended abruptly, and tucked reverently into the jam, which seemed to be his.

"If he would not have risked his life to save the boy," Elspeth interposed hotly, "it would have been because he was thinking of me."

"I should like to believe that thought of you would have checked me," Tommy said.

"I am sure it would," said Grizel.

Mr. Cathro was rubbing his hands together covertly, yet half wishing he could take her aside and whisper: "Be canny; it's grand to hear you, but be canny; he is looking most extraordinar meek, and unless he has cast his skin since he was a laddie, it's not chancey to meddle with him when he is meek."

The doctor also noticed that Grizel was pressing Tommy too hard, and though he did not like the man, he was surprised-he had always thought her so fair-minded.

"For my part," he said, "I don't admire the unknown half so much for what he did as for his behaviour afterwards. To risk his life was something, but to disappear quietly without taking any credit for it was finer and I should say much more difficult."

"I think it was sweet of him," Grizel said.

"I don't see it," said Tommy, and the silence that followed should have been unpleasant to him; but he went on calmly: "Doubtless it was a mere impulse that made him jump into the pool, and impulse is not courage." He was quoting Grizel now, you observe, and though he did not look at her, he knew her eyes were fixed on him reproachfully. "And so," he concluded, "I suppose Captain Ure knew he had done no great thing, and preferred to avoid exaggerated applause."

Even Elspeth was troubled; but she must defend her dear brother. "He would have avoided it himself," she explained quickly. "He dislikes praise so much that he does not understand how sweet it is to smaller people."

This made Tommy wince. He was always distressed when timid Elspeth blurted out things of this sort in company, and not the least of his merits was that he usually forbore from chiding her for it afterwards, so reluctant was he to hurt her. In a world where there were no women except Elspeths, Tommy would have been a saint. He saw the doctor smiling now, and at once his annoyance with her changed to wrath against him for daring to smile at little Elspeth. She saw the smile, too, and blushed; but she was not angry: she knew that the people who smiled at her liked her, and that no one smiled so much at her as Dr. Gemmell.

The Dominie said fearfully: "I have no doubt that explains it, Miss Sandys. Even as a boy I remember your brother had a horror of vulgar applause."

"Now," he said to himself, "he will rise up and smite me." But no; Tommy replied quietly;

"I am afraid that was not my character, Mr. Cathro; but I hope I have changed since then, and that I could pull a boy out of the water without wanting to be extolled for it."

That he could say such things before her was terrible to Grizel. It was perhaps conceivable that he might pull the boy out of the water, as he so ungenerously expressed it; but that he could refrain from basking in the glory thereof, that, she knew, was quite impossible. Her eyes begged him to take back those shameful words, but he bravely declined; not even to please Grizel could he pretend that what was not was. No more sentiment for T. Sandys.

"The spirit has all gone out of him; what am I afraid of?" reflected the Dominie, and he rose suddenly to make a speech, tea-cup in hand. "Cathro, Cathro, you tattie-doolie, you are riding to destruction," said a warning voice within him, but against his better judgment he stifled it and began. He begged to propose the health of Captain Ure. He was sure they would all join with him cordially in drinking it, including Mr. Sandys, who unfortunately differed from them in his estimation of the hero; that was only, however, as had been conclusively shown, because he was a hero himself, and so could make light of heroic deeds-with other sly hits at Mr. Sandys. But when all the others rose to drink the toast, Tommy remained seated. The Dominie coughed. "Perhaps Mr. Sandys means to reply," Grizel suggested icily. And it was at this uncomfortable moment that Christina appeared suddenly, and in a state of suppressed excitement requested her mistress to speak with her behind the door. All the knowing ones were aware that something terrible must have happened in the kitchen. Miss Sophia thought it might be the china tea-pot. She smiled reassuringly to signify that, whatever it was, she would help Mrs. McLean through, and so did Mr. James. He was a perfect lady.

How dramatic it all was, as Ailie said frequently afterwards. She was back in a moment, with her hand on her heart. "Mr. Sandys," were her astounding words, "a lady wants to see you."

Tommy rose in surprise, as did several of the others.

"Was it really you?" Ailie cried. "She says it was you!"

"I don't understand, Mrs. McLean," he answered; "I have done nothing."

"But she says-and she is at the door!"

All eyes turned on the door so longingly that it opened under their pressure, and a boy who had been at the keyhole stumbled forward.

"That's him!" he announced, pointing a stern finger at Mr. Sandys.

"But he says he did not do it," Ailie said.

"He's a liar," said the boy. His manner was that of the police, and it had come so sharply upon Tommy that he looked not unlike a detected criminal.

Most of them thought he was being accused of something vile, and the Dominie demanded, with a light heart, "Who is the woman?" while Mr. James had a pleasant feeling that the ladies should be requested to retire. But just then the woman came in, and she was much older than they had expected.

"That's him, granny," the boy said, still severely; "that's the man as saved my life at the Slugs." And then, when the truth was dawning on them all, and there were exclamations of wonder, a pretty scene suddenly presented itself, for the old lady, who had entered with the timidest courtesy, slipped down on her knees before Tommy and kissed his hand. That young rascal of a boy was all she had.

They were all moved by her simplicity, but none quite so much as Tommy. He gulped with genuine emotion, and saw her through a maze of beautiful thoughts that delayed all sense of triumph and even made him forget, for a little while, to wonder what Grizel was thinking of him now. As the old lady poured out her thanks tremblingly, he was excitedly planning her future. He was a poor man, but she was to be brought by him into Thrums to a little cottage overgrown with roses. No more hard work for these dear old hands. She could sell scones, perhaps. She should have a cow. He would send the boy to college and make a minister of him; she should yet hear her grandson preach in the church to which as a boy —

But here the old lady somewhat imperilled the picture by rising actively and dumping upon the table the contents of the bag — a fowl for Tommy.

She was as poor an old lady as ever put a halfpenny into the church plate on Sundays; but that she should present a hen to the preserver of her grandson, her mind had been made up from the moment she had reason to think she could find him, and it was to be the finest hen in all the country round. She was an old lady of infinite spirit, and daily, dragging the boy with her lest he again went a-fishing, she trudged to farms near and far to examine and feel their hens. She was a brittle old lady who creaked as she walked, and cracked like a whin-pod in the heat, but she did her dozen miles or more a day, and passed all the fowls in review, and could not be deceived by the craftiest of farmers' wives; and in the tail of the day she became possessor, and did herself thraw the neck of the stoutest and toughest hen that ever entered a linen bag head foremost. By this time the boy had given way in the legs, and hence the railway journey, its cost defrayed by admiring friends.

With careful handling he should get a week out of her gift, she explained complacently, besides two makes of broth; and she and the boy looked as if they would like dearly to sit opposite Tommy during those seven days and watch him gorging.

If you look at the matter aright it was a handsomer present than many a tiara, but if you are of the same stuff as Mr. James it was only a hen. Mr. James tittered, and one or two others made ready to titter. It was a moment to try Tommy, for there are doubtless heroes as gallant as he who do not know how to receive a present of a hen. Grizel, who had been holding back, moved a little nearer. If he hurt that sweet old woman's feelings, she could never forgive him-never!

He heard the titter, and ridicule was terrible to him; but he also knew why Grizel had come closer, and what she wanted of him. Our Tommy, in short, had emerged from his emotion, and once more knew what was what. It was not his fault that he stood revealed a hero: the little gods had done it; therefore let him do credit to the chosen of the little gods. The way he took that old lady's wrinkled hand, and bowed over it, and thanked her, was an ode to manhood. Everyone was touched. Those who had been about to titter wondered what on earth Mr. James had seen to titter at, and Grizel almost clapped her hands with joy; she would have done it altogether had not Tommy just then made the mistake of looking at her for approval. She fell back, and, intoxicated with himself, he thought it was because her heart was too full for utterance. Tommy was now splendid, and described the affair at the Slugs with an adorable modesty.

"I assure you, it was a much smaller thing to do than you imagine; it was all over in a few minutes; I knew that in your good nature you would make too much of it, and so-foolishly, I can see now — I tried to keep it from you. As for the name Captain Ure, it was an invention of that humourous dog, Corp."

And so on, with the most considerate remarks when they insisted on shaking hands with him: "I beseech you, don't apologize to me; I see clearly that the fault was entirely my own. Had I been in your place, Mr. James, I should have behaved precisely as you have done, and had you been at the Slugs you would have jumped in as I did. Mr. Cathro, you pain me by holding back; I assure you I esteem my old Dominie more than ever for the way in which you stuck up for Captain Ure, though you must see why I could not drink that gentleman's health."

And Mr. Cathro made the best of it, wringing Tommy's hand effusively, while muttering, "Fool, donnard stirk, gowk!" He was addressing himself and any other person who might be so presumptuous as to try to get the better of Thomas Sandys. Cathro never tried it again. Had Tommy died that week his old Dominie would have been very chary of what he said at the funeral.

They were in the garden now, the gentlemen without their hats. "Have you made your peace with him?" Cathro asked Grizel, in a cautious voice. "He is a devil's buckie, and I advise you to follow my example, Miss McQueen, and capitulate. I have always found him reasonable so long as you bend the knee to him."

"I am not his enemy," replied Grizel, loftily, "and if he has done a noble thing I am proud of him and will tell him so."

"I would tell him so," said the Dominie, "whether he had done it or not."

"Do you mean," she asked indignantly, "that you think he did not do it?"

"No, no, no," he answered hurriedly; "or mercy's sake, don't tell him I think that." And then, as Tommy was out of ear-shot: "But I see there is no necessity for my warning you against standing in his way again, Miss McQueen, for you are up in arms for him now."

"I admire brave men," she replied, "and he is one, is he not?"

"You'll find him reasonable," said the Dominie, drily.

But though it was thus that she defended Tommy when others hinted doubts, she had not yet said she was proud of him to the man who wanted most to hear it. For one brief moment Grizel had exulted on learning that he and Captain Ure were one, and then suddenly, to all the emotions now running within her, a voice seemed to cry, "Halt!" and she fell to watching sharply the doer of noble deeds. Her eyes were not wistful, nor were they contemptuous, but had Tommy been less elated with himself he might have seen that they were puzzled and suspicious. To mistrust him in face of such evidence seemed half a shame; she was indignant with herself even while she did it; but she could not help doing it, the truth about Tommy was such a vital thing to Grizel. She had known him so well, too well, up to a minute ago, and this was not the man she had known.

How unfair she was to Tommy while she watched! When the old lady was on her knees thanking him, and every other lady was impressed by the feeling he showed, it seemed to Grizel that he was again in the arms of some such absurd sentiment as had mastered him in the Den. When he behaved so charmingly about the gift she was almost sure he looked at her as he had looked in the old days before striding his legs and screaming out, "Oh, am I not a wonder? I see by your face that you think me a wonder!" All the time he was so considerately putting those who had misjudged him at their ease she believed he did it considerately that they might say to each other, "How considerate he is!" When she misread Tommy in such comparative trifles as these, is it to be wondered that she went into the garden still tortured by a doubt about the essential? It was nothing less than torture to her; when you discover what is in her mind, Tommy, you may console yourself with that.

He discovered what was in her mind as Mr. Cathro left her. She felt shy, he thought, of coming to him after what had taken place, and, with the generous intention of showing that she was forgiven, he crossed good-naturedly to her.

"You were very severe, Grizel," he said, "but don't let that distress you for a moment; it served me right for not telling the truth at once."

She did not flinch. "Do we know the truth now?" she asked, looking at him steadfastly. "I don't want to hurt you-you know that; but please tell me, did you really do it? I mean, did you do it in the way we have been led to suppose?"

It was a great shock to Tommy. He had not forgotten his vows to change his nature, and had she been sympathetic now he would have confessed to her the real reason of his silence. He wanted boyishly to tell her, though of course without mention of the glove; but her words hardened him.

"Grizel!" he cried reproachfully, and then in a husky voice: "Can you really think so badly of me as that?"

"I don't know what to think," she answered, pressing her hands together, "I know you are very clever."

He bowed slightly.

"Did you?" she asked again. She was no longer chiding herself for being over-careful; she must know the truth.

He was silent for a moment. Then, "Grizel," he said, "I am about to pain you very much, but you give me no option. I did do it precisely as you have heard. And may God forgive you for doubting me," he added with a quiver, "as freely as I do."

You will scarcely believe this, but a few minutes afterwards, Grizel having been the first to leave, he saw her from the garden going, not home, but in the direction of Corp's house, obviously to ask him whether Tommy had done it. Tommy guessed her intention at once, and he laughed a bitter ho-ho-ha, and wiped her from his memory.

"Farewell, woman; I am done with you," are the terrible words you may conceive Tommy saying. Next moment, however, he was hurriedly bidding his hostess good-night, could not even wait for Elspeth, clapped his hat on his head, and was off after Grizel. It had suddenly struck him that, now the rest of the story was out, Corp might tell her about the glove. Suppose Gavinia showed it to her!

Sometimes he had kissed that glove passionately, sometimes pressed his lips upon it with the long tenderness that is less intoxicating but makes you a better man; but now, for the first time, he asked himself bluntly why he had done those things, with the result that he was striding to Corp's house. It was not only for his own sake that he hurried; let us do him that justice. It was chiefly to save Grizel the pain of thinking that he whom she had been flouting loved her, as she must think if she heard the story of the glove. That it could be nothing but pain to her he was boyishly certain, for assuredly this scornful girl wanted none of his love. And though she was scornful, she was still the dear companion of his boyhood. Tommy was honestly anxious to save Grizel the pain of thinking that she had flouted a man who loved her.

He took a different road from hers, but, to his annoyance, they met at Couthie's corner. He would have passed her with a distant bow, but she would have none of that. "You have followed me," said Grizel, with the hateful directness that was no part of Tommy's character.

"Grizel!"

"You followed me to see whether I was going to question Corp. You were afraid he would tell me what really happened. You wanted to see him first to tell him what to say."

"Really, Grizel —"

"Is it not true?"

There are no questions so offensive to the artistic nature as those that demand a Yes or No for answer. "It is useless for me to say it is not true," he replied haughtily, "for you won't believe me."

"Say it and I shall believe you," said she.

Tommy tried standing on the other foot, but it was no help. "I presume I may have reasons for wanting to see Corp that you are unacquainted with," he said.

"Oh, I am sure of it!" replied Grizel, scornfully. She had been hoping until now, but there was no more hope left in her.

"May I ask what it is that my oldest friend accuses me of? Perhaps you don't even believe that I was Captain Ure?"

"I am no longer sure of it."

"How you read me, Grizel! I could hoodwink the others, but never you. I suppose it is because you have such an eye for the worst in anyone."

It was not the first time he had said something of this kind to her; for he knew that she suspected herself of being too ready to find blemishes in others, to the neglect of their better qualities, and that this made her uneasy and also very sensitive to the charge. To-day, however, her own imperfections did not matter to her; she was as nothing to herself just now, and scarcely felt his insinuations.

"I think you were Captain Ure," she said slowly, "and I think you did it, but not as the boy imagines."

"You may be quite sure," he replied, "that I would not have done it had there been the least risk. That, I flatter myself, is how you reason it out."

"It does not explain," she said, "why you kept the matter secret."

"Thank you, Grizel! Well, at least I have not boasted of it."

"No, and that is what makes me —— " She paused.

"Go on," said he, "though I can guess what agreeable thing you were going to say."

But she said something else: "You may have noticed that I took the boy aside and questioned him privately."

"I little thought then, Grizel, that you suspected me of being an impostor."

She clenched her hands again; it was all so hard to say, and yet she must say it! "I did not. I saw he believed his story. I was asking him whether you had planned his coming with it to Mrs. McLean's house at that dramatic moment."

"You actually thought me capable of that!"

"It makes me horrid to myself," she replied wofully, "but if I thought you had done that I could more readily believe the rest."

"Very well, Grizel," he said, "go on thinking the worst of me; I would not deprive you of that pleasure if I could."

"Oh, cruel, cruel!" she could have replied; "you know it is no pleasure; you know it is a great pain." But she did not speak.

"I have already told you that the boy's story is true," he said, "and now you ask me why I did not shout it from the housetops myself. Perhaps it was for your sake, Grizel; perhaps it was to save you the distress of knowing that in a momentary impulse I could so far forget myself as to act the part of a man."

She pressed her hands more tightly. "I may be wronging you," she answered; "I should love to think so; but-you have something you want to say to Corp before I see him."

"Not at all," Tommy said; "if you still want to see Corp, let us go together." She hesitated, but she knew how clever he was. "I prefer to go alone," she replied. "Forgive me if I ask you to turn back."

"Don't go," he entreated her. "Grizel, I give you my word of honour it is to save you acute pain that I want to see Corp first." She smiled wanly at that, for though, as we know, it was true, she misunderstood him. He had to let her go on alone.

Chapter XII

In Which a Comedian Challenges Tragedy to Bowls

When Grizel opened the door of Corp's house she found husband and wife at home, the baby in his father's arms; what is more, Gavinia was looking on smiling and saying, "You bonny litlin, you're windy to have him dandling you; and no wonder, for he's a father to be proud o'." Corp was accepting it all with a complacent smirk. Oh, agreeable change since last we were in this house! oh, happy picture of domestic bliss! oh-but no, these are not the words; what we meant to say was, "Gavinia, you limmer, so you have got the better of that man of yours at last."

How had she contrived it? We have seen her escorting the old lady to the Dovecot, Corp skulking behind. Our next peep at them shows Gavinia back at her house, Corp peering through the window and wondering whether he dare venture in. Gavinia was still bothered, for though she knew now the story of Tommy's heroism, there was no glove in it, and it was the glove that maddened her.

"No, I ken nothing about a glove," the old lady had assured her.

"Not a sylup was said about a glove," maintained Christina, who had given her a highly coloured narrative of what took place in Mrs. McLean's parlour.

"And yet there's a glove in't as sure as there's a quirk in't," Gavinia kept muttering to herself. She rose to have another look at the hoddy-place in which she had concealed the glove from her husband, and as she did so she caught sight of him at the window. He bobbed at once, but she hastened to the door to scarify him. The clock had given only two ticks when she was upon him, but in that time she had completely changed her plan of action. She welcomed him with smiles of pride. Thus is the nimbleness of women's wit measured once and for all. They need two seconds if they are to do the thing comfortably.

"Never to have told me, and you behaved so grandly!" she cried, with adoring glances that were as a carpet on which he strode pompously into the house.

"It wasna me that did it; it was him," said Corp, and even then he feared that he had told too much. "I kenna what you're speaking about," he added loyally.

"Corp," she answered, "you needna be so canny, for the laddie is in the town, and Mr. Sandys has confessed all."

"The whole o't?"

"Every risson."

"About the glove, too?"

"Glove and all," said wicked Gavinia, and she continued to feast her eyes so admiringly on her deceived husband that he passed quickly from the gratified to the dictatorial.

"Let this be a lesson to you, woman," he said sternly; and Gavinia intimated with humility that she hoped to profit by it.

"Having got the glove in so solemn a way," he went on, "it would have been ill done of me to blab to you about it. Do you see that now, woman?"

She said it was as clear as day to her. "And a solemn way it was," she added, and then waited eagerly.

"My opinion," continued Corp, lowering his voice as if this were not matter for the child, "is that it's a love-token frae some London woman."

"Behear's!" cried Gavinia.

"Else what," he asked, "would make him hand it to me so solemn-like, and tell me to pass it on to her if he was drowned? I didna think o' that at the time, but it has come to me, Gavinia; it has come."

This was a mouthful indeed to Gavinia. So the glove was the property of Mr. Sandys, and he was in love with a London lady, and-no, this is too slow for Gavinia; she saw these things in passing, as one who jumps from the top of a house may have lightning glimpses through many windows on the way down. What she jumped to was the vital question, Who was the woman?

But she was too cunning to ask a leading question.

"Ay, she's his lady-love," she said, controlling herself, "but I forget her name. It was a very wise-like thing o' you to speir the woman's name."

"But I didna."

"You didna!"

"He was in the water in a klink."

Had Gavinia been in Corp's place she would have had the name out of Tommy, water or no water; but she did not tell her husband what she thought of him.

"Ay, of course," she said pleasantly. "It was after you helped him out that he telled you her name."

"Did he say he telled me her name?"

"He did."

"Well, then, I've fair forgot it."

Instead of boxing his ears she begged him to reflect. Result of reflection, that if the name had been mentioned to Corp, which he doubted, it began with M.

Was it Mary?

That was the name.

Or was it Martha?

It had a taste of Martha about it.

It was not Margaret?

It might have been Margaret.

Or Matilda?

It was fell like Matilda.

And so on. "But wi' a' your wheedling," Corp reminded his wife, bantering her from aloft, "you couldna get a scraping out o' me till I was free to speak."

He thought it a good opportunity for showing Gavinia her place once and for all. "In small matters," he said, "I gie you your ain way, for though you may be wrang, thinks I to mysel', 'She's but a woman'; but in important things, Gavinia, if I humoured you I would spoil you, so let this be a telling to you that there's no diddling a determined man"; to which she replied by informing the baby that he had a father to be proud of.

A father to be proud of! They were the words heard by Grizel as she entered. She also saw Gavinia looking admiringly at her man, and in that doleful moment she thought she understood all. It was Corp who had done it, and Tommy had been the looker-on. He had sought to keep the incident secret because, though he was in it, the glory had been won by another (oh, how base!), and now, profiting by the boy's mistake, he was swaggering in that other's clothes (oh, baser still!). Everything was revealed to her in a flash, and she stooped over the baby to hide a sudden tear. She did not want to hear any more.

The baby cried. Babies are aware that they can't do very much; but all of them who knew Grizel were almost contemptuously confident of their power over her, and when this one saw (they are very sharp) that in his presence she could actually think of something else, he was so hurt that he cried.

Was she to be blamed for thinking so meanly of Tommy? You can blame her with that tear in her eye if you choose; but I can think only of the gladness that came afterwards when she knew she had been unjust to him. "Thank you, thank you, thank you!" the bird sang to its Creator when the sun came out after rain, and it was Grizel's song as she listened to Corp's story of heroic Tommy. There was no room in her exultant heart for remorse. It would have shown littleness to be able to think of herself at all when she could think so gloriously of him. She was more than beautiful now; she was radiant; and it was because Tommy was the man she wanted him to be. As those who are cold hold out their hands to the fire did she warm her heart at what Corp had to tell, and the great joy that was lit within her made her radiant. Now the baby was in her lap, smiling back to her. He thought he had done it all. "So you thought you could resist me!" the baby crowed.

The glove had not been mentioned yet. "The sweetest thing of all to me," Grizel said, "is that he did not want me to hear the story from you, Corp, because he knew you would sing his praise so loudly."

"I'm thinking," said Gavinia, archly, "he had another reason for no wanting you to question Corp. Maybe he didna want you to ken about the London lady and her glove. Will you tell her, man, or will I?"

They told her together, and what had been conjectures were now put forward as facts. Tommy had certainly said a London lady, and as certainly he had given her name, but what it was Corp could not remember. But "Give her this and tell her it never left my heart"—he could swear to these words.

"And no words could be stronger," Gavinia said triumphantly. She produced the glove, and was about to take off its paper wrapping when Grizel stopped her.

"We have no right, Gavinia." "I suppose we hinna, and I'm thinking the pocket it came out o' is feeling gey toom without it. Will you take it back to him?"

"It was very wrong of you to keep it," Grizel answered, "but I can't take it to him, for I see now that his reason for wanting me not to come here was to prevent my hearing about it. I am sorry you told me. Corp must take it back." But when she saw it being crushed in Corp's rough hand, a pity for the helpless glove came over her. She said: "After all, I do know about it, so I can't pretend to him that I don't. I will give it to him, Corp"; and she put the little package in her pocket with a brave smile.

Do you think the radiance had gone from her face now? Do you think the joy that had been lit in her heart was dead? Oh, no, no! Grizel had never asked that Tommy should love her; she had asked only that he should be a fine man. She did not ask it for herself, only for him. She could not think of herself now, only of him. She did not think she loved him. She thought a woman should not love any man until she knew he wanted her to love him.

But if Tommy had wanted it she would have been very glad. She knew, oh, she knew so well, that she could have helped him best. Many a noble woman has known it as she stood aside.

In the meantime Tommy had gone home in several states of mind-reckless, humble, sentimental, most practical, defiant, apprehensive. At one moment he was crying, "Now, Grizel, now, when it is too late, you will see what you have lost." At the next he quaked and implored the gods to help him out of his predicament. It was apprehension that, on the whole, played most of the tunes, for he was by no means sure that Grizel would not look upon the affair of the glove as an offer of his hand, and accept him. They would show her the glove, and she would, of course, know it to be her own. "Give her this and tell her it never left my heart." The words thumped within him now. How was Grizel to understand that he had meant nothing in particular by them?

I wonder if you misread him so utterly as to believe that he thought himself something of a prize? That is a vulgar way of looking at things of which our fastidious Tommy was incapable. As much as Grizel herself, he loathed the notion that women have a thirsty eye on man; when he saw them cheapening themselves before the sex that should hold them beyond price, he turned his head and would not let his mind dwell on the subject. He was a sort of gentleman, was Tommy. And he knew Grizel so well that had all the other women in the world been of this kind, it would not have persuaded him that there was a drop of such blood in her. Then, if he feared that she was willing to be his, it must have been because he thought she loved him? Not a bit of it. As already stated, he thought he had abundant reason to think otherwise. It was remorse that he feared might bring her to his feet, the discovery that while she had been gibing at him he had been a heroic figure, suffering in silence, eating his heart for love of her. Undoubtedly that was how Grizel must see things now; he must seem to her to be an angel rather than a mere man; and in sheer remorse she might cry, "I am yours!" Vain though Tommy was, the picture gave him not a moment's pleasure. Alarm was what he felt.

Of course he was exaggerating Grizel's feelings. She had too much self-respect and too little sentiment to be willing to marry any man because she had unintentionally wronged him. But this was how Tommy would have acted had he happened to be a lady. Remorse, pity, no one was so good at them as Tommy.

In his perturbation he was also good at maidenly reserve. He felt strongly that the proper course for Grizel was not to refer to the glove-to treat that incident as closed, unless he chose to reopen it. This was so obviously the correct procedure that he seemed to see her adopting it like a sensible girl, and relief would have come to him had he not remembered that Grizel usually took her own way, and that it was seldom his way.

There were other ways of escape. For instance, if she would only let him love her hopelessly. Oh, Grizel had but to tell him there was no hope, and then how finely he would behave! It would bring out all that was best in him. He saw himself passing through life as her very perfect knight. "Is there no hope for me?" He heard himself begging for hope, and he heard also her firm answer: "None!" How he had always admired the outspokenness of Grizel. Her "None!" was as splendidly decisive as of yore.

The conversation thus begun ran on in him, Tommy doing the speaking for both (though his lips never moved), and feeling the scene as vividly as if Grizel had really been present and Elspeth was not. Elspeth was sitting opposite him.

"At least let me wait, Grizel," he implored. "I don't care for how long; fix a time yourself, and I shall keep to it, and I promise never to speak one word of love to you until that time comes, and then if you bid me go I shall go. Give me something to live for. It binds you to nothing, and oh, it would make such a difference to me."

Then Grizel seemed to reply gently, but with the firmness he adored: "I know I cannot change, and it would be mistaken kindness to do as you suggest. No, I can give you no hope; but though I can never marry you, I will watch your future with warm regard, for you have to-day paid me the highest compliment a man can pay a woman."

(How charmingly it was all working out!)

Tommy bowed with dignity and touched her hand with his lips. What is it they do next in Pym and even more expensive authors? Oh, yes! "If at any time in your life, dear Grizel," he said, "you are in need of a friend, I hope you will turn first to me. It does not matter where your message reaches me, I will come to you without delay."

In his enthusiasm he saw the letter being delivered to him in Central Africa, and immediately he wheeled round on his way to Thrums.

"There is one other little request I should like to make of you," he said huskily. "Perhaps I ask too much, but it is this: may I keep your glove?"

She nodded her head; she was so touched that she could scarcely trust herself to speak. "But you will soon get over this," she said at last; "another glove will take the place of mine; the time will come when you will be glad that I said I could not marry you."

"Grizel!" he cried in agony. He was so carried away by his feelings that he said the word aloud.

"Where?" asked Elspeth, looking at the window.

"Was it not she who passed just now?" he replied promptly; and they were still discussing his mistake when Grizel did pass, but only to stop at the door. She came in.

"My brother must have the second sight," declared Elspeth, gaily, "for he saw you coming before you came"; and she told what had happened, while Grizel looked happily at Tommy, and Tommy looked apprehensively at her. Grizel, he might have seen, was not wearing the tragic face of sacrifice; it was a face shining with gladness, a girl still too happy in his nobility to think remorsefully of her own misdeeds. To let him know that she was proud of him, that was what she had come for chiefly, and she was even glad that Elspeth was there to hear. It was an excuse to her to repeat Corp's story, and she told it with defiant looks at Tommy that said, "You are so modest, you want to stop me, but Elspeth will listen; it is nearly as sweet to Elspeth as it is to me, and I shall tell her every word, yes, and tell her a great deal of it twice."

It was not modesty which made Tommy so anxious that she should think less of him, but naturally it had that appearance. The most heroic fellows, I am told, can endure being extolled by pretty girls, but here seemed to be one who could not stand it.

"You need not think it is of you we are proud," she assured him light-heartedly; "it is really of ourselves. I am proud of being your friend. To-morrow, when I hear the town ringing your praises, I shall not say, 'Yes, isn't he wonderful?' I shall say, 'Talk of me; I, too, am an object of interest, for I am his friend.'"

"I have often been pointed out as his sister," said Elspeth, complacently.

"He did not choose his sister," replied Grizel, "but he chose his friends."

For a time he could suck no sweetness from it. She avoided the glove, he was sure, only because of Elspeth's presence. But anon there arrived to cheer him a fond hope that she had not heard of it, and as this became conviction, exit the Tommy who could not abide himself, and enter another who was highly charmed therewith. Tommy had a notion that certain whimsical little gods protected him in return for the sport he gave them, and he often kissed his hand to them when they came to the rescue. He would have liked to kiss it now, but gave a grateful glance instead to the corner in the ceiling where they sat chuckling at him. Grizel admired him at last. Tra, la, la! What a dear girl she was! Into his manner there crept a certain masterfulness, and instead of resisting it she beamed. Rum-ti-tum!

"If you want to spoil me," he said lazily, "you will bring me that footstool to rest my heroic feet upon." She smiled and brought it. She even brought a cushion for his heroic head. Adoring little thing that she was, he must be good to her.

He was now looking forward eagerly to walking home with her. I can't tell you how delicious he meant to be. When she said she must go, he skipped upstairs for his hat, and wafted the gods their kiss. But it was always the unexpected that lay in wait for Tommy. He and she were no sooner out of the house than Grizel said, "I did not mention the glove, as I was not sure whether Elspeth knew of it."

He had turned stone-cold.

"Corp and Gavinia told me," she went on quietly, "before I had time to stop them. Of course I should have preferred not to know until I heard it from yourself."

Oh, how cold he was!

"But as I do know, I want to tell you that it makes me very happy."

They had stopped, for his legs would carry him no farther. "Get us out of this," every bit of him was crying, but not one word could Tommy say.

"I knew you would want to have it again," Grizel said brightly, producing the little parcel from her pocket, "so I brought it to you."

The frozen man took it and held it passively in his hand. His gods had flown away.

No, they were actually giving him another chance. What was this Grizel was saying? "I have not looked at it, for to take it out of its wrapping would have been profanation. Corp told me she was a London girl; but I know nothing more, not even her name. You are not angry with me for speaking of her, are you? Surely I may wish you and her great happiness."

He was saved. The breath came back quickly to him. He filled like a released ball. Had ever a heart better right to expand? Grizel, looking so bright and pleased, had snatched him from the Slugs. Surely you will be nice to your preserver, Tommy. You will not be less grateful than a country boy?

Ah me! not even yet have we plumed his vanity. But we are to do it now. He could not have believed it of himself, but in the midst of his rejoicings he grew bitter, and for no better reason than that Grizel's face was bright.

"I am glad," he said quite stiffly, "that it is such pleasant news to you."

His tone surprised her; but she was in a humble mood, and answered, without being offended: "It is sweet news to me. How could you think otherwise?"

So it was sweet to her to think that he was another's! He who had been modestly flattering himself a few moments ago that he must take care not to go too far with this admiring little girl! O woman, woman, how difficult it is to know you, and how often, when we think we know you at last, have we to begin again at the beginning! He had never asked an enduring love from her; but surely, after all that had passed between them, he had a right to expect a little more than this. Was it maidenly to bring the glove and hand it to him without a tremor? If she could do no more, she might at least have turned a little pale when Corp told her of it, and then have walked quietly away. Next day she could have referred to it, with just the slightest break in her voice. But to come straight to him, looking delighted —

"And, after all, I am entitled to know first," Grizel said, "for I am your oldest friend."

Friend! He could not help repeating the word with bitter emphasis. For her sake, as it seemed to him now, he had flung himself into the black waters of the Drumly. He had worn her glove upon his heart. It had been the world to him. And she could stand there and call herself his friend. The cup was full. Tommy nodded his head sorrowfully three times.

"So be it, Grizel," he said huskily; "so be it!" Sentiment could now carry him where it willed. The reins were broken.

"I don't understand."

Neither did he; but, "Why should you? What is it to you!" he cried wildly. "Better not to understand, for it might give you five minutes' pain, Grizel, a whole five minutes, and I should be sorry to give you that."

"What have I said! What have I done!"

"Nothing," he answered her, "nothing. You have been most exemplary; you have not even got any entertainment out of it. The thing never struck you as possible. It was too ludicrous!"

He laughed harshly at the package, which was still in his hand. "Poor little glove," he said; "and she did not even take the trouble to look at you. You might have looked at it, Grizel. I have looked at it a good deal. It meant something to me once upon a time when I was a vain fool. Take it and look at it before you fling it away. It will make you laugh."

Now she knew, and her arms rocked convulsively. Joy surged to her face, and she drove it back. She looked at him steadfastly over the collar of her jacket; she looked long, as if trying to be suspicious of him for the last time. Ah, Grizel, you are saying good-bye to your best friend!

As she looked at him thus there was a mournfulness in her brave face that went to Tommy's heart and almost made a man of him. It was as if he knew that she was doomed.

"Grizel," he cried, "don't look at me in that way!" And he would have taken the package from her, but she pressed it to her heart.

"Don't come with me," she said almost in a whisper, and went away.

He did not go back to the house. He wandered into the country, quite objectless when he was walking fastest, seeing nothing when he stood still and stared. Elation and dread were his companions. What elation whispered he could not yet believe; no, he could not believe it. While he listened he knew that he must be making up the words. By and by he found himself among the shadows of the Den. If he had loved Grizel he would have known that it was here she would come, to the sweet Den where he and she had played as children, the spot where she had loved him first. She had always loved him-always, always. He did not know what figure it was by the Cuttle Well until he was quite close to her. She was kissing the glove passionately, and on her eyes lay little wells of gladness.

It was dusk, and she had not seen him. In the silent Den he stood motionless within a few feet of her, so amazed to find that Grizel really loved him that for the moment self was blotted out of his mind. He remembered he was there only when he heard his heavy breathing, and then he tried to check it that he might steal away undiscovered. Divers emotions fought for the possession of him. He was in the meeting of many waters, each capable of whirling him where it chose, but two only imperious: the one the fierce joy of being loved; the other an agonizing remorse. He would fain have stolen away to think this tremendous thing over, but it tossed him forward. "Grizel," he said in a husky whisper, "Grizel!"

She did not start; she was scarcely surprised to hear his voice: she had been talking to him, and he had answered. Had he not been there she would still have heard him answer. She could not see him more clearly now than she had been seeing him through those little wells of gladness. Her love for him was the whole of her. He came to her with the opening and the shutting of her eyes; he was the wind that bit her and the sun that nourished her; he was the lowliest object by the Cuttle Well, and he was the wings on which her thoughts soared to eternity. He could never leave her while her mortal frame endured.

When he whispered her name she turned her swimming eyes to him, and a strange birth had come into her face. Her eyes said so openly they were his, and her mouth said it was his, her whole being went out to him; in the radiance of her face could be read immortal designs: the maid kissing her farewell to innocence was there, and the reason why it must be, and the fate of the unborn; it was the first stirring for weal or woe of a movement that has no end on earth, but must roll on, growing lusty on beauty or dishonour till the crack of time. This birth which comes to every woman at that hour is God's gift to her in exchange for what He has taken away, and when He has given it He stands back and watches the man.

To this man she was a woman transformed. The new bloom upon her face entranced him. He knew what it meant. He was looking on the face of love at last, and it was love coming out smiling from its hiding-place because it thought it had heard him call. The artist in him who had done this thing was entranced, as if he had written an immortal page.

But the man was appalled. He knew that he had reached the critical moment in her life and his, and that if he took one step farther forward he could never again draw back. It would be comparatively easy to draw back now. To remain a free man he had but to tell her the truth; and he had a passionate desire to remain free. He heard the voices of his little gods screaming to him to draw back. But it could be done only at her expense, and it seemed to him that to tell this noble girl, who was waiting for him, that he did not need her, would be to spill for ever the happiness with which she overflowed, and sap the pride that had been the marrow of her during her twenty years of life. Not thus would Grizel have argued in his place; but he could not change his nature, and it was Sentimental Tommy, in an agony of remorse for having brought dear Grizel to this pass, who had to decide her future and his in the time you may take to walk up a garden path. Either her mistake must be righted now or kept hidden from her for ever. He was a sentimentalist, but in that hard moment he was trying to be a man. He took her in his arms and kissed her reverently, knowing that after this there could be no drawing back. In that act he gave himself loyally to her as a husband. He knew he was not worthy of her, but he was determined to try to be a little less unworthy; and as he drew her to him a slight quiver went through her, so that for a second she seemed to be holding back-for a second only, and the quiver was the rustle of wings on which some part of the Grizel we have known so long was taking flight from her. Then she pressed close to him passionately, as if she grudged that pause. I love her more than ever, far more; but she is never again quite the Grizel we have known.

He was not unhappy; in the near hereafter he might be as miserable as the damned-the little gods were waiting to catch him alone and terrify him; but for the time, having sacrificed himself, Tommy was aglow with the passion he had inspired. He so loved the thing he had created that in his exultation he mistook it for her. He believed all he was saying. He looked at her long and adoringly, not, as he thought, because he adored her, but because it was thus that look should answer look; he pressed her wet eyes reverently because thus it was written in his delicious part; his heart throbbed with hers that they might beat in time. He did not love, but he was the perfect lover; he was the artist trying in a mad moment to be as well as to do. Love was their theme; but how to know what was said when between lovers it is only the loose change of conversation that gets into words? The important matters cannot wait so slow a messenger; while the tongue is being charged with them, a look, a twitch of the mouth, a movement of a finger, transmits the story, and the words arrive, like Blücher, when the engagement is over.

With a sudden pretty gesture-ah, so like her mother's! —she held the glove to his lips. "It is sad because you have forgotten it."

"I have kissed it so often, Grizel, long before I thought I should ever kiss you!"

She pressed it to her innocent breast at that. And had he really done so? and which was the first time, and the second, and the third? Oh, dear glove, you know so much, and your partner lies at home in a drawer knowing nothing. Grizel felt sorry for the other glove. She whispered to Tommy as a terrible thing, "I think I love this glove even more than I love you-just a tiny bit more." She could not part with it. "It told me before you did," she explained, begging him to give it back to her.

"If you knew what it was to me in those unhappy days, Grizel!"

"I want it to tell me," she whispered.

And did he really love her? Yes, she knew he did, but how could he?

"Oh, Grizel, how could I help it!"

He had to say it, for it is the best answer; but he said it with a sigh, for it sounded like a quotation.

But how could she love him? I think her reply disappointed him.

"Because you wanted me to," she said, with shining eyes. It is probably the commonest reason why women love, and perhaps it is the best; but his vanity was wounded-he had expected to hear that he was possessed of an irresistible power.

"Not until I wanted you to?"

"I think I always wanted you to want me to," she replied, naïvely; "but I would never have let myself love you," she continued very seriously, "until I was sure you loved me."

"You could have helped it, Grizel!" He drew a blank face.

"I did help it," she answered. "I was always fighting the desire to love you, —I can see that plainly, —and I always won. I thought God had made a sort of compact with me that I should always be the kind of woman I wanted to be if I resisted the desire to love you until you loved me."

"But you always had the desire!" he said eagerly.

"Always, but it never won. You see, even you did not know of it. You thought I did not even like you! That was why you wanted to prevent Corp's telling me about the glove, was it not? You thought it would pain me only! Do you remember what you said: 'It is to save you acute pain that I want to see Corp first'?"

All that seemed so long ago to Tommy now!

"How could you think it would be a pain to me!" she cried.

"You concealed your feelings so well, Grizel."

"Did I not?" she said joyously. "Oh, I wanted to be so careful, and I was careful. That is why I am so happy now." Her face was glowing. She was full of odd, delightful fancies to-night. She kissed her hand to the gloaming; no, not to the gloaming to the little hunted, anxious girl she had been.

"She is standing behind that tree looking at us."

"She is looking at us," she said. "She is standing behind that tree looking at us. She wanted so much to grow into a dear, good woman that she often comes and looks at me eagerly. Sometimes her face is so fearful! I think she was a little alarmed when she heard you were coming back."

"She never liked me, Grizel."

"Hush!" said Grizel, in a low voice. "She always liked you; she always thought you a wonder. But she would be distressed if she heard me telling you. She thought it would not be safe for you to know. I must tell him now, dearest, darlingest," she suddenly called out boldly to the little self she had been so quaintly fond of because there was no other to love her. "I must tell him everything now, for you are no longer your own. You are his."

"She has gone away rocking her arms," she said to Tommy.

"No," he replied. "I can hear her. She is singing because you are so happy."

"She never knew how to sing."

"She has learned suddenly. Everybody can sing who has anything to sing about. And do you know what she said about your dear wet eyes, Grizel? She said they were just sweet. And do you know why she left us so suddenly? She ran home gleefully to stitch and dust and beat carpets, and get baths ready, and look after the affairs of everybody, which she is sure must be going to rack and ruin because she has been away for half an hour!"

At his words there sparkled in her face the fond delight with which a woman assures herself that the beloved one knows her little weaknesses, for she does not truly love unless she thirsts to have him understand the whole of her, and to love her in spite of the foibles and for them. If he does not love you a little for the foibles, madam, God help you from the day of the wedding.

But though Grizel was pleased, she was not to be cajoled. She wandered with him through the Den, stopping at the Lair, and the Queen's Bower, and many other places where the little girl used to watch Tommy suspiciously; and she called, half merrily, half plaintively: "Are you there, you foolish girl, and are you wringing your hands over me? I believe you are jealous because I love him best."

"We have loved each other so long, she and I," she said apologetically to Tommy. "Ah," she said impulsively, when he seemed to be hurt, "don't you see it is because she doubts you that I am so sorry for the poor thing!"

"Dearest, darlingest," she called to the child she had been, "don't think that you can come to me when he is away, and whisper things against him to me. Do you think I will listen to your croakings, you poor, wet-faced thing!"

"You child!" said Tommy.

"Do you think me a child because I blow kisses to her?"

"Do you like me to think you one?" he replied.

"I like you to call me child," she said, "but not to think me one."

"Then I shall think you one," said he, triumphantly. He was so perfect an instrument for love to play upon that he let it play on and on, and listened in a fever of delight. How could Grizel have doubted Tommy? The god of love himself would have sworn that there were a score of arrows in him. He wanted to tell Elspeth and the others at once that he and Grizel were engaged. I am glad to remember that it was he who urged this, and Grizel who insisted on its being deferred. He even pretended to believe that Elspeth would exult in the news; but Grizel smiled at him for saying this to please her. She had never been a great friend of Elspeth's, they were so dissimilar; and she blamed herself for it now, and said she wanted to try to make Elspeth love her before they told her. Tommy begged her to let him tell his sister at once; but she remained obdurate, so anxious was she that her happiness, when revealed, should bring only happiness to others. There had not come to Grizel yet the longing to be recognized as his by the world. This love was so beautiful and precious to her that there was an added joy in sharing the dear secret with him alone; it was a live thing that might escape if she let anyone but him look between the fingers that held it.

The crowning glory of loving and being loved is that the pair make no real progress; however far they have advanced into the enchanted land during the day, they must start again from the frontier next morning. Last night they had dredged the lovers' lexicon for superlatives and not even blushed; to-day is that the heavens cracking or merely someone whispering "dear"? All this was very strange and wonderful to Grizel. She had never been so young in the days when she was a little girl.

"I can never be quite so happy again!" she had said, with a wistful smile, on the night of nights; but early morn, the time of the day that loves maidens best, retold her the delicious secret as it kissed her on the eyes, and her first impulse was to hurry to Tommy. When joy or sorrow came to her now, her first impulse was to hurry with it to him.

Was he still the same, quite the same? She, whom love had made a child of, asked it fearfully, as if to gaze upon him openly just at first might be blinding; and he pretended not to understand. "The same as what, Grizel?"

"Are you still-what I think you?"

"Ah, Grizel, not at all what you think me."

"But you do?"

"Coward! You are afraid to say the word. But I do!"

"You don't ask whether I do!"

"No."

"Why? Is it because you are so sure of me?"

He nodded, and she said it was cruel of him.

"You don't mean that, Grizel."

"Don't I?" She was delighted that he knew it.

"No; you mean that you like me to be sure of it."

"But I want to be sure of it myself." "You are. That was why you asked me if I loved you. Had you not been sure of it you would not have asked."

"How clever you are!" she said gleefully, and caressed a button of his velvet coat. "But you don't know what that means! It does not mean that I love you-not merely that."

"No; it means that you are glad I know you so well. It is an ecstasy to you, is it not, to feel that I know you so well?"

"It is sweet," she said. She asked curiously: "What did you do last night, after you left me? I can't guess, though I daresay you can guess what I did."

"You put the glove under your pillow, Grizel." (She had got the precious glove.)

"However could you guess!"

"It has often lain under my own."

"Oh!" said Grizel, breathless.

"Could you not guess even that?"

"I wanted to be sure. Did it do anything strange when you had it there?"

"I used to hear its heart beating."

"Yes, exactly! But this is still more remarkable. I put it away at last in my sweetest drawer, and when I woke in the morning it was under my pillow again. You could never have guessed that."

"Easily. It often did the same thing with me." "Story-teller! But what did you do when you went home?"

He could not have answered that exhaustively, even if he would, for his actions had been as contradictory as his emotions. He had feared even while he exulted, and exulted when plunged deep in fears. There had been quite a procession of Tommies all through the night; one of them had been a very miserable man, and the only thing he had been sure of was that he must be true to Grizel. But in so far as he did answer he told the truth.

"I went for a stroll among the stars," he said. "I don't know when I got to bed. I have found a way of reaching the stars. I have to say only, 'Grizel loves me,' and I am there."

"Without me!"

"I took you with me."

"What did we see? What did we do?"

"You spoiled everything by thinking the stars were badly managed. You wanted to take the supreme control. They turned you out."

"And when we got back to earth?"

"Then I happened to catch sight of myself in a looking-glass, and I was scared. I did not see how you could possibly love me. A terror came over me that in the Den you must have mistaken me for someone else. It was a darkish night, you know." "You are wanting me to say you are handsome."

"No, no; I am wanting you to say I am very, very handsome. Tell me you love me, Grizel, because I am beautiful."

"Perhaps," she replied, "I love you because your book is beautiful."

"Then good-bye for ever," he said sternly.

"Would not that please you?"

"It would break my heart."

"But I thought all authors —"

"It is the commonest mistake in the world. We are simple creatures, Grizel, and yearn to be loved for our face alone."

"But I do love the book," she said, when they became more serious, "because it is part of you."

"Rather that," he told her, "than that you should love me because I am part of it. But it is only a little part of me, Grizel; only the best part. It is Tommy on tiptoes. The other part, the part that does not deserve your love, is what needs it most."

"I am so glad!" she said eagerly. "I want to think you need me."

"How I need you!"

"Yes, I think you do —I am sure you do; and it makes me so happy."

"Ah," he said, "now I know why Grizel loves me." And perhaps he did know now. She loved to think that she was more to him than the new book, but was not always sure of it; and sometimes this saddened her, and again she decided that it was right and fitting. She would hasten to him to say that this saddened her. She would go just as impulsively to say that she thought it right.

Her discoveries about herself were many.

"What is it to-day?" he would say, smiling fondly at her. "I see it is something dreadful by your face."

"It is something that struck me suddenly when I was thinking of you, and I don't know whether to be glad or sorry."

"Then be glad, you child."

"It is this: I used to think a good deal of myself; the people here thought me haughty; they said I had a proud walk."

"You have it still," he assured her; the vitality in her as she moved was ever a delicious thing to him to look upon.

"Yes, I feel I have," she admitted, "but that is only because I am yours; and it used to be because I was nobody's!"

"Do you expect my face to fall at that?"

"No, but I thought so much of myself once, and now I am nobody at all. At first it distressed me, and then I was glad, for it makes you everything and me nothing. Yes, I am glad, but I am just a little bit sorry that I should be so glad!" "Poor Grizel!" said he.

"Poor Grizel!" she echoed. "You are not angry with me, are you, for being almost sorry for her? She used to be so different. 'Where is your independence, Grizel?' I say to her, and she shakes her sorrowful head. The little girl I used to be need not look for me any more; if we were to meet in the Den she would not know me now."

Ah, if only Tommy could have loved in this way! He would have done it if he could. If we could love by trying, no one would ever have been more loved than Grizel. "Am I to be condemned because I cannot?" he sometimes said to himself in terrible anguish; for though pretty thoughts came to him to say to her when she was with him, he suffered anguish for her when he was alone. He knew it was tragic that such love as hers should be given to him, but what more could he do than he was doing?

Chapter XIV
Elspeth

Ever since the beginning of the book we have been neglecting Elspeth so pointedly that were she not the most forgiving creature we should be afraid to face her now. You are not angry with us, are you, Elspeth? We have been sitting with you, talking with you, thinking of you between the chapters, and the only reason why you have so seldom got into them is that our pen insisted on running after your fascinating brother.

(That is the way to get round her.)

Tommy, it need not be said, never neglected her. The mere fact of his having an affair of his own at present is a sure sign that she is comfortable, for, unless all were well with Elspeth, no venture could have lured him from her side. "Now I am ready for you," he said to the world when Elspeth had been, figuratively speaking, put to sleep; but until she was nicely tucked up the world had to wait. He was still as in his boyhood, when he had to see her with a good book in her hand before he could set off on deeds of darkness. If this was but the story of a brother and sister, there were matter for it that would make the ladies want to kiss Tommy on the brow.

That Dr. Gemmell disliked or at least distrusted him, Tommy knew before their acquaintance was an hour old; yet that same evening he had said cordially to Elspeth:

"This young doctor has a strong face."

She was evidently glad that Tommy had noticed it. "Do you think him handsome?" she inquired.

"Decidedly so," he replied, very handsomely, for it is an indiscreet question to ask of a plain man.

There was nothing small about Tommy, was there? He spoke thus magnanimously because he had seen that the doctor liked Elspeth, and that she liked him for liking her. Elspeth never spoke to him of such things, but he was aware that an extra pleasure in life came to her when she was admired; it gave her a little of the self-confidence she so wofully lacked; the woman in her was stirred. Take such presents as these to Elspeth, and Tommy would let you cast stones at himself for the rest of the day, and shake your hand warmly on parting. In London Elspeth had always known quickly, almost at the first clash of eyes, whether Tommy's friends were attracted by her, but she had not known sooner than he. Those acquaintanceships had seldom ripened; but perhaps this was because, though he and she avoided talking of them, he was all the time taking such terrifying care of her. She was always little Elspeth to him, for whom he had done everything since the beginning of her, a frail little female counterpart of himself that would never have dared to grow up had he not always been there to show her the way, like a stronger plant in the same pot. It was even pathetic to him that Elspeth should have to become a woman while he was a man, and he set to, undaunted, to help her in this matter also. To be admired of men is a woman's right, and he knew it gratified Elspeth; therefore he brought them in to admire her. But beyond profound respect they could not presume to go, he was watching them so vigilantly. He had done everything for her so far, and it was evident that he was now ready to do the love-making also, or at least to sift it before it reached her. Elspeth saw this, and perhaps it annoyed her once or twice, though on the whole she was deeply touched; and the young gentlemen saw it also: they saw that he would not leave them alone with her for a moment, and that behind his cordial manner sat a Tommy who had his eye on them. Subjects suitable for conversation before Elspeth seemed in presence of this strict brother to be limited. You had just begun to tell her the plot of the new novel when T. Sandys fixed you with his gleaming orb. You were in the middle of the rumour about Mrs. Golightly when he let the poker fall. If the newsboys were yelling the latest horror he quickly closed the window. He made all visitors self-conscious. If she was not in the room few of them dared to ask if she was quite well. They paled before expressing the hope that she would feel stronger to-morrow. Yet when Tommy went up to sit beside her, which was the moment the front door closed, he took care to mention, incidentally, that they had been inquiring after her. One of them ventured on her birthday to bring her flowers, but could not present them, Tommy looked so alarming. A still more daring spirit once went the length of addressing her by her Christian name. She did not start up haughtily (the most timid of women are a surprise at times), but the poker fell with a crash.

He knew Elspeth so well that he could tell exactly how these poor young men should approach her. As an artist as well as a brother, he frowned when they blundered. He would have liked to be the medium through which they talked, so that he could give looks and words their proper force. He had thought it all out so thoroughly for Elspeth's benefit that in an hour he could have drawn out a complete guide for her admirers.

"At the first meeting look at her wistfully when she does not see you. She will see you." It might have been Rule One.

Rule Two: "Don't talk so glibly." How often that was what the poker meant!

Being herself a timid creature, Elspeth showed best among the timid, because her sympathetic heart immediately desired to put them at their ease. The more glibly they could talk, the less, she knew, were they impressed by her. Even a little boorishness was more complimentary than chatter. Sometimes when she played on the piano which Tommy had hired for her, the visitor was so shy that he could not even mutter "Thank you" to his hat; yet she might play to him again, and not to the gallant who remarked briskly: "How very charming! What is that called?"

To talk disparagingly of other women is so common a way among men of penetrating into the favour of one that, of course, some tried it with Elspeth. Tommy could not excuse such blundering, for they were making her despise them. He got them out of the house, and then he and she had a long talk, not about them, but about men and women in general, from which she gathered once again that there was nobody like Tommy.

When they bade each other good-night, she would say to him: "I think you are the one perfect gentleman in the world."

Or he might say: "You expect so much of men, Elspeth."

To which her reply: "You have taught me to do it, and now I expect others to be like you." Sometimes she would even say: "When I see you so fond of me, and taking such care of me, I am ashamed. You think me so much better than I am. You consider me so pure and good, while I know that I am often mean, and even have wicked thoughts. It makes me ashamed, but so proud of you, for I see that you are judging me by yourself."

And then this Tommy would put the gas out softly and go to his own room, and, let us hope, blush a little.

One stripling had proposed to Elspeth, and on her agitatedly declining him, had flung out of the room in a pet. It spoiled all her after-thoughts on the subject, and so roused her brother's indignation with the fellow. If the great baby had only left all the arrangements to Tommy, he could so easily have made that final scene one which Elspeth would remember with gratification for the remainder of her days; for, of course, pride in the offer could not be great unless she retained her respect for the man who made it. From the tremulous proposal and the manly acceptance of his fate to his dignified exit ("Don't grieve for me, Miss Sandys; you never gave me the least encouragement, and to have loved you will always make me a better man"), even to a touching way of closing the door with one long, last, lingering look, Tommy could have fitted him like a tailor.

From all which it will be seen that our splendid brother thought exclusively of what was best for Elspeth, and was willing that the gentlemen, having served their purpose, should, if it pleased them, go hang. Also, though he thought out every other possible move for the suitor, it never struck him to compose a successful proposal, for the simple reason that he was quite certain Elspeth would have none of them. Their attentions pleased her; but exchange Tommy for one of them-never! He knew it from her confessions at all stages of her life; he had felt it from the days when he began to be father and mother to her as well as brother. In his heart he believed there was something of his own odd character in Elspeth which made her as incapable of loving as himself, and some of his devotion to her was due to this belief; for perhaps nothing touches us to the quick more than the feeling that another suffers under our own curse; certainly nothing draws two souls so close together in a lonely comradeship. But though Tommy had reflected about these things, he did not trouble Elspeth with his conclusions. He merely gave her to understand that he loved her and she loved him so much that neither of them had any love to give to another. It was very beautiful, Elspeth thought, and a little tragic.

"You are quite sure that you mean that," she might ask timidly, "and that you are not flinging away your life on me?"

"You are all I need," he answered cheerily, and he believed it. Or, if he was in another mood, he might reflect that perhaps he was abstaining from love for Elspeth's sake, and that made him cheery also.

And now David Gemmell was the man, and Tommy genially forgave him all else for liking Elspeth. He invited the doctor, who so obviously distrusted him, to drop in of an evening for a game at the dambrod (which they both abominated, but it was an easy excuse); he asked him confidentially to come in and see Aaron, who had been coughing last night; he put on all the airs of a hail-fellow-well-met, though they never became him, and sat awkwardly on his face. David always seemed eager to come, and tried to rise above his suspicions of Tommy, as Tommy saw, and failed, as Tommy saw again. Elspeth dosed the doctor with stories of her brother's lovely qualities, and Tommy, the forgiving, honestly pitied the poor man for having to listen to them. He knew that if all went well Gemmell would presently propose, and find that Elspeth (tearful at having to strike a blow) could not accept him; but he did not look forward maliciously to this as his revenge on the doctor; he was thinking merely of what was good for Elspeth.

There was no open talk about David between the brother and sister. Some day, Tommy presumed, she would announce that the doctor had asked her to marry him; and oh, how sorry she was; and oh, what a good man he was; and oh, Tommy knew she had never encouraged him; and oh, she could never leave Tommy! But until that day arrived they avoided talking directly about what brought Gemmell there. That he came to see Elspeth neither of them seemed to conceive as possible. Did Tommy chuckle when he saw David's eyes following her? No; solemn as a cat blinking at the fire; noticed nothing. The most worldly chaperon, the most loving mother, could not have done more for Elspeth. Yet it was not done to find her a husband, but quite the reverse, as we have seen. On reflection Tommy must smile at what he has been doing, but not while he is working the figures. The artist never smiles at himself until afterwards.

And now he not only wondered at times how Elspeth and David were getting on, but whether she noticed how he was getting on with Grizel; for in matters relating to Tommy Elspeth was almost as sharp as he in matters that related to her, and he knew it. When he proposed to Elspeth that they should ask Gemmell to go fishing with them on the morrow ("He has been overworked of late and it would do him good") he wanted to add, in a careless voice, "We might invite Grizel also," but could not; his lips suddenly went dry. And when Elspeth said the words that were so difficult to him, he wondered, "Did she say that because she knew I wished it?" But he decided that she did not, for she was evidently looking forward to to-morrow, and he knew she would be shuddering if she thought her Tommy was slipping.

"I am so glad it was she who asked me," Grizel said to him when he told her. "Don't you see what it means? It means that she wants to get you out of the way! You are not everything to her now as you used to be. Are you glad, glad?"

"If I could believe it!" Tommy said.

"What else could make her want to be alone with him?"

Nothing else could have made Grizel want to be alone with him, and she must always judge others by herself. But Tommy knew that Elspeth was different, and that a girl with some of himself in her might want to be alone with a man who admired her without wanting to marry him.

Chapter XV
By Prosen Water

That day by the banks of Prosen Water was one of Grizel's beautiful memories. All the days when she thought he loved her became beautiful memories.

It was the time of reds and whites, for the glory of the broom had passed, except at great heights, and the wild roses were trooping in. When the broom is in flame there seems to be no colour but yellow; but when the wild roses come we remember that the broom was flaunting. It was not quite a lady, for it insisted on being looked at; while these light-hearted things are too innocent to know that there is anyone to look. Grizel was sitting by the side of the stream, adorning her hat fantastically with roses red and white and some that were neither. They were those that cannot decide whether they look best in white or red, and so waver for the whole of their little lives between the two colours; there are many of them, and it is the pathetic thing about wild roses. She did not pay much heed to her handiwork. What she was saying to herself was that in another minute he and she would be alone. Nothing else in the world mattered very much. Every bit of her was conscious of it as the supreme event. Her fingers pressed it upon the flowers. It was in her eyes as much as in her heart. He went on casting his line, moving from stone to stone, dropping down the bank, ascending it, as if the hooking of a trout was something to him. Was he feeling to his marrow that as soon as those other two figures rounded the bend in the stream he and she would have the world to themselves? Ah, of course he felt it, but was it quite as much to him as it was to her?

"Not quite so much," she said bravely to herself. "I don't want it to be quite so much-but nearly."

She did not look up, she waited.

And now they were alone as no two can be except those who love; for when the third person leaves them they have a universe to themselves, and it is closed in by the heavens, and the air of it is the consciousness of each other's presence. She sat motionless now-trembling, exulting. She could no longer hear the talking of the water, but she heard his step. He was coming slowly towards her. She did not look up-she waited; and while she waited time was annihilated.

He was coming to her to treat her as if she were a fond child; that she, of all women, could permit it was still delicious to him, and a marvel. She had let him do it yesterday, but perhaps she had regained her independence in the night. As he hesitated he became another person. In a flood of feeling he had a fierce desire to tell her the truth about himself. But he did not know what it was. He put aside his rod, and sat down very miserably beside her.

"Grizel, I suppose I am a knave." His lips parted to say it, but no words came. She had given him an adorable look that stopped them as if her dear hand had been placed upon his mouth.

Was he a knave? He wanted honestly to know. He had not tried to make her love him. Had he known in time he would even have warned her against it. He would never have said he loved her had she not first, as she thought, found it out; to tell her the truth then would have been brutal. He had made believe in order that she might remain happy. Was it even make-belief? Assuredly he did love her in his own way, in the only way he was capable of. She was far more to him than any other person except Elspeth. He delighted in her, and would have fought till he dropped rather than let any human being injure her. All his feelings for her were pure. He was prepared to marry her; but if she had not made that mistake, oh, what a delight it would have been to him never to marry anyone! He felt keenly miserable.

"Grizel, I seem to be different from all other men. There seems to be some curse upon me that makes me unable to love as they do. I want to love you, dear one; you are the only woman I ever wanted to love; but apparently I can't. I have decided to go on with this thing because it seems best for you; but is it? I would tell you all and leave the decision to you, were it not that I fear you would think I wanted you to let me off."

It would have been an honest speech, and he might have said it had he begun at once, for it was in a passion to be out, so desirous was he that dear Grizel should not be deceived; but he tried its effect first upon himself, and as he went on the tragedy he saw mastered him. He forgot that she was there, except as a figure needed to complete the picture of the man who could not love. He saw himself a splendidly haggard creature with burning eyes standing aside while all the world rolled by in pursuit of the one thing needful. It was a river, and he must stand parched on the bank for ever and ever. Should he keep that sorrowful figure a man or turn it into a woman? He tried a woman. She was on the bank now, her arms outstretched to the flood. Ah! she would be so glad to drink, though she must drown.

Grizel saw how mournful he had become as he gazed upon her. In his face she had been seeing all the glories that can be given to mortals. Thoughts had come to her that drew her nearer to her God. Her trust in him stretched to eternity. All that was given to her at that moment she thought was also given to him. She seemed to know why, with love lighting up their souls to each other, he could yet grow mournful.

"Oh," she cried, with a movement that was a passionate caress, "do you indeed love me so much as that? I never wanted you to love me quite so much as that!"

It brought him back to himself, but without a start. Those sudden returns to fact had ceased to bewilder him; they were grown so common that he passed between dreams and reality as through tissue-paper.

"I did not mean," she said at last, in a tremor, "that I wanted you to love me less, but I am almost sorry that you love me quite so much."

He dared say nothing, for he did not altogether understand. "I have those fears, too, sometimes," she went on; "I have had them when I was with you, but more often when I was alone.

They come to me suddenly, and I have such eager longings to run to you and tell you of them, and ask you to drive them away. But I never did it; I kept them to myself."

"You could keep something back from me, Grizel?"

"Forgive me," she implored; "I thought they would distress you, and I had such a desire to bring you nothing but happiness. To bear them by myself seemed to be helping you, and I was glad, I was proud, to feel myself of use to you even to that little extent. I did not know you had the same fears; I thought that perhaps they came only to women; have you had them before? Fears," she continued, so wistfully, "that it is too beautiful to end happily? Oh, have you heard a voice crying, 'It is too beautiful; it can never be'?"

He saw clearly now; he saw so clearly that he was torn with emotion. "It is more than I can bear!" he said hoarsely. Surely he loved her.

"Did you see me die?" she asked, in a whisper. "I have seen you die."

"Don't, Grizel!" he cried.

But she had to go on. "Tell me," she begged; "I have told you."

"No, no, never that," he answered her. "At the worst I have had only the feeling that you could never be mine."

She smiled at that. "I am yours," she said softly; "nothing can take away that-nothing, nothing. I say it to myself a hundred times a day, it is so sweet. Nothing can separate us but death; I have thought of all the other possible things, and none of them is strong enough. But when I think of your dying, oh, when I think of my being left without you!"

She rocked her arms in a frenzy, and called him dearest, darlingest. All the sweet names that had been the child Grizel's and the old doctor's were Tommy's now. He soothed her, ah, surely as only a lover could soothe. She was his Grizel, she was his beloved. No mortal could have been more impassioned than Tommy. He must have loved her. It could not have been merely sympathy, or an exquisite delight in being the man, or the desire to make her happy again in the quickest way, or all three combined? Whatever it was, he did not know; all he knew was that he felt every word he said, or seemed to feel it.

"It is a punishment to me," Grizel said, setting her teeth, "for loving you too much. I know I love you too much. I think I love you more than God."

She felt him shudder.

"But if I feel it," she said, shuddering also, yet unable to deceive herself, "what difference do I make by saying it? He must know it is so, whether I say it or not."

There was a tremendous difference to Tommy, but not of a kind he could explain, and she went on; she must tell him everything now.

"I pray every night and morning; but that is nothing-everyone does it. I know I thank God sincerely; I thank Him again and again and again. Do you remember how, when I was a child, you used to be horrified because I prayed standing? I often say little prayers standing now; I am always thanking Him for giving me you. But all the time it is a bargain with Him. So long as you are well I love Him, but if you were to die I would never pray again. I have never said it in words until to-day, but He must know it, for it is behind all my prayers. If He does not know, there cannot be a God."

She was watching his face, half wofully, half stubbornly, as if, whatever might be the issue of those words, she had to say them. She saw how pained he was. To admit the possible non-existence of a God when you can so easily leave the subject alone was horrible to Tommy.

"I don't doubt Him," she continued. "I have believed in Him ever since the time when I was such a lonely child that I did not know His name. I shall always believe in Him so long as He does not take you from me. But if He does, then I shall not believe in Him any more. It may be wrong, but that is what I feel.

"It makes you care less for me!" she cried in anguish.

"No, no, dear."

"I don't think it makes God care less for me," she said, very seriously. "I think He is pleased that I don't try to cheat Him."

Somehow Tommy felt uncomfortable at that.

"There are people," he said vaguely, like one who thought it best to mention no names, who would be afraid to challenge God in that way."

"He would not be worth believing in," she answered, "if He could be revengeful. He is too strong, and too loving, and too pitiful for that." But she took hold of Tommy as if to protect him. Had they been in physical danger, her first impulse would have been to get in front of him to protect him. The noblest women probably always love in this way, and yet it is those who would hide behind them that men seem to love the best.

"I always feel-oh, I never can help feeling," she said, "that nothing could happen to you, that God Himself could not take you from me, while I had hold of you."

"Grizel!"

"I mean only that He could not have the heart," she said hastily. "No, I don't," she had to add. "I meant what you thought I meant. That is why I feel it would be so sweet to be married, so that I could be close to you every moment, and then no harm could come to you. I would keep such a grip of you, I should be such a part of you, that you could not die without my dying also.

"Oh, do you care less for me now?" she cried. "I can't see things as clearly as you do, dearest, darlingest. I have not a beautiful nature like yours. I am naturally rebellious. I have to struggle even to be as good as I am. There are evil things in my blood. You remember how we found out that. God knew it, too, and He is compassionate. I think He makes many pitying allowances for me. It is not wicked, is it, to think that?"

"You used to know me too well, Grizel, to speak of my beautiful nature," he said humbly.

"I did think you vain," she replied. "How odd to remember that!"

"But I was, and am."

"I love to hear you proving you are not," said she, beaming upon him. "Do you think," she asked, with a sudden change of manner to the childish, like one trying to coax a compliment out of him, "that I have improved at all during those last days? I think I am not quite such a horrid girl as I used to be; and if I am not, I owe it to you. I am so glad to owe it to you." She told him that she was trying to make herself a tiny bit more like him by studying his book. "It is not exactly the things you say of women that help me, for though they are lovely I am not sure that they are quite true. I almost hope they are not true; for if they are, then I am not even an average woman." She buried her face in his coat. "You say women are naturally purer than men, but I don't know. Perhaps we are more cunning only. Perhaps it is not even a thing to wish; for if we were, it would mean that we are good because there is less evil in us to fight against. Dear, forgive me for saying that; it may be all wrong; but I think it is what nearly all women feel in their hearts, though they keep it locked up till they die. I don't even want you to believe me. You think otherwise of us, and it is so sweet of you that we try to be better than we are-to undeceive you would hurt so. It is not the book that makes me a better woman-it is the man I see behind it."

He was too much moved to be able to reply-too much humbled. He vowed to himself that, whether he could love or not, he would be a good husband to this dear woman.

"Ah, Grizel," he declared, by and by, "what a delicious book you are, and how I wish I had written you! With every word you say, something within me is shouting, 'Am I not a wonder!' I warned you it would be so as soon as I felt that I had done anything really big, and I have. I have somehow made you love me. Ladies and gentlemen," he exclaimed, addressing the river and the trees and the roses, "I have somehow made her love me! Am I not a wonder?"

Grizel clapped her hands gaily; she was merry again. She could always be what Tommy wanted her to be. "Ladies and gentlemen," she cried, "how could I help it?"

David had been coming back for his fly-book, and though he did not hear their words, he saw a light in Grizel's face that suddenly set him thinking. For the rest of the day he paid little attention to Elspeth; some of his answers showed her that he was not even listening to her.

Chapter XVI
"How Could You Hurt Your Grizel So!"

To concentrate on Elspeth so that he might find out what was in her mind was, as we have seen, seldom necessary to Tommy; for he had learned her by heart long ago. Yet a time was now come when he had to concentrate, and even then he was doubtful of the result. So often he had put that mind of hers to rights that it was an open box to him, or had been until he conceived the odd notion that perhaps it contained a secret drawer. This would have been resented by most brothers, but Tommy's chagrin was nothing compared to the exhilaration with which he perceived that he might be about to discover something new about woman. He was like the digger whose hand is on the point of closing on a diamond —a certain holiness added.

What puzzled him was the state of affairs now existing between Elspeth and the doctor. A week had elapsed since the fishing excursion, and David had not visited them. Too busy? Tommy knew that it is the busy people who can find time. Could it be that David had proposed to her at the waterside?

No, he could not read that in Elspeth's face. He knew that she would be in distress lest her refusal should darken the doctor's life for too long a time; but yet (shake your fist at him, ladies, for so misunderstanding you!) he expected also to note in that sympathetic face a look of subdued triumph, and as it was not there, David could not have proposed.

The fact of her not having told him about it at once did not prove to Tommy that there had been no proposal. His feeling was that she would consider it too sacred a thing to tell even to him, but that it would force its way out in a week or two.

On the other hand, she could not have resisted dropping shyly such remarks as these: "I think Dr. Gemmell is a noble man," or, "How wonderfully good Dr. Gemmell is to the poor!"

Also she would sometimes have given Tommy a glance that said, "I wonder if you guess." Had they quarrelled? Tommy smiled. If it was but a quarrel he was not merely appeased-he was pleased. Had he had the ordering of the affair, he would certainly have included a lovers' quarrel in it, and had it not been that he wanted to give her the pleasure of finding these things out for herself, he would have taken her aside and addressed her thus: "No need to look tragic, Elspeth; for to a woman this must be really one of the most charming moments in the comedy. You feel that he would not have quarrelled had he had any real caring for you, and yet in your heart you know it is a proof that he has. To a woman, I who know assure you that nothing can be more delicious. Your feeling for him, as you and I well know, is but a sentiment of attraction because he loves you as you are unable to love him, and as you are so pained by this quarrel, consider how much more painful it must be to him. You think you have been slighted; that when a man has seemed to like you so much you have a right to be told so by him, that you may help him with your sympathy. Oh, Elspeth, you think yourself unhappy just now when you are really in the middle of one of the pleasantest bits of it! Love is a series of thrills, the one leading to the other, and, as your careful guardian, I would not have you miss one of them. You will come to the final bang quickly enough, and find it the finest thrill of all, but it is soon over. When you have had to tell him that you are not for him, there are left only the pleasures of memory, and the more of them there were, the more there will be to look back to. I beg you, Elspeth, not to hurry; loiter rather, smelling the flowers and plucking them, for you may never be this way again."

All these things he might have pointed out to Elspeth had he wanted her to look at the matter rationally, but he had no such wish. He wanted her to enjoy herself as the blessed do, without knowing why. No pity for the Grizel man, you see, but no ill will to him. David was having his thrills also, and though the last of them would seem a staggerer to him at the time, it would gradually become a sunny memory. The only tragedy is not to have known love. So long as you have the experiences, it does not greatly matter whether your suit was a failure or successful.

So Tommy decided, but he feared at the same time that there had been no quarrel-that David had simply drawn back.

How he saw through Elspeth's brave attempts to show that she had never for a moment thought of David's having any feeling for her save ordinary friendship-yes, they were brave, but not brave enough for Tommy. At times she would say something bitter about life (not about the doctor, for he was never mentioned), and it was painful to her brother to see gentle Elspeth grown cynical. He suffered even more when her manner indicated that she knew she was too poor a creature to be loved by any man. Tommy was in great woe about Elspeth at this time. He was thinking much more about her than about Grizel; but do not blame him unreservedly for that: the two women who were his dears were pulling him different ways, and he could not accompany both. He had made up his mind to be loyal to Grizel, and so all his pity could go to Elspeth. On the day he had his talk with the doctor, therefore, he had, as it were, put Grizel aside only because she was happy just now, and so had not Elspeth's need of him.

The doctor and he had met on the hill, whence the few who look may see one of the fairest views in Scotland. Tommy was strolling up and down, and the few other persons on the hill were glancing with good-humoured suspicion at him, as we all look at celebrated characters. Had he been happy he would have known that they were watching him, and perhaps have put his hands behind his back to give them more for their money, as the saying is; but he was miserable. His one consolation was that the blow he must strike Elspeth when he told her of his engagement need not be struck just yet. David could not have chosen a worse moment, therefore, for saying so bluntly what he said: "I hear you are to be married. If so, I should like to congratulate you."

Tommy winced like one charged with open cruelty to his sister-charged with it, too, by the real criminal.

"It is not true?" David asked quietly, and Tommy turned from him glaring. "I am sorry I spoke of it, as it is not true," the doctor said after a pause, the crow's-feet showing round his eyes as always when he was in mental pain; and presently he went away, after giving Tommy a contemptuous look. Did Tommy deserve that look? We must remember that he had wanted to make the engagement public at once; if he shrank from admitting it for the present, it was because of Elspeth's plight. "Grizel, you might have given her a little time to recover from this man's faithlessness," was what his heart cried. He believed that Grizel had told David, and for the last time in his life he was angry with her. He strode down the hill savagely towards Caddam Wood, where he knew he should find her.

Soon he saw her. She was on one of the many tiny paths that lead the stranger into the middle of the wood and then leave him there maliciously or because they dare not venture any farther themselves. They could play no tricks on Grizel, however, for she knew and was fond of them all. Tommy had said that she loved them because they were such little paths, that they appealed to her like babies; and perhaps there was something in it.

She came up the path with the swing of one who was gleefully happy. Some of the Thrums people, you remember, said that Grizel strutted because she was so satisfied with herself, and if you like an ugly word, we may say that she strutted to-day. It was her whole being giving utterance to the joy within her that love had brought. As Grizel came up the path on that bright afternoon, she could no more have helped strutting than the bud to open on the appointed day. She was obeying one of Nature's laws. I think I promised long ago to tell you of the day when Grizel would strut no more. Well, this is the day. Observe her strutting for the last time. It was very strange and touching to her to remember in the after years that she had once strutted, but it was still more strange and touching to Tommy.

She was like one overfilled with delight when she saw him. How could she know that he was to strike her?

He did not speak. She was not displeased. When anything so tremendous happened as the meeting of these two, how could they find words at once?

She bent and pressed her lips to his sleeve; but he drew away with a gesture that startled her.

"You are not angry?" she said, stopping.

"Yes," he replied doggedly.

"Not with me?" Her hand went to her heart. "With me!" A wounded animal could not have uttered a cry more pathetic. "Not with me!" She clutched his arm.

"Have I no cause to be angry?" he said.

She looked at him in bewilderment. Could this be he? Oh, could it be she?

"Cause? How could I give you cause?"

It seemed unanswerable to her. How could Grizel do anything that would give him the right to be angry with her? Oh, men, men! will you never understand how absolutely all of her a woman's love can be? If she gives you everything, how can she give you more? She is not another person; she is part of you. Does one finger of your hand plot against another?

He told her sullenly of his scene with the doctor.

"I am very sorry," she said; but her eyes were still searching for the reason why Tommy could be angry with her.

"You made me promise to tell no one," he said, "and I have kept my promise: but you — —"

The anguish that was Grizel's then! "You can't think that I told him!" she cried, and she held out her arms as if to remind him of who she was. "You can believe that of your Grizel?"

"I daresay you have not done it wittingly; but this man has guessed, and he could never have guessed it from look or word of mine."

"It must have been I!" she said slowly. "Tell me," she cried like a suppliant, "how have I done it?"

"Your manner, your face," he answered; "it must have been that. I don't blame you. Grizel, but-yes, it must have been that, and it is hard on me."

He was in misery, and these words leaped out. They meant only that it was hard on him if Elspeth had to be told of his engagement in the hour of her dejection. He did not mean to hurt Grizel to the quick. However terrible the loss of his freedom might be to the man who could not love, he always intended to be true to her. But she gave the words a deeper meaning.

She stood so still she seemed to be pondering, and at last she said quietly, as if they had been discussing some problem outside themselves: "Yes, I think it must have been that." She looked long at him. "It is very hard on you," she said.

"I feel sure it was that," she went on; and now her figure was erect, and again it broke, and sometimes there was a noble scorn in her voice, but more often there was only pitiful humility. "I feel sure it was that, for I have often wondered how everybody did not know. I have broken my promise. I used always to be able to keep a promise. I had every other fault, —I was hard and proud and intolerant, —but I was true. I think I was vain of that, though I see now it was only something I could not help; from the moment when I had a difficulty in keeping a promise, I ceased to keep it. I love you so much that I carry my love in my face for all to read. They cannot see me meet you without knowing the truth; they cannot hear me say your name but I betray myself; I show how I love you in every movement; I am full of you. How can anyone look at me and not see you? I should have been more careful-oh, I could have been so much more careful had I loved you a little less! It is very hard on you."

The note of satire had died out of her voice; her every look and gesture carried in it nothing but love for him; but all the unhappy dog could say was something about self-respect.

Her mouth opened as if for bitterness; but no sound came. "How much self-respect do you think is left for me after to-day?" she said mournfully at last; and then she quickly took a step nearer her dear one, as if to caress the spot where these words had struck him. But she stopped, and for a moment she was the Grizel of old. "Have no fear," she said, with a trembling, crooked smile; "there is only one thing to be done now, and I shall do it. All the blame is mine. You shall not be deprived of your self-respect."

He had not been asking for his freedom; but he heard it running to him now, and he knew that if he answered nothing he would be whistling it back for ever. A madness to be free at any cost swept over him. He let go his hold on self-respect, and clapped his hand on freedom.

He answered nothing, and the one thing for her to do was to go; and she did it. But it was only for a moment that she could be altogether the Grizel of old. She turned to take a long, last look at him; but the wofulness of herself was what she saw. She cried, with infinite pathos, "Oh, how could you hurt your Grizel so!"

He controlled himself and let her go. His freedom was fawning on him, licking his hands and face, and in that madness he actually let Grizel go. It was not until she was out of sight that he gave utterance to a harsh laugh. He knew what he was at that moment, as you and I shall never be able to know him, eavesdrop how we may.

He flung himself down in a blaeberry-bed, and lay there doggedly, his weak mouth tightly closed. A great silence reigned; no, not a great silence, for he continued to hear the cry: "Oh, how could you hurt your Grizel so!" She scarcely knew that she had said it; but to him who knew what she had been, and what he had changed her into, and for what alone she was to blame, there was an unconscious pathos in it that was terrible. It was the epitome of all that was Grizel, all that was adorable and all that was pitiful in her. It rang in his mind like a bell of doom. He believed its echo would not be quite gone from his ears when he died. If all the wise men in the world had met to consider how Grizel could most effectively say farewell to Tommy, they could not have thought out a better sentence. However completely he had put himself emotionally in her place with this same object, he would have been inspired by nothing quite so good.

But they were love's dying words. He knew he could never again, though he tried, be to Grizel what he had been. The water was spilled on the ground. She had thought him all that was glorious in man-that was what her love had meant; and it was spilled. There was only one way in which he could wound her more cruelly than she was already hurt, and that was by daring to ask her to love him still. To imply that he thought her pride so broken, her independence, her maidenly modesty, all that make up the loveliness of a girl, so lost that by entreaties he could persuade her to forgive him, would destroy her altogether. It would reveal to her how low he thought her capable of falling.

I suppose we should all like to think that it would have been thus with Grizel, but our wishes are of small account. It was not many minutes since she left Tommy, to be his no more, his knife still in her heart; but she had not reached the end of the wood when all in front of her seemed a world of goblins, and a future without him not to be faced. He might beat her or scorn her, but not for an hour could she exist without him. She wrung her arms in woe; the horror of what she was doing tore her in pieces; but not all this prevented her turning back. It could not even make her go slowly. She did not walk back; she stole back in little runs. She knew it was her destruction, but her arms were outstretched to the spot where she had left him.

He was no longer there, and he saw her between the firs before she could see him. As he realized what her coming back meant, his frame shook with pity for her. All the dignity had gone from her. She looked as shamed as a dog stealing back after it had been whipped. She knew she was shamed. He saw she knew it: the despairing rocking of her arms proved it; yet she was coming back to him in little runs.

Pity, chivalry, oh, surely love itself, lifted him to his feet, and all else passed out of him save an imperious desire to save her as much humiliation as he could-to give her back a few of those garments of pride and self-respect that had fallen from her. At least she should not think that she had to come all the way to him. With a stifled sob, he rose and ran up the path towards her.

"Grizel! it is you! My beloved! how could you leave me! Oh, Grizel, my love, how could you misunderstand me so!"

She gave a glad cry. She sought feebly to hold him at arm's length, to look at him watchfully, to read him as in the old days; but the old days were gone. He strained her to him. Oh, surely it was love at last! He thanked God that he loved at last.

Chapter XVII
How Tommy Saved the Flag

He loved at last, but had no time to exult just now, for he could not rejoice with Tommy while his dear one drooped in shame. Ah, so well he understood that she believed she had done the unpardonable thing in woman, and that while she thought so she must remain a broken column. It was a great task he saw before him-nothing less than to make her think that what she had done was not shameful, but exquisite; that she had not tarnished the flag of love, but glorified it. Artfulness, you will see, was needed; but, remember, he was now using all his arts in behalf of the woman he loved.

"You were so long in coming back to me, Grizel. The agony of it!" "Did it seem long?" She spoke in a trembling voice, hiding her face in him. She listened like one anxious to seize his answer as it left his heart.

"So long," he answered, "that it seemed to me we must be old when we met again. I saw a future without you stretching before me to the grave, and I turned and ran from it."

"That is how I felt," she whispered.

"You!" Tommy cried, in excellent amazement.

"What else could have made me come?"

"I thought it was pity that had brought you-pity for me, Grizel. I thought you had perhaps come back to be angry with me —"

"How could I be!" she cried.

"How could you help it, rather?" said he. "I was cruel, Grizel; I spoke like a fool as well as like a dastard. But it was only anxiety for Elspeth that made me do it. Dear one, be angry with me as often as you choose, and whether I deserve it or not; but don't go away from me; never send me from you again. Anything but that."

It was how she had felt again, and her hold on him tightened with sudden joy. So well he knew what that grip meant! He did not tell her that he had not loved her fully until now. He would have liked to tell her how true love had been born in him as he saw her stealing back to him, but it was surely best for her not to know that any transformation had been needed. "I don't say that I love you more now than ever before," he said carefully, "but one thing I do know: that I never admired you quite so much."

She looked up in surprise.

"I mean your character," he said determinedly. "I have always known how strong and noble it was, but I never quite thought you could do anything so beautiful as this."

"Beautiful!" She could only echo the word.

"Many women, even of the best," he told her, "would have resorted to little feminine ways of humbling such a blunderer as I have been: they would have spurned him for weeks; made him come to them on his knees; perhaps have thought that his brutality of a moment outweighed all his love. When I saw you coming to meet me half-way —oh, Grizel, tell me that you were doing that?"

"Yes, yes, yes!" she answered eagerly, so that she might not detain him a moment.

"When I saw you I realized that you were willing to forgive me; that you were coming to say so; that no thought of lowering me first was in your mind; that yours was a love above the littleness of ordinary people: and the adorableness of it filled me with a glorious joy; I saw in that moment what woman in her highest development is capable of, and that the noblest is the most womanly."

She said "Womanly?" with a little cry. It had always been such a sweet word to her, and she thought it could never be hers again!

"It is by watching you," he replied, "that I know the meaning of the word. I thought I knew long ago, but every day you give it a nobler meaning."

If she could have believed it! For a second or two she tried to believe it, and then she shook her head.

"How dear of you to think that of me!" she answered. She looked up at him with exquisite approval in her eyes. She had always felt that men should have high ideas about women.

"But it was not to save you pain that I came back," she said bravely. There was something pathetic in the way the truth had always to come out of her. "I did not think you wanted me to come back. I never expected you to be looking for me, and when I saw you doing it, my heart nearly stopped for gladness. I thought you were wearied of me, and would be annoyed when you saw me coming back. I said to myself, 'If I go back I shall be a disgrace to womanhood,' But I came; and now do you know what my heart is saying, and always will be saying? It is that pride and honour and self-respect are gone. And the terrible thing is that I don't seem to care; I, who used to value them so much, am willing to let them go if you don't send me away from you. Oh, if you can't love me any longer, let me still love you! That is what I came back to say."

"Grizel, Grizel!" he cried. It was she who was wielding the knife now.

"But it is true," she said.

"We could so easily pretend that it isn't." That was not what he said, though it was at his heart. He sat down, saying:

"This is a terrible blow, but better you should tell it to me than leave me to find it out." He was determined to save the flag for Grizel, though he had to try all the Tommy ways, one by one.

"Have I hurt you?" she asked anxiously. She could not bear to hurt him for a moment. "What did I say?"

"It amounts to this," he replied huskily: "you love me, but you wish you did not; that is what it means."

He expected her to be appalled by this; but she stood still, thinking it over. There was something pitiful in a Grizel grown undecided.

"Do I wish I did not?" she said helplessly. "I don't know. Perhaps that is what I do wish. Ah, but what are wishes! I know now that they don't matter at all."

"Yes, they matter," he assured her, in the voice of one looking upon death. "If you no longer want to love me, you will cease to do it soon enough." His manner changed to bitterness. "So don't be cast down, Grizel, for the day of your deliverance is at hand."

But again she disappointed him, and as the flag must be saved at whatever cost, he said.

"It has come already. I see you no longer love me as you did." Her arms rose in anguish; but he went on ruthlessly: "You will never persuade me that you do; I shall never believe it again."

I suppose it was a pitiable thing about Grizel-it was something he had discovered weeks ago and marvelled over-that nothing distressed her so much as the implication that she could love him less. She knew she could not; but that he should think it possible was the strangest woe to her. It seemed to her to be love's only tragedy. We have seen how difficult it was for Grizel to cry. When she said "How could you hurt your Grizel so!" she had not cried, nor when she knew that if she went back to him her self-respect must remain behind. But a painful tear came to her eyes when he said that she loved him less. It almost unmanned him, but he proceeded, for her good:

"I daresay you still care for me a little, as the rank and file of people love. What right had I, of all people, to expect a love so rare and beautiful as yours to last? It had to burn out, like a great fire, as such love always does. The experience of the world has proved it."

"Oh!" she cried, and her body was rocking. If he did not stop, she would weep herself to death.

"Yes, it seems sad," Tommy continued; "but if ever man knew that it served him right, I know it. And they maintain, the wiseacres who have analyzed love, that there is much to be said in favour of a calm affection. The glory has gone, but the material comforts are greater, and in the end —"

She sank upon the ground. He was bleeding for her, was Tommy. He went on his knees beside her, and it was terrible to him to feel that every part of her was alive with anguish. He called her many sweet names, and she listened for them between her sobs; but still she sobbed.

He could bear it no longer; he cried, and called upon God to smite him. She did not look up, but her poor hands pulled him back. "You said I do not love you the same!" she moaned.

"Grizel!" he answered, as if in sad reproof; "it was not I who said that-it was you. I put into words only what you have been telling me for the last ten minutes."

"No, no," she cried. "Oh, how could I!"

He flung up his arms in despair. "Is this only pity for me, Grizel," he implored, looking into her face as if to learn his fate, "or is it love indeed?"

"You know it is love-you know!"

"But what kind of love?" he demanded fiercely. "Is it the same love that it was? Quick, tell me. I can't have less. If it is but a little less, you will kill me."

The first gleam of sunshine swept across her face (and oh, how he was looking for it!). "Do you want it to be the same-do you really want it? Oh, it is, it is!"

"And you would not cease to love me if you could?"

"No, no, no!" She would have come closer to him, but he held her back.

"One moment, Grizel," he said in a hard voice that filled her with apprehension. "There must be no second mistake. In saying that love, and love alone, brought you back, you are admitting, are you not, that you were talking wildly about loss of pride and honour? You did the loveliest thing you have ever done when you came back. If I were you, my character would be ruined from this hour —I should feel so proud of myself."

She smiled at that, and fondled his hand. "If you think so," she said, "all is well."

But he would not leave it thus. "You must think so also," he insisted; and when she still shook her head, "Then I am proud of your love no longer," said he, doggedly. "How proud of it I have been! A man cannot love a woman without reverencing her, without being touched to the quick a score of times a day by the revelations she gives of herself-revelations of such beauty and purity that he is abashed in her presence. The unspoken prayers he offers up to God at those times he gives to her to carry. And when such a one returns his love, he is proud indeed. To me you are the embodiment of all that is fair in woman, and it is love that has made you so, that has taken away your little imperfections-love for me. Ah, Grizel, I was so proud to think that somehow I had done it; but even now, in the moment when your love has manifested itself most splendidly, you are ashamed of it, and what I respect and reverence you for most are changes that have come about against your will. If your love makes you sorrowful, how can I be proud of it? Henceforth it will be my greatest curse."

She started up, wringing her hands. It was something to have got her to her feet.

"Surely," he said, like one puzzled as well as pained by her obtuseness, "you see clearly that it must be so. True love, as I conceive it, must be something passing all knowledge, irresistible; something not to be resented for its power, but worshipped for it; something not to fight against, but to glory in. And such is your love; but you give the proof of it with shame, because your ideal of love is a humdrum sort of affection. That is all you would like to feel, Grizel, and because you feel something deeper and nobler you say you have lost your self-respect. I am the man who has taken it from you. Can I ever be proud of your love again?"

He paused, overcome with emotion. "What it has been to me!" he cried. "I walked among my fellows as if I were a colossus. It inspired me at my work. I felt that there was nothing great I was not capable of, and all because Grizel loved me."

She stood trembling with delight at what he said, and with apprehension at what he seemed to threaten. His head being bent, he could not see her, and amid his grief he wondered a little what she was doing now.

"But you spoke" —she said it timidly, as if to refer to the matter at all was cruel of her —"you spoke as if I was disgracing you because I could not conceal my love. You said it was hard on you." She pressed her hands together. "Yes, that is what you said."

This was awkward for Tommy. "She believes I meant that," he cried hoarsely. "Grizel believes that of me! I have behaved since then as if that was what I meant, have I? I meant only that it would be hard on me if Elspeth learned of our love at the very moment when this man is treating her basely. I look as if I had meant something worse, do I? I know myself at last! Grizel has shown me what I am."

He covered his face with his hands. Strong man as he was, he could not conceal his agony.

"Don't!" she cried. "If I was wrong —"

"If you were wrong!"

"I was wrong! I know I was wrong. Somehow it was a mistake. I don't know how it arose. But you love me and you want me to love you still. That is all I know. I thought you did not, but you do. If you wanted me to come back — —"

"If I wanted it!"

"I know you wanted it now, and I am no longer ashamed to have come. I am glad I came, and if you can still be proud of my love and respect me — —"

"Oh, Grizel, if!"

"Then I have got back my pride and my self-respect again. I cannot reason about it, but they have come back again."

It was she who was trying to comfort him by this time, caressing his hair and his hands. But he would not be appeased at once; it was good for her to have something to do.

"You are sure you are happy again, Grizel? You are not pretending in order to please me?"

"So happy!"

"But your eyes are still wet."

"That is because I have hurt you so. Oh, how happy I should be if I could see you smile again!"

"How I would smile if I saw you looking happy!"

"Then smile at once, sir," she could say presently, "for see how happy I am looking." And as she beamed on him once more he smiled as well as he was able to. Grizel loved him so much that she actually knew when that face of his was smiling, and soon she was saying gaily to his eyes: "Oh, silly eyes that won't sparkle, what is the use of you?" and she pressed her own upon them; and to his mouth she said: "Mouth that does not know how to laugh-poor, tragic mouth!" He let her do nearly all the talking. She sat there crooning over him as if he were her child.

And so the flag was saved. He begged her to let him tell their little world of his love for her, and especially was he eager to go straight with it to the doctor. But she would not have this. "David and Elspeth shall know in good time," she said, very nobly. "I am sure they are fond of each other, and they shall know of our happiness on the day when they tell us of their own." And until that great day came she was not to look upon herself as engaged to Tommy, and he must never kiss her again until they were engaged. I think it was a pleasure to her to insist on this. It was her punishment to herself for ever having doubted Tommy.

Part II

Chapter XVIII
The Girl She Had Been

As they sat amid the smell of rosin on that summer day, she told him, with a glance that said, "Now you will laugh at me," what had brought her into Caddam Wood.

"I came to rub something out."

He reflected. "A memory?"

"Yes."

"Of me?"

She nodded.

"An unhappy memory?"

"Not to me," she replied, leaning on him. "I have no memory of you I would rub out, no, not the unhappiest one, for it was you, and that makes it dear. All memories, however sad, of loved ones become sweet, don't they, when we get far enough away from them?"

"But to whom, then, is this memory painful, Grizel?"

Again she cast that glance at him. "To her," she whispered.

" 'That little girl'!"

"Yes; the child I used to be. You see, she never grew up, and so they are not distant memories to her. I try to rub them out of her mind by giving her prettier things to think of. I go to the places where she was most unhappy, and tell her sweet things about you. I am not morbid, am I, in thinking of her still as some one apart from myself? You know how it began, in the lonely days when I used to look at her in mamma's mirror, and pity her, and fancy that she was pitying me and entreating me to be careful. Always when I think I see her now, she seems to be looking anxiously at me and saying, 'Oh, do be careful!' And the sweet things I tell her about you are meant to show her how careful I have become. Are you laughing at me for this? I sometimes laugh at it myself."

"No, it is delicious," he answered her, speaking more lightly than he felt. "What a numskull you make, Grizel, of any man who presumes to write about women! I am at school again, and you are Miss Ailie teaching me the alphabet. But I thought you lost that serious little girl on the doleful day when she heard you say that you loved me best."

"She came back. She has no one but me."

"And she still warns you against me?"

Grizel laughed gleefully. "I am too clever for her," she said. "I do all the talking. I allow her to listen only. And you must not blame her for distrusting you; I have said such things against you to her! Oh, the things I said! On the first day I saw you, for instance, after you came back to Thrums. It was in church. Do you remember?"

"I should like to know what you said to her about me that day."

"Would you?" Grizel asked merrily. "Well, let me see. She was not at church-she never went there, you remember; but of course she was curious to hear about you, and I had no sooner got home than she came to me and said, 'Was he there?' 'Yes,' I said. 'Is he much changed?' she asked. 'He has a beard,' I said. 'You know that is not what I really mean,' she said, and then I said, 'I don't think he is so much changed that it is impossible to recognize him again.'"

Tommy interrupted her: "Now what did you mean by that?"

"I meant that I thought you were a little annoyed to find the congregation looking at Gavinia's baby more than at you!"

"Grizel, you are a wretch, but perhaps you were right. Well, what more did the little inquisitor want to know?"

"She asked me if I felt any of my old fear of you, and I said No, and then she clapped her hands with joy. And she asked whether you looked at me as if you were begging me to say I still thought you a wonder, and I said I thought you did ——"

"Grizel!"

"Oh, I told her ever so many dreadful things as soon as I found them out. I told her the whole story of your ankle, sir, for instance."

"On my word, Grizel, you seem to have omitted nothing!"

"Ah, but I did," she cried. "I never told her how much I wanted you to be admirable; I pretended that I despised you merely, and in reality I was wringing my hands with woe every time you did not behave like a god."

"They will be worn away, Grizel, if you go on doing that."

"I don't think so," she replied, "nor can she think so if she believes half of what I have told her about you since. She knows how you saved the boy's life. I told her that in the old Lair because she had some harsh memories of you there; and it was at the Cuttle Well that I told her about the glove."

"And where," asked Tommy, severely, "did you tell her that you had been mistaken in thinking me jealous of a baby and anxious to be considered a wonder?"

She hid her face for a moment, and then looked up roguishly into his. "I have not told her that yet!" she replied. It was so audacious of her that he took her by the ears.

"If I were vain," Tommy said reflectively, "I would certainly shake you now. You show a painful want of tact, Grizel, in implying that I am not perfect. Nothing annoys men so much. We can stand anything except that."

His merriness gladdened her. "They are only little things," she said, "and I have grown to love them. I know they are flaws; but I love them because — —"

"Say because they are mine. You owe me that."

"No; but because they are weaknesses I don't have. I have others, but not those, and it is sweet to me to know that you are weak in some matters in which I am strong. It makes me feel that I can be of use to you."

"Are you insinuating that there are more of them?" Tommy demanded, sitting up.

"You are not very practical," she responded, "and I am."

"Go on."

"And you are-just a little-inclined to be senti — —"

"Hush! I don't allow that word; but you may say, if you choose, that I am sometimes carried away by a too generous impulse."

"And that it will be my part," said she, "to seize you by the arm and hold you back. Oh, you will give me a great deal to do! That is one of the things I love you for. It was one of the things I loved my dear Dr. McQueen for." She looked up suddenly. "I have told him also about you."

"Lately, Grizel?"

"Yes, in my parlour. It was his parlour, you know, and I had kept nothing from him while he was alive; that is to say, he always knew what I was thinking of, and I like to fancy that he knows still. In the evenings he used to sit in the arm-chair by the fire, and I sat talking or knitting at his feet, and if I ceased to do anything except sit still, looking straight before me, he knew I was thinking the morbid thoughts that had troubled me in the old days at Double Dykes. Without knowing it I sometimes shuddered at those times, and he was distressed. It reminded him of my mamma."

"I understand," Tommy said hurriedly. He meant: "Let us avoid painful subjects."

"I sit still by his arm-chair and tell him what is happening to his Grizel."

"It is years," she went on, "since those thoughts have troubled me, and it was he who drove them away. He was so kind! He thought so much of my future that I still sit by his arm-chair and tell him what is happening to his Grizel. I don't speak aloud, of course; I scarcely say the words to myself even; and yet we seem to have long talks together. I told him I had given you his coat."

278

"Well, I don't think he was pleased at that, Grizel. I have had a feeling for some time that the coat dislikes me. It scratched my hand the first time I put it on. My hand caught in the hook of the collar, you will say; but no, that is not what I think. In my opinion, the deed was maliciously done. McQueen always distrusted me, you know, and I expect his coat was saying, 'Hands off my Grizel.'"

She took it as quite a jest. "He does not distrust you now," she said, smiling. "I have told him what I think of you, and though he was surprised at first, in the end his opinion was the same as mine."

"Ah, you saw to that, Grizel!"

"I had nothing to do with it. I merely told him everything, and he had to agree with me. How could he doubt when he saw that you had made me so happy! Even mamma does not doubt."

"You have told her! All this is rather eerie, Grizel."

"You are not sorry, are you?" she asked, looking at him anxiously. "Dr. McQueen wanted me to forget her. He thought that would be best for me. It was the only matter on which we differed. I gave up speaking of her to him. You are the only person I have mentioned her to since I became a woman; but I often think of her. I am sure there was a time, before I was old enough to understand, when she was very fond of me. I was her baby, and women can't help being fond of their babies, even though they should never have had them. I think she often hugged me tight."

"Need we speak of this, Grizel?"

"For this once," she entreated. "You must remember that mamma often looked at me with hatred, and said I was the cause of all her woe; but sometimes in her last months she would give me such sad looks that I trembled, and I felt that she was picturing me growing into the kind of woman she wished so much she had not become herself, and that she longed to save me. That is why I have told her that a good man loves me. She is so glad, my poor dear mamma, that I tell her again and again, and she loves to hear it as much as I to tell it. What she loves to hear most is that you really do want to marry me. She is so fond of hearing that because it is what my father would never say to her."

Tommy was so much moved that he could not speak, but in his heart he gave thanks that what Grizel said of him to her mamma was true at last.

"It makes her so happy," Grizel said, "that when I seem to see her now she looks as sweet and pure as she must have been in the days when she was an innocent girl. I think she can enter into my feelings more than any other person could ever do. Is that because she was my mother? She understands how I feel just as I can understand how in the end she was willing to be bad because he wanted it so much."

"No, no, Grizel," Tommy cried passionately, "you don't understand that!"

She rocked her arms. "Yes, I do," she said; "I do. I could never have cared for such a man; but I can understand how mamma yielded to him, and I have no feeling for her except pity, and I have told her so, and it is what she loves to hear her daughter tell her best of all."

They put the subject from them, and she told him what it was that she had come to rub out in Caddam. If you have read of Tommy's boyhood you may remember the day it ended with his departure for the farm, and that he and Elspeth walked through Caddam to the cart that was to take him from her, and how, to comfort her, he swore that he loved her with his whole heart, and Grizel not at all, and that Grizel was in the wood and heard. And how Elspeth had promised to wave to Tommy in the cart as long as it was visible, but broke down and went home sobbing, and how Grizel took her place and waved, pretending to be Elspeth, so that he might think she was bearing up bravely. Tommy had not known what Grizel did for him that day, and when he heard it now for the first time from her own lips, he realized afresh what a glorious girl she was and had always been.

"You may try to rub that memory out of little Grizel's head," he declared, looking very proudly at her, "but you shall never rub it out of mine."

It was by his wish that they went together to the spot where she had heard him say that he loved Elspeth only —"if you can find it," Tommy said, "after all these years"; and she smiled at his mannish words-she had found it so often since! There was the very clump of whin.

And here was the boy to match. Oh, who by striving could make himself a boy again as Tommy could! I tell you he was always irresistible then. What is genius? It is the power to be a boy again at will. When I think of him flinging off the years and whistling childhood back, not to himself only, but to all who heard, distributing it among them gaily, imperiously calling on them to dance, dance, for they are boys and girls again until they stop-when to recall him in those wild moods is to myself to grasp for a moment at the dear dead days that were so much the best, I cannot wonder that Grizel loved him. I am his slave myself; I see that all that was wrong with Tommy was that he could not always be a boy.

"Hide there again, Grizel," he cried to her, little Tommy cried to her, Stroke the Jacobite, her captain, cried to the Lady Griselda; and he disappeared, and presently marched down the path with an imaginary Elspeth by his side. "I love you both, Elspeth," he was going to say, "and my love for the one does not make me love the other less"; but he glanced at Grizel, and she was leaning forward to catch his words as if this were no play, but life or death, and he knew what she longed to hear him say, and he said it: "I love you very much, Elspeth, but however much I love you, it would be idle to pretend that I don't love Grizel more."

A stifled cry of joy came from a clump of whin hard by, and they were man and woman again.

"Did you not know it, Grizel?"

"No, no; you never told me."

"I never dreamed it was necessary to tell you."

"Oh, if you knew how I have longed that it might be so, yes, and sometimes hated Elspeth because I feared it could not be! I have tried so hard to be content with second place. I have thought it all out, and said to myself it was natural that Elspeth should be first."

"My tragic love," he said, "I can see you arguing in that way, but I don't see you convincing yourself. My passionate Grizel is not the girl to accept second place from anyone. If I know anything of her, I know that."

To his surprise, she answered softly: "You are wrong. I wonder at it myself, but I had made up my mind to be content with second place, and to be grateful for it."

"I could not have believed it!" he cried.

"I could not have believed it myself," said she.

"Are you the Grizel ——" he began.

"No," she said, "I have changed a little," and she looked pathetically at him.

"It stabs me," he said, "to see you so humble."

"I am humbler than I was," she answered huskily, but she was looking at him with the fondest love.

"Don't look at me so, Grizel," he implored. "I am unworthy of it. I am the man who has made you so humble."

"Yes," she answered, and still she looked at him with the fondest love. A film came over his eyes, and she touched them softly with her handkerchief.

"Those eyes that but a little while ago were looking so coldly at you!" he said.

"Dear eyes!" said she.

"Though I were to strike you ——" he cried, raising his hand.

She took the hand in hers and kissed it.

"Has it come to this!" he said, and as she could not speak, she nodded. He fell upon his knees before her.

"I am glad you are a little sorry," she said; "I am a little sorry myself."

Chapter XIX
Of the Change in Thomas

To find ways of making David propose to Elspeth, of making Elspeth willing to exchange her brother for David-they were heavy tasks, but Tommy yoked himself to them gallantly and tugged like an Arab steed in the plough. It should be almost as pleasant to us as to him to think that love was what made him do it, for he was sure he loved Grizel at last, and that the one longing of his heart was to marry her; the one marvel to him was that he had ever longed ardently for anything else. Well, as you know, she longed for it also, but she was firm in her resolve that until Elspeth was engaged Tommy should be a single man. She even made him promise not to kiss her again so long as their love had to be kept secret. "It will be so sweet to wait," she said bravely. As we shall see presently, his efforts to put Elspeth into the hands of David were apparently of no avail, but though this would have embittered many men, it drew only to the surface some of Tommy's noblest attributes; as he suffered in silence he became gentler, more considerate, and acquired a new command over himself. To conquer self for her sake (this is in the "Letters to a Young Man") is the highest tribute a man can pay to a woman; it is the only real greatness, and Tommy had done it now. I could give you a score of proofs. Let us take his treatment of Aaron Latta.

One day about this time Tommy found himself alone in the house with Aaron, and had he been the old Tommy he would have waited but a moment to let Aaron decide which of them should go elsewhere. It was thus that these two, ever so uncomfortable in each other's presence, contrived to keep the peace. Now note the change.

"Aaron," said Tommy, in the hush that had fallen on that house since quiet Elspeth left it, "I have never thanked you in words for all that you have done for me and Elspeth."

"Dinna do it now, then," replied the warper, fidgeting.

"I must," Tommy said cheerily, "I must"; and he did, while Aaron scowled.

"It was never done for you," Aaron informed him, "nor for the father you are the marrows o'."

"It was done for my mother," said Tommy, reverently.

"I'm none so sure o't," Aaron rapped out. "I think I brocht you twa here as bairns, that the reminder of my shame should ever stand before me."

But Tommy shook his head, and sat down sympathetically beside the warper. "You loved her, Aaron," he said simply. "It was an undying love that made you adopt her orphan children." A charming thought came to him. "When you brought us here," he said, with some elation, "Elspeth used to cry at nights because our mother's spirit did not come to us to comfort us, and I invented boyish explanations to appease her. But I have learned since why we did not see that spirit; for though it hovered round this house, its first thought was not for us, but for him who succoured us."

He could have made it much better had he been able to revise it, but surely it was touching, and Aaron need not have said "Damn," which was what he did say.

One knows how most men would have received so harsh an answer to such gentle words, and we can conceive how a very holy man, say a monk, would have bowed to it. Even as the monk did Tommy submit, or say rather with the meekness of a nun.

"I wish I could help you in any way, Aaron," he said, with a sigh.

"You can," replied Aaron, promptly, "by taking yourself off to London, and leaving Elspeth here wi' me. I never made pretence that I wanted you, except because she wouldna come without you. Laddie and man, as weel you ken, you were aye a scunner to me."

"And yet," said Tommy, looking at him admiringly, "you fed and housed and educated us. Ah, Aaron, do you not see that your dislike gives me the more reason only to esteem you?" Carried away by desire to help the old man, he put his hand kindly on his shoulder. "You have never respected yourself," he said, "since the night you and my mother parted at the Cuttle Well, and my heart bleeds to think of it. Many a year ago, by your kindness to two forlorn children, you expiated that sin, and it is blotted out from your account. Forget it, Aaron, as every other person has forgotten it, and let the spirit of Jean Myles see you tranquil once again."

He patted Aaron affectionately; he seemed to be the older of the two.

"Tak' your hand off my shuther," Aaron cried fiercely.

Tommy removed his hand, but he continued to look yearningly at the warper. Another beautiful thought came to him.

"What are you looking so holy about?" asked Aaron, with misgivings.

"Aaron," cried Tommy, suddenly inspired, "you are not always the gloomy man you pass for being. You have glorious moments still. You wake in the morning, and for a second of time you are in the heyday of your youth, and you and Jean Myles are to walk out to-night. As you sit by this fire you think you hear her hand on the latch of the door; as you pass down the street you seem to see her coming towards you. It is for a moment only, and then you are a gray-haired man again, and she has been in her grave for many a year; but you have that moment."

Aaron rose, amazed and wrathful. "The de'il tak' you," he cried, "how did you find out that?"

Perhaps Tommy's nose turned up rapturously in reply, for the best of us cannot command ourselves altogether at great moments, but when he spoke he was modest again.

"It was sympathy that told me," he explained; "and, Aaron, if you will only believe me, it tells me also that a little of the man you were still clings to you. Come out of the moroseness in which you have enveloped yourself so long. Think what a joy it would be to Elspeth."

"It's little she would care."

"If you want to hurt her, tell her so."

"I'm no denying but what she's fell fond o' me."

"Then for her sake," Tommy pleaded.

But the warper turned on him with baleful eyes. "She likes me," he said in a grating voice, "and yet I'm as nothing to her; we are all as nothing to her beside you. If there hadna been you I should hae become the father to her I craved to be; but you had mesmerized her; she had eyes for none but you. I sent you to the herding, meaning to break your power over her, and all she could think o' was my cruelty in sindering you. Syne you ran aff wi' her to London, stealing her frae me. I was without her while she was growing frae lassie to woman, the years when maybe she could hae made o' me what she willed. Magerful Tam took the mother frae me, and he lived again in you to tak' the dochter."

"You really think me masterful-me!" Tommy said, smiling.

"I suppose you never were!" Aaron replied ironically.

"Yes," Tommy admitted frankly, "I was masterful as a boy, ah, and even quite lately. How we change!" he said musingly.

"How we dinna change!" retorted Aaron, bitterly. He had learned the truer philosophy.

"Man," he continued, looking Tommy over, "there's times when I see mair o' your mother than your father in you. She was a wonder at making believe. The letters about her grandeur that she wrote to Thrums when she was starving! Even you couldna hae wrote them better. But she never managed to cheat hersel'. That's whaur you sail away frae her."

"I used to make believe, Aaron, as you say," Tommy replied sadly. "If you knew how I feel the folly of it now, perhaps even you would wish that I felt it less.

"But we must each of us dree his own weird," he proceeded, with wonderful sweetness, when Aaron did not answer. "And so far, at least, as Elspeth is concerned, surely I have done my duty. I had the bringing up of her from the days when she was learning to speak."

"She got into the way o' letting you do everything for her," the warper responded sourly. "You thought for her, you acted for her, frae the first; you toomed her, and then filled her up wi' yoursel'."

"She always needed some one to lean on."

"Ay, because you had maimed her. She grew up in the notion that you were all the earth and the wonder o' the world."

"Could I help that?"

"Help it! Did you try? It was the one thing you were sure o' yoursel'; it was the one thing you thought worth anybody's learning. You stood before her crowing the whole day. I said the now I wished you would go and leave her wi' me: but I wouldna dare to keep her; she's helpless without you; if you took your arm awa frae her now, she would tumble to the ground."

"I fear it is true, Aaron," Tommy said, with bent head. "Whether she is so by nature, or whether I have made her so, I cannot tell, but I fear that what you say is true."

"It's true," said Aaron, "and yours is the wite. There's no life for her now except what you mak'; she canna see beyond you. Go on thinking yoursel' a wonder if you like, but mind this: if you were to cast her off frae you now, she would die like an amputated hand."

To Tommy it was like listening to his doom. Ah, Aaron, even you could not withhold your pity, did you know how this man is being punished now for having made Elspeth so dependent on him! Some such thought passed through Tommy's head, but he was too brave to appeal for pity. "If that is so," he said firmly, "I take the responsibility for it. But I began this talk, Aaron, not to intrude my troubles on you, but hoping to lighten yours. If I could see you smile, Aaron — —"

"Drop it!" cried the warper; and then, going closer to him: "You would hae seen me smile, ay, and heard me laugh, gin you had been here when Mrs. McLean came yont to read your book to me. She fair insistit on reading the terrible noble bits to me, and she grat they were so sublime; but the sublimer they were, the mair I laughed, for I ken you, Tommy, my man, I ken you."

He spoke with much vehemence, and, after all, our hero was not perfect. He withdrew stiffly to the other room. I think it was the use of the word Tommy that enraged him.

But in a very few minutes he scorned himself, and was possessed by a pensive wonder that one so tragically fated as he could resent an old man's gibe. Aaron misunderstood him. Was that any reason why he should not feel sorry for Aaron? He crossed the hallan to the kitchen door, and stopped there, overcome with pity. The warper was still crouching by the fire, but his head rested on his chest; he was a weary, desolate figure, and at the other side of the hearth stood an empty chair. The picture was the epitome of his life, or so it seemed to the sympathetic soul at the door, who saw him passing from youth to old age, staring at the chair that must always be empty. At the same moment Tommy saw his own future, and in it, too, an empty chair. Yet, hard as was his own case, at least he knew that he was loved; if her chair must be empty, the fault was as little hers as his, while Aaron — —

A noble compassion drew him forward, and he put his hand determinedly on the dear old man's shoulder.

"Aaron," he said, in a tremble of pity, "I know what is the real sorrow of your life, and I rejoice because I can put an end to it. You think that Jean Myles never cared for you; but you are strangely wrong. I was with my mother to the last, Aaron, and I can tell you, she asked me with her dying breath to say to you that she loved you all the time."

Aaron tried to rise, but was pushed back into his chair. "Love cannot die," cried Tommy, triumphantly, like the fairy in the pantomime; "love is always young — —"

He stopped in mid-career at sight of Aaron's disappointing face. "Are you done?" the warper inquired. "When you and me are alane in this house there's no room for the both o' us, and as I'll never hae it said that I made Jean Myles's bairn munt, I'll go out mysel'."

And out he went, and sat on the dyke till Elspeth came home. It did not turn Tommy sulky. He nodded kindly to Aaron from the window in token of forgiveness, and next day he spent a valuable hour in making a cushion for the old man's chair. "He must be left with the impression that you made it," Tommy explained to Elspeth, "for he would not take it from me."

"Oh, Tommy, how good you are!"

"I am far from it, Elspeth."

"There is a serenity about you nowadays," she said, "that I don't seem to have noticed before," and indeed this was true; it was the serenity that comes to those who, having a mortal wound, can no more be troubled by the pinpricks.

"There has been nothing to cause it, has there?" Elspeth asked timidly.

"Only the feeling that I have much to be grateful for," he replied. "I have you, Elspeth."

"And I have you," she said, "and I want no more. I could never care for anyone as I care for you, Tommy."

She was speaking unselfishly; she meant to imply delicately that the doctor's defection need not make Tommy think her unhappy. "Are you glad?" she asked.

He said Yes bravely. Elspeth, he was determined, should never have the distress of knowing that for her sake he was giving up the one great joy which life contains. He was a grander character than most. Men have often in the world's history made a splendid sacrifice for women, but if you turn up the annals you will find that the woman nearly always knew of it.

He told Grizel what Aaron had said and what Elspeth had said. He could keep nothing from her now; he was done with the world of make-believe for ever. And it seemed wicked of him to hope, he declared, or to let her hope. "I ought to give you up, Grizel," he said, with a groan.

"I won't let you," she replied adorably.

"Gemmell has not come near us for a week. I ask him in, but he avoids the house."

"I don't understand it," Grizel had to admit; "but I think he is fond of her, I do indeed."

"Even if that were so, I fear she would not accept him. I know Elspeth so well that I feel I am deceiving you if I say there is any hope."

"Nevertheless you must say it," she answered brightly; "you must say it and leave me to think it. And I do think it. I believe that Elspeth, despite her timidity and her dependence on you, is like other girls at heart, and not more difficult to win."

"And even if it all comes to nothing," she told him, a little faintly, "I shall not be unhappy. You don't really know me if you think I should love to be married so-so much as all that."

"It is you, Grizel," he replied, "who don't see that it is myself I am pitying. It is I who want to be married as much as all that."

Her eyes shone with a soft light, for of course it was what she wanted him to say. These two seemed to have changed places. That people could love each other, and there the end, had been his fond philosophy and her torment. Now, it was she who argued for it and Tommy who shook his head.

"They can be very, very happy."

"No," he said.

"But one of them is."

"Not the other," he insisted; and of course it was again what she wanted him to say.

And he was not always despairing. He tried hard to find a way of bringing David to Elspeth's feet, and once, at least, the apparently reluctant suitor almost succumbed. Tommy had met him near Aaron's house, and invited him to come in and hear Elspeth singing. "I did not know she sang," David said, hesitating.

"She is so shy about it," Tommy replied lightly, "that we can hear her by stealth only. Aaron and I listen at the door. Come and listen at the door."

And David had yielded and listened at the door, and afterwards gone in and remained like one who could not tear himself away. What was more, he and Elspeth had touched upon the subject of love in their conversation, Tommy sitting at the window so engrossed in a letter to Pym that he seemed to hear nothing, though he could repeat everything afterwards to Grizel.

Elspeth had said, in her shrinking way, that if she were a man she could love only a woman who was strong and courageous and helpful-such a woman as Grizel, she had said.

"And yet," David replied, "women have been loved who had none of those qualities."

"In spite of the want of them?" Elspeth asked.

"Perhaps because of it," said he.

"They are noble qualities," Elspeth maintained a little sadly, and he assented. "And one of them, at least, is essential," she said. "A woman has no right to be loved who is not helpful."

"She is helpful to the man who loves her," David replied.

"He would have to do for her," Elspeth said, "the very things she should be doing for him."

"He may want very much to do them," said David.

"Then it is her weakness that appeals to him. Is not that loving her for the wrong thing?"

"It may be the right thing," David insisted, "for him."

"And at that point," Tommy said, boyishly, to Grizel, "I ceased to hear them, I was so elated; I felt that everything was coming right. I could not give another thought to their future, I was so busy mapping out my own. I heard a hammering. Do you know what it was? It was our house going up-your house and mine; our home, Grizel! It was not here, nor in London. It was near the Thames. I wanted it to be upon the bank, but you said No, you were afraid of floods. I wanted to superintend the building, but you conducted me contemptuously to my desk. You intimated that I did not know how to build-that no one knew except yourself. You instructed the architect, and bullied the workmen, and cried for more store-closets. Grizel, I saw the house go up; I saw you the adoration and terror of your servants; I heard you singing from room to room."

He was touched by this; all beautiful thoughts touched him.

But as a rule, though Tommy tried to be brave for her sake, it was usually she who was the comforter now, and he the comforted, and this was the arrangement that suited Grizel best. Her one thought need no longer be that she loved him too much, but how much he loved her. It was not her self-respect that must be humoured back, but his. If hers lagged, what did it matter? What are her own troubles to a woman when there is something to do for the man she loves?

"You are too anxious about the future," she said to him, if he had grown gloomy again. "Can we not be happy in the present, and leave the future to take care of itself?" How strange to know that it was Grizel who said this to Tommy, and not Tommy who said it to Grizel!

She delighted in playing the mother to him. "Now you must go back to your desk," she would say masterfully. "You have three hours' work to do to-night yet."

"It can wait. Let me stay a little longer with you, Grizel," he answered humbly. Ha! it was Tommy who was humble now. Not so long ago he would not have allowed his work to wait for anyone, and Grizel knew it, and exulted.

"To work, sir," she ordered. "And you must put on your old coat before you sit down to write, and pull up your cuffs so that they don't scrape on the desk. Also, you must not think too much about me."

She tried to look businesslike, but she could scarce resist rocking her arms with delight when she heard herself saying such things to him. It was as if she had the old doctor once more in her hands.

"What more, Grizel? I like you to order me about."

"Only this. Good afternoon."

"But I am to walk home with you," he entreated.

"No," she said decisively; but she smiled: once upon a time it had been she who asked for this.

"If you are good," she said, "you shall perhaps see me to-morrow."

"Perhaps only?" He was scared; but she smiled happily again: it had once been she who had to beg that there should be no perhaps.

"If you are good," she replied, —"and you are not good when you have such a long face. Smile, you silly boy; smile when I order you. If you don't I shall not so much as look out at my window to-morrow."

He was the man who had caused her so much agony, and she was looking at him with the eternally forgiving smile of the mother. "Ah, Grizel," Tommy cried passionately, "how brave and unselfish and noble you are, and what a glorious wife God intended you to be!"

She broke from him with a little cry, but when she turned round again it was to nod and smile to him.

Chapter XX
A Love-Letter

Some beautiful days followed, so beautiful to Grizel that as they passed away she kissed her hand to them. Do you see her standing on tiptoe to see the last of them? They lit a fire in the chamber of her soul which is the home of all pure maids, and the fagots that warmed Grizel were every fond look that had been on her lover's face and every sweet word he had let fall. She counted and fondled them, and pretended that one was lost that she might hug it more than all the others when it was found. To sit by that fire was almost better than having the days that lit it; sometimes she could scarcely wait for the day to go.

Tommy's fond looks and sweet words! There was also a letter in those days, and, now that I remember, a little garnet ring; and there were a few other fagots, but all so trifling it must seem incredible to you that they could have made so great a blaze-nothing else in it, on my honour, except a girl's heart added by herself that the fire might burn a moment longer.

And now, what so chilly as the fire that has gone out! Gone out long ago, dear Grizel, while you crouched over it. You may put your hand in the ashes; they will not burn you now. Ah, Grizel, why do you sit there in the cold?

The day of the letter! It began in dread, but ended so joyfully, do you think Grizel grudged the dread? It became dear to her; she loved to return to it and gaze at the joy it glorified, as one sees the sunshine from a murky room. When she heard the postman's knock she was not even curious; so few letters came to her, she thought this must be Maggy Ann's monthly one from Aberdeen, and went on placidly dusting. At last she lifted it from the floor, for it had been slipped beneath the door, and then Grizel was standing in her little lobby, panting as if at the end of a race. The letter lay in both her hands, and they rose slowly until they were pressed against her breast.

She uttered some faint cries (it was the only moment in which I have known Grizel to be hysterical), and then she ran to her room and locked herself in-herself and it. Do you know why that look of elation had come suddenly to her face? It was because he had not even written the address in a disguised hand to deceive the postmistress. So much of the old Grizel was gone that the pathos of her elation over this was lost to her.

Several times she almost opened it. Why did she pause? why had that frightened look come into her eyes? She put the letter on her table and drew away from it. If she took a step nearer, her hands went behind her back as if saying, "Grizel, don't ask us to open it; we are afraid."

Perhaps it really did say the dear things that love writes. Perhaps it was aghast at the way she was treating it. Dear letter! Her mouth smiled to it, but her hands remained afraid. As she stood irresolute, smiling, and afraid, she was a little like her mother. I have put off as long as possible saying that Grizel was ever like her mother. The Painted Lady had never got any letters while she was in Thrums, but she looked wistfully at those of other people. "They are so pretty," she had said; "but don't open them: when you open them they break your heart." Grizel remembered what her mother had said.

Had the old Grizel feared what might be inside, it would have made her open the letter more quickly. Two minds to one person were unendurable to her. But she seemed to be a coward now. It was pitiable.

Perhaps it was quite a common little letter, beginning "Dear Grizel," and saying nothing more delicious or more terrible than that he wanted her to lend him one of the doctor's books. She thought of a score of trivialities it might be about; but the letter was still unopened when David Gemmell called to talk over some cases in which he required her counsel. He found her sitting listlessly, something in her lap which she at once concealed. She failed to follow his arguments, and he went away puckering his brows, some of the old doctor's sayings about her ringing loud in his ears.

One of them was: "Things will be far wrong with Grizel when she is able to sit idle with her hands in her lap."

Another: "She is almost pitifully straightforward, man. Everything that is in Grizel must out. She can hide nothing."

Yet how cunningly she had concealed what was in her hands. Cunning applied to Grizel! David shuddered. He thought of Tommy, and shut his mouth tight. He could do this easily. Tommy could not do it without feeling breathless. They were types of two kinds of men.

David also remembered a promise he had given McQueen, and wondered, as he had wondered a good deal of late, whether the time had come to keep it.

But Grizel sat on with her unopened letter. She was to meet Tommy presently on the croquet lawn of the Dovecot, when Ailie was to play Mr. James (the champion), and she decided that she must wait till then. She would know what sort of letter it was the moment she saw his face. And then! She pressed her hands together.

Oh, how base of her to doubt him! She said it to herself then and often afterwards. She looked mournfully in her mother's long mirror at this disloyal Grizel, as if the capacity to doubt him was the saddest of all the changes that had come to her. He had been so true yesterday; oh, how could she tremble to-day? Beautiful yesterday! but yesterday may seem so long ago. How little a time had passed between the moment when she was greeting him joyously in Caddam Wood and that cry of the heart, "How could you hurt your Grizel so!" No, she could not open her letter. She could kiss it, but she could not open it.

Foolish fears! for before she had shaken hands with Tommy in Mrs. McLean's garden she knew he loved her still, and that the letter proved it. She was properly punished, yet surely in excess, for when she might have been reading her first love-letter, she had to join in discussions with various ladies about Berlin wool and the like, and to applaud the prowess of Mr. James with the loathly croquet mallet. It seemed quite a long time before Tommy could get a private word with her. Then he began about the letter at once.

"You are not angry with me for writing it?" he asked anxiously. "I should not have done it; I had no right: but such a desire to do it came over me, I had to; it was such a glory to me to say in writing what you are to me."

She smiled happily. Oh, exquisite day! "I have so long wanted to have a letter from you," she said. "I have almost wished you would go away for a little time, so that I might have a letter from you."

He had guessed this. He had written to give her delight.

"Did you like the first words of it, Grizel?" he asked eagerly.

The lover and the artist spoke together.

Could she admit that the letter was unopened, and why? Oh, the pain to him! She nodded assent. It was not really an untruth, she told herself. She did like them-oh, how she liked them, though she did not know what they were!

"I nearly began 'My beloved,'" he said solemnly.

Somehow she had expected it to be this. "Why didn't you?" she asked, a little disappointed.

"I like the other so much better," he replied. "To write it was so delicious to me, I thought you would not mind."

"I don't mind," she said hastily. (What could it be?)

"But you would have preferred 'beloved'?"

"It is such a sweet name."

"Surely not so sweet as the other, Grizel?"

"No," she said, "no." (Oh, what could it be!)

"Have you destroyed it?" he asked, and the question was a shock to her. Her hand rose instinctively to defend something that lay near her heart.

"I could not," she whispered.

"Do you mean you wanted to?" he asked dolefully.

"I thought you wanted it," she murmured.

"I!" he cried, aghast, and she was joyous again.

"Can't you guess where it is?" she said.

He understood. "Grizel! You carry my letter there!"

She was full of glee; but she puzzled him presently.

"Do you think I could go now?" she inquired eagerly.

"And leave me?"

It was dreadful of her, but she nodded.

"I want to go home."

"Is it not home, Grizel, when you are with me?"

"I want to go away from home, then." She said it as if she loved to tantalize him.

"But why?"

"I won't tell you." She was looking wistfully at the door. "I have something to do."

"It can wait."

"It has waited too long." He might have heard an assenting rustle from beneath her bodice. "Do let me go," she said coaxingly, as if he held her.

"I can't understand ——" he began, and broke off. She was facing him demurely but exultantly, challenging him, he could see, to read her now. "Just when I am flattering myself that I know everything about you, Grizel," he said, with a long face, "I suddenly wonder whether I know anything."

She would have liked to clap her hands. "You must remember that we have changed places," she told him. "It is I who understand you now."

"And I am devoutly glad," he made answer, with humble thankfulness. "And I must ask you, Grizel, why you want to run away from me."

"But you think you know," she retorted smartly. "You think I want to read my letter again!"

Her cleverness staggered him. "But I am right, am I not, Grizel?"

"No," she said triumphantly, "you are quite wrong. Oh, if you knew how wrong you are!" And having thus again unhorsed him, she made her excuses to Ailie and slipped away. Dr. Gemmell, who was present and had been watching her narrowly, misread the flush on her face and her restless desire to be gone.

"Is there anything between those two, do you think?" Mrs. McLean had said in a twitter to him while Tommy and Grizel were talking, and he had answered No almost sharply.

"People are beginning to think there is," she said in self-defence.

"They are mistaken," he told her curtly, and it was about this time that Grizel left. David followed her to her home soon afterwards, and Maggy Ann, who answered his summons, did not accompany him upstairs. He was in the house daily, and she left him to find Grizel for himself. He opened the parlour door almost as he knocked, and she was there, but had not heard him. He stopped short, like one who had blundered unawares on what was not for him.

She was on her knees on the hearth-rug, with her head buried in what had been Dr. McQueen's chair. Ragged had been the seat of it on the day when she first went to live with him, but very early on the following morning, or, to be precise, five minutes after daybreak, he had risen to see if there were burglars in the parlour, and behold, it was his grateful little maid repadding the old arm-chair. How a situation repeats itself! Without disturbing her, the old doctor had slipped away with a full heart. It was what the young doctor did now.

But the situation was not quite the same. She had been bubbling over with glee then; she was sobbing now. David could not know that it was a sob of joy; he knew only that he had never seen her crying before, and that it was the letter in her hands that had brought tears at last to those once tranquil and steadfast eyes.

In an odd conversation which had once taken place in that room between the two doctors, Gemmell had said: "But the time may come without my knowing it." And McQueen's reply was: "I don't think so, for she is so open; but I'll tell you this, David, as a guide. I never saw her eyes wet. It is one of the touching things about her that she has the eyes of a man, to whom it is a shame to cry. If you ever see her greeting, David, I'm sore doubting that the time will have come."

As David Gemmell let himself softly out of the house, to return to it presently, he thought the time had come. What he conceived he had to do was a hard thing, but he never thought of not doing it. He had kept himself in readiness to do it for many days now, and he walked to it as firmly as if he were on his professional rounds. He did not know that the skin round his eyes had contracted, giving them the look of pain which always came there when he was sorry or pitiful or indignant. He was not well acquainted with his eyes, and, had he glanced at them now in a glass, would have presumed that this was their usual expression.

Grizel herself opened the door to him this time, and "Maggy Ann, he is found!" she cried victoriously. Evidently she had heard of his previous visit. "We have searched every room in the house for you," she said gaily, "and had you disappeared for much longer, Maggy Ann would have had the carpets up."

He excused himself on the ground that he had forgotten something, and she chided him merrily for being forgetful. As he sat with her David could have groaned aloud. How vivacious she had become! but she was sparkling in false colours. After what he knew had been her distress of a few minutes ago, it was a painted face to him. She was trying to deceive him. Perhaps she suspected that he had seen her crying, and now, attired in all a woman's wiles, she was defying him to believe his eyes.

Grizel garbed in wiles! Alack the day! She was shielding the man, and Gemmell could have driven her away roughly to get at him. But she was also standing over her own pride, lest anyone should see that it had fallen; and do you think that David would have made her budge an inch?

Of course she saw that he had something on his mind. She knew those puckered eyes so well, and had so often smoothed them for him.

"What is it, David?" she asked sympathetically. "I see you have come as a patient to-night."

"As one of those patients," he rejoined, "who feel better at mere sight of the doctor."

"Fear of the prescription?" said she.

"Not if you prescribe yourself, Grizel."

"David!" she cried. He had been paying compliments!

"I mean it."

"So I can see by your face. Oh, David, how stern you look!"

"Dr. McQueen and I," he retorted, "used to hold private meetings after you had gone to bed, at which we agreed that you should no longer be allowed to make fun of us. They came to nothing. Do you know why?"

"Because I continued to do it?"

"No; but because we missed it so much if you stopped."

"You are nice to-night, David," she said, dropping him a courtesy.

"We liked all your bullying ways," he went on. "We were children in your masterful hands."

"I was a tyrant, David," she said, looking properly ashamed. "I wonder you did not marry, just to get rid of me."

"Have you ever seriously wondered why I don't marry?" he asked quickly.

"Oh, David," she exclaimed, "what else do you think your patients and I talk of when I am trying to nurse them? It has agitated the town ever since you first walked up the Marrywellbrae, and we can't get on with our work for thinking of it."

"Seriously, Grizel?"

She became grave at once. "If you could find the right woman," she said wistfully.

"I have found her," he answered; and then she pressed her hands together, too excited to speak.

"If she would only care a little for me," he said.

Grizel rocked her arms. "I am sure she does," she cried. "David, I am so glad!"

He saw what her mistake was, but pretended not to know that she had made one. "Are you really glad that I love you, Grizel?" he asked.

It seemed to daze her for a moment. "Not me, David," she said softly, as if correcting him. "You don't mean that it is me?" she said coaxingly. "David," she cried, "say it is not me!"

He drooped his head, but not before he had seen all the brightness die out of her face. "Is it so painful to you even to hear me say it?" he asked gravely.

Her joy had been selfish as her sorrow was. For nigh a minute she had been thinking of herself alone, it meant so much to her; but now she jumped up and took his hand in hers.

"Poor David!" she said, making much of his hand as if she had hurt it. But David Gemmell's was too simple a face to oppose to her pitying eyes, and presently she let his hand slip from her and stood regarding him curiously. He had to look another way, and then she even smiled, a little forlornly.

"Do you mind talking it over with me, Grizel?" he asked. "I have always been well aware that you did not care for me in that way, but nevertheless I believe you might do worse."

"No woman could do better," she answered gravely. "I should like you to talk it over, David, if you begin at the beginning"; and she sat down with her hands crossed.

"I won't say what a good thing it would be for me," was his beginning; "we may take that for granted."

"I don't think we can," she remarked; "but it scarcely matters at present. That is not the beginning, David."

He was very anxious to make it the beginning.

"I am weary of living in lodgings," he said. "The practice suffers by my not being married. Many patients dislike being attended by a single man. I ought to be in McQueen's house; it has been so long known as the doctor's house. And you should be a doctor's wife-you who could almost be the doctor. It would be a shame, Grizel, if you who are so much to patients were to marry out of the profession. Don't you follow me?"

"I follow you," she replied; "but what does it matter? You have not begun at the beginning." He looked at her inquiringly. "You must begin," she informed him, "by saying why you ask me to marry you when you don't love me." She added, in answer to another look from him: "You know you don't." There was a little reproach in it. "Oh, David, what made you think I could be so easily taken in!"

He looked so miserable that by and by she smiled, not so tremulously as before.

"How bad at it you are, David!" she said.

And how good at it she was! he thought gloomily.

"Shall I help you out?" she asked gently, but speaking with dignity. "You think I am unhappy; you believe I am in the position in which you placed yourself, of caring for someone who does not care for me."

"Grizel, I mistrust him."

She flushed; she was not quite so gentle now. "And so you offer me your hand to save me! It was a great self-sacrifice, David, but you used not to be fond of doing showy things."

"I did not mean it to be showy," he answered.

She was well aware of that, but —"Oh, David," she cried, "that you should believe I needed it! How little you must think of me!"

"Does it look as if I thought little of you?" he said.

"Little of my strength, David, little of my pride."

"I think so much of them that how could I stand by silently and watch them go?"

"You think you have seen that!" She was agitated now.

He hesitated. "Yes," he said courageously.

Her eyes cried, "David, how could you be so cruel!" but they did not daunt him.

"Have you not seen it yourself, Grizel?" he said.

She pressed her hands together. "I was so happy," she said, "until you came!"

"Have you not seen it yourself?" he asked again.

"There may be better things," she retorted, "than those you rate so highly."

"Not for you," he said.

"If they are gone," she told him, with a flush of resentment, "it is not you who can bring them back."

"But let me try, Grizel," said he.

"David, can I not even make you angry with me?"

"No, Grizel, you can't. I am very sorry that I can make you angry with me."

"I am not," she said dispiritedly. "It would be contemptible in me." And then, eagerly: "But, David, you have made a great mistake, indeed you have. You-you are a dreadful bungler, sir!" She was trying to make his face relax, with a tremulous smile from herself to encourage him; but the effort was not successful. "You see, I can't even bully you now!" she said. "Did that capacity go with the others, David?"

"Try a little harder," he replied. "I think you will find that I submit to it still"

"Very well." She forced some gaiety to her aid. After all, how could she let his monstrous stupidity wound a heart protected by such a letter?

"You have been a very foolish and presumptuous boy," she began. She was standing up, smiling, wagging a reproachful but nervous finger at him. "If it were not that I have a weakness for seeing medical men making themselves ridiculous so that I may put them right, I should be very indignant with you, sir."

"Put me right, Grizel," he said. He was sure she was trying to blind him again.

"Know, then, David, that I am not the poor-spirited, humble creature you seem to have come here in search of —"

"But you admitted —"

"How dare you interrupt me, sir! Yes, I admit that I am not quite as I was, but I glory in it. I used to be ostentatiously independent; now I am only independent enough. My pride made me walk on air; now I walk on the earth, where there is less chance of falling. I have still confidence in myself; but I begin to see that ways are not necessarily right because they are my ways. In short, David, I am evidently on the road to being a model character!"

They were gay words, but she ended somewhat faintly.

"I was satisfied with you as you were," was the doctor's comment.

"I wanted to excel!"

"You explain nothing, Grizel," he said reproachfully. "Why have you changed so?"

"Because I am so happy. Do you remember how, in the old days, I sometimes danced for joy? I could do it now."

"Are you engaged to be married, Grizel?"

She took a quiet breath. "You have no right to question me in this way," she said. "I think I have been very good in bearing with you so long."

But she laid aside her indignation at once; he was so old a friend, the sincerity of him had been so often tried. "If you must know, David," she said, with a girlish frankness that became her better, "I am not engaged to be married. And I must tell you nothing more," she added, shutting her mouth decisively. She must be faithful to her promise.

"He forbids it?" Gemmell asked mercilessly.

She stamped her foot, not in rage, but in hopelessness. "How incapable you are of doing him justice!" she cried. "If you only knew — —"

"Tell me. I want to do him justice."

She sat down again, sighing. "My attempt to regain my old power over you has not been very successful, has it, David? We must not quarrel, though" —holding out her hand, which he grasped. "And you won't question me any more?" She said it appealingly.

"Never again," he answered. "I never wanted to question you, Grizel. I wanted only to marry you."

"And that can't be."

"I don't see it," he said, so stoutly that she was almost amused. But he would not be pushed aside. He had something more to say.

"Dr. McQueen wished it," he said; "above all else in the world he wished it. He often told me so."

"He never said that to me," Grizel replied quickly.

"Because he thought that to press you was no way to make you care for me. He hoped that it would come about."

"It has not come about, David, with either of us," she said gently. "I am sure that would have been sufficient answer to him."

"No, Grizel, it would not, not now."

He had risen, and his face was whiter than she had ever seen it.

"I am going to hurt you, Grizel," he said, and every word was a pang to him. "I see no other way. It has got to be done. Dr. McQueen often talked to me about the things that troubled you when you were a little girl-the morbid fears you had then, and that had all been swept away years before I knew you. But though they had been long gone, you were so much to him that he tried to think of everything that might happen to you in the future, and he foresaw that they might possibly come back. 'If she were ever to care for some false loon!' he has said to me, and then, Grizel, he could not go on."

Grizel beat her hands. "If he could not go on," she said, "it was not because he feared what I should do."

"No, no," David answered eagerly, "he never feared for that, but for your happiness. He told me of a boy who used to torment you, oh, all so long ago, and of such little account that he had forgotten his name. But that boy has come back, and you care for him, and he is a false loon, Grizel."

She had risen too, and was flashing fire on David; but he went on.

"'If the time ever comes,' he said to me, 'when you see her in torture from such a cause, speak to her openly about it. Tell her it is I who am speaking through you. It will be a hard task to you, but wrestle through with it, David, in memory of any little kindness I may have done you, and the great love I bore my Grizel.'"

She was standing rigid now. "Is there any more, David?" she said in a low voice.

"Only this. I admired you then as I admire you now. I may not love you, Grizel, but of this I am very sure" —he was speaking steadily, he was forgetting no one —"that you are the noblest and bravest woman I have ever known, and I promised-he did not draw the promise from me, I gave it to him-that if I was a free man and could help you in any way without paining you by telling you these things, I would try that way first."

"And this is the way?"

"I could think of no other. Is it of no avail?"

She shook her head. "You have made such a dreadful mistake," she cried miserably, "and you won't see it. Oh, how you wrong him! I am the happiest girl in the world, and it is he who makes me so happy. But I can't explain. You need not ask me; I promised, and I won't."

"You used not to be so fond of mystery, Grizel."

"I am not fond of it now."

"Ah, it is he," David said bitterly, and he lifted his hat. "Is there nothing you will let me do for you, Grizel?" he cried.

"I thought you were to do so much for me when you came into this room," she admitted wistfully, "and said that you were in love. I thought it was with another woman."

He remembered that her face had brightened. "How could that have helped you?" he asked.

She saw that she had but to tell him, and for her sake he would do it at once. But she could not be so selfish.

"We need not speak of that now," she said.

"We must speak of it," he answered. "Grizel, it is but fair to me. It may be so important to me."

"You have shown that you don't care for her, David, and that ends it."

"Who is it?" He was much stirred.

"If you don't know — —"

"Is it Elspeth?"

The question came out of him like a confession, and hope turned Grizel giddy.

"Do you love her, David?" she cried.

But he hesitated. "Is what you have told me true, that it would help you?" he asked, looking her full in the eyes.

"Do you love her?" she implored, but he was determined to have her answer first.

"Is it, Grizel?"

"Yes, yes. Do you, David?"

And then he admitted that he did, and she rocked her arms in joy.

"But oh, David, to say such things to me when you were not a free man! How badly you have treated Elspeth to-day!"

"She does not care for me," he said.

"Have you asked her?" —in alarm.

"No; but could she?"

"How could she help it?" She would not tell him what Tommy thought. Oh, she must do everything to encourage David.

"And still," said he, puzzling, "I don't see how it can affect you."

"And I can't tell you," she moaned. "Oh, David, do, do find out. Why are you so blind?" She could have shaken him. "Don't you see that once Elspeth was willing to be taken care of by some other person — —I must not tell you!"

"Then he would marry you?"

She cried in anxiety: "Have I told you, or did you find out?"

"I found out," he said. "Is it possible he is so fond of her as that?"

"There never was such a brother," she answered. She could not help adding, "But he is still fonder of me."

The doctor pulled his arm over his eyes and sat down again. Presently he was saying with a long face: "I came here to denounce the cause of your unhappiness, and I begin to see it is myself."

"Of course it is, you stupid David," she said gleefully. She was very kind to the man who had been willing to do so much for her; but as the door closed on him she forgot him. She even ceased to hear the warning voice he had brought with him from the dead. She was re-reading the letter that began by calling her wife.

Chapter XXI
The Attempt to Carry Elspeth by Numbers

That was one of Grizel's beautiful days, but there were others to follow as sweet, if not so exciting; she could travel back through the long length of them without coming once to a moment when she had held her breath in sudden fear; and this was so delicious that she sometimes thought these were the best days of all.

Of course she had little anxieties, but they were nearly all about David. He was often at Aaron's house now, and what exercised her was this-that she could not be certain that he was approaching Elspeth in the right way. The masterful Grizel seemed to have come to life again, for, evidently, she was convinced that she alone knew the right way.

"Oh, David, I would not have said that to her!" she told him, when he reported progress; and now she would warn him, "You are too humble," and again, "You were over-bold." The doctor, to his bewilderment, frequently discovered, on laying results before her, that what he had looked upon as encouraging signs were really bad, and that, on the other hand, he had often left the cottage disconsolately when he ought to have been strutting. The issue was that he lost all faith in his own judgment, and if Grizel said that he was getting on well, his face became foolishly triumphant, but if she frowned, it cried, "All is over!"

Of the proposal Tommy did not know; it seemed to her that she had no right to tell even him of that; but the rest she did tell him: that David, by his own confession, was in love with Elspeth; and so pleased was Tommy that his delight made another day for her to cherish.

So now everything depended on Elspeth. "Oh, if she only would!" Grizel cried, and for her sake Tommy tried to look bright, but his head shook in spite of him.

"Do you mean that we should discourage David?" she asked dolefully; but he said No to that.

"I was afraid," she confessed, "that as you are so hopeless, you might think it your duty to discourage him so as to save him the pain of a refusal."

"Not at all," Tommy said, with some hastiness.

"Then you do really have a tiny bit of hope?"

"While there is life there is hope," he answered.

She said: "I have been thinking it over, for it is so important to us, and I see various ways in which you could help David, if you would."

"What would I not do, Grizel! You have to name them only."

"Well, for instance, you might show her that you have a very high opinion of him."

"Agreed. But she knows that already."

"Then, David is an only child. Don't you think you could say that men who have never had a sister are peculiarly gentle and considerate to women?"

"Oh, Grizel! But I think I can say that."

"And-and that having been so long accustomed to doing everything for themselves, they don't need managing wives as men brought up among women need them."

"Yes. But how cunning you are, Grizel! Who would have believed it?"

"And then — —" She hesitated.

"Go on. I see by your manner that this is to be a big one."

"It would be such a help," she said eagerly, "if you could be just a little less attentive to her. I know you do ever so much of the housework because she is not fond of it; and if she has a headache you sit with her all day; and you beg her to play and sing to you, though you really dislike music. Oh, there are scores of things you do for her, and if you were to do them a little less willingly, in such a way as to show her that they interrupt your work and are a slight trial to you, I —I am sure that would help!"

"She would see through me, Grizel. Elspeth is sharper than you think her."

"Not if you did it very skilfully."

"Then she would believe I had grown cold to her, and it would break her heart."

"One of your failings," replied Grizel, giving him her hand for a moment as recompense for what she was about to say, "is that you think women's hearts break so easily. If, at the slightest sign that she notices any change in you, you think her heart is breaking, and seize her in your arms, crying, 'Elspeth, dear little Elspeth!' —and that is what your first impulse would be — —"

"How well you know me, Grizel!" groaned Sentimental Tommy.

"If that would be the result," she went on, "better not do it at all. But if you were to restrain yourself, then she could not but reflect that many of the things you did for her with a sigh David did for pleasure, and she would compare him and you —"

"To my disadvantage?" Tommy exclaimed, with sad incredulity. "Do you really think she could, Grizel?"

"Give her the chance," Grizel continued, "and if you find it hard, you must remember that what you are doing is for her good."

"And for ours," Tommy cried fervently.

Every promise he made her at this time he fulfilled, and more; he was hopeless, but all a man could do to make Elspeth love David he did.

The doctor was quite unaware of it. "Fortunately, her brother had a headache yesterday and was lying down," he told Grizel, with calm brutality, "so I saw her alone for a few minutes."

"The fibs I have to invent," said Tommy, to the same confidante, "to get myself out of their way!"

"Luckily he does not care for music," David said, "so when she is at the piano he sometimes remains in the kitchen talking to Aaron."

Tommy and Aaron left together! Tommy described those scenes with much good humour. "I was amazed at first," he said to Grizel, "to find Aaron determinedly enduring me, but now I understand. He wants what we want. He says not a word about it, but he is watching those two courting like a born match-maker. Aaron has several reasons for hoping that Elspeth will get our friend (as he would express it): one, that this would keep her in Thrums; another, that to be the wife of a doctor is second only in worldly grandeur to marrying the manse; and thirdly and lastly, because he is convinced that it would be such a staggerer to me. For he thinks I have not a notion of what is going on, and that, if I had, I would whisk her away to London."

He gave Grizel the most graphic, solemn pictures of those evenings in the cottage. "Conceive the four of us gathered round the kitchen fire-three men and a maid; the three men yearning to know what is in the maid's mind, and each concealing his anxiety from the others. Elspeth gives the doctor a look which may mean much or nothing, and he glares at me as if I were in the way, and I glance at Aaron, and he is on tenterhooks lest I have noticed anything. Next minute, perhaps, David gives utterance to a plaintive sigh, and Aaron and I pounce upon Elspeth (with our eyes) to observe its effect on her, and Elspeth wonders why Aaron is staring, and he looks apprehensively at me, and I am gazing absent-mindedly at the fender.

"You may smile, Grizel," Tommy would say, "and now that I think of it, I can smile myself, but we are an eerie quartet at the time. When the strain becomes unendurable, one of us rises and mends the fire with his foot, and then I think the rest of us could say 'Thank you.' We talk desperately for a little after that, but soon again the awful pall creeps down."

"If I were there," cried Grizel, "I would not have the parlour standing empty all this time."

"We are coming to the parlour," Tommy replies impressively. "The parlour, Grizel, now begins to stir. Elspeth has disappeared from the kitchen, we three men know not whither. We did not notice her go; we don't even observe that she has gone-we are too busy looking at the fire. By and by the tremulous tinkling of an aged piano reaches us from an adjoining chamber, and Aaron looks at me through his fingers, and I take a lightning glance at Mr. David, and he uncrosses his legs and rises, and sits down again. Aaron, in the most unconcerned way, proceeds to cut tobacco and rub it between his fingers, and I stretch out my legs and contemplate them with passionate approval. While we are thus occupied David has risen, and he is so thoroughly at his ease that he has begun to hum. He strolls round the kitchen, looking with sudden interest at the mantelpiece ornaments; he reads, for the hundredth time, the sampler on the wall. Next the clock engages his attention; it is ticking, and that seems to impress him as novel and curious. By this time he has reached the door; it opens to his touch, and in a fit of abstraction he leaves the room."

"You don't follow him into the parlour?" asks Grizel, anxiously.

"Follow whom?" Tommy replies severely. "I don't even know that he has gone to the parlour; now that I think of it, I have not even noticed that he has left the kitchen; nor has Aaron noticed it. Aaron and I are not in a condition to notice such things; we are conscious only that at last we have the opportunity for the quiet social chat we so much enjoy in each other's company. That, at least, is Aaron's way of looking at it, and he keeps me there with talk of the most varied and absorbing character; one topic down, another up; when very hard put to it, he even questions me about my next book, as if he would like to read the proof-sheets, and when I seem to be listening, a little restively, for sounds from the parlour (the piano has stopped), he has the face of one who would bar the door rather than lose my society. Aaron appreciates me at my true value at last, Grizel. I had begun to despair almost of ever bringing him under my charm."

"I should be very angry with you," Grizel said warningly, "if I thought you teased the poor old man."

"Tease him! The consideration I show that poor old man, Grizel, while I know all the time that he is plotting to diddle me! You should see me when it is he who is fidgeting to know why the piano has stopped. He stretches his head to listen, and does something to his ear that sends it another inch nearer the door; he chuckles and groans on the sly; and I—I notice nothing. Oh, he is becoming quite fond of me; he thinks me an idiot."

"Why not tell him that you want it as much as he?"

"He would not believe me. Aaron is firmly convinced that I am too jealous of Elspeth's affection to give away a thimbleful of it. He blames me for preventing her caring much even for him."

"At any rate," said Grizel, "he is on our side, and it is because he sees it would be so much the best thing for her."

"And, at the same time, such a shock to me. That poor old man, Grizel! I have seen him rubbing his hands together with glee and looking quite leery as he thought of what was coming to me."

But Grizel could not laugh now. When Tommy saw so well through Aaron and David, through everyone he came in contact with, indeed, what hope could there be that he was deceived in Elspeth?

"And yet she knows what takes him there; she must know it!" she cried.

"A woman," Tommy said, "is never sure that a man is in love with her until he proposes. She may fancy-but it is never safe to fancy, as so many have discovered."

"She has no right," declared Grizel, "to wait until she is sure, if she does not care for him. If she fears that he is falling in love with her, she knows how to discourage him; there are surely a hundred easy, kind ways of doing that."

"Fears he is falling in love with her!" Tommy repeated. "Is any woman ever afraid of that?"

He really bewildered her. "No woman would like it," Grizel answered promptly for them all, because she would not have liked it. "She must see that it would result only in pain to him."

"Still——" said Tommy.

"Oh, but how dense you are!" she said, in surprise. "Don't you understand that she would stop him, though it were for no better reasons than selfish ones? Consider her shame if, in thinking it over afterwards, she saw that she might have stopped him sooner! Why," she cried, with a sudden smile, "it is in your book! You say: 'Every maiden carries secretly in her heart an idea of love so pure and sacred that, if by any act she is once false to that conception, her punishment is that she never dares to look at it again.' And this is one of the acts you mean."

"I had not thought of it, though," he said humbly. He was never prouder of Grizel than at that moment. "If Elspeth's outlook," he went on, "is different——"

"It can't be different."

"If it is, the fault is mine; yes, though I wrote the passage that you interpret so nobly, Grizel. Shall I tell you," he said gently, "what I believe is Elspeth's outlook exactly, just now? She knows that the doctor is attracted by her, and it gives her little thrills of exultation; but that it can be love-she puts that question in such a low voice, as if to prevent herself hearing it. And yet she listens, Grizel, like one who would like to know! Elspeth is pitifully distrustful of anyone's really loving her, and she will never admit to herself that he does until he tells her."

"And then?"

Tommy had to droop his head.

"I see you have still no hope!" she said.

"It would be so easy to pretend I have," he replied, with longing, "in order to cheer you for the moment. Oh, it would even be easy to me to deceive myself; but should I do it?"

"No, no," she said; "anything but that; I can bear anything but that," and she shuddered. "But we seem to be treating David cruelly."

"I don't think so," he assured her. "Men like to have these things to look back to. But, if you want it, Grizel, I have to say only a word to Elspeth to bring it to an end. She is as tender as she is innocent, and-but it would be a hard task to me," he admitted, his heart suddenly going out to Elspeth; he had never deprived her of any gratification before. "Still, I am willing to do it."

"No!" Grizel cried, restraining him with her hand. "I am a coward, I suppose, but I can't help wanting to hope for a little longer, and David won't grudge it to me."

It was but a very little longer that they had to wait. Tommy, returning home one day from a walk with his old school-friend, Gav Dishart (now M.A.), found Aaron suspiciously near the parlour keyhole.

"There's a better fire in the other end," Aaron said, luring him into the kitchen. So desirous was he of keeping Tommy there, fixed down on a stool, that "I'll play you at the dambrod," he said briskly.

"Anyone with Elspeth?"

"Some women-folk you dinna like," replied Aaron.

Tommy rose. Aaron, with a subdued snarl, got between him and the door.

"I was wondering, merely," Tommy said, pointing pleasantly to something on the dresser, "why one of them wore the doctor's hat."

"I forgot; he's there, too," Aaron said promptly; but he looked at Tommy with misgivings. They sat down to their game.

"You begin," said Tommy; "you're black." And Aaron opened with the Double Corner; but so preoccupied was he that it became a variation of the Ayrshire lassie, without his knowing. His suspicions had to find vent in words: "You dinna speir wha the women-folk are?"

"No."

"Do you think I'm just pretending they're there?" Aaron asked apprehensively.

"Not at all," said Tommy, with much politeness, "but I thought you might be mistaken." He could have "blown" Aaron immediately thereafter, but, with great consideration, forbore. The old man was so troubled that he could not lift a king without its falling in two. His sleeve got in the way of his fingers. At last he sat back in his chair. "Do you ken what is going on, man?" he demanded, "or do you no ken? I can stand this doubt no longer."

A less soft-hearted person might have affected not to understand, but that was not Tommy's way. "I know, Aaron," he admitted. "I have known all the time." It was said in the kindliest manner, but its effect on Aaron was not soothing.

"Curse you!" he cried, with extraordinary vehemence, "you have been playing wi' me a' the time, ay, and wi' him and wi' her!"

What had Aaron been doing with Tommy? But Tommy did not ask that.

"I am sorry you think so badly of me," he said quietly. "I have known all the time, Aaron, but have I interfered?"

"Because you ken she winna take him. I see it plain enough now. You ken your power over her; the honest man that thinks he could take her frae you is to you but a divert."

He took a step nearer Tommy. "Listen," he said. "When you came back he was on the point o' speiring her; I saw it in his face as she was playing the piano, and she saw it, too, for her hands began to trem'le and the tune wouldna play. I daursay you think I was keeking, but if I was I stoppit it when the piano stoppit; it was a hard thing to me to do, and it would hae been an easy thing no to do, but I wouldna spy upon Elspeth in her great hour."

"I like you for that, Aaron," Tommy said; but Aaron waved his likes aside.

"The reason I stood at the door," he continued, "was to keep you out o' that room. I offered to play you at the dambrod to keep you out. Ay, you ken that without my telling you, but do you ken what makes me tell you now? It's to see whether you'll go in and stop him; let's see you do that, and I'll hae some hope yet." He waited eagerly.

"You do puzzle me now," Tommy said.

"Ay," replied the old man, bitterly, "you're dull in the uptak' when you like! I dinna ken, I suppose, and you dinna ken, that if you had the least dread o' her taking him you would be into that room full bend to stop it; but you're so sure o' her, you're so michty sure, that you can sit here and lauch instead."

"Am I laughing, Aaron? If you but knew, Elspeth's marriage would be a far more joyful thing to me than it could ever be to you."

The old warper laughed unpleasantly at that. "And I'se uphaud," he said, "you're none sure but what shell tak' him! You're no as sure she'll refuse him as that there's a sun in the heavens, and I'm a broken man."

For a moment sympathy nigh compelled Tommy to say a hopeful thing, but he mastered himself. "It would be weakness," was what he did say, "to pretend that there is any hope."

Aaron gave him an ugly look, and was about to leave the house; but Tommy would not have it. "If one of us must go, Aaron," he said, with much gentleness, "let it be me"; and he went out, passing the parlour door softly, so that he might not disturb poor David. The warper sat on by the fire, his head sunk miserably in his shoulders. The vehemence had passed out of him; you would have hesitated to believe that such a listless, shrunken man could have been vehement that same year. It is a hardy proof of his faith in Tommy that he did not even think it worth while to look up when, by and by, the parlour door opened and the doctor came in for his hat. Elspeth was with him.

They told Aaron something.

They told Aaron something.

It lifted him off his feet and bore him out at the door. When he made up on himself he knew he was searching everywhere for Tommy. A terror seized him, lest he should not be the first to convey the news.

Had he been left a fortune? neighbours asked, amazed at this unwonted sight; and he replied, as he ran, "I have, and I want to share it wi' him!"

It was his only joke. People came to their doors to see Aaron Latta laughing.

Chapter XXII
Grizel's Glorious Hour

Elspeth was to be his wife! David had carried the wondrous promise straight to Grizel, and now he was gone and she was alone again.

Oh, foolish Grizel, are you crying, and I thought it was so hard to you to cry!

"Me crying! Oh, no!"

Put your hand to your cheeks, Grizel. Are they not wet?

"They are wet, and I did not know it! It is hard to me to cry in sorrow, but I can cry for joy. I am crying because it has all come right, and I was so much afraid that it never would."

Ah, Grizel, I think you said you wanted nothing else so long as you had his love!

"But God has let it all come right, just the same, and I am thanking Him. That is why I did not know that I was crying."

She was by the fireplace, on the stool that had always been her favourite seat, and of course she sat very straight. When Grizel walked or stood her strong, round figure took a hundred beautiful poses, but when she sat it had but one. The old doctor, in experimenting moods, had sometimes compelled her to recline, and then watched to see her body spring erect the moment he released his hold. "What a dreadful patient I should make!" she said contritely. "I would chloroform you, miss," said he.

She sat thus for a long time; she had so much for which to thank God, though not with her lips, for how could they keep pace with her heart? Her heart was very full; chiefly, I think, with the tears that rolled down unknown to her.

She thanked God, in the name of the little hunted girl who had not been taught how to pray, and so did it standing. "I do so want to be good; oh, how sweet it would be to be good!" she had said in that long ago. She had said it out loud when she was alone on the chance of His hearing, but she had not addressed Him by name because she was not sure that he was really called God. She had not even known that you should end by saying "Amen," which Tommy afterwards told her is the most solemn part of it.

How sweet it would be to be good, but how much sweeter it is to be good! The woman that girl had grown into knew that she was good, and she thanked God for that. She thanked Him for letting her help. If He had said that she had not helped, she would have rocked her arms and replied almost hotly: "You know I have." And He did know: He had seen her many times in the grip of inherited passions, and watched her fighting with them and subduing them; He had seen ugly thoughts stealing upon her, as they crawl towards every child of man; ah, He had seen them leap into the heart of the Painted Lady's daughter, as if a nest already made for them must be there, and still she had driven them away. Grizel had helped. The tears came more quickly now.

She thanked God that she had never worn the ring. But why had she never worn it, when she wanted so much to do so, and it was hers? Why had she watched herself more carefully than ever of late, and forced happiness to her face when it was not in her heart, and denied herself, at fierce moments, the luxuries of grief and despair, and even of rebellion? For she had carried about with her the capacity to rebel, but she had hidden it, and the reason was that she thought God was testing her. If she fell He would not give her the thing she coveted. Unworthy reason for being good, as she knew, but God overlooked it, and she thanked Him for that.

Her hands pressed each other impulsively, as if at the shock of a sudden beautiful thought, and then perhaps she was thanking God for making her the one woman who could be the right wife for Tommy. She was so certain that no other woman could help him as she could; none knew his virtues as she knew them. Had it not been for her, his showy parts only would have been loved; the dear, quiet ones would never have heard how dear they were: the showy ones were open to all the world, but the quiet ones were her private garden. His faults as well as his virtues passed before her, and it is strange to know that it was about this time that Grizel ceased to cry and began to smile instead. I know why she smiled; it was because sentimentality was one of the little monsters that came skipping into her view, and Tommy was so confident that he had got rid at last of it! Grizel knew better! But she could look at it and smile. Perhaps she was not sorry that it was still there with the others, it had so long led the procession. I daresay she saw herself taking the leering, distorted thing in hand and making something gallant of it. She thought that she was too practical, too much given to seeing but one side to a question, too lacking in consideration for others, too impatient, too relentlessly just, and she humbly thanked God for all these faults, because Tommy's excesses were in the opposite direction, and she could thus restore the balance. She was full of humility while she saw how useful she could be to him, but her face did not show this; she had forgotten her face, and elation had spread over it without her knowing. Perhaps God accepted the elation as part of the thanks.

She thanked God for giving Tommy what he wanted so much-herself. Ah, she had thanked Him for that before, but she did it again. And then she went on her knees by her dear doctor's chair, and prayed that she might be a good wife to Tommy.

When she rose the blood was not surging through her veins. Instead of a passion of joy it was a beautiful calm that possessed her, and on noticing this she regarded herself with sudden suspicion, as we put our ear to a watch to see if it has stopped. She found that she was still going, but no longer either fast or slow, and she saw what had happened: her old serene self had come back to her. I think she thanked God for that most of all.

And then she caught sight of her face-oh, oh! Her first practical act as an engaged woman was to wash her face.

Engaged! But was she? Grizel laughed. It is not usually a laughing matter, but she could not help that. Consider her predicament. She could be engaged at once, if she liked, even before she wiped the water from her face, or she might postpone it, to let Tommy share. The careful reader will have noticed that this problem presented itself to her at an awkward moment. She laughed, in short, while her face was still in the basin, with the very proper result that she had to grope for the towel with her eyes shut.

It was still a cold, damp face (Grizel was always in such a hurry) when she opened her most precious drawer and took from it a certain glove which was wrapped in silk paper, but was not perhaps quite so conceited as it had been, for, alas and alack! it was now used as a wrapper itself. The ring was inside it. If Grizel wanted to be engaged, absolutely and at once, all she had to do was to slip that ring upon her finger.

It had been hers for a week or more. Tommy had bought it in a certain Scottish town whose merchant princes are so many, and have risen splendidly from such small beginnings, that after you have been there a short time you beg to be introduced to someone who has not got on. When you look at them they slap their trouser pockets. When they look at you they are wondering if you know how much they are worth. Tommy, one day, roaming their streets (in which he was worth incredibly little), and thinking sadly of what could never be, saw the modest little garnet ring in a jeweller's window, and attached to it was a pathetic story. No other person could have seen the story, but it was as plain to him as though it had been beautifully written on the tag of paper which really contained the price. With his hand on the door he paused, overcome by that horror of entering shops without a lady to do the talking, which all men of genius feel (it is the one sure test), hurried away, came back, went to and fro shyly, until he saw that he was yielding once more to the indecision he thought he had so completely mastered, whereupon he entered bravely (though it was one of those detestable doors that ring a bell as they open), and sternly ordered the jeweller, who could have bought and sold our Tommy with one slap on the trouser leg, to hand the ring over to him.

He had no intention of giving it to Grizel. That, indeed, was part of its great tragedy, for this is the story Tommy read into the ring: There was once a sorrowful man of twenty-three, and forty, and sixty. Ah, how gray the beard has grown as we speak! How thin the locks! But still we know him for the same by that garnet ring. Since it became his no other eye has seen it, and yet it is her engagement ring. Never can he give it to her, but must always carry it about with him as the piteous memory of what had never been. How innocent it looked in his hand,

and with an innocence that never wore off, not even when he had reached his threescore years. As it aged it took on another kind of innocence only. It looked pitiable now, for there is but a dishonoured age for a lonely little ring which can never see the finger it was made to span.

A hair-shirt! Such it was to him, and he put it on willingly, knowing it could be nothing else. Every smart it gave him pleased, even while it pained. If ever his mind roamed again to the world of make-believe, that ring would jerk him back to facts.

Grizel remembered well her finding of it. She had been in his pockets. She loved to rifle them; to pull out his watch herself, instead of asking him for the time; to exclaim "Oh!" at the many things she found there, when they should have been neatly docketed or in the fire, and from his waistcoat pocket she drew the ring. She seemed to understand all about it at once. She was far ahead while he was explaining. It seemed quite strange to her that there had ever been a time when she did not know of her garnet ring.

How her arms rocked! It was delicious to her to remember now with what agony her arms had rocked. She kissed it; she had not been the first to kiss it.

It was "Oh, how I wish I could have saved you this pain!"

"But I love it," she cried, "and I love the pain."

It was "Am I not to see it on your finger once?"

"No, no; we must not."

"Let me, Grizel!"

"Is it right, oh, is it right?"

"Only this once!"

"Very well!"

"I dare not, Grizel, I can't! What are we to do with it now?"

"Give it to me. It is mine. I will keep it, beside my glove."

"Let me keep it, Grizel."

"No; it is mine."

"Shall I fling it away?"

"How can you be so cruel? It is mine."

"Let me bury it."

"It is mine."

And of course she had got her way. Could he resist her in anything? They had never spoken of it since, it was such a sad little ring. Sad! It was not in the least little bit sad. Grizel wondered as she looked at it now how she could ever have thought it sad.

The object with which she put on her hat was to go to Aaron's cottage, to congratulate Elspeth. So she said to herself. Oh, Grizel!

But first she opened two drawers. They were in a great press and full of beautiful linen woven in Thrums, that had come to Dr. McQueen as a "bad debt." "Your marriage portion, young lady," he had said to Grizel, then but a slip of a girl, whereupon, without waiting to lengthen her frock, she rushed rapturously at her work-basket. "Not at all, miss," he cried ferociously; "you are here to look after this house, not to be preparing for another, and until you are respectably bespoken by some rash crittur of a man, into the drawers with your linen and down with those murderous shears." And she had obeyed; no scissors, the most relentless things in nature when in Grizel's hand, had ever cleaved their way through that snowy expanse; never a stitch had she put into her linen except with her eyes, which became horribly like needles as she looked at it.

And now at last she could begin! Oh, but she was anxious to begin; it is almost a fact that, as she looked at those drawers, she grudged the time that must be given to-day to Tommy and his ring.

Do you see her now, ready to start? She was wearing her brown jacket with the fur collar, over which she used to look so searchingly at Tommy. To think there was a time when that serene face had to look searchingly at him! It nearly made her sad again. She paused to bring out the ring and take another exultant look at it. It was attached now to a ribbon round her neck. Sweet ring! She put it to her eyes. That was her way of letting her eyes kiss it Then she rubbed them and it, in case the one had left a tear upon the other.

And then she went out, joy surging in her heart For this was Grizel's glorious hour, the end of it.

Chapter XXIII
Tommy Loses Grizel

It was not Aaron's good fortune to find Tommy. He should have looked for him in the Den.

In that haunt of happier lovers than he, Tommy walked slowly, pondering. He scarce noticed that he had the Den to himself, or that, since he was last here, autumn had slipped away, leaving all her garments on the ground. By this time, undoubtedly, Elspeth had said her gentle No; but he was not railing against Fate, not even for striking the final blow at him through that innocent medium. He had still too much to do for that-to help others. There were three of them at present, and by some sort of sympathetic jugglery he had an arm for each.

"Lean on me, Grizel-dear sister Elspeth, you little know the harm you have done-David, old friend, your hand."

Thus loaded, he bravely returned at the fitting time to the cottage. His head was not even bent.

Had you asked Tommy what Elspeth would probably do when she dismissed David, he might have replied that she would go up to his room and lock herself into it, so that no one should disturb her for a time. And this he discovered, on returning home, was actually what had happened. How well he knew her! How distinctly he heard every beat of her tender heart, and how easy to him to tell why it was beating! He did not go up; he waited for little Elspeth to come to him, all in her own good time. And when she came, looking just as he knew she would look, he had a brave, bright face for her.

She was shaking after her excitement, or perhaps she had ceased to shake and begun again as she came down to him. He pretended not to notice it; he would notice it the moment he was sure she wanted him to, but perhaps that would not be until she was in bed and he had come to say good-night and put out her light, for, as we know, she often kept her great confidences till then, when she discovered that he already knew them.

"The doctor has been in."

She began almost at once, and in a quaking voice and from a distance, as if in hope that the bullet might be spent before it reached her brother.

"I am sorry I missed him," he replied cautiously. "What a fine fellow he is!"

"You always liked him," said Elspeth, clinging eagerly to that.

"No one could help liking him, Elspeth, he has such winning ways," said Tommy, perhaps a little in the voice with which at funerals we refer to the departed. She loved his words, but she knew she had a surprise for him this time, and she tried to blurt it out.

"He said something to me. He-oh, what a high opinion he has of you!" (She really thought he had.)

"Was that the something?" Tommy asked, with a smile that helped her, as it was meant to do.

"You understand, don't you?" she said, almost in a whisper.

"Of course I do, Elspeth," he answered reassuringly; but somehow she still thought he didn't.

"No one could have been more manly and gentle and humble," she said beseechingly.

"I am sure of it," said Tommy.

"He thinks nothing of himself," she said.

"We shall always think a great deal of him," replied Tommy.

"Yes, but ——" Elspeth found the strangest difficulty in continuing, for, though it would have surprised him to be told so, Tommy was not helping her nearly as much as he imagined.

"I told him," she said, shaking, "that no one could be to me what you were. I told him ——" and then timid Elspeth altogether broke down. Tommy drew her to him, as he had so often done since she was the smallest child, and pressed her head against his breast, and waited. So often he had waited thus upon Elspeth.

"There is nothing to cry about, dear," he said tenderly, when the time to speak came. "You have, instead, the right to be proud that so good a man loves you. I am very proud of it, Elspeth."

"If I could be sure of that!" she gasped.

"Don't you believe me, dear?"

"Yes, but-that is not what makes me cry. Tommy, don't you see?"

"Yes," he assured her, "I see. You are crying because you feel so sorry for him. But I don't feel sorry for him, Elspeth. If I know anything at all, it is this: that no man needs pity who sincerely loves; whether that love be returned or not, he walks in a new and more beautiful world for evermore."

She clutched his hand. "I don't understand how you know those things," she whispered.

Please God, was Tommy's reflection, she should never know. He saw most vividly the pathos of his case, but he did not break down under it; it helped him, rather, to proceed.

"It will be the test of Gemmell," he said, "how he bears this. No man, I am very sure, was ever told that his dream could not come true more kindly and tenderly than you told it to him." He was in the middle of the next sentence (a fine one) before her distress stopped him.

"Tommy," she cried, "you don't understand. That is not what I told him at all!"

It was one of the few occasions on which the expression on the face of T. Sandys perceptibly changed.

"What did you tell him?" he asked, almost sharply.

"I accepted him," she said guiltily, backing away from this alarming face.

"What!"

"If you only knew how manly and gentle and humble he was," she cried quickly, as if something dire might happen if Tommy were not assured of this at once.

"You-said you would marry him, Elspeth?"

"Yes!"

"And leave me?"

"Oh, oh!" She flung her arms around his neck.

"Yes, but that is what you are prepared to do!" said he, and he held her away from him and stared at her, as if he had never seen Elspeth before. "Were you not afraid?" he exclaimed, in amazement.

"I am not the least bit afraid," she answered. "Oh Tommy, if you knew how manly ——" And then she remembered that she had said that already.

"You did not even say that you would-consult me?"

"Oh, oh!"

"Why didn't you, Elspeth?"

"I —I forgot!" she moaned. "Tommy, you are angry!" She hugged him, and he let her do it, but all the time he was looking over her head fixedly, with his mouth open.

"And I was always so sure of you!" were the words that came to him at last, with a hard little laugh at the end of them.

"Can you think it makes me love you less," she sobbed, "because I love him, too? Oh, Tommy, I thought you would be so glad!"

He kissed her; he put his hand fondly upon her head.

"I am glad," he said, with emotion. "When that which you want has come to you, Elspeth, how can I but be glad? But it takes me aback, and if for a moment I felt forlorn, if, when I should have been rejoicing only in your happiness, the selfish thought passed through my mind, 'What is to become of me?' I hope —I hope —" Then he sat down and buried his face in the table.

And he might have been telling her about Grizel! Has the shock stunned you, Tommy? Elspeth thinks it has been a shock of pain. May we lift your head to show her your joyous face?

"I am so proud," she was saying, "that at last, after you have done so much for me, I can do a little thing for you. For it is something to free you, Tommy. You have always pretended, for my sake, that we could not do without each other, but we both knew all the time that it was only I who was unable to do without you. You can't deny it."

He might deny it, but it was true. Ah, Tommy, you bore with her with infinite patience, but did it never strike you that she kept you to the earth? If Elspeth could be happy without you! You were sure she could not, but if she could! —had that thought never made you flap your wings?

"I often had a pain at my heart," she told him, "which I kept from you. It was a feeling that your solicitude for me, perhaps, prevented your caring for any other woman. It seemed terrible and unnatural that I should be a bar to that. I felt that I was starving you, and not you only, but an unknown woman as well."

"So long as I had you, Elspeth," he said reproachfully, "was not that enough?"

"It seemed to be enough," she answered gravely, "but even while I comforted myself with that, I knew that it should not be enough, and still I feared that if it was, the blame was mine. Now I am no longer in the way, and I hope, so ardently, that you will fall in love, like other people. If you never do, I shall always have the fear that I am the cause, that you lost the capacity in the days when I let you devote yourself too much to me."

Oh, blind Elspeth! Now is the time to tell her, Tommy, and fill her cup of happiness to the brim.

But it is she who is speaking still, almost gaily now, yet with a full heart. "What a time you have had with me, Tommy! I told David all about it, and what he has to look forward to, but he says he is not afraid. And when you find someone you can love," she continued sweetly, though she had a sigh to stifle, "I hope she will be someone quite unlike me, for oh, my dear, good brother, I know you need a change."

Not a word said Tommy.

She said, timidly, that she had begun to hope of late that Grizel might be the woman, and still he did not speak. He drew Elspeth closer to him, that she might not see his face and the horror of himself that surely sat on it. To the very marrow of him he was in such cold misery that I wonder his arms did not chill her.

This poor devil of a Sentimental Tommy! He had wakened up in the world of facts, where he thought he had been dwelling of late, to discover that he had not been here for weeks, except at meal-times. During those weeks he had most honestly thought that he was in a passion to be married. What do you say to pitying instead of cursing him? It is a sudden idea of mine, and we must be quick, for joyous Grizel is drawing near, and this, you know, is the chapter in which her heart breaks.

It was Elspeth who opened the door to Grizel. "Does she know?" said Elspeth to herself, before either of them spoke.

"Does she know?" It was what Grizel was saying also.

"Oh, Elspeth, I am so glad! David has told me."

"She does know," Elspeth told herself, and she thought it was kind of Grizel to come so quickly. She said so.

"She doesn't know!" thought Grizel, and then these two kissed for the first time. It was a kiss of thanks from each.

"But why does she not know?" Grizel wondered a little as they entered the parlour, where Tommy was; he had been standing with his teeth knit since he heard the knock. As if in answer to the question, Elspeth said: "I have just broken it to Tommy. He has been in a few minutes only, and he is so surprised he can scarcely speak."

Grizel laughed happily, for that explained it. Tommy had not had time to tell her yet. She laughed again at Elspeth, who had thought she had so much to tell and did not know half the story.

Elspeth begged Tommy to listen to the beautiful things Grizel was saying about David, but, truth to tell, Grizel scarcely heard them herself. She had given Tommy a shy, rapturous glance. She was wondering when he would begin. What a delicious opening when he shook hands! Suppose he had kissed her instead! Or, suppose he casually addressed her as darling! He might do it at any moment now! Just for once she would not mind though he did it in public. Perhaps as soon as this new remark of Elspeth's was finished, he meant to say: "You are not the only engaged person in the room, Miss Elspeth; I think I see another two!" Grizel laughed as if she had heard him say it. And then she ceased laughing suddenly, for some little duty had called Elspeth into the other room, and as she went out she stopped the movement of the earth.

These two were alone with their great joy.

Elspeth had said that she would be back in two minutes. Was Grizel wasting a moment when she looked only at him, her eyes filmy with love, the crooked smile upon her face so happy that it could not stand still? Her arms made a slight gesture towards him; her hands were open; she was giving herself to him. She could not see. For a fraction of time the space between them seemed to be annihilated. His arms were closing round her. Then she knew that neither of them had moved.

"Grizel!"

He tried to be true to her by deceiving her. It was the only way. "At last, Grizel," he cried, "at last!" and he put joyousness into his voice. "It has all come right, dear one!" he cried like an ecstatic lover. Never in his life had he tried so hard to deceive at the sacrifice of himself. But he was fighting something as strong as the instinct of self-preservation, and his usually expressionless face gave the lie to his joyous words. Loud above his voice his ashen face was speaking to her, and she cried in terror, "What is wrong?" Even then he attempted to deceive her, but suddenly she knew the truth.

"You don't want to be married!"

I think the room swam round with her. When it was steady again, "You did not say that, did you?" she asked. She was sure he had not said it. She was smiling again tremulously to show him that he had not said it.

"I want to be married above all else on earth," he said imploringly; but his face betrayed him still, and she demanded the truth, and he was forced to tell it.

A little shiver passed through her, that was all.

"Do you mean that you don't love me?" she said. "You must tell me what you mean."

"That is how others would put it, I suppose," he replied. "I believe they would be wrong. I think I love you in my own way; but I thought I loved you in their way, and it is the only way that counts in this world of theirs. It does not seem to be my world. I was given wings, I think, but I am never to know that I have left the earth until I come flop upon it with an arrow through them. I crawl and wriggle here, and yet" —he laughed harshly —"I believe I am rather a fine fellow when I am flying!"

She nodded. "You mean you want me to let you off?" she asked. "You must tell me what you mean." And as he did not answer instantly, "Because I think I have some little claim upon you," she said, with a pleasant smile.

"I am as pitiful a puzzle to myself as I can be to you," he replied. "All I know is that I don't want to marry anyone. And yet I am sure I could die for you, Grizel."

It was quite true. A burning house and Grizel among the flames, and he would have been the first on the ladder. But there is no such luck for you, Tommy.

"You are free," was what she said. "Don't look so tragic," she added, again with the pleasant smile. "It must be very distressing to you, but-you will soon fly again." Her lips twitched tremulously. "I can't fly," she said.

She took the ring from her neck. She took it off its ribbon.

"I brought it," she said, "to let you put it on my finger. I thought you would want to do that," she said.

"Grizel," he cried, "can we not be as we have been?"

"No," she answered.

"It would all come right, Grizel. I am sure it would. I don't know why I am as I am; but I shall try to change myself. You have borne with me since we were children. Won't you bear with me for a little longer?"

She shook her head, but did not trust herself to speak.

"I have lost you," he said, and she nodded.

"Then I am lost indeed!" said he, and he knew it, too; but with a gesture of the hand she begged him not to say that.

"Without your love to help me — —" he began.

"You shall always have that," she told him with shining eyes, "always, always." And what could he do but look at her with the wonder and the awe that come to every man who, for one moment in his life, knows a woman well?

"You can love me still, Grizel!" His voice was shaky.

"Just the same," she answered, and I suppose he looked uplifted. "But you should be sorry," she said gravely, and it was then that Elspeth came back. She had not much exceeded her two minutes.

It was always terrible to Tommy not to have the feelings of a hero. At that moment he could not endure it. In a splendid burst of self-sacrifice he suddenly startled both Grizel and himself by crying, "Elspeth, I love Grizel, and I have just asked her to be my wife."

Yes, the nobility of it amazed himself, but bewitched him, too, and he turned gloriously to Grizel, never doubting but that she would have him still.

He need not have spoken so impulsively, nor looked so grand. She swayed for an instant and then was erect again. "You must forgive me, Elspeth," she said, "but I have refused him"; and that was the biggest surprise Tommy ever got in his life.

"You don't care for him!" Elspeth blurted out.

"Not in the way he cares for me," Grizel replied quietly, and when Elspeth would have said more she begged her to desist. "The only thing for me to do now, Elspeth," she said, smiling, "is to run away, but I want you first to accept a little wedding-gift from me. I wish you and David so much happiness; you won't refuse it, will you?"

Elspeth, still astounded, took the gift. It was a little garnet ring.

"It will have to be cut," Grizel said. "It was meant, I think, for a larger finger. I have had it some time, but I never wore it."

Elspeth said she would always treasure her ring, and that it was beautiful.

"I used to think it-rather sweet," Grizel admitted, and then she said good-bye to them both and went away.

Tommy's new character was that of a monster. He always liked the big parts.

Concealed, as usual, in the garments that clung so oddly to him, modesty, generosity, indifference to applause and all the nobler impulses, he could not strip himself of them, try as he would, and so he found, to his scornful amusement, that he still escaped the public fury. In the two months that preceded Elspeth's marriage there was positively scarce a soul in Thrums who did not think rather well of him. "If they knew what I really am," he cried with splendid bitterness, "how they would run from me!"

Even David could no longer withhold the hand of fellowship, for Grizel would tell him nothing, except that, after all, and for reasons sufficient to herself, she had declined to become Mrs. Sandys. He sought in vain to discover how Tommy could be to blame. "And now," Tommy said grimly to Grizel, "our doctor thinks you have used me badly, and that I am a fine fellow to bear no resentment! Elspeth told me that he admires the gentle and manly dignity with which I submit to the blow, and I have no doubt that, as soon as I heard that, I made it more gentle and manly than ever!

"I have forbidden Elspeth," he told her, "to upbraid you for not accepting me, with the result that she thinks me too good to live! Ha, ha! what do you think, Grizel?"

It became known in the town that she had refused him. Everybody was on Tommy's side. They said she had treated him badly. Even Aaron was staggered at the sight of Tommy accepting his double defeat in such good part. "And all the time I am the greatest cur unhung," says Tommy. "Why don't you laugh, Grizel?"

Never, they said, had there been such a generous brother. The town was astir about this poor man's gifts to the lucky bride. There were rumours that among the articles was a silver coal-scuttle, but it proved to be a sugar-bowl in that pattern. Three bandboxes came for her to select from; somebody discovered who was on the watch, but may I be struck dead if more than one went back. Yesterday it was bonnets; to-day she is at Tilliedrum again, trying on her going-away dress. And she really was to go away in it, a noticeable thing, for in Thrums society, though they usually get a going-away dress, they are too canny to go away in it The local shops were not ignored, but the best of the trousseau came from London. "That makes the second box this week, as I'm a living sinner," cries the lady on the watch again. When boxes arrived at the station Corp wheeled them up to Elspeth without so much as looking at the label.

Ah, what a brother! They said it openly to their own brothers, and to Tommy in the way they looked at him.

"There has been nothing like it," he assured Grizel, "since Red Riding-hood and the wolf. Why can't I fling off my disguise and cry, 'The better to eat you with!'"

He always spoke to her now in this vein of magnificent bitterness, but Grizel seldom rewarded him by crying, "Oh, oh!" She might, however, give him a patient, reproachful glance instead, and it had the irritating effect of making him feel that perhaps he was under life-size, instead of over it.

"I daresay you are right," says Tommy, savagely.

"I said nothing."

"You don't need to say it. What a grand capacity you have for knocking me off my horse, Grizel!"

"Are you angry with me for that?"

"No; it is delicious to pick one's self out of the mud, especially when you find it is a baby you are picking up, instead of a brute. Am I a baby only, Grizel?"

"I think it is childish of you," she replied, "to say you are a brute."

"There is not to be even that satisfaction left to me! You are hard on me, Grizel."

"I am trying to help you. How can you be angry with me?"

"The instinct of self-preservation, I suppose. I see myself dwindling so rapidly under your treatment that soon there will be nothing of me left."

It was said cruelly, for he knew that the one thing Grizel could not bear now was the implication that she saw his faults only. She always went down under that blow with pitiful surrender, showing the woman suddenly, as if under a physical knouting.

He apologized contritely. "But, after all, it proves my case," he said, "for I could not hurt you in this way, Grizel, if I were not a pretty well-grown specimen of a monster."

"Don't," she said; but she did not seek to help him by drawing him away to other subjects, which would have been his way. "What is there monstrous," she asked, "in your being so good to Elspeth? It is very kind of you to give her all these things."

"Especially when by rights they are yours, Grizel!"

"No, not when you did not want to give them to me."

He dared say nothing to that; there were some matters on which he must not contradict Grizel now.

"It is nice of you," she said, "not to complain, though Elspeth is deserting you. It must have been a blow."

"You and I only know why," he answered. "But for her, Grizel, I might be whining sentiment to you at this moment."

"That," she said, "would be the monstrous thing."

"And it is not monstrous, I suppose, that I should let Gemmell press my hand under the conviction that, after all, I am a trump."

"You don't pose as one."

"That makes them think the more highly of me! Nothing monstrous, Grizel, in my standing quietly by while you are showing Elspeth how to furnish her house —I, who know why you have the subject at your finger-tips!"

For Grizel had given all her sweet ideas to Elspeth. Heigh-ho! how she had guarded them once, confiding them half reluctantly even to Tommy; half reluctantly, that is, at the start, because they were her very own, but once she was embarked on the subject talking with such rapture that every minute or two he had to beg her to be calm. She was the first person in that part of the world to think that old furniture need not be kept in the dark corners, and she knew where there was an oak bedstead that was looked upon as a disgrace, and where to obtain the dearest cupboards, one of them in use as the retiring-chamber of a rabbit-hutch, and stately clocks made in the town a hundred years ago, and quaint old-farrant lamps and cogeys and sand-glasses that apologized if you looked at them, and yet were as willing to be loved again as any old lady in a mutch. You will not buy them easily now, the people will not chuckle at you when you bid for them now. We have become so cute in Thrums that when the fender breaks we think it may have increased in value, and we preserve any old board lest the worms have made it artistic. Grizel, however, was in advance of her time. She could lay her hands on all she wanted, and she did, but it was for Elspeth's house.

"And the table-cloths and the towels and the sheets," said Tommy. "Nothing monstrous in my letting you give Elspeth them?"

The linen, you see, was no longer in Grizel's press.

"I could not help making them," she answered, "they were so longing to be made. I did not mean to give them to her. I think I meant to put them back in the press, but when they were made it was natural that they should want to have something to do. So I gave them to Elspeth."

"With how many tears on them?"

"Not many. But with some kisses."

"All which," says Tommy, "goes to prove that I have nothing with which to reproach myself!"

"No, I never said that," she told him. "You have to reproach yourself with wanting me to love you."

She paused a moment to let him say, if he dared, that he had not done that, when she would have replied instantly, "You know you did." He could have disabused her, but it would have been cruel, and so on this subject, as ever, he remained silent.

"But that is not what I have been trying to prove," she continued. "You know as well as I that the cause of this unhappiness has been-what you call your wings."

He was about to thank her for her delicacy in avoiding its real name, when she added, "I mean your sentiment," and he laughed instead.

"I flatter myself that I no longer fly, at all events," he said. "I know what I am at last, Grizel"

"It is flattery only," she replied with her old directness. "This thing you are regarding with a morbid satisfaction is not you at all."

He groaned. "Which of them all is me, Grizel?" he asked gloomily.

"We shall see," she said, "when we have got the wings off."

"They will have to come off a feather at a time."

"That," she declared, "is what I have been trying to prove."

"It will be a weary task, Grizel."

"I won't weary at it," she said, smiling.

Her cheerfulness was a continual surprise to him. "You bear up wonderfully well yourself," he sometimes said to her, almost reproachfully, and she never replied that, perhaps, that was one of her ways of trying to help him.

She is not so heartbroken, after all, you may be saying, and I had promised to break her heart. But, honestly, I don't know how to do it more thoroughly, and you must remember that we have not seen her alone yet.

She tried to be very little alone. She helped David in his work more than ever; not a person, for instance, managed to escape the bath because Grizel's heart was broken. You could never say that she was alone when her needle was going, and the linen became sheets and the like, in what was probably record time. Yet they could have been sewn more quickly; for at times the needle stopped and she did not know it. Once a bedridden old woman, with whom she had been sitting up, lay watching her instead of sleeping, and finally said: "What makes you sit staring at a cauld fire, and speaking to yourself?" And there was a strange day when she had been too long in the Den. When she started for home she went in the direction of Double Dykes, her old home, instead.

She could bear everything except doubt. She had told him so, when he wondered at her calmness; she often said it to herself. She could tread any path, however drearily it stretched before her, so long as she knew whither it led, but there could be no more doubt. Oh, he must never again disturb her mind with hope! How clearly she showed him that, and yet they had perhaps no more than parted when it seemed impossible to bear for the next hour the desolation she was sentenced to for life. She lay quivering and tossing on the hearth-rug of the parlour, beating it with her fists, rocking her arms, and calling to him to give her doubt again, that she might get through the days.

"Let me doubt again!" Here was Grizel starting to beg it of him. More than once she got half-way to Aaron's house before she could turn; but she always did turn, with the words unspoken; never did Tommy hear her say them, but always that she was tranquil now. Was it pride that supported her in the trying hour? Oh, no, it was not pride. That is an old garment, which once became Grizel well, but she does not wear it now; she takes it out of the closet, perhaps, at times to look at it. What gave her strength when he was by was her promise to help him. It was not by asking for leave to dream herself that she could make him dream the less. All done for you, Tommy! It might have helped you to loosen a few of the feathers.

Sometimes she thought it might not be Tommy, but herself, who was so unlike other people; that it was not he who was unable to love, but she who could not be loved. This idea did not agitate her as a terrible thing; she could almost welcome it. But she did not go to him with it. While it might be but a fancy, that was no way to help a man who was overfull of them. It was the bare truth only that she wanted him to see, and so she made elaborate inquiries into herself, to discover whether she was quite unlovable. I suppose it would have been quaint, had she not been quite so much in earnest. She examined herself in the long mirror most conscientiously, and with a determinedly open mind, to see whether she was too ugly for any man to love. Our beautiful Grizel really did.

She had always thought that she was a nice girl, but was she? No one had ever loved her, except the old doctor, and he began when she was so young that perhaps he had been inveigled into it, like a father. Even David had not loved her. Was it because he knew her so well? What was it in women that made men love them? She asked it of David in such a way that he never knew she was putting him to the question. He merely thought that he and she were having a pleasant chat about Elspeth, and, as a result, she decided that he loved Elspeth because she was so helpless. His head sat with uncommon pride on his shoulders while he talked of Elspeth's timidity. There was a ring of boastfulness in his voice as he paraded the large number of useful things that Elspeth could not do. And yet David was a sensible and careful man.

Was it helplessness that man loved in woman, then? It seemed to be Elspeth's helplessness that had made Tommy such a brother, and how it had always appealed to Aaron! No woman could be less helpless than herself, Grizel knew. She thought back and back, and she could not come to a time when she was not managing somebody. Women, she reflected, fall more or less deeply in love with every baby they see, while men, even the best of them, can look calmly at other people's babies. But when the helplessness of the child is in the woman, then other women are unmoved; but the great heart of man is stirred-woman is his baby. She remembered that the language of love is in two sexes-for the woman superlatives, for the man diminutives. The more she loves the bigger he grows, but in an ecstasy he could put her in his pocket. Had not Tommy taught her this? His little one, his child! Perhaps he really had loved her in the days when they both made believe that she was infantile; but soon she had shown with fatal clearness that she was not. Instead of needing to be taken care of, she had obviously wanted to take care of him: their positions were reversed. Perhaps, said Grizel to herself, I should have been a man.

If this was the true explanation, then, though Tommy, who had tried so hard, could not love her, he might be able to love-what is the phrase? —a more womanly woman, or, more popular phrase still, a very woman. Some other woman might be the right wife for him. She did not shrink from considering this theory, and she considered so long that I, for one, cannot smile at her for deciding ultimately, as she did, that there was nothing in it.

The strong like to be leaned upon and the weak to lean, and this irrespective of sex. This was the solution she woke up with one morning, and it seemed to explain not only David's and Elspeth's love, but her own, so clearly that in her desire to help she put it before Tommy. It implied that she cared for him because he was weak, and he drew a very long face.

"You don't know how the feathers hurt as they come out," he explained.

"But so long as we do get them out!" she said.

"Every other person who knows me thinks that strength is my great characteristic," he maintained, rather querulously.

"But when you know it is not," said Grizel. "You do know, don't you?" she asked anxiously. "To know the truth about one's self, that is the beginning of being strong."

"You seem determined," he retorted, "to prevent my loving you."

"Why?" she asked.

"You are to make me strong in spite of myself, I understand. But, according to your theory, the strong love the weak only. Are you to grow weak, Grizel, as I grow strong?"

She had not thought of that, and she would have liked to rock her arms. But she was able to reply: "I am not trying to help you in order to make you love me; you know, quite well, that all that is over and done with. I am trying only to help you to be what a man should be."

She could say that to him, but to herself? Was she prepared to make a man of him at the cost of his possible love? This faced her when she was alone with her passionate nature, and she fought it, and with her fists clenched she cried: "Yes, yes, yes!"

Do we know all that Grizel had to fight? There were times when Tommy's mind wandered to excuses for himself; he knew what men were, and he shuddered to think of the might have been, had a girl who could love as Grizel did loved such a man as her father. He thanked his Maker, did Tommy, that he, who was made as those other men, had avoided raising passions in her. I wonder how he was so sure. Do we know all that Grizel had to fight?

They spoke much during those days of the coming parting, and she always said that she could bear it if she saw him go away more of a man than he had come.

"Then anything I have suffered or may suffer," she told him, "will have been done to help you, and perhaps in time that will make me proud of my poor little love-story. It would be rather pitiful, would it not, if I have gone through so much for no end at all?"

She spoke, he said, almost reproachfully, as if she thought he might go away on his wings, after all.

"We can't be sure," she murmured, she was so eager to make him watchful.

"Yes," he said, humbly but firmly, "I may be a scoundrel, Grizel, I am a scoundrel, but one thing you may be sure of, I am done with sentiment." But even as he said it, even as he felt that he could tear himself asunder for being untrue to Grizel, a bird was singing at his heart because he was free again, free to go out into the world and play as if it were but a larger den. Ah, if only Tommy could always have remained a boy!

Elspeth's marriage day came round, and I should like to linger in it, and show you Elspeth in her wedding-gown, and Tommy standing behind to catch her if she fainted, and Ailie weeping, and Aaron Latta rubbing his gleeful hands, and a smiling bridesmaid who had once thought she might be a bride. But that was a day in Elspeth's story, not in Tommy's and Grizel's. Only one incident in their story crept into that happy day. There were speeches at the feast, and the Rev. Mr. Dishart referred to Tommy in the kindliest way, called him "my young friend," quoted (inaccurately) from his book, and expressed an opinion, formed, he might say, when Mr. Sandys was a lad at school (cheers), that he had a career before him. Tommy bore it well, all except the quotation, which he was burning to correct, but sighed to find that it had set the dominies on his left talking about precocity. "To produce such a graybeard of a book at two and twenty, Mr. Sandys," said Cathro, "is amazing. It partakes, sir, of the nature of the miraculous; it's onchancey, by which we mean a deviation from the normal." And so on. To escape this kind of flattery (he had so often heard it said by ladies, who could say it so much better), Tommy turned to his neighbours on the right.

Oddly enough, they also were discussing deviations from the normal. On the table was a plant in full flower, and Ailie, who had lent it, was expressing surprise that it should bloom so late in the season.

"So early in its life, I should rather say," the doctor remarked after examining it. "It is a young plant, and in the ordinary course would not have come to flower before next year. But it is afraid that it will never see next year. It is one of those poor little plants that bloom prematurely because they are diseased."

Tommy was a little startled. He had often marvelled over his own precocity, but never guessed that this might be the explanation why he was in flower at twenty-two. "Is that a scientific fact?" he asked.

"It is a law of nature," the doctor replied gravely, and if anything more was said on the subject our Tommy did not hear it. What did he hear? He was a child again, in miserable lodgings, and it was sometime in the long middle of the night, and what he heard from his bed was his mother coughing away her life in hers. There was an angry knock, knock, knock, from somewhere near, and he crept out of bed to tell his mother that the people through the wall were complaining because she would not die more quietly; but when he reached her bed it was not his mother he saw lying there, but himself, aged twenty-four or thereabouts. For Tommy had inherited his mother's cough; he had known it every winter, but he remembered it as if for the first time now.

Did he hear anything else? I think he heard his wings slipping to the floor.

He asked Ailie to give him the plant, and he kept it in his room very lovingly, though he forgot to water it. He sat for long periods looking at it, and his thoughts were very deep, but all he actually said aloud was, "There are two of us." Aaron sometimes saw them together, and thought they were an odd pair, and perhaps they were.

Tommy did not tell Grizel of the tragedy that was hanging over him. He was determined to save her that pain. He knew that most men in his position would have told her, and was glad to find that he could keep it so gallantly to himself. She was brave; perhaps some day she would discover that he had been brave also. When she talked of wings now, what he seemed to see was a green grave. His eyes were moist, but he held his head high. All this helped him.

Ah, well, but the world must jog along though you and I be damned. Elspeth was happily married, and there came the day when Tommy and Grizel must say good-bye. He was returning to London. His luggage was already in Corp's barrow, all but the insignificant part of it, which yet made a bulky package in its author's pocket, for it was his new manuscript, for which he would have fought a regiment, yes, and beaten them. Little cared Tommy what became of the rest of his luggage so long as that palpitating package was safe.

"And little you care," Grizel said, in a moment of sudden bitterness, "whom you leave behind, so long as you take it with you."

He forgave her with a sad smile. She did not know, you see, that this manuscript might be his last.

And it was the only bitter thing she said. Even when he looked very sorry for her, she took advantage of his emotion to help him only. "Don't be too sorry for me," she said calmly; "remember, rather, that there is one episode in a woman's life to which she must always cling in memory, whether it was a pride to her or a shame, and that it rests with you to make mine proud or shameful."

In other words, he was to get rid of his wings. How she harped on that!

He wanted to kiss her on the brow, but she would not have it. He was about to do it, not to gratify any selfish desire, but of a beautiful impulse that if anything happened she would have this to remember as the last of him. But she drew back almost angrily. Positively, she was putting it down to sentiment, and he forgave her even that.

But she kissed the manuscript. "Wish it luck," he had begged of her; "you were always so fond of babies, and this is my baby." So Grizel kissed Tommy's baby, and then she turned away her face.

Chapter XXV

Mr. T. Sandys Has Returned to Town

It is disquieting to reflect that we have devoted so much paper (this is the third shilling's worth) to telling what a real biographer would almost certainly have summed up in a few pages. "Caring nothing for glory, engrossed in his work alone, Mr. Sandys, soon after the publication of the 'Letters,' sought the peace of his mother's native village, and there, alike undisturbing and undisturbed, he gave his life, as ever, to laborious days and quiet contemplation. The one vital fact in these six months of lofty endeavour is that he was making progress with the new book. Fishing and other distractions were occasionally indulged in, but merely that he might rise fresher next morning to a book which absorbed," etc.

One can see exactly how it should be done, it has been done so often before. And there is a deal to be said for this method. His book was what he had been at during nearly the whole of that time; comparatively speaking, the fishing and "other distractions" (a neat phrase) had got an occasional hour only. But while we admire, we can't do it in that way. We seem fated to go on taking it for granted that you know the "vital facts" about Tommy, and devoting our attention to the things that the real biographer leaves out.

Tommy arrived in London with little more than ten pounds in his pockets. All the rest he had spent on Elspeth.

He looked for furnished chambers in a fashionable quarter, and they were much too expensive. But the young lady who showed them to him asked if it was *the* Mr. Sandys, and he at once took the rooms. Her mother subsequently said that she understood he wrote books, and would he deposit five pounds?

Such are the ups and downs of the literary calling.

The book, of course, was "Unrequited Love," and the true story of how it was not given to the world by his first publishers has never been told. They had the chance, but they weighed the manuscript in their hands as if it were butter, and said it was very small.

"If you knew how much time I have spent in making it smaller," replied Tommy, haughtily.

The madmen asked if he could not add a few chapters, whereupon, with a shudder, he tucked baby under his wing and flew away. That is how Goldie & Goldie got the book.

For one who had left London a glittering star, it was wonderful how little he brightened it by returning. At the club they did not know that he had been away. In society they seemed to have forgotten to expect him back.

He had an eye for them-with a touch of red in it; but he bided his time. It was one of the terrible things about Tommy that he could bide his time. Pym was the only person he called upon. He took Pym out to dinner and conducted him home again. His kindness to Pym, the delicacy with which he pretended not to see that poor old Pym was degraded and done for-they would have been pretty even in a woman, and we treat Tommy unfairly in passing them by with a bow.

Pym had the manuscript to read, and you may be as sure he kept sober that night as that Tommy lay awake. For when literature had to be judged, who could be so grim a critic as this usually lenient toper? He could forgive much, could Pym. You had run away without paying your rent, was it? Well, well, come in and have a drink. Broken your wife's heart, have you? Poor chap, but you will soon get over it. But if it was a split infinitive, "Go to the devil, sir."

"Into a cocked hat," was the verdict of Pym, meaning thereby that thus did Tommy's second work beat his first. Tommy broke down and wept.

Presently Pym waxed sentimental and confided to Tommy that he, too, had once loved in vain. The sad case of those who love in vain, you remember, is the subject of the book. The saddest of autobiographies, it has been called.

An odd thing, this, I think. Tearing home (for the more he was engrossed in mind the quicker he walked), Tommy was not revelling in Pym's praise; he was neither blanching nor smiling at the thought that he of all people had written as one who was unloved; he was not wondering what Grizel would say to it; he had even forgotten to sigh over his own coming dissolution (indeed, about this time the flower-pot began to fade from his memory). What made him cut his way so excitedly through the streets was this: Pym had questioned his use of the word "untimely" in chapter eight. And Tommy had always been uneasy about that word.

He glared at every person he passed, and ran into perambulators. He rushed past his chambers like one who no longer had a home. He was in the park now, and did not even notice that the Row was empty, that mighty round a deserted circus; management, riders, clowns, all the performers gone on their provincial tour, or nearly all, for a lady on horseback sees him, remembers to some extent who he is, and gives chase. It is our dear Mrs. Jerry.

"You wretch," she said, "to compel me to pursue you! Nothing could have induced me to do anything so unwomanly except that you are the only man in town."

She shook her whip so prettily at him that it was as seductive as a smile. It was also a way of gaining time while she tried to remember what it was he was famous for.

"I believe you don't know me!" she said, with a little shriek, for Tommy had looked bewildered. "That would be too mortifying. Please pretend you do!"

Her look of appeal, the way in which she put her plump little hands together, as if about to say her prayers, brought it all back to Tommy. The one thing he was not certain of was whether he had proposed to her.

It was the one thing of which she was certain.

"You think I can forget so soon," he replied reproachfully, but carefully.

"Then tell me my name," said she; she thought it might lead to his mentioning his own.

"I don't know what it is now. It was Mrs. Jerry once."

"It is Mrs. Jerry still."

"Then you did not marry him, after all?"

No wild joy had surged to his face, but when she answered yes, he nodded his head with gentle melancholy three times. He had not the smallest desire to deceive the lady; he was simply an actor who had got his cue and liked his part.

"But my friends still call me Mrs. Jerry," she said softly.

"But my friends still call me Mrs. Jerry," she said softly. "I suppose it suits me somehow."

"You will always be Mrs. Jerry to me," he replied huskily. Ah, those meetings with old loves!

"If you minded so much," Mrs. Jerry said, a little tremulously (she had the softest heart, though her memory was a trifle defective), "you might have discovered whether I had married him or not."

"Was there no reason why I should not seek to discover it?" Tommy asked with tremendous irony, but not knowing in the least what he meant.

It confused Mrs. Jerry. They always confused her when they were fierce, and yet she liked them to be fierce when she re-met them, so few of them were.

But she said the proper thing. "I am glad you have got over it."

Tommy maintained a masterly silence. No wonder he was a power with women.

"I say I am glad you have got over it," murmured Mrs. Jerry again. Has it ever been noticed that the proper remark does not always gain in propriety with repetition?

It is splendid to know that right feeling still kept Tommy silent.

Yet she went on briskly as if he had told her something: "Am I detaining you? You were walking so quickly that I thought you were in pursuit of someone."

It brought Tommy back to earth, and he could accept her now as an old friend he was glad to meet again. "You could not guess what I was in pursuit of, Mrs. Jerry," he assured her, and with confidence, for words are not usually chased down the Row.

But, though he made the sound of laughter, that terrible face which Mrs. Jerry remembered so well, but could not give a name to, took no part in the revelry; he was as puzzling to her as those irritating authors who print their jokes without a note of exclamation at the end of them. Poor Mrs. Jerry thought it must be a laugh of horrid bitterness, and that he was referring to his dead self or something dreadful of that sort, for which she was responsible.

"Please don't tell me," she said, in such obvious alarm that again he laughed that awful laugh. He promised, with a profound sigh, to carry his secret unspoken to the grave, also to come to her "At Home" if she sent him a card.

He told her his address, but not his name, and she could not send the card to "Occupier."

"Now tell me about yourself," said Mrs. Jerry, with charming cunning. "Did you go away?"

"I came back a few days ago only."

"Had you any shooting?" (They nearly always threatened to make for a distant land where there was big game.)

Tommy smiled. He had never "had any shooting" except once in his boyhood, when he and Corp acted as beaters, and he had wept passionately over the first bird killed, and harangued the murderer.

"No," he replied; "I was at work all the time."

This, at least, told her that his work was of a kind which could be done out of London. An inventor?

"When are we to see the result?" asked artful Mrs. Jerry.

"Very soon. Everything comes out about this time. It is our season, you know."

Mrs. Jerry pondered while she said: "How too entrancing!" What did come out this month? Oh, plays! And whose season was it? The actor's, of course! He could not be an actor with that beard, but-ah, she remembered now!

"Are they really clever this time?" she asked roguishly —"for you must admit that they are usually sticks."

Tommy blinked at this. "I really believe, Mrs. Jerry," he said slowly, "it is you who don't know who I am!"

"You prepare the aristocracy for the stage, don't you?" she said plaintively.

"I!" he thundered.

"He had a beard," she said, in self-defence.

"Who?"

"Oh, I don't know! Please forgive me! I do remember, of course, who you are —I remember too well!" said Mrs. Jerry, generously.

"What is my name?" Tommy demanded.

She put her hands together again, beseechingly. "Please, please!" she said. "I have such a dreadful memory for names, but-oh, please!"

"What am I?" he insisted.

"You are the-the man who invents those delightful thingumbobs," she cried with an inspiration.

"I never invented anything, except two books," said Tommy, looking at her reproachfully.

"I know them by heart," she cried.

"One of them is not published yet," he informed her.

"I am looking forward to it so excitedly," she said at once.

"And my name is Sandys," said he.

"Thomas Sandys," she said, correcting him triumphantly. "How is that dear, darling little Agnes-Elspeth?"

"You have me at last," he admitted.

"'Sandys on Woman!'" exclaimed Mrs. Jerry, all rippling smiles once more. "Can I ever forget it!"

"I shall never pretend to know anything about women again," Tommy answered dolefully, but with a creditable absence of vindictiveness.

"Please, please!" said the little hands again.

"It is a nasty jar, Mrs. Jerry."

"Please!"

"Oh that I could forget so quickly!"

"Please!"

"I forgive you, if that is what you want."

She waved her whip. "And you will come and see me?"

"When I have got over this. It needs —a little time." He really said this to please her.

"You shall talk to me of the new book," she said, confident that this would fetch him, for he was not her first author. "By the way, what is it about?"

"Can you ask, Mrs. Jerry?" replied Tommy, passionately. "Oh, woman, woman, can you ask?"

This puzzled her at the time, but she understood what he had meant when the book came out, dedicated to Pym. "Goodness gracious!" she said to herself as she went from chapter to chapter, and she was very self-conscious when she heard the book discussed in society, which was not quite as soon as it came out, for at first the ladies seemed to have forgotten their Tommy.

But the journals made ample amends. He had invented, they said, something new in literature, a story that was yet not a story, told in the form of essays which were no mere essays. There was no character mentioned by name, there was not a line of dialogue, essays only, they might say, were the net result, yet a human heart was laid bare, and surely that was fiction in its highest form. Fiction founded on fact, no doubt (for it would be ostrich-like to deny that such a work must be the outcome of a painful personal experience), but in those wise and penetrating pages Mr. Sandys called no one's attention to himself; his subject was an experience common to humanity, to be borne this way or that; and without vainglory he showed how it should be borne, so that those looking into the deep waters of the book (made clear by his pellucid style) might see, not the author, but themselves.

A few of the critics said that if the book added nothing to his reputation, it detracted nothing from it, but probably their pen added this mechanically when they were away. What annoyed him more was the two or three who stated that, much as they liked "Unrequited Love," they liked the "Letters" still better. He could not endure hearing a good word said for the "Letters" now.

The great public, I believe, always preferred the "Letters," but among important sections of it the new book was a delight, and for various reasons. For instance, it was no mere story. That got the thoughtful public. Its style, again, got the public which knows it is the only public that counts.

Society still held aloof (there was an African traveller on view that year), but otherwise everything was going on well, when the bolt came, as ever, from the quarter whence it was least expected. It came in a letter from Grizel, so direct as to be almost as direct as this: "I think it is a horrid book. The more beautifully it is written the more horrid it seems. No one was ever loved more truly than you. You can know nothing about unrequited love. Then why do you pretend to know? I see why you always avoided telling me anything about the book, even its title. It was because you knew what I should say. It is nothing but sentiment. You were on your wings all the time you were writing it. That is why you could treat me as you did. Even to the last moment you deceived me. I suppose you deceived yourself also. Had I known what was in the manuscript I would not have kissed it, I would have asked you to burn it. Had you not had the strength, and you would not, I should have burned it for you. It would have been a proof of my love. I have ceased to care whether you are a famous man or not. I want you to be a real man. But you will not let me help you. I have cried all day. GRIZEL."

Fury. Dejection. The heroic. They came in that order.

"This is too much!" he cried at first, "I can stand a good deal, Grizel, but there was once a worm that turned at last, you know. Take care, madam, take care. Oh, but you are a charming lady; you can decide everything for everybody, can't you! What delicious letters you write, something unexpected in everyone of them! There are poor dogs of men, Grizel, who open their letters from their loves knowing exactly what will be inside-words of cheer, words of love, of confidence, of admiration, which help them as they sit into the night at their work, fighting for fame that they may lay it at their loved one's feet. Discouragement, obloquy, scorn, they get in plenty from others, but they are always sure of her, —do you hear, my original Grizel? —those other dogs are always sure of her. Hurrah! Grizel, I was happy, I was actually honoured, it was helping me to do better and better, when you quickly put an end to all that. Hurrah, hurrah!"

I feel rather sorry for him. If he had not told her about his book it was because she did not and never could understand what compels a man to write one book instead of another. "I had no say in the matter; the thing demanded of me that I should do it, and I had to do it. Some must write from their own experience, they can make nothing of anything else; but it is to me like a chariot that won't budge; I have to assume a character, Grizel, and then away we go. I don't attempt to explain how I write, I hate to discuss it; all I know is that those who know how it should be done can never do it. London is overrun with such, and everyone of them is as cock-sure as you. You have taken everything else, Grizel; surely you might leave me my books."

Yes, everything else, or nearly so. He put upon the table all the feathers he had extracted since his return to London, and they did make some little show, if less than it seemed to him. That little adventure in the park; well, if it started wrongly, it but helped to show the change in him, for he had determinedly kept away from Mrs. Jerry's house. He had met her once since the book came out, and she had blushed exquisitely when referring to it, and said: "How you have suffered! I blame myself dreadfully." Yes, and there was an unoccupied sofa near by, and he had not sat down on it with her and continued the conversation. Was not that a feather? And there were other ladies, and, without going into particulars, they were several feathers between them. How doggedly, to punish himself, he had stuck to the company of men, a sex that never interested him!

"But all that is nothing. I am beyond the pale, I did so monstrous a thing that I must die for it. What was this dreadful thing? When I saw you with that glove I knew you loved me, and that you thought I loved you, and I had not the heart to dash your joy. You don't know it, but that was the crime for which I must be exterminated, fiend that I am!"

Gusts of fury came at intervals all the morning. He wrote her appalling letters and destroyed them. He shook his fist and snapped his fingers at her, and went out for drink (having none in the house), and called a hansom to take him to Mrs. Jerry's, and tore round the park again and glared at everybody. He rushed on and on. "But the one thing you shall never do, Grizel, is to interfere with my work; I swear it, do you hear? In all else I am yours to mangle at your will, but touch it, and I am a beast at bay."

And still saying such things, he drew near the publishing offices of Goldie & Goldie, and circled round them, less like a beast at bay than a bird that is taking a long way to its nest. And about four of the afternoon what does this odd beast or bird or fish do but stalk into Goldie & Goldie's and order "Unrequited Love" to be withdrawn from circulation.

"Madam, I have carried out your wishes, and the man is hanged."

Not thus, but in words to that effect, did Tommy announce his deed to Grizel.

"I think you have done the right thing," she wrote back, "and I admire you for it." But he thought she did not admire him sufficiently for it, and he did not answer her letter, so it was the last that passed between them.

Such is the true explanation (now first published) of an affair that at the time created no small stir. "Why withdraw the book?" Goldie & Goldie asked of Tommy, but he would give no reason. "Why?" the public asked of Goldie & Goldie, and they had to invent several. The public invented the others. The silliest were those you could know only by belonging to a club.

I swear that Tommy had not foreseen the result. Quite unwittingly the favoured of the gods had found a way again. The talk about his incomprehensible action was the turning-point in the fortunes of the book. There were already a few thousand copies in circulation, and now many thousand people wanted them. Sandys, Sandys, Sandys! where had the ladies heard that name before? Society woke up, Sandys was again its hero; the traveller had to go lecturing in the provinces.

The ladies! Yes, and their friends, the men. There was a Tommy society in Mayfair that winter, nearly all of the members eminent or beautiful, and they held each other's hands. Both sexes were eligible, married or single, and the one rule was something about sympathy. It afterwards became the Souls, but those in the know still call them the Tommies.

They blackballed Mrs. Jerry (she was rather plump), but her married stepdaughter, Lady Pippinworth (who had been a Miss Ridge-Fulton), was one of them. Indeed, the Ridge-Fultons are among the thinnest families in the country.

T. Sandys was invited to join the society, but declined, and thus never quite knew what they did, nor can any outsider know, there being a regulation among the Tommies against telling. I believe, however, that they were a brotherhood, with sisters. You had to pass an examination in unrequited love, showing how you had suffered, and after that either the men or the women (I forget which) dressed in white to the throat, and then each got some other's old love's hand to hold, and you all sat on the floor and thought hard. There may have been even more in it than this, for one got to know Tommies at sight by a sort of careworn halo round the brow, and it is said that the House of Commons was several times nearly counted out because so many of its middle-aged members were holding the floor in another place.

Of course there were also the Anti-Tommies, who called themselves (rather vulgarly) the Tummies. Many of them were that shape. They held that, though you had loved in vain, it was no such mighty matter to boast of; but they were poor in argument, and their only really strong card was that Mr. Sandys was stoutish himself.

Their organs in the press said that he was a man of true genius, and slightly inclined to *embonpoint*.

This maddened him, but on the whole his return was a triumph, and despite thoughts of Grizel he was very, very happy, for he was at play again. He was a boy, and all the ladies were girls. Perhaps the lady he saw most frequently was Mrs. Jerry's stepdaughter. Lady Pippinworth was a friend of Lady Rintoul, and had several times visited her at the Spittal, but that was not the sole reason why Tommy so frequently drank tea with her. They had met first at a country house, where, one night after the ladies had retired to rest, Lady Pippinworth came stealing into the smoking-room with the tidings that there were burglars in the house. As she approached her room she had heard whispers, and then, her door being ajar, she had peeped upon the miscreants. She had also seen a pile of her jewellery on the table, and a pistol keeping guard on top of it. There were several men in the house, but that pistol cowed all of them save Tommy. "If we could lock them in!" someone suggested, but the key was on the wrong side of the door. "I shall put it on the right side," Tommy said pluckily, "if you others will prevent their escaping by the window"; and with characteristic courage he set off for her Ladyship's room. His intention was to insert his hand, whip out the key, and lock the door on the outside, a sufficiently hazardous enterprise; but what does he do instead? Locks the door on the inside, and goes for the burglars with his fists! A happy recollection of Corp's famous one from the shoulder disposed at once of the man who had seized the pistol; with the other gentleman Tommy had a stand-up fight in which both of them took and gave, but when support arrived, one burglar was senseless on the floor and T. Sandys was sitting on the other. Courageous of Tommy, was it not? But observe the end. He was left in the dining-room to take charge of his captives until morning, and by and by he was exhorting them in such noble language to mend their ways that they took the measure of him, and so touching were their family histories that Tommy wept and untied their cords and showed them out at the front door and gave them ten shillings each, and the one who begged for the honour of shaking hands with him also took his watch. Thus did Tommy and Lady Pippinworth become friends, but it was not this that sent him so often to her house to tea. She was a beautiful woman, with a reputation for having broken many hearts without damaging her own. He thought it an interesting case.

It was Tommy who was the favoured of the gods, you remember, not Grizel.

Elspeth wondered to see her, after the publication of that book, looking much as usual. "You know how he loved you now," she said, perhaps a little reproachfully.

"Yes," Grizel answered, "I know; I knew before the book came out."

"You must be sorry for him?"

Grizel nodded.

"But proud of him also," Elspeth said. "You have a right to be proud."

"I am as proud," Grizel replied, "as I have a right to be."

Something in her voice touched Elspeth, who was so happy that she wanted everyone to be happy. "I want you to know, Grizel," she said warmly, "that I don't blame you for not being able to love him; we can't help those things. Nor need you blame yourself too much, for I have often heard him say that artists must suffer in order to produce beautiful things."

"But I cannot remember," Elspeth had to admit, with a sigh, to David, "that she made any answer to that, except 'Thank you.'"

Grizel was nearly as reticent to David himself. Once only did she break down for a moment in his presence. It was when he was telling her that the issue of the book had been stopped.

"But I see you know already," he said. "Perhaps you even know why-though he has not given any sufficient reason to Elspeth."

David had given his promise, she reminded him, not to ask her any questions about Tommy.

"But I don't see why I should keep it," he said bluntly.

"Because you dislike him," she replied.

"Grizel," he declared, "I have tried hard to like him. I have thought and thought about it, and I can't see that he has given me any just cause to dislike him."

"And that," said Grizel, "makes you dislike him more than ever."

"I know that you cared for him once," David persisted, "and I know that he wanted to marry you —"

But she would not let him go on. "David," she said, "I want to give up my house, and I want you to take it. It is the real doctor's house of Thrums, and people in need of you still keep ringing me up of nights. The only door to your surgery is through my passage; it is I who should be in lodgings now."

"Do you really think I would, Grizel!" he cried indignantly.

"Rather than see the dear house go into another's hands," she answered steadily; "for I am determined to leave it. Dr. McQueen won't feel strange when he looks down, David, if it is only you he sees moving about the old rooms, instead of me."

"You are doing this for me, Grizel, and I won't have it."

"I give you my word," she told him, "that I am doing it for myself alone. I am tired of keeping a house, and of all its worries. Men don't know what they are."

She was smiling, but his brows wrinkled in pain. "Oh, Grizel!" he said, and stopped. And then he cried, "Since when has Grizel ceased to care for housekeeping?"

She did not say since when. I don't know whether she knew; but it was since she and Tommy had ceased to correspond. David's words showed her too suddenly how she had changed, and it was then that she broke down before him-because she had ceased to care for housekeeping.

But she had her way, and early in the new year David and his wife were established in their new home, with all Grizel's furniture, except such as was needed for the two rooms rented by her from Gavinia. She would have liked to take away the old doctor's chair, because it was the bit of him left behind when he died, and then for that very reason she did not. She no longer wanted him to see her always. "I am not so nice as I used to be, and I want to keep it from you," she said to the chair when she kissed it good-bye.

Was Grizel not as nice as she used to be? How can I answer, who love her the more only? There is one at least, Grizel, who will never desert you.

Ah, but was she?

I seem again to hear the warning voice of Grizel, and this time she is crying: "You know I was not."

She knew it so well that she could say it to herself quite calmly. She knew that, with whatever repugnance she drove those passions away, they would come back-yes, and for a space be welcomed back. Why does she leave Gavinia's blue hearth this evening, and seek the solitary Den? She has gone to summon them, and she knows it. They come thick in the Den, for they know the place. It was there that her mother was wont to walk with them. Have they been waiting for you in the Den, Grizel, all this time? Have you found your mother's legacy at last?

Don't think that she sought them often. It was never when she seemed to have anything to live for. Tommy would not write to her, and so did not want her to write to him; but if that bowed her head, it never made her rebel. She still had her many duties. Whatever she suffered, so long as she could say, "I am helping him," she was in heart and soul the Grizel of old. In his fits of remorse, which were many, he tried to produce work that would please her. Thus, in a heroic attempt to be practical, he wrote a political article in one of the reviews, quite in the ordinary style, but so much worse than the average of such things that they would never have printed it without his name. He also contributed to a magazine a short tale, —he who could never write tales, —and he struck all the beautiful reflections out of it, and never referred to himself once, and the result was so imbecile that kindly people said there must be another writer of the same name. "Show them to Grizel," Tommy wrote to Elspeth, inclosing also some of the animadversions of the press, and he meant Grizel to see that he could write in his own way only. But she read those two efforts with delight, and said to Elspeth, "Tell him I am so proud of them."

Elspeth thought it very nice of Grizel to defend the despised in this way (even Elspeth had fallen asleep over the political paper). She did not understand that Grizel loved them because they showed Tommy trying to do without his wings.

Then another trifle by him appeared, shorter even than the others; but no man in England could have written it except T. Sandys. It has not been reprinted, and I forget everything about it except that its subject was love. "Will not the friends of the man who can produce such a little masterpiece as this," the journals said, "save him from wasting his time on lumber for the reviews, and drivelling tales?" And Tommy suggested to Elspeth that she might show Grizel this exhortation also.

Grizel saw she was not helping him at all. If he would not fight, why should she? Oh, let her fall and fall, it would not take her farther from him! These were the thoughts that sent her into solitude, to meet with worse ones. She could not face the morrow. "What shall I do to-morrow?" She never shrank from to-day —it had its duties; it could be got through: but to-morrow was a never-ending road. Oh, how could she get through to-morrow?

Her great friend at this time was Corp; because he still retained his faith in Tommy. She could always talk of Tommy to Corp.

How loyal Corp was! He still referred to Tommy as "him." Gavinia, much distressed, read aloud to Corp a newspaper attack on the political article, and all he said was, "He'll find a wy."

"He's found it," he went upstairs to announce to Grizel, when the praises of the "little masterpiece" arrived.

"Yes, I know, Corp," she answered quietly. She was sitting by the window where the plant was. Tommy had asked her to take care of it, without telling her why.

Something in her appearance troubled the hulking, blundering man. He could not have told what it was. I think it was simply this-that Grizel no longer sat erect in her chair.

"I'm nain easy in my mind about Grizel," he said that evening to Gavinia. "There's something queery about her, though I canna bottom 't."

"Yea?" said Gavinia, with mild contempt.

He continued pulling at his pipe, grunting as if in pleasant pain, which was the way Corp smoked.

"I could see she's no pleased, though he has found a wy," he said.

"What pleasure should she be able to sook out o' his keeping ding-ding-danging on about that woman?" retorted Gavinia.

"What woman?"

"The London besom that gae him the go-by."

"Was there sic a woman!" Corp cried.

"Of course there was, and it's her that he's aye writing about."

"Havers, Gavinia! It's Grizel he's aye writing about, and it was Grizel that gae him the go-by. It's town talk."

But whatever the town might say, Gavinia stuck to her opinion. "Grizel's no near so neat in her dressing as she was," she informed Corp, "and her hair is no aye tidy, and that bonnet she was in yesterday didna set her."

"I've noticed it," cried Corp. "I've noticed it this while back, though I didna ken I had noticed it, Gavinia. I wonder what can be the reason?"

"It's because nobody cares," Gavinia replied sadly. Trust one woman to know another!

"We a' care," said Corp, stoutly.

"We're a' as nothing, Corp, when he doesna care. She's fond o' him, man."

"Of course she is, in a wy. Whaur's the woman that could help it?"

"There's many a woman that could help it," said Gavinia, tartly, for the honour of her sex, "but she's no are o' them." To be candid, Gavinia was not one of them herself. "I'm thinking she's terrible fond o' him," she said, "and I'm nain sure that he has treated her weel."

"Woman, take care; say a word agin him and I'll mittle you!" Corp thundered, and she desisted in fear.

But he made her re-read the little essay to him in instalments, and at the end he said victoriously, "You blethering crittur, there's no sic woman. It's just another o' his ploys!"

He marched upstairs to Grizel with the news, and she listened kindly. "I am sure you are right," she said; "you understand him better than any of them, Corp," and it was true.

He thought he had settled the whole matter. He was burning to be downstairs to tell Gavinia that these things needed only a man. "And so you'll be yoursel' again, Grizel," he said, with great relief.

She had not seen that he was aiming at her until now, and it touched her. "Am I so different, Corp?"

Not at all, he assured her delicately, but she was maybe no quite so neatly dressed as she used to be, and her hair wasna braided back so smooth, and he didna think that bonnet quite set her.

"Gavinia has been saying that to you!"

"I noticed it mysel', Grizel; I'm a terrible noticher."

"Perhaps you are right," she said, reflecting, after looking at herself for the first time for some days. "But to think of your caring, Corp!"

"I care most michty," he replied, with terrific earnestness.

"I must try to satisfy you, then," she said, smiling. "But, Corp, please don't discuss me with Gavinia."

This request embarrassed him, for soon again he did not know how to act. There was Grizel's strange behaviour with the child, for instance. "No, I won't come down to see him to-day, Corp," she had said; "somehow children weary me."

Such words from Grizel! His mouth would not shut and he could say nothing. "Forgive me, Corp!" she cried remorsefully, and ran downstairs, and with many a passionate caress asked forgiveness of the child.

Corp followed her, and for the moment he thought he must have been dreaming upstairs. "I wish I saw you wi' bairns o' your ain, Grizel," he said, looking on entranced; but she gave him such a pitiful smile that he could not get it out of his head. Deprived of Gavinia's counsel, and afraid to hurt Elspeth, he sought out the doctor and said bluntly to him, "How is it he never writes to Grizel? She misses him terrible."

"So," David thought, "Grizel's dejection is becoming common talk." "Damn him!" he said, in a gust of fury.

But this was too much for loyal Corp. "Damn you!" he roared.

But in his heart he knew that the doctor was a just man, and henceforth, when he was meaning to comfort Grizel, he was often seeking comfort for himself.

He did it all with elaborate cunning, to prevent her guessing that he was disturbed about her: asked permission to sit with her, for instance, because he was dull downstairs; mentioned as a ludicrous thing that there were people who believed Tommy could treat a woman badly, and waited anxiously for the reply. Oh, he was transparent, was Corp, but you may be sure Grizel never let him know that she saw through him. Tommy could not be blamed, she pointed out, though he did not care for some woman who perhaps cared for him.

"Exac'ly," said Corp.

And if he seemed, Grizel went on, with momentary bitterness, to treat her badly, it could be only because she had made herself cheap.

"That's it," said Corp, cheerfully. Then he added hurriedly, "No, that's no it ava. She's the last to mak' hersel' cheap." Then he saw that this might put Grizel on the scent. "Of course there's no sic woman," he said artfully, "but if there was, he would mak' it a' right. She mightna see how it was to be done, but kennin' what a crittur he is, she maun be sure he would find a wy. She would never lose hope, Grizel."

And then, if Grizel did not appease him instantly, he would say appealingly, "I canna think less o' him, Grizel; no, it would mak' me just terrible low. Grizel," he would cry sternly, "dinna tell me to think less o' that laddie."

Then, when she had reassured him, he would recall the many instances in which Tommy as a boy had found a way. "Did we ever ken he was finding it, Grizel, till he did find it? Many a time I says to mysel', says I, 'All is over,' and syne next minute that holy look comes ower his face, and he stretches out his legs like as if he was riding on a horse, and all that kens him says, 'He has found a wy.' If I was the woman (no that there is sic a woman) I would say to mysel', 'He was never beat,' I would say, 'when he was a laddie, and it's no likely he'll be beat when he's a man'; and I wouldna sit looking at the fire wi' my hands fauded, nor would I forget to keep my hair neat, and I would wear the frock that set me best, and I would play in my auld bonny wy wi' bairns, for says I to mysel', 'I'm sure to hae bairns o' my ain some day, and —'"

But Grizel cried, "Don't, Corp, don't!"

"I winna," he answered miserably, "no, I winna. Forgive me, Grizel; I think I'll be stepping"; and then when he got as far as the door he would say, "I canna do 't, Grizel; I'm just terrible wae for the woman (if sic a woman there be), but I canna think ill o' him; you mauna speir it o' me."

He was much brightened by a reflection that came to him one day in church. "Here have I been near blaming him for no finding a wy, and very like he doesna ken we want him to find a wy!"

How to inform Tommy without letting Grizel know? She had tried twice long ago to teach him to write, but he found it harder on the wrists than the heaviest luggage. It was not safe for him even to think of the extra twirl that turned an *n* into an *m*, without first removing any knick-knacks that might be about. Nevertheless, he now proposed a third set-to, and Grizel acquiesced, though she thought it but another of his inventions to keep her from brooding.

The number of words in the English tongue excited him, and he often lost all by not confining the chase to one, like a dog after rabbits. Fortunately, he knew which words he wanted to bag.

"Change at Tilliedrum!" "Tickets! show your tickets!" and the like, he much enjoyed meeting in the flesh, so to speak.

"Let's see 'Find a wy,' Grizel," he would say. "Ay, ay, and is that the crittur!" and soon the sly fellow could write it, or at least draw it.

He affected an ambition to write a letter to his son on that gentleman's first birthday, and so "Let's see what 'I send you these few scrapes' is like, Grizel." She assured him that this is not essential in correspondence, but all the letters he had ever heard read aloud began thus, and he got his way.

Anon Master Shiach was surprised and gratified to receive the following epistle: "My dear sir, I send you these few scrapes to tell you as you have found a way to be a year of age the morn. All tickets ready in which Gavinia joins so no more at present I am, sir, your obed't father Corp Shiach."

The fame of this letter went abroad, but not a soul knew of the next. It said: "My dear Sir, I send you these few scrapes to tell you as Grizel needs cheering up. Kindly oblidge by finding a way so no more at present. I am sir your obed't Serv't Corp Shiach."

To his bewilderment, this produced no effect, though only because Tommy never got it, and he wrote again, more sternly, requesting his hero to find a way immediately. He was waiting restlessly for the answer at a time when Elspeth called on Grizel to tell her of something beautiful that Tommy had done. He had been very ill for nearly a fortnight, it appeared, but had kept it from her to save her anxiety. "Just think, Grizel; all the time he was in bed with bronchitis he was writing me cheerful letters every other day pretending there was nothing the matter with him. He is better now. I have heard about it from a Mrs. Jerry, a lady whom I knew in London, and who has nursed him in the kindest way." (But this same Mrs. Jerry had opened Corp's letters and destroyed them as of no importance.) "He would never have mentioned it himself. How like him, Grizel! You remember, I made him promise before he went back to London that if he was ill he would let me know at once so that I could go to him, but he is so considerate he would not give me pain. He wrote those letters, Grizel, when he was gasping for breath."

"But she seemed quite unmoved," Elspeth said sadly to her husband afterwards.

Unmoved! Yes; Grizel remained apparently unmoved until Elspeth had gone, but then-the torture she endured! "Oh, cruel, cruel!" she cried, and she could neither stand nor sit; she flung herself down before the fire and rocked this way and that, in a paroxysm of woe. "Oh, cruel, cruel!"

It was Tommy who was cruel. To be ill, near to dying, apparently, and not to send her word! She could never, never have let him go had he not made that promise to Elspeth; and he kept it thus. Oh, wicked, wicked!

"You would have gone to him at once, Elspeth! You! Who are you, that talks of going to him as your right? He is not yours, I tell you; he is mine! He is mine alone; it is I who would go to him. Who is this woman that dares take my place by his side when he is ill!"

She rose to go to him, to drive away all others. I am sure that was what gave her strength to rise; but she sank to the floor again, and her passion lasted for hours. And through the night she was crying to God that she would be brave no more. In her despair she hoped he heard her.

Her mood had not changed when David came to see her next morning, to admit, too, that Tommy seemed to have done an unselfish thing in concealing his illness from them. Grizel nodded, but he thought she was looking strangely reckless. He had a message from Elspeth. Tommy had asked her to let him know whether the plant was flourishing.

"So you and he don't correspond now?" David said, with his old, puzzled look.

"No," was all her answer to that. The plant, she thought, was dead; she had not, indeed, paid much attention to it of late; but she showed it to David, and he said it would revive if more carefully tended. He also told her its rather pathetic history, which was new to Grizel, and of the talk at the wedding which had led to Tommy's taking pity on it. "Fellow-feeling, I suppose," he said lightly; "you see, they both blossomed prematurely."

The words were forgotten by him as soon as spoken; but Grizel sat on with them, for they were like a friend-or was it an enemy? —who had come to tell her strange things. Yes, the doctor was right. Now she knew why Tommy had loved this plant. Of the way in which he would sit looking wistfully at it, almost nursing it, she had been told by Aaron; he had himself begged her to tend it lovingly. Fellow-feeling! The doctor was shrewder than he thought.

Well, what did it matter to her? All that day she would do nothing for the plant, but in the middle of the night she rose and ran to it and hugged it, and for a time she was afraid to look at it by lamplight, lest Tommy was dead. Whether she had never been asleep that night, or had awakened from a dream, she never knew, but she ran to the plant, thinking it and Tommy were as one, and that they must die together. No such thought had ever crossed his mind, but it seemed to her that she had been told it by him, and she lit her fire to give the plant warmth, and often desisted, to press it to her bosom, the heat seemed to come so reluctantly from the fire. This idea that his fate was bound up with that of the plant took strange possession of the once practical Grizel; it was as if some of Tommy's nature had passed into her to help her break the terrible monotony of the days.

And from that time there was no ailing child more passionately tended than the plant, and as spring advanced it began once more to put forth new leaves.

And Grizel also seemed glorified again. She was her old self. Dark shapes still lingered for her in the Den, but she avoided them, and if they tried to enter into her, she struggled with them and cast them out. As she saw herself able to fight and win once more, her pride returned to her, and one day she could ask David, joyously, to give her a present of the old doctor's chair. And she could kneel by its side and say to it, "You can watch me always; I am just as I used to be."

Seeing her once more the incarnation of vigor and content, singing gaily to his child, and as eager to be at her duties betimes as a morning in May, Corp grunted with delight, and was a hero for not telling her that it was he who had passed Tommy the word. For, of course, Tommy had done it all.

"Somebody has found a wy, Grizel!" he would say, chuckling, and she smiled an agreement.

"And yet," says he, puzzled, "I've watched, and you hinna haen a letter frae him. It defies the face o' clay to find out how he has managed it. Oh, the crittur! Ay, I suppose you dinna want to tell me what it is that has lichted you up again?"

She could not tell him, for it was a compact she had made with one who did not sign it. "I shall cease to be bitter and despairing and wicked, and try every moment of my life to be good and do good, so long as my plant flourishes; but if it withers, then I shall go to him —I don't care what happens; I shall go to him."

It was the middle of June when she first noticed that the plant was beginning to droop.

Chapter XXVII
Grizel's Journey

Nothing could have been less expected. In the beginning of May its leaves had lost something of their greenness. The plant seemed to be hesitating, but she coaxed it over the hill, and since then it had scarcely needed her hand; almost light-headedly it hurried into its summer clothes, and new buds broke out on it, like smiles, at the fascinating thought that there was to be a to-morrow. Grizel's plant had never been so brave in its little life when suddenly it turned back.

That was the day on which Elspeth and David were leaving for a fortnight's holiday with his relatives by the sea; for Elspeth needed and was getting special devotion just now, and Grizel knew why. She was glad they were going; it was well that they should not be there to ask questions if she also must set forth on a journey.

For more than a week she waited, and everything she could do for her plant she did. She watched it so carefully that she might have deceived herself into believing that it was standing still only, had there been no night-time. She thought she had not perhaps been sufficiently good, and she tried to be more ostentatiously satisfied with her lot. Never had she forced herself to work quite so hard for others as in those few days, and then when she came home it had drooped a little more.

When she was quite sure that it was dying, she told Corp she was going to London by that night's train. "He is ill, Corp, and I must go to him."

Ill! But how had he let her know?

"He has found a way," she said, with a tremulous smile. He wanted her to telegraph; but no, she would place no faith in telegrams.

At least she could telegraph to Elspeth and the doctor. One of them would go.

"It is I who am going," she said quietly. "I can't wait any longer. It was a promise, Corp. He loves me." They were the only words she said which suggest that there was anything strange about Grizel at this time.

Corp saw how determined she was when she revealed, incidentally, that she had drawn a sum of money out of the bank a week ago, "to be ready."

"What will folk say!" he cried.

"You can tell Gavinia the truth when I am gone," she told him. "She will know better than you what to say to other people." And that was some comfort to him, for it put the burden of invention upon his wife. So it was Corp who saw Grizel off. He was in great distress himself about Tommy, but he kept a courageous face for her, and his last words flung in at the carriage window were, "Now dinna be down-hearted; I'm nain down-hearted mysel', for we're very sure he'll find a wy." And Grizel smiled and nodded, and the train turned the bend that shuts out the little town of Thrums. The town vanishes quickly, but the quarry we howked it out of stands grim and red, watching the train for many a mile.

Of Grizel's journey to London there are no particulars to tell. She was wearing her brown jacket and fur cap because Tommy had liked them, and she sat straight and stiff all the way. She had never been in a train since she was a baby, except two or three times to Tilliedrum, and she thought this was the right way to sit. Always, when the train stopped, which was at long intervals, she put her head out at the window and asked if this was the train to London. Every station a train stops at in the middle of the night is the infernal regions, and she shuddered to hear lost souls clanking their chains, which is what a milk-can becomes on its way to the van; but still she asked if this was the train to London. When fellow-passengers addressed her, she was very modest and cautious in her replies. Sometimes a look of extraordinary happiness, of radiance, passed over her face, and may have puzzled them. It was part of the thought that, however ill he might be, she was to see him now.

She did not see him as soon as she expected, for at the door of Tommy's lodgings they told her that he had departed suddenly for the Continent about a week ago. He was to send an address by and by to which letters could be forwarded. Was he quite well when he went away? Grizel asked, shaking.

The landlady and her daughter thought he was rather peakish, but he had not complained.

He went away for his health, Grizel informed them, and he was very ill now. Oh, could they not tell her where he was? All she knew was that he was very ill. "I am engaged to be married to him," she said with dignity. Without this strange certainty that Tommy loved her at last, she could not have trod the road which faced her now. Even when she had left the house, where at their suggestion she was to call to-morrow, she found herself wondering at once what he would like her to do now, and she went straight to a hotel, and had her box sent to it from the station, and she remained there all day because she thought that this was what he would like her to do. She sat bolt upright on a cane chair in her bedroom, praying to God with her eyes open; she was begging Him to let Tommy tell her where he was, and promising to return home at once if he did not need her.

Next morning they showed her, at his lodgings, two lines in a newspaper, which said that he was ill with bronchitis at the Hotel Krone, Bad-Platten, in Switzerland.

It may have been an answer to her prayer, as she thought, but we know now how the paragraph got into print. On the previous evening the landlady had met Mr. Pym on the ladder of an omnibus, and told him, before they could be plucked apart, of the lady who knew that Mr. Sandys was ill. It must be bronchitis again. Pym was much troubled; he knew that the Krone at Bad-Platten had been Tommy's destination. He talked that day, and one of the company was a reporter, which accounts for the paragraph.

Grizel found out how she could get to Bad-Platten. She left her box behind her at the cloakroom of the railway station, where I suppose it was sold years afterwards. From Dover she sent a telegram to Tommy, saying: "I am coming. GRIZEL."

On entering the train at Calais she had a railway journey of some thirty hours, broken by two changes only. She could speak a little French, but all the use she made of it was to ask repeatedly if she was in the right train. An English lady who travelled with her for many hours woke up now and again to notice that this quiet, prim-looking girl was always sitting erect, with her hand on her umbrella, as if ready to leave the train at any moment. The lady pointed out some of the beauties of the scenery to her, and Grizel tried to listen. "I am afraid you are unhappy," her companion said at last.

"That is not why I am crying," Grizel said; "I think I am crying because I am so hungry."

The stranger gave her sandwiches and claret as cold as the rivers that raced the train; and Grizel told her, quite frankly, why she was going to Bad-Platten. She did not tell his name, only that he was ill, and that she was engaged to him, and he had sent for her. She believed it all. The lady was very sympathetic, and gave her information about the diligence by which the last part of Grizel's journey must be made, and also said: "You must not neglect your meals, if only for his sake; for how can you nurse him back to health if you arrive at Bad-Platten ill yourself? Consider his distress if he were to be told that you were in the inn, but not able to go to him."

"Oh!" Grizel cried, rocking her arms for the first time since she knew her plant was drooping. She promised to be very practical henceforth, so as to have strength to take her place by his side at once. It was strange that she who was so good a nurse had forgotten these things, so strange that it alarmed her, as if she feared that, without being able to check herself, she was turning into some other person.

The station where she alighted was in a hubbub of life; everyone seemed to leave the train here, and to resent the presence of all the others. They were mostly English. The men hung back, as if, now that there was business to be done in some foolish tongue, they had better leave the ladies to do it. Many of them seemed prepared, if there was dissension, to disown their womankind and run for it. They looked haughty and nervous. Such of them as had tried to shave in the train were boasting of it and holding handkerchiefs to their chins. The ladies were moving about in a masterful way, carrying bunches of keys. When they had done everything, the men went and stood by their sides again.

Outside the station buses and carriages were innumerable, and everybody was shouting; but Grizel saw that nearly all her fellow-passengers were hurrying by foot or conveyance to one spot, all desirous of being there first, and she thought it must be the place where the diligence started from, and pressed on with them. It proved to be a hotel where they all wanted the best bedroom, and many of them had telegraphed for it, and they gathered round a man in uniform and demanded that room of him; but he treated them as if they were little dogs and he was not the platter, and soon they were begging for a room on the fourth floor at the back, and swelling with triumph if they got it. The scrimmage was still going on when Grizel slipped out of the hotel, having learned that the diligence would not start until the following morning. It was still early in the afternoon. How could she wait until to-morrow?

Bad-Platten was forty miles away. The road was pointed out to her. It began to climb at once. She was to discover that for more than thirty miles it never ceased to climb. She sat down, hesitating, on a little bridge that spanned a horrible rushing white stream. Poets have sung the glories of that stream, but it sent a shiver through her. On all sides she was caged in by a ring of splendid mountains, but she did not give them one admiring glance (there is a special spot where the guide-books advise you to stop for a moment to do it); her one passionate desire was to fling out her arms and knock them over.

She had often walked twenty miles in a day, in a hill country too, without feeling tired, and there seemed no reason why she should not set off now. There were many inns on the way, she was told, where she could pass the night. There she could get the diligence next day. This would not bring her any sooner to him than if she waited here until to-morrow; but how could she sit still till to-morrow? She must be moving; she seemed to have been sitting still for an eternity. "I must not do anything rash," she told herself, carefully. "I must arrive at Bad-Platten able to sit down beside him the moment I have taken off my jacket-oh, without waiting to take off my jacket." She went into the hotel and ate some food, just to show herself how careful she had become. About three o'clock she set off. She had a fierce desire to get away from that heartless white stream and the crack of whips and the doleful pine woods, and at first she walked very quickly; but she never got away from them, for they marched with her. It was not that day, but the next, that Grizel thought anything was marching with her. That day her head was quite clear, and she kept her promise to herself, and as soon as she felt tired she stopped for the night at a village inn. But when she awoke very early next morning she seemed to have forgotten that she was to travel the rest of the way by diligence; for, after a slight meal, she started off again on foot, and she was walking all day.

She passed through many villages so like each other that in time she thought they might be the same. There was always a monster inn whence one carriage was departing as another drove up, and there was a great stone water-tank in which women drew their washing back and forward, and there was always a big yellow dog that barked fiercely and then giggled, and at the doors of painted houses children stood. You knew they were children by their size only. The one person she spoke to that day was a child who offered her a bunch of wild flowers. No one was looking, and Grizel kissed her and then hurried on.

The carriage passed and repassed her. There must have been a hundred of them, but in time they became one. No sooner had it disappeared in dust in front of her than she heard the crack of its whip behind.

It was a glorious day of sweltering sun; but she was bewildered now, and did not open the umbrella with which she had shielded her head yesterday. In the foreground was always the same white road, on both sides the same pine wood laughing with wild flowers, the same roaring white stream. From somewhere near came the tinkle of cow-bells. Far away on heights, if she looked up, were villages made of match-boxes. She saw what were surely the same villages if she looked down; or the one was the reflection of the other, in the sky above or in the valley below. They stood out so vividly that they might have been within arm's reach. They were so small that she felt she could extinguish them with her umbrella. Near them was the detestably picturesque castle perched upon a bracket. Everywhere was that loathly waterfall. Here and there were squares of cultivated land that looked like door-mats flung out upon the hillsides. The huge mountains raised their jagged heads through the snow, and were so sharp-edged that they might have been clipped out of cardboard. The sky was blue, without a flaw; but lost clouds crawled like snakes between heaven and earth. All day the sun scorched her, but the night was nipping cold.

From early morn till evening she climbed to get away from them, but they all marched with her. They waited while she slept. She woke up in an inn, and could have cried with delight because she saw nothing but bare walls. But as soon as she reached the door, there they all were, ready for her. An hour after she set off, she again reached that door; and she stopped at it to ask if this was the inn where she had passed the night. Everything had turned with her. Two squalls of sudden rain drenched her that day, and she forced her way through the first, but sought a covering from the second.

It was then afternoon, and she was passing through a village by a lake. Since Grizel's time monster hotels have trampled the village to death, and the shuddering lake reflects all day the most hideous of caravansaries flung together as with a giant shovel in one of the loveliest spots on earth. Even then some of the hotels had found it out. Grizel drew near to two of them, and saw wet halls full of open umbrellas which covered the floor and looked like great beetles. These buildings were too formidable, and she dragged herself past them. She came to a garden of hops and evergreens. Wet chairs were standing in the deserted walks, and here and there was a little arbour. She went into one of these arbours and sat down, and soon slid to the floor.

The place was St. Gian, some miles from Bad-Platten; but one of the umbrellas she had seen was Tommy's. Others belonged to Mrs. Jerry and Lady Pippinworth.

When Tommy started impulsively on what proved to be his only Continental trip he had expected to join Mrs. Jerry and her stepdaughter at Bad-Platten. They had been there for a fortnight, and "the place is a dream," Mrs. Jerry had said in the letter pressing him to come; but it was at St. Gian that she met the diligence and told him to descend. Bad-Platten, she explained, was a horror.

Her fuller explanation was that she was becoming known there as the round lady.

"Now, am I as round as all that?" she said plaintively to Tommy.

"Mrs. Jerry," he replied, with emotion, "you must not ask me what I think of you." He always treated her with extraordinary respect and chivalry now, and it awed her.

She had looked too, too round because she was in the company of Lady Pippinworth. Everyone seemed to be too round or too large by the side of that gifted lady, who somehow never looked too thin. She knew her power. When there were women in the room whom she disliked she merely went and stood beside them. In the gyrations of the dance the onlooker would momentarily lose sight of her; she came and went like a blinking candle. Men could not dance with her without its being said that they were getting stout. There is nothing they dislike so much, yet they did dance with her. Tommy, having some slight reason, was particularly sensitive about references to his figure, yet it was Lady Pippinworth who had drawn him to Switzerland. What was her strange attraction?

Calmly considered, she was preposterously thin, but men, at least, could not think merely of her thinness, unless, when walking with her, they became fascinated by its shadow on the ground. She was tall, and had a very clear, pale complexion and light-brown hair. Light brown, too, were her heavy eyelashes, which were famous for being black-tipped, as if a brush had touched them, though it had not. She made play with her eyelashes as with a fan, and sometimes the upper and lower seemed to entangle for a moment and be in difficulties, from which you wanted to extricate them in the tenderest manner. And the more you wanted to help her the more disdainfully she looked at you. Yet though she looked disdainful she also looked helpless. Now we have the secret of her charm.

This helpless disdain was the natural expression of her face, and I am sure she fell asleep with a curl of the lip. Her scorn of men so maddened them that they could not keep away from her. "Damn!" they said under their breath, and rushed to her. If rumour is to be believed, Sir Harry Pippinworth proposed to her in a fury brought on by the sneer with which she had surveyed his family portraits. I know nothing more of Sir Harry, except that she called him Pips, which seems to settle him.

"They will be calling me the round gentleman," Tommy said ruefully to her that evening, as he strolled with her towards the lake, and indeed he was looking stout. Mrs. Jerry did not accompany them; she wanted to be seen with her trying stepdaughter as little as possible, and Tommy's had been the happy proposal that he should attend them alternately —"fling away my own figure to save yours," he had said gallantly to Mrs. Jerry.

"Do you mind?" Lady Pippinworth asked.

"I mind nothing," he replied, "so long as I am with you."

He had not meant to begin so near the point where they had last left off; he had meant to begin much farther back: but an irresistible desire came over him to make sure that she really did permit him to say this sort of thing.

Her only reply was a flutter of the little fans and a most contemptuous glance.

"Alice," said Tommy, in the old way.

"Well?"

"You don't understand what it is to me to say Alice again."

"Many people call me Alice."

"But they have a right to."

"I supposed you thought you had a right to also."

"No," said Tommy. "That is why I do it."

She strolled on, more scornful and helpless than ever. Apparently it did not matter what one said to Lady Pippinworth; her pout kept it within the proprieties.

There was a magnificent sunset that evening, which dyed a snow-topped mountain pink. "That is what I came all the way from London to see," Tommy remarked, after they had gazed at it.

"I hope you feel repaid," she said, a little tartly.

"You mistake my meaning," he replied. "I had heard of these wonderful sunsets, and an intense desire came over me to see you looking disdainfully at them. Yes, I feel amply repaid. Did you notice, Alice, or was it but a fancy of my own, that when he had seen the expression on your face the sun quite slunk away?"

"I wonder you don't do so also," she retorted. She had no sense of humour, and was rather stupid; so it is no wonder that the men ran after her.

"I am more gallant than the sun," said he. "If I had been up there in its place, Alice, and you had been looking at me, I could never have set."

She pouted contemptuously, which meant, I think, that she was well pleased. Yet, though he seemed to be complimenting her, she was not sure of him. She had never been sure of Tommy, nor, indeed, he of her, which was probably why they were so interested in each other still.

"Do you know," Tommy said, "what I have told you is really at least half the truth? If I did not come here to see you disdaining the sun, I think I did come to see you disdaining me. Odd, is it not, if true, that a man should travel so far to see a lip curl up?"

"You don't seem to know what brought you," she said.

"It seems so monstrous," he replied, musing. "Oh, yes, I am quite certain that the curl of the lip is responsible for my being here; it kept sending me constant telegrams; but what I want to know is, do I come for the pleasure of the thing or for the pain? Do I like your disdain, Alice, or does it make me writhe? Am I here to beg you to do it again, or to defy it?"

"Which are you doing now?" she inquired.

"I had hoped," he said with a sigh, "that you could tell me that."

On another occasion they reached the same point in this discussion, and went a little beyond it. It was on a wet afternoon, too, when Tommy had vowed to himself to mend his ways. "That disdainful look is you," he told her, "and I admire it more than anything in nature; and yet, Alice, and yet — —"

"Well?" she answered coldly, but not moving, though he had come suddenly too near her. They were on a private veranda of the hotel, and she was lolling in a wicker chair.

"And yet," he said intensely, "I am not certain that I would not give the world to have the power to drive that look from your face. That, I begin to think, is what brought me here."

"But you are not sure," she said, with a shrug of the shoulder.

It stung him into venturing further than he had ever gone with her before. Not too gently, he took her head in both his hands and forced her to look up at him. She submitted without a protest. She was disdainful, but helpless.

"Well?" she said again.

He withdrew his hands, and she smiled mockingly.

"If I thought — —" he cried with sudden passion, and stopped.

"You think a great deal, don't you?" she said. She was going now.

"If I thought there was any blood in your veins, you icy woman — —"

"Or in your own," said she. But she said it a little fiercely, and he noticed that.

"Alice," he cried, "I know now. It is to drive that look from your face that I am here."

She courtesied from the door. She was quite herself again.

But for that moment she had been moved. He was convinced of it, and his first feeling was of exultation as in an achievement. I don't know what you are doing just now, Lady Pippinworth, but my compliments to you, and T. Sandys is swelling.

There followed on this exultation another feeling as sincere-devout thankfulness that he had gone no further. He drew deep breaths of relief over his escape, but knew that he had not himself to thank. His friends, the little sprites, had done it, in return for the amusement he seemed to give them. They had stayed him in the nick of time, but not earlier; it was quite as if they wanted Tommy to have his fun first. So often they had saved him from being spitted, how could he guess that the great catastrophe was fixed for to-night, and that henceforth they were to sit round him counting his wriggles, as if this new treatment of him tickled them even more than the other?

But he was too clever not to know that they might be fattening him for some very special feast, and his thanks took the form of a vow to need their help no more. To-morrow he would begin to climb the mountains around St. Gian; if he danced attendance on her dangerous Ladyship again, Mrs. Jerry should be there also, and he would walk circumspectly between them, like a man with gyves upon his wrists. He was in the midst of all the details of these reforms, when suddenly he looked at himself thus occupied, and laughed bitterly; he had so often come upon Tommy making grand resolves!

He stopped operations and sat down beside them. No one could have wished more heartily to be anybody else, or have had less hope. He had not even the excuse of being passionately drawn to this woman; he remembered that she had never interested him until he heard of her effect upon other men. Her reputation as a duellist, whose defence none of his sex could pass, had led to his wondering what they saw in her, and he had dressed himself in their sentiments and so approached her. There were times in her company when he forgot that he was wearing borrowed garments, when he went on flame, but he always knew, as now, upon reflection. Nothing seemed easier at this moment than to fling them aside; with one jerk they were on the floor. Obviously it was only vanity that had inspired him, and vanity was satisfied: the easier, therefore, to stop. Would you like to make the woman unhappy, Tommy? You know you would not; you have somewhere about you one of the softest hearts in the world. Then desist; be satisfied that you did thaw her once, and grateful that she so quickly froze again. "I am; indeed I am," he responds. "No one could have himself better in hand for the time being than I, and if a competition in morals were now going on, I should certainly take the medal. But I cannot speak for myself an hour in advance. I make a vow, as I have done so often before, but it does not help me to know what I may be at before the night is out."

When his disgust with himself was at its height he suddenly felt like a little god. His new book had come into view. He flicked a finger at his reflection in a mirror. "That for you!" he said defiantly; "at least I can write; I can write at last!"

The manuscript lay almost finished at the bottom of his trunk. It could not easily have been stolen for one hour without his knowing. Just when he was about to start on a walk with one of the ladies, he would run upstairs to make sure that it was still there; he made sure by feeling, and would turn again at the door to make sure by looking. Miser never listened to the crispness of bank-notes with more avidity; woman never spent more time in shutting and opening her jewel-box.

"I can write at last!" He knew that, comparatively speaking, he had never been able to write before. He remembered the fuss that had been made about his former books. "Pooh!" he said, addressing them contemptuously.

Once more he drew his beloved manuscript from its hiding-place. He did not mean to read, only to fondle; but his eye chancing to fall on a special passage-two hours afterwards he was interrupted by the dinner-gong. He returned the pages to the box and wiped his eyes. While dressing hurriedly he remembered with languid interest that Lady Pippinworth was staying in the same hotel.

There were a hundred or more at dinner, and they were all saying the same thing: "Where have you been to-day?" "Really! but the lower path is shadier." "Is this your first visit?" "The glacier is very nice." "Were you caught in the rain?" "The view from the top is very nice." "After all, the rain lays the dust." "They give you two sweets at Bad-Platten and an ice on Sunday."

"The sunset is very nice." "The poulet is very nice." The hotel is open during the summer months only, but probably the chairs in the dining-room and the knives and forks in their basket make these remarks to each other every evening throughout the winter.

Being a newcomer, Tommy had not been placed beside either of his friends, who sat apart "because," Mrs. Jerry said, "she calls me mamma, and I am not going to stand that." For some time he gave thought to neither of them; he was engrossed in what he had been reading, and it turned him into a fine and magnanimous character. When gradually her Ladyship began to flit among his reflections, it was not to disturb them, but because she harmonized. He wanted to apologize to her. The apology grew in grace as the dinner progressed; it was so charmingly composed that he was profoundly stirred by it.

The opportunity came presently in the hall, where it is customary after dinner to lounge or stroll if you are afraid of the night air. Or if you do not care for music, you can go into the drawing-room and listen to the piano.

"I am sure mamma is looking for you everywhere," Lady Pippinworth said, when Tommy took a chair beside her. "It is her evening, you know."

"Surely you would not drive me away," he replied with a languishing air, and then smiled at himself, for he was done with this sort of thing. "Lady Pippinworth," said he, firmly-it needs firmness when of late you have been saying "Alice."

"Well?"

"I have been thinking — —" Tommy began.

"I am sure you have," she said.

"I have been thinking," he went on determinedly, "that I played a poor part this afternoon. I had no right to say what I said to you."

"As far as I can remember," she answered, "you did not say very much."

"It is like your generosity, Lady Pippinworth," he said, "to make light of it; but let us be frank: I made love to you."

Anyone looking at his expressionless face and her lazy disdain (and there were many in the hall) would have guessed that their talk was of where were you to-day? and what should I do to-morrow?

"You don't really mean that?" her Ladyship said incredulously. "Think, Mr. Sandys, before you tell me anything more. Are you sure you are not confusing me with mamma?"

"I did it," said Tommy, remorsefully.

"In my absence?" she asked.

"When you were with me on the veranda."

Her eyes opened to their widest, so surprised that the lashes had no time for their usual play.

"Was that what you call making love, Mr. Sandys?" she inquired.

"I call a spade a spade."

"And now you are apologizing to me, I understand?"

"If you can in the goodness of your heart forgive me, Lady Pippinworth —"

"Oh, I do," she said heartily, "I do. But how stupid you must have thought me not even to know! I feel that it is I who ought to apologize. What a number of ways there seem to be of making love, and yours is such an odd way!"

Now to apologize for playing a poor part is one thing, and to put up with the charge of playing a part poorly is quite another. Nevertheless, he kept his temper.

"You have discovered an excellent way of punishing me," he said manfully, "and I submit. Indeed, I admire you the more. So I am paying you a compliment when I whisper that I know you knew."

But she would not have it. "You are so strangely dense to-night," she said. "Surely, if I had known, I would have stopped you. You forget that I am a married woman," she added, remembering Pips rather late in the day.

"There might be other reasons why you did not stop me," he replied impulsively.

"Such as?"

"Well, you-you might have wanted me to go on."

He blurted it out.

"So," said she slowly, "you are apologizing to me for not going on?"

"I implore you, Lady Pippinworth," Tommy said, in much distress, "not to think me capable of that. If I moved you for a moment, I am far from boasting of it; it makes me only the more anxious to do what is best for you."

This was not the way it had shaped during dinner, and Tommy would have acted wisely had he now gone out to cool his head. "If you moved me?" she repeated interrogatively; but, with the best intentions, he continued to flounder.

"Believe me," he implored her, "had I known it could be done, I should have checked myself. But they always insist that you are an iceberg, and am I so much to blame if that look of hauteur deceived me with the rest? Oh, dear Lady Disdain," he said warmly, in answer to one of her most freezing glances, "it deceives me no longer. From that moment I knew you had a heart, and I was shamed-as noble a heart as ever beat in woman," he added. He always tended to add generous bits when he found it coming out well.

"Does the man think I am in love with him?" was Lady Disdain's inadequate reply.

"No, no, indeed!" he assured her earnestly. "I am not so vain as to think that, nor so selfish as to wish it; but if for a moment you were moved ———"

"But I was not," said she, stamping her shoe.

His dander began to rise, as they say in the north; but he kept grip of politeness.

"If you were moved for a moment, Lady Pippinworth," he went on, in a slightly more determined voice, —"I am far from saying that it was so; but if———"

"But as I was not ———" she said.

It was no use putting things prettily to her when she snapped you up in this way.

"You know you were," he said reproachfully.

"I assure you," said she, "I don't know what you are talking about, but apparently it is something dreadful; so perhaps one of us ought to go away."

As he did not take this hint, she opened a tattered Tauchnitz which was lying at her elbow. They are always lying at your elbow in a Swiss hotel, with the first pages missing.

Tommy watched her gloomily. "This is unworthy of you," he said.

"What is?"

He was not quite sure, but as he sat there misgivings entered his mind and began to gnaw. Was it all a mistake of his? Undeniably he did think too much. After all, had she not been moved? 'Sdeath!

His restlessness made her look up. "It must be a great load off your mind," she said, with gentle laughter, "to know that your apology was unnecessary."

"It is," Tommy said; "it is." ('Sdeath!)

She resumed her book.

So this was how one was rewarded for a generous impulse! He felt very bitter. "So, so," he said inwardly; also, "Very well, ve-ry well." Then he turned upon himself. "Serve you right," he said brutally. "Better stick to your books, Thomas, for you know nothing about women." To think for one moment that he had moved her! That streak of marble moved! He fell to watching her again, as if she were some troublesome sentence that needed licking into shape. As she bent impertinently over her book, she was an insult to man. All Tommy's interest in her revived. She infuriated him.

"Alice," he whispered.

"Do keep quiet till I finish this chapter," she begged lazily.

It brought him at once to the boiling-point.

"Alice!" he said fervently.

She had noticed the change in his voice. "People are looking," she said, without moving a muscle.

There was some subtle flattery to him in the warning, but he could not ask for more, for just then Mrs. Jerry came in. She was cloaked for the garden, and he had to go with her, sulkily. At the door she observed that the ground was still wet.

"Are you wearing your goloshes?" said he, brightening. "You must get them, Mrs. Jerry; I insist."

She hesitated. (Her room was on the third floor.) "It is very good of you to be so thoughtful of me," she said, "but ——"

"But I have no right to try to take care of you," he interposed in a melancholy voice. "It is true. Let us go."

"I sha'n't be two minutes," said Mrs. Jerry, in a flutter, and went off hastily for her goloshes, while he looked fondly after her. At the turn of the stair she glanced back, and his eyes were still begging her to hurry. It was a gracious memory to her in the after years, for she never saw him again.

As soon as she was gone he returned to the hall, and taking from a peg a cloak with a Mother Goose hood, brought it to Lady Pippinworth, who had watched her mamma trip upstairs.

"Did I say I was going out?" she asked.

"Yes," said Tommy, and she rose to let him put the elegant thing round her. She was one of those dangerous women who look their best when you are helping them to put on their cloaks.

"Now," he instructed her, "pull the hood over your head."

"Is it so cold as that?" she said, obeying.

"I want you to wear it," he answered. What he meant was that she never looked quite so impudent as in her hood, and his vanity insisted that she should be armed to the teeth before they resumed hostilities. The red light was in his eyes as he drew her into the garden where Grizel lay.

It was an evening without stars, but fair, sufficient wind to make her Ladyship cling haughtily to his arm as they turned corners. Many of the visitors were in the garden, some grouped round a quartet of gaily attired minstrels, but more sitting in little arbours or prowling in search of an arbour to sit in; the night was so dark that when our two passed beyond the light of the hotel windows they could scarce see the shrubs they brushed against; cigars without faces behind them sauntered past; several times they thought they had found an unoccupied arbour at last, when they heard the clink of coffee-cups.

"I believe the castle dates from the fifteenth century," Tommy would then say suddenly, though it was not of castles he had been talking.

With a certain satisfaction he noticed that she permitted him, without comment, to bring in the castle thus and to drop it the moment the emergency had passed. But he had little other encouragement. Even when she pressed his arm it was only as an intimation that the castle was needed.

"I can't even make her angry," he said wrathfully to himself.

"You answer not a word," he said in great dejection to her.

"I am afraid to speak," she admitted. "I don't know who may hear."

"Alice," he said eagerly, "what would you say if you were not afraid to speak?"

They had stopped, and he thought she trembled a little on his arm, but he could not be sure. He thought-but he was thinking too much again; at least, Lady Pippinworth seemed to come to that conclusion, for with a galling little laugh she moved on. He saw with amazing clearness that he had thought sufficiently for one day.

On coming into the garden with her, and for some time afterwards, he had been studying her so coolly, watching symptoms rather than words, that there is nothing to compare the man to but a doctor who, while he is chatting, has his finger on your pulse. But he was not so calm now. Whether or not he had stirred the woman, he was rapidly firing himself.

When next he saw her face by the light of a window, she at the same instant turned her eyes on him; it was as if each wanted to know correctly how the other had been looking in the darkness, and the effect was a challenge.

Like one retreating a step, she lowered her eyes. "I am tired," she said. "I shall go in."

"Let us stroll round once more."

"No, I am going in."

"If you are afraid — —" he said, with a slight smile.

She took his arm again. "Though it is too bad of me to keep you out," she said, as they went on, "for you are shivering. Is it the night air that makes you shiver?" she asked mockingly.

But she shivered a little herself, as if with a presentiment that she might be less defiant if he were less thoughtful. For a month or more she had burned to teach him a lesson, but there was a time before that when, had she been sure he was in earnest, she would have preferred to be the pupil.

Two ladies came out of an arbour where they had been drinking coffee, and sauntered towards the hotel. It was a tiny building, half concealed in hops and reached by three steps, and Tommy and his companion took possession. He groped in the darkness for a chair for her, and invited her tenderly to sit down. She said she preferred to stand. She was by the open window, her fingers drumming on the sill. Though he could not see her face, he knew exactly how she was looking.

"Sit down," he said, rather masterfully.

"I prefer to stand," she repeated languidly.

He had a passionate desire to take her by the shoulders, but put his hand on hers instead, and she permitted it, like one disdainful but helpless. She said something unimportant about the stillness.

"Is it so still?" he said in a low voice. "I seem to hear a great noise. I think it must be the beating of my heart."

"I fancy that is what it is," she drawled.

"Do you hear it?"

"No."

"Did you ever hear your own heart beat, Alice?"

"No."

He had both her hands now. "Would you like to hear it?"

She pulled away her hands sharply. "Yes," she replied with defiance.

"But you pulled away your hands first," said he.

He heard her breathe heavily for a moment, but she said nothing. "Yes," he said, as if she had spoken, "it is true."

"What is true?"

"What you are saying to yourself just now-that you hate me."

She beat the floor with her foot.

"How you hate me, Alice!"

"Oh, no."

"Yes, indeed you do."

"I wonder why," she said, and she trembled a little.

"I know why." He had come close to her again. "Shall I tell you why?"

She said "No," hurriedly.

"I am so glad you say No." He spoke passionately, and yet there was banter in his voice, or so it seemed to her. "It is because you fear to be told; it is because you had hoped that I did not know."

"Tell me why I hate you!" she cried.

"Tell me first that you do."

"Oh, I do, I do indeed!" She said the words in a white heat of hatred.

Before she could prevent him he had raised her hand to his lips.

"Dear Alice!" he said.

"Why is it?" she demanded.

"Listen!" he said. "Listen to your heart, Alice; it is beating now. It is telling you why. Does it need an interpreter? It is saying you hate me because you think I don't love you."

"Don't you?" she asked fiercely.

"No," Tommy said.

Her hands were tearing each other, and she could not trust herself to speak. She sat down deadly pale in the chair he had offered her.

"No man ever loved you," he said, leaning over her with his hand on the back of the chair. "You are smiling at that, I know; but it is true, Lady Disdain. They may have vowed to blow their brains out, and seldom did it; they may have let you walk over them, and they may have become your fetch-and-carry, for you were always able to drive them crazy; but love does not bring men so low. They tried hard to love you, and it was not that they could not love; it was that you were unlovable. That is a terrible thing to a woman. You think you let them try to love you, that you might make them your slaves when they succeeded; but you made them your slaves because they failed. It is a power given to your cold and selfish nature in place of the capacity for being able to be loved, with which women not a hundredth part as beautiful as you are dowered, and you have a raging desire, Alice, to exercise it over me as over the others; but you can't."

Had he seen her face then, it might have warned him to take care; but he heard her words only, and they were not at all in keeping with her face.

"I see I can't," was what she cried, almost in a whisper.

"It is all true, Alice, is it not?"

"I suppose so. I don't know; I don't care." She swung round in her chair and caught his sleeve. Her hands clung to it. "Say you love me now," she said. "I cannot live without your love after this. What shall I do to make you love me? Tell me, and I will do it."

He could not stop himself, for he mistrusted her still.

"I will not be your slave," he said, through his teeth. "You shall be mine."

"Yes, yes."

"You shall submit to me in everything. If I say 'come,' you shall come to wheresoever it may be; and if I say 'stay,' and leave you for ever, you shall stay."

"Very well," she said eagerly. She would have her revenge when he was her slave.

"You can continue to be the haughty Lady Disdain to others, but you shall be only obedient little Alice to me."

"Very well." She drew his arm towards her and pressed her lips upon it. "And for that you will love me a little, won't you? You will love me at last, won't you?" she entreated.

He was a masterful man up to a certain point only. Her humility now tapped him in a new place, and before he knew what he was about he began to run pity.

"To humiliate you so, Alice! I am a dastard. I am not such a dastard as you think me. I wanted to know that you would be willing to do all these things, but I would never have let you do them."

"I am willing to do them."

"No, no." It was he who had her hands now. "It was brutal, but I did it for you, Alice-for you. Don't you see I was doing it only to make a woman of you? You were always adorable, but in a coat of mail that would let love neither in nor out. I have been hammering at it to break it only and free my glorious Alice. We had to fight, and one of us had to give in. You would have flung me away if I had yielded —I had to win to save you."

"Now I am lost indeed," he was saying to himself, even as it came rushing out of him, and what appalled him most was that worse had probably still to come. He was astride two horses, and both were at the gallop. He flung out his arms as if seeking for something to check him.

As he did so she had started to her feet, listening. It seemed to her that there was someone near them.

He flung out his arms for help, and they fell upon Lady Pippinworth and went round her. He drew her to him. She could hear no breathing now but his.

"Alice, I love you, for you are love itself; it is you I have been chasing since first love rose like a bird at my feet; I never had a passing fancy for any other woman; I always knew that somewhere in the world there must be you, and sometime this starless night and you for me. You were hidden behind walls of ice; no man had passed them; I broke them down and love leaped to love, and you lie here, my beautiful, love in the arms of its lover."

He was in a frenzy of passion now; he meant every word of it; and her intention was to turn upon him presently and mock him, this man with whom she had been playing. Oh, the jeering things she had to say! But she could not say them yet; she would give her fool another moment-so she thought, but she was giving it to herself; and as she delayed she was in danger of melting in his arms.

"What does the world look like to you, my darling? You are in it for the first time. You were born but a moment ago. It is dark, that you may not be blinded before you have used your eyes. These are your eyes, dear eyes that do not yet know their purpose; they are for looking at me, little Alice, and mine are for looking into yours. I cannot see you; I have never seen the face of my love-oh, my love, come into the light that I may see your face."

They did not move. Her head had fallen on his shoulder. She was to give it but a moment, and then —— But the moment had passed and still her hair pressed his cheek. Her eyes were closed. He seemed to have found the way to woo her. Neither of them spoke. Suddenly they jumped apart. Lady Pippinworth stole to the door. They held their breath and listened.

It was not so loud now, but it was distinctly heard. It had been heavy breathing, and now she was trying to check it and half succeeding-but at the cost of little cries. They both knew it was a woman, and that she was in the arbour, on the other side of the little table. She must have been there when they came in.

"Who is that?"

There was no answer to him save the checked breathing and another broken cry. She moved, and it helped him to see vaguely the outlines of a girl who seemed to be drawing back from him in terror. He thought she was crouching now in the farthest corner.

"Come away," he said. But Lady Pippinworth would not let him go. They must know who this woman was. He remembered that a match-stand usually lay on the tables of those arbours, and groped until he found one.

"Who are you?"

He struck a match. They were those French matches that play an infernal interlude before beginning to burn. While he waited he knew that she was begging him, with her hands and with cries that were too little to be words, not to turn its light on her. But he did.

Then she ceased to cower. The girlish dignity that had been hers so long came running back to her. As she faced him there was even a crooked smile upon her face.

"I woke up," she said.

"I woke up," she said, as if the words had no meaning to herself, but might have some to him.

The match burned out before he spoke, but his face was terrible. "Grizel!" he said, appalled; and then, as if the discovery was as awful to her as to him, she uttered a cry of horror and sped out into the night. He called her name again, and sprang after her; but the hand of another woman detained him.

"Who is this girl?" Lady Pippinworth demanded fiercely; but he did not answer. He recoiled from her with a shudder that she was not likely to forget, and hurried on. All that night he searched for Grizel in vain.

Chapter XXX
The Little Gods Desert Him

And all next day he searched like a man whose eyes would never close again. She had not passed the night in any inn or village house of St. Gian; of that he made certain by inquiries from door to door. None of the guides had seen her, though they are astir so late and so early, patiently waiting at the hotel doors to be hired, that there seems to be no night for them-darkness only, that blots them out for a time as they stand waiting. At all hours there is in St. Gian the tinkle of bells, the clatter of hoofs, the crack of a whip, dust in retreat; but no coachman brought him news. The streets were thronged with other coachmen on foot looking into every face in quest of some person who wanted to return to the lowlands, but none had looked into her face.

Within five minutes of the hotel she might have been on any of half a dozen roads. He wandered or rushed along them all for a space, and came back. One of them was short and ended in the lake. All through that long and beautiful day this miserable man found himself coming back to the road that ended in the lake.

There were moments when he cried to himself that it was an apparition he had seen and heard. He had avoided his friends all day; of the English-speaking people in St. Gian one only knew why he was distraught, and she was the last he wished to speak to; but more than once he nearly sought her to say, "Partner in my shame, what did you see? what did you hear?" In the afternoon he had a letter from Elspeth telling him how she was enjoying her holiday by the sea, and mentioning that David was at that moment writing to Grizel in Thrums. But was it, then, all a dream? he cried, nearly convinced for the first time, and he went into the arbour saying determinedly that it was a dream; and in the arbour, standing primly in a corner, was Grizel's umbrella. He knew that umbrella so well! He remembered once being by while she replaced one of its ribs so deftly that he seemed to be looking on at a surgical operation. The old doctor had given it to her, and that was why she would not let it grow old before she was old herself. Tommy opened it now with trembling hands and looked at the little bits of Grizel on it: the beautiful stitching with which she had coaxed the slits to close again; the one patch, so artful that she had clapped her hands over it. And he fell on his knees and kissed these little bits of Grizel, and called her "beloved," and cried to his gods to give him one more chance.

"I woke up." It was all that she had said. It was Grizel's excuse for inconveniencing him. She had said it apologetically and as if she did not quite know how she came to be there herself. There was no look of reproach on her face while the match burned; there had been a pitiful smile, as if she was begging him not to be very angry with her; and then when he said her name she gave that little cry as if she had recognized herself, and stole away. He lived that moment over and over again, and she never seemed to be horror-stricken until he cried "Grizel!" when her recognition of herself made her scream. It was as if she had wakened up, dazed by the terrible things that were being said, and then, by the light of that one word "Grizel," suddenly knew who had been listening to them.

Did he know anything more? He pressed his hands harshly on his temples and thought. He knew that she was soaking wet, that she had probably sought the arbour for protection from the rain, and that, if so, she had been there for at least four hours. She had wakened up. She must have fallen asleep, knocked down by fatigue. What fatigue it must have been to make Grizel lie there for hours he could guess, and he beat his brow in anguish. But why she had come he could not guess. "Oh, miserable man, to seek for reasons," he cried passionately to himself, "when it is Grizel Grizel herself you should be seeking for!"

He walked and ran the round of the lake, and it was not on the bank that his staring eyes were fixed.

At last he came for a moment upon her track. The people of an inn six miles from St. Gian remembered being asked yesterday by an English miss, walking alone, how far she was from Bad-Platten. She was wearing something brown, and her boots were white with dust, and these people had never seen a lady look so tired before; when she stood still she had to lean against the wall. They said she had red-hot eyes.

Tommy was in an einspänner now, the merry conveyance of the country and more intoxicating than its wines, and he drove back through St. Gian to Bad-Platten, where again he heard from Grizel, though he did not find her. What he found was her telegram from London: "I am coming. GRIZEL." Why had she come? why had she sent that telegram? what had taken her to London? He was not losing time when he asked himself distractedly these questions, for he was again in his gay carriage and driving back to the wayside inn. He spent the night there, afraid to go farther lest he should pass her in the darkness; for he had decided that, if alive, she was on this road. That she had walked all those forty miles uphill seemed certain, and apparently the best he could hope was that she was walking back. She had probably no money to enable her to take the diligence. Perhaps she had no money with which to buy food. It might be that while he lay tossing in bed she was somewhere near, dying for want of a franc.

He was off by morning light, and several times that day he heard of her, twice from people who had seen her pass both going and coming, and he knew it must be she when they said she rocked her arms as she walked. Oh, he knew why she rocked her arms! Once he thought he had found her. He heard of an English lady who was lying ill in the house of a sawmiller, whose dog (we know the dogs of these regions, but not the people) had found her prostrate in the wood, some distance from the highroad. Leaving his einspänner in a village, Tommy climbed down the mountain-side to this little house, which he was long in discovering. It was by the side of a roaring river, and he arrived only an hour too late. The lady had certainly been Grizel; but she was gone. The sawyer's wife described to him how her husband had brought her in, and how she seemed so tired and bewildered that she fell asleep while they were questioning her. She held her hands over her ears to shut out the noise of the river, which seemed to terrify her. So far as they could understand, she told them that she was running away from the river. She had been sleeping there for three hours, and was still asleep when the good woman went off to meet her husband; but when they returned she was gone.

He searched the wood for miles around, crying her name. The sawyer and some of his fellow-workers left the trees they were stripping of bark to help him, and for hours the wood rang with "Grizel, Grizel!" All the mountains round took up the cry; but there never came an answer. This long delay prevented his reaching the railway terminus until noon of the following day, and there he was again too late. But she had been here. He traced her to that hotel whence we saw her setting forth, and the portier had got a ticket for her for London. He had talked with her for some little time, and advised her, as she seemed so tired, to remain there for the night. But she said she must go home at once. She seemed to be passionately desirous to go home, and had looked at him suspiciously, as if fearing he might try to hold her back. He had been called away, and on returning had seen her disappearing over the bridge. He had called to her, and then she ran as if afraid he was pursuing her. But he had observed her afterwards in the train.

So she was not without money, and she was on her way home! The relief it brought him came to the surface in great breaths, and at first every one of them was a prayer of thankfulness. Yet in time they were triumphant breaths. Translated into words, they said that he had got off cheaply for the hundredth time. His little gods had saved him again, as they had saved him in the arbour by sending Grizel to him. He could do as he liked, for they were always there to succour him; they would never desert him-never. In a moment of fierce elation he raised his hat to them, then seemed to see Grizel crying "I woke up," and in horror of himself clapped it on again. It was but a momentary aberration, and is recorded only to show that, however remorseful he felt afterwards, there was life in our Tommy still.

The train by which he was to follow her did not leave until evening, and through those long hours he was picturing, with horrible vividness and pain, the progress of Grizel up and down that terrible pass. Often his shoulders shook in agony over what he saw, and he shuddered to the teeth. He would have walked round the world on his knees to save her this long anguish!

And then again it was less something he saw than something he was writing, and he altered it to make it more dramatic. "I woke up." How awful that was! but in this new scene she uttered no words. Lady Pippinworth was in his arms when they heard a little cry, so faint that a violin string makes as much moan when it snaps. In a dread silence he lit a match, and as it flared the figure of a girl was seen upon the floor. She was dead; and even as he knew that she was dead he recognized her. "Grizel!" he cried. The other woman who had lured him from his true love uttered a piercing scream and ran towards the hotel. When she returned with men and lanterns there was no one in the arbour, but there were what had been a man and a girl. They lay side by side. The startled onlookers unbared their heads. A solemn voice said, "In death not divided."

He was not the only occupant of the hotel reading-room as he saw all this, and when his head fell forward and he groaned, the others looked up from their papers. A lady asked if he was unwell.

"I have had a great shock," he replied in a daze, pulling his hand across his forehead.

"Something you have seen in your paper?" inquired a clergyman who had been complaining that there was no news.

"People I knew," said Tommy, not yet certain which world he was in.

"Dead?" the lady asked sympathetically.

"I knew them well," he said, and staggered into the fresh air.

Poor dog of a Tommy! He had been a total abstainer from sentiment, as one may say, for sixty hours, and this was his only glass. It was the nobler Tommy, sternly facing facts, who by and by stepped into the train. He even knew why he was going to Thrums. He was going to say certain things to her; and he said them to himself again and again in the train, and heard her answer. The words might vary, but they were always to the same effect.

"Grizel, I have come back!"

He saw himself say these words, as he opened her door in Gavinia's little house. And when he had said them he bowed his head.

At his sudden appearance she started up; then she stood pale and firm.

"Why have you come back?"

"Not to ask your forgiveness," he replied hoarsely; "not to attempt to excuse myself; not with any hope that there remains one drop of the love you once gave me so abundantly. I want only, Grizel, to put my life into your hands. I have made a sorry mess of it myself. Will you take charge of what may be left of it? You always said you were ready to help me. I have come back, Grizel, for your help. What you were once willing to do for love, will you do for pity now?"

She turned away her head, and he went nearer her. "There was always something of the mother in your love, Grizel; but for that you would never have borne with me so long. A mother, they say, can never quite forget her boy-oh, Grizel, is it true? I am the prodigal come back. Grizel, beloved, I have sinned and I am unworthy, but I am still your boy, and I have come back. Am I to be sent away?"

At the word "beloved" her arms rocked impulsively. "You must not call me that," she said.

"Then I am to go," he answered with a shudder, "for I must always call you that; whether I am with you or away, you shall always be beloved to me."

"You don't love me!" she cried. "Oh, do you love me at last!" And at that he fell upon his knees.

"Grizel, my love, my love!"

"But you don't want to be married," she said.

"Beloved, I have come back to ask you on my knees to be my wife."

"That woman —"

"She was a married woman, Grizel."

"Oh, oh, oh!"

"And now you know the worst of me. It is the whole truth at last. I don't know why you took that terrible journey, dear Grizel, but I do know that you were sent there to save me. Oh, my love, you have done so much, will you do no more?"

And so on, till there came a time when his head was on her lap and her hand caressing it, and she was whispering to her boy to look up and see her crooked smile again.

He passed on to the wedding. All the time between seemed to be spent in his fond entreaties to hasten the longed-for day. How radiant she looked in her bridal gown! "Oh, beautiful one, are you really mine? Oh, world, pause for a moment and look at the woman who has given herself to me!"

"My wife-this is my wife!" They were in London now; he was showing her to London. How he swaggered! There was a perpetual apology on her face; it begged people to excuse him for looking so proudly at her. It was a crooked apology, and he hurried her into dark places and kissed it.

Do you see that Tommy was doing all this for Grizel and pretending to her that it was for himself? He was passionately desirous of making amends, and he was to do it in the most generous way. Perhaps he believed when he seemed to enter her room saying, "Grizel, I have come back," that she loved him still; perhaps he knew that he did not love in the way he said; perhaps he saw a remorseful man making splendid atonement: but never should she know these things; tenderly as he had begun he would go on to the end. Here at last is a Tommy worth looking at, and he looked.

Yet as he drew near Thrums, after almost exactly two days of continuous travel, many a shiver went down his back, for he could not be sure that he should find Grizel here; he sometimes seemed to see her lying ill at some wayside station in Switzerland, in France; everything that could have happened to her he conceived, and he moved restlessly in the carriage. His mouth went dry.

"Has she come back?"

The train had stopped for the taking of tickets, and his tremulous question checked the joy of Corp at sight of him.

"She's back," Corp answered in an excited whisper; and oh, the relief to Tommy! "She came back by the afternoon train; but I had scarce a word wi' her, she was so awid to be hame. 'I am going home,' she cried, and hurried away up the brae. Ay, and there's one queer thing."

"What?"

"Her luggage wasna in the van."

Tommy could smile at that. "But what sent her," he asked eagerly, "on that journey?"

Corp told him the little he knew. "But nobody kens except me and Gavinia," he said. We pretend she gaed to London to see her father. We said he had wrote to her, wanting her to go to him. Gavinia said it would never do to let folk ken she had gaen to see you, and even Elspeth doesna ken."

"Is Elspeth back?"

"They came back yesterday."

Did David know the truth from Grizel? was what Tommy was asking himself now as he strode up the brae. But again he was in luck, for when he had explained away his abrupt return to Elspeth, and been joyfully welcomed by her, she told him that her husband had been in one of the glens all day. "He does not know that Grizel has come back," she said. "Oh," she exclaimed, "but you don't even know that she has been away! Grizel has been in London."

"Corp told me," said Tommy.

"And did he tell you why she had gone?"

"Yes."

"She came back an hour or two ago. Maggy Ann saw her go past. Fancy her seeing her father at last! It must have been an ordeal for her. I wonder what took place."

"I think I had better go and ask her," Tommy said. He was mightily relieved for Grizel's sake. No one need ever know now what had called her away except Corp and Gavinia, and even they thought she had merely been to London. How well the little gods were managing the whole affair! As he walked to Grizel's lodgings to say what he had been saying in the train, the thought came to him for a moment that as no one need ever know where she had been there was less reason why he should do this generous thing. But he put it from him with lofty disdain. Any effect it had was to make him walk more firmly to his sacrifice, as if to show all ignoble impulses that they could find no home in that swelling breast He was pleased with himself, was Tommy.

"Grizel, I have come back." He said it to the night, and bowed his head. He said it with head accompaniment to Grizel's lighted window. He said it to himself as he reached the door. He never said it again.

For Gavinia's first words were: "It's you, Mr. Sandys! Wherever is she? For mercy's sake, dinna say you've come without her!" And when he blinked at this, she took him roughly by the arm and cried, "Wherever's Grizel?"

"She is here, Gavinia."

"She's no here."

"I saw her light."

"You saw my light."

"Gavinia, you are torturing me. She came back to-day."

"What makes you say that? You're dreaming. She hasna come back."

"Corp saw her come in by the afternoon train. He spoke to her."

Gavinia shook her head incredulously. "You're just imagining that," she said.

"He told me. Gavinia, I must see for myself," She stared after him as he went up the stairs. "You are very cruel, Gavinia," he said, when he came down. "Tell me where she is."

"May I be struck, Mr. Sandys, if I've seen or heard o' her since she left this house eight days syne." He knew she was speaking the truth. He had to lean against the door for support. "It canna be so bad as you think," she cried in pity. "If you're sure Corp said he saw her, she maun hae gone to the doctor's house."

"She is not there. But Elspeth knew she had come back. Others have seen her besides Corp. My God, Gavinia! what can have happened?"

In little more than an hour he knew what had happened. Many besides himself, David among them towards the end, were engaged in the search. And strange stories began to fly about like night-birds; you will not search for a missing woman without rousing them. Why had she gone off to London without telling anyone? Had Corp concocted that story about her father to blind them? Had she really been as far as London? Have you seen Sandys? —he's back. It's said Corp telegraphed to him to Switzerland that she had disappeared. It's weel kent Corp telegraphed. Sandys came at once. He is in a terrible state. Look how white he is aneath that lamp. What garred them telegraph for him? How is it he is in sic a state? Fond o' her, was he? Yea, yea, even after she gave him the go-by. Then it's a weary Sabbath for him, if half they say be true. What do they say? They say she was queer when she came back. Corp doesna say that. Maybe no; but Francie Crabb does. He says he met her on the station brae and spoke to her, and she said never a word, but put up her hands like as if she feared he was to strike her. The Dundas lassies saw her frae their window, and her hands were at her ears as if she was trying to drown the sound o' something. Do you mind o' her mother? They say she was looking terrible like her mother.

It was only between the station and Gavinia's house that she had been seen, but they searched far afield. Tommy, accompanied by Corp, even sought for her in the Den. Do you remember the long, lonely path between two ragged little dykes that led from the Den to the house of the Painted Lady? It was there that Grizel had lived with her mamma. The two men went down that path, which is oppressed with trees. Elsewhere the night was not dark, but, as they had known so well when they were boys, it is always dark after evenfall in the Double Dykes. That is the legacy of the Painted Lady. Presently they saw the house-scarcely the house, but a lighted window. Tommy remembered the night when as a boy, Elspeth crouching beside him, he had peered in fearfully at that corner window on Grizel and her mamma, and the shuddersome things he had seen. He shuddered at them again.

"Who lives there now?" he asked.

"Nobody. It's toom."

"There is a light."

"Some going-about body. They often tak' bilbie in toom houses, and that door is without a lock; it's keepit close wi' slipping a stick aneath it. Do you mind how feared we used to be at that house?"

"She was never afraid of it."

"It was her hame."

He meant no more than he said, but suddenly they both stopped dead.

"It's no possible," Corp said, as if in answer to a question. "It's no possible," he repeated beseechingly.

"Wait for me here, Corp."

"I would rather come wi' you."

"Wait here!" Tommy said almost fiercely, and he went on alone to that little window. It had needed an effort to make him look in when he was here before, and it needed a bigger effort now. But he looked.

What light there was came from the fire, and whether she had gathered the logs or found them in the room no one ever knew. A vagrant stated afterwards that he had been in the house some days before and left his match-box in it.

By this fire Grizel was crouching. She was comparatively tidy and neat again; the dust was gone from her boots, even. How she had managed to do it no one knows, but you remember how she loved to be neat. Her hands were extended to the blaze, and she was busy talking to herself.

His hand struck the window heavily, and she looked up and saw him. She nodded, and put her finger to her lips as a sign that he must be cautious. She had often, in the long ago, seen her mother signing thus to an imaginary face at the window-the face of the man who never came.

Tommy went into the house, and she was so pleased to see him that she quite simpered. He put his arms round her, and she lay there with a little giggle of contentment. She was in a plot of heat.

"Grizel! Oh, my God!" he said, "why do you look at me in that way?"

She passed her hand across her eyes, like one trying to think.

"I woke up," she said at last. Corp appeared at the window now, and she pointed to him in terror. Thus had she seen her mother point, in the long ago, at faces that came there to frighten her.

"Grizel," Tommy entreated her, "you know who I am, don't you?"

She said his name at once, but her eyes were on the window. "They want to take me away," she whispered.

"But you must come away, Grizel. You must come home."

"This is home," she said. "It is sweet."

After much coaxing, he prevailed upon her to leave. With his arm round her, and a terrible woe on his face, he took her to the doctor's house. She had her hands over her ears all the way. She thought the white river and the mountains and the villages and the crack of whips were marching with her still.

Chapter XXXI

"The Man With the Greetin' Eyes"

For many days she lay in a fever at the doctor's house, seeming sometimes to know where she was, but more often not, and night after night a man with a drawn face sat watching her. They entreated, they forced him to let them take his place; but from his room he heard her moan or speak, or he thought he heard her, or he heard a terrible stillness, and he stole back to listen; they might send him away, but when they opened the door he was there, with his drawn face. And often they were glad to see him, for there were times when he alone could interpret her wild demands and soothe those staring eyes.

Once a scream startled the house. Someone had struck a match in the darkened chamber, and she thought she was in an arbour in St. Gian. They had to hold her in her bed by force at times; she had such a long way to walk before night, she said.

She would struggle into a sitting posture and put her hands over her ears.

Her great desire was not to sleep. "I should wake up," she explained fearfully.

She took a dislike to Elspeth, and called her "Alice."

These ravings, they said to each other, must have reference to what happened to her when she was away, and as they thought he knew no more of her wanderings than they, everyone marvelled at the intuition with which he read her thoughts. It was he who guessed that the striking of matches somehow terrified her; he who discovered that it was a horrid roaring river she thought she heard, and he pretended he heard it too, and persuaded her that if she lay very still it would run past. Nothing she said or did puzzled him. He read the raving of her mind, they declared admiringly, as if he held the cipher to it.

"And the cipher is his love," Mrs. McLean said, with wet eyes. In the excitement of those days Elspeth talked much to her of Tommy's love for Grizel, and how she had refused him, and it went round the town with embellishments. It was generally believed now that she really had gone to London to see her father, and that his heartless behaviour had unhinged her mind.

By David's advice, Corp and Gavinia did not contradict this story. It was as good as another, he told them, and better than the truth.

But what was the truth? they asked greedily.

"Oh, that he is a noble fellow," David replied grimly.

They knew that, but —

He would tell them no more, however, though he knew all. Tommy had made full confession to the doctor, even made himself out worse than he was, as had to be his way when he was not making himself out better.

"And I am willing to proclaim it all from the market-place," he said hoarsely, "if that is your wish."

"I daresay you would almost enjoy doing that," said David, rather cruelly.

"I daresay I should," Tommy said, with a gulp, and went back to Grizel's side. It was not, you may be sure, to screen him that David kept the secret; it was because he knew what many would say of Grizel if the nature of her journey were revealed. He dared not tell Elspeth, even; for think of the woe to her if she learned that it was her wonderful brother who had brought Grizel to this pass! The Elspeths of this world always have some man to devote himself to them. If the Tommies pass away, the Davids spring up. For my own part, I think Elspeth would have found some excuse for Tommy. He said so himself to the doctor, for he wanted her to be told.

"Or you would find the excuse for her in time," David responded.

"Very likely," Tommy said. He was humble enough now, you see. David could say one thing only which would rouse him, namely, that Grizel was not to die in this fever; and for long it seemed impossible to say that.

"Would you have her live if her mind remains affected?" he asked; and Tommy said firmly, "Yes."

"You think, I suppose, that then you would have less for which to blame yourself!"

"I suppose that is it. But don't waste time on me, Gemmell, when you have her life to save, if you can."

Well, her life was saved, and Tommy's nursing had more to do with it than David's skill. David admitted it; the town talked of it. "I aye kent he would find a wy," Corp said, though he had been among the most anxious. He and Aaron Latta were the first admitted to see her, when she was able once more to sit in a chair. They had been told to ask her no questions. She chatted pleasantly to them, and they thought she was quite her old self. They wondered to see Tommy still so sad-eyed. To Ailie she spoke freely of her illness, though not of what had occasioned it, and told her almost gleefully that David had promised to let her sew a little next week. There was one thing only that surprised Ailie. Grizel had said that as soon as she was a little stronger she was going home.

"Does she mean to her father's house?" Ailie asked.

This was what started the report that, touched no doubt by her illness, Grizel's unknown father had, after all, offered her a home. They discovered, however, what Grizel meant by home when, one afternoon, she escaped, unseen, from the doctor's house, and was found again at Double Dykes, very indignant because someone had stolen the furniture.

She seemed to know all her old friends except Elspeth, who was still Alice to her. Seldom now did she put her hands over her ears, or see horrible mountains marching with her. She no longer remembered, save once or twice when she woke up, that she had ever been out of Thrums. To those who saw her casually she was Grizel-gone thin and pale and weak intellectually, but still the Grizel of old, except for the fixed idea that Double Dykes was her home.

"You must not humour her in that delusion," David said sternly to Tommy; "when we cease to fight it we have abandoned hope."

So the weapon he always had his hand on was taken from Tommy, for he would not abandon hope. He fought gallantly. It was always he who brought her back from Double Dykes. She would not leave it with any other person, but she came away with him.

"It's because she's so fond o' him," Corp said.

But it was not. It was because she feared him, as all knew who saw them together. They were seen together a great deal when she was able to go out. Driving seemed to bring back the mountains to her eyes, so she walked, and it was always with the help of Tommy's arm. "It's a most pitiful sight," the people said. They pitied him even more than her, for though she might be talking gaily to him and leaning heavily on him, they could see that she mistrusted him. At the end of a sweet smile she would give him an ugly, furtive look.

"She's like a cat you've forced into your lap," they said, "and it lies quiet there, ready to jump the moment you let go your grip."

They wondered would he never weary. He never wearied. Day after day he was saying the same things to her, and the end was always as the beginning. They came back to her entreaty that she should be allowed to go home as certainly as they came back to the doctor's house.

"It is a long time, you know, Grizel, since you lived at Double Dykes-not since you were a child."

"Not since I was a child," she said as if she quite understood.

"Then you went to live with your dear, kind doctor, you remember. What was his name?"

"Dr. McQueen. I love him."

"But he died, and he left you his house to live in. It is your home, Grizel. He would be so grieved if he thought you did not make it your home."

"It is my home," she said proudly; but when they returned to it she was loath to go in. "I want to go home!" she begged.

One day he took her to her rooms in Corp's house, thinking her old furniture would please her; and that was the day when she rocked her arms joyously again. But it was not the furniture that made her so happy; it was Corp's baby.

"Oh, oh!" she cried in rapture, and held out her arms; and he ran into them, for there was still one person in Thrums who had no fear of Grizel.

"It will be a damned shame," Corp said huskily, "if that woman never has no bairns o' her ain."

They watched her crooning over the child, playing with him for a long time. You could not have believed that she required to be watched. She told him with hugs that she had come back to him at last; it was her first admission that she knew she had been away and a wild hope came to Tommy that along the road he could not take her she might be drawn by this little child.

She discovered a rent in the child's pinafore and must mend it at once. She ran upstairs, as a matter of course, to her work-box, and brought down a needle and thread. It was quite as if she was at home at last.

"But you don't live here now, Grizel," Tommy said, when she drew back at his proposal that they should go away; "you live at the doctor's house."

"Do I, Gavinia?" she said beseechingly.

"Is it here you want to bide?" Corp asked, and she nodded her head several times.

"It would be so much more convenient," she said, looking at the child.

"Would you take her back, Gavinia," Tommy asked humbly, "if she continues to want it?" Gavinia did not answer.

"Woman!" cried Corp.

"I'm mortal wae for her," Gavinia said slowly, "but she needs to be waited on hand and foot."

"I would come and do the waiting on her hand and foot, Gavinia," Tommy said.

And so it came about that a week afterwards Grizel was reinstalled in her old rooms. Every morning when Tommy came to see her she asked him, icily how Alice was. She seemed to think that Alice, as she called her, was his wife. He always replied, "You mean Elspeth," and she assented, but only, it was obvious, because she feared to contradict him. To Corp and Gavinia she would still say passionately, "I want to go home!" and probably add fearfully, "Don't tell him."

Yet though this was not home to her, she seemed to be less unhappy here than in the doctor's house, and she found a great deal to do. All her old skill in needlework came back to her, and she sewed for the child such exquisite garments that she clapped her hands over them.

One day Tommy came with a white face and asked Gavinia if she knew whether a small brown parcel had been among the things brought by Grizel from the doctor's house.

"It was in the box sent after me from Switzerland," he told her, "and contained papers."

Gavinia had seen no such package.

"She may have hidden it," he said, and they searched, but fruitlessly. He questioned Grizel gently, but questions alarmed her, and he desisted.

"It does not matter, Gavinia," he said, with a ghastly smile; but on the following Sunday, when Corp called at the doctor's house, the thought "Have they found it?" leaped in front of all thought of Grizel. This was only for the time it takes to ask a question with the eyes, however, for Corp was looking very miserable.

"I'm sweer to say it," he announced to Tommy and David, "but it has to be said. We canna keep her."

Evidently something had happened, and Tommy rose to go to Grizel without even asking what it was. "Wait," David said, wrinkling his eyebrows, "till Corp tells us what he means by that. I knew it might come, Corp. Go on."

"If it hadna been for the bairn," said Corp, "we would hae tholed wi' her, however queer she was; but wi' the bairn I tell you it's no mous. You'll hae to tak' her awa'."

"Whatever she has been to others," Tommy said, "she is always an angel with the child. His own mother could not be fonder of him."

"That's it," Corp replied emphatically. "She's no the mother o' him, but there's whiles when she thinks she is. We kept it frae you as long as we could."

"As long as she is so good to him ——" David began.

"But at thae times she's not," said Corp. "She begins to shiver most terrible, as if she saw fearsome things in her mind, and syne we see her looking at him like as if she wanted to do him a mischief. She says he's her brat; she thinks he's hers, and that he hasna been well come by."

Tommy's hands rose in agony, and then he covered his face with them.

"Go on, Corp," David said hoarsely; "we must have it all."

"Sometimes," Corp went on painfully, "she canna help being fond o' him, though she thinks she shouldna hae had him. I've heard her saying, 'My brat!' and syne birsing him closer to her, as though her shame just made him mair to her. Women are so queer about thae things. I've seen her sitting by his cradle, moaning to hersel', 'I did so want to be good! It would be sweet to be good! and never stopping rocking the cradle, and a' the time the tears were rolling down."

Tommy cried, "If there is any more to tell, Corp, be quick."

"There's what I come here to tell you. It was no langer syne than jimply an hour. We thocht the bairn was playing at the gavle-end, and that Grizel was up the stair. But they werena, and I gaed straight to Double Dykes. She wasna there, but the bairn was, lying greetin' on the floor. We found her in the Den, sitting by the burn-side, and she said we should never see him again, for she had drowned him. We're sweer, but you'll need to tak' her awa'."

"We shall take her away," David said, and when he and Tommy were left together he asked: "Do you see what it means?"

"It means that the horrors of her early days have come back to her, and that she is confusing her mother with herself."

David's hands were clenched. "That is not what I am thinking of. We have to take her away; they have done far more than we had any right to ask of them. Sandys, where are we to take her to?"

"Do even you grow tired of her?" Tommy cried.

David said between his teeth: "We hope there will soon be a child in this house, also. God forgive me, but I cannot bring her back here."

"She cannot be in a house where there is a child!" said Tommy, with a bitter laugh. "Gemmell, it is Grizel we are speaking of! Do you remember what she was?"

"I remember."

"Well, where are we to send her?"

David turned his pained eyes full on Tommy.

"No!" Tommy cried vehemently.

"Sandys," said David, firmly, "that is what it has come to. They will take good care of her." He sat down with a groan. "Have done with heroics," he said savagely, when Tommy would have spoken. "I have been prepared for this; there is no other way."

"I have been prepared for it, too," Tommy said, controlling himself; "but there is another way: I can marry her, and I am going to do it."

"I don't know that I can countenance that," David said, after a pause. "It seems an infernal shame."

"Don't trouble about me," replied Tommy, hoarsely; "I shall do it willingly."

And then it was the doctor's turn to laugh. "You!" he said with a terrible scorn as he looked Tommy up and down. "I was not thinking of you. All my thoughts were of her. I was thinking how cruel to her if some day she came to her right mind and found herself tied for life to the man who had brought her to this pass."

Tommy winced and walked up and down.

"Desire to marry her gone?" asked David, savagely.

"No," Tommy said. He sat down. "You have the key to me, Gemmell," he went on quietly. "I gave it to you. You know I am a man of sentiment only; but you are without a scrap of it yourself, and so you will never quite know what it is. It has its good points. We are a kindly people. I was perhaps pluming myself on having made an heroic proposal, and though you have made me see it just now as you see it, as you see it I shall probably soon be putting on the same grand airs again. Lately I discovered that the children who see me with Grizel call me 'the Man with the Greetin' Eyes.' If I have greetin' eyes it was real grief that gave them to me; but when I heard what I was called it made me self-conscious, and I have tried to look still more lugubrious ever since. It seems monstrous to you, but that, I believe, is the kind of thing I shall always be doing. But it does not mean that I feel no real remorse. They were greetin' eyes before I knew it, and though I may pose grotesquely as a fine fellow for finding Grizel a home where there is no child and can never be a child, I shall not cease, night nor day, from tending her. It will be a grim business, Gemmell, as you know, and if I am Sentimental Tommy through it all, why grudge me my comic little strut?"

David said, "You can't take her to London."

"I shall take her to wherever she wants to go."

"There is one place only she wants to go to, and that is Double Dykes."

"I am prepared to take her there."

"And your work?"

"It must take second place now. I must write; it is the only thing I can do. If I could make a living at anything else I would give up writing altogether."

"Why?"

"She would be pleased if she could understand, and writing is the joy of my life-two reasons." But the doctor smiled.

"You are right," said Tommy. "I see I was really thinking what a fine picture of self-sacrifice I should make sitting in Double Dykes at a loom!"

They talked of ways and means, and he had to admit that he had little money. But the new book would bring in a good deal, David supposed.

"The manuscript is lost," Tommy replied, crushing down his agitation.

"Lost! When? Where?"

"I don't know. It was in the bag I left behind at St. Gian, and I supposed it was still in it when the bag was forwarded to me here. I did not look for more than a month. I took credit to myself for neglecting my manuscript, and when at last I looked it was not there. I telegraphed and wrote to the innkeeper at St. Gian, and he replied that my things had been packed at his request in presence of my friends there, the two ladies you know of. I wrote to them, and they replied that this was so, and said they thought they remembered seeing in the bottom of the bag some such parcel in brown paper as I described. But it is not there now, and I have given up all hope of ever seeing it again. No, I have no other copy. Every page was written half a dozen times, but I kept the final copy only."

"It is scarcely a thing anyone would steal."

"No; I suppose they took it out of the bag at St. Gian, and forgot to pack it again. It was probably flung away as of no account."

"Could it have been taken out on the way here?"

"The key was tied to the handle so that the custom officials might be able to open the bag. Perhaps they are fonder of English manuscripts than one would expect, or more careless of them."

"You can think of no other way in which it might have disappeared?"

"None," Tommy said; and then the doctor faced him squarely.

"Are you trying to screen Grizel?" he asked. "Is it true, what people are saying?"

"What are they saying?"

"That she destroyed it. I heard that yesterday, and told them your manuscript was in my house, as I thought it was. Was it she?"

"No, no. Gavinia must have started that story. I did look for the package among Grizel's things."

"What made you think of that?"

"I had seen her looking into my bag one day. And she used to say I loved my manuscripts too much ever to love her. But I am sure she did not do it."

"Be truthful, Sandys. You know how she always loved the truth."

"Well, then, I suppose it was she."

After a pause the doctor said: "It must be about as bad as having a limb lopped off."

"If only I had been offered that alternative!" Tommy replied.

"And yet," David mused, better pleased with him, "you have not cried out."

"Have I not! I have rolled about in agony, and invoked the gods, and cursed and whimpered; only I take care that no one shall see me."

"And that no one should know poor Grizel had done this thing. I admire you for that, Sandys."

"But it has leaked out, you see," Tommy said; "and they will all be admiring me for it at the wedding, and no doubt I shall be cocking my greetin' eyes at them to note how much they are admiring."

But when the wedding-day came he was not doing that. While he and Grizel stood up before Mr. Dishart, in the doctor's parlour, he was thinking of her only. His eyes never left her, not even when he had to reply "I do." His hand pressed hers all the time. He kept giving her reassuring little nods and smiles, and it was thus that he helped Grizel through.

Had Mr. Dishart understood what was in her mind he would not have married them. To her it was no real marriage; she thought they were tricking the minister, so that she should be able to go home. They had rehearsed the ceremony together many times, and oh, she was eager to make no mistake.

"If they were to find out!" she would say apprehensively, and then perhaps giggle at the slyness of it all. Tommy had to make merry with her, as if it was one of his boyish plays. If he was overcome with the pain of it, she sobbed at once and wrung her hands.

She was married in gray silk. She had made the dress herself, as beautifully as all her things were made. Tommy remembered how once, long ago, she had told him, as a most exquisite secret, that she had decided on gray silk.

Corp and Gavinia and Ailie and Aaron Latta were the only persons asked to the wedding, and when it was over, they said they never saw anyone stand up by a woman's side looking so anxious to be her man; and I am sure that in this they did Tommy no more than justice.

It was a sad day to Elspeth. Could she be expected to smile while her noble brother did this great deed of sacrifice? But she bore up bravely, partly for his sake, partly for the sake of one unborn.

The ring was no plain hoop of gold; it was garnets all the way round. She had seen it on Elspeth's finger, and craved it so greedily that it became her wedding-ring. And from the moment she had it she ceased to dislike Elspeth, and pitied her very much, as if she thought happiness went with the ring. "Poor Alice!" she said when she saw Elspeth crying at the wedding, and having started to go away with Tommy, she came back to say again, "Poor, poor Alice!"

Corp flung an old shoe after them.

Chapter XXXII
Tommy's Best Work

And thus was begun a year and a half of as great devotion as remorseful man ever gave to woman. When she was asleep and he could not write, his mind would sometimes roam after abandoned things; it sought them in the night as a savage beast steals forth for water to slake the thirst of many days. But if she stirred in her sleep they were all dispelled; there was not a moment in that eighteen months when he was twenty yards from Grizel's side.

He would not let himself lose hope. All the others lost it. "The only thing you can do is to humour her," even David was reduced in time to saying; but Tommy replied cheerily, "Not a bit of it." Every morning he had to begin at the same place as on the previous morning, and he was always as ready to do it, and as patient, as if this were the first time.

"I think she is a little more herself to-day," he would say determinedly, till David wondered to hear him.

"She makes no progress, Sandys."

"I can at least keep her from slipping back."

And he did, and there is no doubt that this was what saved Grizel in the end. How he strove to prevent her slipping back! The morning was the time when she was least troubled, and had he humoured her then they would often have been easy hours for him. But it was the time when he tried most doggedly, with a gentleness she could not ruffle, to teach her the alphabet of who she was. She coaxed him to let her off those mental struggles; she turned petulant and sulky; she was willing to be good and sweet if he would permit her to sew or to sing to herself instead, or to sit staring at the fire: but he would not yield; he promised those things as the reward, and in the end she stood before him like a child at lessons.

"What is your name?" The catechism always began thus.

"Grizel," she said obediently, if it was a day when she wanted to please him.

"And my name?"

"Tommy." Once, to his great delight, she said, "Sentimental Tommy." He quite bragged about this to David.

"Where is your home?"

"Here." She was never in doubt about this, and it was always a pleasure to her to say it.

"Did you live here long ago?"

She nodded.

"And then did you live for a long time somewhere else?"

"Yes."

"Where was it?"

"Here."

"No, it was with the old doctor. You were his little housekeeper; don't you remember? Try to remember, Grizel; he loved you so much."

She tried to think. Her face was very painful when she tried to think. "It hurts," she said.

"Do you remember him, Grizel?"

"Please let me sing," she begged, "such a sweet song!"

"Do you remember the old doctor who called you his little housekeeper? He used to sit in that chair."

The old chair was among Grizel's many possessions that had been brought to Double Dykes, and her face lit up with recollection. She ran to the chair and kissed it.

"What was his name, Grizel?"

"I should love to know his name," she said wistfully.

He told her the name many times, and she repeated it docilely.

Or perhaps she remembered her dear doctor quite well to-day, and thought Tommy was some one in need of his services.

"He has gone into the country," she said, as she had so often said to anxious people at the door; "but he won't be long, and I shall give him your message the moment he comes in."

But Tommy would not pass that. He explained to her again and again that the doctor was dead, and perhaps she would remember, or perhaps, without remembering, she said she was glad he was dead.

"Why are you glad, Grizel?"

She whispered, as if frightened she might be overheard: "I don't want him to see me like this." It was one of the pathetic things about her that she seemed at times to have some vague understanding of her condition, and then she would sob. Her tears were anguish to him, but it was at those times that she clung to him as if she knew he was trying to do something for her, and that encouraged him to go on. He went over, step by step, the time when she lived alone in the doctor's house, the time of his own coming back, her love for him and his treatment of her, the story of the garnet ring, her coming to Switzerland, her terrible walk, her return; he would miss out nothing, for he was fighting for her. Day after day, month by month, it went on, and to-morrow, perhaps, she would insist that the old doctor and this man who asked her so many questions were one. And Tommy argued with her until he had driven that notion out, to make way for another, and then he fought it, and so on and on all round the circle of her delusions, day by day and month by month.

She knew that he sometimes wrote while she was asleep, for she might start up from her bed or from the sofa, and there he was, laying down his pen to come to her. Her eyes were never open for any large fraction of a minute without his knowing, and immediately he went to her, nodding and smiling lest she had wakened with some fear upon her. Perhaps she refused to sleep again unless he promised to put away those horrid papers for the night, and however intoxicating a point he had reached in his labours, he always promised, and kept his word. He was most scrupulous in keeping any promise he made her, and one great result was that she trusted him implicitly. Whatever others promised, she doubted them.

There were times when she seemed to be casting about in her mind for something to do that would please him, and then she would bring pieces of paper to him, and pen and ink, and tell him to write. She thought this very clever of her, and expected to be praised for it.

But she might also bring him writing materials at times when she hated him very much. Then there would be sly smiles, even pretended affection, on her face, unless she thought he was not looking, when she cast him ugly glances. Her intention was to trick him into forgetting her so that she might talk to herself or slip out of the room to the Den, just as her mother had done in the days when it was Grizel who had to be tricked. He would not let her talk to herself until he had tried endless ways of exorcising that demon by interesting her in some sort of work, by going out with her, by talking of one thing and another till at last a subject was lit upon that made her forget to brood.

But sometimes it seemed best to let her go to the Den, she was in such a quiver of desire to go. She hurried to it, so that he had to stride to keep up with her; and he said little until they got there, for she was too excited to listen. She was very like her mother again; but it was not the man who never came that she went in search of—it was a lost child. I have not the heart to tell of the pitiful scenes in the Den while Grizel searched for her child. They always ended in those two walking silently home, and for a day or two Grizel would be ill, and Tommy tended her, so that she was soon able to hasten to the Den again, holding out her arms as she ran.

"She makes no progress," David said.

"I can keep her from slipping back," Tommy still replied. The doctor marvelled, but even he did not know the half of all her husband did for Grizel. None could know half who was not there by night. Here, at least, was one day ending placidly, they might say when she was in a tractable mood,—so tractable that she seemed to be one of themselves,—and Tommy assented brightly, though he knew, and he alone, that you could never be sure the long day had ended till the next began.

Often the happiest beginning had the most painful ending. The greatest pleasure he could give her was to take her to see Elspeth's baby girl, or that sturdy rogue, young Shiach, who could now count with ease up to seven, but swayed at eight, and toppled over on his way to ten; or their mothers brought them to her, and Grizel understood quite well who her visitors were, sometimes even called Elspeth by her right name, and did the honours of her house irreproachably, and presided at the tea-table, and was rapture personified when she held the baby Jean (called after Tommy's mother), and sat gaily on the floor, ready to catch little Corp when he would not stop at seven. But Tommy, whom nothing escaped, knew with what depression she might pay for her joy when they had gone. Despite all his efforts, she might sit talking to herself, at first of pleasant things and then of things less pleasant. Or she stared at her reflection in the long mirror and said: "Isn't she sweet!" or "She is not really sweet, and she did so want to be good!" Or instead of that she would suddenly go upon her knees and say, with clasped hands, the childish prayer, "Save me from masterful men," which Jean Myles had told Tommy to teach Elspeth. No one could have looked less masterful at those times than Tommy, but Grizel did not seem to think so. And probably they had that night once more to search the Den.

"The children do her harm; she must not see them again," he decided.

"They give her pleasure at the time," David said. "It lightens your task now and then."

"It is the future I am thinking of, Gemmell. If she cannot progress, she shall not fall back. As for me, never mind me."

"Elspeth is in a sad state about you, though! And you can get through so little work."

"Enough for all our wants." (He was writing magazine papers only.)

"The public will forget you."

"They have forgotten me."

David was openly sorry for him now. "If only your manuscript had been saved!"

"Yes; I never thought the little gods would treat me so scurvily as that."

"Who?"

"Did I never tell you of my little gods? I so often emerged triumphant from my troubles, and so undeservedly, that I thought I was especially looked after by certain tricky spirits in return for the entertainment I gave them. My little gods, I called them, and we had quite a bowing acquaintance. But you see at the critical moment they flew away laughing."

He always knew that the lost manuscript was his great work. "My seventh wave," he called it; "and though all the conditions were favourable," he said, "I know that I could run to nothing more than little waves at present. As for rewriting that book, I can't; I have tried."

Yet he was not asking for commiseration. "Tell Elspeth not to worry about me. If I have no big ideas just now, I have some very passable little ones, and one in particular that —" He drew a great breath. "If only Grizel were better," that breath said, "I think Tommy Sandys could find a way of making the public remember him again."

So David interpreted it, and though he had been about to say, "How changed you are!" he did not say it.

And Tommy, who had been keeping an eye on her all this time, returned to Grizel. As she had been through that long year, so she was during the first half of the next; and day by day and night by night he tended her, and still the same scenes were enacted in infinite variety, and still he would not give in. Everything seemed to change with the seasons, except Grizel, and Tommy's devotion to her.

Yet you know that she recovered, ever afterwards to be herself again; and though it seemed to come in the end as suddenly as the sight may be restored by the removal of a bandage, I suppose it had been going on all the time, and that her reason was given back to her on the day she had strength to make use of it. Tommy was the instrument of her recovery. He had fought against her slipping backward so that she could not do it; it was as if he had built a wall behind her, and in time her mind accepted that wall as impregnable and took a forward movement. And with every step she took he pushed the wall after her, so that still if she moved it must be forward. Thus Grizel progressed imperceptibly as along a dark corridor towards the door that shut out the light, and on a day in early spring the door fell.

Many of them had cried for a shock as her only chance. But it came most quietly. She had lain down on the sofa that afternoon to rest, and when she woke she was Grizel again. At first she was not surprised to find herself in that room, nor to see that man nodding and smiling reassuringly; they had come out of the long dream with her, to make the awakening less abrupt.

He did not know what had happened. When he knew, a terror that this could not last seized him. He was concealing it while he answered her puzzled questions. All the time he was telling her how they came to be there, he was watching in agony for the change.

She remembered everything up to her return to Thrums; then she walked into a mist.

"The truth," she begged of him, when he would have led her off by pretending that she had been ill only. Surely it was the real Grizel who begged for the truth. She took his hand and held it when he told her of their marriage. She cried softly, because she feared that she might again become as she had been; but he said that was impossible, and smiled confidently, and all the time he was watching in agony for the change.

"Do you forgive me, Grizel? I have always had a dread that when you recovered you would cease to care for me." He knew that this would please her if she was the real Grizel, and he was so anxious to make her happy for evermore.

She put his hand to her lips and smiled at him through her tears. Hers was a love that could never change. Suddenly she sat up. "Whose baby was it?" she asked.

"I don't know what you mean, Grizel," he said uneasily.

"I remember vaguely," she told him, "a baby in white whom I seemed to chase, but I could never catch her. Was it a dream only?"

"You are thinking of Elspeth's little girl, perhaps. She was often brought to see you."

"Has Elspeth a baby?" She rose to go exultantly to Elspeth.

"But too small a baby, Grizel, to run from you, even if she wanted to."

"What is she like?"

"She is always laughing."

"The sweet!" Grizel rocked her arms in rapture and smiled her crooked smile at the thought of a child who was always laughing. "But I don't remember her," she said. "It was a sad little baby I seemed to see."

Chapter XXXIII
The Little Gods Return With a Lady

Grizel's clear, searching eyes, that were always asking for the truth, came back to her, and I seem to see them on me now, watching lest I shirk the end.

Thus I can make no pretence (to please you) that it was a new Tommy at last. We have seen how he gave his life to her during those eighteen months, but he could not make himself anew. They say we can do it, so I suppose he did not try hard enough; but God knows how hard he tried.

He went on trying. In those first days she sometimes asked him, "Did you do it out of love, or was it pity only?" And he always said it was love. He said it adoringly. He told her all that love meant to him, and it meant everything that he thought Grizel would like it to mean. When she ceased to ask this question he thought it was because he had convinced her.

They had a honeymoon by the sea. He insisted upon it with boyish eagerness, and as they walked on the links or sat in their room he would exclaim ecstatically: "How happy I am! I wonder if there were ever two people quite so happy as you and I!"

And if he waited for an answer, as he usually did, she might smile lightly and say: "Few people have gone through so much."

"Is there any woman in the world, Grizel, with whom you would change places?"

"No, none," she said at once; and when he was sure of it, but never until he was sure, he would give his mind a little holiday; and then, perhaps, those candid eyes would rest searchingly upon him, but always with a brave smile ready should he chance to look up.

And it was just the same when they returned to Double Dykes, which they added to and turned into a comfortable home-Tommy trying to become a lover by taking thought, and Grizel not letting on that it could not be done in that way. She thought it was very sweet of him to try so hard-sweeter of him than if he really had loved her, though not, of course, quite so sweet to her. He was a boy only. She knew that, despite all he had gone through, he was still a boy. And boys cannot love. Oh, who would be so cruel as to ask a boy to love?

That Grizel's honeymoon should never end was his grand ambition, and he took elaborate precautions against becoming a matter-of-fact husband. Every morning he ordered himself to gaze at her with rapture, as if he had wakened to the glorious thought that she was his wife.

"I can't help it, Grizel; it comes to me every morning with the same shock of delight, and I begin the day with a song of joy. You make the world as fresh and interesting to me as if I had just broken like a chicken through the egg shell." He rose at the earliest hours. "So that I can have the longer day with you," he said gaily.

If when sitting at his work he forgot her for an hour or two he reproached himself for it afterwards, and next day he was more careful. "Grizel," he would cry, suddenly flinging down his pen, "you are my wife! Do you hear me, madam? You hear, and yet you can sit there calmly darning socks! Excuse me," he would say to his work, "while I do a dance."

He rose impulsively and brought his papers nearer her. With a table between them she was several feet away from him, which was more, he said, than he could endure.

"Sit down for a moment, Grizel, and let me look at you. I want to write something most splendiferous to-day, and I am sure to find it in your face. I have ceased to be an original writer; all the purple patches are cribbed from you."

He made a point of taking her head in his hands and looking long at her with thoughts too deep for utterance; then he would fall on his knees and kiss the hem of her dress, and so back to his book again.

And in time it was all sweet to Grizel. She could not be deceived, but she loved to see him playing so kind a part, and after some sadness to which she could not help giving way, she put all vain longings aside. She folded them up and put them away like the beautiful linen, so that she might see more clearly what was left to her and how best to turn it to account.

He did not love her. "Not as I love him," she said to herself, —"not as married people ought to love; but in the other way he loves me dearly." By the "other way" she meant that he loved her as he loved Elspeth, and loved them both just as he had loved them when all three played in the Den.

"He would love me if he could." She was certain of that. She decided that love does not come to all people, as is the common notion; that there are some who cannot fall in love, and that he was one of them. He was complete in himself, she decided.

"Is it a pity for him that he married me? It would be a pity if he could love some other woman, but I am sure he could never do that. If he could love anyone it would be me, we both want it so much. He does not need a wife, but he needs someone to take care of him-all men need that; and I can do it much better than any other person. Had he not married me he never would have married; but he may fall ill, and then how useful I shall be to him! He will grow old, and perhaps it won't be quite so lonely to him when I am there. It would have been a pity for him to marry me if I had been a foolish woman who asked for more love than he can give; but I shall never do that, so I think it is not a pity.

"Is it a pity for me? Oh, no, no, no!

"Is he sorry he did it? At times, is he just a weeny bit sorry?" She watched him, and decided rightly that he was not sorry the weeniest bit. It was a sweet consolation to her. "Is he really happy? Yes, of course he is happy when he is writing; but is he quite contented at other times? I do honestly think he is. And if he is happy now, how much happier I shall be able to make him when I have put away all my selfish thoughts and think only of him."

"The most exquisite thing in human life is to be married to one who loves you as you love him." There could be no doubt of that. But she saw also that the next best thing was the kind of love this boy gave to her, and she would always be grateful for the second best. In her prayers she thanked God for giving it to her, and promised Him to try to merit it; and all day and every day she kept her promise. There could not have been a brighter or more energetic wife than Grizel. The amount of work she found to do in that small house which his devotion had made so dear to her that she could not leave it! Her gaiety! Her masterful airs when he wanted something that was not good for him! The artfulness with which she sought to help him in various matters without his knowing! Her satisfaction when he caught her at it, as clever Tommy was constantly doing! "What a success it has turned out!" David would say delightedly to himself; and Grizel was almost as jubilant because it was so far from being a failure. It was only sometimes in the night that she lay very still, with little wells of water on her eyes, and through them saw one-the dream of woman-whom she feared could never be hers. That boy Tommy never knew why she did not want to have a child. He thought that for the present she was afraid; but the reason was that she believed it would be wicked when he did not love her as she loved him. She could not be sure-she had to think it all out for herself. With little wells of sadness on her eyes, she prayed in the still night to God to tell her; but she could never hear His answer.

She no longer sought to teach Tommy how he should write. That quaint desire was abandoned from the day when she learned that she had destroyed his greatest work. She had not destroyed it, as we shall see; but she presumed she had, as Tommy thought so. He had tried to conceal this from her to save her pain, but she had found it out, and it seemed to Grizel, grown distrustful of herself, that the man who could bear such a loss as he had borne it was best left to write as he chose.

"It was not that I did not love your books," she said, "but that I loved you more, and I thought they did you harm."

"In the days when I had wings," he answered, and she smiled. "Any feathers left, do you think, Grizel?" he asked jocularly, and turned his shoulders to her for examination.

"A great many, sir," she said, "and I am glad. I used to want to pull them all out, but now I like to know that they are still there, for it means that you remain among the facts not because you can't fly, but because you won't."

"I still have my little fights with myself," he blurted out boyishly, though it was a thing he had never meant to tell her, and Grizel pressed his hand for telling her what she already knew so well.

The new book, of course, was "The Wandering Child." I wonder whether any of you read it now? Your fathers and mothers thought a great deal of that slim volume, but it would make little stir in an age in which all the authors are trying who can say "damn" loudest. It is but a reverie about a child who is lost, and his parents' search for him in terror of what may have befallen. But they find him in a wood singing joyfully to himself because he is free; and he fears to be caged again, so runs farther from them into the wood, and is running still, singing to himself because he is free, free, free. That is really all, but T. Sandys knew how to tell it. The moment he conceived the idea (we have seen him speaking of it to the doctor), he knew that it was the idea for him. He forgot at once that he did not really care for children. He said reverently to himself, "I can pull it off," and, as was always the way with him, the better he pulled it off the more he seemed to love them.

"It is myself who is writing at last, Grizel," he said, as he read it to her.

She thought (and you can guess whether she was right) that it was the book he loved rather than the children. She thought (and you can guess again) that it was not his ideas about children that had got into the book, but hers. But she did not say so; she said it was the sweetest of his books to her.

I have heard of another reading he gave. This was after the publication of the book. He had gone into Corp's house one Sunday, and Gavinia was there reading the work to her lord and master, while little Corp disported on the floor. She read as if all the words meant the same thing, and it was more than Tommy could endure. He read for her, and his eyes grew moist as he read, for it was the most exquisite of his chapters about the lost child. You would have said that no one loved children quite so much as T. Sandys. But little Corp would not keep quiet, and suddenly Tommy jumped up and boxed his ears. He then proceeded with the reading, while Gavinia glowered and Corp senior scratched his head.

On the way home he saw what had happened, and laughed at the humour of it, then grew depressed, then laughed recklessly. "Is it Sentimental Tommy still?" he said to himself, with a groan. Seldom a week passed without his being reminded in some such sudden way that it was Sentimental Tommy still. "But she shall never know!" he vowed, and he continued to be half a hero.

His name was once more in many mouths. "Come back and be made of more than ever!" cried that society which he had once enlivened. "Come and hear the pretty things we are saying about you. Come and make the prettier replies that are already on the tip of your tongue; for oh, Tommy, you know they are! Bring her with you if you must; but don't you think that the nice, quiet country with the thingumbobs all in bloom would suit her best? It is essential that you should run up to see your publisher, is it not? The men have dinners for you if you want them, but we know you don't. Your yearning eyes are on the ladies, Tommy; we are making up theatre-parties of the old entrancing kind; you should see our new gowns; please come back and help us to put on our cloaks, Tommy; there is a dance on Monday-come and sit it out with us. Do you remember the garden-party where you said-Well, the laurel walk is still there; the beauties of two years ago are still here, and there are new beauties, and their noses are slightly tilted, but no man can move them; ha, do you pull yourself together at that? We were always the reward for your labours, Tommy; your books are move one in the game of making love to us; don't be afraid that we shall forget it is a game; we know it is, and that is why we suit you. Come and play in London as you used to play in the Den. It is all you need of women; come and have your fill, and we shall send you back refreshed. We are not asking you to be disloyal to her, only to leave her happy and contented and take a holiday."

He heard their seductive voices, they danced around him in numbers.

He heard their seductive voices. They danced around him in numbers, for they knew that the more there were of them the better he would be pleased; they whispered in his ear and then ran away looking over their shoulders. But he would not budge.

There was one more dangerous than the rest. Her he saw before the others came and after they had gone. She was a tall, incredibly slight woman, with eyelashes that needed help, and a most disdainful mouth and nose, and she seemed to look scornfully at Tommy and then stand waiting. He was in two minds about what she was waiting for, and often he had a fierce desire to go to London to find out. But he never went. He played the lover to Grizel as before-not to intoxicate himself, but always to make life sunnier to her; if she stayed longer with Elspeth than the promised time, he became anxious and went in search of her. "I have not been away an hour!" she said, laughing at him, holding little Jean up to laugh at him. "But I cannot do without you for an hour," he answered ardently. He still laid down his pen to gaze with rapture at her and cry, "My wife!"

She wanted him to go to London for a change, and without her, and his heart leaped into his mouth to prevent his saying No; yet he said it, though in the Tommy way.

"Without you!" he exclaimed. "Oh, Grizel, do you think I could find happiness apart from you for a day? And could you let me go?" And he looked with agonized reproach at her, and sat down, clutching his head.

"It would be very hard to me," she said softly; "but if the change did you good ——"

"A change from you! Oh, Grizel, Grizel!"

"Or I could go with you?"

"When you don't want to go!" he cried huskily. "You think I could ask it of you!"

He quite broke down, and she had to comfort him. She was smiling divinely at him all the time, as if sympathy had brought her to love even the Tommy way of saying things. "I thought it would be sweet to you to see how great my faith in you is now," she said.

This was the true reason why generous Grizel had proposed to him to go. She knew he was more afraid than she of Sentimental Tommy, and she thought her faith would be a helping hand to him, as it was.

He had no regard for Lady Pippinworth. Of all the women he had dallied with, she was the one he liked the least, for he never liked where he could not esteem. Perhaps she had some good in her, but the good in her had never appealed to him, and he knew it, and refused to harbour her in his thoughts now; he cast her out determinedly when she seemed to enter them unbidden. But still he was vain. She came disdainfully and stood waiting. We have seen him wondering what she waited for; but though he could not be sure, and so was drawn to her, he took it as acknowledgment of his prowess and so was helped to run away.

To walk away would be the more exact term, for his favourite method of exorcising this lady was to rise from his chair and take a long walk with Grizel. Occasionally if she was occupied (and a number of duties our busy Grizel found to hand!) he walked alone, and he would not let himself brood. Someone had once walked from Thrums to the top of the Law and back in three hours, and Tommy made several gamesome attempts to beat the record, setting out to escape that willowy woman, soon walking her down and returning in a glow of animal spirits. It was on one of these occasions, when there was nothing in his head but ambition to do the fifth mile within the eleven minutes, that he suddenly met her Ladyship face to face.

We have now come to the last fortnight of Tommy's life.

Chapter XXXIV
A Way is Found for Tommy

The moment for which he had tried to prepare himself was come, and Tommy gulped down his courage, which had risen suddenly to his mouth, leaving his chest in a panic. Outwardly he seemed unmoved, but within he was beating to arms. "This is the test of us!" all that was good in him cried as it answered his summons.

They began by shaking hands, as is always the custom in the ring. Then, without any preliminary sparring, Lady Pippinworth immediately knocked him down; that is to say, she remarked, with a little laugh: "How very stout you are getting!"

I swear by all the gods that it was untrue. He had not got very stout, though undeniably he had got stouter. "How well you are looking!" would have been a very ladylike way of saying it, but his girth was best not referred to at all. Those who liked him had learned this long ago, and Grizel always shifted the buttons without comment.

Her malicious Ladyship had found his one weak spot at once. He had a reply ready for every other opening in the English tongue, but now he could writhe only.

Who would have expected to meet her here? he said at last feebly. She explained, and he had guessed it already, that she was again staying with the Rintouls; the castle, indeed, was not half a mile from where they stood.

"But I think I really came to see you," she informed him, with engaging frankness.

It was very good of her, he intimated stiffly; but the stiffness was chiefly because she was still looking in an irritating way at his waist.

Suddenly she looked up. To Tommy it was as if she had raised the siege. "Why aren't you nice to me?" she asked prettily.

"I want to be," he replied.

She showed him a way. "When I saw you steaming towards the castle so swiftly," she said, dropping badinage, "the hope entered my head that you had heard of my arrival."

She had come a step nearer, and it was like an invitation to return to the arbour. "This is the test of us!" all that was good in Tommy cried once more to him.

"No, I had not heard," he replied, bravely if baldly. "I was taking a smart walk only."

"Why so smart as that?"

He hesitated, and her eyes left his face and travelled downward.

"Were you trying to walk it off?" she asked sympathetically.

He was stung, and replied in words that were regretted as soon as spoken: "I was trying to walk you off."

A smile of satisfaction crossed her impudent face.

"I succeeded," he added sharply.

"How cruel of you to say so, when you had made me so very happy! Do you often take smart walks, Mr. Sandys?"

"Often."

"And always with me?"

"I leave you behind."

"With Mrs. Sandys?"

Had she seemed to be in the least affected by their meeting it would have been easy to him to be a contrite man at once; any sign of shame on her part would have filled him with desire to take all the blame upon himself. Had she cut him dead, he would have begun to respect her. But she smiled disdainfully only, and stood waking. She was still, as ever, a cold passion, inviting his warm ones to leap at it. He shuddered a little, but controlled himself and did not answer her.

"I suppose she is the lady of the arbour?" Lady Pippinworth inquired, with mild interest.

"She is the lady of my heart," Tommy replied valiantly.

"Alas!" said Lady Pippinworth, putting her hand over her own.

But he felt himself more secure now, and could even smile at the woman for thinking she was able to provoke him.

"Look upon me," she requested, "as a deputation sent north to discover why you have gone into hiding."

"I suppose a country life does seem exile to you," he replied calmly, and suddenly his bosom rose with pride in what was coming. Tommy always heard his finest things coming a moment before they came. "If I have retired," he went on windily, "from the insincerities and glitter of life in town," —but it was not his face she was looking at, it was his waist, —"the reason is obvious," he rapped out.

She nodded assent without raising her eyes.

Yet he still controlled himself. His waist, like some fair tortured lady of romance, was calling to his knighthood for defence, but with the truer courage he affected not to hear. "I am in hiding, as you call it," he said doggedly, "because my life here is such a round of happiness as I never hoped to find on earth, and I owe it all to my wife. If you don't believe me, ask Lord or Lady Rintoul, or any other person in this countryside who knows her."

But her Ladyship had already asked, and been annoyed by the answer.

She assured Tommy that she believed he was happy. "I have often heard," she said musingly, "that the stout people are the happiest."

"I am not so stout," he barked.

"Now I call that brave of you," said she, admiringly. "That is so much the wisest way to take it. And I am sure you are right not to return to town after what you were; it would be a pity. Somehow it" —and again her eyes were on the wrong place —"it does not seem to go with the books. And yet," she said philosophically, "I daresay you feel just the same?"

"I feel very much the same," he replied warningly.

"That is the tragedy of it," said she.

She told him that the new book had brought the Tommy Society to life again. "And it could not hold its meetings with the old enthusiasm, could it," she asked sweetly, "if you came back? Oh, I think you act most judiciously. Fancy how melancholy if they had to announce that the society had been wound up, owing to the stoutness of the Master."

Tommy's mouth opened twice before any words could come out. "Take care!" he cried.

"Of what?" said she, curling her lip.

He begged her pardon. "You don't like me, Lady Pippinworth," he said, watching himself, "and I don't wonder at it; and you have discovered a way of hurting me of which you make rather unmerciful use. Well, I don't wonder at that, either. If I am-stoutish, I have at least the satisfaction of knowing that it gives you entertainment, and I owe you that amend and more." He was really in a fury, and burning to go on —"For I did have the whip-hand of you once, madam," etc., etc.; but by a fine effort he held his rage a prisoner, and the admiration of himself that this engendered lifted him into the sublime.

"For I so far forgot myself," said Tommy, in a glow, "as to try to make you love me. You were beautiful and cold; no man had ever stirred you; my one excuse is that to be loved by such as you was no small ambition; my fitting punishment is that I failed." He knew he had not failed, and so could be magnanimous. "I failed utterly," he said, with grandeur. "You were laughing at me all the time; if proof of it were needed, you have given it now by coming here to mock me. I thought I was stronger than you, but I was ludicrously mistaken, and you taught me a lesson I richly deserved; you did me good, and I thank you for it. Believe me, Lady Pippinworth, when I say that I admit my discomfiture, and remain your very humble and humbled servant."

Now was not that good of Tommy? You would think it still better were I to tell you what part of his person she was looking at while he said it.

He held out his hand generously (there was no noble act he could not have performed for her just now), but, whatever her Ladyship wanted, it was not to say good-bye. "Do you mean that you never cared for me?" she asked, with the tremor that always made Tommy kind.

"Never cared for you!" he exclaimed fervently. "What were you not to me in those golden days!" It was really a magnanimous cry, meant to help her self-respect, nothing more; but it alarmed the good in him, and he said sternly: "But of course that is all over now. It is only a sweet memory," he added, to make these two remarks mix.

The sentiment of this was so agreeable to him that he was half thinking of raising her hand chivalrously to his lips when Lady Pippinworth said:

"But if it is all over now, why have you still to walk me off?"

"Have you never had to walk me off?" said Tommy, forgetting himself, and, to his surprise, she answered, "Yes."

"But this meeting has cured me," she said, with dangerous graciousness.

"Dear Lady Pippinworth," replied Tommy, ardently, thinking that his generosity had touched her, "if anything I have said ——"

"It is not so much what you have said," she answered, and again she looked at the wrong part of him.

He gave way in the waist, and then drew himself up. "If so little a thing as that helps you ——" he began haughtily.

"Little!" she cried reproachfully.

He tried to go away. He turned. "There was a time," he thundered.

"It is over," said she.

"When you were at my feet," said Tommy.

"It is over," she said.

"It could come again!"

She laughed a contemptuous No.

"Yes!" Tommy cried.

"Too stout," said she, with a drawl.

He went closer to her. She stood waiting disdainfully, and his arms fell.

"Too stout," she repeated.

"Let us put it in that way, since it pleases you," said Tommy, heavily. "I am too stout." He could not help adding, "And be thankful, Lady Pippinworth, let us both be thankful, that there is some reason to prevent my trying."

She bowed mockingly as he raised his hat. "I wish you well," he said, "and these are my last words to you"; and he retired, not without distinction. He retired, shall we say, as conscious of his waist as if it were some poor soldier he was supporting from a stricken field. He said many things to himself on the way home, and he was many Tommies, but all with the same waist. It intruded on his noblest reflections, and kept ringing up the worst in him like some devil at the telephone.

No one could have been more thankful that on the whole he had kept his passions in check. It made a strong man of him. It turned him into a joyous boy, and he tingled with hurrahs. Then suddenly he would hear that jeering bell clanging, "Too stout, too stout." "Take care!" he roared. Oh, the vanity of Tommy!

He did not tell Grizel that he had met her Ladyship. All she knew was that he came back to her more tender and kind, if that were possible, than he had gone away. His eyes followed her about the room until she made merry over it, and still they dwelt upon her. "How much more beautiful you are than any other woman I ever saw, Grizel!" he said. And it was not only true, but he knew it was true. What was Lady Pippinworth beside this glorious woman? what was her damnable coldness compared to the love of Grizel? Was he unforgivable, or was it some flaw in the making of him for which he was not responsible? With clenched hands he asked himself these questions. This love that all his books were about-what was it? Was it a compromise between affection and passion countenanced by God for the continuance of the race, made beautiful by Him where the ingredients are in right proportion, a flower springing from a soil that is not all divine? Oh, so exquisite a flower! he cried, for he knew his Grizel.

But he could not love her. He gave her all his affection, but his passion, like an outlaw, had ever to hunt alone.

Was it that? And if it was, did there remain in him enough of humanity to give him the right to ask a little sympathy of those who can love? So Tommy in his despairing moods, and the question ought to find some place in his epitaph, which, by the way, it is almost time to write.

On the day following his meeting with Lady Pippinworth came a note from Lady Rintoul inviting Grizel and him to lunch. They had been to Rintoul once or twice before, but this time Tommy said decisively, "We sha'n't go." He guessed who had prompted the invitation, though her name was not mentioned in it.

"Why not?" Grizel asked. She was always afraid that she kept Tommy too much to herself.

"Because I object to being disturbed during the honeymoon," he replied lightly. Their honeymoon, you know, was never to end. "They would separate us for hours, Grizel. Think of it! But, pooh! the thing is not to be thought of. Tell her Ladyship courteously that she must be mad."

But though he could speak thus to Grizel, there came to him tempestuous desires to be by the side of the woman who could mock him and then stand waiting.

Had she shown any fear of him all would have been well with Tommy; he could have kept away from her complacently. But she had flung down the glove, and laughed to see him edge away from it. He knew exactly what was in her mind. He was too clever not to know that her one desire was to make him a miserable man; to remember how he had subdued and left her would be gall to Lady Pippinworth until she achieved the same triumph over him. How confident she was that he could never prove the stronger of the two again! What were all her mockings but a beckoning to him to come on? "Take care!" said Tommy between his teeth.

And then again horror of himself would come to his rescue. The man he had been a moment ago was vile to him, and all his thoughts were now heroic. You may remember that he had once taken Grizel to a seaside place; they went there again. It was Tommy's proposal, but he did not go to flee from temptation; however his worse nature had been stirred and his vanity pricked, he was too determinedly Grizel's to fear that in any fierce hour he might rush into danger. He wanted Grizel to come away from the place where she always found so much to do for him, so that there might be the more for him to do for her. And that week was as the time they had spent there before. All that devotion which had to be planned could do for woman he did. Grizel saw him planning it and never admitted that she saw. In the after years it was sweet to her to recall that week and the hundred laboriously lover-like things Tommy had done in it. She knew by this time that Tommy had never tried to make her love him, and that it was only when her love for him revealed itself in the Den that desire to save her pride made him pretend to be in love with her. This knowledge would have been a great pain to her once, but now it had more of pleasure in it, for it showed that even in those days he had struggled a little for her.

We must hasten to the end. Those of you who took in the newspapers a quarter of a century ago know what it was, but none of you know why he climbed the wall.

They returned to Thrums in a week. They had meant to stay longer, but suddenly Tommy wanted to go back. Yes, it was Lady Pippinworth who recalled him, but don't think too meanly of Tommy. It was not that he yielded to one of those fierce desires to lift the gauntlet; he had got rid of them in fair fight when her letter reached him, forwarded from Thrums. "Did you really think your manuscript was lost?" it said. That was what took Tommy back. Grizel did not know the reason; he gave her another. He thought very little about her that day. He thought still less about Lady Pippinworth. How could he think of anything but it? She had it, evidently she had it; she must have stolen it from his bag. He could not even spare time to denounce her. It was alive—his manuscript was alive, and every moment brought him nearer to it. He was a miser, and soon his hands would be deep among the gold. He was a mother whose son, mourned for dead, is knocking at the door. He was a swain, and his beloved's arms were outstretched to him. Who said that Tommy could not love?

The ecstasies that came over him and would not let him sit still made Grizel wonder. "Is it a book?" she asked; and he said it was a book—such a book, Grizel! When he started for the castle next morning, she thought he wanted to be alone to think of the book. "Of it and you," he said; and having started, he came back to kiss her again; he never forgot to have an impulse to do that. But all the way to the Spittal it was of his book he thought, it was his book he was kissing. His heart sang within him, and the songs were sonnets to his beloved. To be worthy of his beautiful manuscript-he prayed for that as lovers do; that his love should be his, his alone, was as wondrous to him as to any of them.

But we are not noticing what proved to be the chief thing. Though there was some sun, the air was shrewd, and he was wearing the old doctor's coat. Should you have taken it with you, Tommy? It loved Grizel, for it was a bit of him; and what, think you, would the old doctor have cared for your manuscript had he known that you were gone out to meet that woman? It was cruel, no, not cruel, but thoughtless, to wear the old doctor's coat.

He found no one at the Spittal. The men were out shooting, and the ladies had followed to lunch with them on the moors. He came upon them, a gay party, in the hollow of a hill where was a spring suddenly converted into a wine-cellar; and soon the men, if not the ladies, were surprised to find that Tommy could be the gayest of them all. He was in hilarious spirits, and had a gallantly forgiving glance for the only one of them who knew why his spirits were hilarious. But he would not consent to remain to dinner. "The wretch is so hopelessly in love with his wife," Lady Rintoul said, flinging a twig of heather at him. It was one of the many trivial things said on that occasion and long remembered; the only person who afterwards professed her inability to remember what Tommy said to her that day, and she to him, was Lady Pippinworth. "And yet you walked back to the castle with him," they reminded her.

"If I had known that anything was to happen," she replied indolently, "I should have taken more note of what was said. But as it was, I think we talked of our chance of finding white heather. We were looking for it, and that is why we fell behind you."

That was not why Tommy and her Ladyship fell behind the others, and it was not of white heather that they talked. "You know why I am here, Alice," he said, as soon as there was no one but her to hear him.

She was in as great tension at that moment as he, but more anxious not to show it. "Why do you call me that?" she replied, with a little laugh.

"Because I want you to know at once," he said, and it was the truth, "that I have no vindictive feelings. You have kept my manuscript from me all this time, but, severe though the punishment has been, I deserved it, yes, every day of it."

Lady Pippinworth smiled.

"You took it from my bag, did you not?" said Tommy.

"Yes."

"Where is it, Alice? Have you got it here?"

"No."

"But you know where it is?"

"Oh, yes," she said graciously, and then it seemed that nothing could ever disturb him again. She enjoyed his boyish glee; she walked by his side listening airily to it.

"Had there been a fire in the room that day I should have burned the thing," she said without emotion.

"It would have been no more than my deserts," Tommy replied cheerfully.

"I did burn it three months afterwards," said she, calmly.

He stopped, but she walked on. He sprang after her. "You don't mean that, Alice!"

"I do mean it."

With a gesture fierce and yet imploring, he compelled her to stop. "Before God, is this true?" he cried.

"Yes," she said, "it is true"; and, indeed, it was the truth about his manuscript at last.

"But you had a copy of it made first. Say you had!"

"I had not."

She seemed to have no fear of him, though his face was rather terrible. "I meant to destroy it from the first," she said coldly, "but I was afraid to. I took it back with me to London. One day I read in a paper that your wife was supposed to have burned it while she was insane. She was insane, was she not? Ah, well, that is not my affair; but I burned it for her that afternoon."

They were moving on again. He stopped her once more.

"Why have you told me this?" he cried. "Was it not enough for you that I should think she did it?"

"No," Lady Pippinworth answered, "that was not enough for me. I always wanted you to know that I had done it."

"And you wrote that letter, you filled me with joy, so that you should gloat over my disappointment?"

"Horrid of me, was it not!" said she.

"Why did you not tell me when we met the other day?"

"I bided my time, as the tragedians say."

"You would not have told me," Tommy said, staring into her face, "if you had thought I cared for you. Had you thought I cared for you a little jot —"

"I should have waited," she confessed, "until you cared for me a great deal, and then I should have told you. That, I admit, was my intention."

She had returned his gaze smilingly, and as she strolled on she gave him another smile over her shoulder; it became a protesting pout almost when she saw that he was not accompanying her. Tommy stood still for some minutes, his hands, his teeth, every bit of him that could close, tight clenched. When he made up on her, the devil was in him. She had been gathering a nosegay of wild flowers. "Pretty, are they not?" she said to him. He took hold of her harshly by both wrists. She let him do it, and stood waiting disdainfully; but she was less unprepared for a blow than for what came.

"How you love me, Alice!" he said in a voice shaking with passion.

"How I have proved it!" she replied promptly.

"Love or hate," he went on in a torrent of words, "they are the same thing with you. I don't care what you call it; it has made you come back to me. You tried hard to stay away. How you fought, Alice! but you had to come. I knew you would come. All this time you have been longing for me to go to you. You have stamped your pretty feet because I did not go. You have cried, 'He shall come!' You have vowed you would not go one step of the way to meet me. I saw you, I heard you, and I wanted you as much as you wanted me; but I was always the stronger, and I could resist. It is I who have not gone a step towards you, and it is my proud little Alice who has come all the way. Proud little Alice! —but she is to be my obedient little Alice now."

His passion hurled him along, and it had its effect on her. She might curl her mouth as she chose, but her bosom rose and fell.

"Obedient?" she cried, with a laugh.

"Obedient!" said Tommy, quivering with his intensity. "Obedient, not because I want it, for I prefer you as you are, but because you are longing for it, my lady-because it is what you came here for. You have been a virago only because you feared you were not to get it. Why have you grown so quiet, Alice? Where are the words you want to torment me with? Say them! I love to hear them from your lips. I love the demon in you-the demon that burned my book. I love you the more for that. It was your love that made you do it. Why don't you scratch and struggle for the last time? I am half sorry that little Alice is to scratch and struggle no more."

"Go on," said little Alice; "you talk beautifully." But though her tongue could mock him, all the rest of her was enchained.

"Whether I shall love you when you are tamed," he went on with vehemence, "I don't know. You must take the risk of that. But I love you now. We were made for one another, you and I, and I love you, Alice —I love you and you love me. You love me, my peerless Alice, don't you? Say you love me. Your melting eyes are saying it. How you tremble, sweet Alice! Is that your way of saying it? I want to hear you say it. You have been longing to say it for two years. Come, love, say it now!"

It was not within this woman's power to resist him. She tried to draw away from him, but could not. She was breathing quickly. The mocking light quivered on her face only because it had been there so long. If it went out she would be helpless. He put his hands on her shoulders, and she was helpless. It brought her mouth nearer his. She was offering him her mouth.

"No," said Tommy, masterfully. "I won't kiss you until you say it."

If there had not been a look of triumph in his eyes, she would have said it. As it was, she broke from him, panting. She laughed next minute, and with that laugh his power fell among the heather.

"Really," said Lady Pippinworth, "you are much too stout for this kind of thing." She looked him up and down with a comic sigh. "You talk as well as ever," she said condolingly, "but heigh-ho, you don't look the same. I have done the best I could for you for the sake of old times, but I forgot to shut my eyes. Shall we go on?"

And they went on silently, one of them very white. "I believe you are blaming me," her Ladyship said, making a face, just before they overtook the others, "when you know it was your own fault for" —she suddenly rippled —"for not waiting until it was too dark for me to see you!"

They strolled with some others of the party to the flower-garden, which was some distance from the house, and surrounded by a high wall studded with iron spikes and glass. Lady Rintoul cut him some flowers for Grizel, but he left them on a garden-seat —accidentally, everyone thought afterwards in the drawing-room when they were missed; but he had laid them down, because how could those degraded hands of his carry flowers again to Grizel? There was great remorse in him, but there was a shrieking vanity also, and though the one told him to be gone, the other kept him lagging on. They had torn him a dozen times from each other's arms before he was man enough to go.

It was gloaming when he set off, waving his hat to those who had come to the door with him. Lady Pippinworth was not among them; he had not seen her to bid her good-bye, nor wanted to, for the better side of him had prevailed-so he thought. It was a man shame-stricken and determined to kill the devil in him that went down that long avenue-so he thought.

A tall, thin woman was standing some twenty yards off, among some holly-trees. She kissed her hand mockingly to him, and beckoned and laughed when he stood irresolute. He thought he heard her cry, "Too stout!" He took some fierce steps towards her. She ran on, looking over her shoulder, and he forgot all else and followed her. She darted into the flower-garden, pulling the gate to after her. It was a gate that locked when it closed, and the key was gone. Lady Pippinworth clapped her hands because he could not reach her. When she saw that he was climbing the wall she ran farther into the garden.

He climbed the wall, but, as he was descending, one of the iron spikes on the top of it pierced his coat, which was buttoned to the throat, and he hung there by the neck. He struggled as he choked, but he could not help himself. He was unable to cry out. The collar of the old doctor's coat held him fast.

They say that in such a moment a man reviews all his past life. I don't know whether Tommy did that; but his last reflection before he passed into unconsciousness was "Serves me right!" Perhaps it was only a little bit of sentiment for the end.

Lady Disdain came back to the gate, by and by, to see why he had not followed her. She screamed and then hid in the recesses of the garden. He had been dead for some time when they found him. They left the gate creaking in the evening wind. After a long time a terrified woman stole out by it.

Chapter XXXV
The Perfect Lover

Tommy has not lasted. More than once since it became known that I was writing his life I have been asked whether there ever really was such a person, and I am afraid to inquire for his books at the library lest they are no longer there. A recent project to bring out a new edition, with introductions by some other Tommy, received so little support that it fell to the ground. It must be admitted that, so far as the great public is concerned, Thomas Sandys is done for.

They have even forgotten the manner of his death, though probably no young writer with an eye on posterity ever had a better send-off. We really thought at the time that Tommy had found a way.

The surmise at Rintoul, immediately accepted by the world as a fact, was that he had been climbing the wall to obtain for Grizel the flowers accidentally left in the garden, and it at once tipped the tragedy with gold. The newspapers, which were in the middle of the dull season, thanked their gods for Tommy, and enthusiastically set to work on him. Great minds wrote criticisms of what they called his life-work. The many persons who had been the first to discover him said so again. His friends were in demand for the most trivial reminiscences. Unhappy Pym cleared £11 10s.

Shall we quote? It is nearly always done at this stage of the biography, so now for the testimonials to prove that our hero was without a flaw. A few specimens will suffice if we select some that are very like many of the others. It keeps Grizel waiting, but Tommy, as you have seen, was always the great one; she existed only that he might show how great he was. "Busy among us of late," says one, "has been the grim visitor who knocks with equal confidence at the doors of the gifted and the ungifted, the pauper and the prince, and twice in one short month has he taken from us men of an eminence greater perhaps than that of Mr. Sandys; but of them it could be said their work was finished, while his sun sinks tragically when it is yet day. Not by what his riper years might have achieved can this pure, spirit now be judged, and to us, we confess, there is something infinitely pathetic in that thought. We would fain shut our eyes, and open them again at twenty years hence, with Mr. Sandys in the fulness of his powers. It is not to be. What he might have become is hidden from us; what he was we know. He was little more than a stripling when he 'burst upon the town' to be its marvel-and to die; a 'marvellous boy' indeed; yet how unlike in character and in the nobility of his short life, as in the mournful yet lovely circumstances of his death, to that other Might-Have-Been who 'perished in his pride.' Our young men of letters have travelled far since the days of Chatterton. Time was when a riotous life was considered part of their calling-when they shunned the domestic ties and actually held that the consummate artist is able to love nothing but the creations of his fancy. It is such men as Thomas Sandys who have exploded that pernicious fallacy...."

"Whether his name will march down the ages is not for us, his contemporaries, to determine. He had the most modest opinion of his own work, and was humbled rather than elated when he heard it praised. No one ever loved praise less; to be pointed at as a man of distinction was abhorrent to his shrinking nature; he seldom, indeed, knew that he was being pointed at, for his eyes were ever on the ground. He set no great store by the remarkable popularity of his works. 'Nothing,' he has been heard to say to one of those gushing ladies who were his aversion, 'nothing will so certainly perish as the talk of the town.' It may be so, but if so, the greater the pity that he has gone from among us before he had time to put the coping-stone upon his work. There is a beautiful passage in one of his own books in which he sees the spirits of gallant youth who died too young for immortality haunting the portals of the Elysian Fields, and the great shades come to the portal and talk with them. We venture to say that he is at least one of these."

What was the individuality behind the work? They discussed it in leading articles and in the correspondence columns, and the man proved to be greater than his books. His distaste for admiration is again and again insisted on and illustrated by many characteristic anecdotes. He owed much to his parents, though he had the misfortune to lose them when he was but a child. "Little is known of his father, but we understand that he was a retired military officer in easy circumstances. The mother was a canny Scotchwoman of lowly birth, conspicuous for her devoutness even in a land where it is everyone's birthright, and on their marriage, which was a singularly happy one, they settled in London, going little into society, the world forgetting, by the world forgot, and devoting themselves to each other and to their two children. Of these Thomas was the elder, and as the twig was early bent so did the tree incline. From his earliest years he was noted for the modesty which those who remember his boyhood in Scotland (whither the children went to an uncle on the death of their parents) still speak of with glistening eyes. In another column will be found some interesting recollections of Mr. Sandys by his old schoolmaster, Mr. David Cathro, M.A., who testifies with natural pride to the industry and amiability of his famous pupil. 'To know him,' says Mr. Cathro, 'was to love him.'"

According to another authority, T. Sandys got his early modesty from his father, who was of a very sweet disposition, and some instances of this modesty are given. They are all things that Elspeth did, but Tommy is now represented as the person who had done them. "On the other hand, his strong will, singleness of purpose, and enviable capacity for knowing what he wanted to be at were a heritage from his practical and sagacious mother." "I think he was a little proud of his strength of will," writes the R.A. who painted his portrait (now in America), "for I remember his anxiety that it should be suggested in the picture." But another acquaintance (a lady) replies: "He was not proud of his strong will, but he liked to hear it spoken of, and he once told me the reason. This strength of will was not, as is generally supposed, inherited by him; he was born without it, and acquired it by a tremendous effort. I believe I am the only person to whom he confided this, for he shrank from talk about himself, looking upon it as a form of that sentimentality which his soul abhorred."

He seems often to have warned ladies against this essentially womanish tendency to the sentimental. "It is an odious onion, dear lady," he would say, holding both her hands in his. If men in his presence talked sentimentally to ladies he was so irritated that he soon found a pretext for leaving the room. "Yet let it not be thought," says One Who Knew Him Well, "that because he was so sternly practical himself he was intolerant of the outpourings of the sentimental. The man, in short, reflected the views on this subject which are so admirably phrased in his books, works that seem to me to found one of their chief claims to distinction on this, that at last we have a writer who can treat intimately of human love without leaving one smear of the onion upon his pages."

On the whole, it may be noticed, comparatively few ladies contribute to the obituary reflections, "for the simple reason," says a simple man, "that he went but little into female society. He who could write so eloquently about women never seemed to know what to say to them. Ordinary tittle-tattle from them disappointed him. I should say that to him there was so much of the divine in women that he was depressed when they hid their wings." This view is supported by Clubman, who notes that Tommy would never join in the somewhat free talk about the other sex in which many men indulge. "I remember," he says, "a man's dinner at which two of those present, both persons of eminence, started a theory that every man who is blessed or cursed with the artistic instinct has at some period of his life wanted to marry a barmaid. Mr. Sandys gave them such a look that they at once apologized. Trivial, perhaps, but significant. On another occasion I was in a club smoking-room when the talk was of a similar kind. Mr. Sandys was not present. A member said, with a laugh, 'I wonder for how long men can be together without talking gamesomely of women?' Before any answer could be given Mr. Sandys strolled in, and immediately the atmosphere cleared, as if someone had opened the windows. When he had gone the member addressed turned to him who had propounded the problem and said, 'There is your answer-as long as Sandys is in the room.'"

"A fitting epitaph, this, for Thomas Sandys," says the paper that quotes it, "if we could not find a better. Mr. Sandys was from first to last a man of character, but why when others falter was he always so sure-footed? It is in the answer to this question that we find the key to the books, and to the man who was greater than the books. He was the Perfect Lover. As he died seeking flowers for her who had the high honour to be his wife, so he had always lived. He gave his affection to her, as our correspondent Miss (or Mrs.) Ailie McLean shows, in his earliest boyhood, and from this, his one romance, he never swerved. To the moment of his death all his beautiful thoughts were flowers plucked for her; his books were bunches of them gathered to place at her feet. No harm now in reading between the lines of his books and culling what is the common knowledge of his friends in the north, that he had to serve a long apprenticeship before he won her. For long his attachment was unreciprocated, though she was ever his loyal friend, and the volume called 'Unrequited Love' belongs to the period when he thought his life must be lived alone. The circumstances of their marriage are at once too beautiful and too painful to be dwelt on here. Enough to say that, should the particulars ever be given to the world, with the simple story of his life, a finer memorial will have been raised to him than anything in stone, such as we see a committee is already being formed to erect. We venture to propose as a title for his biography, 'The Story of the Perfect Lover.'"

Yes, that memorial committee was formed; but so soon do people forget the hero of yesterday's paper that only the secretary attended the first meeting, and he never called another. But here, five and twenty years later, is the biography, with the title changed. You may wonder that I had the heart to write it. I do it, I have sometimes pretended to myself, that we may all laugh at the stripling of a rogue, but that was never my reason. Have I been too cunning, or have you seen through me all the time? Have you discovered that I was really pitying the boy who was so fond of boyhood that he could not with years become a man, telling nothing about him that was not true, but doing it with unnecessary scorn in the hope that I might goad you into crying: "Come, come, you are too hard on him!"

Perhaps the manner in which he went to his death deprives him of these words. Had the castle gone on fire that day while he was at tea, and he perished in the flames in a splendid attempt to save the life of his enemy (a very probable thing), then you might have felt a little liking for him. Yet he would have been precisely the same person. I don't blame you, but you are a Tommy.

Grizel knew how he died. She found Lady Pippinworth's letter to him, and understood who the woman was; but it was only in hopes of obtaining the lost manuscript that she went to see her. Then Lady Pippinworth told her all. Are you sorry that Grizel knew? I am not sorry —I am glad. As a child, as a girl, and as a wife, the truth had been all she wanted, and she wanted it just the same when she was a widow. We have a right to know the truth; no right to ask anything else from God, but the right to ask that.

And to her latest breath she went on loving Tommy just the same. She thought everything out calmly for herself; she saw that there is no great man on this earth except the man who conquers self, and that in some the accursed thing which is in all of us may be so strong that to battle with it and be beaten is not altogether to fail. It is foolish to demand complete success of those we want to love. We should rejoice when they rise for a moment above themselves, and sympathize with them when they fall. In their heyday young lovers think each other perfect; but a nobler love comes when they see the failings also, and this higher love is so much more worth attaining to that they need not cry out though it has to be beaten into them with rods. So they learn humanity's limitations, and that the accursed thing to me is not the accursed thing to you; but all have it, and from this comes pity for those who have sinned, and the desire to help each other springs, for knowledge is sympathy, and sympathy is love, and to learn it the Son of God became a man.

And Grizel also thought anxiously about herself, and how from the time when she was the smallest girl she had longed to be a good woman and feared that perhaps she never should. And as she looked back at the road she had travelled, there came along it the little girl to judge her. She came trembling, but determined to know the truth, and she looked at Grizel until she saw into her soul, and then she smiled, well pleased.

Grizel lived on at Double Dykes, helping David in the old way. She was too strong and fine a nature to succumb. Even her brightness came back to her. They sometimes wondered at the serenity of her face. Some still thought her a little stand-offish, for, though the pride had gone from her walk, a distinction of manner grew upon her and made her seem a finer lady than before. There was no other noticeable change, except that with the years she lost her beautiful contours and became a little angular-the old maid's figure, I believe it is sometimes called.

No one would have dared to smile at Grizel become an old maid before some of the young men of Thrums. They were people who would have suffered much for her, and all because she had the courage to talk to them of some things before their marriage-day came round. And for their young wives who had tidings to whisper to her about the unborn she had the pretty idea that they should live with beautiful thoughts, so that these might become part of the child.

When Gavinia told this to Corp, he gulped and said, "I wonder God could hae haen the heart."

"Life's a queerer thing," Gavinia replied, sadly enough, "than we used to think it when we was bairns in the Den."

He spoke of it to Grizel. She let Corp speak of anything to her because he was so loyal to Tommy.

"You've given away a' your bonny things, Grizel," he said, "one by one, and this notion is the bonniest o' them a'. I'm thinking that when it cam' into your head you meant it for yoursel'."

Grizel smiled at him.

"I mind," Corp went on, "how when you was little you couldna see a bairn without rocking your arms in a waeful kind o' a way, and we could never thole the meaning o't. It just comes over me this minute as it meant that when you was a woman you would like terrible to hae bairns o' your ain, and you doubted you never should."

She raised her hand to stop him. "You see, I was not meant to have them, Corp," she said. "I think that when women are too fond of other people's babies they never have any of their own."

But Corp shook his head. "I dinna understand it," he told her, "but I'm sure you was meant to hae them. Something's gane wrang."

She was still smiling at him, but her eyes were wet now, and she drew him on to talk of the days when Tommy was a boy. It was sweet to Grizel to listen while Elspeth and David told her of the thousand things Tommy had done for her when she was ill, but she loved best to talk with Corp of the time when they were all children in the Den. The days of childhood are the best.

She lived so long after Tommy that she was almost a middle-aged woman when she died.

And so the Painted Lady's daughter has found a way of making Tommy's life the story of a perfect lover, after all. The little girl she had been comes stealing back into the book and rocks her arms joyfully, and we see Grizel's crooked smile for the last time.